# COME BY HERE, MY LORD

## *Seen in a Mirror Dimly*

Robert G. Proudfoot

FriesenPress
Suite 300 - 990 Fort St
Victoria, BC, V8V 3K2
Canada

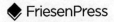

www.friesenpress.com


First Edition — 2020

Edited by Paloma Vita
Edited by Jared Pachan

The author utilized information presented on Wikipedia internet site;1969 to 1975 "Orbit" magazines published by the Zambian Commission for Technical Education and Vocational Training; tourism and government promotional literature such as "Zambia in the Sun" and "Lusaka, Capital of Zambia" ; and historical, ecology, and travelogue books: "So This Was Lusaakas" (Sampson 1971); "Africa Today" (Venter 1975) ISBN 0 86954 023 8; "A Short History of Zambia" (Fagan 1969); and "Zambia Shall Be Free" (Kaunda 1969) SBN 435 900004 8 African Writers Series 4. Maps originated from Collins "Canadian World Atlas" 2003, and National Geographic "Atlas of the World" 1981.



ISBN
978-1-5255-6955-5 (Hardcover)
978-1-5255-6956-2 (Paperback)
978-1-5255-6957-9 (eBook)

*1. FICTION, LITERARY*

Distributed to the trade by The Ingram Book Company

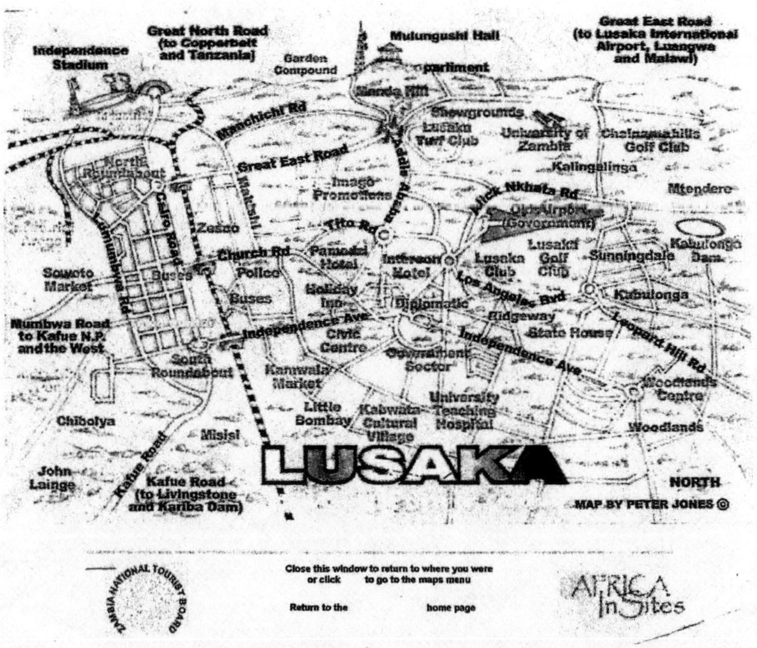


*Lusaka City Map, Africa InSites and Zambia Tourism, 2009.*

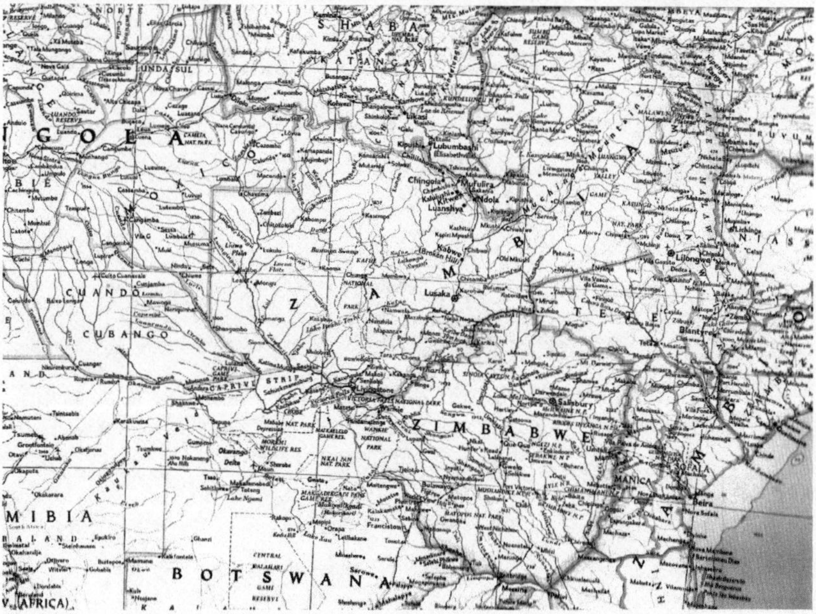


*Map of Zambia and Zimbabwe… of the World 5$^{th}$ Edition, 1981.*

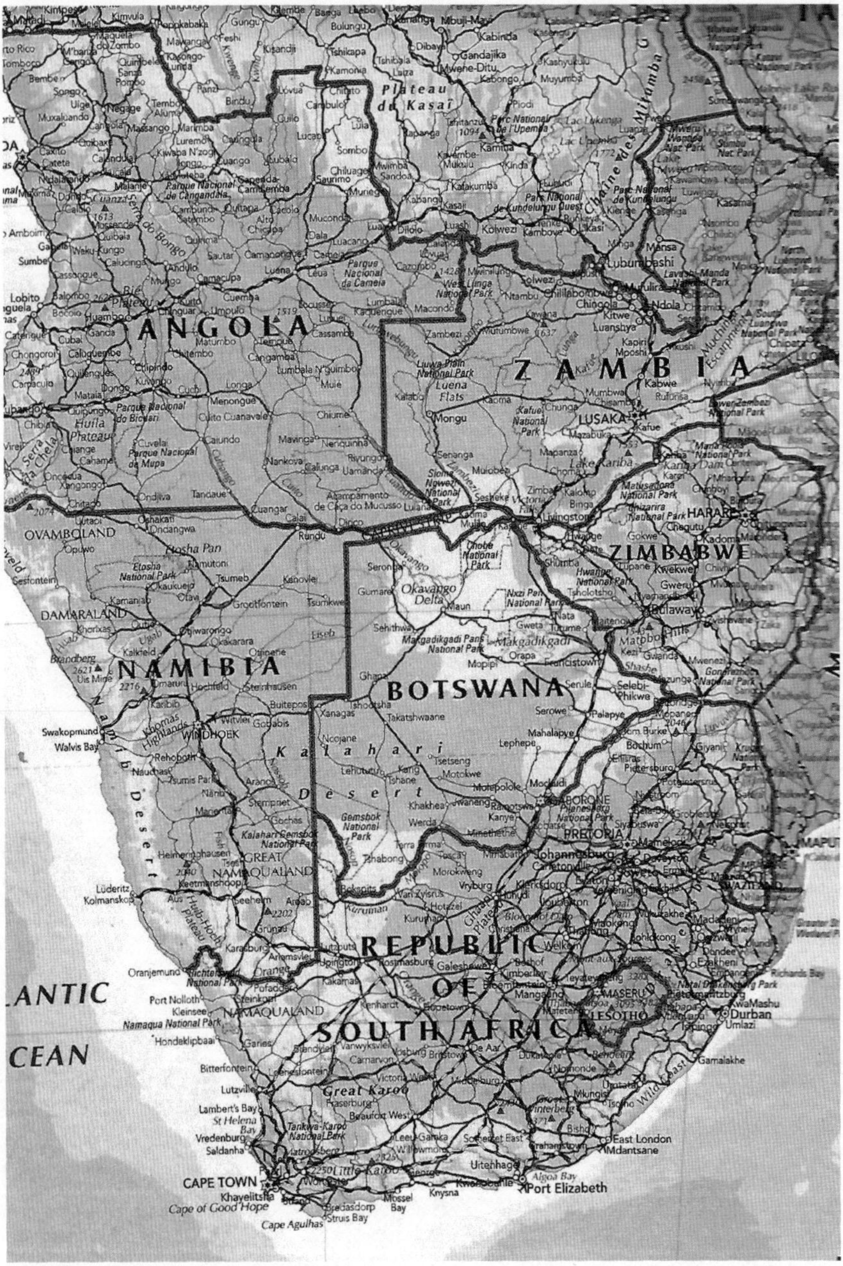


Map of Southern Africa, Collins Canadian World Atlas, 2003.

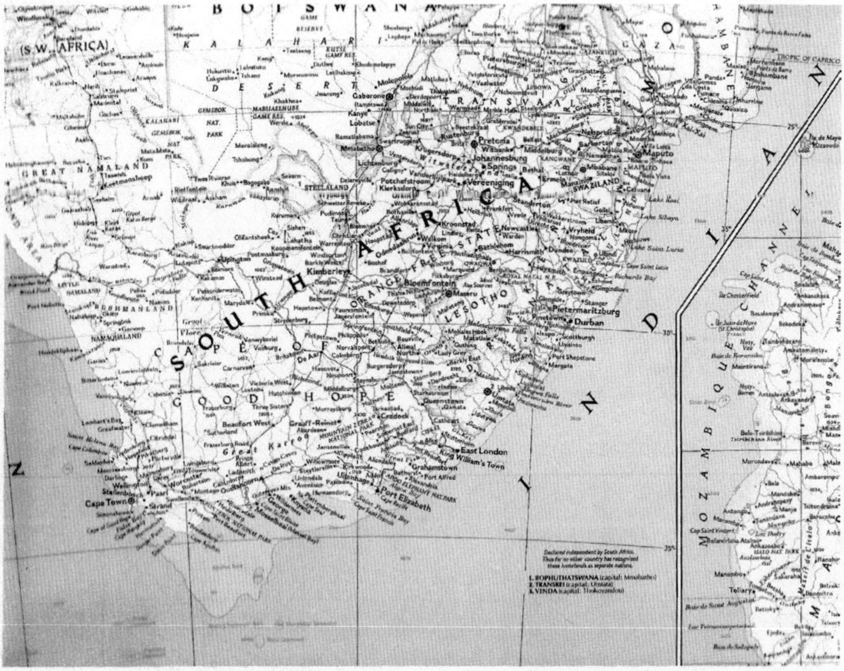


*Map of South Africa, National... of the World 5th Edition, 1981.*

# CHAPTER ONE

"How will I ever capture and organize this tangle of themes and dramas?" griped Orwell Hughes to himself. Frowning at the chicken-scratch that littered his study cubicle, the blonde, sunburnt, University of Zambia freshman muttered, "I don't even have a rough draft cemented, and I'm supposed to present my short story at the UNZA Writers' Club tonight?

"Why can't I get my act together... when all I dream about is to become a world-famous author? On such a rainy, boring afternoon when time and space are my own, I should be fomenting a literary storm! My burning passion is to share unique experiences with the world. For gosh sakes, I've lived enough adventures filled with emotions and struggles during all my globetrotting to spin at least fifty yarns of classical merit. Although I understand this world clearly, it prevents me from chiselling truths into stone. I sometimes wonder why I even bother to write!"

Tormented by his impotent pen, the young, would-be philosopher sighed as he glared out weeping windows at the dreary campus. Drab buildings—like so many cubes and tunnels of concrete—dotted soggy lawns and sailed past bewildered shrubbery to tumble towards the southern African savannah's green ocean that engulfs all things. Orwell gazed deeply into this vast aquarium as far as his eye could see, yet failed to detect the line that partitioned earth from sky.

This high seat of learning, from whose hallowed halls dynamic leaders of young Zambia had emerged, was but a pinhead islet of progressive theorems and scientific technology cast adrift in the depths of ageless myths and mystery. This glistening battleship, upon whose studious decks Orwell was but a stowaway, sailed as much an alien as he was upon the veldt rolling drably beneath its bow. The space-age university seemed descended from Heaven, determined to hold her rain-soaked hills for modern intellect, dialogue, and diplomacy—to be a beacon of hope amid seething conflict and ravenous want. About her festive heights, this amazon of learning strode with pride and ambition for her glorious cause; she smiled benignly upon all who blossomed within the sanctuary of her powerful breast. Orwell held a deep love for the amazon, although in his fruitless times, he observed the university crouching starkly like a prison against an azure sky, and gloomily sensed that he was her helpless prisoner. Nonetheless, Orwell and the institution had forged a grudging friendship out of their mutual isolation and loneliness.

A wry grin pursed Orwell's lips as he mused about how this draughty fortress reminded him of *Habitat,* a unique housing complex made from an inglorious pile of building blocks left over from Montreal's Expo 67. Memories of FLQ[1] letter bombs and the Canadian army arresting Quebeckers without warrant under the *War Measures Act* crowded his suddenly aching brain. Canada refused to be forgotten during his lengthy subtropical stay and awaited his return, somewhere far beyond the soupy northern horizon.

---

1 *Front de Liberation du Quebec* (FLQ): a violent nationalist organization fighting for an independent Quebec that operated in Montreal, Canada during the 1960s and 1970s by sending letter bombs to enemies and blowing up government or public buildings, precipitated the October 1970 Crisis when it kidnapped Quebec Deputy Premier Pierre Laporte and British diplomat James Cross. Prime Minister Pierre Trudeau's federal government invoked the *War Measures Act* in bold response, which gave Montreal police and Canadian armed forces sweeping powers during their search for FLQ operatives and their hostages. Civil liberties were limited, as nearly 500 individuals were detained without bail. The FLQ murdered Laporte, but negotiations led to Cross's release and the kidnappers' exile to Cuba. By 1970, twenty-three FLQ members were in prison, including four convicted of murder.

The *October Crisis* marked a significant loss for the violent wing of the Quebec sovereigntist movement, but it increased support for political means of the French-dominated province to attain independence. The pro-independence *Bloc Québécois* party was the Official Opposition in Parliament during the mid-1990s, while the *Parti Québécois,* which formed Quebec's provincial government in 1976, unsuccessfully proposed two referendums on Quebec sovereignty association with Canada, in 1980 and 1995. The *October Crisis* also was used by Prime Minister Trudeau for transforming the Canadian Military into a force dedicated to assuring our country's internal security, over any military operations against international enemies like communist China or USSR.

Hughes gasped as he glanced at an overhead clock: it was far past time to be scurrying off to his final class for the day, *Africa's Heritage and Future*! In a dither, he scooped his paper and pencils into a battered satchel and raced down the spiral gangway. Running across the library's cavernous lobby, Orwell plowed through a crowd of drenched black students who had streamed indoors to escape the driving rain. His boyish antics amused bystanders as they sipped coffee and marvelled at the white man's hurry, but their "*poly-poly, mzungu*[2]" cajoling went unheeded.

"Time's a-wasting!" Orwell breathlessly declared as he plunged into the downpour and charged across the slippery plaza. He powered into a dark tunnel on the far side, clambered up a stairwell, and sped past classrooms arrayed against the breezeway's open air, fiercely muttering, regardless of who heard him, "Time to come down to earth! Got to stop messing up my mind with this stupid daydreaming!"

He was rain and sweat-soaked, but Orwell shuddered more from the lash of his classroom's bolted door than his clammy state. He was horrendously late! Oh, how he dreaded entering this arena on the best of occasions, let alone now, when his hide was worth nothing!

Professor Ibrahim's scholarly drone abruptly halted and his students' eyes glanced furtively at Orwell as the bedraggled foreigner crept to a desk.

"Hughes, you are inexcusably tardy for class!" growled the stately African doctor, his sudden rebuke nearly causing Orwell to jump out of his skin. Ibrahim glared at the embarrassed youth from where he sat, enthroned like a tribal chief, behind his polished mahogany desk. "Nobody barges unannounced into my realm and casts such arrogant disrespect as you do, insulting both scholars and their mentor!

"You are an insubordinate cur, and shall submit to doing all of us the courtesy now of leaving the room and politely knocking upon our door; then you shall request permission to join our company. Get out and stay out, until you can summon the humility and eloquence to behave like a gentleman!"

Orwell was flabbergasted by this stinging reprimand, but felt powerless to do ought but absorb his humiliation. Stifled snickers from his amused classmates slashed him like a hippo-hide whip, but being the junior son of '*Bwana*'[3] James

---

2 *Poly-poly, mzungu*: 'Slow down, white man', in local Bantu languages.

3 *Bwana:* 'Mister' or 'Sir', a term of respectful endearment in local Bantu languages.

Hughes, *Chargé affairs* at Canada's High Commission, he refused to show his pain. Only dusky Georgina Amadu, the elusive muse of his romantic poetry, gazed upon him with sympathetic eyes—but he perceived to have disgraced her smouldering beauty with his ragged immaturity. Orwell grit his teeth as he silently retreated to the door. He vowed he would prove his manhood—to her and all these baiting whelps!

"Good afternoon, Professor Ibrahim," Orwell solemnly greeted, bowing slightly with eyes respectfully downcast as he re-entered the class. He made a dignified entrance, despite feeling like a cockroach craving to scuttle from sight and mind.

"Professor Ibrahim, Sir!" snarled the old lion, unappeased.

His Muslim fez perched like a crown upon his greying head demanded that this infidel stoop low and pay homage to its regal master. He was no Shrine Circus oriental, speeding around on a scooter in Edmonton's *Klondike Days* parade! Ibrahim, turning livid at the sight of petrified Orwell standing before him, ballooned formidably to his feet.

He railed at this reminder of hated white colonials, oppressors and exploiters, "Do not think, Englishman, that you are superior, and therefore, above greeting your elders with respect and dignity, which is expected in all civilized societies! You shall now properly address me as Professor Doctor Alhaji Abu-Bakr Ibrahim, Sir!"

This hammering rebuke from so proud a peacock nailed Orwell to the concrete floor. He nearly fainted as he nervously bowed low and recited the required mantra before his terrible professor. The young poet's beautiful mind was now so fried that he could barely remember his own name, let alone sing the professor's praises before sidling brokenly into his seat.

The young scholar detested grovelling for mercy and forgiveness at the feet of this bloated egomaniac, but what else could he do? In playing by the elder man's rules, Orwell succeeded only in enraging him. During the next hour, the diplomat's open-minded son was shamefully subjected to a fusillade of vindictive insults, fired relentlessly upon him by this enemy of the immoral western world.

His ogling classmates knew all too well that Professor Ibrahim hounded any student who failed to measure up to his rigid view of what was noble and valuable in man. As though his primitive sport was part of their course curriculum, Orwell's wooden peers attentively settled in, to be nurtured by today's manhunt.

Nobody dared appear vexed or complacent; none in this captive audience was so foolish as to express amusement at Orwell's expense, for anyone who stepped out of line was in danger of taking the *mzungu*'s[4] unenviable place in the arena. It *was* this foreigner's turn to be cut down to size! After months of hiding in the background, trying to fit in, it was whitey's time to be tried by fire! As a token aftermath of their cast off colonial master, he deserved to be put in his place!

Flustered by his brutal loss of face, Orwell slumped dejectedly in his chair as Ibrahim continued to lambaste him.

"Englishman, I have not yet given you permission to sit down! Where are your manners, insolent boy?"

Blushing beet red and rolling his blue eyes in chagrin, Orwell longed for a swift end to his undeserved torment. Yet, in solemn obedience, he stiffly stood up again to acknowledge the command. He clutched a crucifix strung around his neck that Alicia MacDonachie, a family friend and pal to his little sister JJ, had fashioned for him from used shoe nails of her riding pony to celebrate his being saved by Jesus Christ. Emboldened by the faith, lovingly taught by his mother that he was not alone, the targeted student seized a trace of courage and spoke up to Ibrahim.

Defying all logic but his own, he blurted out, "Excuse me, Sir, but I'm *not* English."

"You display much arrogance, stripling! Too much, I say!"

Shaking his ancient head in disgust, Ibrahim sat back down on his throne. From that seat of power, he scrutinized his victim of the moment. Then, his manicured finger stabbing darkly in Orwell's direction, he pronounced, "With your defiance, you must be a Rhodesian spy—or a South African agent. Look students, a blonde and strapping Afrikaner farm boy has stumbled into your all-black classroom!"

This resentful accusation provoked Orwell's fellows to regard him with deep mistrust, even veiled hatred. Assuming that he belonged to these enemy White tribes who illegally oppressed the African peoples south of the Zambezi River, the spellbound onlookers gaped incredulously at Hughes' irritable reply.

"If I heralded from Salisbury or Pretoria, which I do not, I certainly would not be attending this university! I am a native of Canada, a neutral land known

4 *Mzungu*: Bantu term for 'European', 'white man', or 'foreigner'.

for its impartiality and fairness that gives development assistance and peace-keeping troops to nations such as Zambia or Cyprus, which she generously provides—to the hilt! Now, can I receive your stamp of approval?"

"You lie, boy!" roared the professor as he sprang to confront his unrepentant student. Neither Ibrahim nor his classmates had the foggiest inkling as to where Canada was, Orwell sadly perceived as he struggled to maintain his composure. Like a dramatic actor, Ibrahim ranted on, "With your fair complexion, blonde curls and Nordic eyes, you must be Scandinavian. Behold, a savage Viking invades my classroom!"

Baffled by this comic buffoonery, Orwell was nonetheless growing tired of their weird game; hoping to reason, he summoned all the patience he could muster and slowly reiterated, "Doctor Ibrahim, I am Canadian! I am not South African, nor Rhodesian, nor Swedish, nor American, nor even a stubborn holdout from the British colonial era in Zambia. Furthermore, I do not identify with the imperialistic values of John Bull's bygone Empire.

"Having lived in Lusaka for five vital years, I have tried to learn—even here in your class—the issues facing Africans in their efforts to participate in the global community. I believe that Zambians suffered under the colonial regime; I understand their desire for independence and self-government. It is the proper evolution—just too long in happening—and I applaud the spirited determination by which all those involved in freedom struggles won nationhood."

"Do you now? How generous of you. Enough of your trite approval, young rogue or I shall cane you as I would a disobedient child!"

Professor Ibrahim was not done with him. The 'old-school' educator broke into his desk drawer and extracted a clean sheet of foolscap[5]. Then, smoothing his robes and straightening his fez, he stealthily approached the bewildered youth who dared do battle with him. He circled his prey, holding him warily at bay with his glaring eyes and toothy smile. To Orwell's utter chagrin, Ibrahim sadistically held up the white paper like a revolver against his sunburned face.

With relished dramatics, Ibrahim scoffed, "Regardless of where you were spawned, Hughes, you are still a white man—the scourge of developing nations. Yet, I am confused. Why should I keep calling you a 'white' man when your skin is clearly red?"

5 *Foolscap*: a size of writing paper formerly standard in Great Britain.

Humiliated beyond rebuttal, Orwell hung his head and waited for the storm to pass. How he wished he could sink into the floor or be beamed up to the *USS Enterprise,* the intergalactic starship of his favourite TV show, *Star Trek* and be among his heroes, Dr. Spock and Captain Kirk. Professor Ibrahim's relentless insults tempted him to despise his parents' Christian teachings of tolerance and humility! Was there no end to his suffering? In all his twenty tempestuous years living with a poet's heart in a harsh and misunderstanding world, this humiliation was the depth of lonely defeat!

His peers, not daring to become the next scapegoat, each sat in silence, a shaken spectator of Ibrahim's cruel demonstration of how to beat down a wrongdoer. Appearing bereft of sympathy, and in an effort to release the tension, the class burst out in laughter at the mention of Orwell's sunburnt skin.

Only Georgina, a beautiful coloured girl whose white British mother was married to an African noble, elegantly held her peace, but even she of the hazel eyes, wavy brown hair, and milk chocolate skin seemed to compound Hughes' agony. Her sympathetic gaze and Alicia's crucifix helped him find the strength to tough out his degradation. In wordless resignation, the young poet took Ibrahim's cheap shot with dignity and composure.

Standing toe to toe with his elder and learned tormentor, despite the cultural affront, the lad suddenly realized that Ibrahim eyes were blue behind his horn-rimmed glasses and that straight hair escaped from his embroidered hat. Aware that such traits were uncommon in a full-blooded African, Orwell's antagonism melted and solidified into renewed self-confidence. The Professor was a foreigner like himself—an expatriate from black Africa's biggest oil producer and most populous nation, Nigeria—dynamically on the rebound after a brutal civil war. He dwelt like a deposed caliph in exile among the Bantu Christians of southern Africa. As a well-educated elder, he commanded the students' respect, like Orwell was elevated among many Africans just by being European, but what had each man done since to earn such grand welcome? Perhaps it was his insecurity that drove Ibrahim to aggressively maintain his presumed pre-eminence over this rabble of local youths. What past miserable hurts and degradations had *he* endured to drive him to assert dominance over a convenient scapegoat like Orwell Hughes?

It was not from himself but by virtue of Christ walking patiently beside him that Orwell was willing to decipher any good in his oppressor. In return,

Ibrahim appeared grudgingly impressed by Hughes' inner light that flickered with patience, humility, and forgiveness. The resilient young Canadian had survived their duel, bloodied but unbowed, whether or not Ibrahim would ever acknowledge his feat.

"I trust you have learned a timely lesson today about punctuality and respect, Master Hughes. You may now take your seat," directed Ibrahim, dispatching him with disdain.

Orwell followed his instructions, grateful to be finally released. He hoped at worst to suffer in obscure silence for the rest of the seminar. As though the young poet had not been pillaged enough, he was later demoralized by the professor choosing to take apart the lad's political science essay. Adding insult to injury, Ibrahim took pains to explain his handiwork for the benefit of all.

"Babbling boy, take note that I exercise clarity and conciseness to make my point. Did I not, from the outset of this assignment, clearly state that I required an essay of less than two thousand words to describe the causes and effects of neocolonialism upon the emerging Black African state? Your masterpiece of verbosity and senseless jargon is fit only for the dustbin! Yet, to emphasize your dire need to improve your rudimentary writing skills, I took extraordinary measures to decipher and grade this jumble of words. After your two thousandth word, which is barely into the body of your ramblings, I terminated my review! By then, I had practically fallen asleep! Hughes, your low mark is intended to encourage you to take stock of your presently unsatisfactory ability to communicate. Your insight and understanding are keen and not without merit, but you somehow fail to put pen to paper in a coherent way; thus, you exhibit the writing habits of a third form schoolboy!"

This harsh critique, composed with severe frankness before the lolling class, hit Orwell like a ton of bricks, causing him more agony and despair than the previous humiliation. He could live with losing face and being somehow court-martialed by a stern professor before peers he feared might resent his very presence in their developing country, let alone their showcase national university. Orwell conceded that these African academics, drilled from childhood with British standards of writing and rote, were more polished than he, a frontier hick, in the classical use of the Queen's English. They were undoubtedly the cream of the student crop from across the republic, aspiring to gain topflight leadership positions in government, industry, judiciary, and academia, while he was just an ordinary guy from Edmonton. He stood apart from his fellows, however, by being a budding writer since early childhood, so how could his literary efforts now be mercilessly ripped to shreds, leaving him in shambles? Orwell begged the stone-faced jury to understand his burning passions: regardless of his privileged station in life, it was he who arduously toiled to be a literary artist, he who harboured lifelong dreams of becoming a famous novelist! Hughes was a stranger here, but was there no recognition forthcoming from his hosts for his own driving ambitions? Did they who would move the Mountains of the Moon[6] not feel his own yearnings to create, yearnings that no pen could truly harness?

"I'm sorry, sir," Orwell finally acknowledged, resigning himself to the void of humiliation. He promised the indifferent forum, "I'll do better next time."

The after-effect of this terrible experience lingered, and Orwell felt ruined for many days to come—if not the entire semester! He laid low in an obscure corner, relieved to be out of sight from Georgina's lovely eyes. Twice in one hour, he had been dealt heavy blows in her presence, yet he somehow continued to learn, if not to live. Could anything dent the armour of the numbing depression which now cocooned him? If only Tracy MacDonachie, his beloved Sunday school teacher (and by chance Alicia's eldest brother), could counsel him on how to carry on with dignity...Tracy won epic battles wherever he struggled: on sports fields, glittering artistic stages, lovers' lanes, politics, or at the forefront of the marathon movements for environmental protection, social justice, and Christian spiritual renewal.

The unsolicited limelight he endured day after day kept Hughes on his toes, and prodded *him* to dig ever deeper into the textbooks from which Ibrahim waged his fervent socioeconomic, political, and historic campaigns for the hearts and minds of his students. While some African students like Cepheus Belo, Winter Banda, and Benjamin Mudenda seemed insulted by the

---

6 *Mountains of the Moon*: ancient and legendary mountain range in East Africa thought by Greek, Roman, and Arab geographers to be the source of the Nile River. James Bruce determined in 1770 that the source of the Blue Nile was associated with Mount Amedamit in Ethiopia, while the tall and glacier-capped, Ruwenzori Mountains in Uganda were determined by James Grant and John Speke in 1862 to be the source of the White Nile. Although controversy developed among more recent geographers, Ruwenzori Mountains remain the most celebrated possibility for Mountains of the Moon because of their snow-capped whiteness and source water for large, semicircular lakes.

bureaucratic imposition of a course about home upon their lofty academic aspirations, Orwell Hughes gladly lapped up the Dark Continent's fascinating tapestry of history, culture, and philosophies daily unfolding into his life. As though a glutton for punishment, and perhaps because he knew that Georgina was often a guest in the Professor's opulent suburban home—just down the leafy boulevard from Hughes House—the young poet had enrolled in Ibrahim's elective classes to learn the venerable African trade languages of Hausa, Zulu, and Swahili. Most days, this adventurous and romantic idealist revelled in his exotic lifestyle, offered to him only by the strange twist of fate of having world-travelling diplomats for parents.

Today, however, Orwell was reduced to a pathetic bundle of nerves. The doctor's officious droning about 'urbanity' and 'mass rural-to-urban migration' bounced off his tired brain like a barrage of rubber balls. His deep hope was that this dark land would finally accept him at face value and embrace him as one who could belong—because he wanted to! It was not Hughes' desire to become a sideshow act when the mysterious haunts of Livingstone, Rhodes, and Burton lay at his eager trekker's feet, beckoning him to explore and understand.

# CHAPTER TWO

GEORGINA FOUND HER FRIEND HIDING in the bus station, staring at the drizzling rain as he waited for his father to pick him up. The station was a dark and deserted hovel, a perfect cave of exile for miserable wretches who had been defeated in the game of life. Orwell hardly recognized her when Georgina arrived, smiling nervously in the doorway. Noticing that she had no *brolly*[7] and that her shoulders shivered under her wet clothes and dripping hair, he moved to make room for her upon the bench. Despite his foul mood, he offered his cardigan to this shy visitor. Georgina smiled, pleasantly surprised, when he not only drew the woollen vest gently over her outstretched arms and her head but unfurled it smoothly down her shapely torso. They lightly embraced, he to welcome her, she to comfort him.

"I never thought I would say it, but I now seriously want to leave Africa," muttered Orwell as Georgina sat attentively beside him. "I was ready to bounce Ibrahim back there!"

"Orwell, you handled yourself very graciously," Georgie cooed in reassurance. "With your cool-headed diplomacy, you put to shame all of us blockheads who mocked you—who enjoyed your suffering!"

"I was a coward, a wimp!" wailed Hughes, kicking the weathered tin wall of the shelter in exasperation. Wild-eyed, he growled at the dusky beauty. "I stood there silently, like a ruddy lamb, and let that *tosser*[8] make sport of my manhood.

---

7 *Brolly*: British word for 'umbrella'.

8 *Tosser*: a British vulgar expression for a 'stupid person'.

I was too timid to rebuke his degrading insults—especially that trash about the paper!

"Darn! Tracy MacDonachie would have died from embarrassment, had he seen me in action today. He taught me to stand up for myself, put my best foot forward. My pal gives me courage and pride. He's the rugged model of perseverance that I look up to. I'm *so-oo-oo* glad Tracy wasn't here today, to see me play the weakling! *Kai*, I let him down!"

"You keep lauding this Tracy person, like he is some god!" chided Georgina. Then, smiling at his Hausa oath of disapproval as she patted his brawny shoulders, his nemesis' pampered houseguest declared with soothing loyalty, "Listen, boy, Tracy should be impressed by your bravery today.

"What else could you have done? Fighting back and cursing your tormentor would have been foolish, if not blatantly disrespectful...Then, you would have played straight into our professor's hands! He'd probably try to have you expelled from UNZA!"

"Just be quiet and keep your nose clean... Roll over and play dead when the bullies are on the prowl... Always give but never seek reward—is this how you survive, Georgina?" demanded Orwell, boiling with anguish. He dismissed her flimsy attempt at solidarity, and drawing upon his own painful experiences to power his philosophies, Orwell bitterly campaigned, "You must understand by now that the two of us are privileged guests in this unpredictable land. We are but phantoms, seen and known by all but accepted by none. We have neither voice nor stake in Zambia's daily tide of human affairs!"

"We? You surely can't mean you and me! Orwell, you know nothing about my situation! Yes, for *you* to be comfortably enrolled in this university—where only the cream of the black student crop ever gains admittance—just because your daddy is here on a diplomatic assignment and you don't want to go home ahead of him—is an honour that must never be abused," she soberly exclaimed, reminding him of the differences between them.

"My diplomatic status notwithstanding, I am fed up with being ridiculed and treated like some kind of scapegoat for Africa's past misfortunes!"

Who was she to lecture him about privilege? What heated his fire now was his underlying frustration that Georgina knew nothing of Canadian culture although she boasted that her white mother had been raised in Canada, albeit the issue of good British stock. He made every effort to cultivate their heritage connection, but Georgina was not willing to indulge his interest in bringing out the Canadian in her. She wished to remain a delicious mystery.

*Where* was this lovely one's white English mother? Surely Mrs. Amadu was not married to so draconian an aristocrat as Professor Ibrahim! Maybe Ibrahim, a devoutly conservative *Alhaji* who read the Quran every day and had made several pilgrimages to Mecca, kept his wife cloistered in *purdah*[9] or had sent her home to the UK on extended family leave so he could focus on the arduous task of educating Zambia's great unwashed! Orwell never saw the professor show any fatherly affection toward Georgina or even suggest that she was anything more than just one of his many pupils. Occasionally, however, Ibrahim addressed Miss Amadu in their Hausa language as *malama* (lady teacher) but decried her as a girl (*yarinya)* if she ever misbehaved in class. Orwell was aware that an entourage of uniformed drivers, bodyguards, or doting aunts from Ibrahim's palatial household chaperoned this attractive young woman against her many eager suitors. Georgina's dedicated admirer had occasionally seen one or more of these well-heeled assistants driving her to or from university, attending her high-society fetes or tennis tournaments, or strolling together about the leafy grounds of Ibrahim's mansion during his clandestine bicycle rides past the heavily guarded gate.

"I'm sorry that life is so rough for you, Orwell," sighed Georgina. Then, not willing to identify with his self-pity and his ultra-deep feelings, lovely Miss Amadu brightened as cheerful memories of garden parties and discotheques flitted past. She sweetly chirped, "I live a better experience in this beautiful land. I enjoy many close friendships and handsome gentlemen flock eagerly about me. My suitors and servants wait upon me hand and foot, treat me as a fairy tale princess. I spend my time playing tennis, shopping for fancy clothes and high-end cosmetics, or sunbathing at the Olympic swimming pool when I am not studying medicine. Who could ask for more?"

"I need a break," cried the exasperated crusader between wrenching coughs. "I seek the carefree peace that you have. How do you make life work so generously in your favour, Georgina?"

---

9 *Purdah*: practice among women in certain Muslim and Hindu societies of living in a separate room or behind a curtain, or of dressing in all-enveloping clothes, in order to stay out of the sight of men or strangers.

"Holding membership in a rich and powerful family has its perks," acknowledged Georgina sheepishly. "Sacrifices and humility are, however, expected more of me than you, my pampered tourist."

"What?" blurted Orwell in disbelief; she was still teasing him! "You are fabulously rich; your daddy is a highly influential educator. You belong to his classic African culture, yet he allows you to freely mingle with the cosmopolitan societies of Europe and America. How sumptuously he coddles you!"

She laughed raucously at Orwell's enumeration of her advantages. Then, unsettled by his fiery gaze, Georgina dared not aggravate his frustrated mood any further. Her frivolous banter took on a more serious tone.

"You have the freedom to come and go as you please, Mr. Man," she playfully admonished as a call to stay positive and thank his lucky stars. She rolled her brown eyes as her pearly smile, cushioned by full red lips, spoke enthusiastically within her expressive face. "You can cultivate strong friendships here if you desire but could, alternatively, pull out of Africa whenever the urge tempts you, while I am tied here by duties that come with the so-called privilege of belonging to the ruling class of my people.

"The government envisions its educated youth as the future of our nation, the generation who will build bridges between its diverse tribes and inspire development of technology in rural areas. Christian southerners are enlisted to toil in the Muslim north and urbanites are shipped to the outlying frontiers. My father, who loves me dearly, nonetheless refuses to spare me from any mundane responsibilities shouldered by my countrymen. I am required to serve in the army, even if we go to war..."

"Southerners, northerners?" quizzed Orwell, a sharp listener well-versed in history, geography, and current affairs. He chirped along with this pretty bird, hoping she would roost in his protective hands, "I hardly consider working in the highly-industrialized and modern Copperbelt to be a hardship. I thought Zambia's regional troubles, if any, were in the west, Barotseland, although I must say that nowadays, defending our southern border against incursions by the Rhodesian army in hot pursuit of black freedom fighters is no picnic. You would be part of the security wall for frontline black states arrayed against the racist, white minority regimes of southern Africa?"

"*Hubba*! I was talking about Nigeria! Remember, Professor Ibrahim and I are

West Africans. He is not my father, but we both come from a much more robust and dynamic place than this backwater country!"

"You are a foreigner like me? Say what?"

"Shh! Don't tell *everyone* our little secret," muttered Ms. Amadu, pretending to be perturbed. Glancing furtively outside the bus shelter, Georgina added, once certain that no other ears were listening, "Once I graduate as a medical doctor, my government will send me straight away to serve in some bush clinic, making me a prime example to the people of its ideal development worker: versatile, teachable, helpful, and willing to work hard in remote locations.

"Do you honestly think for one minute, Orwell Hughes, that the Nigerian power clique, which deals daily with the headache of two hundred million people from twenty ethnic groups, would permit me—a brash slip of a girl—to become highly educated on its coattails, and then begin my professional practice in some posh European hospital? It is true that soaring oil prices have made my country fabulously rich, but we have mounting debts from all our development and from fighting Igbo separatists in Biafra. Daddy wants me to set a good example for our people.

"I will become their token female doctor, labouring hard under austere male authority in the fiery desert of Bornu State, far from the lush green, liberal modernity of Jos Plateau where I grew up. I could catch malaria or yellow fever in the bush. I may likely live in a grass hut. I would have to catch my own fish and prepare my own pounded yam and *egusi*[10] soup. I would also gather my firewood, and even haul water in a jar on my head! Can you see me doing that stunt, Orwell? No way! I have been a pampered princess all my life.

"My father approves of such rigorous training, to toughen me up, to keep me humble and with my feet on the ground. He thinks I spend too much money on fashionable clothing and expensive perfumes! Humph, am I not a beautiful young woman who must keep herself looking well? Is luxuriant frivolity not my calling?"

Then, coyly plaiting her hair, she laughed for her rapt listener who seemed suspicious of her dire predictions so casually cast about. Usually haughty and shallow, Georgina had never before lowered herself to share so intimately with

10 *Egusi*: vernacular name for the seeds of certain cucurbitaceous plants (squash, melon, gourd), which after being dried and ground, are used as a major ingredient in West African cuisine.

him ... Hughes sensed now, as he glimpsed her scowling in reflection of the rain-streaked glass, that she felt nervously vulnerable. He sensed frustration boiling beneath her unusual attempt to chat with him. Did she finally tumble to his romantic interest in her, though he had pursued her day after day on campus? Why did she care? What did she really want with him?

Georgina, not merely flattered by his attention but encouraged that he was truly listening to her, spoke her mind ever more boldly.

"West Africa is aptly called the 'white man's grave', for it is true that the British could not settle in my country like they did in Kenya or Rhodesia. Many whites left Nigeria when the colonial administration quit at independence while my mother not only stayed but also flourished among the vibrant, resilient people she loves. I am also adaptable ... I too can survive ... Here is where I will stay until Daddy secures his position as Nigeria's duly-elected president and then summons me home," she wistfully promised, sweeping the soggy landscape rolling away from their shelter into oblivion with one of her elegant hands.

"I am treated like any other full-blooded Nigerian by the government and courts, but I will never be fully accepted by my fellow citizens as one of their own. I'm no poster girl for mainstream African society nor, as you my friend can plainly see, am I milky white—a frail, lovely *baturiya*[11]. *Hubba*! Unlike you, I have nowhere else to roost except here, my wonderful paradise in exile ... where I presently dwell as a goddess," Georgina sulked, then smiled bleakly, satisfied that she had stymied this deep thinker with some hard realities of her own, realities that he could marvel at but never share, even if their mothers were somehow compatriots. When her distant countryman failed to snap out of his bewilderment, Georgina grew impatient with him. She muttered, shrugging, "So what, you say!"

He gazed into her large, sad eyes as Georgina struggled through an uncommon quagmire of uncertainty, during which she lifted her lovely veil of unflappable confidence and bared her struggling soul to him; Orwell sensed that hurt and resentment caused her melodious voice to falter. It had obviously been taxing for her to share her deep-seated frustrations with a loser like him—she who seemed so at home, so in charge, in this tropical dreamland. Was he so utterly harmless and hopeless in her sight that she could prattle on so freely with

11 *Baturiya*: 'European or white woman' in Hausa language.

no fear of consequences? Had her witnessing his humiliation at the hands of Professor Ibrahim given her hope that she could reveal herself more intimately now to him in this private sanctuary?

"Forgive me, Georgina," Orwell clumsily mumbled, suddenly ashamed of his petty tirades. "It must be extremely difficult for you to be a subjugated minority all of your life."

Orwell consoled his classmate by draping his arm around her shoulders. Rather than slap him or run away, Georgina acknowledged his sincere kindness by smiling and fervently clasping his free hand. His shy gesture of concern revived the lovely goddess from her hypothermic condition; she now glistened with health and seemed ready to melt with relief in the warmth of his embrace. She was so beautiful, and yet seemed starved of genuine love and respect, thought Orwell as if seeing her truly for the first time. Perhaps, he had been cut out of the frozen north and shipped down into this tropical land to be Georgina's knight in shining armour?

Orwell's ecstasy of triumph at getting so close to her was only fleeting, however. Georgina flew out of his grasp like a dainty, multi-coloured butterfly flitting amongst garden flowers.

"Whatever are you getting at, Orwell?" she gently queried. Her dusky smile expressed both dismay and amusement toward his naïve misunderstanding of her situation. "Life in my sun-kissed corner of the world is a joyous fairy tale for me. Who could ask for more? My father says I must stay here to care for our professor, where it is safe and I can flourish, until I at least complete my bachelor's degree.

"You muse about leaving *gaba daya*[12], before the end of this term because of today's insult, but I have no desire to immigrate to dreary England, let alone freeze in your Arctic igloo! Heaven forbids! What would I do there? Hopefully, we shall meet again in paradise, if not on earth."

She chuckled heartily but Hughes was stung by her teasing, for it shattered his romantic aspirations for the dark beauty; realizing that Georgie was mounting a strong defence against his advances, he stayed deaf to inner whisperings that she was really a cunning witch who was spinning him into her web with little white lies. Hughes, frustrated, decided that he was failing to seduce this

12 *Gaba daya*: Hausa language idiom for 'completely'.

elusive vixen because of his own manly inadequacies. He was giving her his best shot at love, but he was obviously made of the wrong stuff, and the harder he strove to discover Georgina's troubled soul, the more distant she became! Was it only he that she took pleasure in tormenting, or did she treat her many other suitors with equal disdain and cast them under her vivacious spell?

"It burns me that all these dudes hover around and vie for you as though you were a precious diamond glittering in their eyes. There is nothing I can do to protect you," stammered Orwell. Against his better judgment, this Romeo in the rough vented his jealous fears for his lovely goddess. "Must you marry a Zambian to stay here, Georgie? I need to know."

Dumbfounded, Georgina searched for even a glint of humour in his downcast face. As usual, the young poet was deadly serious and was trying too hard to win her heart. If she ever agreed, then what would he do with her? Although they were age-mates, he was simply too young, too inexperienced, too poor; she was not ready for such naïve love and a devotion that placed her on a pedestal. Unable to handle his dramatic questioning, Georgina burst out with laughter, so flattered she was by his fervent passions.

Mistaking her jocularity for ridicule, Hughes poured out a wild concoction of ignorant perceptions in his efforts to justify his question. The grapevine gossip was rife with rumours that young African men were enticed by the luscious and forbidden fruits of her exquisite beauty, wealth, and high social standing. The charmed fellow who earned the right to pick such fruit was honoured and envied by his peers. Marriage to a dazzling woman like Georgina Amadu was viewed as a one-way ticket out of misery and poverty of the African bush. It behooved this goddess to defuse the amorous designs of many crooning admirers, to ensure that she made the best decision possible to protect her wonderful life. Georgina was a very tempting pot of gold....

"Orwell, you are a romantic fool, living in some unrealistic love story. Your vivid imagination needs a holiday," giggled Georgina mischievously from behind the fancy hand mirror she had pulled from her purse. Winking now, her sparkling eyes slew his sensibility. Her puckish grin cleverly spirited him far away, heightening his humiliation. "Look, I am happy to live here and rub shoulders with interesting blokes every day. We Africans are all the same, Orwell! I tremble at these bizarre notions of yours! They are so Hollywood!

"If I do take the plunge, as you crazy Canucks say, I'll marry that one good man who truly loves me for myself and whom I chose to love. Some handsome British diplomat or Dutch oil executive could simply arrive from Europe, and sweep me off my feet. Perhaps, a regal ebony stallion in a magnificently embroidered gown and golden *hula*[13] will secure my dowry by trading so many cattle and cowry shells—not to mention providing me with a beautiful brass bed inside a new house—that my father will agree to the marriage. He has already received offers from worthy suitors' parents for my hand. Photographs of me have been widely circulated amongst his tribe. He prefers of course that I marry a Muslim man of means, but promises that he will allow me some choice in this matter—*Baba*[14] is a kind man who has gone far in rearing me by listening to his daughter as well as the voice of my white Christian mother. I am allowed to have many male acquaintances, not only on this campus but in other places throughout Africa—indeed, in many nations around the globe. Who knows what my future will be?

"This much is certain: marriage is not on my list of priorities right now, dear friend. My goal in life is to become a competent medical doctor. I want to be useful in healing and sustaining the lives of many, not only in Nigeria but in *Turai* [15]also—wherever my calling takes me! This high ambition demands years of dedicated study and work in my profession. I am a proud woman's libber, Orwell, who will encourage other African women to spread their wings! What would I do with a husband at this point in my life?"

"Georgina, I was just wondering," offered Orwell, miffed by the casual attitude with which she met his deep feelings. "I don't want to leave you behind in these jungle wilds when our first-year ends. Do I return to Canada on furlough with my family in October and then continue my university education back home? On the other hand, it will be spiritually hard for me to complete my agricultural sciences degree at UNZA with you also studying so close yet unavailable to date. I hope we can become closer, if not now, then down the road. Either way, I want to be your friend. Let's try to be good pen pals, at least."

"I suppose you think we should be bound together in holy matrimony,

13 *Hula*: Hausa for an embroidered cloth hat that many Nigerian men wear.

14 *Baba*: Hausa for 'Daddy'.

15 *Turai*: Hausa for 'Europe', traditional homeland of the white European people (*Turawa*).

simply because our mothers both lived in Canada," teased Georgina. "There is a world of difference between us!"

"I don't know what I think anymore," muttered Orwell, blushing with embarrassment and frustration. Thankfully, he was let off the hook by the timely arrival of his father's crowded Peugeot station wagon. Smiling nervously, Orwell stammered, "Georgina, can we give you a lift?"

"No thanks. I live in residence here, remember?" she impishly reminded him as she arose to accompany her downcast companion to the curb. Glad to accomplish her mission of finding and comforting Orwell after his humiliating debacle by her uncle, she sprightly bubbled, "If I hurry, I can still get back to the cafeteria in time to eat supper with my friends. Goodnight Orwell."

Having delivered the gloomy boy safely to the car, she waved cordially to his smiling father and gawking siblings before taking her leave. The rain had stopped and the leaden skies were suddenly rent by brilliant sunlight, apparently for and because of Miss Georgina Amadu.

*"Au revoir, ma chérie,"* bid Orwell wistfully as he slumped into the back seat beside snickering Suzanne and sweet Janice Joanne (JJ for short). Rick, in the passenger side of the front seat, was oblivious to Orwell's sadness and only momentarily distracted by Georgina's curvy figure, as he engaged their father in a technical discussion on operating a HAM radio.

Orwell, however, treasured Georgina's gift of gentle fellowship. His calf eyes gazed after her graceful gait as she pranced across the parking lot and ascended a hill beyond. Yet, as Bwana Hughes drove through the schoolyard, Orwell became upset at the sight of his vibrant flame being joined by a black Adonis! Arm in arm, this new escort walked proudly with princess Georgina across the emerald lawns, looking burnished in the glory of sunset.

Did Orwell love Georgina because she was created vaguely like him, distantly related to him, and thus seemed within reach? He clenched his teeth in frustration all the way home as he stewed over the glaring mistakes he had made during their encounter. He had been handed a golden opportunity to woo her, but had fumbled it miserably with foolish questions about who the lady could date!

"Dad, I just remembered, I need to attend the Writers' Club meeting tonight. I'll eat supper at the university dining hall. Can you let me out?" Orwell demanded, suddenly hit by a bright idea.

"What? Right here in the middle of this winding, narrow road? I should find a pull-over at least, Son, don't you think?" Bwana Hughes calmly reasoned with the anxious youth even as he continued to drive towards the campus gate.

"Yeah, any place around here is fine. I'll catch the bus home later."

"An hour ago, you were insisting over the phone that someone come to fetch you, pronto," scolded Suzanne, the older of Orwell's two beautiful sisters. Her eyes sparkling like sapphires, this International School daughter of diplomats grinned knowingly as she confronted the passion behind his wishy-washy demands, "Tsk, tsk! Georgie girl must really be on your case. She obviously stood you up!"

"Orly, don't you know that Mom, Suzy, and I worked all afternoon cooking *tandoori chicken* for supper—your favourite meal? It's far yummier than that pumpkin goulash they serve in the university cafeteria. Didn't you have lungs and feet mixed with your fried chicken the last time you ate there?" admonished Janice Joanne, gently washing him with her large, sea blue eyes. She softly touched his arm with her hand, "Besides, you aren't ready yet to present your short story to the other writers. If you go to that meeting now, they'll just chase you all night to show and tell."

JJ offered valid points, Orwell admitted to himself. His little buddy understood him better than anyone else in his family. Suzanne returned to reading her latest *Harlequin Romance* novel, while Richard and Bwana Hughes, now motoring down the Great East Road towards town, expanded their scientific discourse to the Apollo space program. Orwell turned his head around like an owl but he could no longer see Georgina, though he searched diligently for her pink dress floating on the horizon.

Had he been of sharper mind, like Tracy, the young poet would have confidently executed a winning game plan from the outset: dine with Georgina, then attend his Writer's Club meeting as a guest reader. In reality, however, he was beaten on both fronts—Professor Ibrahim had drained all his energy! He was soothed at last by the sight of the heavenly splendour of water colour skies and verdant gardens rolling away in the wake of the passing warship of education, yet Orwell pined to be escorting Georgina rather than fleeing the campus after another turbulent day of hard learning.

# CHAPTER
# THREE

FEBRUARY, EYE OF SUMMER IN the southern tropics, dressed 1974 Lusaka like a verdant Garden of Eden. The sun smiled warmly overhead, but as Richard explained to his younger brother what he had read without attending university, rain fell almost daily now because of the seasonal intertropical convergence of wet winds blowing from three different directions into the low pressure system camped over Zambia: The Congo Air Boundary from the northwest, Southeast Trade Winds from the southern Indian Ocean, and the Northeast Monsoon from the Arabian Sea and the northern Indian Ocean.

At Orwell's home compound as well as in public parks, church yards, and the guarded grounds of schools or government compounds, the sultry summer brought a riot of rainbow colours and wafted lovely perfumes throughout Zambia's sprawling capital city. Robust fruit trees became richly endowed with mangoes, guavas, avocadoes, and paw paws—tropical delicacies of the gods!—only to have excited children climb high in their leafy branches like chattering monkeys to reap the succulent fruit before Orwell could grab a bite!

In Lusaka's highbrow expat neighbourhood east of downtown, where the Hughes clan and Professor Ibrahim lived pampered in luxury, manicured emerald lawns flowed beneath clumps of rain-washed foliage and tumbled over scrubbed stone terraces towards tennis courts and swimming pools. Fountains, fish ponds, and ornate bird baths reflected a humid sky heavily swabbed with cotton. Ornamental shrubs paraded their Sunday dress in the sweltering sunlight, and unfurled blossoms of brilliant red, sun-kissed orange, and loud lemon that danced amid burgeoning green. Parrots and peacocks abounded, some flying overhead and others strutting about, and fluffed their feathers in celebration of summer.

At first glance, this elegant community seemed to be dormant. In reality, it was languidly awaiting Bwana's return from his city office...Madame's arrival from her downtown shopping spree...the noisy entrance of school girls and boys back for lunch from the posh International School...tots rousing from sleep under the watchful eye of their black nannies. The only movement in the front garden was the rhythmic swish of the garden boy's *panga*[16] as he trimmed the lawn. The house boy had already washed the breakfast dishes and polished the wooden parquet floors. He was nearly done hanging out the white family's laundered clothing; after these garments had dried by the sun, he would iron them indoors during the rainy afternoon.

The noon meal was cooked under Madame's astute direction but not by her regal hands. Hearing the groan of metal and the gate boy's jovial greetings as he opened the compound to her returning family, she inspected her appetizing fair with eagle eyes once more. Westminster chimes signalled noon as Madam set the dining room table for a scrumptious lunch of fish chowder and freshly baked cornbread.

One peered behind a bougainvillea hedge to glimpse the vibrancy of life in the servants' quarters at the back of the grounds. There, African children rowdily played among the chickens and banana groves, while their mother boiled maize gruel, and stirred spicy fish and spinach stew over a small charcoal stove. When her friends visited after lunch, but before the daily rain shower, the women sat in the shade crocheting doilies or styling one another's hair with fire-heated metal combs while their babies slept....

Life teamed on Lusaka's leafy city blocks as well as in her surrounding, white-washed townships. These diverse communities were spread apart but all connected by deep drains that overflowed with water every time it rained. Whether following asphalt roads or well-worn foot paths, commuters flocked daily into the city centre to buy staples; work in factories, shops, or offices; busk street side, or barter wares within the sprawling African Market. The African masses got around by foot or bicycles, shared taxis, public transport or private motor

16 *Panga*: type of curved machete used in East and Southern Africa.

vehicles. Many worked in hotels, private clubs and elegant mansions for expatriates or black *nouveaux riches.*

Garden plots of maize and ground nuts, pumpkins, and cow peas sprang forth from the clay-rich red soil and mingled haphazardly with brick buildings, freshly-thatched roundovals, football pitches, and artisan shops. New elephant grass, still used to thatch many a roof, grew taller than man's height and swallowed all that moved within its stand from line of sight. Lordly acacia, flame, and jacaranda trees loomed as giant umbrellas, at times shading the populace from the brilliant sun or otherwise shielding knots of huddled cyclists and pedestrians from downpours. The blood-warm rains also drove angry legions of Matabele ants to the surface, while their termite cousins secured themselves in mud fortresses they built around tree stumps or any piece of softwood lumber left unattended for more than a day. Giant moths, with eye-spots painted on their multi-coloured wings, and armoured centipedes enjoyed the sunlight. After dark, children gleefully scurried to catch for food the flying ants which swarmed around the lamp lights.

Zambia basked in relative tranquility and prosperity, despite armed liberation struggles raging nearby in the Portuguese colonies and rebel Rhodesia. Droughts and famines plagued the countries of the Sahara Desert's southern beach, where endless civil wars plagued Chad and Sudan—misfit nations cobbled together by ignorant colonial masters. Mad dictators festooned themselves with phony medals and ruled like kings over their oppressed masses in other troubled spots dotting the vast Dark Continent—Uganda, Zaire, and Central African Republic—to name a few unsettled countries currently making the news.

Lusaka, one of continent's most modern but fastest growing cities, had been showcased by Zambia to the world in 1970 during the international summit of nonaligned nations. It was gaining a reputation as Black Africa's political capital because of the government's dedication to holding the front line against racism in southern Africa, staying active in the Organization of African Unity, and forging political and economic ties with other nonaligned nations around the world. Zambia's robust economy was buoyed by high world prices for copper; with clever foresight, the GRZ[17] nationalized its mines in 1969 and developed

17 *GRZ*: Government of the Republic of Zambia.

other export routes to the sea coasts—north-easterly through Tanzania to Dar es Salaam and westerly to Lobito in Angola—before the irresponsible 1973 closure of its southern border by Ian Smith's UDI regime[18]. Although the land held much potential for animal husbandry and the cultivation of various agricultural cash crops, copper production remained the dominant industry; record tons of metal bars were smelted—despite the fatal cave-in at the Mufulira mine. Zambia flourished relative to its desperate neighbours, some political theatre aside: former Vice President Simon Kapwepwe[19] and several cronies were detained for ten months, and their newly-formed United Progressive Party (UPP) was banned in 1972 for fomenting opposition to Kaunda's government. Kapwepwe forsook politics and went farming after his release, having been harassed for illegal possession of firearms and falsely accused by government-controlled media of sending people for military training outside the country. Zambia's diverse tribes nonetheless accepted direction from a one-party State embodied by its only President, who passionately espoused humanism, self-sacrifice, and community spirit to make Zambia truly proud and free. Now in its tenth year of independence, the Land of the Golden Eagle enjoyed progress and stability.

Any refugee from Canada's frigid winters should have savoured this story-book paradise but Orwell trudged through these balmy summer days, finding them turbulent and demanding. He was trapped by the enticing mystery of Georgina, dulled by the tormenting quandary of whether or not he should leave Zambia. Doom's Day shadowed him, derided his struggle to test the waters of decision; some days fled past and were lost forever, but on others, he felt like simply going through the motions. Orwell knew that every moment, however

---

18 *Unilateral Declaration of Independence (UDI)*: statement by the Cabinet of Rhodesia made on November 11, 1965, announcing the British colony as an independent country.

19 *Simon Mwansa Kapwepwe* (1922 to 1980): teacher by profession and a leader within the independence struggle through the *Zambia African National Congress* (ANC) and the *United National Independence Party* (UNIP). He served with the UNIP government as Minister of Foreign Affairs (1964 to 1967), and as Ministers of Culture and Local Government, and Vice President (1967 to 1970) for the Republic of Zambia. Simon Kapwepwe's economic policies and campaign to preserve Zambian culture through teaching of indigenous languages in schools differed from President Kaunda's. His political career with UNIP ended when Kapwepwe acknowledged he was leader of the UPP in August, and elected the sole opposition member in parliament in December 1971.

spent, brought him closer to his final exit from Africa. His present life was winding down—return to the forbidding north was on the cusp!

Although he was given another fortnight's grace to ready himself for his long-expected debut at the venerable Writers' Club, Orwell struggled with a complex composition and made flustered excuses to unimpressed club members Cepheus, Benjamin, and Winter. His ambition to pen the perfect, award-winning novel was stifled by the mounting pressure of expediency. He possessed no affinity for performing in a crucible. His disillusionment withheld purpose for his hobby and robbed him of any strength to craft a story. The whole creative project he lived for was becoming a frightful chore. The youngster was distraught to find that his rich communication style was cramped by Dr. Ibrahim's sneering support for factual simplicity. The learned professor had disheartened him with awful judgment in front of Georgina that he was hopeless as a writer! By extension, the master's niece teased his silly efforts to communicate love. Who could give him another opinion?

*****

WHAT a draining week it had been for the young lad slogging down the rugged road of manhood! One Saturday morning during the final week of classes before midterms, he gulped down his maize gruel and mango-jammed toast as he stared through the dining room window at the rain-soaked land. Orwell was bound to ride to campus with his father today, rather than brave the mud and rain on a harrowing bicycle ride. Little did the poet realize that his power cells were only being rested for more arduous tribulations lurking just beyond his view....

His guarded optimism turned to nervous elation when Orwell slid into an empty seat beside Georgina during their morning Calculus lecture. Remembering their recent, affectionate *tête à tête* in the bus shelter, he naively thought he could spur on their love relationship by clasping her hand under the desk, but Orwell had barely claimed his seat before regal Miss Amadu vexed his romantic plans by commanding that he move away! Sheepishly, Orwell obeyed; under the twang of the Aussie math professor and the smugly amused gazes of other students, the foiled lad slunk into an empty desk at the top of the amphitheatre. Mathematics was his worst subject, especially in the netherworld gloom of 7:30 am but Georgina's curt rebuff bewildered him more severely! Hughes went into a zombie-like trance as he struggled through the rest of the day. He was an apt chemistry pupil and thrived on biology, but today he could barely comprehend acid/base reactions or absorb anatomical facts concerning the cockroach as he wrestled with the hurt wrought by humiliation of public rejection.

But the crazy Canuck loved Georgina, so he forgave the vibrant beauty when she waltzed into his luncheon with Benjamin Mudenda, David Sobukwe, and Solomon Chona, to blame tiredness for her earlier slight. Her charm mesmerized the chatting men, and with skillful diplomacy, Georgina healed Orwell's wounded pride and helped him regain his grasp on reality. Sweetly declining his invitation to dine, Georgina sauntered away with her entourage of sophisticated, trendy people after she airily suggested he attend an impending seminar by the *Hare Krishna* sect—that is, if he was open to hearing about other religions. Orwell could also join her trendy clique at a posh discotheque on Friday night, could he be broad-minded enough to forego his Bible study for once!

After *la belle* had gone, Benjamin drew aside her obedient admirer and solemnly cautioned Orwell to not become yoked with darkness; as a follower of Jesus, he should eat his spiritual food instead at the Campus Christian Fellowship! Despite his friend's sage insights, the young poet, smitten by Georgina's comely form and rewarding smile, eagerly swallowed her bait—hook, line and sinker. Miss Amadu made no further sign to encourage this moonstruck courtier, though she knew that Orwell wistfully followed her every move from a respectful distance.

During the lazy afternoon, Orwell took a break from his study books to enjoy a *Big Rock* beer in the dingy campus bar and listen to soul recordings of Aretha Franklin and the hip new Motown sounds of the *Jackson Five,* and *Diana Ross and The Supremes*. Hughes sat down to chat with Molly, his chemistry lab partner, and her friend Diana when an African patron, perhaps miffed that a fresh white boy was socializing with girls outside his circle, belligerently accused him of being a Rhodesian spy. Backed up by three other thugs in mirrored sunglasses, he was adamant that he had seen Orwell rounding up unarmed Black demonstrators recently on the streets of Salisbury[20]. The diplomat's son was stung, but determined to avoid a hopeless altercation, he quietly set down his

20 *Salisbury*: capital city of Rhodesia until 1982, and is now known as Harare, the capital of Zimbabwe.

half-empty tumbler and left the bar. Hughes gritted his teeth and swallowed his pride as he retreated under a hail of verbal insults. He expected his tormentors to follow him outside for a fight, but turning briefly in the doorway to see if they were coming along, Orwell was dismayed to find that they had chummily taken his place beside Molly and Diana.

"Give me a break, Lord. I really don't need this bullshit," Hughes muttered to himself as he wandered sadly across the grassy common.

Tracy would have mopped the floor with those buffoons, but Orwell grimly realized that *he* was no Tracy MacDonachie! He continued to hone the boxing skills his mentor had taught him at the campus gym, but this beardless youth knew he had a long way to improve in body, mind and spirit before he dared claim to be in the same league as that celebrated gladiator!

Orwell felt tired and thirsty now, so he stopped in the canteen to buy a chilled soft drink before heading back to the library. While chuckling over some provocative political posters—likely plastered by his activist pal Cepheus Belo—as he waited in line to purchase a Coke, another student offered to sell Hughes a pouch of raw *dagga*[21]. The damnable weed grew wild in the countryside, but pot and its trippy culture were not his bag; Orwell easily found courage to brush off the trafficker, who quickly melted into the hustle and bustle of the indifferently babbling crowd.

The overhead clock prodded Orwell to keep moving; he would never be late again for African Studies! During one of the professor's less-tantalizing seminars, the sallow atmosphere was spiced up when Orwell's friend Winter Banda was rebuked by the tyrant for wearing short pants and a khaki shirt to class.

"You are an adult, with pride and dignity to preserve! Men who march on the cusp of life need to sharply deck themselves out: wear white collared shirts and dark dress slacks, crisply pressed—not this childish uniform of a schoolboy!" roared the old lion, frustrated that he must continuously mentor such silly cubs in so many extracurricular ways to make them fit for leadership roles in a rapidly transforming Africa.

Hughes cowered in the corner beside an open window, which would provide a quick escape route into the courtyard garden, should he suddenly be noticed to also be dressed in short khaki breeches and shirt, not to mention walking

21 *Dagga*: local Zambian term used to refer to cannabis.

about in sandals with grey knee stockings. Like Winter, Orwell often wore such comfortable attire during the rainy season rather than perma-press polyester to cope with the clinging humidity; such easy attire was socially acceptable to the public outside these snobbish halls of high learning! Painfully identifying with his chum but inwardly thankful that Winter had taken the Professor's heat today, Orwell refused to laugh with the others at Banda's put down.

Yet, Hughes wondered why he stupidly wore his secondary school uniform when class emptied out and Georgina, stylishly dressed in the latest chic fashion, moved quickly beyond his reach as she chatted among her bevy of girlfriends, oblivious to his presence. Maybe, he really was just an immature boy without the means to aspire to her attention—that was why Georgie avoided him more and more, rather than gratefully accept his burning love! The gorgeous, cultured, and grown-up princess obviously shared the same lofty values as her starchy old uncle!

Orwell shelved his bitterness when Winter Banda, a small and bookish youth who relished reading thick textbooks in the library rather than going out to play football or field hockey, caught up and strolled with him away from the academic wing of campus. Winter and Orwell related well on many fronts, including sharing similar taste in clothing and being oppressed in Ibrahim's class. Today they found themselves travelling on a higher plane, discussing literature from the African Writers Series: *Things Fall Apart* and *No Longer at Ease* by Chinua Achebe, Cyprian Ekwensi's *People of the City,* and *Mine Boy,* poignantly written by Peter Abrahams.

"*Things Fall Apart* is my favourite African novel," Hughes enthusiastically declared. "Chinua Achebe is an excellent writer. To date he has written half a dozen books and won three prestigious awards for his works. Some more recent novels like *Arrow of God* and *A Man of the People* are also well known. They all contribute so much to literature! I am glad that you were instrumental in bringing his exciting body of work into the Writers' Club for group study."

"There is no doubt that Mr. Achebe is a serious and disciplined craftsman," added Banda, beaming with pride at such praise from his white friend. He seemed pleasantly surprised that Orwell was willing to listen to the literary voices of Black Africa when he could so easily bury his nose in some mass-marketed British or American book. "He works slowly but carefully, so that he does not need to make copious drafts of his manuscript, like some more flippant writers do. As a master of English language, Achebe tailors his style of prose to fit not only the setting of his book but also the individual characters who enact his themes. In *Things Fall Apart,* the author uses proverbs and images to emphasize the traditional culture so central to his precolonial village story, while the modern, fast paced narrative in *No Longer at Ease* is reflective of urban life."

"Chinua Achebe, in his first book, vividly described traditional Igbo society and how it was shattered by the arrival of European missionaries and traders during the late 1800s. This difficult story was told through the adventures of Okonkwo, the child of a poor man who grew up to become a rich farmer with three wives, as well as great warrior and champion wrestler—one of the greatest men of his time! Okonkwo was a responsible father and a good husband, but unfortunately his character flaws—pride, temper, and inflexible will particularly in matters of tribal honour—caused him to commit suicide in response to the breakdown of his culture.

"The sequel, *No Longer at Ease,* described the adventures of Obi Okonkwo, Isaac by his Christian name and grandson of Okonkwo, in the great metropolis of Lagos, at a time when Nigeria was gaining independence after many years of British colonial administration. Obi, having recently completed his BA degree, returned with high hopes from England to take a plum position with the Nigerian government, but the competing forces of modern urban life and traditional tribal values brought about his professional, social, and moral decline. Our hero was obligated to pay back his steep student loans, but also desired to live up to his high calling. He purchased an expensive car and lived in an upscale flat, on top of regularly sending money home to his family to pay for his younger brothers' education. He wished to marry Clara, but she, although carrying his child, was unacceptable as a wife to his old-fashioned parents because Clara was a descendant of slaves to his Igbo tribe. When Obi informed Clara that their marriage must be delayed, she had an abortion and then left her partner. Demoralized, Obi fell off the wagon: the high-living civil servant accepted bribes to help pay down his mounting debts, but he eventually was caught and set on trial."

"Well done, my friend, a fine summary indeed. Do these tales seem straightforward to you, as a white foreigner?" asked Winter, fascinated by the *mzungu's* rote regurgitation of the plot. "Actually, you are just scratching the surface here, but if you dig deeper, you will find that the story is not so simple after all, Mr.

Orwell. Obi Okonkwo's problems were created because he was part of two conflicting ways of life. He was enriched by the concepts of individualism and personal freedom via his western education, but was also rooted in the collective tribal culture, which didn't differentiate between one's public and private life. Obi belonged to a group and was bound to support that group, rather than operate independently of it.

"Those of his tribe who had funded Obi's education felt that he was then indebted to them; he must use his newly-acquired status to help his relatives advance. Obi, who had deep ties to his people, felt he was honouring his clansmen by riding in a big car, but resented their interference in whom he should marry. What right had others to advise him against marrying Clara because some traditionalists considered her to be taboo? Why should he share their feelings of disgrace? Obi Okonkwo, a modern, intelligent young man invested to succeed, eventually was defeated because he could not reconcile his inner conflict.

"You mustn't laugh, my friend. That those classic novels were written fifteen years ago when we both were children does not negate what they still reflect for many educated Africans who strive to advance within the broader society of our countries today. The opposing ideologies between the individual and the tribe exist side by side in modern Africa, where we struggle to meld the better qualities of traditional and western philosophies into our national game plan."

"I do not laugh. I am trying to understand these concepts, as well as the writers who present them. It is sad that colonialism has caused so much turmoil. Even in James Ngugi's *The River Between,* we learn how the teachings of white missionaries denounced long-established cultural values as pagan and fuelled rather than reconciled the tensions between communities. What is the use of tearing down proven traditions without providing a workable alternative for the people caught in the change?

"I love to hear Professor Ibrahim extol the virtues of great African kingdoms: Asante, Songhay, Kanem Bornu, Lunda, Kongo, Rozwi, Great Zimbabwe, and Zulu—to name only a few that flourished prior to European colonization. Writers like Chinua Achebe can help Africans stay in communion with their ancestral homes while attesting to their modern surroundings. They can help people remember that their traditional societies have profound and beautiful philosophies, great art, poetry, and dignity."

"You are remarkable, sir! You dwell on the romantic past while I struggle with the difficulties of the present. Maybe, you don't want to solve the complex problems of our current world, which must vex you—but *someone* must!"

"Flora Nwapa also wrote an interesting novel called *Efuru,*" Orwell, who had just finished reading the book, deflected their increasingly heavy conversation to a less straining topic.

"Hah, a woman's story, written by a woman about village women," scoffed Banda, who had already distinguished himself as a master debater at the Writers' Club.

"Ms. Nwapa was a highly-educated and accomplished person, but she wrote about customs and beliefs, as well as chronicled the conversations of traditional rural women in eastern Nigeria," Orwell countered, as though he was suddenly the defender of all women, particularly talented and ambitious Nigerian girls like Georgina.

"Although Efuru married and left two husbands and raised her child as a single mother, she was regarded as a good, hardworking woman, a respectful daughter, and a resourceful trader. The author describes in detail many aspects of women's lot: life and death, birth, rearing and circumcision of children, sickness, trading, food preparation, and superstitions—yet did not question them."

"I have nothing to learn from her that I have not already learned from mothers, sisters, and aunties in my own community. Women belong in the kitchen; when they are not cooking, they should be cleaning or looking after children. This university provides educational opportunities to many brilliant ladies, but some forget their purpose in life as they aspire to become like men: doctors, lawyers, teachers, or engineers. That is why one must marry a strong young girl from his village who is satisfied with her secondary school education."

Banda tossed this grenade with conviction, though he smiled with smug satisfaction when the blushing foreigner failed to argue with him on the status of women in society. Zambia was Winter's country, his society; yet, he knew little about Orwell's private life and his own beliefs. He was unaware that Hughes had two teenaged and unmarried sisters whom the *mzungu* loved and respected, and that it was a given that their outspoken views were permitted, their grandiose dreams heard, and broad opportunities provided for advancement by doting parents as cultural norm in the accommodating Canadian context. But one thing Banda could see as clear as day was that this young white man worshipped the ground upon which Georgina Amadu walked, a young woman whom he deemed to be as dangerous as she was beautiful. To engage the Secretary of the Writers' Club in further debate about the equality of women would only amuse him.

"As a guest in your country, I choose to be interested in African culture—past, present, and future," offered the career diplomat's son. "I enjoy our rich sampling of the African Writers Series."

"But these are South Africans, Kenyans, or Nigerians, foreigners like you or coloured Miss Amadu…or Cepheus Belo, our pompous Writers' Club President," snorted Banda with disdain. "He conveniently forgets that we have a lot of local writers, many of them who hone their skills as members of the club. Do we not regularly produce our own anthologies of poems and short stories in *Forum* magazine?

"Look at our own Zambian President. Kenneth Kaunda is quite a musician as well as an Author—he wrote and sings "Tiyende Pamodzi"[22], number one on the Zambia hit parade. Has KK not also provided a profound dissertation about his vision for the country in *Zambia Shall Be Free*? This book is listed near the top of the African Writers Series, but Mr. Belo refuses to consider it for discussion.

"Rather than promote literary development, Belo pollutes our meetings with political harangues critical of the government and foments civil disobedience against the university administration. Cepheus takes his rancour to late-night rallies and plasters provocative posters all over campus. He too is a guest in my country, but chooses to demonstrate against institutions that he knows nothing about! I don't know how we ever voted Cepheus Belo into leadership of the club. He is a loose cannon who should be disbarred from the Writers' Club, before we all get into trouble!"

Orwell, who counted both Cepheus and Winter as his friends but was troubled by their ongoing public dispute, skirted around his companion's loud

22 "Tiyende Pamodzi": patriotic and popular folk song that encouraged Zambians of all tribes to come together in peace and solidarity for the good of their country, and stand strong together against hostile outside forces like colonialism and apartheid that threatened southern Africa. President Kenneth Kaunda sang and promoted "Tiyende Pamodzi" during Africans' struggle for independence from Great Britain and his rise to national leadership. *The Rising Stars*, a Lusaka Boy Scouts musical band, also popularized the song, and performed it during many national and cultural celebrations during the early 1970s.

opinions and took the high road of politely describing what little he knew about the inspiring Christian vision of President Kaunda.

"Dr. Kaunda, who was a stalwart soldier in your peoples' freedom fight for political independence from the British, urges all Zambians to continue the struggle—against poverty, ignorance, hunger, and disease—so as to make a better world where everyone can live with dignity and justice. This struggle will not be over until every new Zambian is born with the chance of a happy, healthy, and proud life."

"We all want to enjoy happiness and be healthy, but what is a *proud* life, Mr. Orwell? It is knowing that one has worked hard, perhaps suffered somehow, to change the world for good. It is knowing that one has given thought and effort into making life better for his children, whatever one's station in life is. Yes, I learned that our President says what he means! I read his recent letter to *Orbit Magazine.*"

"I've read that President Kenneth Kaunda has promised to put a pint of milk and an egg on the breakfast table, and a pair of shoes on the feet of every Zambian. Such lofty goals are really down-to-earth."

"The President speaks intelligently of development on many levels, my friend. He is not, as Cepheus claims, a despot determined to exploit Zambia while crushing her will. We are not children, you see, nor is our President infallible. Much progress with industry, education, infrastructure, and healthcare has been accomplished over the past decade by his regime, but the ingenuity and determination of the people has always been here.

"Cepheus criticizes the one-party state for suppressing dissent but I regard our President as an egalitarian; he believes in the equality of all members of one tribal community—a social norm that existed prior to Europeans coming to Africa. He wishes to return power to the people through his policy of decentralization. Dr. Kaunda has faith in people's capacity to exercise power properly; he respects their natural wisdom, particularly among ordinary rural people who know the time-honoured tradition of egalitarianism. How, then, can I accept Mr. Belo's opinion that Dr. Kaunda is a dictator who will stop at nothing to hold onto the reins of power? The sad thing is, we had a packed house at our last Writers' Club meeting, but only heard that fool's presentation about unfair rules he claims are imposed on students by the university to keep us in line. He made impassioned calls for a sit-in to be staged by all students inside the Administration

Building! Our planned review of *Zambia Shall Be Free* was shelved in favour of that dangerously charged diatribe! Why? Because Belo deems the President's book to be a political manifesto rather than a great fictional novel."

Orwell shrugged his shoulders in dismay as he stopped on the edge of the common lawn rather than continued to walk with Banda into the men's dormitory. He looked tired but spoke earnestly, "I don't know what to say now, but let me ruminate over your concerns while I wait here for my ride home. I'll see you on Monday, Winter."

"Orwell, we missed you at our last Writers' Club meeting. We, in fact, are still waiting to hear the short story you promised to read to us since before Christmas, my friend."

"I've finished my rough draft, but just have a bit more fine-tuning to do before I can read it to the group. After midterms are over, I should be ready to share it," Orwell assured his smiling, owl-eyed friend.

"May we both look forward to that time with relish," Winter replied before taking his leave.

Orwell savoured the reassuring warmth of the setting sun as he waited on the hillside for his father. From his promontory, he saw many students come and go between the university wings, the dorms, and the bus station. Twice, the three musketeers—Ben, Dave, and Solly—ambled past and greeted Orwell with good-natured grins and light-hearted banter. His pals did not have one *kwacha* to share between them for a bus ticket, let alone taxi fare; they always seemed hungry but they could walk effortlessly forever. They had gone to their spartan dormitories and back and were now heading to the dining hall for supper. Molly and Diana also waved at the fool on the hill; all dolled up and acting carefree, Molly informed him that they were going into town for Saturday evening—would he like to follow them? Before Orwell could explain that he was waiting for a ride and would be able to give these charming ladies a lift, Diana exclaimed that their bus was imminently approaching. The two lovelies suddenly dashed away, laughing as they scuttled down the concrete staircase in their black, high-heeled shoes and tight miniskirts.

A battered, smoke-belching autobus trundled into the depot and exhaled several weary students laden with parcels from downtown shopping sprees. Soon crowded again to the hilt with a fresh batch of riders, the coach lurched back onto the road and droned away to the city. Orwell was relieved to not be sentenced to ride the rough and tumble service of Lusaka's transit system. Yet, he was embarrassed to be seen waiting... and waiting. The sun had dropped behind the university's concrete battlements, now silhouetted against the sky. Why was that white boy so foolish, still stubbornly lingering on a grassy bank far from home, passersby might wonder? Did he not have legs? He could walk five miles home today and return by bicycle tomorrow, like most African students did every day.

One passing group of men had no use for this youthful foreigner at their university, and took advantage of Orwell's predicament to make him an object of scorn.

"What are you doing up there, Bwana?" chuckled one of them.

Hughes did not know this heckler from Adam, but he knew that being a blond, blue-eyed *mzungu* made him an obvious topic of gossip for all who attended the campus. The heckler bowed in mock subservience as he asked, "Are you waiting for your driver, Bwana?"

"No, for my father," acknowledged Orwell calmly as he clung tenaciously to his perch. "He should be arriving shortly."

"Your daddy is late, I think," suggested another japing gorilla. "He's probably drinking martinis in the lounge of the Ridgeway Hotel!"

This derisive slam annoyed Orwell; he didn't mind the odd drink, particularly on such a hot, humid day but his family were virtual teetotallers, thanks to his Bible-thumping mother! Steeped in love and respect for God, she taught her four children to find pleasure in the gospel, rather than in the consumption of alcohol. Bwana Hughes kept a modest stash of assorted bottles—whiskies, brandies, and wines—discretely locked and hidden away at Hughes House, to entertain special guests who, like himself, enjoyed the odd social drink, particularly with a celebratory meal. These degrading insults against his hardworking father infuriated Orwell, however remote a figure the statesman was to him. The old bull had coached him well in diplomacy though, he had to admit.

Out of grudging deference for his nonperson status in their land, Orwell remained calm in his response to these bullies. "My father is not a boozer, friends. As we speak, he is driving over here from work at the Canadian High Commission. So, what if my dad is a little late... he'll come."

"Your daddy is still in the bar!"

"My father is not an alcoholic!" snapped Hughes angrily. "Just can it, eh!"

Like a young lion, Orwell sprang wildly to his feet. He snarled threateningly but his bluster only let him down. His baiters smugly cackled in some local dialect as they casually strolled away. They had triumphed over this remnant of the old order; goaded into losing his cool, the young foreigner had simply played the fool! By Monday, word would be drummed throughout the campus, and likely reach even Georgina's daintily jewelled ears, that Orwell James Hughes was a childish hothead.

Maybe his old man had been detained by some pressing work at the embassy; maybe Rick was too busy flying an airplane to come pick him up instead. He could only control his own destiny. Orwell clenched his teeth in frustration against the melting sunset now as he strode across the savannah towards home.

Hughes house was cheerily lit, as though to welcome the straggler from the enveloping darkness of night, but not even a scrumptious meal of *kapenta*[23] stew on rice with collard greens and plantain lightly fried in coconut oil could cheer Orwell up. He had endured too many taunts from fellow students going about their evening pleasures while he had waited on his lonesome for an hour beyond the appointed rendezvous time.

"It must have been one pretty short hour," Richard griped back. "I buzzed over to the university for you when I got word from Dad that he was tied up at work. Orly, I must have arrived just after you left, but then I waited half an hour for you to show up. I didn't know you had already split until some students returning from the tennis court informed me they had met you jogging across the savannah towards town. I think Georgie was among them; she recognized me and put two and two together."

"You were mistaken," Orwell grumbled, suddenly envious as well as distraught. "Georgina plays tennis—damn well, I'll warrant—but I did not see her on the path tonight. She typically spends the weekend in town at her uncle's place. You likely crossed trails with Lovelace, Georgie's roommate."

"Whatever," shrugged Richard irritably. "Those two look a lot alike. Whoever it was, she recognized me as your bro who might be looking for you. Lovelace is a helpful girl."

"What in the hell took you so long, anyway?"

---

23 *Kapenta*: two species of fish (Lake Tanganyika sardine and Lake Tanganyika sprat) living in Lake Tanganyika in Zambia, and a staple of local cuisine.

"I got caught in traffic, *baas*[24]. Don't you know: drivers are always crazy on Addis Ababa Drive at this time of night? I had guys passing me in the ditch or on the meridian, blaring their horns as they wove fearlessly between grid-locked vehicles. We were five abreast on a three-lane road circling the roundabout near the airport!"

"I didn't know you were coming, Rick. I got tired of waiting. I'm always waiting while you and Dad to do your thing!"

Jolted by this ungrateful retort, Bwana Hughes tossed his napkin onto his plate and glared at Orwell through his horn-rimmed glasses.

"Don't be so despondent, Son!" chided the old diplomat. "Richard and I did what we could for you today; you impatiently chose to walk home, although I suppose I should admire your perseverance and ingenuity?

"Fatigue from worry will be your undoing. Are you such a sourpuss that you want to wear a permanent scowl on your face? Life here involves much more than just your daily routine of soap operas. You seem to forget that your life is actually very sweet.

"Orly, you are privileged to be blooming while the world is convulsing in anguish about you! How would you like to be an American boy in 1974, fighting a humiliating, losing battle in the jungles of Vietnam? Could you fare for one day as a white policeman in Rhodesia or South Africa, ordered to use whatever brutal force necessary to control black protestors in their homeland? Would you be willing to risk your health, your very life, lost in the bush defending the giant Carbora Basso dam or the tenuous Benguela Railway lifeline with other hard-bitten Portuguese colonial soldiers from marauding freedom fighters in Mozambique or Angola? Would you rather be a victim of the bloody excesses of Idi Amin? Maybe you could join those sorry Brits in Kampala, who were recently pressganged into paying homage to that mad dictator on bended knee and carried him aloft on a portable throne, on their shoulders! Utterly deplorable!"

"No, I'd rather be swinging from a star," fumed Orwell without restraint, his vivid imagination recalling Bing Crosby's song that urged children not to play hooky from school.

"And so, you should, therefore you are! Instead of enduring a blistering

24 *Baas*: Afrikaans word for 'boss', typically reserved for a white overseer when addressed by an African.

march down some rocky road, you are blessed as you bask in the sunlight of precious adventure and good times," his father continued. "While many of your high school pals back home failed to make the grades needed for higher learning and are now slugging it out as ditch-diggers, grease monkeys, or grocery baggers, you are allowed to greatly expand your academic knowledge as well as learn a highly marketable profession—here in sun-kissed Zambia—at no expense to yourself! Before they can earn a penny in their chosen profession, your native UNZA colleagues will do military service upon graduation—or before, if war comes with Rhodesia and South Africa!

"Even now, while enrolled at an elite post-secondary institution within a foreign land—where every day is an adventure and offers the opportunity of a lifetime—you live in security with your family instead of being forced to return to Canada or attend some austere boarding school in Britain or South Africa, where you would further your education while living in the company of strangers.

"Look at your brother Richard, for God's sake! Although two years older and arguably more marketable than you, he languishes on the shelf waiting for his family to finally leave this tropical paradise. Do you hear Rick bemoaning that he was shafted by contracting malaria at a critical time when he should have written his UNZA entrance exams? No. He accepted his fate and will enroll at the Northern Alberta Institute of Technology when we return to Edmonton this October, but until that day arrives, Rick uses his time productively: he works at a book store on Cairo Road, and has learned how to drive a car like the British. He has also become a licensed pilot! What have you accomplished lately, Orly?"

Put rigorously on the spot, the youth was suddenly purged of his wasteful self-pity and forced to reflect upon his good fortunes. Given some polish and a rag to work with, Orwell became pleasantly surprised by what a little shine could do to refurbish some of his neglected achievements. Orwell was playing defence and goalkeeper for the university field hockey team during its campaign for the national championship. Only a year ago, he and Rick, together with other adventurous sons of the Canadian expat community in Zambia, had climbed Kilimanjaro, Africa's highest mountain! They had been crowned by native porters with heroes' wreaths of mountain flowers in celebration of their gruelling feat. The Hughes boys, who both sang in choir at the multiracial church, had harnessed their artistic talents even further by joining an ecumenical drama troupe to re-enact the Easter story. Orwell was not only acting but had already been on Zambian television with the International School's team of bright young scholars playing *Knowledge Quest.*

Young Hughes also noted the fact that he was in good health and endowed with a sound Christian mind; he held the keys to all the kingdoms of the world. He thus reminded himself he should be thankful for the many undeserved gifts and innocent joys of youth he was blessed with! Why get bummed out with life over one silly little girl who failed to reciprocate his puppy love, or for the fact that he was the odd man out at university? As the High Commission's head diplomat saw it, his moody second son had no time to waste pining for Georgina—or any other frivolous girl for that matter—with university exams looming!

In a rare divergence from public service protocol, James Hughes explained to his gathered family members that his lateness today stemmed from an important embassy staff meeting, where preparations were made to welcome an incoming planeload of Canadian technicians and their families. A chartered *Air Canada* DC-8 jetliner, regarded as rare as snow in Lusaka, would bring fresh troops into the Zambian capital the following month. These newcomers would require detailed orientation and warm friendship from understanding veterans of African life before being shipped off to their posts throughout the country. His family's eager contributions to the welcome wagon, particularly for mothers and youths, would be duly appreciated.

Such a rare assignment as joining a Canadian advisory team should have flattered Orwell immensely... given him something meaty to chew on. Instead, he was painfully reminded afresh that he would soon be leaving Georgina for those tuque-wearing, back-bacon-munching, beer-quaffing hosers in the Great White North! The last thing Orwell wanted to do now was to discuss Canada, but his annoyingly forward-planning old man persisted in building a coffin for his African experience. And, as if they were leaving the Dark Continent forever in October—rather than just taking a three-month break for rest and visits back home, the patriarch contemplated closing the family's local bank account and tying all their loose ends. Friends had already claimed various household and garden effects, and various folks were already lining up to purchase the trusty, Peugeot 404 station wagon. The veiled threats of a heavy door clanging shut upon a vital chapter in Orwell's young life only burdened his sensitive soul.

The lad, who could not really be in love at his tender age and with his lack of experience when it came to romantic affairs, should shut that door and go home, a simple task to perform in Jim Hughes's steely eyes... Trying to read his father's unfathomable mind, Orwell struggled to understand the codes hidden in his long-winded philosophy: was Bwana Hughes forcing his hand, declaring that he was through with Africa, rather than giving him the choice of staying or not? One could hear a pin drop as others listened intently to the head of the household wax eloquent on the upcoming mission, but Orwell despised the idea of more Canucks flying their own jet into Lusaka—maybe meeting him booted on his inglorious way out!

Jim Hughes was dismayed by Orwell's morbid response but he interpreted it as the lad's grief at having to leave Africa. The entire family would miss this tropical haven, not to mention their good friends with whom many exotic adventures had been shared. This was the end of an era; they could savour many precious memories and praise God for having been so privileged to travel together to the frontiers of the earth. Leaving, however, did not mean that friendships must end; rather, it offered respite for reflection and rejuvenation. No doubt, they would each rub shoulders again back home with some Canadians they had befriended on foreign fields. Corresponding with Zambians might be more difficult but one could always write a letter! Drawing together diverse, far-flung nations into a global community through improved air travel and long-distance telephone service, as well as the mutual desires to work and study abroad, the future held opportunities to keep in touch for those who would seize them!

"One's lifestyle can improve through change. I admit that, while some changes for us are inevitable, they will not be easy. Yet, I firmly believe that we grew stronger together as a family by coming here; we will benefit from such enrichment as we get on with our lives in Canada.

"Africa is not our home—we have possessions, family, and history back in our country of origin—Canada, our real country. We came here under contract of loan to Africa but should conditions of that agreement expire, we must return to where we belong. We arrived in Zambia with nothing of this great country and so must finally leave it behind, taking nothing tangible away. Yet, our five-year stay has enriched us beyond our wildest imaginations. We take away many poignant memories and strengthened family ties."

The old man seldom shared his feelings with his children, other than firstborn Richard; today, had the lad been more observant, he would have seen a wistful tear on Jim's craggy face. When Orwell deduced that his father was simply not content for him to stew in his own juices, he struggled to break out by relating his debacle with the hateful African students today in the bar and on the hillside. Who after all, was racist? He had done nothing wrong to provoke their hatred, only wished to belong—even for a few months. To Orwell's dismay, no sympathy or praise was forthcoming from his impassive father. When Orwell sighed and glared out the window at the driveway's single yard light against the black curtains of night, Bwana Hughes chuckled at his rigid views and suggested, with an unusual twinkle in his eye, that he lighten up a tad. The big man knew what he would do!

Was Orwell not an outcast? Was Africa totally indifferent to his looming departure? What would Tracy do? Thank goodness, Benjamin, David, and Solomon remained his supportive brothers in Christ throughout his self-pity and despair. Despite their fellowship, however, they could not solve his dilemmas like Tracy would, were he but to miraculously visit Orwell's remote outpost. Life seemed eternal for the young sailor drifting on the high seas but she was lost to him.

Only in his fervent letters poured out to Tracy late at night could Orwell do justice to his bizarre life in Africa. Tonight, he vividly described to MacDonachie how, as a volunteer labourer for the Lord, he had helped his church build houses and distribute healthy foodstuffs to malnourished squatters in a shantytown below Burma Road. His family had recently accompanied Rev. Beausoleil, the local white preacher, Benjamin, and fellow members of their multiracial congregation on a Sunday excursion deep into the savannah, to witness the baptism and dedication of new Zambian Christians into the presbytery.

Orwell also told his mentor how inspired he was every time he glimpsed the glowing eruption of molten copper slag pouring from mine trains in Kitwe. He then recounted how, during a recent family vacation to Kenya, Hughes had met giant Masai warriors, their regal bodies decked in beads and smeared with ochre, still herding gaunt, long-horned cattle like ghosts across the arid Serengeti Plains. His family had travelled over hundreds of dusty-red East African miles to view Mount Kilimanjaro, the continent's snow-capped majesty. They had handled a treacherous descent into Ngoro Ngoro Crater, the grassy and treed-over mouth of an extinct volcano, to view all manner of wild game living together in its caldera; Orwell breathlessly remembered glimpsing from the heights above, the shoreline of its lake made pink by thousands of flamingoes wading in the shallows. Among the rugged rocks of Olduvai Gorge—man's birthplace according to Dr. Leaky—they had viewed ancient cave paintings that depicted the Sahara Desert as burgeoning with green foliage and diverse species of animals. Near Lake Manyara, the family had naively slept under a grove of giant trees that shed their branches whipped by wind blowing after dark; in the morning the Hughes boys had been shocked to find their campsite littered with tree limbs, many big enough to crush them in their tents, had the wood landed a few feet closer! He then recounted how curious African spectators had studied the white strangers cooking breakfast on a Coleman stove, washing dishes in a pan of soapy water, and smartly breaking camp like they had been at the circus. No sooner had the travellers hit the road than women and children were scavenging for any crumbs left behind and gathering the tree branches for firewood.

Even his stern father knew that all work and no play made children dull. Orwell was encouraged to stay physically as well as mentally fit, playing field hockey, table tennis, and soccer, as well as vigorously working out at the boxing gym. The young poet heartily cultivated his competing artistic side on the church organ and writing short stories, and he and Richard practised devoutly to perform at the city's Easter pageant.

Whether happy or sad, in spite of his struggles to fit in and find love, the young trooper did his best to make the most of his uniquely splendid opportunity to be a big fish in a small bowl. Perhaps Tracy could come swim with him for a while?

# CHAPTER FOUR

Orwell, finally home after another hectic, rainy day at the front, sat solemnly at supper with his family to consume a delicious spread of exotic cooking: spicy chicken and spinach stew served on a maize gruel. He offered nothing to the conversation whirling around him; his dining parents and siblings were like strangers on the dim periphery of his attention. At one end of the table, Jim and Rick were engrossed in a technical conversation about single-engine aircrafts. Both ardent members of the Lusaka Flying Club, Richard vividly detailed his adventurous solo flight of the day north to Kabwe. On Orwell's other side, his sisters rotated like tops as they excitedly speculated over some late Christmas mail that had finally arrived from Canada. These two pestered Orwell to distraction for keys to his memory vaults, as though he was up to date on every acquaintance and relative back home.

This evening, as usual, the young scholar's thoughts focused on the campus, and he yelled at Suzanne and JJ for repeatedly violating his space. His blow-up came suddenly, like a meteor hurtling from outer space—it seared his startled sisters and silenced the rest of the family caught unawares. Orwell was jolted back to reality under the hard glares of his father and brother. He could *not* blot out the din of daily family activity by locking himself in his hermit's cave! He was the strange one who was out of kilter. Suzanne and JJ shrugged at his outburst, wanted to giggle but dared not. From her observer's seat, mother Martha lovingly discerned that Georgina, not her daughters, continued to bewitch her son. When, she inwardly wailed, would this young buck mature enough to tire of that vixen's game?

After an embarrassing pause, the family resumed eating, eager to end the meal and move on to reading their letters. During after-dinner tea, precious mail was distributed to each family member. Christmas cards, adorned with swaddling of snow and Santa Claus images, offered reports from distant friends and relatives from across many time zones—just three months late—better late than never!

Orwell deduced that life in Canada flowed merrily along, on a far more sophisticated level than what his outpost of civilization could offer. Marriage banns from many cousins and family friends were joyously proclaimed amid other lovely news. Some had soared upward in their workplace; others bought impressive suburban homes or lakeside cottages. Others yet spent their easily acquired wealth on Caribbean Sea cruises, Hawaiian real estate, power boats or luxury cars—many had filled their cradles with healthy babies. The worldwide OPEC oil embargo had put a fire under Alberta's oil patch, and its hardworking folk were more than willing to fill that market gap!

Martha gladly received a letter from her aging father, Grandpa McNeil. The homesteader and war veteran, one of many pioneers who had lent their stout hearts and brawny backs to building western Canada, was still keenly on top of his country's current affairs. The Liberals no longer formed a minority government buoyed up by the socialist New Democrats. Led by Prime Minister Pierre Elliot Trudeau, an intellectual Quebecois dandy, the Grits had won the recent federal election—despite being shut out of conservative Alberta and all but annihilated in the West because they refused to understand the farmer and his constant struggle for survival! The feds, bolstered by their perennial majority in the East, paid no heed to the subservience imposed upon Alberta by Ontario and Quebec. Maintenance of unfair railways freight rates for grain and cattle, and a blatant failure to recognize Alberta's great energy potential, were the excesses of pin-striped bureaucrats on Parliament Hill that grieved grassroots folks of the land.

Fuelling his hard-line, right-wing stance, Grandpa McNeil supplied heinous Toronto newspaper clippings that scorned Albertans as red-necked cowpokes or gun-wielding outlaws. These whiners decried as banditry Alberta's courageous demand for world price for her coveted oil and natural gas, not to mention her pledge for a two-tiered pricing system to protect Albertans as producers from the higher export prices. Wild accusations were published in the nation's energy-hungry, industrialized heartland that Peter Lougheed, Alberta's erstwhile premier, was a 'blue-eyed Arab' who threatened to press his province's outlandish demands by cutting off the supply of natural gas to Canadians! McNeil, who had cleared poplar forests and farmed the blue clay gumbo of the Peace River Country, railed against rich Ontario's haughty stand that the West was just a primitive hinterland for the industrial and commercial hub, and should not presume to act aggressively now against millions of true Canadians who had built her. By the same token, however, the stout pioneer gloated to see eastern premiers come crawling to God's country, caps in hand, begging for loans or energy concessions. Much as Grandpa McNeil deplored the hustlers and foreign money now flooding Alberta's oil patch, he remained optimistic that this boom would finally bring the province recognition as a legitimate partner of Confederation and put on the map in all the corporate boardrooms of Toronto and Montreal. Praise the Lord, the Promised Land had finally come of age!

McNeil's politically astute grandson remembered the 1970 *October Crisis*, having read at the time with shock in the *Zambia Daily Mail* about Canada being one of the world's trouble spots! Canada's domestic disputes seemed so petty, so artificial now to Orwell, compared to the age-old struggles always simmering in the African savannah! He could, however, still loudly cheer with his grandfather about their country's hard-fought win over Russia during the 1972 hockey summit series. Yahoo Paul Henderson![25]

A more genteel greeting was next read by Martha from dear Mrs. Bingham, the ancient matriarch of St. Andrew's Presbyterian Church who still clucked over her children flown far from the downtown Edmonton nest. Bless their dignified souls, these little old ladies from the Women's Auxiliary had pooled

---

25 This high-profile, eight-game exhibition series occurred in September 1972 between Team Canada and the Soviet Select all-stars. Canada, historically a power house in international hockey tournaments in what was supposed to be "our" national game, had not won the gold medal at the Winter Olympics since 1952, while the Soviet Union dominated by icing older, more experienced, and arguably professional teams in elite amateur games. Canada withdrew from international play in 1970, but two years later, the world's two ice hockey powers played head-to-head, each represented by their best players, professional or amateur.

The Soviets, backed by their sensational goaltender Vladislav Tretiak, won two games and tied one, losing only once in four games played on Canadian rinks. Shifting to the Soviet Union, the locals won game five, but Canada won the last three games by close scores to narrowly take the series. . Paul Henderson became a Canadian hero by scoring the winning goal in each of the last two games, capping the 6-5 score with 54 seconds remaining in the eighth game, on September 28, 1972.

their resources to send over some seed money, as well as Bibles, encyclopedia, study guides, and several hymn books for the burgeoning multiracial congregation where the Hughes clan now served as missionaries. This blessed gift would arrive in spring in response to Martha's encouraging report of the dynamic spiritual growth by her African brethren. Intended to nurture the pursuit of Biblical wisdom and instill Christ's gospel in new believers who might otherwise return to the pagan rituals of Africa's primeval jungles, this gracious gesture of faith by the mother congregation would be delivered into Hughes' good hands by its own dutiful son and zealous ambassador, Reverend Tracy MacDonachie!

As well-meaning as such outreach was intended to be, the Hughes clan was amused by the naivety displayed by their patrons. The family had moved to a mysterious country, full of jungles teaming with wild beasts and swarming insects, stone-age people dwelling in grass huts, where missionaries trekked through the bush on foot with porters, to spread the flame of Christianity? After five informative years on safari, these Canadian visitors felt that Lusaka had also discovered them, revealing herself in due course as a modern and cosmopolitan city, which boasted modern shops, hotels and amenities, and thousands of automobiles driven by Africans and Europeans alike on wide, paved roads.

Hughes House, like for many upper crust expats who called Lusaka their home away from home, was a rambling stone bungalow with a corrugated tile roof and glass windows, set in beautiful gardens and equipped with modern conveniences: running water, electricity, a telephone line, state-of-the-art appliances, and fashionable furniture. Urban lifestyle was, admittedly, far less secure for most of their hosts, but the Hughes family had generously made their servants' lives as comfortable and prosperous as possible. So much for the American television movies clichés of Africa being all about Tarzan leaping through the trees and lions stalking vast herds of wildebeest across untamed savannah...

That his idol was coming to visit him in Africa was a treat overshadowed by his dismay at hearing this swashbuckling adventurer reduced to an errand boy for well-heeled church folk! Orwell resented MacDonachie's apparent demotion. From Mrs. Bingham's doting praise, one could have concluded Billy Graham was coming to town! To add to Orwell's chagrin, his brother and father roundly scoffed at the choirboy image of Tracy the old biddy portrayed in her glowing letter of introduction.

His dismay was heightened by a frivolously confusing letter written to

Suzanne and JJ from Tracy's little sisters, Kathleen and Alicia. Kathleen—aka Kathy, but no longer Kitty-Cat or Kitty for short to the mesmerized Hughes children—brightly announced that babies born to older siblings Jane and Robert had entered the world bouncing and crying loud. Orwell smiled as Alicia decried Robert's smug notion that Jane and his own wife Mona were fulfilling their female destinies by becoming baby factories. Robert, the second MacDonachie brother, was a consummate entrepreneur, and the manager of hundreds of Hereford beef cattle at the family's ranch in Alberta's northern boreal forest. Not content with his ranching activities, Robert had also set up a saw mill on the ponderosa to manufacture lumber from all the big timber that *Silver Lining Corporation* was clearing to make room for pipelines or well leases. Bruce, as Robert was affectionately nicknamed after a heroic Scottish king by his preaching tycoon father, was cashing in big by cutting survey stakes, pallets, and pipeline supports from waste wood, which he sold back to oil and gas companies operating in his neck of the woods. His own cat skinners also bladed well leases and access roads. Bruce also rented trailers, provided water and cooks, and flew choppers for drilling camps come to sit a spell on *Bonne Chance.*

In a year or so, if their father had his way, Alicia and Kathleen would also earn their 'MRS Degrees' at Prairie Bible Institute. Yuk! A lot of handsome young men already came calling for elder sisters Evelyn and Jane, but Alicia, who loved Jesus, music and sports, wanted no dumb boyfriend to mess up her busy schedule and future plans! Kathleen penned romantic poetry about Xmas sleigh rides and skating parties, and marvelled at the ghostly wonders of night skiing in the mountains. Alicia, not to be outdone by her sibling rival, declared that golden poplar leaves interwoven with green spruce trees in the autumn river valley gave the *Edmonton Eskimos* and University of Alberta *Golden Bears* their bold football colours for another winning fall. For Orwell's information, his 'ever luvin' Esks' had finally gone to the Grey Cup game in 1973, after a 13-year drought, albeit losing to Ottawa Rough Riders! Hank Aaron was poised to break Babe Ruth's all-time home run record in Major Leagues baseball. Godspeed to those Canada geese migrating south over Cherry Crest, lest some trigger-happy MacDonachie male shoot some for Thanksgiving dinner and stuff the rest!

Kathleen was euphoric that she, Alicia, and Tracy were breaking away from the mouldy *MacDonachie Family Singers* to form their own upbeat Christian rock band. Despite their father's disgruntlement, they were performing at folk services or in evening coffeehouses; the trio would soon cut its first record. Wow, the Hughes boys chuckled; bright lights of Broadway were calling!

If only St. Andrew's church could be so vibrant every Sunday morning as it was during such venerable congregational festivals as Christmas, Easter, and *Robbie Burns Night,* Alicia wistfully pined. Speaking of the infamous Scottish bard, his latest birthday celebration had packed the church hall with rollicking clansmen and their Highland lassies, where Burns had been given a lively roasting, in both Gaelic and English, by a guest comedian from Scotland. His rich poetry and ribald accolades to fair maidens had been rousingly toasted, and the normally dour Scottish and Irish congregation sang, with bubbly good humour, his enduring ditty "Auld Lang Syne"! Aromatic haggis had been ceremonially piped in by Tracy and heartily blessed in Gaelic brogue by Mr. MacPhail, before being carved by flashing swords and served to all who could stomach sheep guts and oatmeal. Alicia and Kathleen, exquisitely dressed in the traditional red tartan of the proud Robertson clan, had delighted the audience with skillful Highland dancing over crossed swords and then made people weep for their old country's loss of independence from England by forlornly singing "Skye Boat Song".

Melancholy Scottish songs and ancient traditions had touched the Celtic heart beating in even the proudest Canucks in attendance, except for Alicia's father, who shunned his ethnic roots in favour of the almighty dollar, which knew neither boundaries nor culture. Highland braes, and country jigs and reels had come down to all four MacDonachie girls honestly through their Métis mother Pearl, whose hardy Scottish and Cree forbearers had worked in the fur trade across the Canadian north. Most outspoken and flamboyant among Tracy's womenfolk, Kathleen proclaimed that her enchanted soul danced with William Wallace, Robert Bruce, and Bonnie Prince Charlie to the haunting wails of bagpipes and drumbeats stealing down from the dark Grampian Mountains and across misty lochs, but Kathy was as Canadian as maple syrup or ice hockey!

Again, and again, the two girls gave fervent testimony to the inspiring works of Tracy, their valiant hero. Alicia recounted the midnight service that Tracy had conducted last Christmas Eve within St. Andrew's candlelit sanctuary. How reverently had choirs, orchestra, nativity actors, and scripture readers interwoven under his caring direction united into one family 1,500 worshippers gathered from everywhere to remember the birth of Christ Jesus! Tracy had sung a stirring rendition of "O Holy Night", bringing tears to the eyes and Christmas hope to many souls lost in winter's lonely desert.

Having taught Sunday school to teenagers for years after returning from seminary, Tracy had recently been hired by the old downtown church as its youth pastor. He had long entertained in song, but now used his wide talents to inject new life into the staid music ministry. His exuberant leadership style and the polished skills he passed on to those around him brought many newcomers into the folds of the congregation!

Tracy introduced teen choirs, street witnessing campaigns, and coffee-house ministries to the bustling transient population in downtown Edmonton. Wilderness retreats and province-wide youth conferences were but two of many exciting initiatives he brought to rebuild a viable, loving Christian presence for disenfranchised and distracted kids, who fallen through the cracks of an archaic church system. Although seen by some parents and the more conservative members of the congregation as a modern-day Pied Piper, the hip youth leader had taken their children to see such controversial 'religious' movies as *The Exorcist* and *Jesus Christ Superstar,* to later debrief and discuss them over hot chocolate in someone's comfortable living room.

Even if St. Andrew's had embodied Presbyterian work and witness in Edmonton since the city's founding, the old edifice had become crowded in by new downtown office towers who knew not its illustrious history... and lost hundreds of adherents to satellite congregations recently started in the suburbs. Tracy felt that the esteemed mother congregation had grown staid and that, in order to survive, it should embrace its position as a downtown church by providing hospitality with ministry to the inner city. He was determined to do his utmost to bring Christian revival of glorious proportions to his congregation, city, and denomination! Driven by his need to save the world before Doomsday, Tracy struggled to tread softly and work carefully within the baleful framework outlined by the institution's entrenched power clique, lest his great ambitions betray him by forcing change to come too quickly.

Alicia was known to her readers as Annie Fannie—Fannie for short—thus nicknamed by her father because the auburn-haired, brown-eyed, and freckle-faced child reminded him of a Raggedy Anne doll, although Richard rudely joked with Orwell that the 'Fannie' moniker came from her ample backside! This normally shy and virtuous girl surprised them now with a plethora of vocal opinions as she praised Tracy's decision to sink his boxing ring earnings and musical gigs dollars into legitimate property investments, rather than impulsively blow it on fast cars and fancy living. Tracy, she sighed less charitably, was dutifully building a family with his gorgeous, yet hoity-toity wife.

Stephanie was, in Kathleen's view, the perfect companion for Tracy: she refined his rough edges and groomed him eloquently for his return to public grace. In case memory failed her readers, Kathy proudly reminded everyone that Stephanie was a beautiful Christian lady whose parents were pillars of church and society! Although she was an exceedingly shy and gentle soul, Kathy's sister-in-law was a gifted Sunday school teacher who possessed winning ways with children. She had borne her hunk of a husband three strapping boys in just six years of marriage—not bad for a guy who had vowed to live out his days as a swinging single! As Orwell struggled to decipher the source of Alicia's apparent jealousy, amid the laughter from the alpha males in the audience, Fannie's acidly remarked that her big bro had lost his final bout! While Tracy had always been a fast mover with women, the stunningly beautiful Stephanie made him shine... But now he was dutifully tied down to her, whether he liked it or not!

Kathleen and Alicia then announced a pleasant surprise: they would accompany their superstar brother during his epic African visit! They eagerly awaited the opportunity to view big game animals roaming in the wild jungles round about, and visit the Hughes tribe in its grass huts... that is, if they could pick their friends out from the other black folks! These naïve quips, coming from two sprightly lasses who had been born in Africa to parents who had given years of dedicated service cultivating African missions, was barely uttered when the listeners broke into uproarious laughter amid excited banter about the upcoming visit.

Orwell sat alone, slouched in silent mourning for his free-spirited hero, lamenting Tracy's fatal slide into oblivion. Swarmed by three kids and stuck to some hoity-toity dame who wore white gloves and silk kerchief to play football with her man's youth group... who labelled social pleasures in life like dancing, movies, and playing cards as works of the devil... was Tracy not already dead and buried? The Good Ship MacDonachie, upon who's swift, knife-edge deck Orwell Hughes stood tall as first mate, would sail to exotic lands no more nor master bold adventures upon the high seas of life. All his robust feats, from gorgeous female admirers, to concert hall acclaims and athletic glories were lost but for silent testimony of the countless trophies, medals, and yellowed newspaper clippings mutely displayed in glass cabinets.

Alicia praised God that her brother was born-again, although Orwell could not understand nor rejoice in her enthusiasm in spite of his own devout faith. They both missed the rough and tumble cavalier who was fading into what Alicia gloomily called a gentleman of leisure in chains. They pooh-poohed as frivolous Kathleen's assertion that Tracy was finally growing up: living up to his great potential as a MacDonachie, and taking his proper leadership place as he served society as a Christian of high calling. Both girls loved Tracy dearly, but Orwell solemnly noted that this devious Kitty-and-Fannie team, who long had tormented him, finally disagreed on how their talented brother should live. He was both relieved and disconcerted that Tracy had written nothing to confirm what others rumoured about him.

JJ and Suzanne, ecstatic that their two best friends had accepted their invitation to come for a visit to Africa during the Easter holidays, gladly washed the supper dishes as they started making detailed plans with their mother on how best to host her best friend's two youngest daughters. Bwana Hughes and son Richard retired to the garage to tune up the Peugeot's engine, leaving Orwell to fret alone about the complex mysteries of his life.

# CHAPTER FIVE

"HAVING THE MACDONACHIE GIRLS VISIT will be a breath of fresh air around here! How marvellous it will be to traipse about Lusaka with them—not to mention Stephanie and her rollicking family in tow—showing our guests the exotic sounds and sights of our home away from home. A few strong women at my side to keep you guys in line will be a real treat!" Mom Hughes cheered when Orwell moped about Tracy being saddled with wife and children on his visit. "The men can go flying, play tennis, tinker on their cars, show off their muscles high-diving at the swimming pool... or whatever you guys do—enjoy!

"We ladies will hold luxurious tea parties in the back garden, amid sweet hibiscus blooms and bougainvillea vines, serenaded by polished musicians. Uniformed waiters—resembling my sons—will pamper us by serving tea and crumpets! We'll attend some gala fashion shows at the InterContinental Hotel or organize a fete for the YWCA. For a special treat, I'll take these lovely creatures of charity and grace shopping at the African Market."

Orwell, who had steadfastly kept his nose in his school books for the past six months, naively gathered that his mother's plush itinerary was daily fare for the city's pampered expatriate women. She had never been to fancy women's shows in Canada, let alone in these far-flung tropics, but nothing was too dear when it came to his mother pampering those golden MacDonachie girls! He knew not whether to laugh or cry at her frilly plans until Martha's soft grin clued him in that, deep within her solid Christian sobriety, dwelt a clever sense of humour.

No fan of the young nymphs about to invade his space, Orwell derogatorily howled, as he did yard work with his siblings and mother one brilliant Saturday afternoon. "Kitty-Cat and Annie Fannie haggling with black peasants to buy skewers of mice and dried dragonflies for din-din? I can just see it now! They'd go into shock and wither away!"

"I've heard that expression before," sniffed Suzanne, as she screwed up her sapphire eyes and brushed her brother away like he was some pesky gnat. Orwell gazed back askance at Suzy as she disdainfully added, "Wither away! That's the MacDonachie males' only line, especially around me!"

Orwell took a break from weeding some Calla lilies and mimicked how he thought the finicky princesses would react to Africa by waving his arms and gasping in horror at exotic foods and the weird sights of the local markets and bazaars.

"Don't be so hard on our esteemed guests, Orwell," clucked mother hen. "Tracy, Kathleen, and Alicia are my best friend Pearl's children, whom I love! I will treat them as my own while they are here, as I honour their mother.

"Tracy and his sisters have sung beautifully in church, as well as on Christian radio and television broadcasts, for years. They exude Christ-like hope and inspiration. They are coming as emissaries of St. Andrew's church, bearing gifts and glad gospel tidings to our outpost congregation. I believe we in the far-flung mission fields could sincerely benefit from their testimonies and gospel songs. They'll warm the hearts of my Sunday school children down at the multiracial church."

Orwell was ashen-faced at the suggestion that his hero should further humiliate himself by performing at their church, but it was Suzanne who voiced a rebuttal.

"Humph!" she grunted distastefully, "Kathleen and I will kick up our heels and paint this drab town flaming red! We'll be the life of the party at all the *braais*[26] and discos—I don't care anymore that Kristi Stephenson flaunts her latest, handsome pool boy at me like a gold chain around her neck—even if that two-timing turd used to be *my* boyfriend! Kathy and I will make a big splash with all the hunks at the swimming pool; and if they're nice, those he-men might even get a chance to drive us around town."

"This ballyhoo about bar hopping and pool-side sex orgies is just a foolish pipe dream, Suzanne Marie Hughes, which I am certain the MacDonachies will

---

26 *Braai*: Afrikaans word for a 'barbecue social'.

avoid, and your father and I will disallow!" replied Mrs. Hughes, fiercely scratching dirt against her daughter's rebellious plans.

"Aw, Mom!" Orwell protested the stifling rule of their mother's strict adherence to the establishment as much as her hellfire and brimstone inference that bad acting was being planned, let alone was possible, among young people. Rolling his eyes and sighing under his breath, he out-chorused his overtly rebellious sister in pshawing the Victorian dictatorship ruling them! "The MacDonachies are Christians, Mom, just like us. Tracy is a Sunday school teacher and youth pastor. We're joking... Can't you trust us?"

"Tracy better behave if he is shepherding his sisters so far from home!"

"Who cares about Tracy? Fannie is a naïve prude who can play dolls with my baby sister and keep her out of my face," Suzanne glared derisively at JJ. Big sister chased after little sister now, flashing her electric blue eyes and wagging her finger threateningly, to put JJ on notice in advance. "You better leave Kathy and me alone when we are chatting in my bedroom. I don't want you two bugging us, asking to wear my clothes or play with my jewellery, understand!"

"Then, don't hide my bike when Alicia and I want to go out for a spin! And don't let my pet rabbit out of her cage while we're playing tennis!" JJ shot back.

"You girls are always fighting," Orwell rasped in frustration. "I wish I could stay in residence at the university, so I could find a little peace and quiet."

"I am sure you do... to be closer to your goddess, Georgina Amadu," teased Suzanne. Exacted satisfaction from his reddening face, the teaser added, "Orwell, I've got a strong hunch that our MacDonachie girls have got Georgie beaten by miles in brains and good looks."

"I'll wager those imps will corrupt us brass-buttoned Canadian boys beyond repair. We Canuckleheads don't know how to tame women," snickered Richard, suddenly relishing the opportunity to tangle with Kathleen now that she had most likely ripened into a pretty young woman. He winked sideways at Orwell, "Bro, you know the daughters of preachers or missionaries—they're the worst brats going!"

Orwell rolled his eyes in frustration at this poor excuse for advice on the delicate matter of women. Rick ignored him, and continued to nonchalantly sip his iced lemonade and survey his handiwork to the retaining wall behind the yellow sage beds. His older brother was either totally oblivious to Orwell's tribulation or dismissed it as trifle and moved on. Left to plow his own crooked course,

Orwell glared at Suzy but failed to deflect her teasing comment. She winked impishly and stuck out her tongue at him. Did the sly vixen know some dark secret lurking, like a snake in the grass, to bite him?

A few years back, Orwell remembered getting pulled away from his beloved riverbank, all gussied up, and bundled into his Dad's battered station wagon for a Sunday evening banquet with some snobby church family from a riverside mansion tucked away near the *Storyland Valley Zoo* in Edmonton's exclusive west end. Visits at Cherry Crest were driven by culture and liturgy. Inspirational organ music droned unceasingly from the phonograph...Vivid oil paintings, elegantly potted plants, Persian rugs on marble floors, stuffed animals, and statues of carved wood or alabaster all praised the Creator. He felt that these exquisite artworks scrutinized the children like so many heavenly witnesses whenever they sat quietly on couches in the front reception room, dressed in their Sunday best while the parents conversed, awaiting the master of the house's invitation to dine.

Reverend Wynnard MacDonachie graciously deferred to 'Brother' Jim to offer the dinner grace, but otherwise the renowned evangelist and billionaire entrepreneur dominated the table discussion with rousing travelogues about his exotic business ventures, peppered with deeply scriptural themes. Mrs. MacDonachie's children solemnly ate their meals with downcast eyes and polished etiquette, but Orwell, feeling that the diners were being secretly taped for 'da Rev's' next Bible Hour radio broadcast, furtively scanned the room for hidden microphones. When he wryly noticed that Robert was pretending to be devoutly listening to his father, while secretly tuned into the radio broadcast of his football game via transistor earphone, Robert scowled at this snoop. Blushing and turning away, Orwell caught Annie Fannie studying him with amusement.

After their sumptuous meal, everyone retired to the drawing room to not only sing but also study the Bible. Wynnard again held court. He called upon young adults like Tracy, Robert, or Jane to read the key scripture passage he had chosen for the day. Rev. MacDonachie welcomed questions and passionate debate, but then stamped his own learned interpretation upon God's word. He gathered everyone around the grand piano to dedicate their lives to Jesus and sing with gusto such encouraging revival hymns as "Bringing in the Sheaves" and "Shall We Gather at the River?" These gospel songs were vintage MacDonachie tent revivals soul-savers, though seldom heard during Sunday morning services from the comfortable pews of St. Andrew's.

Alicia happily stood beside Orwell and shared his hymnal during such gatherings. Alicia, wanting to help him, turned pages, found songs, and supportively cued the blushing older lad to any unfamiliar timing. Too humble to flaunt it, Little Missy was an integral part of The *MacDonachie Family Singers*, Edmonton's own finely-tuned, Christian radio and television choir of the 1960s!

On this lovely night shared between good friends, the MacDonachie children's stringed quartet of violins, cello, and double base filled the room with majestic harmony as they richly bowed in concert for their enthralled audience. A polished brass band pealed the woodwork during another fellowship evening; on yet another occasion, Tracy treated everyone to a brilliant piano recital. Only 30 minutes of the children's precious time was required by proud father MacDonachie for show and tell, thank God, after which they were allowed to fade away to other interests awaiting them in secret nooks and crannies around the mansion. A budding musician himself and methodically tutored by Pearl MacDonachie on piano, Orwell was highly impressed by her children's polished output, but he doubted not that much blood, sweat, and tears had been spent perfecting those music acts in the practice studio every night under Wynnard's stern glare and cracking whip.

Orwell, during family get-togethers, was invariably paired with Alvin, a wimpy boy who was deeply lost in his electric trains and stamp collections rather than in exploring riparian forest glades. Richard fared no better! He was shooed in the company of a bespectacled beanpole named Jonathan, whose joy it was to pound away in his room on a miniature piano, like Schroeder from *Peanuts*, the classic tunes of Bach or Mozart while Rick climbed the walls and dreamed of flying spaceships.

James Hughes's sons pined to stay seated as young men of promise beside their father and listen to Wynnard, Tracy, and Robert talk a blue streak about their manly adventures. Tracy endeared himself to Mr. Hughes with his intelligent views on current affairs or social justice; he also engaged in practical, hands-on discussions about engine mechanics, wind power, electric cars, and how to refurbish old farm equipment. Yet, he was a brooding, slouching, shiftless rebel without a plan in the eyes of his father, who felt disappointed by Tracy's failure to build something constructive with his many God-given talents! Small wonder, detractors chirped, when this unruly first born, with his shaggy black hair and hooded, piercing blue eyes, ran with a crowd of unkempt hoodlums, drinking beer and smoking pot, fixing motorcycles or driving hot-rods, boxing, shooting pool, or playing rock music with loud electric guitars rather than serving his parents' many upstanding businesses or fancy house parties. Tracy could not hold a candle to Robert, the household's brush-cut and golden-haired boy, by order and praise of Rev. MacDonachie.

Indeed, Robert was the opposite of his off-beat older brother and diligently followed in his father's footsteps; he was obviously groomed to partner with the tycoon. Robert parroted his father's stern views and bold ambitions. On many social nights, he would go on verbosely about all the money to be made in Alberta's oil patch or boast about going for a sure-fire try-out as a quarterback with the *Edmonton Eskimos*. Robert enthusiastically told all, during yet another adult-males-only billiards game about *Bonne Chance,* the huge ranch he managed up north for some of his dad's big doctor and lawyer friends. Robert boasted how he had invented a machine that chopped poplar saplings into cattle feed, which was a bonus because cows loved poplar... and he was trying to clear the bush of such weeds anyway, to boost the production of spruce and pine for commercial saw logs. Robert also claimed that diamonds, as well as uranium and oil sands, lay waiting to be mined beneath his rugged ponderosa. Orwell, enthralled by his zeal and ingenuity, fell for his sly beckoning and offered to work for this strutting young lord, but Robert, scoffing, told this "*peach-faced boy with hands as soft as a baby's bum to wither away...*"

Suzanne and Janice Joanne patiently read books in the library while the four MacDonachie girls dealt with dinner dishes under the eagle eye of their mother, even as she visited with Mrs. Hughes over tea at the kitchen table. Jane washed as Evelyn put dishes away, but not before their little sisters dried every plate, cup, and eating utensil to a mirror polish. Only after these typically feminine chores were properly done could Jane, the blue-eyed blonde, meet with her fiancé from Bible School to work on her MRS Degree. Evelyn would bury her raven head in a *Harlequin Romance* novel, while Suzanne played her subversive Beatles and Elvis Presley records on the turntable.

Alicia and Kathleen often whisked JJ into some remote corner of the castle to play dolls, but the three brats invariably ended up fighting with Orwell!

"So, what else is new?" moaned Hughes, as Suzy and JJ listened with feigned sympathy. "I should have learned years ago about the wily trouble of a temptress!"

As far back as Orwell could remember, Kitty-Cat and Annie Fannie were double trouble! Despite portraying themselves as pristine ladies to the world, these bratty girls behaved like in-your-face tomboys around the Hughes boys. They fought like lionesses when cornered, and enjoyed teasing their pliable male foes whenever they were forced to play together, whether the battlefield be *Kick the Can* or *Commando* in the woods cladding the Hughes's river valley acreage, table tennis or billiards in the MacDonachie rumpus room, or pounding through supposedly calm board games like *Monopoly, Mouse Trap,* even *Tiddly-Winks* at the lake cottage or church picnic!

"Those conniving MacFemales always get my goat. They secretly plan to beat me and make good on their threats, no matter what I do! Robert laughed at me like I was some feeble piece of shit for getting whipped at ping pong by his 'dumb broad' sisters. My friends howled at me for even learning to smash, loop, push, or chop a white plastic ball over a flimsy net instead of playing the red-blooded, Canadian male game of ice hockey!"

"Our friends like you and Rick a lot, so you'd better be on your toes!" Orwell's impish sisters chimed their warning in unison, while they worked, supposedly together, in the flower gardens of Hughes House.

Rick ignored such threats as childish banter, but his little brother steeled himself for battle. The very idea of becoming wild Fannie's boyfriend terrified him; dark clouds now hovered over his head, threatening torrential rain on an otherwise sunny March afternoon in Lusaka, Zambia.

"Perish the thought!" Orwell rebuked the giggling girls, although he could not forget how Kathleen and Alicia persisted in tagging along whenever he, Richard, and the MacDonachie boys engaged in manly adventures, from river rafting to rock climbing, baseball to fly fishing....

Alicia and Kathleen were endowed with the adventurous MacDonachie spirit, which drove them to follow determinedly where they did not belong—namely in the boys' ambitious footsteps—where they defied Orwell's clumsy efforts to ignore them. Kathleen was a beautiful snob who hated his guts, but Alicia was a more complex girl he managed to get along with, although she had a wild temper and sometimes seemed down-right crazy!

Orwell vowed he never would have noticed this brawny girl with poor eyesight, three years his junior, had Alicia not been JJ's bosom buddy. Janice Joanne idolized her big brother, so he also became Alicia's knight in shining armour. He picked apples and saskatoon berries for them from high in Hughes' fruit trees; patched flat tires on their bicycles; escorted them on river valley hikes and bus rides to the library or swimming pool. He collaborated with them on jigsaw puzzles, watched them tap dance, held their pet rabbits, tied their skates, or played silly board games with them. Alicia was a shy girl, but she placed herself squarely in Orwell's face at odd times and told him her mind—and even dared to argue—bold behaviour forbidden for girls in her fundamentalist Christian family. Orwell made this wallflower laugh, and drew out her well-read knowledge, clever talents for art and sport from behind her sombre, dark-eyed stares. Alicia, amazed and pleased that he listened to her, taught him winning strategies of many games that she learned from Tracy whenever he was home. Orwell enjoyed having Alicia as an ever-willing dance partner at their Church social functions. The young lassie kicked up her heels for the *Highland Fling* and *Virginia Reel,* and carried him through the intricate *Gay Gordons*[27] like nobody's business; let other boys and girls heap scorn at the odd couple! They sat on the sidelines all night, waiting awkwardly for the opposite sex to ask one of them to dance.

Despite his chivalry, Orwell also enjoyed teasing Alicia, even though he felt for her as she was rumoured to have been ripped off from birth. Robert scoffed that his awkward kid sister had been left in a basket on the MacDonachies' mission doorstep while they lived in Nigeria, when only a few days old. She had grown into a reddish-haired, black-eyed, freckled faced, brawny girl—an easy target for rude boys who enjoyed challenging her instant temper. Orwell and his Sunday school mates rowdily stamped their feet in the back of the church recital hall while young Miss MacDonachie squeezed out accordion tunes like a sailor on stage. They whistled while she bounced her Highland dance routines to the

---

27 *The Gay Gordons*: traditional Scottish country dance that is popular at *ceilidhs* and other kinds of social gatherings in Scotland. *The Gay Gordons* dance was popular in the late 19th and early 20th centuries, in which every couple danced the same steps, usually in a circle around the room. Englishman Victor Silvester stated in his 1949 book *Old Time Dancing* that *The Gay Gordons* was created later, between the two World Wars, as part of a wider craze for march-style dances. The name alludes to a Scottish military regiment, the *Gordon Highlanders*.

drone of Tracy's bagpipes. They yanked her pigtails, hid her coke-bottle glasses, pulled away her chair as she sat down, or tripped her to see if white or flowered panties hugged Fannie's round rear. Then the chickens ran away, taunting her to catch them!

On this balmy Saturday afternoon in faraway Africa, Orwell recalled the tenacity of his oft-angry childhood playmate. Alicia never let other kids off the hook if they riled her, and refused to back down from a fight. Long after one who crossed her felt the game was done, Alicia still plotted her revenge. You never knew when or where she would strike back, but by golly that lioness *did,* with strength and ferocity when one least expected her attack! He recalled how Alicia had once played shark in a game of swimming pool tag and chased only him, relentlessly and cunningly, until he collapsed like jelly into her clutches. Or how she had skated down the length and breadth of a skating rink to make him hers, regardless of who else was fair game out there, scraping the boards, or falling on their rears.

Alicia had met him during an intermission at the refreshment table one Sunday eve, after Orwell had nonchalantly tossed a paper airplane at the stage while she performed her Mozart piano recital. The fuming, red-haired *Margaret* to this *Dennis the Menace* had kicked his shin with her buckled shoe to get his attention. Glaring up at her would be tormentor with huge dark eyes, Alicia had exclaimed, *"I know who you are, Oh-well Hughes. I never forget a face, especially an ugly one!"* Then she whipped out a glass of cold water concealed behind her back and splashed him through and through! His cronies cackled at his expense, while several adults smiled in amusement. Alicia left her soaked nemesis speechless as she pranced off, giggling triumphantly with JJ in tow.

"Orly, you'd better watch your mouth when Alicia visits us over Easter," warned Janice Joanne, flashing her haunted brother a wry smile as she handed him a cold glass of lemonade. "She may be prim and proper now, but she has not forgotten how you teased her when all 'Lisa' wanted was to be your pal. You know Lisa is Alicia's preferred nickname, but I've heard you calling her Annie Fannie lately—a name she hates—and tossing out rude comments behind her back.

"She made it amply clear to you years ago not to push her buttons. Don't you remember how Lisa tore up your shirt for calling her that awful Fannie nickname once too often?"

"Yes, and 'Olga the Wrestler' had you pinned helplessly on our front lawn," Suzy added her blazing two-cent's worth. "You turned totally green, man!"

"Don't remind me!" scolded Orwell crossly. "I still have scars from the licking that banshee gave me! Both my shirt and the skin off my chest were torn to ribbons. I missed the *Eskimos* football game that afternoon because of her!"

Fuming now as he recalled that horrible debacle, Orwell turned away from his sisters and resumed weeding with furious vigour; it was good that nobody beaked off at him now! The others chuckled rowdily, but taking their cue from the family gardener, also went back to work. There was plenty of work to be done and daylight was waning. The young poet loved puttering around the verdant tropical garden, but now that his enemy had so brazenly heralded her arrival, he knew his work must finish swiftly, so that he could retreat safely inside his den before nightfall, lest he encounter the lioness hunting him among the shadows outside!

Most fellow males would have ridiculed him without mercy, had they learned, during that dreadful summer of 1968, how a barely teenaged Orwell was not only pounded by a girl but had let her do it! He blamed his humiliation on his father, who had schooled him sternly to never hit a girl. Pleading further in his own defence, Orwell argued to himself that Alicia was bigger than most kids his age… he had been just a runt then, and she could match him. Could she not smack a baseball or throw a dodge ball like any boy on the team?

After Warrior Girl had bushwhacked him with some swift judo moves, Hughes should have tried to fight back, but because she was a girl, he had laid off totally and just did what he could to protect himself. She had refused to let him go until her pent-up fury was drained! What a horrible, humiliating lesson Orwell had endured for simply calling Alicia a name!

He could deal with her flailing fists—even her slicing claws—but he continued to be haunted by her scowling red face and feline eyes bulging beneath her heavy brows, like she was a wild beast, famished, and craving to eat him as prey. What awful words she had uttered, in a harsh voice far older and deeper than her eleven years! Not only had Alicia screamed at him, she had lashed him with chilling oaths, while ripping his shirt like a cat scratches furniture "*Oh-well, you slime, take this… and this… and this!*" and "*How do you like me now, bucko?*" and "*Can't whip a girl your own size now can you, wimp!*" and "*Kiss my big booty if you like it so much!*" and "*I'm gonna whip your butt, Oh-well!*"

While he had writhed on the ground and taken his lumps, mistress Alicia had shown him how deeply he had hurt her feelings and betrayed their special friendship. She had eased up only when he had contritely obeyed her gravelly demands and promised *never* to tease her again.

Suddenly, the fog had cleared and Rick and the girls came running and shouting, frantically followed by their mother. Orwell had felt embarrassed, even as he hoped his rescuers would pull the lioness off him. Alicia sprang up but then awkwardly slumped on the grass, sobbing in shame. *"I am so sorry, Orwell! Mrs. Hughes, I'm not my real self! I was wrong to rip his shirt. Forgive me!"* she blubbered to her stunned hosts.

Orwell hoped to block out his churning memories, but soon, a little helper diligently weeded beside him in the mother-in-law tongues and black-eyed Susan's who could read his mind.

"You and Alicia both said sorry to each other before you were sent to your room and my friend went home bedraggled," JJ reminded Orwell while they kept their noses to the grindstone. "Even though you started that fight, Alicia forgave you—because she trusts that you now understand her better. She gifted you with that crucifix for your baptism, which she fashioned herself during Industrial Arts class from Windchaser's own shoe nail. Remember?"

"Really?" Orwell replied cautiously, uncertain of his release. Any girl who chose carpentry and metal work over sewing and cooking had to be taken with a grain of salt.

"Don't worry, Orly, Alicia has grown up too over the last five years. Just give her another chance," JJ gently assured him. "You really were quite noble, but also humble and kind in the way you behaved toward my friend—Lisa has praised you many times for this in her letters."

This imp must be joking, trying to trip him up, Orwell surmised as he sternly scrutinized his nodding, smiling sister. Yet, the longer he paid her mind, the more he was flooded with queasy recollections long suppressed that he had verbally forgiven Alicia and helped her get up, showing his attacker that he too was distraught and crying as they had looked each other briefly in the face. When he had stammered his own heartfelt apology to Alicia for all his teasing, her wounded heart had melted. She had broken free and fled, head down and sobbing afresh, to the back porch to hide. Orwell recalled that he had wanted to seek Alicia, but was immobilized by his own clumsy inability to deal with weepy girls. He had felt sorry for the unruly brat, who was always being yelled at, spanked, or sent to her room at home for 'acting up', and now would be sorely disciplined for tearing his Sunday shirt! He had been sent to his room to change while his mother and sisters had held a heart-to-heart talk with their distressed young visitor. A phone call had been made to the MacDonachie home, and a short while later, Orwell had seen from his bedroom window Tracy drive up in his hot-rod, scowling behind his dark sunglasses and smoking a cigarette, to fetch Alicia home in disgrace for supper.

"You don't know and probably couldn't care what happened to Lisa after she left that day!"

"I did not see Alicia again for months. How would I know anything?"

"Obviously, she got grounded for what she did! Her parents prevented us from playing together, except on special occasions only when parentally supervised. They bused Lisa up north to work for Robert as ranch kitchen help for the rest of the summer. Come fall, Alicia was placed in some upscale, all-girls' academy across town. Any extra time away from her grindstone of schoolwork and chores was channelled into music or competitive athletics. If ever I saw Alicia at church, it was only briefly during Sunday school class, when we were not allowed to chat—then the MacDonachies flew away home before I could turn around! It was like they didn't want Lisa and I together anymore, but we vowed that not even her parents or frickin' Robert could stifle our friendship. It's sad but true: I have not gone with my friend since, only communicated with her in letters—but Orly, what fun we've had being pen pals and now, Lisa is coming to visit me in Africa! She'll be living and breathing in our house forty days from now!"

"Rains that caused the great Genesis flood lasted forty days!" Orwell blandly reminded her, only to be smacked by JJ's buoyant reply.

"Thank God for rainbows!"

JJ sang happily "Puff the Magic Dragon" to herself, one of the girls' favourite songs that Alicia had performed as a guest celebrity on the children's afternoon TV show *Popcorn Playhouse*. Orwell shuddered meanwhile as he inwardly recalled a weird, chance meeting with the strapping girl, post ripped shirt, in a downtown department store, back in '69 when he was fifteen and Warrior Girl was twelve. His family was preparing to go to Africa on his father's diplomatic assignment, while Alicia was training in table tennis and curling for the Alberta

Winter Games. As he wandered through *Woodward's* department store, on his way to the bus stop, Hughes spied the tall girl admiring earrings in the woman's boutique. Orwell hardly recognized his nemesis, dressed as she was in turtleneck sweater and dark slacks, rather than in some fancy Sunday dress; her rich auburn hair was tied back in a simple ponytail instead of styled in curly ringlets. She had removed her thick glasses and was closely examining some piece of jewellery when he cautiously moved in to stammer a polite hello, but Alicia, for whatever reason... perhaps still smarting from their past battles, flashed Orwell a stern look with her huge ebony eyes. He fled her icy glare down the aisle, around the corner, and up an escalator. It was only after the fugitive reached the top and ducked behind a mannequin that she relented, cracked a sly smile, and waved goodbye....

"I'm glad Tracy is coming here soon, but I need a visit from pesky Alicia and Kathleen now like a hole in the head," railed Orwell, hours later as he helped his mother take down dry clothes from the line and fold them into a large plastic basket. "Why do they have to come now, when I've got a myriad of other issues to deal with? We'll be home in six months, for God's sake! We can rendezvous then."

"I think their visit will do us all some good. I've known you young'uns from those days not so long ago when you were all in diapers," clucked Martha, without missing a beat in the folding department. "Just like your father and I, Wynnard and Pearl MacDonachie have raised their brood wholesomely—from free-spirited Tracy whom you admire, right down to his two sisters whom now you mock—in nurture and admonition of the Lord! You children are of a similar clan, and will help each other grow stronger in your walk with Christ Jesus. I believe that His timing is perfect in every experience for those who fear God. He answers prayers and acts for our best interests, even when we least expect Him to, when we don't understand or see His love for us.

"You kids sent the invitation in earnest and the MacDonachies have responded positively; we are friends, even though we live worlds apart! Orly, I know that your sisters are glad for the promised fellowship of their girlfriends; Tracy, although considerably older and worldlier than you, also wants to come. Is he an answer to your prayers? You guys seem to get along well and thrive on each other's presence. I hope you kids will respond graciously to this gift and make the MacDonachies' visit fun. Your father and I will certainly do our part."

Weighing everything in the balance, Orwell took comfort by what he had heard. He embraced his mother's view to the good life of following that straight and narrow road, with God and His angels as travel mates. If only he could tell her how much he loved her, that he longed to respect her belief in faithful, moral living! How *naive* his mother was, basking in her own pleasant dreams and refusing to speculate what wrong her children were capable of doing!

"Imagine the unthinkable: me, flirting with Kitty or Fannie MacDonachie!" Orwell sighed as he hoisted the pile-high basket smoothly aloft like a weightlifter and carried it on his head into the house for his mother, while she strode ahead to hold open the kitchen door for him. "Those delicious apples may be ripe for picking, but they will stay securely on their tree, as such perfect fruit are not meant to spoil!"

Martha laughed at the wild look on his face, but then offered her knowing response, "It is not you who I worry about, Son. I hope you will set a good example for the other young folks."

Orwell dutifully carried the basket into the laundry room and set it on the bench for his mother. He helped her sort clothing into piles for each member of the household to claim and put away in their own wardrobes. As pleased as he was that his mother appreciated his help, Orwell nonetheless was troubled that she somehow perceived him to be her reliable, upstanding son, incapable of doing wrong. What harm could come about anyway from a pleasant Easter visit by Sunday school friends from back home? With these turbulent thoughts tumbling inside his brain, the young poet grabbed his own pile of clothes and retreated gloomily to his bedroom.

Re-emerging soon after, Orwell briefly surveyed the tranquil world that continued to revolve around him. Rick, who was setting the table for supper while listening to the BBC via a shortwave radio he had recently built from a kit, seemed as far away from any worries as jolly old England was from her former colony. Suzy played Beethoven's "Moonlight Sonata" on the piano, as JJ danced to the lilting music while watering house plants. Bwana Hughes chatted pleasantly with his wife in the kitchen as he chopped veggies for the stew pot. Everyone was so happy!

"Announcements! Announcements! An-now-unce-ments!" Orwell blew his horn for all to hear. "Everybody, listen up. Your clothes are in from the line—please put them away!"

His siblings gazed gregariously at their would-be herald before surprising him by actually checking out what he had told them. Feeling vindicated, Orwell claimed the already well-read *Zambia Daily Mail* newspaper and sat down on the living room couch like a young prince. He pulled the chain on the lamp at his elbow to give a spot of light against the gathering dusk. He rested, aware that he was on tap to wash dishes later that night. Orwell read with great interest about the unfolding Watergate scandal in the US, 'Idiot' Amin's rampages in Uganda, the radical nationalization of commerce under Mobuto in Zaire, and the more sensible Zambianization of industry and institutions at 'home'. Advertisements of the latest Hollywood and Indian movies now playing in town also piqued his interest, while the football scores of the *Kabwe Warriors* and *Mufulira Wanderers* and upbeat reports from tennis and golf tournaments left a pleasant aftertaste.

Caught up in the vibrant spirit of anticipation that was seeping into his family's dull routine, Orwell found his own thoughts filling with hope of Tracy's visit. He imagined his mentor sitting with him now, confident and debonair, as they relaxed, sipping on ice-cold Cokes and munching roasted groundnuts in the cool of the day; Tracy would help him make sense of how to relate with eligible young women, racism, and where his joys and sorrows could fit into the big game of life.

"Who are you talking to, Orly, the walls?" asked Suzy suddenly, from somewhere beyond his view. "You're yakking a blue streak!"

"What?"

Orwell was jolted out of his happy daydreaming by his sisters' laughter. Squinting into dark corners of the room, he finally spied the dainty shapes of Suzanne and JJ as they peered from around the corner of the well-lit kitchen.

"Bro, you provided us with some fantastic dinner theatre," chuckled Richard as he ceremoniously followed the girls, bearing their dinner stew in a large clay bowl. Rick gave him a thumb's up salute as Orwell sheepishly trudged to the table and sat in his designated chair. "You should be in show business. Maybe old Tiptoe will teach you the ropes when he comes to town."

"You two clowns can play ukuleles and sing a falsetto duet as you tip-toe through the tulips together," teased Suzy as she sassily connected Orwell's mentor with *Tiny Tim*, who Tracy had been saddled with by Rev. MacDonachie as a nickname to fight or die over. Johnny Cash's rugged ballad *A Boy Named Sue* came to mind. Her quips orchestrated another bout of sibling laughter at now scowling Orwell's expense.

"Just like you pesky young'uns, Orly is looking forward with eager excitement to our joyful reunion with Alicia, Kathleen, and Tracy", Mom noted sympathetically as she brought in a platter heaped with freshly baked biscuits.

Bwana Hughes, last to arrive, gave his second son a quizzical glance, but kept his comments to himself as he placed the juice pitcher and took his seat as head of the table. He discouraged further heckling of his namesake, not so much by casting a portrait of sobriety to the children, but by asking Orwell to seek God's blessing on the meal.

Orwell fantasized that night of making passionate love with Hollywood stars Raquel Welch and Jane Fonda—even European beauties like Brigitte Bardot and Sophia Loren—having been schooled with charm and confidence by Tracy on how to win the heart of every cinema goddess whose press clippings filled his scrap books. Suddenly, Georgina's beguiling face danced into his dream, surrounded by more seasoned suitors, but daring him to also compete for her attention. Orwell woke up with a start, his heart aching for Tracy, his romantic gladiator, to show him how to woo this fair maiden! Would God really fulfill his heart's desire?

Falling back to sleep, he dreamed about mermaids frolicking in the moonlit sea. They initially took no notice of him as he strolled like Adonis on their storybook beach, and watched these wondrous creatures body surf and race each other as the waves carried them powerfully towards shore. As he waited for them at the finish line, these beauties started to sing and laugh, exuberantly called his name as they waved to him—yet they would not leave the water to meet their admirer.

Out of the corner of his eye, Orwell suddenly glimpsed the flash of a tail and shapely torso of one mermaid swimming powerfully towards him, as though bent upon winning the race and receiving his congratulations. He marvelled at her lithe body gleaming in the quickening twilight, and pined to spirit her away, so that he could embrace her energy and stroke her wild red hair as she serenaded him. When gallantly he came forward to invest this smiling heroine with her gold medal, however, the dream turned dark as Orwell realized that she was haggard with fear, neither a svelte bunny from *Frankie and Annette* beach movies nor his elusive Georgina! Miss Amadu hung back, but failed to help another sea girl with blonde hair who was drowning or being dragged under by some unseen predator of the deep, and was desperately crying out for help. He felt a deep urge to save them all from their unseen enemies and protect their flight to sanctuary. The foremost siren must be Alicia, but how did that once heavy girl become so sleek and lovely? Tracy must have coached her well and trained her rigorously. *Who* was that drowning blonde babe so needy of his rescue? Surely, not one of those shy but hard-working, van der Merwe farm girls from church?

Alicia remained his familiar yet bewildering rival for Tracy's affection. In reality, the amazon would never stoop so low as to seek Orwell's help, even in her worst hour, but what trouble would she inflict upon him instead during her looming visit? Where previously Orwell had found deep peace and freedom in his own lazy aquatics, to dream that this enchantress would clinch her victory against him in Africa was suddenly charge enough to propel him with torpedo speed through life's oceans....

Orwell awoke with a start and found himself drenched with sweat.

"Sweet Lord! What do you want me to do? What are you trying to teach me?" he muttered, confused by the weird turn his dream had taken, yet determined not to wake his brother who slept like a log on the far side of the dark, airy room. "I do not need this crap; I don't understand it! Speak to me God."

Exhausted, he lay heavily in his bed and stared blankly at the curtain that danced in the soft, evening breezes blowing through the open window. He listened intently to crickets singing somewhere beyond the even rise and fall of Rick's blissful snores. His brother reminded distraught Orwell of a pleasure ship floating upon gentle seas.

Lightning did not flash nor did some thunderous voice call out his name from on high, but Orwell smiled as he remembered being taught by Mrs. MacDonachie in Sunday school, Jesus' simple but comforting words, *"Consider the lilies of the field, how they grow; they toil not, neither do they spin: And yet I say unto you that not even Solomon in all his glory was arrayed like one of these. Wherefore, if God so clothes the grass of the field, which today blooms and tomorrow is cast into the oven, shall he not much more clothe you, O ye of little faith?"*

# CHAPTER SIX

ORWELL ARRIVED HOME FROM UNIVERSITY feeling energized yet apprehensive about the night's special social event: his debut as a reader at the university Writers' Club. Intending to look his best, he planned to bathe and change into fashionable evening clothes before supper. He thus barely found time to greet his father and brother, let alone marvel that Bwana Hughes was home early as he hurried past while they sharpened blades of the push mower in the backyard. Orwell chained his bike and went in the house, where supper was barely underway, although the circular wall clock pointed its hands at twelve and five. As he made his way through the kitchen, he encountered his sisters arguing with their mother, but Orwell dared not get involved. He trained his eyes straight ahead and rushed to claim the bathroom.

Fifteen minutes later, young Hughes was back in his bedroom, pulling on terry towel socks and bellbottom slacks. He applied *Brylcreem* to his blond hair, and then slicked it back. He liberally applied roll-on deodorant, and as though ensuring divine protection, hung around his neck the iron crucifix Alicia had given him. Orwell rummaged through his wardrobe looking for the right cotton dress shirt and settled on an open-collared, purple one that would fit the bill nicely. Feeling hip, Orwell marched out of his room in a happy mood, only to have a downer when he found his mother still in the midst of her lecture.

Suzanne pouted bleakly as she spooned a can of herring in tomato sauce into a frying pan. JJ looked flushed as she made sure the rice did not boil over. Mrs. Hughes spoke sternly to both her daughters as she sliced cucumbers into a platter at the table behind them.

"Truly, Suzanne and Janice Joanne, I am glad that some clean, spiritual folk are coming down here to visit, but these vulgar plans of yours to act out while they are here must stop. Our MacDonachies will not go for such foolish behaviour! They are Christian movers and shakers who will inject some much-needed productivity into you lazy kids. Imagine, lounging all day by the swimming pool, listening to rock music, and sipping martinis—entertainment that is totally foreign to Zambia's indigenous people. You're a pack of bored and pampered girls, who behave like fish out of water without all your Canadian amenities!

"Suzanne, you need to watch yourself around young men—like this suave Ali fellow who drives you about in his fancy sports car! Do you intend for Kathleen to joy ride with him also? I want you to bring Ali over to meet us."

"Mom," argued Suzy indignantly. "Ali is Georgina's brother. He came here last Christmas with Orwell's hot date, remember? What about Orly and Georgie?"

"Both your father and I wish to talk with you and Ali, very soon. Do you hear me?"

When Suzanne whimpered a feeble, "Uh-huh." Martha continued, "You have the opportunity of a lifetime here to explore cultures much different from what you know. The MacDonachies, who grew up in Africa for part of their childhood, will be fascinated to be re-immersed in its exotic sights and sounds; they'll surely want to meet your Zambian friends. Take this chance yourselves to get renewed."

Orwell thought his Mom was right on! Zambia's vibrant life was going on outside, for them to explore, but every moment of procrastination brought the Hughes clan toward that fateful day when they would leave this enchanted kingdom. Yes, they were guests in a foreign culture, and Orwell painfully knew that it was nigh impossible to erase all fears and prejudice; sometimes, he wished he could assimilate into mainstream African culture and stay forever with a local wife like Georgina or Molly, but unlike these enthralling lovelies, he was not African and never could be! The youth of Canadian diplomats in Zambia held different interests and experiences from their native age-mates ... At least Orwell could boast that he and his siblings had laboured diligently to count many Zambians among their friends. It was not as easy as his mother would have it, Orwell wished to record.

Benjamin, David, and Solomon were his pals, but could Orwell really envisage the MacDonachies mingling freely at some young peoples' party with these local folks? Their father was a celebrated missionary and business tycoon who had made his fortune foraging the globe while proselytizing for God, but did Tracy and his sisters remember what it truly meant to be African? They had lived as the naïve, pampered children of a white master on his clean and sheltered missionary compound prior to the winds of change blowing across the continent.

To hang around the necks of these visitors the onerous responsibility of leading Lusaka's tight community of wealthy expatriate youth on a whirlwind journey of self-realization and dialogue with indigenous masses was like asking the blind to lead the blind. No doubt, Tracy and the girls would eagerly accept this cultural challenge and burn themselves out in order to succeed, for their ignorant idealism would rush them in where angels feared to tread! Orwell, a student of Africa, failed to unite his white peers and bring the Dark Continent into their hearts—so why ask greenhorns from half a world away to do the impossible? Mom was such a dreamer!

Orwell was jolted back to reality when his father, who had wandered in like a hungry bear snooping for food, flashed a letter under his nose. The lad nearly fainted when he recognized the imposing handwriting of Tracy MacDonachie, his boyhood idol—here was a plum for the evening! Orwell had already heard thrilling rumours of the giant's coming from Mrs. Bingham and the MacFemales, but *here* was the solid promise, penned by the hand of the Master himself!

"Tracy is coming to Lusaka with his sisters at Easter," Orwell duly confirmed what was already common knowledge. Suzy and JJ exchanged wry grins, amused by his effort to make exciting such tiresome repetition. As the herald dug deeper into his airmail, he cheered to find bigger and better news!

"Tracy will cultivate some hot local business opportunities he is following for his dad, but he also wants to learn first-hand, through my eyes and ears, what pressing community development and social justice issues in Zambia need a boost from concerned Christians back home. Our friend is also relying on *me* to show him the interesting cultural festivities and natural history sights in this corner of the globe. He mentions Victoria Falls, Serengeti Plains, Mount Kilimanjaro, and Luangwa Valley for starters!"

"Like, bro, those wonders are hundreds of miles apart!" whistled Rick in awe. "Tracy's travelling in high gear... Is he a rocketeer, flying about by jet-pack?"

"What a showman! MacDonachie puts a finger in every pie that he lays his hands on," quipped Bwana Hughes, happy for his second son, yet appearing dryly amused. He marvelled at this bizarre twist of fate, but had a million questions hovering in the back of his analytical, bureaucratic mind over the legitimacy of Tracy's latest brainstorm. "Like his father, that big wheel is always rolling, making the largest splash possible in every project that he undertakes!

"But I did not think Tracy would be his father's errand boy, although I am certain that Reverend MacDonachie's finely-tuned, evangelistic machine and billions of investment dollars will offer him strong backing. Nonetheless, Tracy is an entertainer—not an entrepreneur—he marches to a different, gentler drummer, and may not be the best choice to investigate opportunities here in Zambia."

"Dad, Tracy is coming here of his own accord. He expresses his own heartfelt interests and concerns as a fellow Christian," insisted Orwell in wild-eyed approval of his mentor. "Neither Tracy nor his sisters claim to represent some big, bad establishment in their bold foray; I think they would loathe such a commission."

"Did you not just mention he was coming to cultivate business opportunities for his father? Without Daddy's support, how does our noble zealot intend to build schools, pipe clean water, or provide tractors and farm chemicals to rural villages from a youth pastor's meagre salary?" Bwana Hughes reasonably inquired.

"Tracy has faith enough to move mountains; he is supported by many diverse folks who also believe that God provides richly to those who ask in faith," Orwell added, his face flushed with devout fervour. His indomitable spirit troubled his father but inspired his mother. Orwell's face shone as he came down from his mountaintop with bold explanation, "Tracy serves God where he is, but he has not always been a mere youth pastor. He made good money as a young man on the oil rigs, then he continued to build his wealth as a professional musician and sportsman. He's done reasonably well—without cow-towing to the *Silver Lining Corporation*—and made lasting friends around the world through those endeavours! They, like me, will help him succeed in his noble plans!"

Jim Hughes had always harboured nagging doubts about the soundness of Tracy's character, but he inwardly rejoiced that Orwell's spirits were soaring again. He could tolerate his renewed enthusiasm for life because the lad had suffered through a long dark night of the soul these last months. At times he had behaved more like some screech owl than his gifted namesake, but Tracy had once more successfully reached out to restore his protégé. What potions did rugged MacDonachie employ to conjure such steadfast loyalty in his deep thinker of a son? What was the purpose of their connection, anyway?

"Please refresh my memory, boy. What did our illustrious mover and shaker do that Canadians should remember him by?" Bwana Hughes dared ask.

"My God, Dad—get with the program!" scolded Orwell. "Tracy loved ice hockey. He was good enough to play for the *Edmonton Oil Kings* and would probably have made it to the NHL, had his dad let him practice on Sundays—an unpardonable sin in Rev. MacDonachie's Bible! He then laboured tirelessly as a pianist and glee club singer for the man's old-time religion programs, which paid off later when Tracy performed professionally with pop, rock, or gospel bands at dance halls or nightclubs, albeit at his father's displeasure.

"Tracy not only excelled academically, but was an all-around athlete throughout high school and Bible college, where he did track and field as well as played baseball, basketball, and—as mentioned—hockey. He once showed me all the trophies and medals he had won at various events, which filled a glass case that would cover the length of our living room! As you know, he won many cash bonspiels in men's curling, too! He was also a provincial table tennis champion, and a successful amateur boxer at seminary; it was in boxing that Tracy turned pro."

"From the way you talk, Orwell, it's a wonder your friend had any time to study, let alone eat and sleep, with all his demanding extracurricular activities. I understand why Tracy never graduated: he burned himself out playing sports! Athletics, writing, music, girls—all good pursuits of course, but they should be taken in moderation, like one glass of red wine with supper!" pontificated Bwana Hughes. And pointing his finger at his flustered second son, the man of the house declared, "I don't want the same thing to happen to you, Son. Your focus at the moment should be university; successfully finish your studies and write your exams. Those other interests you cultivate have merit, but in the crunch, field hockey, creative writing, and girlfriends are secondary—window dressing if you like. I don't want you needlessly burning your candles at both ends. Don't blow your opportunities, Orly—like Tracy did!"

Feeling overburdened by his old man's lecture, Orwell backed further and further down the kitchen wall until he was bent awkwardly over the arborite counter top. Taking exception at this last unwarranted swipe at his friend, however, Orwell rose up indignantly.

"Dad! Tracy was ranked by the international boxing federation as one of the world's top heavy-weight pugilists when he retired from the ring two years ago. He beat the majority of other contenders of his era, and was in line for a shot at the world title. Had my friend been a bit younger and better connected, Tracy 'Iron Horse' MacDonachie instead of George Foreman would be fighting Muhammad Ali in *The Rumble in the Jungle* later this year! Just imagine, I could be in Kinshasa, Zaire, cheering him on!"

"So, what happened to him?"

"Tracy's fortunes ran a little dry some years ago, which is why everyone figured that Iron Horse was washed up. Tracy certainly proved his detractors wrong over the years! His days of ring glory may have faded somewhat with time, but I'll bet that Tracy could still make a comeback if he chose to. For sure, he'd make short work of the Zambian champion, Leopard Milongwe, who claims to represent all Africa and boasts to be the number one contender among the world's heavy-weights. Milongwe is just some stiff for Tracy to knock over on his way back to the top!"

By now, the kitchen was reverberating with laughter at Orwell's furious defence of his illustrious hero. Orwell could not take much ribbing when his sensitive nerves were being touched, and Jim's quizzical look only made things worse, though he insisted he had simply wanted a clarification of Tracy's credentials. Nobody missed the fact that Orwell was enjoying a vital high.

This moved Martha's mothering instinct, but she asked the wrong question when she tried to rescue her embattled lad, by wondering whether Stephanie and her boys were coming to Lusaka to cheer their man on. Martha found inspiration in this Florence Nightingale, whom she imagined to be balm for Tracy's tempestuous life, though Orwell and Alicia jointly dismissed Stephanie as an albatross around their hero's sea-faring soul. Martha and her son had a brisk debate as to whether Tracy and Stephanie were a match made in Heaven. To Orwell's chagrin, the wild rover was viewed as a very fortunate man indeed to be married to such a wonderful woman, in the discerning eyes of Martha Hughes and other wise matrons of St. Andrew's church.

"Mom, I don't see any reference to the wife and kids in this cable," he muttered, trying to conceal his relief, after having meticulously re-read Tracy's letter.

Besides, the fight game was no place for wives or children, particularly when they had been raised in the church and knew nothing about the real world! Stephanie was a fish out of water in Tracy's rough and tumble circles! Better to leave her securely in her bubble, nursing her babies and reading her Bible, than to haul her and kids into the wild, insect-infested jungles of southern Africa to cringe as her stud pulverized another boxer! Had not Stephanie and her plush family vowed to end Tracy's mighty stake in this so-called violent and vainglorious sideshow? Imagine, a high-society Christian saint married to a callous rogue who beat up other men for money and praise; she bid to keep her wild man locked in a cage! No music, art, or church service could erase the brutal fact that Tracy was a fighter. Orwell sensed that Tracy would never redeem his sport in the disapproving eyes of Stephanie's high church, when all she wanted was for him to be born-again as a mild-mannered dandy and returned to seminary! His wife could not accept Tracy's ministry to the poor and oppressed, as long as athletics remained in his blood!

"I'm shocked that Reverend MacDonachie would allow his young, virgin daughters to travel so far from home in the dangerous company of his rebel son Tracy, so I'll be a monkey's uncle if Stephanie and her boys are part of his road show!" groused Orwell.

"Maybe Tiptoe kidnapped his siblings, aiming to bring them down here as wampum to secure one of his dad's shifty business deals!" Richard guffawed from the peanut gallery. Orwell glared at his brother, but he was the only diehard Tracy fan who saw no humour in Richard's teasing banter. "Who knows? Perhaps, Kitty-Cat and Annie Fannie are meant to behave as bodyguards for our jolly Sunday school teacher."

Enraged by these slights, Orwell stamped after Richard as he, having drawn the curtain on this pointless discussion, swaggered out of the kitchen to watch television until supper was served. Orwell attacked his unsuspecting brother in the living room, fists flailing and screaming to extract an apology for the illustrious Tracy. Cushions flew and the couch nearly collapsed under the weight of the two wrestling brothers, opposite as night and day. Although Orwell was the wildcat aggressor, he still made no impact on cool dude Rick, who swiftly beat this foe into submission. Rick had gained mastery over his unrepentant little brother by the time JJ and Suzy raced to ringside.

Bwana Hughes behaved more like a stampede wrestler than a career diplomat as he broke up the short-lived donnybrook.

"Cool it, you punks, or I'll tan both your hides!" growled the old bull. "If this is how Tracy gets you all worked up, he shan't be coming here!"

He threw Rick aside and pulled rumpled but snarling Orwell off the floor. He then glowered sternly at Rick, who backed off without a word, combing his barely disturbed hair. Spinning Orwell around like a top to face him, Jim demanded, “Son, we will talk about this later...if you still intend to dash off to your Writers’ Club tonight, we’d better get cracking and finish dinner.”

Orwell was surprised that his father cared a whit about his Writer’s Club meeting. Indeed, Bwana Hughes had recently been pushing him to shelve his foolish artistic notions for good in favour of finishing his studies and turning to a real trade like carpentry, bricklaying, or auto mechanics, to fall back on in case of hardship. Passionate to be an author, Orwell recomposed himself and confirmed his unpopular choice.

“Yes, I want to go—I must attend this meeting!” the young poet vowed as they made their way back to the dining table. “Dad, tonight is my turn to read one of my works to the members.”

“One of your works?” scoffed his dad, unconcerned by his son’s feelings. Winking slyly at Richard, who nonchalantly straightened his collar before the wall mirror, Jim sighed, “Which novel is it this time?”

“It’s that drivel about the night watchman we hired during your trip last year to Sudan,” piped up tricky Dick, smiling in the mirror at his deflated brother. “Orly couldn’t get any decent story written in time, so he’s bringing that skeleton out of his closet again.”

“Man, it’s a darn good yarn!” retorted Orwell, stung afresh by his faithless detractors. “Look, my secondary school English teacher gave me a top grade, called it a masterpiece. She remarked that my literary style and perception showed much promise.”

“Perhaps, but a writer’s salary—if there *is* such a thing—won’t put food on your table or clothe your family. I’ve heard that your Writers’ Club is really a front for hotbed political rebellion…You’re supposed to be studying tropical agriculture out there at UNZA, not plotting thrillers?” pressed Bwana Hughes, showing concern as he stared at Orwell over his glasses. “Orly, this guard story could be judged by your colleagues as a satire of their local African society—not social justice as you see it through youthful, untrained eyes. Remember, your exposé sheds an uncomplimentary light upon Lusaka’s society and institutions—particularly the national police force. You pit yourself against your listeners, so that you come out smelling like roses at their expense! That's a dangerous line to follow over here.

"Will your peers even relate to your feelings of being a stranger in their strange land, as you portray in your critique? Such might seem very alien and obscure to them—the experience of spoiled or even bigoted expat to your proud and learned African novelist friends. If you value those hard-won friendships, you want to be careful not to provoke the club members by tossing them a hot potato!"

"But Dad," argued Orwell defensively. "It's a true story; our experiences had a profound influence on my life, and should be shared. I must honour my feelings."

"I know what I would do!" declared Jim, thoroughly unimpressed by his son's entreaty.

It seemed obvious to Orwell that his father wanted him to obediently scrap his daring idea, and back down like any normal kid would do. Then again, as the old codger often acknowledged, Orwell was no normal kid! He stubbornly made his own way and liked to learn the hard way about life at the school of hard knocks. Meanwhile, all Jim wanted was for his sons to tap into his storehouse of wisdom and experience, so as to avoid the unnecessary and painful mistakes of youth. Yes, thank you Dad, but Orwell was frustrated time and time again that his authoritarian father deigned not to spell out his wishes or verbalize his advice. He was a strong, proud, and silent man who spoke in riddles if at all to those who followed in his footsteps. Orwell was stubborn enough to hold his ground.

"Dad, we'd better go over to the campus *tout de suite*. My meeting starts in 30 minutes," snapped Orwell as he fidgeted in his chair behind his empty plate. Orwell had wolfed down his supper in order to beat the clock and get to the Writer's Club meeting on time, while Jim and Richard dawdled over their meal amid avid discussions about the latest test flight of the new supersonic, jumbo jetliner, the *Concorde*—awesomely made in collaboration between England and France.

"Why all the hype? The damn thing looks like a giant Canada goose, for God's sake," Orwell fumed, fed up he was being painted into a corner by his overbearing father and brother.

"Don't gun me, boy! You're just a whippersnapper, so keep your opinions to yourself and don't interrupt," lectured Jim as the women squirmed uncomfortably in the suddenly heated atmosphere. Much as they hated washing dishes, JJ and Suzy scurried into the scullery when called away by Mother hen. Oblivious to their retreat, Jim demanded, "Orly, how do you propose to get to your blessed gathering?"

"By car, of course," grouched Orwell. The young poet gave Rick a stern glance as he arose impatiently from the table.

"But how, Orly, do you intend to drive to the campus? It's twenty miles away by tarred road and nightfall has come, precluding that you ride your bike *sans* light," continued Bwana Hughes, trying to reason with his fuming offspring while scrutinizing his every nervous word and gesture. "You don't know anything about handling a motor vehicle."

"I thought you were going to drive me, Dad..." trailed Orwell, fit to be tied.

Did his austere old man demand a pound of flesh as well as total submission before he would stoop to humour his son? Feeling his pride and dignity seeping away, Orwell could no longer conceal his exasperation. Despite floundering like a fish on the beach, the lad had the gall to rasp, "I thought that's what you meant by, 'we should get cracking' earlier. And why don't you guys teach me how to drive? If you could simply put enough faith in my abilities, I'd get my goddam driver's licence! Then, you wouldn't have to chauffeur me around like some stupid child!"

Put-off by this missile charging so unexpectedly from under a paper cup, Bwana Hughes tossed his car keys to Richard and gruffly commanded, "Here, Rick, take this kid out of my hair! Glory be, three drivers and two cars in this household surely ought to be enough!"

"Good luck, Orly," whispered Martha, planting a warm kiss on her son's forehead as he fled from the bungalow. Smiling sympathetically, she reassured him, "I understand your passion for the arts, because it flows in my veins too, and I also hunger to harness such passion for good. We budding authors should stick together and encourage each other.

"And dear, be careful out there; stern and pragmatic as your dad is, he has your best interests at heart. He loves you and cares deeply for your endeavours. Father holds a sound argument concerning your short story about the guard that should be heeded. Listen to his sage words of wisdom, my lad."

Orwell took in his mother's soothing words and the soft look in her eyes, but his soul burned with envy when his brother swaggered smoothly past to go fire up the Peugeot station wagon. Little JJ, so often trodden underfoot, rescued Orwell from his anguish. She scurried out from behind her mother's apron strings and gave her brother a warm farewell hug. Her sunny grin drifting upwards from her pixie face wished Orwell *bonne chance* in tonight's uncertain venture; JJ's innocent efforts to bring healing were finally rewarded by the sheepish smile appearing on her big brother's face. Orwell playfully tousled the imp's bouncy brown curls as his mother looked on in amusement and admiration. She was grateful that a glint of humour was finally breaking through his heavy brow.

"Although your father and I don't fully approve of Tracy MacDonachie—nor his high-rolling father—we are very glad that your friend and his sisters are coming to visit us, Orwell," shared Martha hopefully. "Tracy is very special to your heart; his encouragement greatly spurs your own self-confidence. This uplifting attention that Tracy lavishes is a gift that you need from such a successful and ambitious fellow. You have a special treat to look forward to, I dare say!"

"Thanks Mom," Orwell replied, appreciating her gentle encouragement. He grinned as he darted away.

For Orwell, his long-awaited evening of reckoning now held no hidden anxieties, but promised only breathless anticipation towards Tracy's glorious coming. His spirits buoyed and his Adrenalin pumping at the thought of his mentor watching over him like a guardian angel, Orwell dove into the car through the passenger door that Richard had sullenly thrown open. Clearly, this gymnastic feat startled his elder brother, who gazed incredulously at his beaming passenger as they sped away. Bwana Hughes joined his wife on the porch and smoked his pipe pensively as they watched the Peugeot drive off. Even Suzanne, reading on the couch, took passing notice through a crack in the Venetian blinds. What did it all mean?

# CHAPTER SEVEN

ORWELL HUGHES SHEEPISHLY ENTERED THE darkened campus amphitheatre just as the first author began reading his manuscript. There was no place for Orwell to hide from his peers, but nobody dwelt upon him other than sigh or flack him with disgruntled tongue clacks as he tripped past several well-dressed listeners and slid into a shadowy pew high in the back. The lonely foreigner recognized Benjamin Mudenda, his loyal Zambian friend, transfigured behind the podium, addressing a large and attentive gathering of fellow Africans. Hughes was immediately distraught that he had arrived late at Ben's defence, but a warm nod from the elegant bard welcomed Orwell into his realm of literary magic. This uplifting stroke of acknowledgement helped to allay the lad's uncertainty as to his status and purpose in this forum. Reassured that he was welcomed to stay, Orwell inhaled the dynamic literature of new Africa.

Benjamin Mudenda was a devout Christian who walked his faith talk; he led UNZA's Campus Christian Fellowship and was choirmaster where Hughes attended church. This medical student had nearly completed his first degree, and would be leaving Zambia come October for a hospital residency in the UK. Standing nattily attired in a pinstripe suit before his esteemed literary colleagues, Mudenda already spoke with a polished Oxford accent. His owlish eyes floated majestically behind horn-rimmed glasses; his handsome face exuded the wisdom and confidence of a master philosopher. Ben was one of Orwell's earliest friends made on campus, but the beardless schoolboy stood in awe beneath his regal authority. Ben was a seasoned actor, and liked to create first-rate drama when he read on stage! This artist's esteem and proven maturity thwarted

Orwell's literary courage, and at times instead of inspiring him, made him feel deeply inadequate.

Benjamin smacked of London high society in dress and manners but his novel spoke eloquently of his youth, steeped in the ageless tribal values of his rural *boma*[28]. Like the majestic golden eagle that soars and swoops as it hunts in the wild Zambezi River valley, Benjamin rode the winds of imagination and gathered away his rapt audience. With poetic grace, he bore his listeners across the abyss of the modern world, back to his fertile Bantu homeland and tribal heritage. How coherent and soulful were Ben's simple lines of thought! Vivid scenes and powerful emotions came alive in the still semi-darkness of the amphitheatre. The drama he unfolded followed the mysterious rhythm of ancient Bible chronicles, but there was nothing scriptural about the black magic and animist legends he cleverly wove into the plot! As listeners concentrated upon the entwining storyline, the reader's fluted cadence and ghostly intonation hypnotized, then carried everyone back to bush culture forgotten by time. There, Christianity and western technology were reviled as clumsy intruders rather than embraced as beacons of enlightenment.

Across the vast waters of the Zambezi floodplain, sailed the *Nalikwanda,* splendid royal barge of the *Litunga,* led by the *Natamikwa,* a small fast canoe and attended by a colourful fleet of canoes as the Lozi paramount chief moved his people from Lealui, surrounded by rising water in March, to their winter capital Limulunga waiting dry at the forest edge. The pomp and ceremony of the *Ku-omboka* rang across the expanse of water to the beat of tribal drums, and gathered excited cheers from welcoming crowds of spectators assembled on shore from near and far to view the stately arrival.

Weathered fishermen poled their way upstream in dugout canoes, serenely casting their nets in a languid backwater channel of the floodplain, where flamingoes and herons posed knee-deep in muddy pools and rotund hippos yawned at the cloudless sky. On a rocky shoreline, country women chattered as they vigorously washed their laundry with long yellow cakes of *Sunlight* soap. They came first to the river in the early morning mist bearing clay jars to draw water for drinking and the cooking of maize porridge. A rocky path wound back

---

28 *Boma*: livestock enclosure, but the term extends to include a small fort or a community. This term is used by many languages around the African Great Lakes region, and in Central and Southern Africa.

to a cluster of grass roundovals set in lush mango and banana groves. The eaves-dropping foreigner deduced that village life revolved around a giant *mungongo* tree growing regally beside the great river; the soft wood hewed from its thick trunk was used for making drums and masks. Orwell fancied himself as a care-free ten-year-old, playing with the other boys high amongst the fruit-laden trees. Hughes could smell acrid charcoal smoke in the soft evening breezes as he heard their soft rustling in the tall, leafy *Hyparrhenia* grasses that were used for roof thatching. He viewed with reverence the molten ball of the setting sun dropping into the distance of the misty floodplain, and sweeping its golden rays across the watery expanse and its floating carpet of papyrus reeds....

The boys, who so recently had played with Orwell, underwent the painful ordeal of circumcision and proved themselves in their arduous apprenticeship into manhood. They learned to wrestle and handle spears and knives, as well as heard the oral history of their tribe, and emerged as young warriors in their community. To each was given manly independence and respect; some herded cattle, others cultivated maize and groundnuts, while still others fished or prepared charcoal from smoking piles of earth-covered logs.

"The good old ways of life are swiftly changing, what with the call to modern cities and the lure of quick wealth beckoning from the copper mines. Yet, traditional rural living is a joy to recall," Ben wistfully concluded. He closed his impressive book and returned to his seat under a rain of applause.

Although the stylish narrator had woven his story like a dream for Orwell, he could neither understand nor appreciate its depth and purpose. In truth, he felt belittled by the young African man's ritual of progression from childhood's carefree games into responsible adulthood so integral to tribal society. Nothing in Orwell's own pampered upbringing could draw him to feel on par with the hero of Ben's Barotseland chronicle. He was now three years older than Chola of the river people, but Orwell still regarded himself as a virgin youth dismissed by his unsympathetic father and belittled by his macho older brother. Gaining no words of wisdom from *his* austere sire, the desperate youth sought purpose where he had been rocked in Africa's bosom for five years as her apt pupil, yet again found himself wanting.

He was vexed by the frenzied drum revels, pagan fertility rites, and fabled ceremonies that invoked dark powers or honoured the advent of puberty that seemed to him as shadowy as the subtropical night—their weird incantations warred against his searching Christian soul. If only Mudenda could explain the significance of these tongue-twisting, vernacular titles for animals, gods, spirits, and big men of his tribal hierarchy, cried Orwell from the deep... Then, he could claim to be in tune with his reader. Was Orwell the only 'tourist' in the crowd who failed to understand?

Orwell suddenly shivered, aware that he was scrutinized by a dark figure who eerily materialized beside him, seemingly out of thin air. Daring to look this arrival in the eye, Hughes recognized the animated face of Cepheus Belo, flamboyant president of the Writer's Club.

"Enjoying the presentation, Master Hughes?" Belo inquired, his pearly teeth gleaming like polished piano keys in a darkened room. Their strong line and the whites of his eyes were all Hughes could discern in this gloomy light. Out of the shadows, Cepheus darted like a striking cobra to unnerve Orwell with reptilian assurance, "I searched for you earlier, concerned that our guest speaker for tonight had missed the meeting."

"Can't get off that easily, Master Cepheus... I've been lurking back here this whole time, plotting my strategy!" chuckled Orwell, though clumsy in his bid to master a casual air.

Belo slyly beckoned Hughes, like the spider to a fly, to take his turn at the podium. "I understand that you have prepared a powerful exposé about rampant corruption flourishing within our traffic police force, inflicted upon otherwise good young men by systemic injustice, like abysmally low pay and brutal training. Thank you for shedding light upon this deplorable situation!"

"You wish... Actually, I developed a story based around our family's experience with a rogue night watchman."

"Oho, a *mai garde*—a bad one to boot!" chortled Cepheus. This social agitator gleefully accepted Orwell's correction, but went on chattering about his own volatile agenda. "Certainly, corruption in the face of hunger cries out to be addressed. You jestingly describe patrolmen as yellow fevers! Is it because they wear yellow uniforms, or plague motorists like a dreadful disease?"

"A combination of both, although I haven't pinpointed which is more important," murmured Orwell shyly, embarrassed by his comrade's boisterous laughter. He squirmed when someone clacked his tongue indignantly at their unruly behaviour. On stage, the new reader nervously paused to drink a glass of water while waiting for his restless audience to simmer down. Orwell whispered to Belo in concerted effort to quiet him. "Cepheus, what are you thinking? Policemen here wear dark uniforms; certainly, they are not required to direct traffic, what with robot signals installed at major intersections."

His Eminence scowled, appearing insulted that this smart white youth intimated that, being Nigerian, he was confused over the uniform colours of Zambian policemen. Belo's glare shredded his bluff, purposely ungluing this rookie orator. Needing to retreat and rebuild his confidence, Orwell desperately offered, "Ben is a good storyteller as well as an excellent author."

"He'll pass," yawned Cepheus indifferently, seeming to find more inspiration in his luminous wristwatch than in the speaker. In response to the lad's silent dismay, the President offered his terse critique. "Benjamin's work is an entertaining fairy tale; I'd call it escapist pulp fiction! It is good that Mr. Mudenda is studying to become a doctor, for he will never make a profitable living as a novelist!"

Orwell was floored by this rude assessment of his best friend by their guild's leader. When he failed to challenge Cepheus, however, Orwell was smothered by the latter's flashing grin of triumph. The Canadian expat apparently fascinated Cepheus much more than did the tale being spun at the podium. Pantherlike Belo took sinister delight in gauging his quarry's reaction to his provocative remarks.

He suddenly asked, "Master Hughes, did you understand Ben's tale?"

"Not really, though I certainly desire to," confessed Orwell apologetically. "Ben spun many fascinating tales about his village upbringing while we sat together, eating maize gruel with our hands and dipping it in a tangy, pumpkin leaves relish laced with peppers, cow peas, and smoked fish at the university cafeteria. He marvelled at my ability to eat native foods in the traditional way."

"You don't say!" chided Cepheus, suspecting ridicule in Orwell's voice.

"But I simply can't identify with the cultural experiences Ben just shared in his stories," stammered Orwell in disillusionment. "I'm just a stupid *mzungu*, eh?"

"Come, come, sir! Don't think so poorly of yourself. You are a fellow within our esteemed brotherhood of literary artists and thus, most welcome here," admonished his rapt listener, apparently vexed by Orwell's unseemly outburst. Yet, by so patronizing the flustered youth, Cepheus only succeeded in scorning him.

"Don't belittle yourself because you can't identify. We writers of the world over are a special breed. We each have experienced a unique and gifted history, which behooves our desire—indeed our *duty*—to share what we have learned with others.

"Let me tell you this: I, a Black African, find tribal customs cumbersome if not obsolete in the new society we progressives are building. I am ignorant of those ancient concepts Ben focuses on in his story—they are *not* part of the culture of my tribe! I have buried my forefathers' wearisome traditions; I abhor tribalism and see it as a cancer on the emerging Black African state. I espouse a modern Marxist-Leninist ideology for Africa, to which all member countries must cling, not only to stem political breakdown along tribal lines, but also to repel further encroachment by multinational corporations and Western imperialists. What, you find my revelations inconceivable? Why?"

"I forget about the diverse backgrounds of most Africans around me, and assume that everyone here grew from similar roots and traditions, even if you do not share all the same language," blurted Orwell, immediately ashamed by the foolishness of his stereotypical view.

He hoped that Cepheus would become incensed and run off in a huff, leaving him alone for good, to enjoy what remained of the evening; instead, he gazed at him incredulously, appeared wounded by the unwitting insults the dolt had blurted out. When Belo spoke, he became at once a polished orator; his stinging lecture pierced forth as a weapon of war. Orwell, fearing that their unseemly outburst would disturb further readings, retreated quickly from the amphitheatre, hotly pursued by his would-be educator.

"Master Hughes, yes, there are many native dialects spoken in my country, but English has been converted from a lash of colonial oppression into that convenient bridge by which we modern Nigerians communicate, both amongst ourselves and with the outside world. Who can deny that English has become the language of international diplomacy, travel, and commerce?

"As for your ignorant concept that all Africans share a common jungle lineage, I compare it to an equally preposterous notion that every White man is British!" declared Belo contemptuously in the hallway. "Look at all the different Caucasian nations that ravaged Africa during the past four hundred years: Belgium, Britain, France, Germany, Italy, Portugal, and Spain—to name just a few invaders alphabetically, though not in order of demerit!

"The founding peoples of your own nation bear this out... British and French settlers continue to bicker over language long after they fenced the indigenous people onto reservations. Your *October Crisis* of 1970 featured letter bombs and kidnappings that led to an assassination, which sparked a reactionary clampdown by the military on all the French people of Quebec! Fascinating stuff, but how do you explain these outrageous human rights abuses in your homeland to the UN, sir?"

"No one usually cares about Canadian affairs," muttered Orwell sarcastically. "Besides, I am Canadian-born, and neither French nor English. My family has lived in Canada for 250 years and even boasts a hint of native ancestry, somewhere way back. Did I not explain myself clearly in Ibrahim's class?"

"Well, aren't we holy!" jeered Cepheus, bowing in mock reverence. Hardening suddenly, he roared into a tirade against all *mzungus*. "You might be Canadian-born, but you are not a 'native' Canadian, therefore you are an unwelcome colonizer on somebody else's land—I believe they are called Eskimos and red Indians by white people, which astonishes me since your aboriginal tribes originally migrated to North America from the Orient, not India.

"I know what an Indian is, Master Hughes! They came here in the pockets of their British overlords and now run all the small shops across Africa—except in Uganda that is, where President Idi Amin rightfully expelled the lot of them two years ago for cheating his people. Many of these purged foreigners fled to Canada and the UK, where the sons of British colonials took them in. And why do you think these dispersed Indians did not go home to India?"

"Because India is not their home anymore after having lived many generations abroad, just like Scotland is not my home anymore. The Scottish side of my family has not lived in the old country since Bonnie Prince Charlie was defeated by the English at the Battle of Culloden in 1745! My mother's ancient community is now a pile of rocks and her people are scattered throughout the world—Canada, West Indies, US, Australia, New Zealand—a real diaspora!"

"All former British colonies ..."

"I understand the Celtic people of Ireland and Scotland predate the English on their shared islands by centuries, but they all came from somewhere else—the Celts from the Danube region spread throughout Europe from Spain to Ireland; English came from Germanic tribes like the Angles and the Saxons. More ancient Pict tribes wore feathers and painted their faces blue. Some

Scottish men still wear kilts and are scorned by refined English gentlemen as being wild—like in that old song "Donald Where's Your Trousers?""

"I've never heard that song, Mr. Orwell. Can you please sing it for me?"

"I only know the chorus since I'm really not Scottish or English anymore, as I have been trying to explain," backpedalled Hughes, laughing nervously. When Belo glared, not getting his drift, Orwell jovially suggested, "Anyway, moving right along... Modern humans supposedly all came out of Africa, so we likely all share some genetic similarities that fade racial lines."

Cepheus, sensing that this bizarre white youth was attempting to entertain as well as inform him, laughed out loud at his joke that he could actually be part Black African. What would the apartheid racists of South Africa think of such a proposition—that their racial percentages used in classifying persons were useless after all, and that they themselves had a dash of colour in their ancestral closet? Orwell appreciated the feedback but did not understand what Cepheus found so funny. Hughes felt confident however that he had come to a suitable stopping point, and politely stated that he wished to return to official club business, but Cepheus detained him, showing an unhealthy interest in his history and asked that he continue with his account. Orwell, although frustrated by the task, reluctantly complied.

"Having fought the English fruitlessly for a millennium, the Scots finally were brought into union with their victorious foe in 1707. They were then forbidden to speak their Gaelic language; Scottish lairds were forced to intermarry and adopt English ways. During the *Highland Clearances,* numerous small crofters were uprooted and sent packing, as their gardens were seized for large-scale sheep ranches by decree of the new order. Like many of their clansmen, my ancestors sailed to Nova Scotia, where they took up farming, fishing, or coal mining, albeit still within the rule of a British colony. Others opened up the wilderness further west, working in the fur trade; the Scots were valued for their hardiness by the Hudson Bay Company—they managed quite well in the harsh interior country. Some married indigenous women and learned native languages and cultures. Later, after peace treaties were signed between local tribes and the Canadian government representing the British head of state—Queen Victoria at the time—an influx of settlers into ceded western lands helped build a new country as farmers and tradesmen."

"Mr. Orwell?" baited Cepheus glibly. "You seem to be blushing now, as though embarrassed by this recounting of the history of your people that potentially makes you a man of colour. You can't be allowed in South Africa!"

"Maybe as an honorary white man, considered like the Japanese are."

"Do you know the names or tribes of your native ancestors, Mr. Orwell?"

"No sir, I don't know who they were, when, or how they lived. Some of these brave ingenious women were *country* wives who weren't married in a church or even buried in regular graveyards," admitted Orwell humbly, jealous of Alicia and Tracy who boasted traditional names, could speak Cree and Michif, flew the Infinity flag, and occasionally wore colourful sashes as *bona fide* members of the Alberta Métis Nation. They were truly Canadian-made. "Most family members of my grandparents' generation won't discuss those supposed skeletons in our closet, but it doesn't bother me that I might have a trace of aboriginal ancestry—I am proud of even what little I could have. It secures my legitimate place in Canada after more than 250 years of development—what Alicia derisively calls exploitation. *She* demands that I listen when my indigenous ancestors beg me in dreams to learn about them and correct the social injustices they suffered—that their descendants continue to suffer, even in so tolerant a society as Canada's."

"Who is Alicia?"

"My junior sister's friend. She plans to visit us in Lusaka during Easter."

"She is too young to sound so harsh," judged Cepheus on flimsy evidence. "Is Alicia really such a bossy woman that you must obey her? Will you marry Alicia?"

"God, I hope not!" Orwell swore as he brusquely replied. "Alicia is a nice girl but we are just casual friends, and she's kind of young for me."

"Intellectually, perhaps, but Alicia is old enough to bear children and keep your house clean. Kanuri girls of my village were traditionally married at age twelve. I know who my mother is, though my father was a wealthy Muslim chief who had fou*r* wives and forty children. I know the names of all my brothers who have the same father and mother. My family is very large and esteemed in my community, going back many generations prior to Nigeria being awkwardly cobbled together by that detestable British imperialist, Lord Lugard[29]," Cepheus, puffed up with haughty pride, stoutly informed Orwell.

---

29 *Frederick John Dealtry Lugard,* 1st Baron Lugard (1858 to 1945): first British Governor of Nigeria (1914 to 1919), after governing Southern and/or Northern Nigeria Protectorates from 1900 to 1914. During his leadership, Lugard suppressed slavery within Nigeria, and developed the state's infrastructure.

Starting in 1894, Lord Lugard secured treaties between African rulers and the Royal Niger Company that

"I'm a '*Heinz 57*' mongrel myself," confessed Hughes, feeling like dust shaken off the ornately braided sandals of Malam Belo—Sahelian prince, clever intellectual, and world traveller. "My grandfather was a Scottish labourer with grade eight education; he married a teacher of English background from one of Prince Edward Island's leading families. That unusual coupling, together with some Irish, French, German, and Mi'kmaq mixed in, muddles my ethnicity—but that's Canada, eh—a diverse, multicultural society where everyone nicely gets along. I'm Canadian, not some hyphenated person."

"Excellent my dear friend ... but what does the Red Man think of your claim? Is Canada a real country to him or just a rock that presses him against a hard place? He suffers while you prosper. Europeans stole his land and denigrated his culture across the board, on a scale never witnessed before colonists came to the Americas. The same treachery was played in Africa by Europeans."

This criticism touched a nerve in the diplomat's son, who accepted that his life was blessed at the expense of others, but whose heart was heavy by what little he knew about the native people in his own country, let alone Africans that currently served him. Orwell did not feel personally responsible, but did not accept the exploitive status quo of stratified races and countries; he dreamed of starting over properly and righting every historic wrong perpetrated by his race. He impulsively blurted out what little he knew.

"The Native peoples of Canada claim they have lived on Turtle Island—which is how they call our land—since the Great Creator made the world. My understanding is that ancestral hunters-gatherers of the modern Cree and Blackfoot tribes came across a land bridge over the Bering Strait from Asia while Ice Age glaciers were retreating—10,000 to 15,000 years ago—when prehistoric woolly mammoths and sabre-tooth tigers still roamed the land. First

---

established British sovereignty. In 1897, he organized the native West African Frontier Force to defend Nigeria against French aggression, until 1899, when disputes with France were settled. Lugard led successful military campaigns against traditional rulers like the Sultan of Sokoto or the Emir of Kano, and during the Adubi War; some uprisings he brutally put down, including at Satiru during the Mahdi rebellion of 1906. During the 1920s to 1940s, Lugard served as British representative on the *League of Nations Permanent Mandates Commission,* where his anti-slavery activism influenced Great Britain to reform exploitation of cheap native labour throughout its colonies. He promoted indirect British rule and later, native rule in Africa, yet wished to keep Britain's superpower status intact.

Nations came first, followed a few thousand years later by the Inuit. That's an eternity compared to my paltry two centuries of historical presence, yet I know zilch about precolonial native history. It's mainly oral testimony given by elders on reserves, and not stuff written down in history books or taught in school.

"The Inuit and the various Indian tribes are historic enemies, but why they hate one another, man, I don't know. Samuel Hearne, an Englishman who sought copper mines and the Northwest Passage to help the northern expansion of the fur trade on behalf of the Hudson Bay Company, witnessed a massacre of Inuit by Chipewyan Indians in 1771. And only God knows what happened to *Dorset Man*, a different race altogether who lived in the Canadian Arctic centuries ago but is now extinct.

"The Cree and Blackfoot traditionally fought every year, but through efforts of the great Cree Chief Maskepetoon, they also made their own peace treaty last century near Wetaskiwin, the 'Hills of Peace'. Thanadelthur, a Dene woman previously captured by the Cree, negotiated peace between Dene and Cree warriors in 1715, and helped establish regular trade relations between the Dene people and the Hudson Bay Company English operating in northern Canada."

"Ah, yes—the English!" blurted Belo with sarcastic relish. He chuckled at Orwell's grimace as he spat out tongue-twisting aboriginal names he had only read in the white man's history books. He could see the lad's wealth of knowledge had been recently acquired, as though crammed from some politically-correct history book, and merely regurgitated like a parrot trying to impress real anthropologists. Belo questioned his sincerity to respect it, as he discerned, "You enjoy history Mr. Orwell, but you have so much to learn—from others' viewpoints that are so often dismissed by authorities who oppress them."

"Which is why I count myself privileged to be able to learn about African history from Professor Ibrahim. It's amazing how different tribes moved around here, taking over each other's territory for a while and creating great societies before getting bounced by someone else, in just a few decades sometimes. These cultures were strong and clever, but they were also ruthless and demanding. Europeans were not the only invaders Zambia saw!

"Look at how the expansion of the Zulu nation under King Shaka in South Africa during the 1820s and 1830s caused the neighbouring Sotho group, Makololo, to migrate northward into Barotseland, where they subjugated the Lozi people for 20 years before being overthrown. Some Zulu princes who quarrelled with Shaka left Zululand and made conquests elsewhere in southern Africa: Shagane conquered and absorbed the Tsonga people in southern Mozambique; Ngoni warriors destroyed the Changamires' Rozwi kingdom in Rhodesia before settling in the highlands around Lake Malawi. After raising havoc with African tribes in the high veldt of South Africa but being defeated by the invading Boers near Pretoria, the Ndebele Zulus retreated northward into Rhodesia, where they took charge of the local Shona people of the Zimbabwean Plateau, who previously had been subjects of the Rozwi Kingdom. The Ndebele lordship of Shona continued for years; after the advent of Britain's colony in Southern Rhodesia, African politics were split between these two tribes. They remain bitter rivals today."

"Remember, much of this turmoil was exasperated by Afrikaner settlers, who were hungry for farmland. The African tribes round about came into conflict among themselves over the remaining grazing land that the Boers did not control. Africans refer to this turbulent time of violence and destruction as the 'Time of Troubles'," Cepheus drolly reminded Orwell, wanting him to hear the *rest* of the story and making quotations marks in the air for emphasis with his upraised hands. He then sternly taught this apt pupil from his own history books. "Africa is balkanized because of self-interested, European aspirations over the past five hundred years!

"These locusts swarmed into Africa, arrogantly laying claim to huge tracts of land and ravaging all nature in their path. No understanding was sought for history, culture, or governments of the inhabitants. First, slave traders took away our young men and women; then, Christian missionaries vilified our time-honoured religious and cultural values in favour of their own convenient theory that the sons of Ham were called by God to be hewers of wood and drawers of water for white Christians. Vassal states were artificially created, backed by superior armed might, using convenient geographic boundaries, and manipulating the pre-existing animosities between different tribes; thus, the crafty colonial powers solidified their plans for the long-term exploitation of Africa and its riches. Intruders, having disenfranchised us, fought over our endowments as though they waged some high-stakes chess match in a royal, European drawing room, far away from *our* misery. These visionary empire builders—like Lord Lugard—claiming to be agents of development and holiness, imposed their stuffy institutions upon every African man, woman and child as they crushed us under their heel. Such carpetbaggers created enduring havoc for us. They stole our land, made us subservient, then cut us loose to sink or swim at independence, amid the turbulently unfamiliar seas of enforced Cold War alliances and an unfair world marketplace. We were left to salvage a future out of chaos in our own lands!"

His tone softening, now that he had demoralized his enemy, Cepheus concluded, "Today, Benjamin, you, and I attend the same university and enjoy the fraternity of this venerable writer's guild, but history teaches us that we should *not* be friends. How can I understand the essence of Ben's childhood? Why should I want to? And do you think your jottings can teach me anything noble? Although I am a patient, open-minded person, Master Hughes, do you see how hard it is for me to bury our hatchet?"

"I don't know what to say!" stammered Orwell dismally, suddenly feeling the full weight of guilt for the entire history of the Colonial era settle on his sagging shoulders. Such humble admission pleased Belo, even if only temporarily. Grasping at straws in the wings of the auditorium where they had retreated to not disturb the reading underway, Orwell was eager to conclude this impromptu trial and return to sanctuary next door with some redemption, so he tapped into a daring brainwave. "I figure that tribal animosities were a scar from the past, which would seem petty and obsolete in light of modern values and healing ointment of Christ's gospel."

His idea, however well-meaning, came off with such insulting glibness that it only rekindled Belo's ire.

"Not in Northern Ireland, would you agree? The flame of 'the Troubles' burns yet again between Roman Catholics and Protestants... Not in Nigeria, my friend, where Christians and Muslims are unrelenting rivals ...You talk like my old teacher at missionary school—you must be one of his disciples, although I hope you are more sensible than him! He espoused very dangerous ideas; he behaved like a devil in zealous efforts to pacify Africa's many impressionable youths through salvation in Jesus Christ. This evil man continues to reach out across the seas from his brilliant citadel through weekly Christian radio broadcasts, but I refuse to listen anymore to his malarkey! It is no accident that I can't remember his name—I refuse to pay any attention to this oppressor who caned me for speaking my native language and lowered my grades for refusing to adopt the Christian name he had chosen for me.

"Fortunately, Master Hughes, you understand and care more about Africa than does my enemy, though he was born and raised on this continent. You willingly listen and learn; you discuss rather than ram your views down our throats with the almighty powers of God and money as your authority."

Orwell longed to make a break for freedom but when he gazed incredulously at his accuser, Cepheus held him back with further discourse. Belo heaved a sigh before diving into his own gospel, "Alas, political fractions are built along tribal lines throughout Black Africa today, Master Hughes. I have met many a cabinet minister, civil servant, entrepreneur, and military officer who lives under the daily pressure to favour his tribe over an outsider. Tribal roots appear to sustain even our most forward-thinking leaders, causing onlookers to simplistically consider them corrupt."

"But Cepheus, we are all one in God's eyes, whether one follows the Lord, Yahweh, Gichi Manitou, or Allah," argued Orwell with maverick insight. "Our Supreme Being has created all humans equally in His holy image. Ben, a devout Christian, is one of the most loving and humble people I know."

"Ben may be baptized in the blood of the Lamb, but there is no glory for Christ in his story. Our friend writes of the old ways...values and traditions born in the dawn of time and proven by Lozi ancestors long before the coming of Schweitzer or Livingstone. You can't take heritage from a man; it is branded upon his soul...though many so-called missionaries like my childhood oppressor have labelled our grassroots beliefs as being satanic!" countered Cepheus with sarcastic gusto.

Orwell was aggrieved that he had stumbled into an even stronger trap set by this fiery soldier for liberation and empowerment of the masses. Cepheus was a relentless debater, stuffed to the gills with revolutionary opinions and emboldened by self-righteous determination to overturn the power elites. There was no placating him, let alone defeating him! Even if Belo's wrath was off-base, his arguments seemed well-founded—even bulletproof to his captive listener! This seasoned agitator came out smelling like roses in his rant, whereas the one on the receiving end felt he must repent for the white man's inherent evil on his knees, by hearing and accepting every word from Belo as just and true. Only by surrendering totally to whatever judgment the older man doled out, could Orwell escape the flamboyant haranguer who seemed to find intimate pleasure in listening to the unabating racket of his own voice!

Despite the narration in progress next door, this tenacious battler erupted yet again to bring his points home.

"Tribalism and religious strife are two of Africa's most wearisome ills, Master Hughes. Civil wars in Nigeria, Chad, Zaire, and Sudan are bloody testimony to these continuing heartaches!" ranted Cepheus, his eyes wide and blazing in the shadows. "I wish Professor Ibrahim would focus on these brutal realities instead of feeding us cake about what could be, were his students all rich and powerful like he is! That foolish man should be sacked!

"In the past, Christian missionaries tried to destroy our venerable cultures without offering a workable alternative. Do you realize, Master Hughes that despite Prophet Muhammad—peace be upon Him!—bringing Allah's final message to the world over five hundred years after the birth of Prophet Jesus, son of Mary, Islam spread into Nigeria centuries before Christians ever came to our shores?

"Were I President of Nigeria, religious holidays would be banned and all proselytizers of any stripe prevented from entering my country. Only foreigners offering skills and money to help develop our infrastructure for the betterment of the Nigerian peoples would be welcome. Religious fundamentalists hold people back. No wonder Marxism is being eagerly embraced! The *Communist Manifesto* still offers hope and a new direction to our troubled world by levelling the playing field for all citizens."

Cepheus now towered over a flabbergasted Hughes, lambasting him with his fiery rhetoric. Deeply uneasy in the shadow of this soap box activist, Orwell was fed up with his silver-tongued tirades. Like a wounded grizzly, he became uncharacteristically ugly in his bid to escape. Had Orwell been more assertive and less diplomatic he would have socked Cepheus with a well-timed left hook for polluting his literary development with selfish need to preach and hang some massive guilt trip on him. Orwell reminded him that he had not journeyed into the storyteller's club to become mired in a heated political debate. This was supposed to be a gentlemen's hour dedicated to sharing the lasting gifts of creative writing but Orwell's good friends, Benjamin Mudenda and Winter Banda, were snubbed by his repugnant sideshow. If Cepheus claimed to be a devout patron of African literature, why did he abuse his position of power to spew empty speeches that exulted utopian ideologies as magic remedies for Africa's complex and age-old troubles? He had made some key points that made Orwell re-examine his own position on the topic, but wasn't this enough whipping for one night? Why should Cepheus continue to spew his mind-numbing political shoptalk? It must take a backseat to the splendour of storybook Africa!

Having said his piece, Orwell darted past Belo and made a beeline for the auditorium. When Cepheus ran ahead of him and blocked the door, Hughes found no option left but to stand and fight.

"Look, Cepheus," he muttered bluntly, baring his teeth at his obnoxious pursuer. "I totally agree that severe problems ravage modern Africa due to its continued exploitation by western industrial nations...Canada is no picnic either! Get off my case and stop indicting me as the root cause of all your problems! Instead of bitching about the unending list of ills and casting blame upon others, it is high time that progressive African thinkers, movers, and shakers like yourself work to solve those issues. I know you can do it! You have all the tools to do a proper job!"

"I've worked my fingers to the bone to bring my continent prosperously into the 20th Century," growled Cepheus, stung by Orwell's apparently self-righteous brush off. "Yet, I am only one player in the global community. I can only do so much on my end to ensure equality and cooperation in the international arena. My greatest struggle lies in opening the blind eyes of indifferent First World folks like you to the glaring schisms between north and south that continue to nourish poverty, ignorance, malnutrition, and violence in underdeveloped nations.

"When will you lobby your Prime Minister to pressure Canadian banks and companies to pull their investments out of racist South Africa? Why won't you give me a fair price for my copper or buy my cotton and coffee instead of catering to powerful companies who run huge plantations at the expense of landless subsistence farmers? I want my soil to grow food to feed my own hungry children, not be covered with tobacco and sugar cane so that you can sweeten your coffee or smoke your favourite brand of cigarettes. Master Hughes, when will you acknowledge your role in unjustly keeping me poor?"

Orwell was just as flabbergasted by Cepheus's rant as the latter was with the foreigner's refusal to listen. Hughes cared little that he had poked the orator's bloated pride—it was high time that this pompous radical become educated in the harsh realities of life! Cepheus was not an elected member of government but a privileged foreign student like himself, training to become a civil engineer. Orwell deemed that Cepheus should leave affairs of state to the government and finish his studies, so that he could get into the work field, dirty his hands, and challenge his mind building roads and constructing bridges to help his people, particularly isolated backcountry folks, to progress.

Orwell seethed inside as he fled from livid Cepheus, down the stairwell, and back into the auditorium. He had not realized that someone had shut this door to muffle the drone of their voices. Hughes banged clumsily into the barrier, and fumbling to open it, rattled the heavy latch more desperately than he ever would have outside Ibrahim's class. Stumbling inside the hall, Orwell nearly fell into the lap of an astonished spectator sitting nearby. He apologized fervently as he groped his way through the crowd and found an empty seat.

Orwell looked bogus as Cepheus was nowhere in sight! Ashen-faced and sweating profusely, he immediately recognized that his sudden re-entrance from a heated backroom argument had not only nullified the now-forgotten reader but grievously disturbed the audience. The lecture hall was reverberating with clacking tongues and disapproving murmurs as irritated faces swivelled in search of the troublesome bat in the belfry. Some fussbudget went so far as to halt the speaker on the podium in order to publicly rebuke Orwell for his grossly discourteous conduct. Demoralized by the interruption of his cleverly spun yarn, Aloysius could do ought but sip water and stare at the floor.

Orwell, ashamed for having whipped the assembly into an uproar, wished he could morph into a mouse to scurry into some dark hole, but he muzzled his pride, woodenly remained seated, and apologized in the hope he could redeem himself.

"Mr. Moderator, I saw Mr. Belo chasing Mr. Hughes down the stairwell," declared the same member who had shut the door. "They were shouting at each other!"

"That being the case, I suggest that our esteemed President also apologize for his unseemly behaviour," Winter Banda judiciously ruled on behalf of the riled throng. When Cepheus failed to respond, Banda rose from his seat and scanned the room. Unable to find Cepheus anywhere in their midst, the moderator sternly demanded, "Where is he? Mr. Cepheus Belo, stand and account for your disturbance!"

Although Orwell had been hotly pursued by Belo, he had not actually seen him re-enter the auditorium. Cepheus, one clever cat with nine lives, had noted in advance that the door was closed and stopped short before Orwell barged into it. He had reversed direction and gone down the other stairwell. As angry calls that he show himself reverberated throughout the crowd, Cepheus brazenly entered the well-lit stage from the main entrance at the bottom of the room.

Pretending ignorance of any discord, the president smiled serenely and waved blithely at the protesting audience. While Cepheus relished this limelight as a golden opportunity to defend his self-trumpeted views, he took raucous calls for an apology as an affront to his honour. The club had voted this elegant blowhard into office year after year because of his literary prowess, but he was well known for his ego. Cepheus, Orwell marvelled, seemed as Teflon-coated as the illustrious Tracy MacDonachie; he too was born to govern! Oddly enough, Hughes would never have been able to serve such an arrogant man, though he would follow Tracy anywhere… He knew why he was in the doghouse, yet was relieved by Belo's arrogant capacity to acquire all the heat for himself.

"Mr. Banda!" Belo chided. "This club is reserved for gentlemen and scholars, and is founded upon principles of professional etiquette. I refuse to be scolded like a beardless juvenile by the likes of you! You are the one behaving like a child!"

"Me? Och, this argument is pointless!" exclaimed Winter Banda. Throwing up his arms in theatrical dismay, Banda appealed to the exasperated listeners for sympathy. He demanded, "What can we do if our president scorns the comfort, intelligence, and literary aspirations of this club. Mr. Belo is a tyrant, who should be purged forthwith from our midst!"

"Gentlemen!" interjected Benjamin, rising like a mountain of reason amid the hubbub of mudslinging and ego bashing. "Aloysius has more to read to us! I for one was engrossed in his science fiction story about secret agents investigating treachery among the crew of an international space mission, but his reading has been spoiled by your outburst. Why should Aloysius bother with us anymore tonight?"

Brought back to reason by this wise reminder, the crowd suddenly hushed in recognition of its foolishness. Heeding his call for a return to sanity, the membership rallied around Mudenda, an esteemed curator of fine literature and the embodiment of the club's love for creativity. They chanted, "Yay Ben! We want Aloysius!"

Grieved that he had somehow slighted his brother in Christ, Orwell grabbed hold of this outpouring of support for this pillar of the faith by joining in the chants for Benjamin Mudenda to chair the meeting. The elegant bard, visibly touched by this vote of confidence, came forward as though too dignified to remember any invasion of chaos into his beautiful realm. Calling Aloysius Tembo back on stage, Ben's quiet strength of character anchored him as they turned the tide.

Cepheus was forced to sit down and give back the limelight to a junior author whose space-age espionage writings he dismissed as frivolous. While Aloysius eagerly resumed his story, Orwell listened to the far out science fiction offered by his peer writer and tried to learn from the fellow rookie how to read while keeping this tough crowd entertained—*he* was the next victim to be sacrificed!

*****

ORWELL was roused from his musings by eager calls for him to come down from the rafters to share his story on stage. Orwell was astounded by the rollicking, unrelenting interest of his peers! While he craved to publish his fervent voice, he felt completely lost as to how he could satisfy their appetite for enlightenment. Hughes was a high-profile stranger among them—at times loved, hated, admired, or ignored... He reminded his Zambian hosts of their cast-off British master on top of being the son of a powerful white expatriate, although Hughes was the first to admit that he did not speak the Queen's English and remained an outsider to white Africans, critical albeit embarrassed by what little he knew of them. He identified more sympathetically with modern Black African society!

Hughes hesitated, clinging to the safety of the shadows as he contemplated his fate. What right had these lolling wolves to probe his mind and glean everything unique and special to Orwell Hughes, the sideshow freak! His number was up—if he failed to go for the gusto now, Orwell had no business calling himself an author! As he made his way to the podium, he was roundly welcomed by Benjamin Mudenda, who urged listeners to put their hands together and acknowledge this refreshing writer from abroad.

Before he reached the reader's platform, as he bounced self-consciously down the aisle, his papers spilled haphazardly from his briefcase that was left swinging open in his hand! Reddening at Belo's smile of wry amusement, Orwell frantically gathered the dense handwriting before genuine friends like Benjamin could read his contrary thoughts, and rushed past Mudenda to take his turn at the podium holding his crumpled manuscript tightly against his breast as if it was a baby just rescued from a fire.

The crowd was impressed that their esteemed host had parachuted a stand-up comedian into its forum to entertain during intermission! Orwell's striped bellbottoms, platform shoes, and fluorescent beach shirt, not to mention his unruly mop of blonde hair, set him apart as a hippie among this conservative crowd. That he seemed nervously out of place was obvious, but Hughes smiled bravely as he opened his briefcase and neatly laid his manuscript on the lectern. Peering out at the waves of spectators, Orwell smiled at his peers and prepared to read his piece.

From the moment he had entered the auditorium, Orwell had mulled over how best to present his satire piece to these friends—who could quickly become his victims if not his enemies! What had begun as a disquieting prick of doubt in his mind had brewed into a raging gale as he had fiercely argued with himself whether or not he should ignite a powder keg on his first public foray into authorship. Bowing to common sense, Orwell finally decided to release his exposé to the four winds and wistfully allow it to escape into obscurity. This was best, his staid father would agree; the raucous assembly might well have run Orwell out of town for his slam against an African night watchman struggling to better himself as a teacher.

"I don't have any story to read you tonight. Sorry, guys," confessed Hughes unabashedly. He shrugged meekly and kept his resolve when some of his peers expressed disbelief or jocularly tempted him to prove himself.

Orwell's manuscript told how a native guard had behaved like a thug rather than the protector he was sworn to be. He had fallen asleep nightly on the job at the Hughes family compound. Suzanne had awoken from a bad dream, only to face the brute leering through her bedroom window. He had also skulked about in shadows like some petty thief, bareheaded and dressed in civvies. During his week of assignment, the guard had entertained unsavoury guests in the evenings who accompanied him on his rounds. He was working on the unhappy night when the family's garage was swept clean by thieves. Orwell's tale drew the conclusion that the guard had either stolen their goods or had been bribed to act as an accessory to the crime.

The young philosopher's tale was meant to highlight his disillusionment that a person in whom trust had been placed to protect the household during his father's diplomatic travels abroad proved to be a robber. Why had Bwana Hughes not found enough confidence in his two brawny sons to look after his women and property? Something was wrong with this picture! The family would have fared better without the guard's unsettling presence. Orwell's chronicle presented a grim lesson on petty crime and corruption, which he saw as a festering weakness in native society. Impoverished in mind and body, the urban African was viewed as a shadowy parasite feeding upon wealthy Europeans, his unwanted guests but sustainers of his economy!

As Orwell took a sip of water from a glass Aloysius had poured for him from a flask on the podium, he shuddered at the power of the bitter words he had wisely censured. Orwell concluded that his sensitive listeners were bound to view his experience in an entirely different and more realistic light. Undoubtedly, they would justify the guard's antics as the results of fatigue and stress, which he was forced to endure in his diligent effort to feed his extended family. Had Orwell not recognized this guy the following week, guarding the main gate to Zambia's High Court house?

Europeans had long exploited Africa for her abundant resources, so whatever scraps Africans could glean with their wits from beneath the sumptuous table of these foreign opportunists, were well-deserved. What were four bicycles to these regal expats, anyway? They could buy new ones in five minutes with their loose change. For jobless squatters who languished in misery of their shantytown, dwelling in shacks made of squashed oil drums and pilfered bricks, while he sipped mineral water on ice in the flower garden of a shining hilltop mansion, tomorrow only came for survivors. Orwell frowned at the irony that the guard had made off with his heist scot-free...Ironically, he had seen a young black man being chased through the downtown market and nearly beaten to death by an 'instant justice' mob for allegedly stealing a bicycle from an African shopkeeper. The level of hardship he saw around him troubled Orwell, and as a member of the powerfully rich First World, he felt embarrassed to speak of his own petty problems to those who knew poverty and hunger on a first name basis.

"My dear friend, you won't escape your duties so easily," chided Cepheus from the depths of the gallery. Orwell searched in vain for Belo as he continued to rail, "You have shared our company for almost a year and have yet to substantiate your fervent claim that you are, in fact, a writer! Are we to assume therefore that you are a pretender?"

"I am an author!" growled Orwell fiercely. Then, mincing no words, he declared, "Sometimes, because of my background, I feel that I don't belong here. How can we relate when we live in different worlds, even if in the same city?"

"Sir, we are a rainbow brotherhood of literary artists, an energetic guild that draws no barriers between those who craft the written word. Amongst our ranks are men and women of many tribes, creeds, and professional aspirations: Bemba and Lozi, Muslims and Christians, socialists and lords of free enterprise, whites and blacks, coloured and Indian! A veritable United Nations we are, and our varied backgrounds set aside, we are one club of writers!"

Cepheus disapproved of Orwell's self-pity. The club president rose from his seat and encouraged the tongue-tied speaker to share his written musings with the gathered assembly.

"It is a unique honour to have you, our esteemed Canadian visitor, share our abiding love of penmanship," encouraged Cepheus. "We can and should learn from one another, that we might better understand each other. You have heard of the famous *Mbari Club* in Ibadan?"

"I know that Ibadan is a large city in western Nigeria, where the prestigious *International Institute of Tropical Agriculture* is located. The traditional practice of alley farming—intercropping vegetables or grains between rows of nitrogen-fixing trees—was researched there, with cooperation from the University of Ibadan's agricultural faculty and funding by the *Ford Foundation*. I hope to visit the place someday as I continue agricultural studies at UNZA."

"Yes, yes," Belo conceded, as Orwell spouted off a tangent. He then filled in the gaps on the lad's reply. "Ibadan is a very progressive city, where traditions are celebrated in today's terms. The *Mbari Club,* through its diverse and eclectic membership, promotes modern African art and literature. Chinua Achebe, author of *Things Fall Apart* and Nobel Prize-winning dramatist Wole Soyinka, helped Ulli Beier, a German professor lecturing at Ibadan's University College, found this creative group in 1961, during an exuberant time when many African nations were becoming independent. When Fela Kuti, today's Afro beat artist *extraordinaire,* was named as the new band leader of the *Mbari Club,* the venue became a magnet for artists from all over Africa, America, and the Caribbean. In 1957, Professor Beier also co-created *Black Orpheus,* the first African English language magazine. Alas, this European promoter of African arts no longer lives in Nigeria, and the *Mbari Club* disbanded before I could become a member.

"I believe, however, that our eminent Writers' Club here at UNZA can confidently carry the torch that *Mbari Club* tossed us. We publish our own top-drawer anthologies in *Forum* and we are an influential think tank for Zambia's socioeconomic and political affairs. You see, Mr. Orwell, how important you are to helping our local efforts succeed?"

"Hear, hear!" enjoined Banda, "And what have you to say for yourself, thou envoy from the rich and powerful Americas? Please enlighten us. Who are you and why did you choose to study in Zambia's university?"

"What shall I say?" countered Orwell, feeling put on the spot. "I am not sure about sharing my background and experiences...I don't know if you can identify with them!"

"We are not so different after all—every man is created equal in God's sight," professed Benjamin, humility resounding in his gentle voice, "Perhaps, He brought you into this determined but suffering land; He placed you in our midst—to learn, grow, and work with us as we walk together, even if for only one year. You seem to be up for this task, with His help.

"Whether humans recognize Him or not, the Lord firmly holds the rudder of history in His mighty hands and will carry out His master plan, despite the follies of men. The Bible testifies to God's leadership in the lives of people whom He chose to be the instruments of His labour. Jehovah has appointed a time and a season for everything, and brings rain upon good and evil as He pleases. God's ways are too wonderful for man to fully comprehend. Although He wishes the best for those who truly fear Him, the Lord will not permit His children to fully discover all the righteousness He operates in their lives, until that glorious day when He shall draw us to His bosom in Heaven.

"You belong to Christ, my friend, because you believe that He has redeemed you through His teachings, death, and resurrection. God hears your prayers when you call faithfully upon His name. Surely, our Lord has given you a role—indeed, to each of us who believe—to be salt and light to this weary world for the furtherance of His Heavenly kingdom, wherever you may be. Through His gifts and your desire for excellence—not only in athletics, music, and writing—but also in diplomacy, understanding, and justice, you glorify Him. To love God and glorify Him is what matters here, Orwell, not the differences in culture, skin colour, religion, and social standing that presently overwhelm you. Wealth and power will pass, governments will fail, but Christ's healing gospel remains forever as a testimony of grace for mankind.

"Let go of your fears and imagined inadequacies; be part of us tonight. I understand why you assert that you have no story to share with us now...but I don't believe you. Your predicament may be a blessing in disguise."

Ashen-faced with amazement and shame, Orwell soaked up Ben's fervent testimony and was dumbfounded by his encouragement. In a rare move of trust, he had shared his guard story with Ben a few days prior. He had become upset then by Ben's apprehensions about reading the controversial piece to the club, and had vowed to his mentor's concerned face that he would carry out his plan, come hell or high water! Rather than ridicule Orwell's present plight, the elegant writer now honoured him for growing wise enough to see the light.

"Ben must be brimming with Christ's love," marvelled Hughes, bewildered by his supporter's reassuring smile.

Mudenda was a mighty disciple for Jesus, Hughes realized, a lump building in the back of his parched throat. Ben seemed to be the only other person in the room now, an angel bringing him a message from God while the others faded from his view, frozen in time.

"We writers shape the lives of our readers," continued Benjamin, his armour shining as he addressed the audience. "The Lord appoints certain people to walk with each one of us that we may turn to Him by way of their testimony and example. Had it not been for the faith and inspiration of people He placed in your life, Orwell, you might not be following Christ today...But I have sermonized too long already, yet dare to ask you this: who is a person in your circle that you feel has shaped your life, and *why*? Let such testimony be your story tonight."

Flustered as he was, Orwell was encouraged by Ben's sincere witness and gently prompting hand. Hughes' heart soared as he gazed upon this rock who loved him as a friend. How much Orwell looked up to Ben and found inspiration in his fearless witness, he could not rightly express, but the lad grasped the fierce desire for Godly embrace of all people as the power driving this pious man. Like Tracy MacDonachie, Orwell marvelled, Mudenda possessed the eloquence of heavenly prophets and the crystal-clear faith needed for spreading the gospel. Yet, Tracy had always taught his protégé to stay bold for the Lord without wearing religion on his shirtsleeve...So, what now, Tracy?

"Jesus Christ has made a big impact upon my life," declared Orwell solemnly, yet trembling like an aspen tree in a stiff breeze. He held back from naming his earthly mentors, lest he glorify them ahead of the One who gave life to all creation. "From scriptures, I draw upon His example for my encouragement and guidance."

The entire university knew of Orwell Hughes simply because he was the only blonde, blue-eyed youth on campus. Benjamin Mudenda had tried his best over the past turbulent year to keep Orwell strong in the Lord, but it was Tracy MacDonachie who had brought the thoughtful youth into personal relationship with Jesus. What a rejuvenating elixir Hughes had quaffed then—it had unlocked the entire world to him!

"Who is Jesus Christ?" demanded one voice in the audience. "Tell me young chap, is your daddy a missionary?"

Staving off this obvious jab, Orwell solemnly declared, "Jesus Christ is the Son of God!"

"What I meant, dear fellow..." continued his challenger, "Who is Jesus Christ in *your* life?"

Hughes blushed, suddenly realizing he had no personal insights with which to substantiate his pat answer. Orwell wished to please his conscience with some charitable sacrifice, but knew he had spoken from the shallowness of his mind. He was now challenged to do the impossible: prove the power and authenticity of his faith. Was this club member expecting him to call down fire from Heaven to consume the podium, like Elijah had done with the evil priests of Baal? These doubting Thomases and evolution believers were crying for a miracle before they would believe in Almighty God. Orwell lacked Benjamin's faith, which was so powerful it could toss mountains into the sea!

Perhaps this detractor was a firebrand member of the Watch Tower sect...Or maybe an atheist or Muslim looking for a religious debate? With so many cults and traditional religions flourishing in the land, it was no wonder that Christmas and Easter were not recognized as statutory holidays! In so many ways, despaired Orwell, he was part of a precarious minority!

Much as he was aflame for the Lord, Hughes was afraid to pound the desktop and hurl a hellfire sermon from his podium—like Benjamin could among his people! Orwell recalled an event when he had proclaimed to fellow students that Jesus Christ was the only way to Heaven, and all other religions were no more than cults of Satan. Orwell had paid the price for his zealous claim by becoming mired in a no-win argument with some Islamic students, who had attacked his every argument with valid points from the Quran in favour of Allah and His prophet, Muhammad. They had made Orwell look weak in his knowledge of Christianity and the Bible—a hypocrite worse than an unbeliever! He had vowed to never again allow divergent spiritual voices to bewilder him!

Stymied as to where to go from here, he surmised it was time to quickly tap dance off stage. Where was that shepherd's crook when you needed it? The lad had no guns left to subdue his challengers, as Tracy would have done with charming impunity. Ashamed of his failure, Orwell's scouted the wings for an exit sign, but all he could decipher was Benjamin rising to bat for him yet again. Hughes waived his brother off this time, refusing to take his helping hand against those who questioned God. Just when Orwell was about to give up, an idea from on high popped into his tired brain.

"Jesus Christ is the One who inspires me," he testified, pausing to breathe deeply. Orwell then spoke of Tracy MacDonachie with the newfound eloquence he had prayed for. "The Lord has worked His gospel in my life through a mentor who has grown into a dear friend. I was introduced to the path of Christ by my Sunday school teacher, and He has shaped my life ever since!"

"It isn't that I discount the fervour of your faith or that of your beloved mentor; rather, I quest to meet an honest Christian. Why do you believe?

"Gentlemen, my father left our rural village to work in the South African gold mines and never came back, abandoned my mother to raise us seven children by the sweat of her brow. My uncle took me in after my mother died of yellow fever. When I was still a small boy, he found an opportunity for me to advance: I was given to one of his friends to work as cook's helper for some Scottish missionaries in Southern Rhodesia. We lived in a grass hut in the back garden of their splendid house up-country from Gwelo. The blessed old Madame, who thought I was a bright lad, spent painstaking hour after hour in her parlour, teaching me how to read and write her English language. She and her husband were kind to me in an austere way as they brought me up as a proper lad of the British Empire. They took me further under their wing and sent me to a British boarding school when I could not gain admission to a secondary school in the colony—my homeland! Upon graduation from ordinary and advanced levels programs, I completed my formal education at a fine British university, covered by the expense and encouragement of my patrons. Now, I am a professor of natural sciences at this African university, where I presently teach chemistry to up-and-coming students like yourself, Master Hughes."

Professor Muzorewa, having identified himself with a flourish that evoked gasps of awe and applause from the audience, stared at Orwell and Benjamin as they listened intently to him from the podium. Orwell sagged at this revelation, but Benjamin buoyed him up with a discrete hand on his shoulder and encouraged him to work with Professor Muzorewa yet a little longer, who wanted to learn from as well as teach these young men of faith.

"Do you astute fellows think that God's hand was upon me? As a child servant of white missionaries, I was taught that God did not live in trees nor dwell on hills; He lived in the Holy Bible from which white missionaries preached at their church. I read those scriptures many times and took them to heart, yet I believed that God is everywhere—not only in manmade temples but also in the majesty of His creation—the natural world. I am convinced that the Great Creator made and loves every living thing. If He created us all in His own image, let me ask you this, Mr. Hughes? Could Christ have been black skinned?"

"I've never thought about it before, but I suppose that Jesus could be a black man," offered Orwell, too dumbfounded by Muzorewa's suggestion to oppose it. "Your journey, Sir, testifies how God watches over you."

Growing up, all the pictures of Jesus he had seen in Bibles, hospital rooms, in the plethora of religious artworks, or at Christmas had depicted a blonde, blue-eyed Caucasian man. But was not Jesus of Nazareth, son of Mary, a brown-eyed, black-haired, and olive-skinned fellow from the Middle East? The nativity scene set up last Christmas at Lusaka's multiracial church was cast with black Africans—except for one of the three wise men visiting from Europe. Hughes remembered having seen an image of the Saviour portrayed with braided hair, almond eyes, and high cheekbones hanging on the cross inside a Roman Catholic Church during a native pilgrimage that he, along with Tracy, their little sisters Alicia and JJ, and Mrs. MacDonachie had made to wade into the sacred, healing waters of Lac Saint Anne, located an hour's car ride but years past, northwest of Edmonton.

During a piano lesson at Cherry Crest, Mrs. MacDonachie informed her dumbfounded pupil that some of the early Christian missionaries to Canadian natives were themselves indigenous! She told him about Joseph Brant, a Christian and Mohawk war chief who aligned with the British in Ontario during the latter 1700s and operated a school for Six Nations[30] children. Other examples were John Sinclair, a local Cree, and Henry Steinhauer, an Ojibwa from Ontario, who worked among the Plains Cree as Bible translators. And there was also Charles Pratt, a lay teacher for the Church Missionary Society of London who brought Christianity and agriculture to his Cree and Assiniboine peoples in Saskatchewan's Touchwood Hills in the 1860s. Alicia grinned from ear to ear as her mother related to the two children how Sophia Mason, the Cree wife of Methodist missionary William Mason, had helped her husband and fellow missionary James Evans translate hymns and catechism for the Cree believers.

Orwell expressed no problem with such images because they spoke of the Creator's inclusive love for all humanity. What better way to reach people than to testify the Gospel of Jesus Christ through believers who not only understood their culture and language but looked like them!

In spite of his willingness to entertain these thoughts, Orwell could barely conceal his growing weariness with this heavy debate as he replied, "Christ said he was the Shepherd for all humankind, not me. I am simply defending Him as my Lord and Saviour. Without Jesus in my life, I am nothing!

"I am a Christian," Orwell declared with a joy that made Cepheus scowl, Winter flinch, Professor Muzorewa nod in salute, Aloysius take notes, and Ben, beam with pride. "I am young in the faith and have many frailties, but Tracy MacDonachie, my best friend back in Canada, is an active disciple of God. His walk is a fervent testimony that God is mightily alive in this world. In Sunday school, or during sports and outings of our church's youth group, Tracy showed me the Lord's love and majesty. I am honoured to hail Tracy as my older brother in faith!"

Orwell's heart rose into his throat as he related how a mature boxer come playboy with connections in the fields of entertainment, fine arts, social activism, and professional sports, was so dear to him. Tracy MacDonachie was living proof that Christians could be debonair, fierce, or jovial; resourceful and successful; radical and artistic—and still dutifully read scripture, serve on church committees, and attend Sunday worship services—be boldly in the world but not of it! Thanks to him, Christians were seen as real people with dreams and

30 *Six Nations*: Mohawk, Cayuga, Onondaga, Oneida, Seneca, and Tuscarora Iroquois nations. It is also the name for the largest reservation in Canada, located in southern Ontario.

talents, not just as losers to be ridiculed as naïve, hypocritical, and ultra-pure. Orwell found courage in Tracy's fervent testimony and felt blessed to call him a friend!

Although born into great wealth, this champion of the little man had overcome many hang-ups, and chosen to build community rather than join his father's business pursuits. He was blessed with talents more valuable than gold! The giant's indomitable spirit had driven him to victory after bloody victory in the professional boxing ring, but Tracy was gentle and loving with children, and anyone who was weaker than him. He played piano and sang bass as anchor to The *MacDonachie Family Singers*, a well-known Christian family choir the world over, yet also was a highly-sought entertainer in nightclubs, on radio and TV.

The MacDonachies were seen as aristocrats in rustic Alberta and also served as pillars of its church and society, although *none* were doctors, lawyers, engineers, or statesmen with degrees mounted on the wall. By wit and muscle, the family had made its fortune in grassroots enterprises—grain farming, cattle ranching, and farm machinery—before branching into more urbane services like hotels, taxicabs, trucking, and sporting goods. They were currently junior players in offshore oil, gas and mining sectors but were growing by leaps and bounds, blessed by clean living under Christ. They moved easily in both urban and rural circles and rubbed shoulders—breaking down any differences with grace and charm—with people of all religious backgrounds and social classes.

While Reverend MacDonachie's son Robert now operated the family business empire, the fiery evangelist continued to live his noble dream of radio and television ministry. Many in Orwell's audience surely had heard Rev. MacDonachie preach his weekly sermons broadcast around the world? Did they know that he had been a decorated military padre during the Korean War? He had also been a church planter in Nigeria, where he had been born to long-term Christian missionaries. Young Reverend MacDonachie had honed his skills in Canada by preaching on street corners and at tent meetings, shepherding church congregations large and small. Throughout his turbulent pilgrimage, this giant among men never lost sight of his purpose: to spread the gospel and make a better world for those less fortunate. He generously shared his God-given wealth to fund charities and projects that improved the lot of humanity, such as the full-service hospital and mission school near Maiduguri, Nigeria started by the Rev's father. Tracy followed his father into ministry rather than commerce by pastoring wayward youths and street people in the inner city.

Despite such regal bearing, this gifted family had opened its heart to the Hughes gang, poor cousins who lived on the wrong side of the tracks, because Martha Hughes and Pearl MacDonachie were bosom buddies since teachers' college. The families also attended the same church—a traditional Scottish and Irish congregation with generations of ministry in Edmonton. Pearl and Martha, students in the big city who had both been raised on northern Alberta farms, had found a meaningful spiritual home away from home at St. Andrews; they encouraged their families to stay plugged into the serene downtown church, to serve and find sanctuary. Even though Rev. MacDonachie was a business tycoon, while James Hughes became a world-travelling diplomat, they were not alone; both were anchored by their loving wives and enriched by bright children. In Christmas letters, Rev. MacDonachie intimated that his family was inspired by the humble faith and stalwart service of the Hughes clan; they felt a loving affinity for these genuine folks of the cross. Jim Hughes, a reflective man who wrapped his emotions in plenty of diplomatic red tape, would have his loved ones say the same about the MacDonachies.

During Orwell's formative years, Tracy had been an intriguing older guy lurking on the periphery of the lad's technicolor world. Not one to spend much time with little kids, he held court in the MacDonachie garage with his leather-jacket gang, smoking joints, jamming on electric guitars, working over fin-tailed cars with all their gleaming chrome, punching heavy bags bearing a devilish rendition of Prime Minister Trudeau's face...Tracy was also a daredevil, enthralled by extreme thrills like hang-gliding, driving jeeps on sand dunes or amphibian cars in the river, flying small planes or air balloons. Before he got married, MacDonachie cruised Jasper Avenue draped with gorgeous dames in his shiny sports car, radio blaring and ragtop down.

Rumour had it that Tracy had been ingloriously shipped home from seminary for questioning the established church doctrine. The troubled young man was simply spinning his wheels and seeking purpose in his life. He was feared by the young Sunday school boys as some kind of ogre. Orwell and some of his friends would mount attacks against Tracy, chasing him with snowballs and insults through the labyrinth of stairwells and hallways of the church, daring him to catch and wrestle them boyishly into submission. As he graduated into double digits, however, Orwell realized that Tracy actually had a huge soft spot for the kids. One Sunday noon, Tracy caught the boys mischievously hurling popsicle sticks and 'fossilized' Girl Guide cookies at departing parishioners from a third story window. Rather than fink on them to their parents or church authority, Tracy had challenged them to meet him on a vacant lot across the street for scrub baseball.

MacDonachie, sensing that these wild boys needed mentoring as well as supervision, toned them down by making interesting use of their restless energy. He organized a snow shovel brigade to clear sidewalks during the winter, fashioned his young charges into eager busboys or polite dispensers of coffee and tea at congregational socials; helped them to pick up garbage left on church grounds during the summer—in short, gave them a purpose other than hanging around bored while their parents chatted and got their caffeine fixes after worship service. Orwell took the decisive step of asking his father, then the Sunday school superintendent, to invite Tracy to teach his grade nine class, the last hurdle for kids to clear before they could graduate into full membership within congregational life.

"Tracy took his calling seriously and redeemed himself in the eyes of detractors who felt that this rebel son would only turn kids into hooligans. He proved to be an excellent teacher and advocate for young people still seeking a place in the church during the '60s' restless and changing times. He brought dry scriptures to life with vivid retelling of Bible stories and refreshing images of Heaven for today. He replaced the tired pump organ with the modern sound of guitars and drums. Gospel songs and reader's theatre became integral parts of his lesson.

"Rather than wash his hands of us, Tracy developed a vibrant youth ministry that extended beyond our graduation Bibles and public recitations of scriptures that were usual Sunday school fare. Under his tutelage, a dusty storage room was turned into a cool clubroom, as we painted the walls with groovy fluorescent colours, brought in some old couches and a record player, hung hip posters of our favourite rock stars, put in a black light...like, made the room ours. Raucous volleyball and basketball games again echoed within the church's underused gymnasium. Hot chocolate nights and wiener roasts followed skating or toboggan parties. During hot summer afternoons, the MacDonachies' backyard swimming pool became the perfect playground for happy, splashing kids. Hayrides and campfire sing-alongs were also fun, but summer camps at Sylvan Lake and the ski trips to Jasper's Marmot Basin were awesome, radical outings!"

Tracy especially endeared himself to teenagers by passing down his passion for athletics and fine arts. He encouraged a youth choir to sing gospel hymns accompanied by their own guitars and to dramatize Bible stories with modern themes and props during Sunday evening folk services inside the ancient cathedral's ornate sanctuary, in newer but smaller sister congregations, or downtown coffeehouses. Tracy meticulously schooled a few apt pupils, Orwell among them, in the science of pugilism; when he saw their promise, he engaged them in amateur boxing tournaments around the province. It was never MacDonachie's intention that nice church boys turn into prizefighters, only that they become confident, learn how to defend themselves, and keep physically fit.

If only hockey leagues had discouraged Sunday morning practices, then Orwell could have both enjoyed church and jumped on the bandwagon of Canada's national game. Yet again, Tracy made room in his busy schedule to coach a boy's hockey team from St. Andrew's and motivated them to play well and exhibit true sportsmanship. How great it was to win for such a motivator and celebrated champion!

"These are my glowing memories of Tracy MacDonachie, who will be coming to visit us in Lusaka this Easter!" Orwell, on the stroke of ten, closed his eulogy to his mentor and friend.

The forum fellow writers might not identify with Orwell's playful childhood, nor understand his abiding love for a rich white family and an ancient cathedral, but they recognized how compassion and justice, comradery and zest for good life embodied in Tracy MacDonachie had rubbed off on this young expat. Orwell Hughes, Tracy's eager protégé, had risen to the occasion; with Professor Muzorewa, Benjamin, Cepheus, Aloysius, and Winter, the assembly arose in unison to applaud Orwell's heartfelt speech, which was more compelling than any manuscript he could have read that night. He passed the acid test by sharing a slice of his life with these tough philosophers, and now took his rightful place among them. Orwell's once heavy heart soared to freedom; he openly with gratitude as he embraced forgiving and uplifting Ben.

Hughes did not know then that this strange evening would mark his last appearance at the Writers' Club; as such, he was leaving on a winning note. Fumbling to stay abreast of such critical minds from the outset, perhaps to hobble himself forever, would not have made this victory so sweet.

# CHAPTER
# EIGHT

ORWELL, EMBOLDENED BY HIS OUTPOURING about Tracy at the Writers' Club, followed the desires of his turbulent heart rather than heeded his father's strict rules or Ben's wise counsel, by accepting Georgina's challenge to think outside his box...expand his horizons...and plunge into unknown waters. To prove his desire for her, he did what Tracy would: be where Georgina was.

UNZA students' union unveiled an exotic treat for its study-weary cohort during the first week of March: an evening seminar by some touring yogis of the *Hare Krishna* faith. Against their parents' better judgment, Orwell and Richard joined the crowd of curious and impressionable youths for an adventure into the mysterious aura of eastern religion. Georgina, resplendent with her entourage of fellow seekers, also graced the packed house. When she smiled from across the room, acknowledging that he had accepted her mission to learn about other faiths, the younger Hughes euphorically concluded that he could set aside his Christian understanding for one night. *Here* was where the action was!

Colourful portraits of Lord Krishna—the mighty, blue-skinned god-prince—adorned the space, driving the chariot of his friend Arjuna, or playing the flute in lush forests surrounded by deer and peacocks. His monks, clad in orange robes and all sporting shaved heads but for a ponytail, provided an entertaining diversion to the drudgery of the rainy season and classroom assignments. The Hare Krishnas ran a short film that exuded their carefree and peaceful, vegetarian lifestyle, and the joy of being devotees to their chosen deity. The whole event was interspersed by excerpts from the sacred Hindu poem *Bhagavad-Gita* and deeply resonating chants of praise and admonition to Lord Krishna, all sung in Sanskrit—the ancient sacred language of India. They fervently distributed plates of their delicious vegetarian foods piously prepared, together with glossy pamphlets espousing spiritual enlightenment. The monks also taught their powerful chants, sung while counting *malas*—a kind of rosary—of japa beads they wore around their necks. Clay markings on their foreheads, called *tilakas*, signified they belonged to Lord Krishna.

It was a fantasy to taste and savour, but many in the impressionable crowd, including lovely Georgina, were dazzled by promises of good karma and liberation of the soul from their present dark age. Devotees would be raised to a higher level of spiritual consciousness by renouncing the pointless vanities of the world and beginning their pilgrimage back to Godhead. Many students danced blissfully and sang with the priests to the transcendental beat of drums, mimicked the intricate hand gestures—*mudras*—and repeated the great mantra to Krishna, so that they might share in His creative energy.

Orwell, however, was oppressed by what he saw as the shadowy indoctrination of a cult. His stomach felt queasy and a headache throbbed within his doubting mind as he feared that the tasty morsels so pleasantly served had been previously sacrificed to idols or spiked with mind-bending drugs by these smiling monks, who now beckoned him with glassy eyes! Orwell was beleaguered most severely by Georgina's pleasant acceptance of these bizarre festivities. How readily she and her entourage were spirited away into some distant realm wherein he could never follow! Glancing furtively at Rick, he sensed that his brother, while playing cool, was on the same wavelength as him for once! These doubting Thomases quietly slipped away...but Orwell found no peace.

Georgina's would-be lover was tormented how she had embraced the Hare Krishnas but ignored his standing invitation to attend weekly Christian gatherings on campus. She extolled her mother as a devout handmaiden of the Lord, but only occasionally did Professor Ibrahim's voluptuous guest drag her lovely body into Sunday services at the multiracial church. Her excuse: she claimed to follow Muhammad while Hughes followed Jesus, so never would they find common ground, although Professor Ibrahim comforted Orwell by teaching that Islam, Christianity, and Judaism all sprang from the same monotheistic roots, and together with Hinduism and Buddhism, formed the 'great' world religions—all of which valued peace, justice, humility, and human dignity. Orwell would have better understood if the coloured beauty practised her uncle's Muslim faith, but Georgina preferred to attend residence parties and booming dances where most religious people were awkward outsiders. Was Islam just her convenient crutch?

Orwell slept restlessly that night, yet was surprised to find the object of his affection also attending African Studies class early the next day. Georgina looked tired, though intelligently answered every question that Professor Ibrahim presented her. She boasted not about her exploits, but broached his own impressions of the Hare Krishnas when she briefly greeted Orwell on the sunlit plaza after class.

"I learned a lot, although I did not achieve enlightenment," Hughes admitted, causing Georgina to giggle at what she perceived to be a joke. He did mean it however, and he told so to the bobbing little imp who looked at him from behind her sunglasses with a wide, blissful smile, "Thanks for encouraging me to come along."

"You are most welcome, sir. Thank you for coming. I gained enough understanding of Hare Krishna to count it as an authentic sister religion rather than some sinister cult. I found last evening to be exotic—full of freedom and entertainment. Dare I say, I was enthralled like a tourist by the ageless mysteries of India? Many Westerners seek spiritual enlightenment from Eastern philosophies when science and technology fail them—look how *The Beatles* have embraced sitar music and the teachings of Maharishi Mahesh Yogi! North American and European young people backpack around the Himalayas in search of truth and peace...

"For some, Hare Krishna provides spiritual answers, but for me, the seminar was just a polite introduction to this faith, not a crusade! For the record, Orwell Hughes, I did not convert—I was not taken by force or brainwashed overnight! I am still a Muslim and stronger in my faith, although one who is now more tolerant of other voices. Did not Jesus claim that He had other sheepfolds to tend besides his own flock? Who am *I* to wear blinders or pretend to be deaf to the joys and sorrows of my neighbours when I am a modern citizen of a vibrant, multicultural world?"

Orwell gazed incredulously at Georgina, admiring her all the more for such open embrace of others. This beauty seemed so genuine in her respect and care, so determined to be inclusive; she came across as pleasant and positive, who never preached nor condemned—unlike those fundamentalist, evangelical MacDonachies or even his own devoutly Christian mother! Georgie rightly deserved her popularity, for it came from her lovely character as well as her appearance! He repressed as selfish his welling complaint that this goddess should grant him more personal attention. He did not think Georgina was including him as best she could....

"I believe that you also benefited from attending the Hare Krishnas' seminar. Christian boy, your education is expanding remarkably. I am glad to help you grow in any small way that I can," Lady Amadu assured him. Daring him to travel even further out of his safe planet in quest of knowledge of her, she coyly asked, "Shall you honour me with a dance or two on Friday night?"

"For you, Georgie girl, I'll do anything!" Orwell blurted out with ultra-chivalrous promise. "We'll dance the night away."

"Until tomorrow, then," she airily lilted as she waved goodbye and skipped down the stairway that led to the women's dorm. Surrounded by high concrete walls rigged with broken glass battlements and guarded at the narrow entrance, they both knew that no one could invade her private space once she entered it.

Orwell troubled himself throughout the next two days, battling emotions that ranged from worry over how he would dance up a storm with Georgina, to whether or not he should show at all. He liked pop and rock 'n' roll music—even high life and soul—but his memories of junior high school sock hops were rather threadbare, given that he had been a small boy who was afraid of girls, and had spent his time reading books in his classroom instead. He had danced a few times with Alicia at church socials but did not need to impress her! Annie Fannie was always there for him, tolerated his clumsiness, and took initiative to lead on the dance floor. He had finally found his nerve to initiate during International School dances, although most girls gave him just one chance or would refuse him altogether, only to be happily swept away by the next young man standing in line. Even Canadian girls like Kristi Stephenson, with whom he interacted regularly at High Commission parties, played mind games with him. Was he such a bad dancer? Was he so ugly that women would not give him a chance? He wasn't asking to date anyone, after all, only move to the music for a few minutes of fun. Contemporary music was sometimes hard to dance to but people still did their thing and tried to enjoy themselves. Hip fans tuned into band concerts found the beat—no matter what.

After he had pestered her for months, Georgina was now finally calling him out, and she expected him to comply with her summons. Perhaps, she really desired his company rather than simply teased him. Orwell vowed to learn what the lady had in mind and where he really stood with her. His crazy heart needed answers!

Richard, surprising his little brother for the second time in a week, accompanied Orwell on his quest. Bwana Hughes, unconvinced by their promise to not drink and drive, dropped his sons on campus at 8:30 p.m., having pounded into their ringing ears that they must be home by midnight! Darkening the door of the discotheque, the Hughes boys found it jumping with the blare of popular music and filled with partiers grooving to the beat.

As his eyes adjusted to the darkened blueish light, Orwell glanced around him, scanning for familiar faces. At first, he did not recognize anybody, but made out some cool cats boogying in the middle of the dance floor while countless others watched from the margins. Some ate and drank as they chatted amicably at tables. Everyone was enjoying the homegrown Afro-rock hits of *Osibisa, Fela Kuti,* and *Johnny Clegg,* which skillfully blended African drums with western jazz, rock, traditional soul, and a sprinkling of Caribbean salsa and calypso. Spicy aromas of blackened chicken, samosas, and sweet potato fries wafted through a breezeway from cooking fires on the back patio.

Not spotting Georgina in this largely black party crowd, Orwell thought to blow the joint, but then he spied Dr. Otis—a highly-published agricultural research scientist and multilingual interpreter for many international conferences—dressed in a flowery tunic and enthusiastically dancing up a storm with several fellow professors and students. Jillian Burgess, an economics post-graduate from America, smiled in recognition as she passed by with her two adoring coloured boyfriends, Fabian and Rollo in tow. He knew Benjamin would not be caught dead at such a lowbrow affair, but Orwell felt more at home when he glimpsed David and Solly dancing with fellow church choristers, Yvonne and Lalitha, and saw Winter and Aloysius chowing down on a heaping platter of barbecued chicken with several other Zambians at a table down the line. When Winter recognized his shy writer friend, he jovially waved him over to join the feast; Orwell did his best to thread his way through the rollicking crowd but was held up by other well-wishers. He good-naturedly suspended his move for now, and shouted to Winter above the festive commotion that they would meet later.

"I'll buy you a Coke," Orwell offered his brother, whose face wrinkled into a smile as he reminded him that any money he had was an allowance from their old man. Orwell shouted back above the din, "We need to get in closer to the action, man. I don't want to stand out any more than necessary."

"Okay," sighed Rick, letting his brother lead. "I'm your guest."

Orwell blushed at his comment as he cautiously escorted his older brother gingerly through the writhing, sweaty crowd. Everyone around was a blur to him until Molly suddenly moved into his path. Her eyes and teeth gleamed with excitement beneath her flowing mane of black curly hair.

"Come play with me, Orwell," she huskily suggested with a broad smile, clasping both of his hands in hers. His serious chemistry lab partner now looked the nightclub cutie as she dragged him enthusiastically onto the crowded dance floor. She kept encouraging him, "I think you dance very well to *Afrobeat*—you must almost be African now!"

"Thanks," gulped Hughes. "Here we go!"

Pleased that Molly had plucked him from the crowd and wished to dance with him, Orwell followed his exuberant friend though he really knew nothing about her night life or her dance style. Leading the way through the gyrating throng to some open space, Molly sashayed in rhythm to the drum beat. Hughes, stumbling in his efforts to mimic her energetic gait, struggled to keep up. Molly was shorter and curvier than Georgina and she enjoyed flaunting her shapely figure. Her powerful legs glistened in the light and her generous buttocks quivered deliciously under her tight miniskirt with every move she made. This normally strait-laced classmate who regularly attended mass at the Roman Catholic Church was now enticing Orwell to play with her. He turned back to glance at Rick and reassure him that he would return sometime later, and was impressed to find that his brother had joined Molly's chic friend, Diana on the dance floor.

"Orwell, over here!" Molly hailed from somewhere ahead. She giggled at his clumsy efforts to reach her. When they finally joined and he bent low to hear her in the din of the music, Molly asked, "Is that tall, dark-haired white man your brother? Don't worry about him, Orwell, he is now dancing with Diana. Please, keep dancing with me."

Orwell smiled at her invitation and blushed at the thought of embracing her luscious, exotic body and holding her hands as he struggled to lead her about—find their beat. Molly reassured his concerns by stepping back and boogying to the music as she felt it, happy and free. Staying with her friend, Molly encouraged him to do his own thing as it came naturally to him.

They danced thus together for several numbers. Glancing around him from time to time, hoping to catch Georgina's eye, Orwell discovered that he and Molly were following the trend; everyone was dancing individually in one large gyrating group, rather than cozily coupling up. An appreciative roar from the crowd called Orwell to look incredulously at Richard, who was performing back flips and push-ups in time to Diana's groove. They had the moves! Somebody dubbed Orwell's brother James Brown[31], to the applause of many. Orwell relaxed; there was obviously no set pattern to this dancing thing—one simply did what felt cool.

Molly and Diana danced as much with each other as with their dutiful male partners. Although these soul sisters moved intermittently between Orwell and Richard, they seemed happily bound to one another as they artfully swayed, twisted, and shimmied in space. They stayed in place, yet their every muscle and limb responded smoothly to the lively music. Orwell and Richard found themselves aroused by such sensuous choreography.

"You move well, without a care," Molly complemented Hughes during a break as they sipped on chilled coca colas. She shared some giggles as they recalled how he flailed his arms about, kicked his legs, and swivelled his hips like

---

31 *James Joseph Brown* (1933 to 2006): often called the 'Godfather of Soul', was an American singer, songwriter, dancer, musician, record producer, and band leader, who over a fifty-year career, influenced the development of several music genres. Starting in the late 1950s and peaking during the 1960s, Brown and his rhythm and blues (R&B) group *Famous Flames* produced such hits as: "Please, Please, Please"; "Try Me"; "Papa's Got a Brand-New Bag"; "I Got You (I Feel Good)"; and "It's a Man's, Man's, Man's World"; and built a reputation as a tireless live performer.

During the late 1960s, James Brown took an 'Africanized' approach to music making that influenced development of funk music. By the early 1970s, he had produced such hit records with the *JBs* as: "Get Up (I Feel Like a Sex Machine)"; and "The Payback". He became noted for songs of social commentary, including his 1968 hit "Say It Loud—I'm Black and I'm Proud".

Brown recorded seventeen singles that reached No. 1 on the *Billboard* R&B charts; he also isranked No. 1 in the Top 500 R&B artists from 1942 to 2004, and seventh on *Rolling Stone's* list of its one hundred greatest artists of all time. He was, in 2013 and 2017, inducted into the National R&B Hall of Fame as an artist and then a songwriter. Brown was also inducted into the Rock and Roll Hall of Fame and Songwriters Hall of Fame.

Elvis the Pelvis, to the pounding drums and peals of trumpets and saxophones. "Orwell, you are such a fun boy to dance with!"

"I try," Orwell winsomely replied, taking her observations in stride. Believing that they were simply having some good fun together, he entertained his friend by taking a hearty swig of his drink, draining the Coke bottle in one gulp to quench his parched throat. When he could speak again, he gasped, "I enjoyed dancing with you, Molly. We made a good pair out there together, did we not?"

"Certainly, and we shall dance again later, I hope," Molly offered as she laid down her empty pop bottle on the bar counter top. "Thank you, Orwell."

She smiled broadly, then strolled away buoyantly, arm in arm with Diana.

"Nice girls—maybe some promise there," Richard noted with a grin to Orwell as their gal pals rejoined the big dance. "Did you make plans with them for a future date? Did they pass you an address where we can get some tail later tonight?"

"Do you have to be so crude, man? You're grody to the max. I like Molly. She is a nice girl but she's just having fun, not looking to get laid. I'm not crazy. You can get expelled from this university for having illicit sex!" scolded Orwell, shocked and dismayed by his brother's raunchy comment. He suddenly glimpsed Georgina chatting with several young people at a nearby table. "Really Rick, I've got another girl on my mind. There's Georgie now. Let's say hello."

Orwell and Richard sauntered over to Georgina's table. She looked up from an intimate conversation with her roommate Lovelace, and smiled in the newcomers' direction. Although there was nowhere for these handsome studs to sit, Georgina congenially beckoned for Orwell to stand beside her.

"You have finally arrived, my friend. It is good to see you here at last," gushed the campus queen, as she regally clasped Orwell's hand in hers.

Georgina introduced her young friend and his brother to other handsome, well-dressed students in her party, all of whom Orwell and Richard dutifully greeted in turn. Though he could barely remember their names or faces, Georgina's inner circle all jovially acknowledged her admiring white knight.

"Likewise, my dear, but we've been here for an hour already. Richard and I have danced a set of tunes already," Orwell informed her, mystified that they had not crossed trails until now.

"Really?" she parried, her black eyes twinkling. "Then, you are surely ready for me by now. Listen! The Beatles' *White Album* is on—just for you! Come along, Lovelace; help me entertain Orwell and his bro."

The two lovely girls bounced to their feet and made their way to the dance floor. Orwell, having pulled Georgina's chair aside as she stood up, won an approving smile from the dark beauty. Their gleaming eyes met, for she stood nearly as tall as he did with her high heels on. The movement of her graceful figure, clad in a silk blouse and trendy midi skirt, sent a wave of floral fragrance as they walked happily hand in hand onto the dance floor.

Orwell's pinnacle of happiness wilted when black cat Cepheus Belo crossed his path.

"Master Orwell Hughes, then it is you after all! I am so glad to see you here, enjoying the dance in the company of this beautiful young lady," Belo exclaimed. Dressed in a flowing gown and embroidered cap that helped him stay cool in this sweaty den, Cepheus bowed low to greet Orwell's date in the Hausa *lingua franca* of their West African homeland, "Good evening, Miss Amadu. How is your family?"

"Everyone is well, sir," Georgina replied solemnly, refusing to look Cepheus in the eye. This exiled foe of her father's government should not be allowed to hold her in detention. He would rule her, though her 'old-school' countryman looked awkwardly out of place and utterly lost in front of her. Troubled enough that he was hindering her from kicking up her heels to "Ob-La-Di Ob-La-Da", she discretely cautioned Orwell, "This prowling lion does not belong here. What does he want with us?"

"Is the Professor well?"

"Yes, sir, he is doing fine."

"Thank you, I am glad to hear of your news, *Malama*. Someday, if you continue to do well in your medical studies, I will be required by convention to address you as Doctor Amadu," Cepheus offered with musical pleasantry.

Georgina warily nodded, but said nothing more to this agitator as she clung tightly to her escort, for she sensed Belo's underlying rage seething against her. A Muslim warrior blown too far south from the Sahara Desert with the dusty Harmattan Wind, Cepheus looked Georgina up and down, offended by her flowing black hair, antimony eye shadow gracing her bright brown eyes, silver earrings and beaded necklace, high-heeled shoes and svelte western dress that immodestly left uncovered her athletically toned arms and legs. Her head was not respectfully covered with the traditional Muslim *hijab*! Why did she adorn herself for this Christian white man, an infidel from the imperialistic West?

Georgina felt, from the first time she met him years ago in her uncle's house, that this sad excuse for a countryman had judged her as a spoiled girl who played the harlot. Having spent his youth in the traditional way prescribed by his religion and tribe, rote-learning the Quran by firelight and doing odd jobs and begging for food by day before being adopted by conservative Christian missionaries concerned for his soul, Belo believed that even upscale Muslim females of Georgina's station should be properly married and raising children in some rich Alhaji's house. Georgina wished to educate this prehistoric Malam Belo that she was not only a devout servant to Allah and a follower of the Prophet Muhammad—peace be upon Him—but a modern, liberated woman with God-given talents to help make the world a better place for all to live in... with love, peace and joy.

Cepheus smiled triumphantly at the obvious nervousness he caused her, as he left her to squirm while he addressed his fellow writer, "I much enjoyed your dissertation the other night at our club meeting, Mr. Orwell. You spoke very passionately about your mentor Tracy MacDonachie, who I understand will do us all the honour of a visit here to Lusaka at the end of this rainy season, during your Christian festival of Easter. Am I correct, sir?"

"On all accounts, Cepheus," Orwell replied, beaming, as he assured both Nigerians, "I happily anticipate Tracy's visit. I am honoured that he wishes to look me up in this wonderful place. You, my friends, must meet him when he comes."

"I wish to learn more about Mr. MacDonachie...I definitely want to meet this legend of a man who so inspires you!" Belo declared in all seriousness, though he appeared to be on the verge of ridiculing Orwell as some underling. "I feel that I have already met him—perhaps I have, actually. When Tracy MacDonachie comes, I will know for certain, for I do not easily forget people whom I have experienced in past times. Then, God willing, my peace of mind will return. Do you perchance have Rev. MacDonachie's photograph to show me, Mr. Orwell?"

"Not on me, but there are some photos of Tracy and his talented singing family at my house," Orwell proudly answered. "Why don't you pay me a visit sometime, Cepheus, and we will look at some memorabilia together?"

Georgina also pricked up her ears in interest and piped in, "You've never shown me any memorabilia!" pouted Georgina. "Surely, Orwell, I should also be invited, but ahead of Mr. Belo, to view your impressive musical collection. We only scratched the surface when my brother Ali and I visited your family last Christmas."

"Certainly, my dear, you are most welcome to grace us with your presence whenever you wish, but I am especially thrilled to invite you over the Easter holidays, to meet Tracy and his sisters, Kathleen and Alicia," Orwell promised Georgina, blushing at the spark in her huge dark eyes that suddenly reminded him of Alicia in all her angry splendour. Orwell continued, "If Easter is too far away and you are in agreement, I could bring my *MacDonachie Family Singers* album to where you stay on weekends with Professor Ibrahim."

"We will talk more about this after our dance. Let us go now and have some fun, sir," Georgina smiled appreciatively as she prodded Orwell along. In passing, she triumphantly dismissed Cepheus with a brief, "Have a good evening, Malam Belo."

The Sahelian prince, determined not to be outdone by this vixen, detained Orwell a little longer. Intrigued that Hughes was willing to suffer at being tugged away by a girl, he trotted out a petition, "I wish to review that manuscript you brought but chose not to read the other night at the Writers' Club. You have told me a few juicy tidbits about the guard you once employed and I would like to read all the gory details myself. In fact, they much interest me."

"I will lend you the manuscript next week," Orwell shouted over his shoulder above the buoyant din of *The Beatles'* "Back in the USSR", even as Georgina vigorously pulled him along. "Mind me though, it's for your eyes only."

Cepheus nodded at his reply and grinned with sinister pleasure as he giggled, "Excellent, Master Hughes. Enjoy the rest of this evening—if you dare!"

Orwell and Georgina totally got down into their dancing then as they shared a suite of chart-topping pop, rock, R&B, and disco numbers: "Joy to the World" and "Black and White" from *Three Dog Night*; *Mungo Jerry's* "In the Summertime"; "Power to the People" from John Lennon; "Cecilia" by *Simon and Garfunkel*; a couple of peppy instrumentals like "Little Arrows" from *Hammond-Hazelwood*; and "Hey Tonight" by J.C. Fogerty. Another popular number was "Baby Come Back" by *The Equals*—an interracial, British pop-rock band that had recently toured Zambia—all put on the turntables during the following hour, seemingly for their special enjoyment by the talented DJ. After a well-deserved break, *The*

*Beach Boys* came on with "Help Me Rhonda" and "Barbara Ann", and *Credence Clearwater Revival* kept pace with "Bad Moon Rising" and Proud Mary". Contemporary black American artists like Wilson Pickett with "In the Midnight Hour" and "Hey Jude", and the *Supremes* with their "Come See About Me" and "You Can't Hurry Love" were also featured. The exotic couple entertained their peers, leading the pack in tribute to hits twisting with Chubby Checker, wrapping a long human chain about the room for *Grand Funk*'s "Loco-Motion" and energetically rock 'n' rolling during Chuck Berry's "Sweet Little Sixteen" and "Johnny B. Goode".

For Orwell, this night was sweet to savour; his heart soared when he realized that Georgina was also enjoying their fun. He could see it in her soft eyes and broad grins, and by the energy she exuded in making every dance come alive for him. Georgie, a tennis star as good as Aussie aborigine Yvonne Goolagong[32], showed off her powerful and curvaceous body as she moved tirelessly in perfect time to various genres. Like Molly, Georgina could really shake her booty, but she seemed more refined; this coloured goddess felt soft and cool and smelled of *Chanel No 5* whenever they affectionately brushed against each other. Over drinks that Georgie let him buy, the healthy, sun-kissed girl chattered sweetly with him about many various topics; she laughed easily, and freely touched his arm to emphasize a point. He could feel her hand intimately clasping his as they strolled to and from the dance. Georgina was becoming a close friend after all; she gladly accepted his company....

Miss Amadu, as though reading his mind, suddenly made it clear that he should cool his heels and not claim her as his own! Their main event wound down as Hughes patiently stood aside or danced on his own or with others, when Lovelace or Gladwyn showed up to whisper secrets in Georgina's ear. He good-naturedly agreed if other males like Joseph, Edward, and even Rick cut in to take the popular beauty for a spin. Georgina returned to him after a few bars of music or during the next song, but she played along with each new partner

32 Evonne Goolagong Cawley (1951 - ), an Australian aborigine, was a former world #1 tennis player (1976) and one of the world's leading players during the 1970s and early 1980s. She won fourteen Grand Slam titles, including seven singles (at Wimbledon, and Australian or French Opens), six women's doubles and one mixed doubles championships. Ms. Goolagong Cawley recorded eighty-two singles titles and won 704 of 869 total professional matches; she was inducted into the International Tennis Hall of Fame in 1988.

and received his attention for as long as she wished, in carefree oblivion of what Orwell might be doing meantime. There was no need for him to hover over Georgina; it would actually be foolish to do so, since there were many young men fluttering around this special gal, eager to earn her favour.

Georgina also sensed that the handsome white man was well-liked by many young ladies on campus, so could also have his pick of dance partners. Black girls appreciated that this gentle giant accepted them all as friends, regardless of colour or cultural differences. He admired their exotic beauty and was intrigued by their different backgrounds and stories. Indeed, Lovelace, Molly, Diana, and Gladwyn took turns keeping him busy whenever Georgina flitted away with her next dance partner.

Orwell felt honoured by all the sweet girls frolicking with him, but he was tossed another curve ball when Cepheus suddenly showed up on the dance floor with him. At first, Hughes thought that the eclectic Nigerian might engage him in some tiresome dialogue about the gross immorality of western music, but when he just kept gyrating with him, Orwell did not know what to do. At first, he felt embarrassed that Cepheus thought him gay, but his ladies-in-waiting politely made way for the chief; indeed, they softly clapped when Orwell sheepishly humoured him for more than one agonizing minute of artistic interaction. Georgina encouraged Orwell to play along, while she sashayed past with Joseph—she did not however return to her Canadian admirer after this interaction!

Afterwards, Cepheus grabbed Orwell's right hand in his and bid they walk together to the bar for a cold beer. He refused to explain his actions further; as the music was too loud for them to talk comfortably without shouting, Hughes dumbly complied like a lamb being led to slaughter. Cepheus bought two bottles of local brew after which, at his artful instruction, they drained their frothy beverages with flexed right arms intertwined in a ritual of male bonding. Orwell found himself staring at a beautiful gold ring glinting on Belo's elegant finger, strongly cast yet daintily woven.

In a moment of reflection, he remembered that it was common for virile, heterosexual African men to hold hands as they casually strolled on campus or about town. His five years in Zambia taught him that such affection was a sign of friendship, trust, and mutual respect between males; nothing sexual intended! Homosexuality was a crime, but was it not culturally appropriate for African men or women to socialize separately at parties? Women and children often sat apart from their men folk in church or at official functions. Orwell had observed many new and interesting things, yet he found Cepheus' advances upon his space ominously threatening!

"Thank you, my friend Mister Orwell, for truly you are my friend—the one dear friend I count upon here at this detestable University of Zambia!" Cepheus applauded him. "You understand me; you care for all Africa and her people!"

"My faith and upbringing teach me to care!" Orwell replied, sounding more defiant than intended. "I want to learn. I want to share. I want to get along. Mutual understanding and respect between people are what make the world go around."

"Indeed. You remind me of Canada's late Prime Minister, Lester Pearson, the great UN peacekeeper who resolved the 1956 Suez Canal crisis in Egypt," Cepheus declared. He gazed wistfully at his companion and prophesied, "Mr. Orwell, someday you will serve mankind as a diplomat or mediator. I believe you will save many people with your patience and sensitivity."

His eyes exuded intelligence, while his long, regal face appeared handsome in the dim light of the club. Although dark brown skinned and curly-haired, he did not carry the flattened nose and thick lips that Orwell naively associated with Negroid people. Rather, Cepheus' features looked vaguely Caucasian save for the colour of his skin grown dark against the scorching sun, and that three razor scars sliced down each cheek identified him as belonging to the Kanuri tribe. Orwell fancied him to be some fabled desert prince from the *Arabian Nights*, or perhaps one of the Wise Men who had visited the infant Jesus. He seemed ageless, immortal. Cepheus dropped no hints, but enjoying Orwell's speculation, he determinedly remained a cleverly unsolved mystery to the searching lad.

"I am going now, Mr. Orwell. The noise and confusion of this flesh pot troubles my soul," he informed him as he arose abruptly to leave. Whether Cepheus was drunk, Orwell could not tell, but this sudden movement caused him to stumble.

"Let me help you," Orwell offered, quickly moving with concern to support him, lest Belo fall headlong to the floor.

"*Bature*[33], you are free to come or go as you wish. Do not be concerned with

---

33 *Bature*: Hausa word meaning 'white or European' man.

my minor difficulties," Cepheus rasped as he struggled against Orwell to regain his composure.

"I see that you are unwell. Let me help," insisted Orwell kindly, trying to calm his troubled companion.

"Please remember then to supply me with your manuscript at our earliest convenience. I also wish meet your friend, Mr. Tracy MacDonachie, so that I too may be enriched by him and therefore come to terms with my own checkered life. Do you agree with me on these accounts, Mr. Orwell?"

"I understand, and will do my best to help you."

Leaving the club unnoticed by his brother, Georgina or any of his friends, Orwell cautiously walked a teetering Cepheus up the stairs and down the hall, stopping when he stopped, stepping where he trod, and hospitably talking to him only as required to keep Cepheus lucid.

"I will visit the men's room now, Mr. Orwell, to relieve and freshen myself. My head is clearing, and I think I can manage independently from this juncture," Cepheus declared as they reached a small sitting area with washrooms located nearby. He nodded appreciatively as he shuffled away, "Thank you, Mr. Orwell, for your most generous assistance."

"You're welcome, President Belo," Orwell replied, good-naturedly saluting the Writers' Club's grand poohbah. They both laughed. "I will sit here for a few minutes and take a break. If you need anything, just call me."

"I hear you. Have a good evening."

They respectfully parted ways. After Cepheus disappeared into the bathroom, Orwell sat down on one of the benches in the open-air vestibule across the hall. Although he was suddenly tired, on top of struggling with the many confusing images from the momentous evening, Orwell strove to stay alert as he waited twenty minutes in vain for Cepheus to re-emerge. Several people came and went, some of whom nodded or gazed curiously at the white man, but Hughes did not see the flamboyant magus again. With mounting concern, he finally entered the bathroom himself to investigate. The wily fox was nowhere to be found!

Was Belo a ghost? Had the President rubbed his magic ring and slipped away through an air vent or a floor drain? Had he stolen to freedom in disguise, Orwell wondered as he stomped out of the loo, totally frustrated. After scouring the empty, concrete hallways in vain, Orwell glanced at an overhead clock—it was twenty to twelve, for God sake! His enchanted night was over; he had wasted it trying to placate confusing folks who cared less about him!

Orwell rushed back to the dance hall to find Rick and hopefully, get a final squeeze or even a smile of appreciation from Georgina. Sifting through the writhing crowd, he glimpsed Molly first, chatting with her favourite friend in dark glasses while she sat on his knee with a beer in her hand. On the floor, Rick was whirling like a dervish between Diana and Lovelace. Georgina, her jacket on and a fancy purse slung over her shoulder, appeared to be leaving the action, escorted by Joseph and Edward.

"Let's go for coffee, Georgina," Orwell offered when she passed where he was plopped on a bench. Anguished by her glazed eyes and sensual smile as he rose to accost her, Orwell added, "I've got to talk to you."

"Really?" she airily quizzed, teasing him by suggesting he could follow her to the women's powder room if it was urgent. When he refused to share her lilting laughter, Georgina vexed him all the more with her lame excuse. Gesturing to her friends hovering in the shadows, Georgina assured him, "I'm in good hands to journey home safely, when I decide to leave. Go home yourself, Christian, you look tired—I'd better stay behind with the other lost people!"

Georgina headed on her way but her soft rebuke cut Orwell deeply, causing him to reel with guilt and despair. How could Georgina scoff at his determined faith when two great religions flourished in her parents' home? Perhaps he had played too purely and had alienated her with his stance. What awful thing had he said or done to so deeply offend her? How could he return into her good graces? Orwell simply could not reach Georgina, for all his effort. And who were those men who entertained her? Why did Georgina trust them more than Orwell, and enjoy their companionship over his? Now, they served as bodyguards and had earned the exotic beauty's gratitude by deflecting Orwell's attempt to invite her. If only this would-be crusader could rescue his wayward girl and reclaim her for God....

The rattled young poet stumbled out of the discotheque. He pay-phoned his father to request a ride home for himself and his brother. Humiliated, he admitted to Bwana Hughes that his engagement with the disco crowd and loud music had ended on an unsettling note, which confirmed his father's austere advice that rock music and dancing in crowded, smoky nightclubs were idle diversions not worthy of his keen mind. James Hughes, to Orwell's relief, expressed no victory in hearing his son's halting admission, and he agreed to fetch his sons to bring them home.

While huddled in the bus shelter, listening half-heartedly to Richard mooning over beautiful Lovelace, Orwell questioned his own fundamental beliefs and the gutless way by which he surrendered Georgina to her bodyguards. His racing imagination conjured awful scenes of his beloved dove being sacrificed to some dark spirits of music land. Where was she now...was she safe? Hughes had been warned that he had no business soliciting the affections of Black or Asian women, many of whom were more beautiful than Georgina could ever hope to be! Molly found Orwell pleasing and would date him at the drop of a hat. Could he muster the fortitude to cultivate a genuine yet seemingly forbidden friendship with her? How could he give up his dogged pursuit of the unattainable, mulatto woman whom he foolishly thought he knew and understood? Georgina treated him as a boyish admirer, an amusing plaything; he did not exist to her as a real contender, despite his intense efforts to woo her. Encouraged by the goddess herself, many rivals defied him and pursued her with equal ardour. In the end, it always came down to her choice of friends, her right to do as she pleased. Did it matter to Georgina that Orwell Hughes could leave on a morning plane, and be lost to her forever? He seriously doubted that he and Georgina were meant to ever be together.

There was no justice in life, Orwell bemoaned. What else could he do now but pray for God's help? He hoped God's answer would be found in Tracy.

# CHAPTER NINE

Orwell's pessimistic outlook was opened by the prospect of Tracy's upcoming visit, which like a magic pen made him view the world again as vibrant—full of hope and expectation. Balmy sunshine returned as the rainy season ended, bursting his doldrums, disillusionment, and weariness. As when he had first encountered Africa in 1969, the young poet bonded afresh with all he experienced, his golden head in the fluffy clouds, where he saw battleships and animals rather than leaden rain. He glimpsed Heavenly glory in every glowing sunset, and found peace in the soft greenery of fading summer. Africa smiled in sweet acknowledgement upon Orwell as he promised to shower his coming guest with her mysterious finery.

"How jolly has Orwell become!" marvelled friends and family. "About time!"

Pleased by his transformation, nobody dared question him lest they upset the applecart. Orwell refused to divulge the secret of his newfound happiness, except that he trusted better days lay ahead. Only his mother knew the depth of his desperation; savouring this bloom, she refused to pluck it from the vine.

The rejuvenated youth wrote often to his faraway hero, telling MacDonachie about his uplifting church music and school athletics, and commenting on burning issues of social justice, race relations, and religious turmoil—not to mention his desire to win the heart of a certain young woman who played hard to get. Until the recent letter announcing his visit, Tracy had never replied. Orwell, although disappointed, had accepted The Great One's silence as him being too busy to write petty little letters as he roamed over this grand universe, doing more important things for the Lord.

Thus, when word finally came down like manna from Heaven that Tracy was planning an actual visit, the ecstatic lad thought his hero would march into Lusaka at any moment, laud his accomplishments, and solve all his irritations. He not only expected bold MacDonachie to pour out entertainment to overflowing...but help Orwell enter into manhood, to gain the approval of Bwana and Richard Hughes, and bushwhack the ignoramuses on campus who tormented him for being foreign and thus evil. Georgina Amadu would finally see him as dating material, not a simple child!

"Tracy will show me how to woo that willowy vixen," Orwell vowed, as he penned yet another emotionally-charged tome to his mentor.

Made quietly confident by the promise in waiting, Orwell continued to befriend Georgina, but refused to chase her anymore with the same reckless abandon. What was the use? Why embarrass her, when she retained her divergent tact of avoiding anything but the most casual interaction with her sworn admirer?

Georgina did her best to reduce any risk of an impromptu encounter, yet they now ran into each other more often than not. She now occasionally attended Sunday worship services at his church. When Orwell chose to sit with Dave and Solly, Joachim and Beatrice Phiri, or the van der Merwe girls rather than Georgina, he sometimes caught her quizzically glancing his way, hoping that he might smile back at her. Orwell was left puzzled by such behaviour. As a sports aficionado, Orwell attended her tennis matches and thus watched Georgina play Zambia's best at the Lusaka Club or on UNZA's clay courts, but he let other admirers rally around the star and only carried her racquets when the moment felt right. Hughes sauntered ahead or followed behind, chatting with others, sometimes carrying another girl's gear as players and fans strolled along the winding, stony path back to the dorms after a meet. While she pretended to be unaware of Orwell's affection, Georgie appreciated his growing maturity and sent him mixed messages that gave him hope, as she continued to smile and engage with him after he had put away his useless butterfly net during those final, churning weeks of semester.

Rather than find disappointment by pursuing her, Orwell chose to savour his better memories of Georgina until Tracy arrived. He had been impressed from the get-go by the wide understanding of geography, history, art, and literature she had displayed a year ago when they had competed on opposing secondary school teams during the televised *Knowledge Quest* play downs. Orwell's expat team had lost by the narrowest of margins to her Zambian side in the final when confronted with a raft of questions tapping deeply into local knowledge, but Georgina had humbly admitted to him afterwards that her team had been given an honest run for its money.

They had prepared together for the Ordinary Level exams at the end of Form VI, under the same private tutor—a dowdy British professor lady who demonstrated the mechanics of pulleys, levers, and prisms in the cluttered kitchen of her rambling old farmhouse on the edge of town. Edith Halliwell had even used her own children as well as some of the houseboy's brood as components of complex mathematical equations, dramatized among overgrown flowerbeds and rough-cut grass in her jungle-like garden. Dr. Halliwell was a brilliant physicist who taught UNZA students and had written the physics textbook that Orwell and Georgina studied from, but one would not know it from looking at the state of her house...or her children...*man,* were they shabbily attired! Barefoot, unkempt, haystacks for hair—they came to church sloppily dressed, in cardigans and knickers fit for some hike in Luangwa Valley Game Park! Since Professor Halliwell was a widow and did not employ a nanny, supervision of this half-wild brood—at least in public—fell to Sylvia, her eldest daughter, who always looked harried and sternly prim and proper when she was in charge, in stark contrast to the usual jovial mood displayed by the popular UNZA engineering student who enthusiastically gave her all to the Campus Christian Fellowship. Orwell and Georgina had shared many secret laughs while learning physics from Professor Halliwell.

At first, he had wrongly assumed that this beautiful young woman was Zambian, and had been raised in one of the teeming townships sprawled below his elite hilltop neighbourhood, or maybe hailed from a local rural village. It was not until he accepted a ride home from Professor Ibrahim one hot Saturday noon after his African Studies class did Orwell learn that Georgina lived like a mysterious princess among beautiful gardens and elegant stone archways behind the protective walls of Ibrahim's colonial mansion. The esteemed educator had found the youngsters chatting amicably outside Georgina's cinderblock dorm when he, rather than his driver, had come to pick her for the weekend. Georgie had turned quiet during the ride into the city, demurely deferring to the menfolk as they discussed affairs of the continent in Hausa—her language! She seemed perturbed when Orwell gladly accepted the Professor's unexpected invitation to dine rather than take his leave when he was dropped at the curb outside the gate of Ibrahim's compound. Georgina had played dutiful server, bringing cold drinks into the drawing room for the men while they reviewed the Professor's pet academic peeves: 'Unity or Poverty', 'Africa in Social Change', and 'African Political Systems'. Complaining of fatigue, she had then retired to her bedroom for the afternoon, leaving Orwell to engage her uncle.

Presented with a simple meal of hard-boiled eggs, sweet rolls, fresh fruit, and tea, Orwell had dined alone while his Muslim host prayed before retiring to the back porch to read his mail. What a unique meal it had been, sitting alone in a strange mansion, his plate regularly replenished by a uniformed butler who was at Orwell's beck and call! An egg, he learned, could be opened with aristocratic etiquette by being daintily set in a silver cup and beheaded with an ornate guillotine-like tool. When he had eaten his fill, Orwell rang the bell for the butler to clear away the dishes. He had then politely thanked the professor for his fine hospitality and strolled home.

Georgina had joined the Hughes family for dinner last Christmas. The princess, together with her globetrotting, playboy brother Ali, and Orwell's good friend Benjamin Mudenda, had enjoyed a sumptuous holiday fare of roast goose with steamed sweet potatoes, spinach and baby carrots, freshly baked sourdough biscuits, and mango-orange marmalade. After the meal, everyone had gathered in the parlour to sing Christmas carols to Orwell's piano accompaniment. Georgina had led the group in a soulful rendition of "Kumbaya My Lord", the only Christian song that she knew! Georgie bashfully explained to her encouraging Canadian hosts that she and fellow primary students back home in Nigeria had often sung this missionary tune during chapel or at special school assemblies—the words meant 'Come by Here, My Lord' in pidgin English....

Everybody had then strolled onto the front lawn, where they had engaged in a vigorous 'snowball fight' using cotton batting for ammo: what a midsummer's daydream for young people seeking fellowship! Ali and Suzy, JJ and Benjamin, had played lawn darts with Orwell and Georgina; the players had taken a special liking to one another that tamed their competition into a collaboration sweetened with laughter and friendly banter. JJ had enjoyed big Ben's gentle attention, but while being too strict with her own regimen to fall for boyfriends, she was quite the romantic pixie where others' hearts were concerned; Janice Joanne had played matchmaker between Orwell and his glorious lady friend!

Orwell, pretending to be manly, scolded his impish sister for prying into the affairs of her elders, but ignoring such bluster, JJ encouraged the young poet to show Georgina how his lush garden grew. Indeed, Georgina had adorned her wavy black hair with beautiful flowers for Orwell to admire while he pushed her on the swing in the cool of the day. How gleefully she had laughed…They had pleasantly chatted, her exquisite milk chocolate face aglow seemingly only for him! He had fallen in love, but Georgina was beyond his reach even then, so the young poet had refrained from wading in too deep, choosing instead to hold back and hope for tomorrow, as was socially acceptable across such diverse boundaries as theirs.

*****

ORWELL, surrendering his troubles to God and placing his hope in Tracy, focused now on what God had given him to do, rather than on his own desires. He maintained top-drawer scholastic grades, but refused to become some recluse who spent every spare hour studying mathematics or writing essays in the library. He cultivated his male African friends—Benjamin, Solomon, David, Winter, and Cepheus. He dutifully took his turn at distributing food stuffs in shantytown for the church's Social Action Committee, with Mr. Granger and his shy Afrikaner nieces, Katrina and Andrea, plus young Zambian men like Crispin, Daniel, Godfrey, and Fwanya. Together with Ben, Solly, Dave, Sylvia, and other volunteers from Campus Christian Fellowship, Orwell raised funds for an adult literacy program by collecting pledges and walking twenty miles through Lusaka one balmy Sunday afternoon. He felt free to serve God fully, since the anguish of unrequited love no longer pulled him down—life was fun, not a bust! Orwell chose to enjoy each day for itself, no matter what!

The young poet was filled with daydreams about reconnecting with Tracy. What amazing adventures they would share as he entertained MacDonachie with the exotic highlights of his adopted world. Hughes could hardly wait to show his idol some impressive trophies of his own, but he also needed help in mastering new challenges that he had set for himself...and not just with Georgina!

He would make his acting debut in Lusaka's ecumenical Easter pageant during Tracy's visit...Orwell had been dutifully practising with his group of fellow Christian artists under the masterful direction of Mrs. Veronica

Musakanya, a church friend who was also Zambia's Minister of Art, Culture & Antiquities. In spite of this, he laboured now against growing stage fright as the Big Night approached. Tracy would not only be watching from the gala audience to encourage him, but the seasoned star of stage and screen, who understood and shared Orwell's theatrical aspirations, would help his nervous tutee learn his lines and train his voice.

He could also envision Tracy cheering him on as he played goalkeeper for the UNZA field hockey team in its stretch drive toward the national collegiate championship. Orwell was sure that his advocate would see his worth and persuade the team's coach and captains that he deserved to be starting goalie, not warm the bench and play second fiddle. Although Orwell did whatever was asked of him to help the team win, he spent most of the season blocking shots on the practice pitch. He had also perfected his complex defensive techniques, diligently honed his own ball-blocking skills, and had rigorously followed an exercise routine of long-distance running through the savannah to maintain his physical endurance and mental sharpness. He was ready to play at any position at all times, in case the call came to participate in the big game where Tracy would be watching.

Yet, Orwell despaired that the time left was so short before Tracy's arrival! Feeling inadequately prepared to host his hero, he nurtured a driving ambition to present himself fit for all faculties before his mentor. Obsessed with achieving excellence , Orwell devoured his textbooks, meticulously completed his remaining assignments, and paid all the attention due to his professors' lectures. Thank the Lord, he would be done with school and on vacation when Tracy arrived for Easter! Orwell planned to ace every test and then give his undivided attention to his guest. Concerned he was not fit but perceived as lazy, Orwell purged himself of all complacency and demanded that his family members do the same rigorous service. If Orwell had been performing well beforehand in field hockey, boxing, table tennis, and soccer, receiving Mr. MacDonachie's letter made him feverishly train his body through a gruelling, iron man regimen of daily weightlifting, jogging, and cycling to make up for any previous slacking.

*****

ORWELL arose early one Saturday morning in late March to the majesty of the red sun stealing upwards through the umbrella silhouettes of acacia and jacaranda trees. The daily rebirth of this ancient god gilded the cactus, sisal, and aloe gardens, and washed the dark lawns with a crimson glow. Rains had bathed these verdant landscapes the previous evening; morning mists floating away sprinkled down dew freshly scented by flowers.

"Praise God! It's good to be alive; treasure this miracle of returning hope!" Orwell exclaimed, breathing in the heady aromas wafting on the balmy breeze as he cranked open the windows and dressed to meet the day.

"Why, because Tracy is en route?" murmured a groggy voice across the boys' bedroom.

Rick stared incredulously as his crazy brother jogged past his mosquito net. Moaning as he shielded his eyes with a pillow from the dazzling sunlight, Rick rolled over to salvage his sleep.

"That lazy bones has no concept of my joy! Tracy is flying halfway around the world, just to see me; he's my special friend!" boasted Orwell as he shadow-boxed with his reflection in the hallway mirror. Good fortune was his, at last!

Padding exuberantly into the empty living room, Orwell sat on the plastic shell chair—vowing to linger only long enough to lace up his sneakers before heading out for a run—but he soon reclined on the sofa, surveying his beautiful kingdom as he played his parents' *MacDonachie Family Singers* record on the phonograph, and basked in the angelic renderings of Christendom's beloved gospel hymns. Orwell relished the peaceful hush of the still sleeping household as a sanctuary that amplified Nature's outdoor symphony of songbirds, doves, and roosters. He was mesmerized by the playful shadows of the pepper trees dancing in the breeze on the whitewashed porch walls, inspired by the gracefully waving leaves and colourful petals of the giant protea flowers as they nodded good day greetings to him from their beds further down the sidewalk. Was his sensitive side showing? Women would applaud it but what would Tracy think?

As he listened, Orwell pored over the image featured on the glossy record jacket and was enthralled by the likeness of MacDonachie's handsome baritone standing tall against the majestic background of rugged, snow-capped Rocky Mountains wrapped in autumn gold. The young poet breathed in the pristine alpine air as he marvelled at how lovely Jane and Evelyn appeared in their black evening gowns. Their lilting voices intertwined sweetly with the rich harmony of the four brothers, so elegantly attired in white tuxedoes—but wait, who on God's green earth were the other two lovelies who completed the happy family portrait? As he read the names mentioned in the group's bio, Orwell was amazed at how much Alicia and Kathleen had grown and blossomed into goddesses of beauty and grace!

The Lord, against all odds, had given Tracy two gorgeous young travel mates for his mission to Africa! Remembering, with a pang of guilt cutting through his awe, how in the not-so-distant past he had obnoxiously teased Alicia and received her tempestuous ire in response, Hughes suddenly felt afraid, very afraid for his future as he snapped off the music and launched into his morning jog.

Tug, the family's German shepherd, waited patiently on the doorstep to indulge in his daily moment of glory; he eagerly bounded after his master as Orwell started down the leafy street. Balmy morning air caused wings to sprout on Orwell's heels, and he felt buoyed as he ran vigorously through the already bustling city. Nothing better than a short run before his one boring class of the weekend, and to limber up for a vital play-off hockey match later that afternoon... Orwell was eager to take on all opposition before breakfast!

Unaware of his impact on curious passersby, the blonde muscular athlete flew like an angel down the grassy, tree-lined meridian of Independence Avenue. He respectfully honoured from afar the President's State House, a colonial mansion of red brick and marble pillars that stood among manicured lawns and shady trees, like Tara from *Gone with the Wind*. He fancied that a platoon of black servants waited primly upon Zambia's First Family and their guests—the official list occasionally including his own parents—inside the gracious halls or among the splendid grounds of that grand residence. The clip of a military band playing the Zambian national anthem that opened and ended the daily TV broadcasts, had been filmed behind the State House.

Further along his circuit, Orwell saluted the beautiful stained-glass windows of the Anglican Cathedral and the imposing stone lions that guarded the red brick High Court. The multi-storied Civic Centre appeared to be waiting for people like an ocean liner moored at harbour. Dreaming of lovely sea cruises that he might take someday, Orwell considered stopping in for breakfast at the five-star, InterContinental Hotel, like wild rover Tracy would do on a whim, but he then remembered that he was just a jobless expatriate student with a dog, running down the road. Heading homeward, the pair passed several diplomatic missions, including the Canadian High Commission where Bwana Hughes was already toiling at his desk. Orwell dared not beg money off his old man today, knowing how busy he was, preparing for the incoming jet-load of Canadians recruited to contribute to Zambia's progress. They rounded the towering stone Cenotaph but stayed as far as possible away from the heavily guarded Government Secretariat—hulking nearby with its array of cream-coloured archways and giant golden eagle ornament glistening in the sun—without breaking stride, lest he or his dog provoke watching soldiers to question his presence!

Tug enthusiastically bounded ahead or trotted behind his beloved master, but was never too far away to return to heel at Orwell's call. Hughes was encouraged by Tug's high spirits and knew he would never outrun his canine mate. Like Tracy, Tug raced with pleasure against man or beast. Tug hated to be left behind during family outings. Could he be seen as anything else but family...be anywhere else but be with his friends? Whenever he was left behind, unchained in the yard, Tug would leap over the gate and pursued the car until he overtook his unsuspecting humans—then, giggling with embarrassment and awe, they invited him into the vehicle as soon as they could pull over.

During his turbulent lifetime, Tug had gone through many masters, but none had subdued him nor kept their end of the bargain. Tug had learned early in his life to steal meat from the local grocery store. It amused Orwell that in all the Asian shops protected by barred windows, armed guards, and concrete walls crowned with jagged glass against the poor black man, one stray dog could play the stealthy thief! Why should Tug not turn up his nose and refuse to eat some bland gruel handed him by his keeper when he could fetch a prime beefsteak any time he pleased?

Tug also felt ultimate humiliation when the Hughes household required him to bathe. He always hid before the tub of warm, soapy water arrived in the yard. When finally cornered, and dragged piteously as if through Hell itself, this mighty canine would endure his torment with much indignity, only to rub off that hated soap in the mud at the first moment of freedom. Orwell often wished he could dispense entirely with this biweekly ritual, but was brutally reminded of the need to keep the dog clean when ticks migrated into the virgin territory of his own groin. After all, Tug was an adventurer, and thus a bearer of all manners of creepy crawlies from Africa's untamed undergrowth.

Tug had earned the hatred of neighbouring dogs because he strode free. On this sunny Saturday morning in upscale suburbia, the loyal dog followed his human, deaf to the loud taunts and provocative barks of watch dogs kept behind the fences along their route. Tug ignored the cacophony as he paraded past with his head held high, his eyes gazing straight ahead and his bushy tail proudly flying like a flag...Tug was a take-charge showman, Orwell marvelled—the amazing Tracy M of his canine world!

Their feeling of sheer freedom inspired Orwell to whistle a church hymn as they bounded up the hill. His eagle eye took in everything without missing a beat. Roosters crowed while children played among banana groves, clustered about the servants' quarters hidden behind great white mansions of bygone Empire glory. Reggae music danced out of radios, as women chattered happily where they cooked over charcoal fires. An African judge, robed in black and crowned in a curled white wig, left his palatial home for the High Courthouse, riding in a polished, government-issue Mercedes Benz car driven by a uniformed chauffeur. At the entrance of another estate, the gate boy manned the barrier while his white madam and her native cook wheeled past en route to the European supermarket.

A cloud suddenly came over Orwell as he paused in front of Ibrahim's spiked wrought iron gate. In a few short hours, after they had attended African Studies class together, the girl he loved would be returning to this palatial sanctuary for the weekend, but the young poet would not be dining or even riding with her. She might swim in the pool or stroll about the lush grounds during the sun-kissed afternoon, perhaps dance in town for the evening with her trendy friends or entertain them with table tennis, billiards, and card games over finger foods and soft drinks at the house. Orwell assumed the professor had already left for UNZA, as he could not see his Citroen parked on the driveway but *lo,* a green Volkswagen beetle was stationed outside the garage and a gleaming Rolls Royce limousine that he had never seen before rested under the canopied carriage way. What esteemed visitors was the rich Nigerian household hosting this weekend? Had Georgina's phantom father come with a handpicked suitor, to whisk Orwell's beloved away forever? Had playboy brother Ali blown in for some wild house party with his high-class pals where Hughes, a lowly boy from down the road, was not invited? Orwell wanted to brood upon his undeserved misfortunes a little longer, but when a guard suddenly emerged from the shrubbery and leered at him through the gate bars, he was startled and jogged towards home.

The neighbouring lot west of Hughes House was overgrown with woody thickets and breast-high grass, behind whose screen a shabby house stared out through dark, vacant windows. Its once grand decor had been pilfered long ago and the haunted place was now abode to bats, snakes, and rats—not to mention the occasional human squatters. Rumour had it that Lusaka's white Police Chief had previously lived in that eyesore when it was still beautiful, but the old Brit had abandoned the place, lock, stock and barrel when his wife, caught home alone, had been beaten during a violent burglary. How could such a tragedy have occurred without galvanizing the neighbourhood, if not the Canadians newly arrived next door? As Orwell and Tug raced up the driveway of their own tranquil home, he mused at how much life he heard and smelled travelling his circuit that the rich expats strove to shield from outsiders behind steel gates, armed guards, and great thorn hedges—barriers that, apparently, were of little deterrent to foxes bent on ravaging the hen house!

Iron Man and his best friend powered into their yard while the family was polishing off breakfast. Tug drank thirstily from his bowl and then chowed down on a pile of bones that JJ had set out for him. Orwell doused himself with a watering can he had filled at the garden spigot before he charged ravenously indoors. Unaware that the houseboy laughing at his antics from the kitchen window had set his family abuzz, wet-down Orwell slid into place at the dining room table and tied into a heaping bowl of fruit salad while eyes were fixed with amusement upon him.

"What?" Orwell finally demanded of his pesky little sisters, who giggled and winked at him while he tried to dine. The imps didn't answer, but chortled together as they boisterously ran off to their rooms. Orwell cared not! He had a big day awaiting him, with school and field hockey calling him to battle.

*****

Rafik Patel, UNZA's regular goalie, arrived at the big game with his arm in a sling, but young Hughes had backstopped well enough during practice scrimmages to replace him for the sudden-death play-off game against the local army squad. Nobody knew that Orwell had starred as a shutout goalie for Tracy's team in Edmonton church leagues, so his teammates thought him crazy to eagerly accept the call to stand in against a military barrage—a dangerous position that no player dared wrest from him today!

The soldiers played a rugged, high-speed game; their forwards were crack marksmen and the defence took no prisoners when they went into the pits against the intellectual bums from the university! Not expected to win—let alone score—the normally cocky students were tried by fire that sultry Saturday afternoon! Engulfed with their subdued fans by legions of troops and equally baleful residents from the local base, the young academics were roundly out-played and out-muscled by the well-drilled favourites. They were trained harder than raw recruits upon a spongy turf hidden behind the garrison's barbed wire and armoured vehicles.

This severe test became Orwell's big chance to shine. Thriving between the pipes, he deftly guarded his crease as ten men on this lonely pitch. Throughout this decisively one-sided affair, Hughes looked like a moving target in a midway shooting gallery. Orwell made several brilliant saves, including blocking at point-blank range a cannon shot that should have beaten him. Only because their white goalkeeper magically stonewalled all enemy strikers were the beleaguered college boys able to knot a scoreless tie in regulation and then break the deadlock by shoot out. Orwell's heroic sacrifice encouraged his fellows to grasp an upset victory!

Shellacked by a hurtling wooden ball, this arduous test nonetheless proved strangely therapeutic for his troubled soul. His many bruises and frayed nerves were soothed by the fact that he demonstrated undeniable courage for all to see. Tracy would have been proud of his stellar effort! He knew that his mentor had not yet embarked upon his epic safari, but in fleeting moments of reprieve from enemy onslaught, Orwell wistfully envisioned MacDonachie standing tall and confidently, cheering with the crowds of spectators. Surely, his mentor's indomitable spirit strode with him on his lonely quest, and rejoiced with him for his hard-won victory.

The game was barely finished before Orwell's teammates hoisted him on their sweat-drenched shoulders and cheering campus supporters swarmed out of the woodwork to mob these underdog winners. Rather than pressgang him into service, some enemy strikers gathered around Orwell to congratulate his astounding effort. A newspaper reporter, impressed by his performance, asked Orwell for a quote. Benjamin, David, and Solomon came striding up, spiffily attired in new suits like three young lords, to congratulate their friend.

If Hughes felt honoured by this uncommon swell of acknowledgement, he was dumbfounded when Georgina dashed across the field to hug him! He could nearly speak by the time this butterfly waved goodbye and flitted away with her giggling girlfriends Jasmine and Lovelace. Such a bewildering experience did not ruin him however; gazing after the chauffeured limousine driving off in the distance, Orwell took this unexpected interaction as a good omen.

Suzanne, JJ, and Richard emerged from the throng to shower him with affection. Orwell was incredulous that his self-certain brother and shy sisters would come all the way to the game field just to watch him play. JJ squealed with delight as she jumped into her hero's lap. He was deeply moved to hear his siblings publicly laud his winning effort. Tracy was not present to witness his heroics, but Hughes felt his luck had obviously changed for the better since the glad tidings of MacDonachie's momentous coming had reached his ears. Truly, Orwell was small fry in comparison to his mentor, but who could blame him on this royal day for daring to dream that he was following in footsteps of The Great One?

In the cool of the day, as Orwell trekked out of Kabwata Township, crossed Burma Road and toiled up the hill towards his home, his drained energy was rejuvenated by Tug's exuberance and the light-hearted companionship of his siblings. They were joined on the rocky red path by Benjamin, Solomon, and David, who were heading back to campus, having enjoyed a leisurely Saturday afternoon of window shopping and a sudden-death sports game. The fashionable young men joked with Orwell about Professor Ibrahim's stern classroom decorum as they noted his ripped hockey shorts, rumpled knee socks, and soiled jersey. They won the impressionable hearts of Orwell's suddenly tongue-tied sisters with their gentle manners and congenial smiles.

Unfortunately, these gallant gentlemen were literally driven away by Tug's menacing growls! The same watchdog, who tail-wagged to even the strangest of white folk, could not be persuaded to accept Orwell's cohorts, who happened to be African, no matter how harshly he was disciplined. Rick spewed a blue streak as he strapped on the leash and dragged the brute ingloriously toward home. Suzanne sharply tore away from her admirers, and followed her older brother without looking back. Humbly escorting his friends to a nearby bus station, Orwell apologized for damage done to them, and died a thousand deaths in his spirit.

"What will you do for the Easter holidays?" Orwell softly inquired.

Benjamin reminded him that, as choir master, he must be on tap for all the services at their Trinity Lutheran church. Solomon would weed a vegetable garden that he kept behind the swimming pool, while David promised to take advantage of the relatively quiet campus to study for his final exams. Orwell, hearing lonely hesitation in their voices, discerned that these good friends made no plans to go home or visit kin in Lusaka; they had precious little money to do anything to celebrate the festive resurrection day. Their loved ones must live in the back country, far from this spacious, tree-lined boulevard and its polished caravan of weekend touring cars. Orwell felt sorry for the lovely trio, but lost as to how he might adequately minister to their needs. An UNZA bus approached now as the setting sun called everyone home for supper.

"Will you all come for Easter dinner at our house?" piped up tagalong Janice Joanne, out of the blue. "We could have an Easter egg hunt and play volleyball in the garden. Mom will be cooking a traditional ham to feed our special friends—Tracy, Kathleen, and Alicia MacDonachie who will visit from Canada—but there'll be oodles of food for other greeters. Will you come too?"

These young men about town...these educated future leaders of Africa were pleasantly taken aback by her invitation, so innocently offered to feast together in the Lord. Orwell was embarrassed by his sibling—who obviously had a crush on his friend Ben—but he inwardly beat himself for failing to be the bearer of good will. Janice Joanne was old enough to be wife to any of these friends in their traditional cultures. She had stepped forward to save the day so naturally with easy grace when Orwell, who sought to be suave and cool, had frozen and not known what to say. The four men were flabbergasted by the novel idea of sharing Easter across cultures...JJ's spiritual brainwave—it was right on!

Orwell marvelled at how JJ totally looked and behaved like his mother! Both women served the Lord diligently...and passionately rose to the occasion when they saw a need. Mother Hughes had once rushed onto railroad tracks in front of an oncoming train to scoop eight-year-old Suzy to safety when nine-year-old Orly had impatiently abandoned rather than escorted his dawdling sister back from the toilet to where their family picnicked and built sand castles on White Rock's ocean beach. She had also charged into Sandy Lake from the porch of their rented cottage to save baby JJ from drowning after she had fallen off the wharf under his very nose! Orwell grieved his youthful obliviousness when he remembered these childhood misadventures. He could be a man now, if only he could learn to seize the moment like these strong women intuitively did, so that he too could stand up and be counted when the Lord called his name....

Benjamin gazed, stoically amused, into the young woman's starry blue eyes and suddenly broke into laughter. Bowing gallantly and reaching a hand to her, the gentleman declared, "Little One, I shall be glad to dine with you and your gracious family! My mates and I thankfully accept your hospitality!"

"Hear, hear!" chanted Dave and Solly in agreement.

"I also count it an honour to meet your special friends, the children of esteemed Reverend Wynnard MacDonachie—particularly Tracy his firstborn son who, I understand from Mr. Orwell, is also a faithful brother of the cloth," added Benjamin, gently holding hands with Orwell and JJ as they escorted him onto the bus. "Miss Janice, do you know that I recently purchased a record album cut by The *MacDonachie Family Singers* from *Blessings*, the largest Christian book and music shop in Lusaka? What wonderful songs they share from God! Your friends come highly recommended by your brother, indeed by many of our Christian colleagues who have heard them sing on shortwave radio."

"From *Blessings*, where our brother Richard works? I am glad you made the purchase, Mr. Mudenda; you heard the angel voice of Alicia, my best friend."

"Yes, most assuredly I have. I believe when you say that Miss Alicia sings like an angel, and I can see why she's your best friend. I hope, Miss Janice, that you will introduce this fine young lady to me during our Easter festivities together," broached Ben, nearly causing JJ to swoon in the warmth of his handsome smile. Then, turning to Orwell, he fervently shared, "Ever since I heard your stirring ode to Tracy MacDonachie at the Writers' Club, I have prayed for an opportunity to meet this mighty man of God.

"I believe that Reverend Tracy will bless the burgeoning Christian community in Lusaka, at Trinity Church and on the UNZA campus—not only by bearing rich greetings and words of inspiration from his father, but also by encouraging southern Africa's searching minds with his own vital ministry. Mr. Orwell, I have heard Reverend Tracy preach powerfully from the Bible on his father's radio broadcasts. I felt spiritually refreshed by his poignant speeches on social justice and jubilee that have made their way into daily Bible commentaries for African believers. For us who struggle every day to obtain our daily food, and suffer in the threatening shadows of racist regimes, Reverend Tracy's liberation theology strikes a harmonious chord. I thank God to meet one of His high priests so early in my own lifetime!"

They parted ways through the traditional ritual of farewell handshakes.

Orwell smiled clumsily, still not used to his limp grip, followed by clasping of thumbs and an affectionate embrace. The smiling black trio waved at him through the window of the departing coach and blew kisses in the gathering darkness to darling JJ, leaving Orwell mesmerized by their zest for life when they owned so little material wealth. They showed no sign of awkwardness, although Orwell felt ashamed of his own lethargic efforts to emulate the generous hospitality they gave him with no strings attached.

He was a hero this day and on the eve of mountaintop experiences galore to come with Tracy MacDonachie. Something told him, however, that his skinny kid sister and her best friend would also walk with him on the highest heights as well as through the lowest valleys that he could not yet see.

# CHAPTER
# TEN

AT PRACTICE, A SCANT THREE days after performing heroics against the troops, 'Mr. Goalie' learned that he had been struck from the team roster for the upcoming semi-final game against Northern Training College, Ndola. His teammates had mysteriously forgotten how Orwell had helped them advance, now that Rafik Patel was healthy again. Returned into the good graces of the club's top brass, Rafik was reinstated to backstop the team going forward, and hopefully lead them all the way to win at the national colleges' championship! No job was left for crushed Orwell Hughes...Even the roles of equipment attendant, water boy, and bench warmer were filled! Hughes wished to travel with the team to Ndola, so he could suit up and be ready to go into battle if any player got sick or went down, but now he saw no hope of participating, or contributing to the cause in any way—an awful thought when Tracy would be in the stands for the big game!

Orwell and Rafik were friends; they understood and respected each other on and off the field. Orwell would never deprive this devout Muslim and stolid son of long-time merchants his opportunity to shine; he only wished that he too could be allowed to play! Perhaps they could each take one half of the match? Orwell was content to be assigned to any position, because he knew he could contribute everywhere, but the powers that be had no further use for his talents.

"Don't be glum, Orwell old chap!" jovially admonished Sanjay, captain of the university side. "You helped secure a place in the Final Four for us, it's true, and we're all very grateful, I am telling you! You received the best experience this year with regular practice at UNZA—the best team in the league! Experience is never wasted, my friend. Next year, your strong apprenticeship will allow you to take over from Rafik, who graduates in April."

"That's if I attend this university next year!" gnashed Orwell, seared to the core by such logical but unsatisfactory reasoning. Were these hockey lords, like his dad, forcing his hand? Weariness from their hard-fought scrimmage frazzled his nerves as, huddled with the club heavies under leaden evening skies, Orwell pleaded to salvage his rapidly-sinking case. "Whether I should continue my degree here or in Canada is as yet undetermined. I like Zambia alright, but I am not sure I want to commit to four more years right now in order to graduate from UNZA, since my father's diplomatic tour may not keep him in Lusaka that long. So, fellows, I'm still in a quandary as to my own educational future...I do hope to figure it out while we're back home on furlough, but at this point, I don't know if I will even be around here to play next year—Like Rafik, I might be gone for good this April, which is why playing now matters to me!"

He hoped his listeners would relate rather than judge, but when Sanjay, Joachim and several of the other brown or black teammates looked askance at the flustered white youth, Orwell snapped, "Damn it guys, I've come out to *every* practice, *every* game and given my best effort every single time! I deserve to play somewhere in the semis—it may be my last chance!"

Sanjay exchanged furtive glances with the other team officers, but Rafik, who seemed embarrassed by the whole display, hung his head and said nothing. The solemn physicist was a hapless pawn in this power play, but he could not hide his gratitude for his timely reinstatement. Passing over the mute Rafik, Sanjay sought support from Joachim Phiri, his burly black assistant.

"Rafik has been our keeper for three years now," Phiri stoically explained, his prestige swiftly fading in Orwell's eyes because of his collusion in the foul plot. "We never intended for you to replace Rafik, only that you should substitute for him while he struggled to regain his confidence. Now, Rafik is back—and in good time too!"

"Let me play on defence then," suggested Orwell. "I can play back line quite well."

They looked at him dubiously, as though silently disputing his claim. How humiliating it was to bargain for favours from guys who obviously hated him! Where was Tracy when he so desperately needed his sharp negotiating skills? What would MacDonachie think of his foolishness? He knew that his mentor would wisely tell him that it was better to simply walk away from these clods than to beg like a buffoon for fleeting moments of playing time. Yet, as Tracy pointed out during more than one pep talk, Orwell always felt like the grovelling weakling, the inadequate performer who needed to be cut—even if he had single-handedly won the last game for his side. Could he stitch a silk purse from a sow's ear? And why throw pearls to swine?

Joachim, sensing Orwell's sadness as he trudged off the darkening pitch, did his best to explain the club's dilemma as he walked beside him.

"The roster has already been submitted to the tournament organizers. There simply is no room for extra players, Mr. Orwell. Even if we fielded you as a substitute, the opposing teams would cry foul."

"Yeah, sure," muttered Hughes unconvinced, as he continued to make his exit without even a backwards glance. Was this how he would go, with just a shirt on his back and not a penny to his name, if he quit the country altogether in October?

"With our shoestring budget, we can't afford to have tag-a-longs. You know that our next game is being staged in Ndola, which calls for a bumpy, six- hours ride to the Copperbelt. We must pay for our own meals and provide hotel accommodation for every team mate. Ndola is an extravagant mining city, Mr. Orwell."

"Whatever. Good luck at the big game, Joachim!"

Crestfallen, Orwell roughly mounted his bicycle and rode away, but he was barely out of the park when he heard a pounding noise rapidly coming up the tarmac behind him. Phiri was suddenly loping beside him, racing him like a cheetah. Hughes was unnerved to see the flash of his white, saucer eyes and large teeth in the darkness, but as Orwell decided to confront him, he realized that Joachim was pleading with him to stop, to understand, without getting angry.

"Excuse, sir! Excuse me! Young man, you are an excellent player, an honourable sportsman, so I am very sorry."

"For what?" demanded Orwell hoarsely, pumping his legs to flee, still hurt as he lashed out at his perceived tormentor.

"Everything is possible in Africa, particularly if God is present; if there is a will, a way can be found," prophesied the capable elder brother of Beatrice Phiri, Orwell's choir friend and a solid member of the Trinity United Lutheran Church.

Orwell's fever broke when, under the ghostly yellowish glow of a sodium vapour street lamp, far from the practice fields and smug team captains, this

Christian Zambian athlete in action, admonished him with open arms to be patient, put faith in good things. He listened, incredulous that Joachim truly wanted him to support the team in spirit, even though given no opportunity to play. They still needed him at practice scrimmages on UNZA's pitch so that the strikers had another goalkeeper to test their mettle on before heading to Ndola. He made a positive impact on the team, no matter what happened from this day forward....

"Amen. May God protect our journey," Orwell responded solemnly in *ciBemba*. He hurt too much inside to rejoice at this point! What could he show Tracy now?

Joachim, surprised by the white foreigner's command of vernacular language, laughed and lightly met the other's hand in a gesture of good will. Hughes could hear *ciBemba* better than Sanjay and Rafik, who were both Zambian natives; he made greater effort to understand Africa and Africans than white missionaries or university professors who had made a career of teaching his people how to live. "Well done, my friend. May you sleep well tonight."

"Until tomorrow morning," replied Hughes appreciatively, bidding adieu.

Despite this enlightening encounter, Orwell still fled homeward on his long-horned steed, driven by angry disillusionment. His eyes locked like flint on the red, grass-walled path twisting before him, he bounced recklessly over rocky knolls, pounded washboard flats, and churned through greasy wadis like an overwound eggbeater. A late summer rainstorm threatened, but this warrior was neither concerned for his own health nor for the well-being of pedestrians who might be in his way. When a pack of squatters failed to clear the path, Hughes grimly powered through them. With his bell loudly clanging and his headlight casting a bouncing beam upon the scattering women and children, he felt a power surge at their chaotic flight to safety.

Racing the driving curtain of rain, Orwell pedalled relentlessly through narrow, garbage-strewn alleys and over open drains reeking with sewage. The bureaucratic beehive of Mulungushi House suddenly disappeared like the sun during an eclipse as he zoomed past and careened down Nationalist Road beneath the wind-tossed canopy of the flamboyant trees. Security lights blazing within the walled gardens of expatriate mansions and sports clubs turned into so many wet blurs. Rain blasted his face and soaked his grass-stained uniform, lashing him onward. Drenched by the time he reached home, Orwell carelessly dismounted at the gate and clambered his bicycle up the long gravel driveway under the grimly scrutinizing gaze of the torch-wielding guard. His family barely recognized this wild man when he demanded entry into their warm, well-lit home.

Orwell made his way to the bathroom and quickly washed the muck from this body, then changed into clean clothes, and took his place at the crowded dining room table. Although he was mollified by the succulent fare of spicy chicken on rice, he still ached from rejection's bitter sting.

"Those jerks weeded you off their team because they're jealous of your splash of glory," growled Richard, egging Orwell on as he enthusiastically devoured his food. Having listened with uncommon patience to his kid brother's lengthy complaints, Rick pointed his half-eaten drumstick like a microphone at flustered Orwell as he proudly declared, "You won that last game for them, bro, and they know it, but these field hockey veterans are embarrassed that some sunburnt schoolboy from Alberta showed them up!"

"I wouldn't get too worked up about this little tempest in a tea pot, Son," ruled Bwana Hughes, staring sombrely at Orwell through the steam of his aromatic chicory coffee. "You've more than proven yourself to that shallow-hearted gang. Perhaps they went fishing to see whether I or the High Commission might finance their expensive hockey junket on the Copperbelt, but when—thank *God*—you didn't bite, well, the rich white kid was scratched from the team roster!"

"I doubt that's what happened. I paid my dues, Dad, just like anyone else!"

Jim Hughes nodded dourly but remained cynically unconvinced—he had become hardened by years of dealing with a slew of diverse characters, each with their own selfish—or at least self-serving—agenda. He admired his son's stalwart athleticism and collaborative spirit, but winced inwardly at his propensity to naively embrace each person who crossed his path at face value. Such a headstrong good-heart, difficult to advise intellectually, was ripe for being bruised by rough handling. Nonetheless, there might be a teaching moment in Orwell's debacle.

Wading yet again into the rough waters where Orwell floundered, Jim admonished him, "If cavalier exclusion is how those hockey boys repay you for your dedication, don't waste another moment on them. If I were you, Orly, I'd focus on passing your impending final exams. That's where the action really is."

"It's not fair!" blurted Orwell. His face turned red with anger as he savagely hacked a slice off his mango and stuffed it down his throat. Nearly choking on juicy yellow pulp, he gasped, "Why do I always get shortchanged?"

"You don't always, dear, although when it seems so, it's most likely because you don't demand your own way," suggested Martha, smiling sympathetically at her distraught son after Jim, sighing in resignation, went back to his meal. "You happen to be a Christian gentleman, fair and congenial, eager to please, and happy to be at peace with your neighbours as far as it depends on you. Look at Rafik—he now has an opportunity to participate in this championship because *you* made room for him. You live rightly by dying to yourself. I admire those good fruits of character that God has endowed you with by His Holy Spirit. Never belittle the good that He does for you."

"Mom, I hate being so weak! I despise myself for it; Tracy will make those creeps pay for their treachery. He intended to view the big game in style, but now what? Nobody messes with my friend!"

"Orly, might doesn't make right," JJ admonished. To her big, scholarly brother's dismay, the little brat countered MacDonachie's 'aggressive' teachings with a lilting Bible quote (Luke 6:27-36). "*'Love your enemies and do good to them. If one slaps your cheek, turn and offer him your other cheek. If your foe takes your cloak, do not withhold your coat from him. Do unto others as you would have them do unto you. Love your enemy and do good, without expecting anything in return'*... and he may become your friend, like Joachim is."

"I know that, you dumb kid," grumbled Orwell. "Stop bugging me!"

"Yeah, Miss Priss! We don't need to be preached at, especially by some pigtailed squirt who knows nothing!" berated Suzie out of the blue, perturbed by the child's presumed' authority. "Don't be another Annie Fannie!"

"Suzanne Marie!" scolded Martha, incensed by her teenager's haughty retort. Suzy would do anything—even pick a fight with JJ—to get out of washing the dishes! "You, of all my children, could benefit immensely from the Lord's instruction. Remember, it is God and not yourselves whom you serve. Jesus teaches us to *'Be merciful, even as God is merciful to us all. The Lord is kind, even to the selfish and ungrateful and will greatly reward those who love them.'"*

Out of love and respect for his mother and baby sister, Orwell glumly embraced their holy advice, but his feelings smarted by the seemingly insensitive direction the impromptu family tribunal had taken. Their no-nonsense guidance spelled defeat for his utopian dream of athletic prowess. And if a young man could not dream, then was life was even worth living?

Was it really true that his own flesh and blood were his most loyal companions? Their fervent words were difficult to digest because they would be unpalatable to Tracy MacDonachie. Oh, how Orwell hoped that this gallant knight would pluck him from his fetid backwater, and transport him on the glorious road to adventure and chivalry. Well, this young page would await his squire patiently, though all his fretting and distractions made this task more arduous than walking barefoot through hot coals or sleeping on a bed of nails.

"I wouldn't push my luck with that show-boater, Orly," advised his father, gazing at his starry-eyed son with hooded eyes. "Tracy has obviously influenced you in many good ways, but he may yet prove to have frailties of character that would make your head spin...He reminds me of a used car salesman!"

The stuffy diplomat's opinion of MacDonachie as a smooth-talking crook, which was somehow meant as cautionary teaching, caught Orwell off guard and made his chin visibly drop. Yet, this greasy image loosed a cascade of laughter from the other family members around the table. Sensing the lad's deep embarrassment, Jim tapped Orwell's bewildered shoulder and encouraged him to reach for a higher plane of excellence.

"Be your own man, Orly!" the master declared. "Don't put Georgina and Tracy—who are imperfect humans just like you—on pedestals and expect them to play out your fantasies like Hollywood movie stars. You seem to be living in your novel these days...It's not healthy, boy!"

"That Portuguese lady living next door thinks Orly is insane, the way he's always jabbering to himself when working in the garden," teased Suzy, jumping in again from the hallway with her two-bits worth of trivia. "Orly, don't you know that Mrs. Rodriguez is afraid of you?"

This onslaught of judgments slammed headlong into Orwell, fuelling his defiance against his father's superficially sound reasoning, as he failed to see what right this old bull had to condemn his hopeful outlook on life.

To be fair, his father had earnestly endeavoured to bring Tracy MacDonachie in from the cold, all while harbouring sober reservations about the young renegade from the beginning. Why did a loudmouthed playboy hang out with kids half his age, filling their impressionable minds with psychedelic gobbledygook, instead of working a decent job and tending to his own family like any normal, middle-aged man should?

"Dad, what is so wrong with caring about today's youth, bewildered as we are with the all-powerful establishment?"

Jim Hughes, with a motion of his up-held hand, commanded Orwell to halt his blustery spouting so that he might learn common sense from his father.

"Tracy and his sisters are travelling into this tropical paradise as short-term tourists—as our family's guests in Zambia—am I correct?"

"Yes, and I am honoured to host them!"

"So, you should be, Son," patiently acknowledged the defiant boy's sire. "Tracy, Kathleen and Alicia are good friends to you kids, as well as the children of dear friends of your mother and I. They gladly accepted our invitation to visit us here, halfway around the world from their home!"

Orwell, taken aback that his high and mighty statesman appreciated the point he had just made, relaxed just enough so he could begin to really listen to what the old codger had to say—which made Jim drop the other shoe even more loudly.

"Three MacDonachie young people are venturing abroad, but they, while following gingerly in the bold footsteps of their grand old man, are nonetheless making their own extraordinary journey! Not through mere coincidence but by diligent research on their part as well as ours, they are privileged to enjoy the rare opportunity of being included as passengers on a chartered *Air Canada* jet flying to Zambia for the first time ever...It's a champagne flight without booze, in case Rev. MacDonachie should ask! Brother Wynnard would suffer insult to hear that his children are travelling at reduced fares subsidized by the Canadian taxpayer. Yet, as our special guests really do number among diplomatic workers, they are also giving up Easter celebrations at home to serve abroad. We at the Canadian High Commission take pride in accommodating our MacDonachie guests like royalty, for we understand better than those wandering troubadours how they are celebrities of highest degree: integral members of a family troupe of world-famous radio/television entertainers—Canada's own *von Trapp Family*[34] singers, if you like! We must do our best to welcome these VIPs. The

34 *Von Trapp Family Singers*: Austrian family singing group made famous by the 1959 Rogers & Hammerstein Broadway musical *The Sound of Music*, which also became a movie in 1965, based on the 1949 book *The Story of the Von Trapp Family Singers*. Baroness Maria, a former novice in a Roman Catholic

MacDonachies are heavenly talented, but they have also toiled rigorously to achieve their high stature. Orwell, let me follow suit of my wife and daughter to quote scriptures for your unique pleasure, '*To whom much is given, of him shall be much required: and to whom men have committed much, of him they will ask the more.*'"

"Jesus taught this truth in His parable about the wise and faithful steward; we read it in Luke 12:42 to 48," devoutly replied Orwell as he diligently followed his father's philosophical discourse long after Rick's eyes glazed over and Suzanne squirrelly hightailed to her bedroom.

"Well done, sir! You ought to go to seminary and become a preacher instead of spinning your tires in the mud, studying tropical agriculture—what with you being a city slicker from Canada and all," cracked Jim. "Raised on the farm myself, I learned all there was to know about soil from behind the wheel of a tractor. You, my good lad, you have a golden memory! Guard it well, so that you may go far. I remember how flawlessly you memorized Bible passages in Sunday school, when you were knee-high to a grasshopper. Reverend MacDonachie is so impressed with your interest in God's word that he wants to recruit you for reading scriptures at his revival meetings. I'll take your word that I was quoting Luke 12:42 to 48, but don't expect me to remember that passage five minutes from now!"

"An apt verse, especially for us rich folk in the First World," nodded Orwell woodenly, struggling to find the humour which had Jim and Rick suddenly shaking their sides with laughter.

Just as suddenly, the first secretary to the High Commissioner resumed his sombre schoolmaster's stance.

"Tracy, Kathleen, and Alicia know full well they have a rich and influential father, but my friend Wynnard pulled no strings to ensure that his children be pampered in any way during their safari...Rev. MacDonachie respects Canada's diplomatic mission but believes, without shadow of a doubt, that his precious

---

religious order, married wealthy and heroic Georg Ritter Von Trapp, a widower with ten children. The family became well-known musicians in Austria, performing at prestigious Salzburg Music Festival. A decorated Austrian naval officer, Baron Von Trapp's refusal to join Nazi Germany's navy on the eve of World War II forced the family to flee to USA, where they continued to sing in public and eventually purchased a resort in New England.

little daughters will be held in good hands over here, living under the solid roof of Jim and Martha Hughes!"

"What about Tracy?" begged Orwell anxiously, "He's the ambassador!"

"That big contender is a self-made man, but I doubt he loves his sisters more than himself!"

"He's a pretender, more like!" scoffed Rick. "Despite his nickname, 'Tiptoe's' skulked around the block more than a few times! Never fear, Orwell, we'll take care of Annie Fannie and Kitty-Cat, whether their blowhard brother shows up or not."

"Do you hear me well so far, Son? Are you catching my drift?" demanded Jim, his face flushed with frustration at Orwell's naïve allegiance to his hero. "Listen carefully boy, for now a thorn is stuck hard into the flesh to irritate our celebration. While the Canadian diplomatic community is excited about the prospect of so many countrymen joining us here in our pleasant home away from home, we are also burdened with Tracy's bizarre requests to reserve extra seats, ensure an abnormally large luggage compartment, provide vegetarian meals onboard, and to travel by night—all to accommodate a diverse entourage of friends who will accompany him on his epic safari. And his on again, off again flight plans are holding up the expedition's departure date, making it nigh impossible to plan a decent airport reception and dinner party for our incoming service people!" decried Jim, breaking diplomatic silence on what was becoming a tempestuous saga of procrastination, negotiation and uncertainty. "Why does an honoured family visitor whose official mission, incidentally, is to deliver a small donation of money, hymnals and Bibles to a needy congregation here on behalf of our Canadian church, insist upon calling the shots?

"Just why is my friend's eldest son bent upon bringing along an unknown cast of characters to this impoverished nation? Tracy demands that we help a certain Mr. Thompson obtain a tourist visa, but he won't divulge the purpose of this stranger's visit or what the man does for a living. It was difficult to obtain a visa for Tracy's acquaintance because the guy apparently has a criminal record! Needless to say, Tracy was not impressed with my reticence; he pushed me all the harder to pave the way for Mr. Thompson, even pompously suggesting that some personal remuneration could be arranged for my efforts!"

"How insulting!" shouted Rick with disgust on behalf of their old man, who felt that such shady dealings were beneath his dignity to acknowledge, let alone contemplate. "That's unadulterated graft, man. Orwell, your pal crossed the line when he tried to bribe Dad! We aren't in Mexico or Nigeria, for God's sake, where corruption is part of doing business!"

Bwana Hughes let Rick lecture Orwell while he glared sternly at his fidgeting second son, hoping that the numbskull would understand the severity of Tracy's tampering. When Orwell protested these wild accusations in a staunch defence of his mentor, the normally pleasant but tight-lipped diplomat wearily realized he would have to keep trying to educate him, and thus decided to divulge what shenanigans involving his own people had been going down lately behind the inviting doors of Canada's mission.

"The High Commission keeps getting updated wires from MacDonachies' agent, informing us of their latest demands and requests, as well as the expanding size of their retinue. The MacDonachie entourage seems to be growing every day, stacked with all sorts of cameramen, lawyers, bodyguards, hair stylists, fitness directors, reporters, choreographers and fans...all of whom Tracy insists upon booking into the mix! Are Wynnard's children planning some sort of gala concert? I have no idea, Orwell...Only a week ago, your hallowed mentor requested that the government provide him with two limousines and make arrangements for his staff to be accommodated in five-star hotels during his stay in the capital city. I complied, only to be tersely informed by his agent that Mr. MacDonachie was so put out with the 'sub-standard' quality of these lodgings that he will likely not come at all! We made every effort to appease his outrageous concerns, for reasons that I simply fail to comprehend in the all-revealing light of day. Tracy has refused so far to confirm his travel plans! I hope that no legitimate traveller gets bounced off the flight because of Tracy's haphazard game of musical chairs. He and his idiotic agent hijacked the show instead of graciously accepting our hospitality."

"Who is demanding so much?" probed Orwell, rocked at hearing this wild news. He muttered his own misgivings in answer, "Tracy has no agent; he doesn't need some gofer paving the way for him. Must be that spoiled brat Alicia or her snob of a sister who are making crank calls behind Tracy's back! Girls can be such a royal pain in the butt! They should just stay home with their dollies in Lotus land. I invited Tracy!"

"Dad already told you, it's Tracy and his agent who are causing this ruckus!" growled Rick, exasperated with how thick and dense his kid brother could be.

"You invited Tracy here all right, but you know nothing about him. You should have checked him out before opening our house to that thug. Tracy's just fooling around with you now, Orwell!"

These jeers hit the young poet like a ton of bricks. If true, then Tracy was embarrassing Canada abroad—at Easter no less—by bringing along a motley crew of hangers-on to Zambia and making outlandish demands all over the place, like to the High Commission? And his mentor and only friend was now pouting over details like hotel rooms and cars...And even threatened not to come? His dad and brother had to be liars, just out to hack Tracy down!

"I can't take this bullshit!" roared Orwell, "I'm outta here!"

He stormed out of the kitchen, and slamming the door of his bedroom behind him, threw himself onto his cot in the throes of deep frustration. His father and brother, jolted by his childish antics, sent JJ, who, concerned for Orwell, anxiously begged for him to open his door.

But Orwell summarily dismissed her, "Beat it, you little errand twerp! Bother me again and I'll spank you!"

He would not be interrupted, even by his innocent and caring sister as he desperately, furiously, scribbled an urgent letter to Tracy. Before sealing his lengthy petition and stuffing it in his briefcase for secure mailing from campus the following day, he poured out his heart and soul, begging The Great One to stay the course they had planned.

Jim and Rick had each other and seemed content to exclude 'Little Orly' from their manly activities as though he were some hopeless stooge. This exclusion smacked as bizarre to Orwell, given that the latter was the spitting image of his father and a perfect complement to his brother. Yet, this second born was an artistic dreamer whom the real Hughes men folk regarded as a freaky threat to their scientific approach to life. They seemed jealous of their poet who was able to use his brain to earn passage to the local African university and gain new horizons, experiences, and friends beyond their stifling sphere of influence. This feudal baron and his knightly heir showed annoyance that their court jester was able to overcome their taunting jibes by hopping aboard the 'Good Ship MacDonachie' and escaping into the magical haven of Cherry Crest. Did not these hard-line pragmatics understand that their callous refusal to accept him drove Orwell to flee deeper into his refuge of dreams? Orwell liked his mother and sisters well enough, but being women, they could not satisfy the longings of his complex and romantic soul.

Only Tracy could provide the swashbuckling camaraderie that Orwell craved, though he tormented himself when he failed to love his own family with the same, unrequited fervour he reserved for MacDonachie. Orwell even dared to intimate that his hero loved him and reciprocated such manly devotion, yet loathed the base suggestion, whispered in the dark by his idiot siblings, that he was gay. He resented being slapped by such a demeaning label, for he considered himself to be a complex individual who was too multi-faceted to be so easily defined. Like Tracy, Orwell believed he could achieve greatness in any course he followed. Was he not a champion athlete, an accomplished student, an aspiring artist and musician, a fervent believer in God? Tracy was his brother! Brave MacDonachie would come; he must come!

*****

BLOCKBUSTER news broke across the continent that Africa's heavy-weight boxing champion had signed a fat contract to fight an upcoming white contender, right in Orwell's adopted city of Lusaka. This might have been an obscure bout by North American standards, but it locally became the heart of excited, anticipatory conversations wherever active men or boys gathered. Such illustrious names as Battling Siki[35] and Dick Tiger[36] had already given Africa its

35 *Amadou M'Barick (Baye) Phal* (1897 to 1925), known to the boxing sport as 'Battling Siki' reigned as world light-heavyweight champion for approximately seven months from September 1922 to March 1923. He defeated several prominent European fighters, including Harry Reeve and Marcel Nilles, before challenging and defeating Frenchman Georges Carpentier for the title on September 24, 1922. Born into a poor Muslim family in St. Louis, Senegal, Phal went to France as an eight-year old in the company of German dancer (Mme. Fauquenberg) who, travelling on an ocean liner, had found him at the harbour and asked him to show her the city before they boarded the docked boat to continue to Marseilles. He met Paul Latil in Marseilles, who taught him how to box and got him into professional matches. During the First World War, Phal fought as a French citizen with the Eighth Colonials at Toulouse and became a decorated corporal, but was wounded in the Battle of the Somme in 1916. He continued to fight after the war in Europe and in United States. He had a common-law relationship with a Dutch woman, Lyntje Van Appelterre, but married Lillian Werner in 1925. Battling Siki was killed during a street brawl in New York.

36 *Richard Ihetu* (1929 to 1971), known as 'Dick Tiger', was a Nigerian-born professional boxer who held the British Commonwealth middleweight title in 1960 and subsequently held the world middleweight

champion gladiators, but homegrown Leopard Milongwe was fervently billed by the government press as gifted with the prowess to fight his way for Zambia into the enduring chronicles of the world's mightiest men. Stirring news articles and international boxing magazines now filled every news rack in the capital, giving credence to such boasts by predicting that this skilled pugilist—who had been raised in the rough and tumble Copperbelt mines district—was poised to propel himself into the upper echelon of the heavy-weight class.

Leopard's upcoming fight was gleefully touted as the 'Battle of the Century' because it pitted a proud son of Africa on his own turf against an undefeated Caucasian opponent, at a time when white minority regimes oppressed black millions with escalating brutality. This upcoming set-to would mark Milongwe's last preliminary fight before moving on to the sport's main events—battling the best pugilists that England and America could offer. Milongwe, never one to mince words, cared little who his next foe was—a white bloke from Canada you say—as long as the soon to be endangered fellow was worthy of pitting his skills and experience against one on his way to glory. That this representative of the colonial powers was more than a mere stepping stone, in fact a world-class boxer with solid credentials—who had already fought against Ali, Foreman, and Frazier—was bait enough to fill Independence Stadium and force the global prizefighting community to take notice!

Leopard Milongwe, Africa's 'Great Black Hope', was lavishly depicted in partisan local media as the epitome of manhood in all its rugged glory. His sizable strength was displayed before admiring crowds jammed into his spartan training quarters or along the routes of his arduous road training. With his brawny back laced to a marble slab, Milongwe leisurely reclined between workouts

(1962 to 1966) and light heavyweight (1966 to 1968) boxing titles. Dick Tiger fought many top contenders of his era, including middleweights Gene Fullmer, Joey Giardello, Emile Griffiths, and Rubin Carter, and light heavyweights Jose Torres, Nino Benvenuti, Frank dePaula, and Bob Foster. Tiger retired in 1970 with a record of 60 wins, 19 losses and three draws. He was inducted into the International Boxing Hall of Fame in 1991, and was named 'Fighter of the Year' by *The Ring Magazine* in 1962 and 1965, and *Boxing Writers Association of America* in 1962 and 1966. An ethnic Igbo, Dick Tiger served as a Lieutenant in the Biafran army during the Nigerian Civil War; for this action he was banned by the Nigerian government but the ban was lifted in 1971, shortly before Tiger died of liver cancer in December 1971. He was described in numerous accounts as a solid, decent and un-nuanced person.

while eager sparring partners wielded sledgehammers to smash concrete blocks against his massive chest. He boldly advertised his Herculean immunity to punishment by eating light-bulbs and heaving engine blocks before his frenzied mob of supporters. Like a zebu determinedly plowing a field, the boxing champ strained his powerful frame to lift pallets piled high with 100-pound sacks of maize flour or cane sugar.

Although revered as a jungle 'man-eater', Leopard Milongwe dined with the President at State House, where he carried himself like an English gent, in his fashionable black tie and tailed tuxedo. Giggling children and doting grandmothers flocked around him wherever the local hero strolled through Lusaka's African Market or teeming townships. He was young, handsome, and as yet unblemished by his gruelling sport. Leopard Milongwe was a rising star, a ruggedly handsome model for the developing country's youth to look up to; a national hero who embodied hope for a young nation troubled by many growing pains.

Meanwhile, minimum press coverage was allotted to the white opponent in this great slugfest. Initially, nobody was prepared to name the sacrificial lamb, let alone pen articles about his background or boxing career. How Orwell wished that the giant-killing Canuck who would soon face the deified Leopard Milongwe could be Tracy MacDonachie rather than rugged George Chuvalo[37]—the Canadian champion and legitimate world contender whose courage and endurance he greatly admired nonetheless....He worried that the challenger would turn out to be some bum of the month handpicked for a shellacking, simply because he was white! Orwell wondered why Tracy and George

---

37 *George Chuvalo (1937 - )*: Canadian heavy-weight boxing champion from 1956 to 1960, then again from 1968 to 1979. Over twenty-two years, he earned a record of 72 wins, 19 defeats, and two draws during a 93-bout career, but was never knocked down. Chuvalo fought gallantly against many of the world's best heavy-weight boxers of his era, including Ernie Terrell, to whom he lost in fifteen rounds for the World Boxing Association world heavy-weight title in 1965. Chuvalo challenged Muhammed Ali twice: for the world heavy-weight boxing title on March 29, 1966 but lost in a fifteen-round decision; and on May 1, 1972, but lost in a twelve-round decision for the North American Boxing Federation title. Ali regarded George Chuvalo as one of the toughest boxers he ever fought. George Chuvalo was inducted into the Canadian Sports Hall of Fame in 1990. He became an outspoken opponent of recreational drug usage; several members of his family died from drug overdoses and/or the pain of loss.

had never duked it out for the Canadian championship belt, but as an amateur boxer himself, he believed Tracy when his trainer explained that he had cobbled his success in high-profile, big-money bouts in England and America; Tracy, fighting strategically, had risen so high that there was no need to conquer the small Canadian ring. As the day of reckoning approached without the mysterious challenger being named, Orwell's vivid and hopeful imagination convinced him that 'Iron horse' MacDonachie might be taking another shot at glory. His polished hero—not some punch-drunk palooka—deserved the opportunity to tame the brash, roaring Leopard!

"Tracy was a natural," Orwell excitedly hyped himself and anyone else who cared to listen with this mantra.

Although his hero had recently retired at 33 years of age, MacDonachie had battled as hard as any of his peer contenders—Chuvalo, Quarry, Bonavena, Norton, Ali, and of course the two Fs (Frazier and Foreman). He had beaten ranked fighters the world over and amassed fifty-five victories, while steadfastly going the distance and proving himself more than worthy with only three fifteen-round defeats and two draws during his impressive sixty-bout career. Instead of dutifully following the currently scripted game plan whereby some villainous cracker was crushed by the heroic African underdog, the surprisingly resilient MacDonachie would pound Leopard Milongwe into submission before knocking him out; not only was Tracy bigger and stronger, his wealth of experience and skills would reduce his opponent to the rank of journeyman!

Tossing into the dust bin his father's wild speculation that Tracy was some obnoxious shit disturber intent on disrupting incoming Canadian workers' travel plans to Zambia, Orwell revelled in his hero's quest and built his apology in his own vivid mind. "'Iron horse' is a star athlete who deserves nothing less than the red-carpet treatment usually afforded to foreign dignitaries visiting this outpost of civilization! Tracy's fame rates an official airport welcome and a black-tie dinner reception at State House! His visit warrants a police-escorted motorcade down Lusaka's main thoroughfares, while polished military bands play *O Canada* and cheering crowds wave Canadian flags beneath jaunty portraits of their accomplished guest!"

That Orwell's adopted country was ill-informed about Tracy was understandable, but he lamented the fact that few Canadians in his expatriate circle knew or cared who MacDonachie was. Yet, after hearing the stirring ode he gave at the discerning Writers' Club, both Benjamin and Cepheus expressed keen interest in meeting The Great One. Ben grew enthusiastic about Orwell's special friend to the point of inviting the Christian envoy to address the burgeoning community of believers on campus, and purchasing The *MacDonachie Family Singers'* latest album, which had mysteriously turned up in Lusaka record shops.

Taking the zealous Orwell aside one evening after a particularly inspiring prayer and praise meeting, however, Benjamin admonished him that, although the MacDonachies soared as angels above the drab mundanity of the world, he should fix his impressionable eyes upon Jesus, mankind's true source of hope and strength, instead as on some boxing idol. Orwell must understand, first and foremost, that Christ was God's gift of salvation; His Holy Spirit dwelt in the hearts of all believers who invited the Lord into their lives. Orwell, despite his friend's impending visit, must continue to hear the wails of the hungry with such clarity to become God's instrument of peace to redress the socioeconomic disparity between rich and underdeveloped nations. Mudenda praised God for obedient harvesters like Wynnard and Tracy, whom he also desired to emulate, but the studious future pastor pointed out to his idealistic young friend that the Lord alone was worthy of glory and honour. God had given the MacDonachies all their talents and riches for good use; they were simply His instruments and vessels for blessing creation and thus upholding His holy name. So, it was with all believers, lest anyone should boast.

"Not by works that we mortals have done but what God is doing every day in the world He has created, is how He brings His plans to fruition," Ben solemnly advised.

Orwell did not fully comprehend the poignant thoughts of this black disciple; indeed, he now had no time at all to chase curve balls being thrown his way! Anxiously, Hughes despaired that the great and glorious day of Tracy's coming was virtually upon him. He would madly erase the fleeting hours left, however, convinced that Tracy was already marching into his flailing life to restore it to vibrant health.

# CHAPTER ELEVEN

Tracy did not reply to Orwell's impassioned letters, nor was he there to acknowledge the grand welcome his disciple had so meticulously planned when Kathleen and Alicia, flying excitedly so far from home, disembarked with dozens of other white folks from a Canadian jetliner that effortlessly glided into Lusaka International Airport one dry April afternoon.

With anxious thrills coursing through his body, Orwell searched from the observation deck for this athletic mentor among a flock of travel-weary countrymen, standing at attention on the sun-drenched runway as a polished military band played "Come and Sing of Zambia, Proud and Free" and "O Canada", and the Zambian Minister of Advanced Education, flanked by the Canadian High Commissioner, officiated the welcome. After the luggage was unloaded, the newcomers hauled their suitcases into the terminal like so many ants crossing the tarmac – their first hurdle upon entering this strange, new land.

Young Hughes ran excitedly down the stairs into the bustling Arrivals section, but no tall prince jovially waved at him from the billowing crowd, nor did any MacDonachie reach out to vigorously shake his hand after breezing through the Customs gate. Had Tracy grown a beard and worn shades to go incognito? Had he ducked into a washroom to let the crowds thin before their diplomatic meeting, or was he playfully hiding behind some marble pillar, just to tease him?

MacDonachie, whose charm and confidence were legendary, was invisible among the raw recruits buzzing around James Hughes and his assistants Michelle and Geoffrey, who patiently answered dozens of anxious questions about their lodging, travel arrangements, upcoming employment, Easter parties, and other seemingly trivial items that First Officer Hughes, now basking in his glory, soothingly assured were all arranged and would unfold properly in due time. In spite of one red-faced, heavy-set guy who marched around like a male peacock, crowing complaints about the lousy trip while ordering his brow-beaten wife and tired kids to hurry-up with their slew of suitcases, the High Commission gave a cordial welcome to each fragile person placed in its care as he or she trickled into port, still blitzed from having flown across ten time zones through noisy and exotic airports, spent sleepless nights on random hotel beds, and eaten plastic-wrapped meals on the go, all to endure a gruelling, medieval-style interrogation by African Customs at journey's end.

"Dad, where are *our* friends?" Orwell and JJ, worry etched across their faces, dared broach the diplomat during a brief lull—a mere half hour into the marathon welcome exercise.

"They'll be along shortly, like everyone else on the passenger list," promised Jim from his command post beside the Canadian flag planted in the middle of the room.

Bwana Hughes stayed cool as a cucumber despite the myriad details he had to keep straight in his mind. Everything was developing as best it could, but Jim, despite his meticulous preparations, knew full well that neither he nor Canada was in control. Tedious hours more would elapse before everyone was checked through! He sternly advised his children to be seen and not heard, at least around him. "Meanwhile, be useful to all our guests, as we discussed previously."

Orwell desperately clung to his hope that Tracy would yet appear, envisioning him politely standing by his sisters at the back of the queue. Yet, his hope painfully dimmed as the hours dragged on and the noisy Customs room continued to spit out stamped and approved newcomers he knew not from Adam or Eve.

Suzanne and JJ, working beside their mother as charming hostesses, did their bit by festooning people with roses. A couple of sapphire-eyed, platinum-blonde 'sisters', looking wan, spaced out, and ready to crash, nonetheless blushed and giggled at such a welcoming gesture. They giddily introduced themselves as Brandi and Karlee; they presented a chatty breath of fresh air after the likes of the pompous oaf, Dr. Philip Walker, who blusterously preceded them with his exhausted wife, hippie sons, and two pint-sized daughters in tow! Orwell and Richard did their bit to help smooth the way, toting luggage and ushering hapless strangers into waiting taxis. Many passengers—even supposedly highly-educated adults who were meant to be adventurous and world-wise—were still dressed in dowdy winter garb and hauled unnecessary piles of personal effects from the affluent homeland they had so recently left as they gawked and chattered about their strange surroundings like aliens landing on Earth for the first time. They seemed to bond quickly, like newborn babes, as the Hughes boys tucked them into car seats, negotiated their fares, and double-checked their accommodations in fluent pidgin English with their drivers to ensure they comfortably completed the journey into town.

Somewhere close to midnight, Orwell was roused from a fitful sleep by some gospel hymn being energetically played on the piano—except there were no musical instruments in this dingy airport! He must be in church or at Cherry Crest, singing after a sumptuous meal with the MacDonachies in their ornate drawing room. Dragging himself awake, Orwell blinked and rubbed his eyes as they moved about the nearly empty cavern, searching for the lovely tune. He glimpsed a faraway glow, like a train's headlight shining in the darkness. This beacon of hope was cautiously moving forward, seeking him out rather than gliding past or standing still. Enthralled at this spectacle, he watched where the curtain had been torn in two, and beheld two young women cautiously approaching with small torches in hand, looking lost and wanting to be found.

"*Yoo-hoo*! Here *they* are!" cheered JJ and Suzanne, as the Hughes ladies jumped off couches where they too had been dozing or reading. The locals rushed forward exuberantly to welcome the MacDonachie lasses with much clapping of hands and warm hugs. Although remaining shyly aloof, Orwell recognized "We're Marching to Zion" as that wonderful hymn swirling about the women as they revelled, "Finally, you're here! Alicia! Kathleen! Last but not least! It's a dream come true!"

"It is a dream, but we are really here! Let the bells ring and the banners fly," gushed Kathleen melodiously, triumphant over her travelling ordeal.

Having already shed her swaddles of sweaters and corduroys for a light tropical dress, the tall and shapely blonde with electric blue eyes appeared refreshed and ready to enjoy her holidays. Like some fashion model or airline stewardess arrived on a champagne flight from London, she sported a sassy flight bag strapped over one tanned shoulder and pulled her tiny suitcase on wheels with her other hand. Kathleen removed her chic Polaroid sunglasses with flair and tossed her shimmering mane of golden hair—a colour as rare as bullion in these parts.

Then, turning back to check on her drab sister, who was weighed down with gear like some pack mule but followed steadily behind, Kathleen remonstrated, "We are all here in one piece, ready for some fun...I believe."

"Oh, yes!" affirmed Alicia loudly, perspiring profusely and gritting her teeth in determination as she laboured under her heavy load. "Our papers and bags are in order. I made sure of that!"

While their train idled, the burly red-head gently set down a bulging trunk she had carried in one hand and the designer guitar case, from the other. Alicia adjusted a heavy rucksack on her back; she then paused to straighten her cat's eye glasses, which had become crooked and smudged from all the jostling with containers and the bustle of fellow travellers. Her precious windows to the world were already cloudy after only a few hours in the tropics, Orwell smirked as Alicia removed her glasses and fiercely wiped them clean with a cloth she kept handy in her skirt pocket. She flashed a shy smile at Orwell, but the shine of her large, ebony eyes beneath fine dark eyebrows revealed joy mixed with fatigue, and even a hint of sadness in their gaze.

Orwell gulped at the beauty he had never before noticed on the stocky, myopic girl. As he watched with fascination from his leaning post, safely beyond the bevy of joyous women, Alicia blubbered to sympathetic Mrs. Hughes, "Thank you so much for waiting! I was worried you guys would be gone home by now, having given up on us!"

"Never, my dear," cooed Martha as she hugged the distraught teenager. "Patience is a virtue, as is a good sense of humour."

"We'd have waited all night if necessary!" vowed JJ, in a manner that coaxed a feeble smile from her stolid friend. "I've got a ton of neat things to show you, and lots of girl things to talk about with you, Lisa."

"I can't wait to learn all about it," giggled Alicia sleepily.

"You've got so much to learn, baby girl!" chided Kathleen, giving her younger sister an affectionate pat on the back. When Alicia frowned, Kitty meowed like her mother, "I can see how tired you are, with all we've endured in the past seventy-two hours. Let's get to bed now...After all, tomorrow is another day."

"We'll get you ladies home now, before we shut this place down with all our chattering," directed Mrs. Hughes, noting that the kiosks were now dark and barred shut.

As if on cue, airport janitors began mopping the marble floors behind them in the waning light. The Hughes party, having helped all the deplaned workers make their way safely through the airport, now escorted their own grateful billets into the fragrant African night.

"Where are my two young men?" Mrs. Hughes cued Orwell and Richard to show her best friends' daughters how helpful and polite they had become.

Richard, who was attracted to the vivacious Kathleen like a bear to honey, chivalrously carried her suitcase and opened every door for the smiling poster girl. His newly adopted, lady's man manners surprised Suzanne as he chatted effortlessly with Kathleen, asking about the fabulous Miss MacDonachie's travel highlights so far, and inquiring about the latest news of all the hot movie stars and rock bands from back home.

"Lisa, let me at least carry your guitar," insisted JJ, grabbing the rigorously packaged musical instrument before Alicia could. "You've got too much to haul as it is!"

"That's Kathy's guitar," corrected Alicia, flashing a glare of frustration after her pampered sister. Her huge rucksack shifted and she listed like some huge ocean liner as she struggled to pick up the trunk.

"Now I have nothing to balance this iron bale with! Oof, ugh! Oh, Cowabunga!" Alicia MacDonachie muttered in despair as she awkwardly plopped herself down, lest she lose her balance and fall. "I gotta calculate a new mathematical formula for hauling what's left of our belonging…unless," she smiled craftily to those who still loitered around her, "Some strong guy around here can lend me a hand with this trunk."

Orwell sidled over, showing interest in the less flashy sister, now that the ice had broken and she revealed herself, not as a battle axe, but as a vulnerable person with real feelings and fears. Yet, he still searched every nook and cranny of the shadowy hallway behind them in vain for Tracy, and finally clued in to Alicia's teasing request when JJ shouted, "Hey that's you, poet dreamer! Lend this poor woman a hand!"

"Who, *moi*? Oh, sorry, girls," Orwell stammered, blushing in sudden embarrassment as he jump-started into action. He played his part well, and recited with relish, "Of course, I'll help... I would do anything for my kid sister's best friend, Miss Alicia Pearl Rose MacDonachie!"

As the lad clambered over, his muscular arms spread wide like crab pincers, Alicia squealed as she lifted her ample bottom off the trunk and jumped to safety before he grabbed the box by its side handles and heaved it skyward like a weightlifter. Miss MacDonachie giggled appreciatively, and her black, oriental eyes gleamed with admiration as her powerful helper placed the trunk effortlessly on his square shoulder, and steadying it with his arms, marched briskly towards the exit.

"We better follow that masked man, *tout de suite*, JJ!" Alicia joked gleefully to her co-conspirator as though Orwell was some burglar heisting a safe towards an idling getaway truck.

The two girls raced boisterously after Orwell—JJ clutching Kitty-Cat's expensive guitar flat against her chest with both hands and Alicia hauling her rucksack like an infant strapped on her back. The laughing girls nearly tumbled over the trunk now sitting abandoned on the sidewalk as they clattered past Orwell through the glass door which their porter gentlemanly held open for them. While Orwell chuckled at the clumsy girls, they turned their silliness into a game by congratulating each other for having run such a fine race, all to reach the finish line in a tie. His amusement was tinged with concern, however, when Alicia carefully set down her rucksack and smoothed her rumpled blue dress. Producing a mirror from inside her pack, she coyly applied balm to her lips and readjusted the butterfly clips holding back her surge of auburn hair. Pleased that he watched her, 'Big Bertha Butt' gave Hughes a knowing look before skipping back into his startled presence.

"You seem so tall and mighty for a studious young poet," declared Alicia breathlessly. Bowing low, she acknowledged his gallantry with a shyly extended hand, "Thank you for your help, kind sir."

"You are most welcome, Lady Alicia," replied Orwell, in the mannerly way his parents had taught him. "But I certainly don't mind helping you, or any other person in need."

"It's nothing, Lisa," boasted Janice Joanne on Orwell's behalf. "When we were building houses for needy people with our church, I saw him haul empty 45-gallon drums on his back to the water pump, and roll them back full to where others were mixing cement to lay the bricks. And Orly can carry a 100-pound flour sack on each shoulder home from the market like African men do. He does all our garden work: waters plants, weeds flower beds, turns the compost heap, cuts the grass with a scythe...And he lifts weights, rides his bicycle to and from university, skips rope (both girls laughed), does calisthenics, and jogs three miles a day, all to stay in shape and keep up with those bionic black guys playing soccer and field hockey. Orly's built like Hercules, Lisa!"

"Don't exaggerate, you pixie cheerleader," Orwell begged JJ, shaken by Alicia's unblinking doe-like gaze, her eyes shining with admiration. Smiling gingerly, the shy lad broke her trance by loading her belongings politely into the trunk of the family car and finally daring to ask, "By the way, Alicia, what is this ton of bricks I'm hauling into the car for you—a set of encyclopaedias?"

"It's just a bunch of boring girl clothes, packed around my violin!" she loftily informed him, suddenly miffed that he should ask about her personal belongings. Concerned, even though he had treated her precious fiddle with kid gloves until now, that he had just slammed the trunk on it, Princess berated, "Careful with the merchandise! Don't you remember, 'Oh-well', that I bow a Stradivarius for The *MacDonachie Family Singers*?"

"Not your accordion? Aw shucks, Alicia," Orwell pretended to be glum as he joshed with the berating lass, trying in vain to make her laugh, "I was looking forward to you bringing *Excalibur* to Africa."

"*Excalibur* is a dear musical friend, but my accordion became extra weight at the last minute when I had to stuff our travel trunk instead with some old church books that Tracy was supposed to bring from the Women's' Missionary Society. That guy; I tell you!" she sighed, rolling her eyes in frustration. As Orwell opened the car door for JJ and Alicia, Miss MacDonachie advised her astute listener with knowing sympathy, to rest his case. "By the way, Orwell, you can stop looking for him tonight. Tracy isn't here; he didn't make our flight!"

"Why not? Where is he?" demanded Orwell insistently.

"I have no idea," she sang a tune of airy sarcasm.

Paranoid that she was now being flippant and callously baiting him as of old, Orwell grabbed her arm to make sure Alicia understood the real anguish burning in his face. Hughes haltingly begged, "When will Tracy be here? Is he even coming?"

"I don't know, Bucko, nor do I care!" Alicia snapped in exasperation, stepping on his sandaled foot with her wooden clog to force him to release her. Ramming him sideways with her ample hips, Alicia slammed the door behind her and burrowed into the car, where she claimed a safe seat beside JJ before Orwell knew what hit him.

"You think you're pretty clever, eh Annie?" Orwell snapped, clearly upset as he ripped open the door and slid into place. "With all your nifty judo moves, you forgot to push down the old button. Our African cars don't have power door locks yet. You can't ditch me that easily!"

When she realized that this problem male was determined to tag along, rather than go quietly with his parents, who were now driving past in a sleek embassy car, Alicia half-heartedly protested, "Golly geez, I get all the luck!"

Orwell and Alicia glared at each other for a moment, then stared rigidly ahead in cross-armed silence, embarrassed to be jammed together like sardines inside a vehicle that was otherwise abuzz with Kathleen's chatter, who was regaling Suzanne, JJ, and Richard with saucy tales from her recent Banff ski trip with movie stars and hockey celebs. Soon, however, the frustrated silence of the other two subdued everyone else riding with them into town.

"Princess Alicia, you are being *really* immature, especially after making us wait all this time while you horsed around out there! What's got Your Highness this time?" scolded Kathleen.

"I am going through high-tension anxiety withdrawals," Alicia retorted. Just when mortified Orwell thought she would spill the beans about his overt longing for Tracy, the feisty young girl yowled about some other ordeals, "Those wicked Customs cops dumped our suitcases in front of the other passengers and rifled through our clothing like we were smuggling diamonds...."

"...Or drugs, I know!" chimed Kathleen indignantly. "How embarrassing; Fannie started crying when one big mamma jokingly threatened to tear the stuffing out of your rabbit angel toy. I thought James Bond was your hero—don't you remember that crooks smuggle gems and microfiche inside dolls in all the spy movies?"

"I was afraid she would hurt Bathsheba!"

"She wasn't gonna do anything bad to your dolly, you big baby! If I had known you were packing stuffed animals along, I'd have put a stop to it long ago. Because of your tantrum, those pigs confiscated our passports! They tossed our underwear into a filthy basket and whisked their booty into a side room, so that some pervert could get his jollies feeling my bra with rubber gloves!"

"Or inspect my flowered panties under a microscope!" Alicia sobbed to her petrified listeners. "I thought one of those gorillas would smash my violin! He shook it like some cheap jack-in-the box."

"Well, another guy opened my camera, ruining the film I had started to shoot on our London layover!" growled Kathleen. "Which reminds me, Sue, can I buy new film here?"

"I'll buy you some, Kathy," promised Richard, soothing her with a debonair smile. "I know just the place, a swinging hot shop in the heart of Lusaka."

"Humph!" complained Suzanne disparagingly. "If you mean *Fototek*, all those bozos sell is black and white film that looks blurred when it gets 'washed'! Everything in the Third World is below par; I can hardly wait to get back home to the comforts of civilization."

"We came here to see something new and exotic," Kathleen coolly reminded her hostess. "I know we won' be disappointed."

Rather than take the comment in stride and look for ways to impress her jet-lagged friend, the ever-sensitive Suzanne unfortunately felt Kitty's remark as a slap in the face. Richard added to the sting when he relit Kathleen's scintillating smile by again promising to replace her spoiled film, as though he could do many, much greater feats than this—anything in short—to cater to the pampered beauty queen.

Alicia, sensing a sudden rift between the two older girls, diffused the situation, even if only momentarily, by interjecting her own first impressions.

"I am so glad they gave us our passports back, all stamped for clearance into Zambia—*in the Sun,*" sighed Alicia, recalling the uplifting tourist marketing slogan. Shaking and pale from the trip, her dark eyes gazing hopefully at Orwell, she stammered, "I am sure the worst part of our trip is over: that Customs ordeal and those plate-sized moths flying around my face as I slogged my way across the molten tarmac... Everything else will be sunshine and roses."

Orwell nodded, despite aching for Tracy in his heart. The uplifting gospel piece *Bringing in the Sheaves* lilted about his relieved guests, now relaxing in the safety of their hosts' presence, helped him cope with the sharp disappointment. Refusing to read Tracy's inexplicable absence as a bad omen, Orwell continued to hope and pray for deliverance by the hand of his beloved swashbuckler. Sticking to his guns, he turned a blind eye to any and all warnings, stubbornly taking them in stride as little hurdles to overcome in his strange but privileged life. Everything was meant to strengthen his character in preparation for that great day when he would finally, after a stalwart climb, make it to the glorious summit of his life's mountain...

On their first night back in Africa after a lifetime spent in Canada, the travel-weary MacDonachies were grateful to simply sink into their beds after learning where the bathroom was, and found it satisfactorily equipped with a functioning flush toilet and both hot and cold, clean running water for sink and bathtub. Their bags were good-naturedly carried from the car into the inner sanctum by Orwell and Richard, who then respectfully left the young ladies alone, to settle in and get reacquainted amongst themselves. JJ alertly reminded the porters to bring the luggage into her and Suzy's respective bedrooms, correcting the lads' 'shallow' thinking that their guests would stay in the seldom used guest room at the far end of Bwana Hughes's *boma*! After Orwell and Rick retired sheepishly, JJ and Alicia delightfully disappeared into the young'uns' bedroom, while Suzanne formally introduced her digs to Kathleen.

Quickly shedding their grimy clothes and luxuriating in the joy of bathing in hot, clean water, the newcomers donned their cotton nighties and settled in for the night. Alicia and Kathleen postponed their sleep only long enough to devour a midnight snack of yogurt and fruit with their female hosts. They slept restfully for the few remaining hours of darkness and well into the next day, assured that there were no mosquitoes, spiders, or snakes to contend with—at least not indoors—and content that the sprawling stone house was comfortably cool and safe.

# CHAPTER
# TWELVE

JJ AND SUZANNE RELUCTANTLY LEFT their sleeping beauties and attended secondary school soon after sunrise, but were pleased to find the MacDonachies refreshed, dressed, and playing a rousing game of *Bridge* on the living room carpet with Richard and Orwell when they returned at 1:00 p.m. After lunching on Mom's rice and spicy beans, cooled with a garden salad prepared by Kathleen and Alicia, all the girls went out to play.

Suzanne and Kathleen rode to the swimming pool on their bicycles, purportedly to cool off in the deep, clear water, but their true intention was to sunbathe and meet muscular young studs. Richard, releasing the object of his affection to her flight of fancy, logged four hours of solo piloting in a Flying Club Cessna aircraft. Since Annie Fannie expressed her fear of heights and was stubbornly shy about exposing her luscious figure in public, she and JJ went cycling about the neighbourhood.

Orwell lent his bicycle to Alicia, but felt too lethargic after last night's marathon to jog behind her or work all afternoon in the garden—which had already received his green thumb attention in the coolness of the morning, while she had slept-in like a princess! Having spent a restless night himself, pining for Tracy and Georgina, and worrying needlessly about phantom university exams that he had already aced into oblivion, Orwell's only wish was to either spend some time writing his never-ending story or sleep on the couch. But Mrs. Hughes had something else in mind; sensing that he was depressed, she recruited her listless son to help cart the welcome wagon to all the Canadian newcomers lodged into various hostels around the city.

Orwell was glad to pitch in, and was rewarded for his care by an odd interaction with platinum-haired and sapphire-eyed Karla Eve of the lily-white Bryant tribe. Karlee had been the only deplaning Canadian who had allowed him to carry her bags, and thanked him for helping her get into the taxi... She had looked rather good by night with her pretty face and curvaceous body, but after opening the door in the light of day, barefoot and still clad in pyjamas—slept-in, squinting, dishevelled, and grumpy—to greet the upbeat welcome wagon for afternoon tea, Karlee sulked in a corner while her parents and twin older brothers, Jim and John, chattered with Orwell and Mrs. Hughes about their exotic first day in Zambia. Her family sucked up its tiring, multi-time zone journey and engaged their seasoned visitors, but Karlee yawned copiously and hid her baggy, bloodshot eyes behind some worn, colonial-era book she had plucked off the shelf. Quickly bored with the dusty tome, she left the room under a cloud, yet grinned at Orwell who offered her a tentative smile as she trundled off. Karlee did not return—even to say goodbye and thank you for coming—but Orwell returned her parting wave, and sensed that she watched him leave from the deck chair on a remote porch across the courtyard, where she demurely smoked a cigarette.

The extended Hughes family reconvened after sunset for a scrumptious supper of roast chicken with sweet potato and collard greens, prepared by Martha and her four daughters. Richard and Bwana Hughes puttered about the garage, servicing the Toyota, but Orwell chose to stay indoors, helping the women get the meal on. The ladies had a gay old time as they buzzed around in the scullery, chatting, singing, and bringing each other up to speed on various church friends back home. They kidded their only male helper, who had developed an unusually feminine interest for kitchen duty of late. Orwell drained and mashed potatoes for Alicia to spoon into the serving bowl, while the admiring girl bothered him with small talk.

Once the splendid meal was served, the men folk led the table conversation. Pilot Richard reported back to base, boasting how he nailed a textbook aerial reconnaissance over sugar cane and cotton fields in the Kafue floodplains, south of Lusaka. After commending this accomplishment, Mr. Hughes shared his astute insights into current national and international affairs. US President Richard Nixon, who had visited Mao in China and Brezhnev in Moscow, faced impeachment at home for obstructing justice in what was being called the Watergate scandal. The UN barred South African delegates from the general assembly because of their government's racist apartheid policy. Diplomats turned deaf ears to Israel's continuing struggle to exist after the Yom Kippur War, yet slapped Israel's face by allowing PLO leader, Yasser Arafat, to speak of Palestinians' oppression in their Israeli-occupied homeland.

Orwell, who was avoiding eye contact with Tracy's curious and chatty sisters—whom he received as ill-conceived replacements for the great prince himself—tried to impress them by debating his father on how the CIA-inspired overthrow of Chile's Marxist government brought into power a brutal military regime. OPEC oil embargoes were strangling the economies of First World nations—particularly that of Israel, a good friend of the US. An independent Mozambique spelled trouble for white rule in Rhodesia and South Africa. Ethiopia's Emperor Haile Selassie, the venerable Lion of Judah, failed to stave off food riots that unceremoniously ended a monarchy whose dynasty stretched back to the Queen of Sheba!

"Those are all very interesting conundrums, Son," dourly acknowledged elder Hughes after this enthusiastic youth's tirade. Without arguing or lecturing his foaming-at-the-mouth social justice fighter, the diplomat simply asked him, "Okay, so, what would you do to solve them Orly? I mean it, how?"

Caught off guard, Orwell scrambled for plausible answers under the hopeful gaze of his cheerleading little sister and her plump, four-eyed sidekick seated across the table. Even they could not wait forever, and so piped in to break the silence.

"Wow, the Queen of Sheba is from the Bible! She visited King Solomon!" exclaimed JJ, daring to break into this male's only club. Glancing furtively at Alicia and finding that her friend was listening so intently that her glasses seemed pinned to her furrowed brow, JJ rescued her with a nudging question, "What's been happening in Canada lately, Lisa?"

"Pardon me?" stammered the honours politics, geography, history, social justice student.

Blushing now that all eyes were turned on her, but determined to show poise and intelligence before her hosts, Alicia deftly sorted through memories of her suddenly remote homeland. She solemnly articulated, mindful to defer to Bwana Hughes should the career diplomat wish to clarify anything, that Quebec prepared to legislate French as the only official language in *La Belle Province,* while neighbouring New Brunswick chose instead to officially embrace both French and English.

Having gained a nod of approval from smiling Bwana Hughes, Alicia then offered plums to his daughters and sons in turn while continuing her account of Canadian news. "The first female recruits will soon be training to join the ranks of our Royal Canadian Mounted Police, and that snazzy *Bricklin* SV-1 sports car—you know, Richard, the one with those space-age gull-wing doors—has started assembly in St. John. The *Bricklin* will be so exciting to drive!"

She also reminded Orwell that Hank Aaron, a black American baseball player, was poised to break Babe Ruth's lifetime record of 714 home runs in the Major Leagues.

When the patriarch found no reason to interject, and Orwell listened intently to her words while shyly watching her, Alicia beamed with pride and vindication as she continued, emboldened, "And Ralph Steinhauer was appointed Lieutenant Governor of Alberta just this month. Chief Steinhauer of Saddle Lake Reserve is the first native person to become a Queen's representative in Canadian history!"

"That is an important development whose time has come—long overdue, in fact," concurred Orwell. Bwana Hughes nodded in stolid agreement.

"Only fifteen years ago were Indians even given the right to vote in Canada! That's also when native children started attending public schools in Edmonton, instead of taking classes on their reserves or in those horrid residential schools run for the federal government by missionaries or priests. You know, our native people carried passbooks until the 1960s to travel off their reservations, like black folks still must do today in South Africa."

"Fannie, you were just a baby living in Africa as a pampered missionary kid in the early Sixties," cajoled Kathleen, to make her sister lighten up and to cover her own discomfort. "Who told you this crazy stuff about our natives?"

"Mom tells me many stories about how the other side lives when I am alone with her, Blondie...So do Grandma and her friends, whenever Evelyn and I visit the Métis in Paddle Prairie," retorted Alicia, dark eyes flashing defiantly at her blue-eyed sister. "We'd have gay old chatters as we baked bannock and cooked moose stew on Gran's wood stove in her log cabin."

"That was after Robert took you up north to do hard time at *Bonne Chance* for ripping Orwell's shirt to ribbons in a fit of rage, eh Fannie!" declared Kitty with gleeful wickedness.

"Yes, it was!" hissed Alicia, glaring dagger eyes at her two-faced sister.

"Kathleen, you promised—cross your heart and hope to die—not to bring up my sordid past on this trip!"

"I crossed my breast, not my heart! A doctor wannabe like you should know the difference," sassed the older MacDonachie flippantly, drawing stunned laughter from Richard and Suzanne.

"That's not fair!" rasped the younger MacDonachie, rolling her eyes in annoyance. She seemed on the verge of tears as she looked away from her staring audience, and around the room in search of an exit. Alicia whimpered at Orwell when she caught him suddenly staring down at his supper, "I am sorry, Orwell, that I scratched you and tore your shirt. I'm sorry I sat on you...I hope I didn't hurt you too much."

"I mend quickly," Orwell replied, with a kind smile breaking across his rugged face. "That fight we had was a long time ago, but as I recall, we forgave each other and made up before you went home, so it's water under the bridge."

Now that everyone was laughing at rather than rubbing in her infamous tantrum, Alicia finally grinned as she divulged, "At least I looked in on Grandma once in a while. Burning sweet grass, and learning about medicinal plants and traditional foods from the land was far more interesting than washing dishes and cleaning bunkhouses for Robert's gross cowpokes!"

"Robert still complains about how often you lazy bones snuck off the ranch!" insisted Kathleen, determined not to be upstaged. "You and Evelyn were just a couple of lay-abouts, hardly worth your keep, so I've heard tell!"

"Hmm, here I am, eagerly learning all about Africa, but what do I know about the first peoples of my own country?" confessed Orwell, playfully breaking up the latest sibling argument brewing amongst Tracy's catty sisters. "Can you tutor me about Métis cooking and medicine, Miss A. P. R. MacDonachie?"

"Oh-well, you are one weird dude. Are you just being polite, glib, or what?" needled Kathleen, a smirk plastered across her elegant face. "Don't pussyfoot around my adopted, half-breed sister! We're all native Canadians here!

"Most Canadian boys don't think like you—they're all glued to the boob tube right now for the Stanley Cup play-offs! Expansion teams are challenging the Original Six for hockey supremacy: The Broad Street Bullies from Philly just took out *New York Rangers*, for Heaven's sake! Boston's next, Bobby Orr and Phil Esposito or not! Quality of play in the *National Hockey League* has been watered down, according to Robert, with all these funky new teams joining, and stars like Bobby Hull and Gordie Howe jumping to the rival *World Hockey Association*. That upstart is playing Russia later this year, but our Brucey Goosey worries we'll get spanked!"

"We should beat the Reds handily, with those big stars leading the charge," predicted Orwell confidently, making Alicia smile by bugging Kathleen and muddling through his own version of every Canadian boy's despair at the apparent demise of the NHL. "Bobby Hull and Gordie Howe are living hockey legends! They've written books, appeared on commercials and cereal boxes... My heroes sold out to the WHA, became turncoats? NY *Rangers,* all speed and finesse, got clocked by a bunch of goons? I hope my *Boston Bruins* hang in there... Please Bobby Orr, don't let this be the end of all the glory!"

"Your food is getting cold, Orwell," chided Rick, noting that Kathleen had started to yawn. Alicia grinned as the bookish lad went over the top—as usual—in expressing himself fully on yet another issue. "Better gobble up those sweet orange spuds your girlfriend cooked for you."

Orwell and Alicia both gave smugly triumphant Rick their darkest glares, while Suzanne, JJ, and Kathleen razzed such odd affection and rubbed their fingers vigorously together over the unlikely sparkers.

"Come on now kids, stop being so thin-skinned; it's all harmless fun!" Martha jovially admonished Orwell and Alicia as Bwana Hughes looked on with a twinkle in his eyes, "Please eat up, everyone! I want clean plates and an empty table!"

The crew caught her drift and went to work on their meals. After the dishes were washed, the girls held court in the drawing room, bubbling effervescently about all that they had seen and done in the community earlier that day. Alicia and JJ displayed some curved, brown seed pods they had collected, and even shook them like maracas as they performed "La Bamba" for the gringos. They recounted, in vivid details, coming across some African ladies harvesting a small urban garden behind a private, whites-only tennis court. The foreign girls were treated to some bush mangoes and roasted locusts after helping the flattered local women husk maize, pile pumpkins into baskets, and play with their children.

Suzanne and Kathleen, proudly sporting their new tans, chattered about these neat wire cars they had tried, after swimming. Intricately fashioned with diverse bits of scrap wire, and steered by wired rubber wheels mounted on long push rods, such contraptions were true works of art and ingenuity—not mere toys. After the girls had stopped to gawk at them admiringly, some African boys had vigorously bartered with them, as they played the *Indianapolis 500*. The girls had also watched some senior boys rumbling through a rugby match at the International School; Orwell, who had played the rugged game in secondary school and followed the mighty New Zealand *All Blacks*, Australia *Wallabies* and South Africa *Springboks*, related when Suzy and Kathy marvelled at how the players endlessly battled on the muddy field without wearing pads!

At 8:30 pm, Bwana Hughes broke the fun by concluding that all good things must come to an end. Claiming that he needed some time *in camera* with Mrs. Hughes to discuss such fascinating topics as new staff, the crusty old diplomat suggested that the children find some quiet activities to do before retiring for the night.

"Your friends have come to us from across ten time zones faster than the speed of sound—I am sure they're still adjusting, and must be tired," admonished the wise old household head, appealing to his eldest son when Rick gazed at him askance as some establishment stooge toting outdated concepts. "Remember how long it took you ragamuffins to acclimatize to your new surroundings during your first month in southern Africa? We want Alicia and Kathleen to be happy campers down here, now don't we?"

"You bet!" responded Rick dutifully, though his frown betrayed some level of frustration. "After all, tomorrow's another day, and only three sleeps left until Good Friday."

"I had a splendid time dancing at the ball tonight, but I better retire soon before I turn into a pumpkin," lilted Kathleen facetiously, biting her rebellious tongue and showing her hosts uncommon obedience and gratitude that would have made her parents proud. She even yawned and looked oddly weary as she instructed her sister, "Fetch our photo album, Fannie; Mr. Hughes, is it okay if we just sit around the kitchen table for a few minutes and quietly look at some of our recent family pics?"

"Dad, we'll be quiet, honest! Please?" begged Suzy, winsomely beaming at her father.

"All right," Bwana Hughes relented, impressed by the cooperation between these normally stubborn girls. He smiled tightly as he pointed to the clock on the wall, "But only half an hour more, and keep your noise down to a dull roar, please, so that your mother and I can talk in the den."

No sooner had Bwana Hughes given his blessing that Alicia bounded down the hallway to her bedroom to get the photo albums. Orwell took this opportunity to disappear for the night, but Kitty-Cat cleverly trapped him in the corner, making him tarry instead with the sly promise that he would soon see Tracy.

# CHAPTER THIRTEEN

ORWELL AROSE BEFORE DAWN THE following morning, after a fitful sleep. Unable to enjoy his sisters' guests, he felt a sudden urgency to get back into his own uplifting rhythms, which he had suspended for them. He must successfully complete his academic studies and perform the ecumenical Passion play! Pining for Georgina, those strange girls living in his house and challenging him to get to know them better were nothing but a distraction...And what about Karlee, an intriguing newcomer who connected with him, but was moody and smoked? Try as he might, he could not find his groove as his mind stormed with nagging questions: why, how, and where was Tracy delayed? Was he, rightly pissed off by crazy Hughes dramas, coming at all?

In his roiling distress, the anxious lad conjured up countless lame reasons for his mentor's troubling absence, and ultimately blamed himself for Georgina's determined boycott. Why had he been so foolish to invite such a proud and determined heathen to a Biblical drama...let alone desired her beguiling presence at the festive table of the risen Lord? He had driven Georgina away with his zealous faith, just as he did not belong—him the bogus white student—on a coloured campus. Not only had the pouty, paranoid lad failed every exam in his worst nightmares, but had missed so many new classes that he was unable to complete his assignments. Professor Ibrahim had even petitioned the Chancellor's office for the immediate expulsion of such an unruly student! Alicia, who seemed so tuned into him to both feel his pain and revel in his joys, admonished Orwell like Mary Magdalene did Jesus in Jesus Christ Superstar, "'*not to turn onto problems that upset you... everything's all right, yes everything's fine.*'" She was clearly taken with him, but what could he do with a homely, immature girl like her?

"Lord, what are you trying to tell me?" this doubting Thomas beseeched God as, instead of easing reverently into the special Easter season with his extended family, he cycled anxiously over to UNZA to ascertain if he was still enrolled for the upcoming semester.

Perchance he would find Georgina there ready to be wooed all over again, rather than hearing she had married or was holidaying abroad, since his Lord had planted her so vibrantly in his life. Vexed and troubled by Satan, Orwell inquired of the *One Who Sees and Knows All Things*. "Is she Your will for me today? I must talk to her or go mad with anguish!"

Hughes found the campus dark and deserted, but unfazed, he diligently searched for familiar faces in the canteen, around the dorms, on the central plaza. Saluting passersby but finding no one of interest, this young-man-on-a-mission prowled hallways of the central academic building, peered into empty classrooms, studied refurbished bulletin boards, greeted staff and faculty, and gabbed casually with fellow students he met en route. At last he arrived at the austere general office of the School of Agricultural Sciences, which stared forbiddingly back at him like a prison. To his relief, Hughes, Orwell found passing grades beside his name for every class he had attended during the previous academic year! He was, as per usual, running solidly in the middle of the pack—not great for a diplomat's son, especially one who had regularly won academic awards back home—but not bad, once he realized that he was competing with the cream of Zambia's crop at the only university in the land.

"Yes, you are most definitely here with us again, Master Hughes. I have just now typed your name on the class list for Animal Husbandry 300," reassured Reuben, a pleasant young African clerk smartly dressed in starched white shirt and black trousers. Looking up from his typewriter to converse with his red-faced visitor, Reuben divulged, then admonished him, "Classes shan't resume until another fortnight, after Easter holidays have past, and may yet be delayed indefinitely due to labour unrest fomenting on campus. I certainly hope that student radicals don't get involved! Anyway, you need not tarry here today. Go home, sir. Enjoy your wonderful Christian festivals with your church and family."

Greatly relieved, Orwell returned home feeling strong and confident. He arrived late for breakfast, but having already achieved much this day, he entered the crowded dining room singing *Tiyende Pamodzi,* which encouraged people to peacefully gather to eat and celebrate.

Orwell was about to spoon an inviting guava chunk from his bowl of homemade fruit cocktail when Bwana Hughes briskly collared him in front of his wide-eyed female admirers, "You've got fifteen minutes before the car leaves, Son. What's with you, moseying into breakfast so late after a leisurely spin on your bicycle? I say, old chap, no classes today? Are you enjoying a holiday?"

"I already cycled onto campus as per usual, in time for my first lecture of the day—at 7:30 a.m. that is!" young Hughes explained, trying to appear responsible before Kitty-Cat, the demure Barbie doll and Annie Fannie, who admired him with large dark eyes, her auburn hair tied back like flattened ears on a young rabbit doe. Hoity-toity Kathleen, likely suffering from a high fashion hangover, seemed mildly put out, but gracefully restrained her tongue—unlike Suzanne who sassily stuck hers out at Orwell when he quipped, "You babes should still be sleeping by this brisk hour! Hah! Hah!

"I found the theatre dark and empty. After making discrete enquiries, I realized that I was not dreaming: classes are really over for this term, and I have successfully passed into the second year of my Bachelor of Agricultural Sciences degree program! We will likely not reconvene as scheduled in a fortnight, however, unless a strike by support staff is settled. I heard rumours about some student unrest brewing on a back burner."

"How insightful, little brother," mocked Rick, lest the young ladies become impressed by big-talking Orwell. He should listen to the radio, read the newspapers more often, to get the scoop instead of making house calls. Kitty giggled at her man's ability to rattle his kid brother.

"I thought student sit-ins went out of style with the 1960s!" sighed Jim, grimacing at his politely listening guests as he crisply folded his newspaper. As he was about to leave the rag for the houseboy gathering up their breakfast dishes, a bold headline carelessly fell out, announcing that the high-stakes international boxing tournament everyone was eagerly awaiting, would be splendidly staged at Lusaka's Independence Stadium on May 2nd. The greying diplomat vaguely glanced at the article, then dismissed it with a sigh, "Oh, it's just that local strongman, Leopard Milongwe, boasting again about his magnificent muscles and daring other gladiators from around the world to come down here and duke it out with him, to be the next Hercules. What balderdash!"

"My brother Tracy should take on this Leopard man!" sniggered Kathleen, winking at Rick who was admiring her goddess beauty from across the table. "Tiptoe's always looking for a fight!"

"Kitty, you're being too catty", warned Alicia as she glanced sideways and wagged her finger at her sister. While Kathleen's sky-blue eyes narrowed coldly, Alicia instructively set the record straight, "Tracy doesn't need to scrap with anyone; he might break his hands! They're expensively insured, you know, so that he can play piano with the *Edmonton Symphony Orchestra*."

"So, he can honky-tonk in bars," Kathleen retorted, derisively sweeping her elegant hand out far beyond her own dainty nose. "Fannie, your schnoz is getting longer than Pinocchio's!"

The other youngsters lingering around the table broke out in laughter, amused at the siblings' barbed banter. Alicia, blushing and glaring, clumsily bumped the table and made the dishes tinkle when she reared up like a bull in a china shop at her taunting sister. JJ and Suzy wiped off their grins and watched intently now, eager to learn some fine points on how sisters should squabble. Alicia, breaking into a sweat, embarrassed at having spilled Bwana's coffee, refused to entertain the others further; she clamped her thick lips shut and gripped her ample hips with big hands in a tenacious effort to restrain herself from wading into a fist-fight, then and there.

"Oh, Richard," meowed Kitty-Cat, smiling with beguiling charm. Jumping at an opportunity to escape, she sweetly suggested to her eager attendant, "Can we go see those lovebirds in the backyard that you so eloquently extolled to me last night."

Alicia's dark eyes were fiercely beautiful, Orwell marvelled to himself as the tall, burly girl continued to stand and glare without the cover of her thick glasses through the open French windows, where her gorgeous sister promenaded airily outside with Richard. She smiled in shy appreciation, however, when she caught Orwell looking fondly at her, draped in her plain schoolgirl's jumper, rather than admiring Kathleen's trim figure, revealed through her satin blouse and skin-tight midi skirt. Maid Alicia humbly reassembled Bwana Hughes' cup and saucer and mopped up the spilled coffee with her napkin.

"That's okay dear—it was an accident," Mrs. Hughes whispered, coming to Alicia's aid.

Orwell and Alicia both then grabbed for the compelling news article still lying folded on the table, but Bwana Hughes, surprised that either youngster should show the slightest interest in such vainglorious violence as boxing, declared that everyone was now excused from the table.

"I must go to the High Commission this morning and tend to our new staff, Richard, so you are the designated driver for the family in my stead." Jim solemnly briefed his oldest son from the sundeck, like a preacher at his pulpit, although Richard seemed more eager to stroll in the back garden a bit longer on this fine sunny morning with young and blooming Kathleen.

"I'd love for you to show us around town, Rick," purred Kitty as she briefly released her admirer so that he could attend to his familial duties.

Bwana Hughes, preparing to drive away in his Mercedes Benz, entrusted Rick with car keys to the Peugeot station wagon. He prodded Orwell, who had retrieved the newspaper and was poring over the boxing article while Alicia read it aloud from behind his broad shoulders, "Son, instead of frittering your morning away reading about something as seedy as a fight game, I suggest you accompany your mother and sisters—and our gorgeous MacDonachie lasses, of course—to the African Market. Mother is going to cook up a stellar Easter feast for Sunday and needs to shop for it, so I understand. You can show your harem the sights, carry groceries, be a bodyguard... You know, do useful, manly things."

"*C'est la vie,*" obeyed Orwell, flashing happy Alicia a sidewise grin. She watched in awe as he discretely instructed the houseboy in the man's own language to leave the journal on his bedroom study desk after he himself had read the news. Bouncing deftly back to English, Orwell spoofed to any of the females who would listen, "I'm da man! Look out girls, here come da man doin' man things!"

"Did I miss something?" quizzed Bwana Hughes, at those who tittered amongst themselves while they milled about in the cobblestone foyer, choosing funky sun hats and slipping on leather sandals for their outing. When nobody answered him, Bwana sighed, "Oh well, it can't be that important. I'll see you folks later. Have a good day!"

"I guess I could use a day off from the books. Thank God, tomorrow's my concert!" said Orwell congenially.

"I really need your help today, Son," confirmed Martha, appreciative of Orwell's revived sense of humour and the unlikely *she* who sparked him now with eager questions about his concert. Mrs. Hughes winked at Alicia until the blossoming wallflower grinned broadly, before speaking further to them both, "I want to treat some special friends of the family to baked Easter ham, with all the trimmings—pineapple, cloves, honey—to celebrate a very special day. Orwell, we have two fine ladies here already; I've also heard so much through the grape vine about Benjamin, Solomon, and David that I am most eager to host your fine young men as well."

"Has JJ been sighing about those suave campus dudes again?" chuckled Suzanne, as she clasped her hands and aped her sister in a swoon. "*'Oh mommy, I can hardly breathe when I see such beautiful boys… I think I'm in Heaven!'*"

"Quit teasing me!" indignantly blurted Janice Joanne, blushing beneath her stiff brimmed bonnet. Her pigtails swung like rag dolls dancing in the breeze as she explained for Alicia, "Those guys Orwell knows from university are very polite and dress real snazzy, but they never have enough to eat. Nobody cooks for them!"

"JJ and Suzanne are such wonderful sisters, I would be honoured to show them to my friends," crooned Orwell, making Alicia giggle.

Hughes, for his next trick, grabbed up a decoratively woven grass tote bag in each hand and briskly strode to the front door ahead of Alicia, Suzanne and JJ like their bell-hop. The girls, meeting his implied challenge, laughed and bumped him aside as they ran ahead to grab the coveted window seats in the station wagon that Rick and Kathleen had purring while they awaited stragglers. Martha followed sedately at a distance, reviewing her long list of foodstuffs she needed to buy to feed the crew.

"Whoa now, settle down, you punks!" rebuked Rick, using his newly-acquired authority to lay down the law against immature children jostling each other to pile first into the vehicle. "This is how it's going to be: Mom and Kathleen will ride in front with me, and the rest of you will seat yourselves in the back, in orderly fashion. You'll have to double up—JJ being the smallest, will sit on someone's lap!"

"Aw Rick, don't play such the big shot. I'm nearly grown up now!" protested Janice Joanne, embarrassed in front of her age-mate Alicia. "Look, I'll prove it."

JJ looked like a pipsqueak in comparison to the robust MacDonachie girl, but she nonetheless sidled forward and gestured to her jovial friend playfully to stand back to back so she could show that they were evenly matched. Engineer Rick remained firmly unconvinced.

"Fannie, hop onto Orwell's lap," Kathleen dared, "Just don't squish him or make him hatch!"

"I'll not sit on any boy's lap, thank you!" vowed Alicia, scowling back. She then showed her naivety, despite her best intentions to appear worldly, as she blurted out moral warning, "I understand from Robert that it can lead to dancing!"

"Okay," replied Kathleen slowly, pretending to respect this obviously bizarre notion. She had a hard time repressing her laughter when Rick cackled heartily at Alicia's inadvertent joke. Kitty, gleaming when Rick affectionately encircled her slim waist with his arm, giggled as she playfully admonished Miss Frown Face to loosen up, "Someday, you and Reverend Robert will have to show me where in the Bible you read that dire threat."

"Anyone stuck on top of another would block the rear-view mirror, which would be dangerous with all these reckless drivers whizzing around the streets. Besides, there's lots of room on this back bench—for each of us," observed Orwell, sympathetically taking up the cause of the two younger girls. JJ and Alicia listened with renewed hope as he suggested, "Why get all hot and bothered? If we all squish together just a little, we can all fit side by side...."

Suddenly, Tug raced among them from out of nowhere and bounded into the car, where he took his self-appointed place, regally attentive, in the middle of the back seat.

"Or maybe not..." Orwell added, incredulously staring at the presumptuous pet. While Alicia beckoned to Tug, Orwell tried unsuccessfully to reason with the dog king to *sortie*. "You sure about this, pal? Not this time, okay. Come out of there, please Tug, come out!"

"My Gawd, Orwell, you've got to show that mangy pooch who's boss! Of course, he can't come with us to the African Market—or enter any store for that matter!" declared Rick in frustration. He strode fiercely to the other side, ripped open the door, grabbed Tug roughly by the collar, and dragged him yelping and kicking from the car. He sent him ingloriously packing to his doghouse with a couple of slaps upside the head. As Kathleen stood admiringly and rubbed his shoulder, Rick berated his younger sibling, "You see how it's done? Easy as pie! Okay then, let's stop messing around and motor on out of here."

Rick opened his left driver's door for Kathleen and bid her to seat herself.

"You want me to drive? But I don't have a driver's licence yet," she informed him with rare innocence swimming in her huge blue eyes, even as she complied. "I've been learning already back home under Robert's guidance, so I'm quite careful behind the wheel—not your typical bimbo blonde, but I'll need help negotiating this crazy traffic—oh, Rick," Kitty laughed foolishly as she stopped short, noticing her error, "Why didn't you tell me the steering wheel was on the *right* side? We're still British over here! Now, I feel like an airhead!"

"You aren't one...so don't feel bad, Kathy," Richard told her as he slid confidently into the driver's seat beside her. "Things are different here but not so strange that you can't adapt."

"Well said, Son. You would know," chirped Martha as she sat beside Kitty, assuring her that Richard was a very patient and understanding young man. "We are going to have a gay old time, driving around town today."

Suzanne, JJ, Alicia, and Orwell childishly sang "Four in the Bed and the Little One Said" as they climbed into the back seat one by one, slid over methodically, and conscientiously made room for one another to fit on the back seat. Orwell and Suzanne rolled down their windows halfway, to ensure that everyone could breathe and expand to normal size. Just before the backdoor shut, Tug snuck into the well at Orwell's feet. The young man grimaced at his canine friend and nudged Alicia, who was pressed against him. She smiled in pleasant surprise, but shared his secret rather than tattled on him to the driver, who was by then serenely engrossed in piloting their packed sardine ship. Alicia, JJ, and Suzanne broke into excited girl talk on various topics while Rick, absorbed with pointing out special landmarks and activities to an enthralled Kathleen, blissfully drove down the hill towards the vibrant city.

As they trundled along, Orwell pined for Tracy and wished his mentor was the one squished beside him and listening to his own travelogue, instead of being saddled with the task of babysitting MacDonachie's overgrown brat of a kid sister. Her flowery perfume enveloped him and her ropy hair swished his face every time she moved her head to glimpse the vivid scenery passing by. Still, he must admit one thing: Alicia was good at keeping his secret about the stowaway dog. She also was true when speaking her mind, and her eyes revealed a depth she otherwise hid to her entourage.

"I would like to jog with you and Tug in the mornings," she resolutely informed Orwell. "I belong to a long-distance running club in my private, all-girls school back home, and I am in better shape than you think. I like many sports—basketball, soccer, hockey, baseball, tennis on clay as well as tables—but I too must keep fit, even while vacationing. We'll see who sleeps in! Let me run with you!"

"Okay, you're on! We pull out tomorrow at sunrise!" Orwell issued his own bold challenge.

"Pick me too, Orly. You promised," reminded JJ buoyantly from where she sat on Alicia's other side. Alicia gave her a strange look, as though worried that JJ would make the proverbial three-is-a-crowd adage rather than the two good company she was hoping for.

"I called uncle already," gasped Orwell in muffled agreement as the two girls leaned on him heavily whenever the car turned sharply left and right.

"Alright!" chimed JJ, as they girlishly pretended to play bongo drums together in triumph over their ever-agreeable playmate. Suzy made a quirky face in response to the immature antics of these children, while Orwell laughed and enjoyed their fun. Suzanne pouted, "Whatever!" as she too was being jostled back and forth as she tried to check her antimony eyeliner using her pocket mirror.

They pleasantly motored along a broad carriageway lined with leafy jacaranda and flamboyant trees, under which pedestrians and cyclists also streamed toward the central market place. Piloting over a bridge that spanned the railroad tracks, Rick explained that new diesel locomotives would soon pull loads of imported manufactured goods from, and transport copper bars to, Dar es Salaam in neighbouring Tanzania, using the new line built by the Chinese—aptly called the *Great Freedom Railway*—rather than obsolete, coal-fired engines now seen belching black smoke as they chugged along the old southern route down to the Indian Ocean at Beira, travelling through enemy Rhodesian and Portuguese territories. Passenger train traffic between Zambia and Tanzania was about to boom! Orwell added that many of his university friends had left to study railway engineering in Mao's China...Cepheus Belo came to mind, if he didn't get arrested for sedition!

They soon arrived wide-eyed into a modern urban hub that boasted glistening office towers, cosmopolitan boutiques, trendy theatres, and fine eateries fronting many tree-lined streets bustling with vehicles, vendors, and shoppers from all ages and all walks of life. Although obscurely named after *Lusaakas,* a skilled Lenje elephant hunter who had lived in the area many years ago, Lusaka had grown dynamically in the past 50 years: from a dusty colonial village built on land granted by a Lenje tribal chief to the first white settlers for cultivating maize, into a town, then a city, and finally into this vibrant and progressive, national capital!

"We'll park here," announced tour guide Rick as he brought the Peugeot to a halt beneath an umbrella-like tree. He explained to Kathleen their shopping itinerary while others already threw open their doors and stepped from the car, "It's a little walk, my dear, but you'll enjoy embracing many new sights and sounds. Let me escort you! Lusaka's more cosmopolitan than Edmonton."

His chivalry was interrupted when frisky Tug bounded from his hiding to race about, barking excitedly and jumping up with muddy paws to lick his travel mates, paying particular attention to the fresh, brightly dressed MacDonachie women! Rick and Orwell exchanged bewildered glances, but Alicia surprised both of them by being a good sport. She laughed and danced with Tug until he lost his two-footed confidence and whimpered with many arm licks to be let down. Rick saw red when Tug began sniffing up the tight dress of his Kitty-Cat.

"Pew! Get off me, you lewd animal!" yowled Kathleen when the furry brute stole a sloppy kiss from her.

"What! How did he get here?" demanded Mom Hughes.

Putting two and two quickly together as they both rushed to grab Tug, Rick rasped at Orwell. "I told you: no dogs allowed on this venture! Now do you see why?"

"I do, I really do!" reiterated Orwell in tired subservience. "I came prepared this time."

Providing a shield so that Rick could not punish the anxious animal, Orwell bent down and clipped Tug's collar to a leash he had retrieved from one of the carrying baskets. When Orwell grasped the looped handle securely, Tug meekly resigned himself to his restriction in exchange for the joy of accompanying his master.

"I don't know, Orwell, I am worried about him making a scene; Tug will just get in the way."

"Not with me walking beside him," Orwell audaciously promised everyone while they looked on with sardonic disbelief. He offered a proviso, "Tug obviously wants our company, and I promise, if he does not behave, I'll bring him back to the car forthwith and lock him inside until we are done shopping. Can you guys work with us on this?"

They all nodded but with various levels of confidence. Not wanting to start a parade, Orwell suggested that Mom and Rick open the way, while he and Tug would leisurely stroll along behind the shoppers. As if responding to the crack of some imaginary starter's pistol, Kitty and Suzy dashed into the nearest women's dress shop to search for chic skirts and bathing suits, while Mom and Richard debated which food stall in the market they should start with. Orwell wondered whether certain simple truths would dawn upon self-centred Kathleen, under the incredulous gaze of the locals, who could not help but stare at her: winter was nearly here, and decent women did not so overtly flaunt their sexuality in public!

"Let's meet back at the car in one hour, okay?" suggested Rick, before disappearing from view, shackled in Kathleen's grip. He shrugged at his brother like one of Bambi's friends in love.

"Hmm, is my bro Flower or Thumper, I wonder?" Orwell mused to himself as he ambled along, fully enjoying his bachelor's freedom.

Martha and the two younger girls darted into a bookstore. Expecting to glimpse these avid bookworms immersed in their various choices of literature when he sauntered past the display window, Orwell shook when Alicia and JJ jumped out from some hiding place near the door.

"Surprise! Here we are!" they yelled at the flabbergasted young man in jarring unison. "Where are you going, Oh-well?"

"To market, to market, to buy a fat hog!" rhymed Orwell clownishly, to calm his frazzled nerves. "Home again, home again, jiggery-jog!"

"We've already bought our book together; we'll take turns reading to each other during more reflective moments," announced JJ proudly, displaying Alan Paton's famous South African novel *Cry, the Beloved Country* against the white pinafore of her blue cotton dress.

"Hey, that's my kind of book! It's very poetic, almost Biblical in language, although the plot is as sad as it is thought-provoking. Paton was deeply concerned for his beloved country; he warned South Africa in 1948[38] of many

38 *Alan Paton* (1903 to 1988): South African school teacher, prison reformer, politician and writer. He published *Cry the Beloved Country* in 1948, the same year as the victory by the *National Party* led by DF Malan, together with their political ally the *Afrikaner Party*, over the *United Party*, led by General Jan Smuts in

dangers to come if the oppression of apartheid was not lifted...But I digress. Maybe we three pundits can read from it together some evening."

"That would be fun," replied Alicia politely, pleased that she had so caught his attention that he wanted to spend quality time reading with her. Then, inexplicably turning devious, she gleefully razzed Orwell, "And you were saying, Mr. Da Man that we are mere Valley Girls who would shop 'til we dropped? What do you say now?"

"You've only visited your first store of the morning," observed Orwell wryly as he walked ahead. "We'll compare notes at the end of the day."

"Okay, Mr. Da Man," battled Alicia, loudly slapping the sidewalk with her sandals as she strode briskly beside her startled friend. She seemed to tower over him as she played, "If you are so clever, Mr. Da Man, answer my riddle! I spy, with my little eye, something that is red . . . ."

"It must be the printed dress of that African woman, the one with her baby tied on her back, strolling ahead of us with a sewing machine balanced on her head," he of the eagle eye replied quickly and confidently.

"Her? I have more imagination than that!" retorted Alicia haughtily.

"You mean the red Volkswagen beetle driving up the street beside us?"

"Fuchsia, in fact! No, although I wish I could be driving such a swell car."

"How about those red flowers so vividly blooming in yonder baskets overhanging the boulevard? No? Then, you must be referring to those fire engine-red flowers still blooming in the flame trees."

"You are getting colder, Oh-well, frigidly cold in fact!" scoffed Alicia, energetically swinging her big hips and strong arms and causing her lush female forms to jiggle provocatively as she power-walked beside him. She winked back at JJ, who seemed equally stumped as she struggled to keep up. "Think, sir, as you look around you; and try harder!"

"I know! You must be referring to the red stripe in the Zambian flag flying over the post office beyond the traffic robot. Did you know that red represents the blood shed by African freedom fighters during the struggle for independence from their British colonial masters?"

---

South Africa's general election. The new, Afrikaner-dominated, white minority government swiftly imposed its policy of *apartheid* for separate development of races. The *National Party* governed until 1994, when Nelson Mandela's *African National Congress* took power in South Africa's first one-man, one-vote election.

"Really? Nice try, bucko!" snorted Miss MacDonachie, unimpressed by his fount of trivial knowledge. "Guess again!"

"What about Tug's red tongue? He's really getting thirsty, lolling it out there like a carpet in this sweltering heat! Am I even close?"

"Nope."

"Lisa, here's the drugstore I was telling you about. We can buy new film for your sure-shot camera, maybe find some neat postcards to send to your mom and friends back home," interrupted JJ as she pointed to a busy little print shop whose frontage displayed racks festooned with all manner of vivid big game posters and bold, silk-screened T-shirts sporting reproductions of Victoria Falls and Mount Kilimanjaro. Out of yawning windows danced *The Archies* sprightly tune "Sugar, Sugar".

"Hey, I know that song—it's one of my favourites! I love reading the *Archie* comic strip in the Saturday funnies," chattered Alicia airily as she smoothly ducked into the shop following JJ, "I'm like Betty, the decent practical gal, but then I get bounced whenever Veronica, that raven-haired vixen comes primping along! Kathleen reminds me of Veronica, even if she's really blonde, because she always gets her guy—no matter how dumb she acts."

"What about me? Don't I count?" protested Orwell from where he stood restraining Tug, suddenly feeling drained and left out. "I'm sun-bleached blonde too, though not by choice!"

Little did he realize what blessing in disguise it was to not follow this babbling chick talk, drowned out by a lorry rattling past on wobbly tires, piled high with flour sacks and spewing acrid black exhaust from its stack. The budding women's libbers, on the other hand, heard his bleating complaint all too well.

"Well, what about you?" teased Alicia, giving her discarded plaything a sweet grin. She instructed him, "Go for a stroll around the block; we'll be waiting for you at this door by the time you pass by again."

"I'm not that fast; there are too many interesting pitfalls around here, especially with this unpredictable pet as my familiar. I'm a little preoccupied now, but I'd love to read about the upcoming *Rumble in the Jungle* between Foreman and Ali over in Kinshasa, Zaire—although it's certainly not as big or reachable as the Leopard Milongwe fight here in town. Maybe there'll be some fresh news today about who Leopard's daring white opponent actually is. Can't you imps at least buy me some chewing gum and a boxing magazine?"

"Imps?" derided Alicia, glaring and huffing at Orwell in fake offence. JJ shook her head in mock perturbation, in concert with MacDonachie's pouty protest, "I thought we were fairies at the very least!"

"Or, if you can, sis, please splurge for the latest *Classic Comic*? I think *King Solomon's Mines* is due out. Aw, come on!" he pleaded when she turned around and made a funny face suggesting civil disobedience. "You read them too—this is for both of us! Just sign out one or two of my comics at a time from now on then instead of taking ten, so I know who has them and where they are."

"I prefer the latter choice, Oh-well," declared Alicia righteously. She furtively signalled to her purse. "I'm also impressed that you maintain a library. Maybe I can cash in a traveller's cheque here to pay for your next good read."

"Aren't you going to tell me the answer to your riddle?"

"No way, Jose! If you can't figure it out, I won't tell you the answer, simple though it is."

"Be that way then, see y'all later," sighed Orwell in resignation. He gasped after glancing at his wristwatch, "I'd say you've got fifteen minutes left before we should head back to meet the others at the car, so don't doddle in there!"

Alicia bent down and whispered something rude, seemingly at Orwell's expense in JJ's ear, after which they both giggled richly and sashayed into the store. He was left behind, unable to follow these puzzling creatures because of Tug, but as he stared at his sunburned face in the window front, he suddenly realized what was *red*! It didn't matter that he wore fashionable platform shoes, striped bellbottom trousers, and a sky-blue vest over his navy cotton shirt; those broads still found a way to tease him. Embarrassed at the sunburnt redness of his face, Hughes scowled dully now at the girls' carefree, almost cavorting activities, and wondered with painful chagrin as to why Tracy stayed away, but sent his mouthy sister to torment him instead. Where the hell was The Great One?

"Orwell Hughes!" hailed a cheerful voice on his blind side. "Good morning! How are you this fine day, my friend?"

Whirling around, Orwell froze like a deer in the headlights to be come face to face with the cleverly bespectacled, broadly smiling, and impeccably tailored Cepheus Belo. Striding over with feline fluidity, and showing respect without fear for little Tug, the eloquent leader of the Writers' Club warmed Hughes' heart with an exuberant hand shake. Tug, playing his role well, heeled crisply at attention and did not bark.

"Top of the morning to you, sir!" saluted Cepheus, touching hands again. "What, Mr. Orwell, are you doing here on this busy street, in front of this fashionable shop, on such a fine Tuesday morning as today?"

"I'm just walking my dog," replied Hughes vaguely.

"In the heart of the city? My good man, you should be strolling your magnificent pet along some leafy suburban lane or, better still, in an open park. The king of the African Market will absolutely bar your entry at the gate! Come now! Don't tell me you intend to go into this fancy shop with your furry companion," Cepheus feigned dismay. Laughing raucously, he let his vivid writer's imagination describe Orwell's worst nightmare. "You would be angrily driven off by the proprietor's hired men, and chased down the street by a mob. You'd beg to be handed over to the police, whom I know you equate with the scourge of malaria!"

Unnerved by Belo's rambling fiction, Orwell bid him to reign it in with solemn explanation, "In truth, sir, I am waiting here for my sister while she buys camera film. She will soon be coming out to join me."

"I didn't know you had a sister, Master Hughes. Is she also blonde-haired and blue-eyed?"

Orwell, baffled by this question so casually tossed by such an esteemed gentleman, had to stop and think for a moment at the last time he had looked deeply into JJ's delicate little face. When he shook his head, embarrassed, Cepheus quipped, "The young lady must be beautiful. Can you show me her photograph?"

"Better still, I can introduce you to Janice Joanne in person. Here she comes now!" Hughes announced buoyantly with sweeping hand gestures, having inhaled some of the chief writer's legendary effervescence.

Emerging into the blinding sunlight, blissfully unaware that they were under scrutiny, the merrily chattering girls pranced up to their male admirers.

"Sorry Brother," groaned JJ as she collided with Orwell's barrel chest. The slim, brunette pixie seemed much younger than seventeen, especially when compared with dark Alicia, who towered over her despite their same age.

"Oh, fiddlesticks!" Alicia gasped as she in turn nearly stumbled over her dainty friend. Readjusting her glasses, she blushed at Orwell—the cause of the near-collision—as she handed him his precious *King Solomon's Mines* comic.

Orwell lit up at the sight as Cepheus stared critically at these blooming yet rough-around-the-edges females, particularly the tall and robust MacDonachie.

She, shyly aware of his piercing attention, stooped down to buckle her sandals, which had loosened during the kerfuffle.

"Dear ladies," Orwell suavely made introductions. "Allow me to introduce Mr. Cepheus Belo, my good friend and fellow writer. We are both struggling university students with the clear intention of becoming famous authors. Cepheus, meet my sister, Janice Joanne and her age-mate who is presently visiting us from Canada, Miss Alicia Pearl Rose MacDonachie."

JJ, always pleased to meet her brother's friends—strange and colourful characters one and all—gaily shook hands with this impeccable gentleman, but Alicia did not quickly follow suit. Hughes, acting gallantly, gently took Alicia by the hand and helped her to her feet when she seemed suddenly more interested in petting Tug, who had moved in to lick her face while she squatted girlishly at his eye level. Still, she smiled broadly and responded obediently when Orwell reached to her with such charm. She refrained from robustly shaking hands or speaking boldly in her usual tom-boyish way, as if believing herself to be on par with men—like Cepheus pictured most brash American women did. Instead, keeping her head bowed respectfully in deference to the stately black gentleman's superior age and calling, Alicia politely curtseyed for Mr. Belo.

"I understand that you purchased some film for your camera, Miss Hughes?" commented Cepheus to his friend's sister. "Will darkroom technicians wash your negatives into colour or black and white photos when you have finished snapping this roll of film?"

"Colour, of course!" boldly pshawed JJ, impressing shy Alicia by so forwardly expressing her opinions in the company of men. "Black and white snapshots are simply too grey for me!"

"Did you buy much film today for your camera?" Cepheus continued, trying not to chuckle too loudly at her unintentional joke.

"I certainly did, Mr. Belo, as did Lisa. We are not professional shutterbugs yet, but with dear Lisa visiting, we want to take many photographs to document our special journey together."

"Your name is *Lisa*, Miss MacDonachie?"

"No, I'm Alicia."

"I see," noted Cepheus, tickled by the discovery; he made a noble effort to draw an intelligent conversation out of this shy and aloof diamond in the rough. "Lisa is your nickname or your second name?"

"You should not be so impertinent, sir, as to ask after my personal names, especially at first glance," the amazon suddenly rebuked her observer, who then seemed taken aback by her sharp correction. "Suffice it to say, I am called by many names, some which I treasure, but others I loathe...Orwell knows."

"You are well-versed in African culture, Miss MacDonachie, such that you must have visited my peoples' continent before," surmised Cepheus, still cheer ful, but treading more softly now. He glanced at Orwell for support, but the lad, a frivolous grin plastered on his face, could only watch in dumb amusement.

"I was born near Maiduguri in Nigeria, West Africa."

"Was your father a colonial administrator, or a celebrated hunter of big game? Or perchance a businessman with considerable means and a well-developed taste for exotic adventures?"

"He is the latter, that's for sure," sighed Alicia sardonically as she rolled her large brown eyes in mocked chagrin, causing Orwell and JJ to giggle. "I am the youngest daughter to long-serving Christian missionaries; you see, my father was also born in Gwoza and my grandfather is buried there. Although I am white, Africa colours my being."

"That is very interesting!" exclaimed Cepheus happily. "I too was born in Bornu, albeit among Muslims. Since coming of age and learning to think independently, I embraced Communism, which transcends religious lines to champion the vital cause of oppressed people everywhere. We nonetheless appear to be related, to some degree."

"Yes, we are all part of God's wonderful creation."

"We both revere God and follow His just moral teachings for living here on earth. We treat one another with kindness and respect. Maybe you and I can explore this common ground further sometime down the road, *Malama*... My friend Mr. Orwell seems anxious to go now. I too must run some pressing errands, but I would certainly enjoy talking with you young ladies again."

Alicia smiled coyly, appearing vaguely pleased by Belo's interest in her. Shy and respectful, however, the single girl avoided his piercing eyes. She primly ventured, "If my hosts agree to organize such an opportunity."

Young Hughes, having observed this odd encounter with as much enjoyment as bewilderment, nervously felt called upon to arrange a place and a date for his ward to receive a worthy gentleman caller. He coughed and sputtered into action like an old car being fired up after a long rest in someone's back yard.

"If you don't mind partaking in our Easter festivities on the weekend, Cepheus, you are welcome to join us for good food and fellowship. Ben plans to attend, as do some of my other good friends on campus: Solomon and David..."

"Georgina Amadu and her brother Ali, are also invited," interjected JJ with the flourish of one who announced VIPs arriving at the royal palace. "Miss Amadu will be the guest of honour...at least in the eyes of men!"

"My goodness, the latter are fellow Nigerians—and Muslims too—feasting with you Christians! I shall be in splendid company then, what with articulate Mr. Benjamin and the beautiful, charming *Malama* Amadu on the official guest list. Ah yes, many men swoon whenever she waltzes into their midst like a garden of summer flowers."

He suddenly put Orwell on the spot with a ruthlessly astute observation, "I believe, my dear Orwell, that the fancy lady has also cast her charming spell upon you. Miss MacDonachie, your friend's brother seems to have become a very prolific poet since she first smiled at him."

"It's not because of her. I have always loved to write," protested Hughes, flustered that nobody seemed to believe him. "JJ, you know that!"

"I know how dreamy you become whenever you think of Georgie girl," teased his little sister, mischievously rubbing her two index fingers together like fire sticks to spark him, "Shame on you, Orly! Brother's got a girlfriend!"

"I do not—not Georgina at least. We're just casual friends," argued Orwell vigorously. "The mighty queen of the campus comes and goes as she pleases, and bestows her graces on whomever she chooses. But if Georgina has agreed to partake in our humble Easter feast, so be it! I'm glad to host her."

Cepheus laughed and clapped his hands uproariously at Orwell's outburst, but Alicia stood back, frowning at the lavish description of another girl. Although he did not understand why then, Orwell sensed that she was mad at him; as much as he wished to brighten her mood, he was unsure as to how to proceed.

"Cepheus, the women can entertain themselves with music and parlour games, while the men folk will be at leisure to discuss worldly affairs in our own quarters," Orwell, wanting to look sharp and savvy once he had caught his breath, promoted the Sunday social in sedately traditional terms to Belo, yet revealed himself as a crass male chauvinist to the two budding feminists. "I'm certain you will be able to enliven our conversations with your fount of knowledge and famous wit."

"Indeed, then I shall be delighted to come. I enjoy discussing many issues, particularly with our prophetic Benjamin Mudenda, an eloquent writer but a respectful listener who behaves fairly with me even though he follows Jesus, son of Mary. Christians, Muslims and Jews are all brothers of the same Book—that is to say, we share many noble truths and a mighty scriptural heritage! Abraham is our shared prophet and pillar of obedience. Would you not agree, Malama Alicia?"

"I understand where you are coming from, sir," soberly acknowledged MacDonachie as she painfully remembered her father's zealous efforts to win for Christ "*pagan slaves to the cult of Islam*". She cautioned the intellectual gentleman nonetheless. "But I must ponder this idea awhile before answering you. Perhaps, when you visit me at my friends' home on the Sunday of my risen Lord, we can discuss it further...that is, if you can tolerate a strong female voice in your manly palaver."

"May I snap a picture of you and Miss Hughes as a memento of our meeting?" suggested Cepheus, congenially changing the topic without answering Alicia's question. "It has been such a pleasure to meet both of you!"

"Please do," JJ tinkled. Smiling at her less forward friend, she could see by her blushing smile that Alicia was also flattered by this uncommon male attention heaped upon her. She tapped MacDonachie's strongly planted sandal with her own slender foot to encourage her to primp cleverly for the camera, "I think we can handle being flashed, eh Lisa-babe? Orwell's friend is just being polite. The nice man is not stealing our souls or passing us out to prospective courtiers, the police, or anyone naughty, is he?"

"I believe you are right, JJ!" Alicia giggled nervously as she ran her hand down her pony tail to ensure that it still flowed neatly along the back of her neck. Glancing furtively at Orwell, as though seeking his approval for such a risqué display, she muttered with dark humour, "We wouldn't want our pictures to get into the wrong hands."

JJ confirmed that Alicia was on board, fished into her purse for her compact camera and handed it to beaming Cepheus. She then snagged her self-conscious friend by the waist and energetically pulled her close for a playful pose, urging Alicia to smile, "Come on, say cheese!"

"Yes, thank you! You are indeed movie stars!" chortled Belo as he took a slew of shots of JJ and Alicia while they wandered back toward the car to rendezvous with the rest of the Hughes party. "You are so absolutely fine!"

Orwell observed that Belo would certainly have been long gone, had they met alone—unless he really wanted something off of him, like his guarded manuscript, which he eagerly had taken for review already, but conveniently kept forgetting to return!

Meanwhile, 'Bertha' and 'Twiggy' cutely smiled and held hands for *Mwaiseni's* looming department store; they then posed extravagantly and made goofy clown faces against a wrought iron fence. JJ clenched a freshly picked sprig of hibiscus flowers in her teeth as she and Alicia deftly tangoed beneath the dancing elephant sign at *National and Grindlays* bank. One photo, taken against a pleasing backdrop of flower gardens, showed Orwell closely flanked by two lovely admirers; each looped one hand lovingly through the crooks of his elbows, while he held onto Tug, regally seated in front of them.

The girls draped themselves lavishly across some rich person's limousine, pretending to be foreign models of a high-class fashion magazine, while Orwell joked in the vernacular with the uniformed driver, and bought him an ice-chilled soda as a small *dashe*[39] for allowing their play. Hughes realized too late to that he was talking to Georgina's chauffeur, and the parked car was Professor Ibrahim's Rolls Royce; without missing a beat, he continued to hand out cold Schweppes orange drinks he bought from a smiling street vendor to everyone who had stopped by to watch the impromptu photo shoot!

The rambunctious crew could not move on before Miss Amadu and her brother Ali returned from their morning shopping spree. Ali, swanky dressed in a brushed denim safari suit, sauntered slightly in the lead, a radio tuned to African *Highlife* in one hand and a wicker bag of sundry dry goods, in the other. Georgina followed, carrying brightly wrapped parcels filled with clothes and stationery for the upcoming university term. She was dressed in a new, blue and white striped cardigan, a sky-blue midi skirt, and a knitted blue cap pulled cutely over her forehead.

Georgina almost looked like a girl today, but she really was a vivaciously attractive and full-figured woman who, even at twenty Orwell fantasized, could most certainly please a man if this was her desire. The gorgeous lady smiled and

39 *Dashe*: vernacular for a modest bribe, often needed to get something done.

happily waved at Orwell when she noticed him witnessing her movie-worthy approach from afar with a wistful gaze. Georgie knew she was God's blessed answer to his fervent prayers.

Alicia hastily retreated behind a fig tree to get a better view of the new arrivals, grimly sensing that this attractive newcomer was the beguiling siren that enticed Orwell's heart.

"She stoops to conquer," quoted Cepheus wryly as he joined Alicia on her vantage point. Belo, scowling as he watched the spectacle with his new lady friend, muttered to her under his breath, "This yellow man who escorts Her Highness, he is a rich philanderer who embarrasses our people as he pilfers our nation's wealth and prestige!"

Alicia, vaguely smiling, ignored Belo as she continued to assess what was really happening between Orwell and this beguiling beauty. Cepheus could stomach the banter no longer, for he sensed that the setting was about to change decidedly for the worse. He seized his opportunity to make a graceful exit before Georgina and Ali could stake their countryman claim upon him.

"I am leaving now, Malama," Cepheus discretely resolved, politeness in his voice belying fury burning in his heart and urgency clouding the features of his face. "I entrust you presently to the fair protection of Mr. Orwell, as I still have other errands to run in this part of town. I relish nonetheless meeting you again on your appointed day for the upcoming religious festivities."

Belo, softly shaking hands about the circle, bid pleasant adieu to each of the tarrying party, "Goodbye Miss Hughes and Miss MacDonachie. I enjoyed escorting you about our vibrant city, photographing you, and soaking up your pleasant company like sunshine. Until we shall feast together—God willing—may you both have good health and happiness. I bid you adieu as well, Mr. Orwell; you have been most enlightening today. May God carry us safely to Sunday afternoon, sir, when I will again talk with you and Mr. Benjamin. Your dog has been most peaceful with me."

He then fluidly took his leave, smiling back occasionally like some Cheshire Cat as he strolled away. As Alicia glanced after him, she thought that Cepheus cut an imposing figure even when overdressed in his formal attire. She would have liked to share her observation with Orwell, but was dismayed to find that he had eagerly moved forward to bow in homage before the amused Georgina.

Envious of his overt loyalties, Alicia turned back to look upon Cepheus, but he had mingled into the crowds and was gone.

"Hello, what's going on here?" Ali demanded in not serene Oxford English as he strode into the scene while shaking his car keys impatiently like some rich young ruler. Getting no answers from the wannabe movie stars that had suddenly turned to stone, the master browbeat his Coca Cola-guzzling chauffeur, "I say, Joseph, do you know these people?"

"Ali, don't keep such a stiff upper lip; you are only half British," playfully admonished Georgina. Smiling generously, she warmly embraced the flabbergasted Orwell like some long-lost friend. When Ali gazed askance at his sister's forward behaviour with the strange white youth, Georgina boldly jogged his memory. "Don't you remember Orwell Hughes, Brother? This fine gentleman is my fellow student. We've both been to his house for Saturday afternoon tea."

"I've never laid eyes on that lamentable bloke in my life!" stormed Ali, fiercely inspecting his uncle's luxury car for damage. Pointing out an almost invisible patch of reduced polish on the front fender, he declared to his frivolous sister, "I shall call a policeman forthwith to arrest the blackguard for vandalizing our property!"

"For goodness sake's, we all played lawn darts at the Hughes compound during your last visit, only three months ago...at Christmas time! Remember? You even made a point of demonstrating to our hosts the intricate differences between North American baseball and English cricket, which was fun until you broke Mr. Hughes's bedroom window with a badly hit ball!"

"I did? Are you certain the batsman was not my servant?"

"I saw you do it with my own eyes, sir—in fact, I was the unfortunate bowler who tried to hit the wicket behind you. You defended your bails very well but I never forget a face!" JJ chimed deliciously, throwing caution to the wind and joining in the fray.

"Oh yes, well, Orwell Hughes then you are—you must be, of course. Excellent affair, a very polite and thoughtful host, I might add," recollected Ali sheepishly, softly taking Orwell's calloused hand in his while covering his own butt with officious comedy. Finding some spare congeniality in his pockets for this rabble-rouser so soon after reaming him out for touching his uncle's antique Rolls Royce, Ali confessed. "Sorry, Orwell old chap... I didn't recognize you at first. How are you, sir? And who could this attractive young lady be but your sister Suzanne?"

"Janice Joanne to you, Mr. Ali; the little white girl is growing up!" replied the vivacious brunette with gleaming blue eyes, tickled pink that this handsome mulatto man mistook her for Suzy. To skirt the flurry of questions regarding her beautiful sister, JJ effervescently pulled Alicia into the sunlight from where she had brooding against a tree, detachedly sipping her orange juice, and keeping Tug calm. "And I am doing well, thank you—fabulously well now that my special friend, Alicia MacDonachie, is visiting me from Canada."

"How ya doin', Hanoi Jane?" Ali twanged in badly-attempted American, assuming that the burly, unsophisticated visitor was your typically liberated, loudmouthed, braless female from Hollywood. He was taken aback when Miss MacDonachie curtsied shyly from afar before his prestigious personage like the polite schoolgirl she really was, rather than flaunting her curves or boldly pumping his hand as he expected.

When Alicia whispered solemnly that she was fine, the playboy student who had attended various venerable European universities, remarked in a suavely condescending way, "Well, we certainly *are* chatty today."

"Alicia MacDonachie is your name?" questioned Georgina, intrigued that this seemingly dull and homely school girl kept avoiding her gaze. "Where have I heard such a regal name before? Let me see...Why, of course, you are of that famous singing family I so often hear praising the Lord in our women's dormitory late at night!"

"I play my part to the best of my ability, using the musical talents that God gave me," replied Alicia quietly but guardedly, not appreciating the limelight that the more glamorous and experienced woman brazenly shone upon her.

"This is very commendable, but how do you pay your way in this world?"

"I still live at home where I attend high school, but I also do yard work and clean house for my parents, who are getting on in age," admitted Alicia self-consciously. "During the summer, I cook at my brother's cattle ranch."

"You are a working girl," snorted Ali, his interest waning even further for this roughhewn servant so unlike the dainty fashion models, royalty, and movie stars he pursued at high-society playgrounds in the Alps and Riviera. His handsome chocolate face feigning a frown as he pointed out her apparent confusion, Amadu then asked the dismayed girl for an explanation, "I thought that rich American celebrities employed a platoon of lackeys to do their menial household tasks. That way, you are free to enjoy...the finer things in life."

Meanwhile, Georgina light-heartedly showcased Orwell Hughes the bounce in her curvy body by playing peek-a-boo behind a sweet frangipani sprig in her bonnet. The latter followed Georgie girl's every word and gesture like some worshipping fan as she circled the newcomer who dared intrigue her.

"My dear Alicia, are you related to Tracy MacDonachie, the wonderful athlete and teacher that Orwell boasts as his best friend, who is supposedly coming here to southern Africa to visit him soon? Mr. MacDonachie's heroic feats have been enthusiastically related by Orwell for many weeks now. Surely his arrival is imminent—he may be marching through the Lusaka International Airport as we speak!"

"My brother Tracy will soon be among us," asserted Alicia, nodding towards her friend to buoy up his sagging faith. Her dark eyes flashing within her otherwise plain features, MacDonachie glanced at Orwell, "Then, I will be able to celebrate with Tracy and my dear friends just like you, Georgina, are doing now with your brother Ali. We're all strangers here—except for Mr. Joseph, perhaps. My own fellowship will be complete when my straggling brother finally holds me securely in his arms."

Orwell watched silently, enthralled, as the two women gazed at each other, with stern looks at first, which then softened with the wistful understanding of each other's loneliness, and the love they bore for a few loyal supporters who remained near to their hearts.

"How true. I wish you well in your quest," affirmed Georgina pleasantly after this moment of soul-searching reflection. Touching Alicia gently on the shoulder to release her from the trance of intense scrutiny, the socialite uttered a reverent blessing upon the other's hope, "May Allah bring Malam Tracy alive and well into your presence—even during this important Christian festival, if such is His pleasure!"

JJ had been sweetly chirping on the sidelines with Ali in apparent oblivion to the exchange between Alicia and Georgina, but the tears now glistening in her large blue eyes revealed her response to this fervent intertwining of sisterly souls by the Lord.

"Amen, and thank you," Alicia and Orwell replied gratefully, their spirits refreshed.

Turning to her would-be courtier, Miss Amadu coyly invited, "Orwell, my big brother wants to go. Can we give you folks a lift somewhere? Our car is more than large enough for all of us."

Orwell—who wished he could rest like a loaf of freshly baked bread in her bejewelled and sweetly scented hands—candidly explained his situation.

"Well, we are frightfully late now to rendezvous with the rest of my family, who are expecting us at the south end of Cairo Road—you know, near the roundabout with all the flags of the Nonaligned Nations. It would be nice if you could bring us there, but we are three more people...and my dog as well!"

"It's no bother, really," Georgina assured him, "Ali doesn't mind."

"If you're quite done wasting time, then, please step into our luxury ship for a few magic moments as we ferry you to your destination," muttered Ali briskly to Orwell. Calling his driver to take the wheel, he crisply ushered the women through the rear door, and tempted them to comfortably settle onto the plush, crushed velvet cushions.

Ali joked as he invited Orwell and Tug to sit beside him on a separate bench among the gleaming redwood trim and polished brass ornaments of their magic carpet, "Let those silly hens do their incessant clucking about their frivolous interests. We shall engage in manly discourse without being distracted by womanly charms."

"Thank you, Ali. Yes, let's!" agreed Hughes, honoured that the regal older brother of his flame, so well-versed with the sporting life, endorsed him as a manly friend.

"So, how do you find this big affair?" Ali asked Orwell about what the impressionable white youth might think of his rare luxury automobile as they drove in style along Cairo Road. His roving eyes gleaning for sight of attractive women, Mr. Amadu could just as easily have sought fleeting entertainment from a new joke or solicited Orwell's comments about the swinging night life in Lusaka.

"Your limo is a marvel, a true palace on wheels," exuberantly exclaimed Hughes. "Such finish and decor are never seen on ordinary cars. It suits you well, Ali for you are a wealthy, successful man-about-town, who entertains his guests with nothing but the most exquisite style!"

"Ah, no, you flatter me because you like my little sister!" teased Ali.

"No, I mean it. Your limousine has trappings I've only glimpsed in spy movies: a well-supplied bar with fine cigars and expensive liqueurs, state-of-the-art colour television set and stereo record player...Until this very moment, I had only dreamed of riding in a Rolls Royce."

"Is that so? You mean that the talented son of the Canadian High Commissioner's executive director dares to claim he has never ridden inside the most luxurious of all automobiles? Are you not chauffeured to every *haut monde* party of the diplomatic jet-set? I thought all white men in North America were accustomed to Porsches, De Loreans, and Corvette Stingrays."

"Some very rich folks may drive a Mercedes Benz or Cadillac, possibly own a Jaguar, and more often a Corvette, but not us: we are no higher in standing than your run-of-the-mill, middle-class schmucks from Canada, where I ride the bus or pedal my bicycle from 'Eh to Zed'. We have no chauffeur, Ali. Perhaps my brother Richard or I may drive the family Peugeot to a social event."

"A *Peugeot*? *Hubba*! Such rib-jarring rattletraps are best used for taxis in Africa. A dozen passengers can be crammed into such a vehicle for rough, cross-country travel!" chirped Ali. He gazed seriously at his blushing guest as he declared, "I hardly believe you do not own a fashionable sports car by now. How can you not have Rolls Royce in Canada's fleet, my lad?"

"This is my first time, honest—I'm a virgin in the luxury department!"

"A virgin! How *gauche*!" Ali guffawed, not caring if the women overheard. It seemed that he was teasing his impressionable captive about Georgina instead of the limousine as he gestured playfully towards their female company, "Isn't she beautiful? Do you really like her?" he whispered now provocatively in Orwell's ear.

"I admire Georgina", Orwell whispered back, blushing at the honest truth welling up in his heart. "Meeting your sis has been the most wondrous highlight of my life. I am tickled that she wants to know Alicia."

"So, you also desire Miss MacDonachie? Is loving two beautiful women at once not living dangerously?" quipped Ali. "You are not a Muslim! We are allowed to keep four wives!"

"Georgina and Alicia are good friends of mine. I am too young to be fully engaged to either one—or to any other girl, for that matter!"

"You lie, Orwell! Thoughts of girls dance around your brain!" chastised Ali, scoffing at his immature longings. "Put your manly efforts into dealing with more substantial problems than those butterflies drinking nectar in the back seat! I was referring to the OPEC embargo."

"OPEC? What on earth does that stand for?"

"*Kai*! *Organization of Petroleum Exporting Countries—OPEC*!" Ali hissed, educating him on a subject that Orwell, when in his right mind, could usually speak volumes about. Sliding over until he loomed within inches of his suddenly worried companion, Ali's light brown face almost looked reptilian as he glared at Hughes. "My home country Nigeria, along with Gabon, Ecuador, Venezuela, Iran, and several Arab countries, sharply increased the world price for oil last year. As a powerful bloc, we forced a fair price for this vital commodity from opulent consumer nations in Europe and North America. With the increased revenues, Nigeria will be able to feed and care for its booming population. We will soon be able to pay off our suffocating national debts, build new roads and hospitals, expand our industries, improve educational opportunities, and upgrade the military. Nigerians will finally reclaim our power as the leader of Black Africa. The setbacks our country suffered during its recent civil war will be rectified."

"All these things should come to pass", acknowledged Orwell, blandly supportive. "It is just and appropriate."

"Oil-guzzling Europeans and North Americans complain of being put over the barrel, so to speak. Does this jolt of reality not trouble you?"

"We all need to wake up and understand how people really live in the world around us. Canada, particularly the province of Alberta where I come from, is very well-endowed in fossil fuels. My country may now be challenged to develop more intensely its own oil fields, particularly the Athabasca tar sands. We could also look more seriously at alternative fuel sources: wind power, hydrogen, solar energy, alcohol, hydroelectricity, biofuels... but we should also sell our second or third car at a fair price to someone who has none, and then choose instead to walk, cycle, or use public transport to stay physically fit and reduce air pollution, particularly in cities. That's 'Participaction', man! There are many blessings to be discovered within a crisis."

Ali frowned and shook his head at Orwell. Since the future of his country depended on OPEC, his hungry attitude stood in contrast to Orwell's blissfully optimistic innovations. Feeling righteously insulted, it was small wonder that the spoiled prince did not toss this young fool out on the street right now. Showing admirable restraint, however, Ali fell silent and tuned his attention to the more pleasant and surprisingly intellectual conversation of the women seated behind them.

"What are you studying at university, Georgina?" asked Alicia with interest.

"Medicine, of course!" replied Miss Amadu, her stalwart conviction completely at odds with her happy-go-lucky charms that attracted all manner of men like moths to a flame. Her passion showed when she hotly declared, "I want to help my people maintain their health and overcome the diseases that afflict us and sap our strength—cure preventable maladies like measles and whooping cough that needlessly take our children before their time."

"I also want to be a medical doctor," MacDonachie shared, pleased that they shared such ambitious career goals—as well as other matters of interest that she was now too shy to discuss. "I also hope to contribute to my society in this manner."

"Great minds think alike, eh my magnificent princess? What, Mairam, you don't think I know what your middle name means in *Bere Barici*[40]? Maybe, we shall work together someday for those tall ladies with the fancy plaited hairdos who struggle in the broiling sands of the Lake Chad basin," Georgina laughed, gently brushing Alicia's large hand with her own dainty one, made even more beautiful by her pink amethyst ring and intricately woven, rhinoceros hair bracelets. "Mairam, I could turn you into a Kanuri woman today by painting a tapestry on your hands with henna."

"Maybe," agreed Alicia believing, despite her secret difficulties, in the hope that God still worked in mysterious ways. She added, belying her inner passions, "But becoming Kanuri takes more than a little tattoo—the linguistic, religious, and cultural immersion learned over many years of hardship will only scratch the surface of my birthplace for me. I somehow must earn the right to belong there, just as here or even in Canada, where I am growing up on the fringe of society. I certainly welcome any opportunity, however, to come back to Africa for a longer stay."

"Or we could build our careers together in Britain—or even Canada. Who knows?" Georgina's sweeping whimsical speculations prodded Alicia toward happiness and enjoyment of life. As the familiar, green Peugeot station wagon

---

40 *Bere Barici*: language of the Kanuri people of northeastern Nigeria, whom the dominant *Hausawa* call *Bere Bari*.

came into view, Georgina brought the fantasy journey to an end by announcing, "Here we are ladies, safely arrived at your destination!"

The luxury vehicle glided smoothly to a stop at the appointed meeting place. Orwell alighted first on the asphalt, and with chivalrous aplomb, helped his sister and her grateful friend out from the shaded, air-conditioned coach into the bright, hot sunlight of the bustling midday. Pleasant good-byes and thank yous were exchanged, delightfully mixed with gay promises to meet again for an Easter Sunday feast. Ali, remaining hidden in the Rolls, asked JJ to greet her sister for him. Then, like royal celebrities, he and Georgina were whisked away to their fairy tale palace in the polished black limousine.

Others in the Hughes shopping party, who had been waiting far beyond the appointed time, now emerged crossly from under the trees and took umbrage with these nonchalant arrivals.

"It's about time!" remonstrated Suzanne to the bubbly trio, shaking her fist at them. "You guys are lollygagging being tourists and all, but you forgot something! Don't you remember? We've got more stops to make, but since you're an hour late and heat has become unbearable for some of us, we're just going home now!"

"I'm melting," pouted Kathleen to Rick within her sister's earshot as he dutifully began opening doors, rolling down windows and ushering folks inside the Peugeot. "If I had known we'd be waiting this long, I'd have already put on that airy cotton dress I bought—right here behind a beach towel if necessary, like those brash German dames did yesterday at the pool! Thank goodness, I'm wearing these new sandals now instead of high heels, or I'd have blisters all over my feet."

Her complaints rolled off many deaf ears, but then Kitty turned prickly at Alicia, "What did you splurge on, Annie Fannie—a fancy comb, an ice cream cone—a romance novel perhaps?"

Alicia, who refused to answer by her slave name, glared indignantly at her sister as they loaded up and pulled into traffic.

"Our stroll was fun! We bought the poignant story *Cry the Beloved Country*, about social injustice in South Africa, which is very topical," informed JJ to the grouchy group on behalf of her cohort. "We also bought camera film. Some handsome student friend of Orwell's spent a whole roll photographing us."

"So, he can market lewd pictures of you on the black market! Fannie, just who *was* that cool cat who seemed too happy to shower you with undue attention as you all cavorted across town?" taunted Kathleen, smiling devilishly back at Alicia who, remaining stubbornly silent and looking out the window, refused to engage her as they drove along. "Did you get his name and address, so you can be his pen pal after this safari is over, and you return to the old grind back home? For God's sake, Fannie, he's a white slaver or some pimp preying on dumb, bored, rich girls vacationing far from home!"

Orwell anxiously raised his hand to speak in defence of Cepheus, but Kathleen blatantly ignored him. When Janice Joanne gazed blithely at their tormentor, pretending to be clueless, the platinum blonde growled, "Don't play stupid with me, you smart-aleck girls! Three of the new Canadian workers we flew down here with—Fannie, you recall Mildred, Charlotte, and Barbara I'm sure, since you lectured me in front of them for having a glass of wine with my meal—well, those busybodies accosted me on the street today with wild claims that you posed suggestively for some overdressed black gangster while Orwell, your dimwitted escort, looked on with blasé acquiescence!"

"It's not his fault! Stop blaming Orwell for every bad thing you imagine, Kitty-Cat!" snapped Alicia. "He and Mr. Belo behaved like proper gentlemen around JJ and me today, which is more than I can say for many high-society guys you and I both know, including our own brothers! Take Robert, for example...."

"Enough!" yelled Kathleen in exasperation. "Keep your mouth shut if you have nothing good to say, especially about family members who aren't here to defend themselves against your lies!"

"Look who's talking!" Alicia retorted. Kathy wanted to fight back, but feeling a sting of truth in this rebuke, fell silent as she abruptly practised what she preached to her younger sister. Despite winning their scrap, Alicia blushed as she testified to the vinyl seat in front of her. "*I* enjoyed socializing with Mr. Belo, Ali and Georgina—all of whom highly regard Orwell as their friend, and so do I."

She smiled sweetly now at the young man beside her as he took in her uncommon show of praise. Orwell was touched by the unexpected honours Alicia heaped upon him, but finding no adequate words of response, only offered a nervous smile in her direction.

"I encouraged our shy friend to play along," JJ said, sticking her neck out for Alicia. Never lost for words, she broke the tension by tickling her listeners.

"Sissy, you must be more careful," chastised Suzanne. "Not every friendly person you meet in this world is kind and honest. Why are you smiling? Doesn't any well-meaning advice from more mature women sink into your brain?"

"Ali and Georgina Amadu just gave Orwell, Lisa, and I a dream ride in their Rolls Royce," cheered JJ, relishing their deluxe experience in defiance of the berating chatter of the overbearing older girls. Her joy stopped their mouths as if she had plugged them with corks. "We lounged on soft oriental cushions and sipped chilled colas in air-conditioned comfort as we listened to Tom Jones and the Motown sounds of *Diana Ross* and the *Jackson Five*. Ali thought I was you, Suzy—he flirted with me! Can you believe it? Ali thinks I've grown up."

"What a dope head!" exclaimed Suzanne indignantly, embarrassed now that Kathleen was gazing curiously at her. Her sapphire eyes gleamed nonetheless as she mulled over this interesting tidbit. At length she slyly inquired, "Did our high-roller lady's man enquire about me?"

"Oh, nothing much. He got to know me a little better, but spent most of his time talking to Orwell about...well, you know, male stuff! Georgina and Alicia found out they share some interesting goals in common—no, not you, Orwell!" laughed JJ when the young poet looked quizzically at her. "These two both want to be doctors! Maybe they'll work together somewhere...at some rugged ends of the earth or… on the cutting edge of medical research!"

Alicia smiled appreciatively and sat back as they drove along, soaking up her yappy girlfriend's chatter. Orwell and his mother nodded appreciatively but Richard just drove, his clenched teeth grinding within his zipped mouth, still put out by the disruption in their schedule. The older girls clucked in exasperation at such elaborate day dreams, to say, "That'll be the day."

Back home, the girls took advantage of the afternoon siesta to get their beauty sleep, while Richard went flying to clear his head. Martha spent time in the back courtyard deliberating with Orwell, trying to pin down with him the final guest list for Sunday dinner as they reviewed sober repercussions of inviting so many.

"How much more food should we buy?" she pointedly asked him.

"We need to get that Easter ham of course, but halal meat dishes should be prepared too, now that Cepheus, Georgina, and Ali are coming—devout Muslims all who believe pork to be unclean," was the young poet's thoughtful reply. "Which means that beef, fish, or chicken should be added to the menu."

"Will everyone get along, what with their diverse cultures and views, and us celebrating a Christian holiday?"

"It will be a good mix, as most invitees have met at least one other guest somewhere before, and seem to connect well. Even Benjamin and Cepheus agree to disagree! What is truly sweet is that all of them know me."

"How do you plan to entertain so large a gathering?"

"We'll play some parlour games: I've got croquet and lawn bowling stuff. Anyway, that's JJ's department, Mom—she's the social butterfly who's charmed everyone into coming. JJ has been working up a few ideas for ice breaker mixers, which I think will be highly entertaining, to hear Alicia and her laughing in their bedroom last night. Benjamin loves to sing, and can play the guitar as well as Kitty-Cat. As for musical back-up, you know we've got two world-class artists staying under our roof right now!"

"Should we not also invite the new Canadian workers and their families, at least the ones who are stationed in Lusaka? They must be quite homesick by now, and are likely looking for social outings where they can get their words out. Karla Eve Bryant and her twin brothers might enjoy some fun—Karlee especially, who's feeling isolated here so far, at least according to her mother. Being twenty-two, she's a bit old for the International School, so she's taking Grade Thirteen by correspondence and could benefit from a tutor, especially in English and Math, at which both you and Richard excel. So, should we not be more hospitable to our countrymen—go for the gusto, as you declare in sports challenges?"

"Karla Eve seems nice enough to me, Mom, but the girls have not taken to her, and I'm feeling a tad isolated myself, with all the estrogen already perfuming our house! As far as tutoring, I can occasionally help Karlee with her homework after Alicia and Kathleen leave in a week or so," added Orwell, surprised that the curvy and morose Bryant girl was slightly older than him. What had happened to her? Why was she here, game to live in Zambia for the next four years, when she had nothing to do and nowhere to plug into?

He suddenly refocused, lest his mother's sympathy for Karlee sidetrack him from doing his best for their current guests of honour: Tracy and Georgina.

"This party will be different from the staid, family-oriented gatherings the High Commission hosts. Ours is a multiracial group of young people, in whose midst new Canadians would suffer like fish out of water! I'm sorry if I've set the bar high, but I want to gather and entertain my special friends for one final time before I leave for good."

"You don't know the hour or reason," Martha cautioned his tragic exit. Focusing on the task at hand, she demanded, "When will your invitations end, when is enough?"

"I am done, Mom! But I still hope Tracy will show up," replied Orwell intensely. "He would be the cherry on the sundae. I so want him to meet my Zambian friends, to appreciate the people I know. Even if none of the others came, I would be satisfied if Tracy ate Easter dinner with me. It will deeply distress me if he stands me up. Please pray to God that Tracy makes it here."

"I do, Orly, I do. But only God knows where Tracy is. I certainly can't deliver him to you. I'm amazed that you balance him against all of your other friends put together. Perhaps they are less worthy in your eyes, but please, don't use them to salve your pain. Son, you remind me of the rich man in Jesus' parable who filled his banquet hall with the poor and downtrodden when his invited wedding guests refused to come!"

"Aw shucks, Mom, you're not being fair. You know I love these people, and they are neither poor nor downtrodden," wailed Orwell sheepishly.

"I don't mind you opening your home to so many people Orly, but how will we accommodate everyone to the extent that all will enjoy our fellowship?"

"This is the biggest day in my life, Mom! All the important people I know will be there. I will do my best to help make our festival a blessing to everyone, and God will also be present at our table," promised Orwell with unshakable faith. "We can eat outside on lawn chairs. We'll organize a variety of social activities, maybe rotate through a schedule of events. The Lord will prepare people's hearts and minds, but I will do whatever you and Dad want to make things happen and ensure everyone has a grand time!"

"Son, you absolutely must help, starting now to see this epic event through. All of Hughes House will be expected to work hard in preparation," insisted Martha.

Until then, Orwell had not considered his mother's litany of worries, having been so wrapped up in his own joys and concerns. She normally did not complain, and remained eerily serene through all their socializing, but now he saw where the rubber hit the road! She was a Trojan when it came to entertaining folks, which made her the perfect match for eclectic Bwana Hughes.

"I still must buy heaps more groceries and a variety of meats, Orly. We'll go back to market on Thursday to fill this huge order of ingredients;. I hope there is still decent choice in foodstuffs to be had. You will help carry things. Our family picnic planned for *Munda Wanga* botanical gardens is postponed, as you kids need Saturday to clean up your digs, and get the living room and yard in order. There are many chairs to place and a grand table to set for our guests on feast day. Kathleen and Alicia will also be expected to pitch in wherever helping hands are needed. I am certain that they will cheerfully cooperate—all you kids were well brought up!

"Remember: prior to hosting our household festivity, we will attend a very busy church service on Sunday morning, when Kathleen and Alicia will present their gifts to the congregation. Doubtless our guests of honour will be nervous and high strung, so you must be extra patient and loving to those girls. Remain courteous and attentive, congenial but nonpartisan in hosting your friends—no matter what happens for you personally!"

"You'll see me stalwartly on duty, Mom. My hands, as well as my head and strong back, are already on deck," promised Orwell fervently. He gave her a hug. "I admire your resourcefulness, and am grateful for your patience."

"You are learning so much these days, Orwell," his mother sighed. She was proud of his manly determination, yet worried for his youthful innocence. Then, glancing at the setting sun and noting the lateness of the hour, she whistled, "We'd better get supper on. Your father will soon be home, famished."

*****

Orwell had—in his own romantic poetry at least—already rubbed shoulders with the stars, but later that same evening, after Bwana Hughes released the youths from the table, Richard set up his telescope on the patio, so that the children could peer more deeply into the brilliantly glittering heavens.

Rick was pleased that both MacDonachie women were interested in astronomy. They *oohed* and *aahed* as he helped them explore the craters of the moon, pointed out the Red Planet, and brought sharply into focus Saturn playing hula-hoop with all its gorgeous rings. They cheered at stars, which although only dimly flickering, finally reached across billions of miles and were found, no longer dusty specks lost in unknown galaxies. With pleasure, Orwell drew the shapes of several impressive southern constellations: *Carina,* the keel of the Argonauts' ship; *Centaurus* the mythical man-horse, on whose prancing foreleg shone Alpha Centauri, the closest star to the sun; *Scorpius* the Scorpion with

Antares blushing on its back; and the Dog Star, twinkling with dazzling brilliance, brighter than all other heavenly bodies on the nose of *Canis Major*.

"But I don't recognize any of these objects," Kathleen sighed as she stared skyward. "I can't see Orion's jewelled belt. Where has the Great Bear ambled off to? I can't even find that daring "W" woman, *Cassiopeia*."

"Silly, those constellations belong in the Northern Hemisphere. Look at the moon! It is curved upside down, like I saw during our flight from Khartoum," giggled Alicia, pointing at the silvery crescent bowing before them.

She strangely remarked how, in its dancing with a nearby star, she was reminded of the Red Crescent counterpart to the International Red Cross relief agency, as well as the flags of various Muslim countries.

"Sure," was Kitty's dubious reply, pointing to her sister's weirdness rather than intellect. After a pause, she orchestrated her own more stimulating conversation. "In Greek mythology, Cassiopeia was the wife of Cepheus, King of Ethiopia, and mother of Andromeda and Atyminius by Zeus, the King of the Gods.

"Cassiopeia boasted that she and her daughter were more beautiful than the Nereids, mermaids who were daughters of Nersus, a sea god. The Lord of the seas, Poseidon, in his wrath at this defamation, sent a monster to devastate the land, then had Andromeda chained to a rock in the sea, exposed to that monster. Perseus freed Andromeda and married her with Cassiopeia's blessing, but the mother later reneged on her agreement and disrupted the wedding festivities. Perseus then turned Cassiopeia into stone. For further revenge, Poseidon placed Cassiopeia in the northern heavens as a constellation, where at times, she appears to be hanging upside down."

"Now that is quite the legend!" remarked Richard, enamoured by the comely teller. He took Kathleen gently by the hand, and pointed her view into the gap between the house and mango trees to the north. There, appearing to scratch the northern horizon, were five bright stars that he helped Kathy connect, to form an M. "I see *Cassiopeia*, sitting in her chair!"

"She's conversing with *Ursa Major*."

"You mean the *Big Dipper*?" quipped Rick, remembering all the navigation signs in the northern stars learned from his youth, while becoming a Queen's Scout. "The two stars forming its dipper that are opposite the handle form a straight line that points due north, towards the North Star, which as you can see, appears to be hiding somewhere in the ground beyond the horizon."

"How clever you are!" cooed Kathleen, smiling in rich acknowledgement of his wisdom. She laughed when he put his arm around her slim waist. "It's rather chilly out; I'd have asked you to fetch my sweater, were you less brave."

"I read the signs—not just of the Zodiac," Richard stated impressively. "And I aim to please."

"Hey, Orwell, where is the *Southern Cross*?" Alicia queried as she witnessed this budding romance. Wanting to enjoy some manly affection herself, Alicia called upon the second Hughes boy to display his knowledge. "I understand that sailors use it for navigation down here."

Hughes, despite all happy the chatter and gentle music swirling around him, seemed oblivious to Alicia's question as he inwardly mourned Tracy's absence. Why did he refuse to write him even a brief air mail explanation for his delay? And, for that matter, why was Georgina feeling so gay today?

The brooding youth was jolted from his melancholy when Alicia sidled towards him like the moon passing the earth to eclipse the sun; her buxom silhouette blotted out the yard light behind her, darkening his view. Orwell could not defend himself when she playfully pinched him to see if he was alive or simply another stone lawn ornament bewitched to haunt him.

"Boo!" Alicia spooked him. His would-be tormentor smile was tinged with unusual wickedness in the glow of a torch she clownishly held against her face as she made a ghoulish mask to make him laugh. Alicia rasped deeply, "I, the sea witch, demand you to speak, *Oh-well*!"

"It's that kite-like constellation sometimes called *The Crux*, see? It's lying on its side in the middle of the sky, under the *Centaur's* feet," Orwell replied obediently, not daring to reveal his shocked amusement, lest she take his laughter wrongly. He knew Alicia was playing, all in good fun, though he wondered in the back of his head whether she really understood the power of the spirit world, particularly among the ancient animists of this strange land wherein they all inexplicably found themselves.

"You have answered well, mortal man, so you shall live," the sea witch sombrely declared. "For your cooperation, Oh-well, I grant you safe passage."

"Your most beautiful and honoured majesty, can you please tell me where Tracy is?" broached Orwell sadly.

Confronted by her sudden fierce look, he stepped back in preparation to flee, thinking that she had found his flattery insulting and would behead him forthwith. Yet Alicia, who was more human than her appearance betrayed, perceived underlying kindness in his flowery words.

"Right from your own quivering lips, you called me beautiful!" exalted 'Big Bertha', clasping her hands together and holding them, like a mink stole, close to her throat. Grinning broadly and mellowing from a witch into a pretty-faced wrestler, Alicia loudly conferred with JJ to make sure she had heard right, as though such an uplifting adjective had never been hung with all those horse collars around her rippling neck. "Did you hear your brother, JJ?"

"I certainly did," chimed Janice Joanne, as she cavorted with Alicia to celebrate the occasion in a mock Highland dance around the much-embarrassed Orwell Hughes. Then she clapped hands with her friend, "I didn't think my brother had it in him to speak such terms of endearment to any girl, despite his flair for romantic penmanship. It's okay, Orwell. You are here now among good friends."

"Where is Tracy?" cried Orwell, falling out of role play and begging for enlightenment.

"I don't know what to tell you anymore!" Alicia emphatically replied. Her winsome smile twisted into a bitter cocktail of sadness and frustration at her inability to satisfy this blockhead. Becoming distraught, Alicia suddenly fled the scene, followed by frowning JJ; Orwell tossed in their wake, lost more at sea than before.

"What was that all about? Have you got something juicy to tell me, Oh-well?" Kathleen asked mischievously, mimicking Alicia as she bandied about her kid sister's teasing nickname for the dumkopf, while Rick laughed carelessly at their childish antics.

"Nothing," muttered Orwell in frustration at such a bizarre end to an otherwise fine evening. He hung his head and slipped into the darkness.

# CHAPTER FOURTEEN

ORWELL DID NOT AGAIN LAY eyes on tempestuous Alicia Pearl Rose MacDonachie until well into the next day. She even stood him up for their appointed sunrise run! Aware of the rift, JJ glared sullenly at Orwell as they silently ate breakfast at diagonal corners of the large teak table, leaving the pleasant morning conversation to their parents and older, unaffected siblings. Suzanne and Richard entertained Kathleen briefly before the two Hughes girls biked to school, and Richard took Kathleen for an invigorating game of tennis.

Orwell trudged alone through his morning jog as though his feet were encased in cement. Returning home early, limping and under a cloud of despair, he sought refuge in the garden, where he hoped to gain some wisdom from the trees that had lived on their patch of ground for eons and had seen many troubled young men struggle with life. He stood under the jacaranda tree, enjoying the fresh morning breeze singing among its crown of strong, far-reaching limbs. Her once verdant greenery was wistfully yellow, what with the cool dry season already stealing upon the land. On happier days, Hughes climbed high into the embrace of this great mother tree, which burst into mauve flowers in spring, provided a leafy umbrella during summer's torrid rains, gave pod shakers for music and games in winter, and always encouraged him to play among her branches.

Today, however, Orwell contented himself with bagging the disc-like seed pods carelessly dropped beneath the skirt of her branches, lest his friends visiting in five days condemn his untidy garden. Orwell prepared to dispose the organic refuse into his compost pit, but then his great leafy friend gently reminded him that JJ and Alicia liked to make music with her offspring and could also use them in their seed mosaic art being prepared for Easter. Hughes opted to place the seed pods on the patio table for the girls' project before wandering into the back yard.

On his way to the banana groves beyond the servants' quarters, Orwell set down his machete and respectfully greeted the houseboy's wife and her lady friends, seated on mats in her spotlessly swept courtyard, chattering happily as they nursed their babies and crocheted intricate lace doilies. He, conversing as best as he could in local vernacular that nonetheless amazed his listeners, complemented Mrs. Joseph on her garden's various bumper crops: maize, squash, sweet potatoes, cowpeas, spinach, okra, peppers, bitter tomatoes and garden eggs — all fruiting in different beds, yet sharing the same hilly plot of fertile red ground. Emboldened by his communicating effort, the women asked after his new white ladies, from where they had come, and whether he would marry one or both of them soon. When Orwell shook his head vigorously, the amused ladies invited his guests to come over for tea someday, to learn the art of making doilies while they had their hair plaited. As Orwell softly bid adieu, Mrs. Joseph advised him to check the banana grove and take what fruit was left, before the neighbourhood children ate everything like locusts.

Orwell promptly followed her advice, yet wondered why people called these succulent banana plants 'trees' while he looked up the tall, celery-like stalks and searched beneath floppy, papery, elephant-like ears in secret places where clusters of ripe bananas hung down like outstretched fingers from ropy vines. His diligence was rewarded when he spied an appealing yellow bunch suspended in the heart of the grove. Hughes grabbed the vine tautly and cut it loose with a precise slice from his machete. He wistfully thought of Harry Belafonte, singing *Banana Boat Song* with carefree sway of the sunny West Indies.

As Orwell bent to pick up his booty, he felt the sudden pang of being watched! He looked carefully around but did not spot anyone intruding upon his Garden of Eden. No curious children peered at him through slots in the back, brick wall nor heckled him like monkeys from the limbs of the large acacia tree spreading over his yard from behind that wall. Seemingly miles away, Joseph's kids played ball on the freshly cut grass between the servants' quarters and Bwana's house; the African women fraternized over their morning tea oblivious to him or the chills running up and down his spine. Orwell, peeking over neatly clipped bougainvillea hedges and patches of cactus, frangipani, and hibiscus, glimpsed Joseph hanging laundry on the clothesline behind the main house. This placid scene seemed normal as day on the Hughes compound, so Orwell concluded that his cloak and dagger worries must be due to his sometimes-over-active mind, as he slung the banana bunch over his shoulder and made back for home, carrying the machete blade-down in his other hand.

Orwell heard the screen door to the kitchen slam shut as he stepped through an archway entwined with red and yellow trumpet vines, but seeing no one, assumed that Joseph had just gone back indoors to begin ironing bed sheets or polishing hardwood floors. His attention was distracted as mango, avocado, papaya, and guava trees now sweetly beckoned him to pause and eat their last, best fruits of the season. He took two baskets and a ladder from the tool shed, and scaled each tree in turn to glean what fruits remained as a present to please his lady friends.

Orwell climbed high in the guava tree, softly manoeuvring like a cat among the branches and reaching heavenward to grab the most upward fruits, when he heard banjo music, sounding in his vivid imagination like a brook merrily flowing through sun-dappled forest glades...or angels laughing as they sailed upon their clouds through sunlit skies. Stopping to listen, he recognized not only the tune but heard a rich female voice singing "Sweet By and By". Enraptured, yet wondering how such inspiring melody could be playing in his garden, Orwell remembered that the youngest member of *MacDonachie Family Singers* was presently alone with him as his guest.

He crept down from his tree with the guavas he had picked and put away his ladder. Then, gathering up his bounty of diverse fruits, Orwell breathlessly followed the music along the walls of his rambling house. Rounding the corner, he discovered Alicia singing with profound conviction on the patio, where she nimbly flailed on his father's prized, 5-string banjo! Sporting a stone-washed denim sash that hung over one of her strong, tanned shoulders and swooped down to her bare foot firmly planted on a stool that she had hauled out from the living room, she performed as if on stage at Nashville's *Grand Old Opry*, one leg bent at the knee to accommodate the banjo. Her long auburn hair hung shaggily across her broad back, drying in the mid-morning sun after some waterfall she must have enjoyed bathing in. Alicia appeared untamed and magical rather than overweight and awkward as she tenaciously followed the sheet music clipped onto her music stand. She played as fervently as any sophisticated concert musician, entertaining the flowers and trees while taking no notice of Orwell's intrusion as he crouched at her periphery. No sooner did the first song fade away than Alicia turned the page and waded stalwartly into "Jesus Like a Shepherd Lead Us".

"She's not wearing her glasses!" he suddenly rationalized with a smirk. "That's why Alicia can't see me!"

Hughes reclined suavely on the grass for a few minutes while the verdant nearsighted musician, totally adsorbed in her art, entertained him apparently unaware of his presence. No doubt about it, Miss A. MacDonachie exuded talent beyond measure; she did not *need* to read her notes, as this valued accompanist at church camps and tent meetings knew all the beloved, old-time gospel hymns by heart! Her large ebony eyes did not blink as they gazed fiercely upon her score from beneath strongly-arched eyebrows on her impassioned face. She was beautiful—in a wild, stormy sort of way—certainly not some dainty waif like other white girls he saw flitting about the International School or tanning their slim bodies at exclusive sports clubs or swimming pools. Alicia`s complexion was not lily white either; like his beloved Georgina, she was an exotic coloured product of mixed races—an interesting love history to explore! He saw First Nation features in her dark curved eyes, high cheek bones, and strong nose sloping from her long forehead. Yet, as he listened to her eloquently praise of their Lord, Orwell boyishly thought that Alicia *must* be more soft and girly than the rugged natives profiled at the end of Canadian TV viewing or on the *Chicago Blackhawks'* uniform, worn by Bobby Hull before his hockey idol had sold out to the rival WHA! But *that* was another story....

When Alicia poured out "Keep on the Sunny Side", another country gospel classic, without pausing to acknowledge him, Hughes grew restless at listening so long in obscurity, and decided it was time for him to go back to work. She paid him no heed when he stood up and stretched his limbs. Frustrated by her stern aloofness and confused that he, rather than she, should overstay their welcome, he left Alicia the fruit offering on the lawn and slunk away behind the hedge. He vowed to never again listen to her music, but instead suffer in glorious solitude in his own sanctuary, as he did hard labour turning the compost heap.

Alicia carefully stowed the banjo and wildly replayed her repertoire on her fiddle in jaunty oblivion to Hughes' mad theatrics as he waddled past, unrolling a garden hose that he had hooked up to the faucet. Better prepared than not, he would haughtily inform Her Highness—should she stoop to ask. Once the compost pit emptied and refilled, he planned to thoroughly wet down the organic house and yard wastes recycled between layers of earth. Maybe he should douse that giant velveteen rabbit also, turn her into a real person! Orwell japed at her like a clown as he strode by yet again, this time toting a shovel and pitchfork, but Alicia's recital boldly continued without her taking any notice of him.

Orwell, angry at Mairam's undeserved neglect—or so he thought—took out his frustration on the compost heap. He furiously forked away the fresh surficial leaves, grass clippings, weeds, small branches, and peelings and stockpiled them aside, later to be placed in the pit once he cleaned it out. Feeling exonerated now that he was finally sweating and covered with grime, Orwell dug rigorously into the dirt layer and pulled it into another pile. He laboured until the compost heap was level with ground and pungently decomposing organics were separated from soil.

Orwell could not determine exactly when the violin music finally stopped, but he suddenly felt that uneasy sensation again: *something*—be it man or beast—was watching him! He planned to box well if forced to fight, or run like the wind if he could avoid this unnamed foe, but as the queasy knot in his stomach tightened, Orwell lost confidence in his own strength. His silent, invisible stalker threatened more ominously its intentions to act maliciously rather than simply study him from some secret vantage point.

He heard a rustling sound, like somebody running through the grass, but glancing furtively up, Hughes saw only that a breeze was billowing the pale green leaves of overhanging pepper trees and caressing their drooping spikes of black seed balls. He was suddenly alerted to the distinctive smack of a stone hitting the brick wall behind the banana grove, but still saw nothing hostile as he peered towards that barrier through the dusty gloom of his work place. Out of the corner of his eagle eye, Orwell glimpsed another human dart behind the bougainvillea hedge somewhere near the lovebird cage. Noting with trepidation that the normally clamorous birds were now strangely silent and that their hutch stood some 30 metres away, yet not in clear line to the wall, Orwell marvelled at the accuracy and strength of his opponent's hurl. He must not dwell on trajectory physics for too long; from the sandaled feet that periodically appeared under the hedge, he surmised that this predator moved stealthily towards him. Sooner or later they would meet; then what evil would he face?

"Who are you? What do you want?" Hughes demanded, first in English then in *ciBemba,* as he stood fast at the drip line of the pepper trees, holding his shovel like a drawn sword. The sandaled feet stopped, then disappeared... Nothing moved or spoke save the breeze, which whispered no secrets into his anxiously craned ears. Orwell dared blurt out his most desperate hope, "Tracy is that you, playing hide and go seek with me? Show yourself, god dammit—if you are man enough!"

A tennis ball, cleverly lobbed as a decoy from the middle of the hedge, bounced onto the ground in front of him. Orwell moved to fetch it, when suddenly the bronzed head and stout shoulders of Alicia MacDonachie, laughing hysterically as she reared herself up to full height and girth, emerged like some warrior goddess over the hedge.

"Do I have you worried, Bucko?" the amazon taunted wickedly as she marched out from hiding and posed like a boxer on the grass he had recently so finely scythed, her fists brazenly cocked for battle. "What shall I do with you now, Oh-well my feeble mortal man?"

"Please have mercy upon me, your majesty," stammered Orwell, playing his role with gusto, his heart pounding with fear as he noted how trim and strong was this gladiator princess.

Grinning savagely, and glaring madly at him from shadowed eyes that jumped out piercingly without any glasses to shield them, she did not reveal what horrible fate she had in store for her intended victim—but the myopic menace would have to catch him first!

Orwell stealthily slunk beneath the pepper tree as he tried to trick her by throwing back his voice to where he had been. "I am just a dust-caked labourer, surely of no concern to royalty such as you."

"Sir Dust-Caked Labourer, you are of utmost concern to me, since I need your guidance. I am all alone and lost in these strange woods without my winged horse *Windchaser* or *Excalibur,* my magic accordion," Alicia deviously spun more yarn for her web as she made a beeline to her quarry's new location, like some sinister and unblinking black widow due to feast.

He dodged her initial advance, but she danced skillfully with him however he tried to elude her. Alicia, ebony eyes sparkling and ivory teeth flashing, pursued Orwell relentlessly, yet as though toying with him, delayed touching his body so plastered with uncouth grime. This hunting lioness could see him plainly,

Orwell realized with a sinking heart, but why did she keep her powerful hands hidden behind her back, as if hiding a weapon much worse than her claws?

Alicia finally backed Orwell against a tree trunk, where she pinned him for the kill. He, noting with trepidation the triumphant gleam in her eyes, worried that this mysterious foe might kiss him passionately while he was caught in her iron grip. Orwell gulped, but followed Alicia's strong hands as she held them clasped as in prayer at her waist, then sailed them deftly up her firm, hourglass torso. Cleverly opening her hands near her heaving chest, she released into the charged space between them a large, multi-coloured moth that she had managed to catch and gently hold alive, just for this beguiling purpose! Grinning broadly at her stunned admirer, Alicia parted her hands and out-spread them as though readying to take flight herself.

Delicately balancing before her stunned prey, Alicia bathed him in the twin dark pools glistening within delicately laughing eyelid folds, then softly dried him with the plush crimson robes of her smiling lips. She bowed her head so he noticed the fancy butterfly clips holding her bouncy dark hair. Her full face danced happily from side to side, swishing her hair like a dress lifting to reveal dream-catcher earrings fluttering on her ear lobes. She smelled pleasantly of wild flowers and her braless breasts, pressing succulently against her faded Levi dress, presented Alicia as a sexually awake young maiden, brimming with promise and desire, who needed only a guiding male hand to bloom.

"You are now a strong, handsome man," she acknowledged with husky awe. She puckered her lips as though to plant a huge, wet kiss on Orwell's chiselled face, but when he closed his eyes to duck away, an exultant laugh escaped her, "... But I have grown too!"

Alicia met him face to face, but for all her raw power, she could only reach up to his chin.

"Hey! No fair! You're standing on tiptoe while I'm still flat-footed on the ground!" Orwell pointed out as he wrestled her playfully into a clinch, so that she could not further entice him.

Alicia and Orwell laughed together as her secret was revealed. She, pretending to be disturbed by his attempt to control her, playfully kicked his shin but stumbled when he nimbly stepped aside. He, not wishing for even such a scrappy brat as Mairam to fall into his decaying compost heap, swiftly caught her in his strong arms. She laughed gleefully as he set her gently on her feet, but her adoration quickly curdled into wrath when he could not resist releasing her with a slap to her ample backside.

"Now, *that* was insulting", Alicia growled as she turned, with balled fists belligerently hugging her hips, to face the now nervously grinning Orwell. "Spanking me is a far worse offence than calling me Annie Fannie! Do you remember, mortal man, how I dealt with you the last time you called me thus?"

"I do, Alicia, and I remain abjectly sorry for my indiscretions. I slipped then, as now! Teasing you because of how the Good Lord has wonderfully fashioned you was totally bogus then, as it is today," Hughes apologized breathlessly. He gently placed his other shoe on the ground as quickly as he could, trembling at the horrible thought of being flayed alive by this riled lioness, "I also forgive you for testing me."

"You forgive me?" said huntress demanded haughtily. Then, giving her head a shake, Alicia the Contrite returned with her lower lip quivering in chagrin, recognizing that he had granted her mercy rather than taken advantage of her provocative display. "Thank you, my prince. I behaved badly on that awful day long ago when, in a fit of rage, I tore your new Sunday clothes. I got severely punished by my folks for such a regrettable outburst.

"As you know, I was grounded from playing with JJ for months. Father sent me to boot camp—or should I say *Bonne Chance,* his frigging ranch in the north woods—to cook and clean for a gang of uncouth wranglers for the rest of that summer. I was shoved rigorously into my traces: studied in a private, all-girls' school through junior high, followed by six months of Bible School—to fashion me into a fine, Christian lady of grace—then on to finishing school. No parties, boyfriends, dances, or gifts until I learned the errors of my wicked ways and repented of them!

"You don't know this, but I was viciously belt-spanked on my bare bottom by Robert the day after my run in with you! With Alvin and Jonathan obediently holding me down, that chicken liver took his brutal liberty out on me when Dad and Tracy were away from the house! My parents had already discussed the harsh terms of my grounding with me, and I had agreed to them. Why did Robert need to rub salt into my wounds? Am I so evil that I deserved such a thrashing?"

"Bob is not your father; nobody should beat you like that! Loss of friends and privileges is a far more teaching form of punishment," grimly acknowledged

Orwell, his heart aching at this revelation. "I did not ask for you to suffer such harsh consequences just for tearing my shirt, especially when I egged you on! You are a good person, Alicia...a fellow believer in Jesus. I'm inspired by your horseshoe nail crucifix gift, and thank you for it!"

"I've waited six years to apologize to you, Orwell," she cried openly despite his gratitude, her head bowed as she appealed to him with open palms. "And I do now, as God is my witness, seek your forgiveness."

"I said then, as today, Alicia: I forgive you. I really do," insisted Hughes, taking her trembling hands gently in his, offering her a hug of sympathy and understanding. He chastised himself in remorse. "I was just as much to blame as you were, my friend; I was duly given a sound licking with Mom's wooden spoon for my folly before being sent to bed for the rest of the day!"

"It's not altogether uncalled for if a righteous man spanks me when I'm truly bad," the well-reared daughter of Reverend MacDonachie softly admitted, as they shook hands in truce. Then, flashing him a grim warning, she vowed, "But no man, not even my father or brother or—God forbid—a husband, holds the right to beat me just for sport. I will protect myself like a warrior against such stone-age abuse!"

Then, with a hopeful smile, Alicia shyly intimated for his ears alone. "If, however, my decent Christian friend desires to caress me lovingly in private once we are married, I consider such tenderness to be pleasure and honour, particularly if all touching is done with mutual love and respect."

"You are a strange girl!" gulped Orwell incredulously as JJ and Suzy came marching up the yard, insistently calling them for lunch. He thankfully quipped, "We're both saved by the bell!"

She flashed him one last smile and then, both proudly smudged with dirt, they emerged from the pepper trees, and strolled to meet their gobsmacked friends. The Hughes girls gawked in disbelief at the incredible sight!

"I see you clearly, even better without my glasses, Orwell," Alicia informed her amazed male friend as they ambled across the grass. Giving him a powder puff punch to the shoulder, she affectionately berated him, "Do you honestly believe that I didn't see you watching me when I was practising church hymns on the patio earlier this morning? I not only observed you admiring me, but I found both the seed pods and the baskets of fruit that you gave me. I squirrelled them indoors for all of us to enjoy."

"How can you view anything without your glasses?" her escort begged to know as he marvelled at how leisurely she glided her way through life today without her vital windows.

"It's my secret, Oh-well. Perhaps shall I divulge the simple truth to you someday, but only after you have honestly tried to learn it on your own. I have many secrets wrapped about me that you could unravel," she replied mysteriously, with a devious grin. Then, leaving Orwell blinking with confusion in the sunlight, Alicia exuberantly hailed her dear girlfriend, "Hey JJ, did you see the delicious little cornucopia, all washed and neatly arranged on the dinner table? Orwell gathered it all for us as a love offering."

She slipped her strong hand tenderly into his and waxed eloquently to her receptive listener as they walked through the archway, "Now, JJ and I can complete our seed mosaic, and the entire family will enjoy a bouquet of sweet edibles. You are so kind! I believe, Orwell James Hughes, that you are the best male friend I know!"

"This praise is indeed an honour!" Orwell assured her, touched by tears brimming joyfully in her huge ebony eyes.

He inwardly hoped, however, that the blossoming virgin would take him with many grains of salt, all in good fun, and not become foolishly infatuated with him—or any other flawed man for that matter—at such an impressionable time in her young life. Despite appearing to be much older and wiser, he suddenly craved a bolt to freedom, if only to tease this lovey-dovey out of her daydreams. Held fast by chivalry however, yet unable to perform his duty with Tracy's confident air, Orwell stammered finally to the happy maiden like a peach-faced schoolboy, "What can I say? What can I do but accept you?"

She affectionately squeezed his hand. All should have been strawberries and cream from that moment forward, but no sooner had Alicia led her willing captive through the kitchen doorway than they were confronted by fuming Kathy. Brashly dressed in a red halter top and checkered hot pants, she seemed bent on caning the dynamic duo for a multitude of sins.

"Where have you been, my wild things, baking mud pies?" demanded the big sister, her blue eyes piercing both delinquents as she tapped the toe of her high-heeled shoe menacingly on the slate tile floor. When Alicia tried to escape, Kathleen not only blocked her desperate flight to the bathroom but prevented both grime-covered mongrels from contaminating the noon meal already served in the dining room. "Did they taste good, Orwell, better than what mommy makes?"

"A tad gritty but edible," Hughes dared to tease his glowering age-mate, emboldened by the euphoria brought about by his recent exchange with Alicia.

"Sir, you shall scrub yourself outside with lye soap and a scouring brush!" murmured Kitty, who remained icily unamused as she dispatched him forthwith to the garden hose. "You look like *Pigpen* from the *Peanuts* comic strip, and smell like a sty too!"

Kathy then took dirt-streaked Alicia firmly by the arm and marched her to the bathroom, like she had just been arrested. As Orwell bucket-washed himself under their window, he could not help but hear the elder MacDonachie girl arguing with her sister as she made her presentable.

"You are too old to be playing tomboy, Fannie; it's high time you started acting like a young lady. Take off that loin cloth and get in the tub! If you want to wear a skirt instead of cut-off blue jeans, then I applaud you Fannie, but you can do much better than act like that mute cave woman from *Planet of the Apes*! Where is your *Laura Ashley* cotton dress? You look good in dresses; they flatter your God-given curves."

"Kitty-Cat, say what you mean! Fannie is plump, especially in her bottom," grated Alicia, frowning at her model-thin sister who studiously admired her nakedness. Alicia wrapped her large hands and long arms modestly around her body, complaining as she splashed into the steaming water, "I can't always hide my shape with baggy clothes. I've tried all kinds of rabbit food diets and exercise routines. I swim; I cycle; I play a ton of sports to stay in tip-top shape but still my big, fat rear keeps jiggling around whenever I move! And now that I've hit puberty, my breasts are swelling into melons.

"Why can't I be thin and lithe like you, Kitty-Cat? Like all those glamorous fashion models strutting on the runways in Paris, New York, and Milan? Where does *Vogue* Magazine find such skinny women?"

"You are beautiful, Fannie. Let the world see and admire your wholesome beauty—but in proper ways!"

"If you really think so and want me to believe, stop calling me 'Fannie'! I hate that wink-wink, slap-in-the-backside, dog-tag that Dad and Robert gave me."

"Just like I rebel against being called 'Kitty-Cat' or 'Kitty'! Such boorish names label me as a sex kitten—a *slut* to some lads! As we previously discussed, I go by Kathy or Kathleen, my Christian name. Remember that!"

"Am I some donkey with no feelings to you, too?"

"Of course not! You are a clever young woman with joys and sorrows, just like me but you, Alicia, are the true beauty!" Kathy insisted, embarrassed at having to revise her message as she scrubbed her sister's strong shoulders with a cloth, "I am as tall as you, but just more svelte. Don't be ashamed of your looks, Alicia. You are my buxom sister, and just as attractive. That's why I spent time and money on this trip making you look fashionable."

"Okay! Fine, Kathy, buxom I might be, but that floating ensemble of handkerchiefs you wrapped me in makes me look like a cross between a hippie and a go-go dancer! Peep holes at my stomach and shoulders, slit seams under my arms...my bare legs wink at all the guys whenever I walk. I'm no sex symbol!"

"It's an *Ossie Clark* creation, dearie—he designs for celebrities like Bianca Jagger, Mick's wife! Having silk chiffon flow over your body as you dance lightly is becoming and tantalizing, without being vulgar. I bought one for me too—we'll parade around fancy-style at all the parties."

"I'm no party girl, Kitty; I don't want to attract all manner of boys panting after my body. While I am okay with loose fitting jumpers, my butt is too big for that other stuff you would have me wear, like that fancy *Irish Spring* dress you bought me in London! I told you this a million times, but still I squirmed into it for modelling, just to keep you sane at Harrods."

"Like an ape you did! Honestly, Princess, you have no fancy dresses of your own, just hand-me-downs from the rest of us MacDonachie women that you've either torn or are too proud to wear...because you won't receive charity, being so grown-up and all.

"I made a real effort to find something elegant that suited an innocent girl like you who enjoys the country life. The dainty flounces, ruffles, puff sleeves, and high neck of your floor-length gown may be Victorian—not unlike you Alicia—but these *Laura Ashley* features are still very chic in today's 'anything goes' society. Mrs. Hughes and her daughters have never seen the likes, out of touch as they are with current North American and European fashions, but they nonetheless concur that the intricately crocheted tapestry banding your sleeves and bordering your collar will be well received by the stately women in their church, so I hope you will wear your new green gown with pride on Easter

Sunday. It's designed for special occasions and the tropical heat, because it's made from soft cotton, not polyester or *spandex*, God forbid! It was your special birthday present from me—sweet seventeen and never been kissed!"

"I *am* sorry, Kathleen. You have become a sophisticated, fashionable woman; I too want to behave like a lady, even if I'm still growing up. I enjoyed a luxurious bubble bath this morning—I even shampooed and curled my hair—with the intention of lounging about in a patio deck chair like the spoiled princess everyone says I am, sipping a cool fruit drink and reading my latest *Harlequin Romance* novel. Instead, I practised our songs while you were away having fun, playing tennis with Richard."

"Hmm...that was a waste because now I have to wash your hair again to make you presentable—while everyone else is waiting on us for lunch!" Kathleen bemoaned as she ran fresh water into a bowl. Her voice softened passive-aggressively as she mimicked her mother bathing them as children, "Mommy is going to wet down your hair. Now close your eyes, Princess; here comes the shampoo!"

Then, smacking some shampoo into her palm, she bent over and began to knead the scented lather through Alicia's soaked dark hair while the latter gingerly held her head in place. Kathleen muttered with agitated voice, "Your hair feels like a mop! Lordy, girl, hold still! You aren't under the guillotine!"

"Ouch! You are rubbing my skull raw!"

"I'm washing your hair, so just be thankful, you silly goose! Sure, I played tennis for two hours and worked up a sweat, but then I bathed and dressed appropriately, in time for the lunch hour. As usual, Fannie, you did things backwards, and compulsively—with no thought for the time or how you affect others! Where is your wristwatch? If you could just stay clean for two hours, instead of playing in the dirt like a rascal, you wouldn't be stuck with me now!"

"Ow! I've got soap in my eyes! Give me a towel!"

"Let me rinse your hair first, Princess, then I'll get you a towel. Here comes the water," Kathleen announced, sweetly coy. A cascade splashed over Alicia's head and ran down the length of her hair. Clean rinse water was drawn from the tap and poured over her again.

"That water is scalding hot, Kitty-Cat!"

"Stop complaining, you big baby—just remember that I love you and want the best for you," Kathleen gruffly soothed her little sister as she poured several more bowls of rinse water over her head. Finally, she offered, "Dry off with this towel. It's a beautiful, fluffy thing—like you, Princess."

"I had the best of intentions, but then a beautiful, giant butterfly flitted across the yard and lovebirds sang in the aviary that sweetly beckoned me. I saw this strong, handsome man working in the garden and went to help him. For a moment, I felt like Mary Magdalene come at daybreak Easter Sunday with incense to sweeten the tomb of our risen Lord; like Mary, I spoke with the gardener—who really was Jesus, though I couldn't tell until He opened my eyes by gently calling my name! Then I saw Orwell, smiling and admiring me. That young man is a great gardener! I only meant to watch what he was doing, momentarily from afar, maybe learn a thing or two about tending tropical fruit trees and flowers. I went to him and engaged him in a game of hide and seek.

"I totally forgot what I was wearing during our little game. And then we got carried away and got down and dirty," she acknowledged as she vigorously towelled herself dry. Accepting clean underwear, knee socks and a blue skirt that Suzanne hurriedly brought in from her closet, along with an urgent message from Bwana Hughes that everyone was famished from waiting overtime for them at the table, so to please hurry. The princess flippantly concluded to both of her incredulous attendants, "I'll quickly dress now and get out there, if you gals don't mind leaving me in peace."

"I won't! I can't! Fannie, you need to take care of your clothes, especially your new *Laura Ashley* gown I want you to model for our hosts, instead of this drab school girl uniform! I found it hidden in your closet, sloppily hung on a hook and now it's all wrinkled! Are you trying to ruin that expensive but fashionable gown, just to spite me? I didn't say anything until now, but I am getting really annoyed at your self-centredness," snapped Kathleen, having listened patiently to her sister ramble on far too long, and was now bursting in anger. "Why does Mom spoil you so much, Annie Fannie? Has she never taught you how to use a washing machine or iron your clothes? Do you even know what a clothes line is?"

"Spoiled...Me?" replied Alicia dully above the din of the stiff cotton rustling in her ears as it was pulled tightly over bouncy hair and smooth skin, polished long fingernails clicking as they twisted buttons through eyelets to furiously close the back of a plain blue skirt.

"Okay, so you aren't a girlie girl, but if you don't take interest in female fashion and presentation—not to mention the things men expect of us, like laundry, housekeeping, and cooking—you will become an old maid!

"Fannie, I think you are cleverer and more observant than you let on. You get away with far too much at home because you're Daddy's baby girl! You may act dumb and come across as rough around the edges to chase people away, but I think you are quite the schemer. You have this knack for conning folks, particularly stupid boys like Orwell, into becoming your slaves!"

Scrutinizing her sister as if she had committed a cardinal sin, Kathleen interrogated over her soiled denim as Alicia sat contrite on the rim of the tub, her eyes on the floor, "I see Orwell's grubby hand prints all around your waist and the small of your back. I wasn't even allowed to be looked at, let alone touched, by any strange male when I was your age. Were you two lamebrains mud wrestling or what?"

Orwell, who had finished his own scrub and was listening with burning ears to this amusing female banter under their window as he towelled off, took Kitty's dark insinuation as his cue to leave. Dreading Alicia's frank answer, he stole quickly up the lawn and entered the house before he could hear more, but not even one so adroit could leave the scene without a trace. The pail he had used fell where he dropped it and thudded against the brick wall of the house.

"Hey, what was that?" inquired Kathleen, immediately suspicious of the strange noise outside. She tore away the curtain of the bathroom window and cranked the glass pane open, but saw only the overturned pail lying below her when she stuck her head out. The would-be detective cried out in dismay, "Have we got a peeping Tom on our block? Some jerk just heard a lot of deeply personal information! I hope for your sake and his that Orwell is not that guy!"

"Girl talk doesn't interest him!" sardonically critiqued Alicia. "Remember, he has two sisters...One is a blabbermouth, but the other acts like a bitch these days. Kitty, I think you need to get back in sync with Suzanne and try to be her friend. Be careful how you cultivate a relationship with Richard. Suzy feels left out!"

"Humph! What do you know about relationships, child?" snorted Kathleen haughtily. "Suzanne and I don't see eye to eye on anything. I don't know her anymore. I can't reach her. She has drastically changed in the past five years. Richard, on the other hand, is a very receptive host to me. Besides, we are talking about you and Orwell, missy, so don't change topics. Do you really think he is the right kind of guy for you? I've got my eye on him!"

"We did nothing wrong, so don't be so zealous! Orwell is not exactly a strange male to the MacDonachies, if you bother to recall how close our families are. We are long-time friends, which is *why* you and I are here in this tropical paradise right now! Orwell is a genuinely nice guy who is also very handsome and strong—my God, woman, he's like steel!"

"A steel trap more like...that can't catch a flea! On the other hand, maybe he is too nice—and you know what they say: nice guys finish last! Who cares! A beautiful, smart lady like you can wrap such boys around her finger, even if the guy is Hercules!"

"Orwell takes time to have fun and interact with me intelligently. He would never do anything bad to me—unlike some of those two-faced creeps you flirt with at parties! Maybe that's why Dad nicknamed you 'Kitty-Cat'—he knows you enjoy being a sex kitten!"

"You stop insulting me right now!" shouted Kathleen, slapping her angrily. "You apologize, Fannie, or we are going to have a real problem here, real fast!"

"I'm sorry if I hurt your feelings, but I am telling my heartfelt concerns and warning you to clean up your act," Alicia gnashed through clenched teeth, her face red with defiance as well as from the blow. When Kathleen refused to listen, but kept glaring at her, Alicia pointed her nose heavenward in a pouty huff and announced coolly, "We're very late to lunch now, so if you'll be so kind as to let me pass...."

"I should have bought you a bar of soap for your birthday instead of that dress!" crossly muttered Kathleen. Digging her claws into her sister's arm to restrain her, she seethed, "One of those funky soap bars scented with roses or strawberries would fit the bill quite well. It might clean your brain as well as your body."

"I will take care of my dress after lunch," promised Alicia, deceptively docile in her most civil effort to be released without physically throwing Kathleen off her arm. "Maybe Orwell can help me, him being so handy and all."

Laughing boisterously to choke back exasperation against her livid sister, Alicia begged, "Let me go, super babe, pretty please...with a cherry on top?"

"All right, go!" Kathleen dismissed this truant and obnoxious child as she pointed her rigidly towards the dining room. Nipping at Alicia's heels, she briskly meted out her punishment, "After lunch and once you've appropriately cleaned your grubby dress, you shall report to me at 3:30 pm sharp on the front lawn, where you will pay for your rudeness by performing one hour of community service: practising our special violin/guitar duets with me for the Easter service. Don't try my patience any further by showing up late!"

"Or what?" retorted Alicia, turning back to challenge her elder sister, making Orwell and every other patiently-seated Hughes wait a bit longer in expectation of Kathleen's vital answer before they could say grace and finally begin to eat together.

"If you play well, we will go later tonight to watch the Easter story unfold, as performed by Richard and Orwell together with their troupe in some city-wide Christian pageant held at the Anglican Cathedral...Otherwise, you can just stay home and do chores like Cinderella."

"Oh, *yeah*! I'm going to the ball tonight!" cooed Alicia, defiance gleaming in her feline eyes, for Orwell's benefit in the steely presence of her disapproving sister. From his place at the meal table, princely Hughes was impressed both by Alicia's resolve and her comely transformation as she matched wits with Kathleen.

As much as all were curious to learn more about how the odd couple—Orwell and Alicia—had spent their morning together, every member of Hughes House was much too hungry and grumpy to even think about talking. Each ate his or her fill quietly intently; the only sounds were chomping teeth and the clink of cutlery on the china plates. Allotting an extra half hour to mealtime to mitigate their unfashionable lateness, Bwana Hughes soberly excused everyone at 2:30 pm. He retired to his den to read his mail; Martha and the girls cleared the table and washed dishes.

While Suzanne and JJ completed their homework and Richard leisurely read his *Popular Mechanics* magazine on the deck, Mrs. Hughes walked Kathleen and Alicia through the process of washing the younger MacDonachie girl's dresses, Africa-style. When the wash load was done, Orwell dutifully hung garments on the clothesline to dry in the brilliant afternoon sun. Unlike defiant Alicia, however, he fulfilled his hard labour as penance for them both under the scrutinizing eye and critical tongue of Kathleen, who refused to let this eavesdropping, mud-wrestling buffoon off the hook for leading her gullible sister astray!

*****

Orwell and Richard, cowed by Kathleen's ire and made more anxious about their looming show now that the MacDonachie girls—seasoned performers on radio and television—would be among the spectators, sped downtown like jail breakers to pick up new dress shirts and trousers their mother had ordered from the tailor. The harried young men lost interest in the forced musical practice of their guests; it was girls' business, prissy *prima Dona* stuff! By the catty manner in which Alicia and Kathleen snarled at each other when they left, Orwell and Richard half expected the spoiled rich brats to start a screaming match or bang out their frustrations on the piano if not on each other!

Amazingly, the boys returned on time, mission accomplished, to be greeted by wonderful bluegrass gospel music rolling across the lawn. Standing side by side like two twangy angels, Alicia passionately fiddled while Kathleen sang and briskly strummed her acoustic guitar. Alicia's rich alto harmonized sweetly with her sister's ethereal soprano; for variety, they sometimes took turns singing solo. Other verses were deftly played instrumentally or belted out *a cappella* with enthusiastic audience participation, visiting such timeless gospel favourites as: "Do Lord"; "What A Friend We Have in Jesus"; "I'll Fly Away"; "On an Uncloudy Day", "Everlasting Arms" and "Jesus Saves!". The late afternoon sun gently bathed the MacDonachies with the Lord's pleasure, just beyond the tranquil shade of the jacaranda tree, wherein sat an appreciative audience on lawn chairs or mats: Bwana and Mrs. Hughes, Suzanne and JJ, some expatriate neighbours, Joseph and his family, several of Mrs. Joseph's friends, and a host of community children.

Their earlier sibling tiff healed by inspiring music and the blessings of grace and fellowship, Kathleen encouraged their audience to add their voices to the gospel band on the chorus. Alicia asked if there were any special numbers they would like to share.

"Can we sing "Rifted Rock"?" Orwell piped up, from the mat where he sang and clapped with other youth.

Kathleen's radiant smile froze as she stared at him quizzically. She subtly sought guidance from Alicia, but finding none, shook her head, embarrassed that she did not know the words to his unfamiliar tune. Suzanne unhelpfully mustered a few titters from the audience when she asked her brother why he wanted that dumb song.

Orwell solemnly defended his choice, "Its lyrics are encouraging to me because they mention how God always walks with us, even in difficult times, and that in Him we have divine protection. I identify with the fervent hope that the hymn writer expresses."

"Why, thank you Orwell, so do I," affirmed Alicia, smiling broadly at him. Without checking with Kathleen, she asked, "For those who don't know it well, can you lead us into "Rifted Rock"?"

"Well, uh-er, I'm not much of a singer," he waffled, turning beet red before these polished musical talents on loan from The *MacDonachie Family Singers*. "I can't carry a tune for more than ten seconds."

"You are too modest, sir," Alicia encouraged him playfully, without taking no for an answer. "I hear you *tra-la-la-ing* in the shower, and I listen to you belt out "We Shall Overcome" or "Blowing in the Wind" while you work in the garden. You're a church organist and chorister, so I know you aren't shy to perform, Orwell. Come up here and help us get started. Hum a few bars; we'll knit the tune together in no time."

"Okay, I'll try anything once," gulped Hughes, struggling to his feet on rubber legs and shuffling self-consciously forward under the beaming smile of his hostess.

Awed to share the stage with these professionals, he felt every eye on him and every ear waiting to hear him squawk. Orwell turned his back on the audience like a rank amateur and lowered his eyes to Alicia as he blurted the words to her, "*In the Rifted Rock I'm resting, Safely sheltered I abide. There no foes nor storms molest me, While within the cleft I hide....*"

"Talk to the audience, Orwell," she giggled, sweeping her large but elegant hands at the people seated behind him. "Please speak the words slowly and clearly, so they can remember them and sing along."

After Hughes faced and repeated the first verse to those assembled on the lawn before him and they echoed back, his unexpected mentor gently asked him, "Please sing those beautiful words again as best as you remember the tune?"

As Hughes sheepishly complied, his stage fright gradually eased when he heard Alicia not only singing softly with him but deftly using his father's borrowed banjo to cover him. She quickly picked up the tune by ear, in the right key, and stayed with him through the first verse and chorus. Honoured to share this piece so dear to his heart, Hughes sang enthusiastically now—his deep bass provided depth to the melody rather than the braying growls or monotone chants he had been fearing. He heard Alicia's beautiful voice collaborating joyously with his, felt her large dark eyes admiring him through tinted shades clipped over her heavy glasses as he sang with her under the brilliant afternoon sun. Kathleen hesitantly joined in, but then her angelic soprano soon soared like they had been harmonizing for years. Some listeners sang fervently along, becoming a mass choir rather than an audience looking for inspiration on the midweek hump.

Alicia smiled with him, more devoutly this time, as they hit with reverent gusto the final bars of "Jesus, Blessed Rock of Ages, I will hide myself in Thee". Orwell smiled back, but in the intimacy of their shared gaze, both innocent flirts shyly lowered their eyes.

Orwell concluded, even as he cast Alicia a nod of wondering acknowledgement, "She already knows my piece by heart—like any other song in her repertoire. Yet, she cleverly strung me along, got me involved to expose my talents. She knows that I am able and willing to do my part. I bet I will be called upon again and again to sing with her now. Maybe some of the MacDonachie artistry will dust off on me; I may learn something helpful. This could be fun...."

The faith that Alicia and Orwell shared brought merit to their rediscovered friendship, yet he worried that he did not know where it would lead them. Alicia was blooming vigorously, but she was only a child: awkward and unpredictable, a sometimes-crazy girl who could easily weigh heavily upon him. God should show him how to handle Alicia. Tracy—wherever that rogue was today—must help him make it through the weekend!

"Yes, Georgina, I am not obsessed with you lately—at least not since noon," Orwell lamented to himself as he sang through to the end of his inspirational music alongside Alicia.

In a daze from the buzz of performing, Orwell heard his father speak about being spiritually moved by this wonderful time of fellowship. He, as the esteemed headman of the compound, brought the impromptu recital to a close by pleasantly thanking the beaming daughters of his good friends, Wynnard and Pearl MacDonachie, for leading the hymns. Bwana Hughes officially welcomed them to Zambia on behalf of the Canadian High Commission as well as all who had gathered in his yard to hear them play. Obviously uplifted in his heart, the normally austere diplomat wished everyone God's richest blessings for Easter.

"Before we go our various ways, friends," he remarked. "In closing, I would like my second son to give thanks to our Lord. Orly, could you please pray?"

Orwell was not surprised that he, rather than Richard, should be called upon to offer the benediction. Rick followed in his scientific father's footsteps, but wise in his own eyes, kept religion to himself, rather than wore his views fervently on his sleeve like his younger brother did. Bwana Hughes chose, however, to talk about Christian topics with Orwell James, his other son but namesake during those rare private moments when he was profoundly sad, happy, or distressed. Orwell was his father's deputized spokesman on spiritual matters because he wished to discuss matters of faith. Orwell knew his Bible well; he believed that God spoke words of wisdom and inspiration for daily living through nature, angel visitations, and current events, as well as by preachers or the scriptures—even in these modern times of high technology and secular deities. One had only to be open to hear and believe in that still, small, yet clear Voice.

Smiling bashfully, the young poet came forward again; yet, when he stood tall among them and asked everyone to bow their heads, he prayed with unfettered conviction. He was pleased to connect with God, his first love. Orwell praised the Lord for His many blessings and the talents He liberally bestowed upon the assembled people, and asked for mercy and grace to continue to work in their lives. He thanked God for the privilege of having the MacDonachies among them, who had travelled from so far away to become special guests of his community. With unabashed bewilderment and grief, however, Orwell also lifted up the name of Tracy, who must still be out there somewhere but was missing....

His heart sank even further when he heard Alicia sobbing within his unanswered prayer. Orwell, wanting to comfort her without knowing how, quietly thanked Jesus when he opened his eyes to glimpse JJ hugging Alicia and whispering sweet encouragement in her ear. Alicia, rather than growing quiet, changed her tune to one of laughter amidst sorrow and, with JJ's help, began to sing "Take My Hand, Precious Lord", which drew other singers in, but caused acerbic glares and orders to hush emit from their stern older sisters. Orwell blanched when fierce-eyed Kitty-Cat caught him staring at her. She looked as if she would eat him alive! Could not she and Suzy just sing along, like the others? Orwell, joining the majority - who suffered and sought God's help on various fronts - continued to sing hopefully; and altogether they rolled the beseeching hymn to its completion, like a steadily surging wave, across the yard.

He invoked the closing *Amen* like an evangelist, his hands raised and eyes fervently clamped shut—daring to reopen them once the ceremony over, in hope that Kathleen had been pacified or gone strolling with Rick. Orwell temporarily lost sight of Alicia as the green, freshly cut lawn became brilliantly coloured by children trotting boisterously away, teenagers rolling up mats and folding chairs, and adults wishing each other Easter blessings before moving casually towards home for supper. He happily watched many people, black and white with shades in between, thank the MacDonachies for sharing their music, and be graciously received by these young but seasoned performers.

Other folks greeted Orwell to express appreciation for his own spiritual offering.

"I often hear you singing as you toil in the garden, young Master Hughes, but today I realize that you are a trained chorister," chuckled Mrs. Rodriguez, as she introduced her husband, an owlish, grey-haired diplomat who was seldom seen in the neighbourhood.

Senhor Rodriguez broke into a smile as he added, with soft articulation that belied a great inward drive to deal with much misery, "Ah yes, my dear, but he also a fine public speaker. *Bon jia, senhor*[41]. Thank you for your prayers—you would make an excellent priest, were you to choose such a spiritual vocation...or a great diplomat, like your *pai*[42]. All the world needs God's help these days...and so do we, as we bid you farewell."

Although this sad announcement hit him like a ton of bricks, Orwell, a current affairs buff despite his pampered 20 years, suddenly understood why Senhor Rodriguez and his wife were pulling up stakes to travel home to Portugal. The veteran ambassador had been urgently recalled to Lisbon following the fall of Caetano's government, lame duck successor to the austere, long-entrenched Salazar dictatorship that originally had appointed him to Zambia. Portugal's hard-line colonial regime had been toppled by 'flower power'—just the other day—in a bloodless coup d'état! Demanding urgent social reform at home as well as abroad, weary of fighting unwinnable wars against three guerilla forces in Angola as well as *Frelimo* in Mozambique, the Portuguese had abandoned their African colonies of 450 years, overnight, to tempestuous independence.

After their guests departed, Orwell smiled as he spied Alicia and Kathleen packing away their instruments, yet he shuddered with nervous energy as he

41 *Bon jia, senhor*: Portuguese for "Good afternoon, sir."

42 *Pai*: Portuguese for 'father'.

strode across the yard to lend a hand. The celebrity girls, looking tired and still out of sorts with each other, smiled briefly in his direction when the boy scout dutifully asked if he could help. They said nothing, but disclosed by stiff reaction that they would certainly not allow their precious instruments to be carried by some lout. Bearing their own loads, they strode determinedly towards the house.

"Thank you," offered Alicia meekly, flashing him an appreciative smile as Orwell ran ahead and held open the door for the spent musicians. "You are gentle, mortal man."

She wearily trudged inside and went down the hall towards her bedroom without another pause. Her sister followed close behind.

"You are an eager beaver, Oh-well, I grant you that!" Kathleen muttered smugly in passing, what he must accept as gratitude for this time of day. She gazed back as she rounded the corner of the living room, but then it was Suzanne and Richard, rather than the lowly doorman, who gained her attention. "You two can bring those things to my room. Come along."

"Gotcha," assured Rick as he respectfully followed her, delicately carrying one folded music stand under each arm.

Somewhere in the tight squeeze of the shady stone hallway, this charming servant gave Kathleen's provocatively swaying rump a pinch to prove his point, which made her laugh rowdily, "Tricky Dicky, you surely caught a piece of me!"

Orwell blushed to imagine such a daring scene with the high-bred, youngest daughter of Canada's foremost Christian leader...Alicia would slap him silly!

"Orwell, you should grab your chance to bathe first", advised Suzanne as she passed her brother carrying two folded lawn chairs. "Be quick, so Richard can jump in next. Don't blow your chance or you'll be waiting for two hours while we girls use the facilities. Then, you'll arrive late at the church for make-up and costume fitting."

"Right-oh", obeyed Orwell, taking his sister's thoughtful direction as a tip for his services. "I'm off to powder my nose then, Miss."

*****

ORWELL'S joy in the Lord bubbled up effervescently during the Easter play later that evening at the Anglican Cathedral, an imposing edifice of stone and stained-glass glimmering hopefully on this sombre Ash Wednesday evening.

He and Richard, fiercely dressed in armour, played their parts brutally well as Roman soldiers who scourged and nailed Jesus to the cross; having roughly thrust Him up, they cast lots for his seamless garments. Later, Orwell became the Gentile who recognized Jesus as the Son of God when, in darkness and tempest of noonday, he saw Him surrender His Spirit. After Jesus had arisen, Orwell sang solo, in heartfelt testimony as a watchman on the city wall, "Go Tell It on the Mountain, that Jesus Christ Is Lord."

Alicia and JJ, enthralled by his warm fervour as well as his perfect on-key timbre, saluted with champion hand clasps as they grinned radiantly at him from the depths of the sea of viewers.

"Orwell, you were stellar! Give us five, man!" his two groupies cheered as they broke through the happy throng and congratulated the smiling, blushing performer with exuberant slaps on his outstretched palms during the gala reception held after the show, when actors and audience of all colours and denominations mingled over fruit punch and biscuits in the crowded, buzzing church foyer.

Alicia admired the bronzed youth now comfortably decked out with slim-waist navy trousers and an open-necked, fluorescent shirt. She liked how he bathed in euphoric afterglow of the highly-acclaimed show. Smiling brightly, Alicia sprightly exclaimed, "You are my hero, Orwell," then playfully begged, "Pretty please, can I have your autograph?"

"Why certainly, Miss," the buoyant actor, given by his brush with celebrative role play, humoured his surprising, elegant young admirer. He used a borrowed fountain pen to write his signature with flourish on the handbill that she shyly offered to him.

This strapping lass was definitely not Georgina, the lithe goddess who was somewhere else, but here Alicia was, the thrilled servant girl who had fulfilled her chores to attend the show. Like Cinderella, was she not really a princess?

Alicia's ebony eyes sparkled and her flowing auburn hair shimmered in the light; she had hooked him by cleverly replacing her usual dress with a more fashionable one and softening her look with an appealing array of feminine adornments. He knew her flowery scent, but gazing appreciatively at how the young lady bloomed in her silky butterfly wings, delicately applied rose lip-stick and black eyeliner, tinkling earrings and delicate cross necklace, Orwell felt tempted to ask his fan, "I'm glad that you enjoyed our little play. I did not catch your name, but have we not met before? You look familiar, vivacious yet elegant...sophisticated..."

"My name is Mairam", she revealed with a mischievous wink. Then, placing the treasured, autographed brochure between her large but feminine hands like she was marking a special passage in her Bible, Alicia closed the book and clasped her praying hands reverently against her heaving breasts. With a dainty curtsey she briefly presented a shapely, butterscotch leg before the apple of her eye and his amused fellow actors, as she cooed, "Oh, thank you so much, Mr. Hughes. I enjoyed tonight's performance. You all are incredible, simply marvellous!"

The celebrity of the night gazed incredulously as, nudging each other and laughing melodiously, JJ and Alicia flew away like fairies, to study the now personalized program more intimately in some nook or cranny within the cavernous stone cathedral. Their childlike antics entertained many onlookers—particularly Madame Musakanya, the pageant's artistic director. Splendidly dressed in golden robes intricately printed with floral designs of red and black and an elegant, golden headdress, she glanced with renewed interest at Orwell, and even jovially quizzed him on how he should come to have such a novel following of young girls fluttering around him.

Another stir suddenly rippled through the crowd, and light-hearted banter turned to intrigue. Alicia lingered and become an informed bystander, but shuddered when she spied her gorgeous sister—regally attired and blissfully at ease among these artsy-fartsies in her flawless make-up, expensive perfumes, and fantastic fashions of blue and white—sashaying forward with handsome Richard holding her gloved hand; the pair were dutifully followed by Suzanne, a beautiful lady in waiting. Waves of people fomenting around them parted with awed respect as these distinguished emissaries from another planet glided past.

"You performed splendidly tonight, Oh-well", graciously acknowledged Kitty-Cat as she offered the flabbergasted youth her elegant hand. A giggle escaped from her serene face as she confessed, "I did not realize until late this afternoon that you could sing, but now your acting abilities are even more outstanding. Your talents, although long hidden, are beginning to show.

"You certainly were one authentic brute on stage tonight, my lad—the singing centurion! You rated a lead role, more refined of course, but as per usual, you do what you are told! I understand you were even wearing make-up for this part—is this your first time, soldier boy?"

While Alicia screwed up her face in dismay, Kathleen's quip evoked laughter from everyone else within earshot. Orwell tried to be jovial, but he was swiftly rendered speechless. Such a compliment—even if backhanded—coming from one as beautiful and theatrically accomplished as Miss Kathleen Beulah MacDonachie was music to his ears; yet blushing Orwell, as well as many performers hovering about them, could not help feel sting amidst her praise.

Madame Musakanya came to the defence of her soldiers against the pompous *prima donna*. "As did all my actors, Orwell and Richard Hughes worked very diligently to perfect their parts. They became faithful warriors obeying orders of the authorities of their day, yet they were passionate in their brutal work as they understood it would exalt the power of their Lord, today. Hopefully you were able to see, young lady, that Mr. Orwell in particular was not just some mindless fighting machine; he rose above his stereotype and repented when his heart was pierced by the death of our Saviour!"

"I'm glad they didn't break their own legs, even if they broke those of Jesus!" muttered Kathleen in sardonic response, refusing to relent. Nobody laughed at her brilliant stage joke.

"Madame Musakanya, I beg your pardon, but I don't think you've met Miss Kathleen MacDonachie, our family's special guest from Canada here for Easter holidays," explained Richard, diplomatically smoothing both women's ruffled feathers. "She is the daughter of our country's most famous Christian evangelist. Kathleen has performed, both as a singer and actress, in many religious festivals—not to mention that she also contributes with the renowned *MacDonachie Family Singers* on radio and television! Kathleen and her junior sister Alicia—that red-haired girl in the flowery silk dress yonder who is fluttering around my brother—will perform in our church on Easter Sunday."

"You came all the way from Canada to sing in one of Lusaka's churches?" exclaimed Madame Musakanya. Nodding politely at each MacDonachie lass in turn, the esteemed, government-appointed purveyor of fine arts appeared flattered by their magnanimous generosity and effort. "Trinity United Lutheran Congregation of St. Luke is certainly honoured by your presence! I earnestly wish to listen as you grace us on Sunday, my fellow artistes."

"We, Madame—Janice Joanne and I who are younger sisters to Richard and Orwell—invited our girlfriends to visit us here in Zambia. It was on a whim actually and with only a faint hope of being possible, but look how good things happen when friends really care about one another," added Suzanne, stepping out from the shadows to join the conversation.

Suppressing selfish pangs that Tracy was not his friend, since he refused to visit and Georgina held some grudge against him because she did not attend his play, Orwell admired his sister. Her comely shoulders, left bare by her blue evening gown but adorned by the amethyst/malachite necklace she was wearing, accented her elegance as Suzy rose to the occasion and politely explained their situation to the high and talented Zambian lady, Joshua her nattily attired industrialist husband, and many other intently listening onlookers. "St. Luke and our church back home partner on some mission and social action projects in Zambia. Alicia and Kathleen were invited by St. Luke to play for the congregation during the Easter celebration, so it only made sense to invite them to join us for this occasion."

"I see, indeed," purred the stage director who, despite her leadership in government as well as in the local cultural and religious circles, was humbly pleased to learn something new and exciting from so many up-and-coming young leaders of tomorrow. "I know you, Miss Suzanne Hughes, but you have enlightened me. I am so pleased that you all have shared the evening with our theatrical company. I hope you enjoyed the play?"

"I really did, Madame Musakanya—it was totally awesome!"

The dignitary laughed richly, appreciating heartfelt praise offered by this pretty white girl with gleaming blue eyes and wide smile, wearing a fashionable, ankle-length blue gown, yet acting so mod and cool, proudly displaying her jagged hairdo dyed floridly pink!

The art maven, widening their circle, inquired of Alicia and JJ, "How about you young ladies? Did we reach you as well?"

"Most definitely, Madame. I have read my Bible many times and heard many sermons from a lot of preachers—including my father, God bless him—but the truth of Christ's death and resurrection as re-enacted tonight refreshes my faith. Thank you," Alicia acknowledged graciously, emboldened by Suzy's effort.

She bowed slightly, her soulful eyes gazing heavenward from beneath her arched eyebrows as she shyly clasped the grand dame's hands within hers, in humble gratitude for all the ingenuity and hard work that had been spent by so many, bringing this wonderful show to fruition. The Hughes girls nodded enthusiastically in agreement.

Not wishing to appear isolated, aloof or hostile, Kathleen joined the chorus. Richard and Orwell beamed with pride at her growth, but the prima donna inwardly laughed at them as she cleverly bided her time from deep inside her own mind. What did these little boys know about the ways and means of a high-society lady like her?

# CHAPTER FIFTEEN

THE NEXT MORNING, MRS. HUGHES raced to the market early to purchase the remaining items of meats and spices on her list. She preferred the company of her reliable sons, but when Alicia got wind of the shopping expedition right after her sunrise jog with Orwell, she lobbied to come along. Soberly attired in a cotton pink dress, white blouse, and sandals when she met her hostess by the front door, this willing helper promised Mrs. Hughes that she would stick to her like glue and carry all shopping bags as required. Orwell did not want Alicia to be a millstone around his neck during such a vital mission, but he reluctantly followed suit when his mother nodded to the proposition. As part of the crew, Alicia happily marched down the sidewalk beside her hero, and helped him put grass-weaved shopping bags and an ice-filled cooler into the boot. They quickly piled into the car, and drove toward downtown before any other tag-alongs appeared.

While Richard drove along familiar roadways with quiet deliberation and his mother strategized her shopping spree, Mairam reclined like a touring princess in the back seat beside Orwell. She enjoyed the breezy spaciousness of her ride and relished being the sole young female in the absence of yackety-yak JJ, Kathleen's refined brilliance, or Suzy's disparaging sneers. The young lady also was also flattered by the shyly respectful, yet easy manner by which her friend Orwell conversed and accepted her.

Rather than chatter frivolously or saddle him with riddles, Princess Mairam asked pertinent questions today to gain clarity on her many keen observations. Why were uniformed police standing on pedestals, directing traffic with gloved hands at some intersections while other ones were regulated by lights? How did so many cyclists, scooter taxis, and pedestrians—many weighed down with bulging and teetering loads—manage to stay alive on these chaotic thoroughfares when every rule of the road was disobeyed, if any existed at all? How did so many erratic drivers obtain their licences in the first place, when they couldn't read or write; why were none arrested for careless manoeuvres? Why were uniformed labourers sweeping street gutters with brooms or washing windows with bucket and sponge below the benign gaze of modern office towers or between parades of glistening automobiles? Where did workmen find water downtown, to serve various flower arrangements along Cairo Road with their long-nosed watering cans? Why were there so many beggars loitering on street corners in the midst of so much prosperity? Where did the beggars spend the night? Why did all white people and some rich Africans bask in the lap of luxury while these ragged folks languished in misery in their own country? Why were armed guards stationed at every bank, department store, and palatial home? Why did those buildings sport heavy iron bars on their windows and broken glass cemented on top their protective walls?

Orwell patiently answered every question, impressed that such a rich celebrity from abroad should care about social justice in Zambia. Alicia listened intently, honoured that he took the time to allay her concerns. Southern Africa, Orwell explained from his point of view as well as from what he had learned from those in the know—Benjamin, Winter, Cepheus, Solomon, and David, plus Professors Ibrahim and Muzorewa to name a few—was really quite modern in the western sense, but still retained ancient cultural ways and means. People were innovative and resilient as they struggled to find balance between unity and poverty, progress and sustainability.

Africans quickly learned how to implement technologies that Europeans brought with them, but they still encountered many gaps and breakdowns. Manufactured spare parts and repair tools were often in short supply, so one had to improvise to ingeniously solve problems on the spot. Lusaka was full of young men and women who had left their rural communities in search of jobs and progress, but not everyone found fulfillment, hence some of the poverty. If only they could believe that manual jobs, particularly associated with food production, were still important to make the economy self-sufficient. Although some snobbish intellectuals might refuse to do piecework themselves, they could hire others—particularly young people—to complete such mundane yet vital tasks and thus keep the new economy chugging along. Unemployment was low because labourers were always found somewhere, willing to work, to feed their families. No government-instituted social safety net existed here nor did welfare programs, pension plans, or unemployment insurance help needy people, like in Canada.

In the extended family system of traditional society, adults raised children, but then the children looked after their elders as well as their own offspring when the former could no longer make a living. This time-honoured security was not always on-seat in large urban centres, however, where one had to make ends meet by finding employment, exercising talent and wit to get ahead… As for beggars like the compassionate princess saw trawling for alms outside banks, the European supermarket, and trendy shops, these too were making their living; it was not a matter of laziness, but because they were either blind, lame, or somehow deformed, and therefore had no other avenue available to them. The poor were acutely visible, but even they kept a society.

Rick became frustrated by the drone of unproven philosophies being spewed in response to the barrage of questions emanating from the back seat. Irritated that Kathleen had feigned sickness and chosen to hang out with Suzanne today rather than shop with him, Rick finally lobbed a cannon ball over the *Green Peace* ship sailing behind his head.

"Man, Orwell! You're really outdoing yourself to answer all those mind-boggling questions. Why didn't you just sleep in, Annie Fannie? I thought you never went anywhere without JJ. I never knew how gabby you really are until now!" Rick, choked by his brother's suffering to provide social commentary to satisfy Alicia's endless curiosity but wanting peace and quiet while he drove, gruffly kyboshed their conversation.

"I have other friends to help when JJ is not well," Alicia sweetly sang her response.

She and Orwell exchanged hopeful smiles when he glanced quizzically her way. Refusing to rise to any provocation on such a lovely day, she offered no more fuel to the fire Rick sought to ignite. Instead, Alicia shrugged whimsically at her detractor's reflection that sardonically grinned at her in the rear-view mirror. Moments later, however, she wildly turned tables on both Hughes boys!

"Orwell, look! Tug is chasing us!" Alicia whooped gleefully, pointing to a dark form hurtling in hot pursuit between busy lanes of traffic. To the young men's utter chagrin, she cranked her window open and shouted boisterous encouragements, “Come on Tug, you can do it, boy! What a greyhound you are!”

While they stalled momentarily at a traffic robot[43], Tug jumped aboard through the open window and took his rightful place beside his appalled master.

“You caught up to us, Tug! What heart you have, what drive!” praised Alicia as she rubbed him down. To his master she exclaimed, “Orwell, you have a magnificent animal here—far more than just a mere circus dog: Tug is your best friend! He loves you—he stops at nothing to be with you! Such loyalty!”

“That’s nothing”, boasted Orwell, daring to impress his friend who seemed to love his dog as much as she sought to please him. “Tug can steal wrapped steaks from the most heavily guarded butcher shops.”

“I wonder *who* taught him that clever trick.” Alicia teasingly inferred.

“Tug absolutely shan’t come to the market!” growled Richard. He glared menacingly at these backseat stowaways as he shoulder-checked, veered abruptly out of the mad traffic flow and bounced to a halt on the busy road’s pot-holed shoulder. “I told you, Orwell, to tie up that flea-bitten mutt long before we left the yard. Don’t you ever learn? We’re not moving any further until we figure out how to deal with this fucking problem.”

“Maybe, Tug can stay in the car while we shop, as a deterrent to would-be thieves—and please watch your language,” suggested Mrs. Hughes, wincing at Richard’s rough speech.

“Alright,” Rick relented with a sigh of exasperation, remembering the gross number of times that groceries had been pilfered in broad daylight from fellow expatriates within the bustle of the city’s commercial heart. “Tug’s a good guard dog; he’ll protect our loot.”

Orwell preferred to take his dog on-leash into the market place, but knowing how his mother now depended upon his utmost attention, he knew hers was the best solution for the current shopping mission. Tug was thus left in the family car, none too happy with the situation and bounced anxiously while hanging his head out the gap of the cracked window, loudly barking protests and gasping for air.

The Hughes party ventured into ZCBC’s vast, air-conditioned supermarket in search of specialty foodstuffs. As was reportedly the case with other shops in

43 *Traffic robot*: British word for traffic signal lights.

town, this elite department store was abnormally packed today with people of all stripes who had queued up since dawn on sheer rumour, to purchase scarce stocks of cooking oil that had finally been trucked over the Hell Run from Dar es Salaam. Mrs. Hughes, blessed with many options for preparing food, could forego this staple of the African's kitchen, but even expatriates were lucky to snap up today's dwindling shelf supplies of sugar, flour and soap. Orwell smugly pointed out for Alicia an exotic cache of Quebec maple syrup, tagged with exorbitant price per tiny bottle of liquid gold. Under the baleful gaze of armed store guards, Orwell, Richard, and Alicia carried hampers full of milk, eggs, jam, cheese, and soups purchased by their mother, who went on to buy several freshly-butchered chickens and cuts of beef hung for display by the meat vendors. A prize Easter ham that caught her eye was decisively purchased by the elegant diplomat's wife before many gaping onlookers, who would never be able to afford such rich fare in a *month* of Sundays! Little did they know how many people—white and black—Mrs. Hughes would feed with that ham!

"Do you have any dog meat for sale?" inquired Orwell boldly of the head meat cutter, as Alicia looked on, impressed by his interaction with the locals. He gathered that Tug deserved some choice bones and beef scraps for his trouble of guarding the car, but could not fathom the quizzical look that paralyzed the steward's jolly ebony face.

"Dog meat is boys' meat, young Bwana," chuckled the butcher at length, gesturing Hughes towards a side door dark with natives buying flesh under the counter at apparently cheaper quality. "Dog meat is not for you, young Bwana!"

Orwell blushed as the whole floor seemed to erupt in laughter. The young man looked to Rick for some reassurance, but his older brother glared back and sidled away, embarrassed by the unwanted attention.

It was only when they were back in the car on the way to their next stop at the African Market that Orwell dared to ask what he had done wrong.

"I suppose that butcher thought you really wanted to buy the meat of a dog," philosophized his understanding mother, while her sons and their female guest listened intently. "Some Africans probably eat such animals, particularly when there is little else in the larder. Many locals don't consider dogs to be pets; they also purchase cuts of meat that we consider inferior from the butcher when they can't afford luxuries like beef tenderloin or Easter ham."

Orwell gulped as he gazed sadly at Tug, then struggled with the horrid concept of eating such a fine friend for supper. Yes, rich expatriates like himself were truly blessed when they dwelt in palaces and dined sumptuously in this poor country. He was an alien here, yet all his physical needs were well taken care of. No wonder, hungry peasants gazed enviously at his pampered splendour...They assumed that he was materially rich because of his white skin; and they were right! It seemed so unfair, so beyond his power to control for their just inclusion. Orwell's already lavish standard of living in the world stage had been much improved—yet not by his doing—when he had been transplanted abroad.

How embarrassing it was for Orwell to be uplifted so high by the less fortunate, yet expected to dedicate his life and wealth for them! Very few of his social stature in Canada employed servants—not even the likes of the MacDonachies, who disdained being spoiled by their privilege; they revelled in charity and acts of kindness, but insisted on doing all their chores themselves, with patent can-do resourcefulness. Yet, here in this tropical paradise, Orwell was treated with kid gloves by gardeners, houseboys, and guards—all happily hired for a pittance! It was selfish of him to hoard their work by maintaining the yard himself, but the lad wanted to be useful and stay fit as he cared for lovely nature...How his white peers ridiculed him as daffy!

Whenever he toiled, Orwell fancied himself to be one of those swashbuckling British colonials portrayed in adventure novels by Kipling, Burton, Stanley, and Haggard. The young poet despised the ease by which he lived, and unearned privileges that still lingered as trappings of a bygone colonial empire: white mansions staffed with platoons of fawning black servants; exclusive memberships at the Flying Club, tennis courts, and golf courses; first class, 'American-calibre' education at a private school for children of foreign diplomats, experts, and missionaries; segregation of races at church and community socials; paternalistic catering by Zambians to moneyed tourists from the Northern Hemisphere... Was not Lusaka north of the Zambezi River? Orwell, who firmly believed that he should earn any royal treatment given him by the locals—and suffered on a daily basis at the thought he did not measure up—had resisted as best as he could the pitfalls of expatriate society, for the past five years. Some white kids living in Lusaka took their privilege for granted but he would not disappoint Tracy, maverick and soon to be arriving social justice activist, by giving in now....

Orwell was roused from his emotional wrangling by Rick's curt demands, shouted from afar, that he get out of the car. They had parked in a garbage-strewn lot near the open-air market; his brother, mother, and Alicia already gathered at the gate, gawking at him as they impatiently awaited his companionship. Sheepishly, Orwell slid out, but then was nearly bowled over as Tug lunged against the door in a frantic bid to escape the confinement of the car.

"No, you don't, Tug!" snapped Orwell, struggling to his feet and shoving the car door shut against its prisoner. "You can't follow us where dogs are pariah. Stay here and guard our provisions!"

Hughes dutifully ensured that all doors were locked, but his soft heart wept for his friend inside who was wailing as though he was condemned to cruel entombment. Filled with compassion at the creature's sad eyes and wincing as his feet desperately scraped against the windshield, Orwell braved Rick's impatient glare by stalling yet a bit longer to roll open two windows enough to supply Tug with a cross breeze of fresh air against the billowing midday heat. Then Hughes obediently trotted after his colleagues as they ventured, enigmatic strangers, into the vibrant heart of Lusaka.

Here wafted the pungent reality of African commerce, emerging relentlessly from behind the office towers and polished western banks. Here the nation's tribes mingled to barter a sea of garish and vibrant goods, according to traditional protocols as ancient and mysterious as the land itself. Countless rickety stalls, each featuring its own product and seasoned hawker, hugged the edges of a labyrinth of dusty narrow lanes, jammed with buyers and sellers of every ware imaginable.

The succulent fruits of the recently ended rainy season—sweet yellow paw paws and banana clusters, juicy red mangoes, purple avocadoes hiding creamy green butter, and rough lemons the size of grapefruit—brimmed for the picking from grass baskets. Sweet potatoes, pumpkins, soybeans, and cowpeas; cassava and groundnuts; sugar cane and rice; tomatoes, onions, hot peppers, and garden greens were measured and weighed in calabash bowls and quickly made their way from bulk piles into hand bags. Fifty-pound sacks of dried rice or maize were carried through the market in wheel barrows or balanced on someone's head. Sun-dried *kapenta* sardines from Lake Tanganyika were haggled over and sold wrapped in newspaper. Garlic, cloves, black pepper, ginger, curry, and other exotic spices scented the air. Hill-grown tea, freshly shipped from estates near Lake Malawi, lay neatly packed in shiny wooden chests, boasting rich, aromatic flavours not found in the more sophisticated international marketplaces of the

Western world. Charcoal, woven grass mats, galvanized iron tubs, and paraffin candles were all borne by local shoppers as they moseyed toward buses and taxis lined patiently under the spreading acacia trees at the far end of the square.

A clever partnership was seen at play in a prime location under a shade tree beside the market's main water tap: while one jaunty youth greased down your hair with Vaseline, another industrious fellow flashed his comb and scissors as your barber. A third one wore a colourful bandana and played soulful Miriam Makeba and Aretha Franklin tunes from his ghetto blaster as he cheerfully shined your shoes with an impressive selection of leather dyes. Another vendor sold cigarettes that he rolled himself, using the country's finest homegrown tobacco.

The African Market was a chaotic, eclectic bazaar where one must sample the wares and barter to be accepted. For all their involvement in fine arts and international diplomacy, the Hughes party learned more here about theatre and psychology than in all their years spent singing on the airwaves or reading science books. Sweaty, tired, and laden with tote bags and shopping baskets full of fresh fruits and vegetables, everyone craved a cold drink to quench their thirst as they made their way back to the car.

As they ambled along the shady boulevard, the Europeans saw one street vendor after another hawking all manner of curios: wood-carved elephants, chess sets, and African heads; brightly decorated fabrics; thumb pianos and dipper gourds with intricately pyrographed designs; elephant hair bracelets and green malachite pendants. Others balanced plates of bananas or mangoes on their heads and, behind them, more curbside entrepreneurs lined up with foot-long bars of yellow soap, pocket mirrors, shoes, watches, or cigarettes. One well-dressed salesman, purportedly representing a souvenir shop of high repute, showed rare samples of costly items: ivory figurines inlaid with ebony, giraffe tail fly swatters, ostrich plume pens, zebra or lion skin rugs, and dustbins hollowed from elephant feet....

Orwell did his best to shepherd Alicia through these vibrant characters using grace and humour, but Miss MacDonachie seemed mesmerized by their exotic merchandise and the lilting spiel of any hawker who accosted her. Tracy's inexperienced sister knew nothing of the real value of things nor how to play the barter game which was expected here. She cluelessly flashed American dollars around like some Las Vegas blackjack dealer, and would have liberally bought a gift for every shirttail relative back home from each of these fast-talking traders, to help them feed their families at Easter, until Mrs. Hughes gently asked Alicia how she would carry everything back to Canada?

The savvy souvenir salesmen who knew an easy mark when they saw one, followed Alicia back towards the car and continued to entice her with outrageous deals until even she faltered at the piddly prices being hustled for some of their items, but in the end, they got more than *they* bargained for! Indeed, their dogged persistence was rewarded by a stern lecture about protecting endangered species from the ardent environmentalist. Incensed that elephants were still being slaughtered for their ivory tusks and feet—to store umbrellas of all things!—Alicia bought very little in the end. Heeding the softly persistent advice of her hostess, she decided to shop around a little more.

After purchasing iced 'milksicles' to quench their thirst from a bicycle vendor with a large grin, the four white companions came into view of their car. Even from a distance, Orwell and Richard sensed that something was dreadfully amiss with the Peugeot; Tug could not be seen in the windows, red tongue lolling jauntily over strong white teeth, bounding up and down as he excitedly barked his greetings. Upon further inspection, they finally glimpsed him, cowering on the floor boards, pathetically looking up from a strange soup bone he had obviously been chewing with relish. He almost appeared drugged as he sheepishly wagged his limp tail after his owners began boarding the car. Their once filled grocery bags that had been left in his care on the back seat were now crumpled, torn, and depleted. They suddenly realized that the front windshield was missing, surgically removed in fact and probably looted for resale nearby while one of the carjackers clad in a fine suit paraded as the owner. The straw that broke the camel's back was the cooler full of choice meat missing from the picked-open yawning boot!

"Mom, all our food has been stolen!" gnashed Orwell, warily inspecting the damage. "Looks like a professional job too—no clues...and I will be surprised if we find any fingerprints."

After bribing Tug, thieves had also selectively swiped salt, cooking oil and milk, yet had taken great pains to place back the apparent dregs of their booty in bags and to leave the car doors shut like they had found them. The Hughes boys were red-faced now as they glared angrily at the bystanders indifferently shuffling past. Out there were thieves posing as innocents who had robbed their household of a hard-earned Easter feast! Enraged beyond caution, Orwell and

Rick vowed to find and punish the evil culprits who had so brazenly violated them and jeopardized their upcoming feast!

Orwell spied a dirty, shifty-eyed youth smugly watching their debacle as he lounged against a nearby wall, and immediately assumed that this punk had done the foul deed.

"Hey you, where did you take our groceries?" yelled Orwell, glowering murderously at the youth. "What kind of drug did you give my dog?"

As though he was deaf, the shabby youngster silently picked himself up and ambled away. Another man trotted by, glancing askance at Orwell as though the young white man was out of his mind. Orwell, incensed by what he perceived as acts of defiance, shouted after the unresponsive suspects in broken *ciNyanja*[44], "Come back in once, you thieves!"

"Orwell, shut your mouth and get in the car, this instant!" ordered Mrs. Hughes. Deep hurt and embarrassment blazed in her dark eyes as she held the door for him. She boarded only after he had grudgingly piled into the car, and she had closed the door tightly behind him. Once the car moved like a dune buggy along the boulevard, the diplomat's wife sternly confronted her fuming sons, "You two are supposed to be following in your father's footsteps as role models for dignity and justice. What will you accomplish by all that racket? Are you fomenting a riot?

"I know that you are both angry and frustrated—as am I—but do you want to make other people on the street feel just as bad? It is dangerous and cruel to call someone a thief, without being certain of his guilt. Without proof, we have no right to pass such judgment on anyone. We may hurt that person now, but also label him forever as a thief. Do you care about this, boys? Two wrongs do not make a right!"

For once, neither Rick nor Orwell had anything to say. As the crew drove silently homeward under a cloud of gloom, buffeted by insects and an ill wind, Orwell mulled over the tragedy and realized how poorly Tug had performed in his vital task of guard dog. The spineless mutt had let them down for a measly soup bone! He, who roamed the city as a king in dog's clothing and could outrun and outsmart men as well as beasts, had weakened to accept a petty bribe while strangers burgled the master's car entrusted in his care. Tug was a chump,

44 *ciNyanja*: a Bantu language spoken typically by Africans hailing from eastern Zambia or Malawi.

a dumb fool, Orwell bitterly concluded! He glowered at the humiliated animal and refused to accept its conciliatory lick. Hurt and confused, Tug sighed mournfully and hung his head in shame. When they arrived home, Orwell dealt punitive blows, what he saw as justice, and chained the disgraced canine in the yard; he vowed to never take Tug running again!

Alicia and JJ fearfully hung back, yet curiously watched this punishment meted out from their hideout behind the carport. When Orwell was through venting his wrath, he steamed past them and entered the house, slamming the screened kitchen door behind him. His glaring glance tossed in the girls' direction had been returned by their own fierce smiles; he frowned but did not question why these do-gooders carried fresh food and water for the prisoner. Staring through the window blinds from within the sanctuary of his shadowy bedroom, Orwell was amazed to see Alicia and JJ behaving like angels of mercy as they comforted downcast Tug. A lump clogged his throat when he remembered how, during his own humiliating retreat from the market, Tracy's kid sister had softly touched him with a sympathetic hand and cooled his rage with caring smiles, after he had been dressed down by his mother for failing to be a good example.

"What do you mean, Son? Now, you don't want your university friends to be our guests over Easter Sunday?" demanded Jim as the extended family sat together around a crackling camp fire that evening, pensively rehashing the day's market debacle over a simple meal of tea, cheese, and sourdough buns. Almost comically, Bwana Hughes reminded his dismal namesake, "Invitations have already been given, Orwell; we can't disinvite our guests, and everyone is gearing up for a jolly Resurrection Party."

"I would be utterly embarrassed to bring my friends over here—who are much less fortunate than me—and provide nothing to feed them," lamented Orwell. "And how am I supposed to tell Benjamin that some of his countrymen stole our prize Easter ham while we were patronizing the African Market for him?"

"They don't need to know the gory details", countered Martha with feisty determination. "It was not our ham...and yes, we have other food to eat, plenty of it. I won't let anyone starve.

"We will honour your friends with our best hospitality regardless of this little setback; nobody will complain about the food because they care about you. They look up to you because they see how well you respect them, Son. On short notice, many will gladly share in the fellowship of our special festival—even if there is nothing to eat but tea and bread! Did not Jesus feed 5,000 men with just two fish and five loaves? We will do our best to host our guests!"

"Hey, everyone, we'll have a *braai*! Let's barbecue those spicy South African *boerewors*[45] you still have in the freezer, Mom!" bubbled JJ, the only ray of sunshine in the otherwise sombre lot. "We could also have an Easter egg hunt, play some fun party games like *Twister* or ping pong. We could sing camp songs around the fire. Orly can play the piano—maybe pluck a duet with Alicia—I will if you won't! There's still plenty of fun to be had!"

"If you don't mind banjo, fiddle, or guitar, Kathy and I can help accompany the sing along," offered Alicia politely. She nudged her less-enthusiastic sister into showing their hosts the good old MacDonachie spirit of collaboration. "We can even pick some bluegrass tunes."

"I've heard tell that the banjo originated in Africa, and the traditional instrument was brought to America by slaves," quipped Bwana Hughes, voting *aye* on Alicia's positive idea.

Hope brewing within his heart that Tracy, the finest picker of them all, might heed the call and show up, Orwell chirped, "You know *Oh Susannah,* about that love-sick dude who came from Alabama with a banjo on his knee…"

"My father preaches that the Bible discourages dance music, especially during such a holy affair as Easter," Kathleen drubbed. She blushed with embarrassment when the Hughes young folk, who often enjoyed lively fetes with African and other expatriate kids, stared dully at her. She quickly came around, however, boldly chortling as Richard smiled upon her, "But when da Rev ain't listening, Fannie and I can strike up just about any tune we want...if no one tells!"

"Why not play *Name that Tune*?" Rick chuckled in collaboration.

"Now, that's my cup of tea!" declared Jim, tipping his steaming china cup to the ladies of the house. "It's what you call humbling yourselves and having a grand old time using what you've got. Each of us is very privileged, I might add, to have such abundance gained through the people who sit together here tonight, as well as those who will come to visit us on Sunday.

"So, thieves stole our *piece de resistance*...You were all able to ride rather than

45 *Boerewors*: type of sausage which originated in South Africa, and an important part of South African cuisine. The name is derived from the Afrikaans words *boer* "farmer" and *wors* «sausage».

hike those five long miles home because they did not steal the Peugeot, which I might add, would fetch a pretty penny as a taxi on Zambia's black market! And yes, it could be that some low-lives are gorging themselves on roast ham and beef tonight as we speak...At least, they too will be able to celebrate this happy victory of Christ over death with a fine meal."

"I hope the crooks weren't Muslims. I'd hate to see that ham get chucked in the garbage!" grumbled Orwell, his heavy mind brooding on Georgina and Ali.

"I doubt such rich food will be wasted in any event," Jim cautioned him against bitterness. "I'll bet that none of us here have ever been as poor or hungry as those clever pilferers are. Maybe God can bring good for them out of our present misery. We'll learn something from this set back and make the best of it. Now, let's all get moving with that spirit of giving God has instilled in each of us."

Every one listened intently to the diplomat's sensible wisdom and learned much food for thought from his resilient attitude. His exhortations got people chatting about good times ahead, and what each could do to enhance the celebration.

# CHAPTER SIXTEEN

Easter weekend dawned joyously as Christians throughout the land gathered in their various places of worship—be they gothic cathedrals, mud-walled chapels, or a spot of shady ground beneath a mango tree—to remember the suffering, death, and resurrection of Jesus. With the rainy season over and the cool, dry winter still weeks away, the weather cooperated splendidly to bathe Lusaka in balmy sunshine. Expatriate students, home for the holidays from European boarding schools, graced the public swimming pools and private tennis courts to earn their tans. Picnickers flocked to *Munda Wanga,* while game parks along the Kafue and Luangwa rivers and the five-star resort hotels overlooking Victoria Falls gained a sudden influx of adventure seekers. The Zambian President attended an elaborate Easter service in the Anglican Cathedral; at an afternoon reception hosted by State House for hundreds of invited dignitaries from various faith communities, KK encouraged his people, on the $10^{th}$ year since national independence, to uphold the all-inclusive and edifying spirit of humanism. For those who preferred more radical discourse, Evelyn Hone College presented a provocatively engaging commentary on current international affairs, played to the rock opera music of *Jesus Christ Superstar*.

These pleasant celebrations were all missed by the Hughes household, who spent most of Friday and Saturday toiling like beavers in preparation for their Easter Sunday feast. Alicia and Kathleen rolled up their sleeves as well to make ready, touched that their hosts worked so hard to prepare a grand reception for them as visiting dignitaries, yet acted curious, even a little put out that Sunday's big bash seemed geared to celebrate others from Orwell's local club—and during the Sabbath? Like, what was all the buzz?

To assure these sensitive missionaries that party participants really were Christians...but that they were essential to the church service, the younger Hughes showed the guest performers where they would be singing on Sunday by taking Kathleen and Alicia to the Good Friday service held early morning at their own church. This being a last-minute decision, the MacDonachies jumped hastily from the breakfast table and flew into a tither about their unbrushed hair and lack of adequate attire. While Orwell and Richard waited impatiently on the front porch for the girls to get their act together, Bwana and Mrs. Hughes left home quickly but separately, duty-bound to serve their church and grimly content to leave the high-maintenance MacDonachie damsels in their sons' capable hands! The young people were grumpy and running late when they finally wheeled down the road.

Orwell, who misunderstood how such rich and talented daughters of the world-famous Reverend MacDonachie had any worries, still took it upon himself to play the dutiful host. Yet, he inwardly gnashed his teeth and felt increasingly put upon by these high-strung stars who cluttered his own busy agenda with so many petty demands and issues! Were these celebrities not feeling pampered enough by their peers who waited upon them hand and foot, now drove them to church in style in a sleek limousine loaned from the High Commission—since the plain family Peugeot was in the shop, getting a new windshield? Alicia and Kathleen seemed blind to the reality that the world did not revolve around them, and behaved in demanding ways for being raised in such a devout household!

Orwell had his own mega worries—a big party with no feast to impress his university friends or win the heart of Miss World, aka Georgina Amadu! He also stewed over the possibility that lovely Georgina might be attending church today—but with whom: Joseph or Edward...Jasmine, Lovelace, Gladwyn? Her gigolo bro Ali or, Heaven forbid, their intellectual uncle from the Dark Side?... How would his upbeat university friends even relate to the MacDonachies, let alone enjoy becoming acquainted these haughty royals?

Orwell could not glimpse the professor's Rolls Royce motoring ahead of them down the tree-lined and aptly named Church Road, nor had Ibrahim's opulent limousine already taken a choice, shady spot under the flamboyant trees among gleaming vehicles parked before the whitewashed church when they arrived on African time—fashionably late! A voice broke through to his raging spirit, as Alicia sweetly sang "One more river to cross, sweet Jesus" (not

"One toke over the line, sweet Jesus" as he wished in his absurd frame of mind!) to calm the edgy crew as they trundled up the packed, red-earth walkway and joined revelling believers still crowding into the arched brick entrance of the church. Was Miss A. MacDonachie really a witch who could read his mind?

Six tardy, downcast, but dressed-to-the-nines, white teenagers could not hope to slip in without causing curious heads to turn and faces to smile in friendly acknowledgement as they were ushered into a front-row pew. Surrounded by believers of all ages, colours, and backgrounds within this cross-shaped sanctuary, the newcomers smiled bashfully and shared blessings with all as they settled in for this bittersweet service. Joachim and Beatrice Phiri, the Musakanya and Halliwell 'tribes', along with several Zambian peers from youth group, UNZA, and choir, cheerily noticed that the Hughes kids escorted their promised visitors. Orwell nodded greetings across the worship podium to Mrs. Granger and her sombre South African nieces, Katrina and Andrea, who chose to remember Jesus' crucifixion at multiracial Trinity church rather than worship with other Afrikaner farmers at their Dutch Reformed Church outside of Lusaka. Having joined Trinity's youth group and visited at Hughes House, these shy, hardworking girls gazed curiously at the glorious MacDonachies, but the van der Merwes were not the only blonde, blue-eyed girls in church today, Orwell noted as he and Karla Eve exchanged pleasant smiles. Kathleen, yet another—although come from a higher plane—stared from down their pew at Rick's flirtatious younger brother, wondering what so many women saw in him!

The focus of attention thankfully shifted from the blushing late arrivals to the front of the pulpit, where the Zambian worship leader now admonished everyone to rise. The pipe organ exhaled under Mr. Rosebury's deft hands, as he began mass singing of the gathering hymn "Stand Up, Stand Up for Jesus!"

Pastor Serge Beausoleil, a stocky, unassuming Frenchman who was ordained in the US, comically reminded Orwell of Fred Flintstone; he nonetheless touched his heart with a meaningful reflection about how God sacrificed His only Son for the salvation of the entire world. Pastor Beausoleil reiterated Jesus' claim that there is no greater gift of love than this: to lay down one's life for friends. What would the world be like today if Jesus had not obeyed His hard calling? How would life be for each person gathered in the sanctuary today? Would life even matter?

"Who are our friends?" he asked the congregation, "Would any one of us seated here be willing to sacrifice our time and talents, let alone our very being, to save the life of another person whom we cared about, let alone one we considered inconsequential or even, perish the thought, an enemy? Can we love another person as much as possible, as much as is needed to sustain them, like Christ Jesus first loved each of us? Who are each of us called to love?"

Pastor Beausoleil illustrated his point by retelling the story of Konrad, the old gardener at a church he attended in St. Louis, and how God's love enabled him to endure harassment by a gang of thugs. These hoodlums verbally abused the gardener, stole his meagre belongings, vandalized his property, and occasionally roughed him up! They assumed Konrad was a soft target for their weekly kicks because he was some bottom-of-the-social-ladder immigrant. They had no idea that Konrad had been a high-ranking officer in the German *Wehrmacht* during World War II, who had been decorated but killed many men while performing his duty for the Fatherland, although he himself had been raised in a Christian home.

Konrad, like most soldiers, had suffered terribly in war, but had survived and come to America in 1950 to begin a new life. He never forgot his faith and sought God's forgiveness for the cruelties he had inflicted upon others. The love and forgiveness that God freely bestowed on Konrad bolstered him in his struggle with the gang. The thugs were amazed that this old codger would smile and greet them in a friendly manner, rather than fight or call the police each time they assaulted him. Eventually some gang members tired of their game and relented, but Rico, the gang leader, remained adamant that the 'old Nazi kraut' should be broken.

"Rico led a raid on Konrad's home late one Saturday night after the gang had been out drinking and roaring around town in their big-winged convertible. They burst into Konrad's home, and as they ransacked his cabin, found a locket, which they stole. The old man confronted the thieves, but was unable to persuade Rico to give back the locket. Rico shoved Konrad down to the floor, stomped on him, and then led his hooligans triumphantly from the hovel. They knew or cared not that the locket belonged to Konrad's dear mother; they were unconcerned for the old man's condition. Konrad died alone that night of a heart attack, though some would say that, unable to sleep, he died of a broken heart!" related Pastor Beausoleil, his voice breaking and his eyes flashing with emotion.

"While studying at seminary, I attended the church for which Konrad had worked all those years, trimming hedges, watering and weeding flower beds, cutting lawns. He kept the grounds neat and colourful for the parishioners, but few of us knew that his personal life was far less than idyllic until after his funeral, when the police conducted their investigation. Nobody saw how those hoodlums had tormented him; Konrad never complained about them to the congregation or police. The authorities were unable to make any arrests for what seemed to be a simple case of property damage. The outrage dwindled away into obscurity with passing of time.

"You may wonder how I learned what really happened to Konrad. Since I was a foreign student with poor English and not a penny to my name during the mid-1960s, I lived on a shoe string. I worked odd jobs to pay my way through school, but the church where I worshipped, seeing my destitution, eventually hired me as their gardener.

"One afternoon, while watering flowers in front of the church, I was approached by a well-dressed, clean-cut young man, who had been watching me sombrely from a street corner some distance away. He asked me where the old gardener was. When I said that Konrad Siefert had died, the young man turned white as a ghost and fled. It struck me as curious at the time, but I forgot the incident, what with all my own concerns; adjusting to a new country and doing well in my studies kept me busy as I worked in the yard, earning my daily bread. The young man returned the next day to say hello and greeted me subsequently several times throughout that summer, always cordial but brief. By then, he knew that I was a priest and therefore to be trusted. One afternoon, my acquaintance tarried long enough to tell me that he had once known Konrad, and was very sad that 'the old kraut' had passed away.

"I sensed that this troubled fellow had more to say, so I put down my tools and offered him a cup of coffee. I invited him into the rectory to chat, since Konrad's old cabin had become a tool shed by then and was no fit place to entertain guests! The young man insisted that we walk down to the local café instead for a brew...his treat! He gave me an offer I could not refuse," Pastor admitted sheepishly, garnering laughter. "Over a cup of coffee in some noisy, hole-in-the-wall bistro, this spiffy but troubled stranger confessed to me that he and fellow hoods had previously tormented Konrad for kicks. He felt responsible for the gardener's death, and had been haunted ever since by his own evil, dished out without cause, toward such a gentle old man. He told me as we parted for the last time that his name was Rico.

"Although he could not bring Konrad back to life to make restitution, Rico wanted me to understand that he had quit the gang, stopped drinking, and cleaned up his life. This repentant young man had gone to night school to complete Grade Twelve, and then had taken industrial training to obtain his ticket as an auto mechanic. He had married a nice Catholic girl and was father to a lovely little daughter. His wife treasured the locket he had lifted from Konrad's house, but it bothered Rico every time she wore it. He loved Jody too much, and was afraid to tell her how he had acquired the trinket, lest she turf him, then turn him in to the cops. Life was good now, but he was troubled by his dark past. He could not understand how things turned out so well for him after all the harm he had done to Konrad and many others during his gang years.

"Why did you mistreat Mr. Siefert so badly?" I asked Rico, who looked too gentlemanly for me to imagine him as a thug. I wanted to slap him, then make citizen's arrest, but I felt God's love swell in my heart and chose to hear him out instead.

"Rico soberly confided, '*Because he looked like a loser, a weakling, a nobody—how wrong I was! That feeble old guy was a better man than I will ever be. He had been a decorated war hero to his people, but he never fought back against us – I thought Konrad was just a useless old fool – but I was the fool. Konrad was kind and loving, even to me – he didn't deserve the crap we put him through. He had repented from his past and become a good man – I hated his gentleness! Now I see how stupid I was! I just wish he was still alive, so that I could make amends.*'

"It is because Konrad believed that God loved and forgave him that he was able to love Rico in turn. Konrad loved his enemy and did good for him; thus, he was the instrument by which God was able to finally reach Rico. Rather than have Rico punished, Konrad suffered for him. He eventually laid down his own life for his tormentor, since he could not force the young man to change with direct confrontation.

"God, rather than obliterate humankind as we deserve for our countless transgressions, also gave us freedom when creating us. He chose to provide a way for our salvation, through the death and resurrection of His only begotten Son, Jesus Christ. Jesus was obedient to his Father even through death—nailed to a cross after being mocked and scourged by His enemies—that all who believe might be saved. There is wonderful hope for us in the love of our Lord. Thanks be to God for His mercy and grace bestowed upon us. May God grant us understanding in His message to us today. Amen."

A refreshing peace wafted through the sanctuary, touching all who sat together in humble reflection. Orwell believed that God spoke directly to him, though he could not see into the future. He dared not summarize the mind of God or put Him in a box to do as he thought his life should transpire. Alicia, solemn as ever, had tears in her eyes. Indeed, all who sat in their bench, as well as many who faced or flanked them, seemed deeply moved by the pastor's sermon.

Perhaps it was God's blessing that came with giving up something to Him and helping others during the Lenten season that helped soothe Orwell's anxious heart, but he felt pleased to wear his horseshoe nail crucifix, privileged to sit beside and introduce to his congregation the happy young lady who thoughtfully celebrated with him his commitment to Christ. He was inspired to hear Alicia sing melodiously with him—how they had sung together as children after Sunday dinner in Rev. MacDonachie's riverside mansion. She shared his pleasure, though she still knew all the hymns better than he did! Georgina, for all her allure, because she was a Muslim, would never be able to share with him this little pleasure! Tantalizing Miss Amadu was not here again today at the Cross of Jesus, but then, he could never interest her in discussing matters of any religion, let alone exploring his own precious faith. She would not be yoked by fundamentalism to any man!

After the service, Orwell introduced Alicia and Kathleen to Benjamin. They found the dedicated choir conductor and youth leader busy stacking music sheets into a filing cabinet within his cubbyhole of an office, but Benjamin was never too busy to meet Orwell and his friends, especially women!

"I am pleased and honoured to be greeted by the beautiful sisters of Mister Orwell's mentor, Rev. Tracy MacDonachie," Mudenda warmly assured the young ladies as he clasped their hands. "You are most welcome in Zambia. Orwell has spoken highly of you both many times—and of your brother and father, of course. How fare these two esteemed pastors?"

"My father is doing well, Mr. Mudenda. He continues to preach God's word with Bible authority on Sunday evening radio broadcasts," replied Alicia sweetly, as she curtseyed politely in her prim dress. She kept her abundant auburn hair humbly covered with a headscarf (even if it made her look like a pirate, Orwell teased) and avoided eye contact in deference to the older and more accomplished, yet regally handsome church leader. "Our brother is also doing well, although he was unable to travel here with us due to unforeseen circumstances. I believe however that Tracy is somewhere en route; his journey is in God's hands. How is your family?"

"We are all well, thank you," replied Mudenda, placidly vague as always, when it came to his personal affairs.

Benjamin was impressed by the humility and gentle faith of this young maiden, yet seemed amazed by Kathleen; the exotically beautiful older sister with her flowing blonde hair and miniskirt, was so tall that she stood up to him, brazenly engaging him with her piercing blue eyes.

"You call *Tracy* Orwell's mentor? That clown can't even bring himself to sing with us on Easter Sunday!" scoffed Kathleen. "I guess Tracy's fledgling protégé will have to perform in his august place whenever we find ourselves in need of male harmony—there's no one else at such short notice. Look Orwell, you do have a purpose after all!"

"We have already practised together, and will continue to do so. Orwell is an amazing talent, sir—he fits into our repertoire as smoothly...as a silk glove slips onto the smooth hand of a princess. He sings Tracy's parts *better* than my brother ever will," promised Alicia, effervescently touting Hughes to Benjamin to gain his approval even though the amused conductor was already convinced of Orwell's sterling musical abilities.

Benjamin, smiling broadly and chatting easily with the young dignitaries, handled the situation with tact, while many other issues and concerns swirled through his bright mind.

"Yes, it will be wonderful for Mr. Orwell to sing with you delightful ladies. I expect that he would partake in the event, since Orwell is an excellent chorister, being a strong member of the bass section of our local choir. He also plays organ and piano well, whenever called upon. In fact, Orwell's brother and sisters collaborate regularly with us as choir members. Richard, Suzanne, Janice Joanne, and Orwell stand as an excellent family of singers, although they blend enthusiastically into our little company here to bolster the weekly liturgical music."

"The *Hughes Family Singers*...hmm, that's got a nice ring to it. Maybe we could open on stage for the MacDonachies someday...if we ever get as good as them!"

mused Orwell, teasing dour Kathleen and Alicia. "Eh, what d'ya say, dolls?" he added with a nudge to each of the young women at his side.

"In your dreams, Bucko!" giggled Alicia, with a twinkle in her eyes.

"Fat chance, Oh-well!" Kathleen added, deflating his budding dreams of a singing career at their side. Benjamin, unfamiliar with such playful joshing among white folks, seemed concerned by their apparent animosity towards one another, and how they suddenly two-stepped, hand in hand, out of his office. He decided to stroll along with them.

"We are a rainbow band here, my friends! The multiracial character of our choir allows us to explore a wide variety of music with many instruments—we even use steel drums brought to us by one member who hails from the West Indies. We enjoy the instruments and hymns that European missionaries brought to Africa, but also sing some of the old, familiar gospel tunes in the vernacular tongue, and use our own peoples' hide drums, gourd xylophones, thumb pianos, and a variety of traditional shakers in accompaniment. Young ladies, Mr. Orwell can sing in *ciBemba*![46] After learning for five years, he sings like a Zambian now!"

"This is all very interesting, but Benjamin, we really need to discuss our Easter recital with you," declared Kathleen, cutting to the chase. "Fannie and I have six songs ready to go. How would you like these numbers arranged within the order of service? I understand that we are also speaking from the pulpit, so I suggest we sing after we are introduced. Since this sanctuary is cross-shaped, I think we should position ourselves below the pulpit and sing to the audience in front and on either side. I noticed that nobody uses microphones in this place... Will you have some sound equipment available for us on Sunday? How are the acoustics here for string instruments?"

"Miss MacDonachie, you have surely raised many important items for consideration," assured Benjamin, smiling although looking at her with glassy eyes, mesmerized by her flurry of details. This implied to dismayed Kathleen that he had not made any accommodations to date for this important event, but would somehow cobble a game plan together over the holiday. Mudenda promised, "I will certainly do my best to cover all these issues."

"When? Our performance is in two days! We have worked very hard to polish a class act and have come from far away to deliver it. You are getting a

46 *ciBemba*: the language of the Bemba Bantu people of northern Zambia.

concert of the highest quality for free, but we still owe our fans a stellar effort. Our vocals must be strategically placed to ensure best projection. We also have expensive instruments to lug in here," Kathleen lectured on, realizing that she was dealing with an incompetent stage hand.

"I most certainly will take your concerns under advisement to Pastor Beausoleil and the church elders, Miss MacDonachie," Benjamin quietly promised. Although darkly insulted, he sensed that nervousness drove the seasoned singer's tirade. Kitty reminded Orwell of Jesus' friend Martha, who was always busy in the kitchen while her sister Mary (Alicia) eagerly sat at the master's feet, learning from him. Ben brightened as he shared, "As Mr. Orwell knows, we amateur musicians at Trinity are honoured by your magnificent gesture to visit us in our humble home. We have been busy preparing since the start of the rainy season for your participation in worship with us. We have also diligently worked through two favourite numbers that we wish for you fine ladies to sing with us, as guest members of our choir."

"You'll have a blast, Lisa!" JJ piped up enthusiastically. "We always do!"

"I second the motion!" chorused Suzy and Rick in stereo in a rare show of solidarity, from where Orwell's siblings patiently waited under a tree for him to arrive with their guests, but they were dismayed as this bizarre commotion spilled out of the church. Kathleen grimaced in frustration, but Alicia, covering for her, asked with interest, "Benjamin, what songs would you like us to sing with you guys?"

"Since you ask, Miss Alicia, they are "Low in the Grave He Lay" and "Battle Hymn of the Republic"," replied Mudenda with pleasure.

"Those pieces are as old as the hills!" pouted Kathleen dismissively. " Get in the groove, my man; as Bob Dylan's folk song goes, '*The times, they are a changing*'...Look, we brought a whole case load of contemporary Christian music."

Benjamin could not hide his disappointment. Suddenly looking pale and feeling faint, the normally sharp Kathleen excused herself and slipped away, escorted by Richard, who had been watching her meltdown from the wings. As they trudged towards the car, she spilled for him her deep worries about the upcoming concert.

Kathleen threatened to pack up and go home as she cursed her jackass, deadbeat brother for leaving her alone to get everything organized with a bunch of backwater morons bent on 'winging it'. Rick calmly listened to her rant before gently promising his feverishly suffering Kathy while he drove her home that all good things would fall into place as they always tended to do down here, even if one must give in to trusting unknown possibilities.

After glowering in exasperation at her fleeing sister, Alicia mellowed back into a Christian school girl again as she graciously returned to Orwell and Benjamin. Alicia promised in congenial MacDonachie can-do to Ben's earnest proposal, making him smile with her small, embracing reply, "We will sing with you anyway, with joy and humility, however is best. Thank you so much for including us."

As he and his sisters chatted amicably in the church yard with Benjamin and Alicia, long after the service ended, Orwell was glad that his good friends took an immediate shine to one another, but admitted it was too bad he had to whisk the girls back to the house, so they could get on task of party preparations. Benjamin politely declined to join them for lunch today, since he was already coming to their home for Easter Sunday, but Ben still gallantly offered to carry Alicia back to Hughes House now by motorcycle, after which he would branch to visit his auntie in Kabwata for the rest of Good Friday. Alicia, noticing JJ's envious pout and recognizing in her own heart that she hardly knew this charming fellow, shyly declined. As Orwell, his sisters, and Alicia walked towards home, he happily predicted that two friends, Ben and Alicia, would have much more to talk about come Sunday—leaving him free to entertain Georgina!

*****

WITH the city closed down on Friday afternoon, many demanding chores got done without secular distractions once all the youths were home to pick up the slack. Rick and Orwell toiled outside: raking and mowing lawns; clipping hedges; weeding gardens; watering flower beds; whitewashing stone borders along the driveway and around flowering shrubs; picking up doggy-do; and cleaning the aviaries. The girls, working indoors and thus relatively protected from heat and grime, listened to inspirational music as they baked cinnamon hot cross buns, prepped food for the Sunday feast, and decorated hard-boiled Easter eggs.

The two brothers were putting away their tools and planning to take a well-earned siesta, when an impressive feminine delegation met them in the garden.

Suzanne bore a fancy tray laden with festive buns and ice-chilled juice. JJ spread out a picnic blanket where all the youths could sit in the shade to eat and parley. Alicia carried a bucket of hot, soapy water in one hand and towels in the other. Handing these cleaning implements to the puzzled lads, she balefully directed them to scoot around the corner and make themselves presentable. Kathleen brought up the rear, carrying a thick black binder securely under her arm, with an air of urgency and importance. After they pleasantly shared a well-earned meal, Kathleen informed each peon of his or her vital mission and how to perform it.

"Alicia and I need your help practising some mod Christian songs we brought from Canada to perform during the Easter church service. We want to hear how these songs sound here, sung in a group setting with instrumental back-up. As you learn these pieces, you can also help us choose the best ones for Sunday. Any questions?"

"When do we start?" asked Orwell, eager to help, but still looking grimy in spite of a hasty sponge bath as he snacked on his third bun. "Can I quickly change into some clean clothes?"

"You've got fifteen minutes, Oh-well. Get on the stick. Go!" ordered Kathy, sending him off on the double. "What about you, Richard?"

"You gals look so sharp while I feel like a bush ape by comparison—practically naked—no fresh threads on me!" Rick howled like Tarzan.

"Well, then, my handsome lover boy, you'd better get more suitably attired. We'll no doubt see you both in the living room in a jiffy!"

Siestas went out the window but, if anyone felt tired now after a few chores, they found an hour of rigorous choral practice led by taskmaster Kathleen Beulah MacDonachie utterly exhausting! Toiling under her sharp command but accompanied dexterously on the piano by Orwell, the fledgling young peoples' choir learned to fly. Kathleen, mercifully, stopped short at rehearsing so much and jumping headlong into the pieces that risked them risked going hoarse. She exercised foresight and a technique handed down by her father, the grand poohbah of music maestros! First, they bent and stretched, then massaged one another's shoulders before adopting a posture that was both straight and comfortable. They sang out "Jesus Loves Me" using their lungs and diaphragms, not just through their mouths and throats; they rolled their "r"s, crisply pronounced "k", "g", and "ch", and held onto their "t"s and "d"s. They then covered the scales, going up or down a semi-tone with each iteration. Orwell gave a mini-seminar on using the *Do-Re-Mis* to read sheet music and harmonize tunes. When his clownish verbosity drew laughter from the others, he repented under Kathleen's fierce direction by leading everyone to sing the familiar "Doe a Deer, a Female Deer" from *The Sound of Music.*

Finally, energized and raring to go, the choir tore through several old-time gospel favourites, for which Bwana and Mrs. Hughes enthusiastically joined in, filling the house with vigorous handclapping and inspiring melody. "Bringing in the Sheaves" and "In the Sweet Bye and Bye" rolled on like the mighty Zambezi River, but such proven, old-time gospel hymns were already minted by Rev. Wynnard MacDonachie's evangelistic crusades, beautifully shared around the world by *MacDonachie Family Singers,* and adopted by zealous African flocks. Just starters for today's set, however, these classics had *not* brought new age, musical explorer Kathleen back to Africa!

Her sapphire eyes flashing and her high cheek bones rosy with fervour, the young but accomplished musical director introduced her hosts blessedly lost on safari to radically new and catchy Christian tunes that had just been penned, she exuberantly declared, within the last decade: "I am the Light of the World"; "He's Everything to Me", by Ralph Carmichael; "Put Your Hand in the Hand"; "Everything Is Beautiful"; "We'll Understand It In the Sweet By and By"—even that hard rock special "Spirit in the Sky" by Norman Greenbaum hit the charts!

"I love how the harmony on the "Spirit" song is just belted out, but we don't have any electrical guitars to grind," Orwell pointed out ruefully, having just sweated bricks to accompany the singers through the raft of unfamiliar pieces. "I don't think Ben would go for screeching heavy rock, anyway."

"No doubt, he'd prefer "We Shall Overcome" or "Amen", being black and standing on the front line against apartheid," retorted Kathleen defiantly. She had not expected anyone in this blissful little troupe to question her ideas, but Orwell was obviously a special case. Did he really mean to be a stumbling block?

"America's Civil Rights Movement, not to mention the struggle here for independence against the British, is still pretty fresh in people's minds. Reverend Martin Luther King, although dead, is a hero to many in Black Africa who feel downtrodden. Our brethren will appreciate "We Shall Overcome" more intuitively than "Down by the Riverside", which is more of a protest song against the Vietnam War, although I am moved by both songs. Peace making and social justice go hand in hand in my book. Reverend King's nonviolent approach to civil disobedience was amazing, as was Gandhi's, don't you think? Civil disobedience can become necessary to change the status quo; if we just sit back, enjoying life, without pressing society and governments to respect the rights of all citizens, I don't know how the winds of change will ever blow toward justice in southern Africa. I hope peaceful resolution can work in Rhodesia and South Africa now that the time for an end to white minority regimes is approaching. Brutal guerilla wars and the siege mentality of reactionary whites—with their colonial mindset that they can form a majority simply by killing blacks or excluding them from their areas are hopeless—will lead to more bloodshed."

Alicia was impressed by her friend's fervent desire for social justice, but Kathleen lost patience with his highjack of her agenda. "As I was saying, Oh-well, before you so rudely interrupted me, these new Christian songs are all on our wish list for singing on Sunday, but Benjamin is being a royal stick in the mud with his choices! Benny, Pastor 'Beautiful Sunlight' and the church elders don't want to upset anyone's sensitivities, let alone rock their boat. What is so wrong with God's simple message for equality that is epitomized in "Everything is Beautiful"?"

"Red and yellow, black and white...All are precious in His sight...Jesus loves the little children of the world," intoned Richard, in an effort to support frustrated Kathleen. "We chirped that happy little ditty when we were all Sunday school tykes; now, I know the rest of it, quite a neat message, really. *Everything* is beautiful—we *all* are, each in our own way. That's cool, man. I vote with two hands that we sing it on Sunday, even if Ben won't agree."

"Me too," added Suzanne daringly, putting up her hand with two fingers spread in a hip V-salute. Was she for peace or civil disobedience, worried the church organist, by virtue of playing, part of the establishment? "Songs like that encourage everyone, no matter who you are."

"Me three!" JJ squeaked.

Everyone laughed except the rigid conductor. She of the celebrated *MacDonachie Family Singers* felt this bunch was glibly patronizing her, when only she really cared about how they performed and what they sang. Obviously, these inexperienced singers knew nothing of her great personal sacrifice and the collaboration required to succeed at the highest level of musical presentation!

"Jim Nabors beautifully croons that tune on a Christmas album we picked up while on leave in Canada. Would you believe he's the same guy who played that

US Marine clown, *Gomer Pyle* on a television comedy show during the 1960s?" offered Orwell as another tidbit of trivia, still ignorantly striving to quench Kathleen's simmering wrath. "If you give me a moment, Kathy, I'll fetch Jim Nabors' record and play it for us. I'm amazed that a man who plays a misfit can also be such a good singer."

Without waiting for her approval, he raced to the music cupboard. Alicia giggled at Orwell's unintentional buffoonery, but Kathleen raced after him and blocked his path. Backed against the polished teak music cupboard, she clapped her hands as she mischievously exclaimed, "Oh-well, you are too brave!"

Kathy was envious that someone this awkward harboured so many intelligent insights about a wide range of topics. She saw how he desired to support her, engage her as an equal, but Kathleen was too proud then to let Orwell into her life. She called him as she sternly marched back to the group, lest he derail her process utterly. "Come along, my lad. We'll play your record later—okay?"

"S'all right," muttered Hughes, as he hustled back to the piano.

The choir slogged through fresh, new Christian music like "Lord of the Dance", "They that Wait Upon the Lord", "Seek Ye First the Kingdom of God" and a soulful tune about Jesus the carpenter that the MacDonachies liked from having heard it play lately on country gospel radio. Even after they had learned each number to her relative satisfaction, Kathleen was not happy. Tired and on edge, the song leader complained that, from this fruitful repertoire she and Alicia had diligently gathered, the two sisters had hoped to entertain the local faithful brimming at St. Luke's; yet, like Cain, her offering was unacceptable. Even though she considered herself to be a serious contemporary artist, to prove that she was also a willing team player in Benjamin's old-time religion band, Kathleen duly finished the practice by running through both "Low in the Grave He Lay" and "Battle Hymn of the Republic".

By the time that brilliant sun dropped beneath the western horizon, Dame MacDonachie hinted that she felt they were ready to sing in public, yet she trudged scowling into the dining room where Martha Hughes was cheerily serving supper.

The troupe of young people did come together and responded well under her direction; they had sung angelically, Kathleen reassured herself as she filled her plate from savoury dishes being passed around the table. While they enjoyed eating together, however, this worry wort's angst stole away her own joy. Was their conviction authentic or did they simply want to impress her, so that she would finally let them rest? Had they listened at all when she had uncharacteristically stooped to reveal her inner struggle? Everything would go smoothly and unfold as it should, she pouted, if only Tracy followed through on his responsibilities to lead their mission instead of leaving his kid sisters holding the bag! In her torment, Kathy sensed that Orwell cared more about her feelings than did her flame Richard—but what had she to do with him?

*****

"WHERE will you set up the board games to play with your guests on Sunday evening?" Martha Hughes, amusement twinkling in her eyes, asked her second son as he topped his plate of fried rice with spicy fish stew. "And in what room do you intend to hold this dance that the girls have been chattering about for hours?"

"Dance?" gulped Orwell, suddenly queasy as he glanced around at several smiling females. Remembering that Georgina loved dancing, Hughes reasserted himself as project leader. Alicia stared with amazement at him as he said without missing a beat, "I thought of using our gardens for most afternoon events—you know, croquet, volleyball, lawn darts, and the likes. We could dance on the deck; it would be a swell place to hold our refreshment bar too.

"Yes...might as well keep everything outdoors. I need to set up the phonograph in the corner where the electrical outlets are, you know, under the awning...Balloons and streamers should be hung overhead just before the guests arrive Sunday."

"That should work, Orwell, as long as the night air doesn't get chilly," noted Martha.

"We have no room inside the house for doing the twist or shaking all over to loud rock music—not even if Rick and I clear out our bedroom—which ain't gonna happen! Maybe we should dance in the afternoon," Orwell pondered his mother's concern like Plato's *Thinker*.

"Nobody wants to dance in daylight, man! Everything looks too real and bright; there's no atmosphere," billowed Kathleen from across the table, where she and Suzy had been smugly observing Orwell make it up as he went along, while they nibbled at their food like pretty birds.

When the boy and his mother looked quizzically at her, Kitty explained with the flair for an interior decorator, "People dance at night, but look at that yellow brick road you call your deck! A naked yellow security light over the French windows worries me—it's too loud for a party and just attracts moths. We need to create a groovy mood here, people! Candle lanterns cast a soft, romantic glow for slow waltzes, but what about rock and roll? Do you guys own any black lights—or a strobe light, perhaps?"

Just when Orwell appeared stumped, Suzanne and Richard came moseying out of the woodwork with helpful ideas.

"I have two lava lamps in my bedroom that we can use for night time party decorations," offered Suzy brightly. "I just finished cleaning the glass."

"Splendid," concluded Madame Hughes, nodding in confirmation with her collaborators. "I think we have the dance hall covered...that is, if you kids don't mind dancing on a brick floor."

"I'll probably catch my high heels in the cracks!" pouted Kathleen. "They'll break and knock me over."

"Lordy, girl!" Alicia suddenly admonished her prissy sister. "Just pretend you're at a high school sock hop. Like, you can do anything on hardwood, Kitty-Cat: bunny hop, loco-motion, twist, mashed potato, watusi, or rock and roll. You're an ace dancer whether you've got fancy ballroom slippers on, or kicked them off for jiving. I've seen you dance barefoot!"

Alicia's buoyant pep talk trailed away into a dull whisper as she added, "I was never allowed to do anything so sinful. I don't even know how to dance."

"You used to tap dance like Ginger Rogers, wowing the audience with your energy and rhythm, looking so cute in your bouncy curls, fairy dress, nylons, and top hat. You'd toss your baton high in the air and break into a huge grin when you caught it, as if to say '*I told you so! I got this*!'" said Kathy sweetly to cheer up her sister as Rick dutifully refilled his girl's glass with more lime cordial.

"Kitty-Cat, I was ten years old then and a cute little Minnie Mouse kid!" grumbled Alicia. The black-rimmed spectacles she wore made her look like a raccoon bandit as she plastered mango chutney on her bread. "Even Dad approved of my pixie performance, as long as there was no hot boy who tapped danced with me."

Ever eager to please, Rick, pampering Kathleen to the max, massaged her shoulders and coaxed his purring kitten to relax in his care after a hard day at the office, while she sipped on her drink and smiled serenely at other diners: her friends and supporters. Alicia, miffed that nobody addressed *her* complaints, glared at the sensual energy of their connection with disdain; it seemed to her that Kitty-Cat enticed Rick to work all the harder by displaying just enough of the tanned cleavage of her luscious breasts over her low-cut blouse as a mouth-watering feast for his calf eyes. Before long, he would be peeling those succulent ripe fruit to eat....

"Alicia, do you and Kathleen still perform that Highland dance where you step over crossed swords as kilted lassies to Tracy's bagpipes for *Robbie Burns' Night*?" recalled Orwell with pleasure. "You did dainty but intricate footwork."

"That was our traditional Scottish culture on display, Bucko!" Alicia sternly replied, perhaps a bit perturbed that he would not fawn over her like his well-trained brother did Kathy. "I'm too tall now and out of practice; it hurts my knees to bounce around like a young doe."

She was slow to join her sister who was now holding court with Richard, Suzanne, and their parents in the living room for after dinner tea. Instead, Alicia lingered at the dinner table to brood over her troubles and half-eaten meal, with no small amount of self-pity, yet within sympathetic earshot of Orwell and JJ who, concerned about her moodiness, tried their best to console the haughty princess.

"Surely, Lisa, you enjoyed dancing all those jigs and reels, and all the round and square dances with Orly and me at church socials," reasoned JJ with a winsome grin. She pleaded with the frowning, unblinking, sullen girl to relish the good times of their childhood. "We were so full of vim and vigour then, tripped the light fantastic doing the *Bird Dance*—all three of us!"

"Your old man, who claimed in his temperance sermons that violins were precious cultural instruments of high society, sawed the old fiddle like nobody's business; you came off the floor to accompany him on *Excalibur*! He called the square dances and even dressed the part in red checkered shirt and blue jeans, complete with cowboy boots and kerchief. I remember that Rev. MacDonachie wore a black felt cowboy hat and played the banjo and guitar; you made your daddy happy by following his calls so well, Alicia. He always asked you, not one of your sisters, to demonstrate unfamiliar routines for beginners—which usually entailed me coming along as your willing partner! I thought guys were supposed to lead the girl along, but you knew splendidly well how to do the old-time country and western dances. Cheer up, Alicia. You can dance!"

"That was child's play, Oh-well! Look at me! I am seventeen years old—a high school senior! I'm an urban girl, a modern girl. I want to dance the popular, cool dances like normal young women my age do...but I don't know how," she moaned, frustration sharpening her retort. "I want to enjoy this dance you've planned for your friends, but I'm afraid I'll look like some dumb ox out there. Maybe I'll save you all the embarrassment...just hide in my room and read a book."

"Please, don't do that," begged Orwell, consternation etched on his red face. Despite being peeved by her high-maintenance needs, he tried to rationally explain his dilemma to the brooding princess, "We only have five girls for six guys...Besides," he grinned, "Rick and I typically don't dance with our sisters!"

"Well, well, so now it's out in the open!" declared JJ indignantly. She caused Alicia to giggle as she tossed Orwell a live firecracker of her own. "You're not my type anyways, bro—I like the dark and handsome guys!

"We'll teach you, Lisa—you just go onto the dance floor with the rest of us and bounce around to the beat," explained JJ as she now hopped energetically around her downcast friend. "Make your own moves, and follow the music any way you feel. If the music's loud and the lights are blinking away, you shake your booty, twist around, and throw out your limbs. If the lamps are glowing softly or the room is packed with dancers, you glide slowly in place in some guy's arms. You see, Lisa, it doesn't matter so much *how* you dance. Nobody's an expert! We're all doing our own thing with rock or popular music, and feeling groovy. Just kick up your heels, and have fun!

"Orwell's a good dancer—all the university chicks find him irresistible! He's Elvis, James Brown, and Tom Jones all rolled into one cool dude. If you want to dance real swell, my brother can show you how!"

"I am? I can?" gulped Orwell, as JJ gazed upon him with glee while Alicia's shiny, dark pools gleamed her hope and admiration. He was caught between a rock and a hard place!

Shy and self-conscious too, Orwell knew that his dancing skills were nothing to write home about, though he would have loved to be a suave and handsome Casanova who impressed beautiful women—particularly Georgina—on the big dance floor of life. Despite his clumsiness, he would do his utmost to perform.

Did not candlelight dinners and romantic melodies woo women's hearts, and potentially lead to torrid bedroom adventures, which were the stuff of fantasy for every young male in his prime?

Yet, he must also try to understand Alicia's despair. God surely required him to honour this family friend, and she did not seem so formidable now that her big brown eyes were filled with honour that *he* might take her out for a spin and teach her how to dance. With her knight in brilliant armour guiding her, the shy princess believed she would learn how to perform all her steps flawlessly, in time to the beat. Sensing that she was counting on him now, Hughes vowed inside that he would make time for awkward, shy and needy Alicia—maybe during an intermission—just to show everyone, Georgina in particular, that he was a proper host. This was the right thing to do, and would earn him points with the belle of the ball.

Yet, how would it look to Georgina, he wondered with trepidation, if she saw him flirting with another girl? Would the beautiful maiden even care that Orwell—her stooge, valet, and wannabe suitor—was paying attention to a homely, awkward female too far below her station to be considered a rival? Would Lady Georgina be jealous and stamp away in a huff, or would she applaud his interest in helping their mutual friend feel part of the group? After all, Georgina liked Alicia too—making Alicia happy would please the love of his life. Orwell smiled shyly, not betraying this train of thoughts as he gracefully accepted his mission, "I sure can and I will!"

"Just make sure you remove the grass mats before you start all your fancy footwork. I don't want them to catch on fire," instructed Mrs. Hughes from her comfortable seat on the sofa besides Bwana Hughes. They all shared a laugh.

When Alicia blushed at him and hurried with JJ from his presence, Orwell thought he had embarrassed her. However, the two young ladies returned in a twinkling of an eye, Alicia bearing for him a tray laden with a cup of steaming Darjeeling tea and a delicately arranged assortment of cheeses and crackers. She smiled shyly in his direction and gave a deep bow, as she offered these goodies to her friend. Touched by her kind gesture, Orwell graciously partook of the enticing fare from the young maiden whom he promised against his better judgment to sponsor. Winking at him as he gawked incredulously after her, Alicia coyly bid her liege to follow her and JJ as they glided into the living room, where the others were blissfully snacking before a crackling hearth fire and enjoying the play.

*****

ALICIA found Orwell again later that evening as he fussed with decorations, fiddled with furniture, and sorted through his records alone on the deck in a frazzled effort to prepare just the right atmosphere for the great garden party he anxiously wanted. Hearing a piano gospel tune playing joyfully in the background, Hughes looked up and was startled to find Alicia standing in the French windows. How long this she had been watching him, Orwell could only learn by asking.

"Hours and hours," she sweetly teased, laughing merrily triumphant that he finally acknowledged her presence. Encouraged by his smile, Alicia brazenly stepped over the threshold and joined him on the deck. When he welcomed her in, she offered a compliment to his artful preparations, and flirtatiously asked as she gaily advanced towards him, "I spent a long time secretly admiring you work from afar, mortal man; since you last set eyes on me, I slipped into something more comfortable. Do you see a change in me? And do you approve, Mr. Man?"

Orwell swore that he had recently glimpsed this budding goddess—just minutes ago—dully clad in a long print dress, her hair tied in a ponytail and her heavy glasses obscuring the lovely features of her face...Alicia now strode regally towards him, her now uncovered eyes gleaming, her pearly teeth grinning beneath a cascade of fiery hair; she wore well-fitting blue jeans and a turtleneck sweater against the cool night air. Such casual attire befitted such a liberated, down-to-earth *Canadienne* as Ms. Alicia MacDonachie...but Orwell could not help but do a double take at the sight of his tantalizing companion! He rarely saw African girls wearing pants, except the odd prostitute on a street corner in Lusaka, and he had never laid eyes upon this saucy version of Alicia, given that he had not seen her sprout into a woman over the past five years apart—except for her recent loin cloth performance—so long ago now in his crazy life! Alicia's hip-hugging denim advertised her bottom as provocatively round, bouncy and protruding in contrast to her slim waist and long, shapely legs. Her braless breasts heaved deliciously against her sweater. This dream female was fearfully but wonderfully made for his eyes only; he shuddered as he gazed admiringly upon her! Who was she, really?

"What are you doing out here on your own, Orwell? Why are you labouring so diligently? Who are you trying to impress at this late hour?" Alicia teasingly quizzed him. "Can I help you?"

Why did this young lioness find him so interesting, yet so amusing, Orwell wondered as he nervously rose to his feet to meet her, lest she devour him?

"I'm just touching up the deck for the party", Orwell stammered like a kid who had been caught with his hand in the cookie jar. "How does it look to you, Alicia? Do you think we'll have fun in here on Sunday?"

Standing comfortably beside him, Alicia gazed about the space, critically appraising its decorative layout with her keen, almost fierce eyes. She frowned occasionally but nodded appreciatively at the bulk of his handiwork.

"Well, since you asked, Orwell," she replied with a burst of self-importance, giving him a sideways glance, "I think you've done an awesome job here. You are very creative and hospitable. I feel that our party will be totally groovy."

"But?" replied Orwell, sensing that she harboured suggestions.

"I would move that table to the other side of the deck. I suppose you intend to use it for refreshments, but if that's the case, the table is a tad bit inaccessible in its present location: it's stuck in a corner abreast to the stairs. People won't readily see it there, but if they do, they may think you're trying to fatten them up with junk food right off the bat!"

"Okay, I'll move the table to the other side. You've picked a good location, Alicia, near the French windows where we can easily replenish snacks and refill the punch bowl from the kitchen. I was planning to put pop bottles in an ice bath under the table anyways; they'll stay cooler now in the shade."

Hughes obediently went over to the table while Alicia playfully two-stepped to the other end, eager to help him move it. He nodded in appreciation as they each picked up an end, but Orwell quickly learned that she had a radically different trajectory in mind and method of carrying furniture than he did; it was not easy, but they came to an agreement before expending too much energy at loggerheads. Alicia fussily wanted to first move a chair and three crates full of pop bottles out of the way, to clear just a bit more space for the table. She then neatly centred the table over the ice box and in line with the awning. Even while gnashing his teeth, Orwell made numerous little adjustments dutifully for the opinionated decorator over the next half hour: increased the heights or relocating attachment points for streamers and balloons; ensured bottle openers, tongs, matches, serviettes, and clean barbecue utensils were on hand; repositioned the record player and speakers so nobody bumped against them while they danced or visited the snack bar; taped down all electrical cords to minimize tripping hazard; and rearranged the deck chairs, repeatedly, to equally space them out in such a way that guests need not sit under hanging flower baskets or face the blinding afternoon sun. For someone who never partied, fancy pants Annie Fannie suddenly had all the right answers for this newbie host!

He nearly signed his own death warrant when presented with the perfect opportunity to kick if not swat her fat derriere in gleeful rebellion as Alicia rummaged through a box of balloons, he had inflated to hang around the deck. Intently inspecting the colours and shapes of these decorations, she seemed oblivious to how he admired the curvaceous lines of her tightly sheathed buttocks, which gaily danced with every move she made.

"You've got a marvellous assortment of balloons here: yellow bananas, red strawberries, and balls of bright orange. Some balloons have funny faces on them, others have Mickey Mouse ears. I see some long blue or green caterpillars in this box. Orwell, you must have worked your lungs overtime blowing up all these balloons. No wonder you passed on playing *Pit* with the rest of us! My, what energy you have—and nimble fingers too! You've tied these balloons really well—I didn't know you had it in you, since you were all thumbs at Sunday school and always tied yourself in knots instead of the balloons!" kidded Alicia boisterously. When he did not respond, she felt something was amiss and demanded, "Hey, are you listening to me?"

Orwell tried to avert his eyes when she suddenly glanced sharply his way, but it was too late. Alicia had caught him red-faced, fascinated by her bottom. He thought he was a goner when she blushed at the sight of the bulge in his groin area, but then Alicia surprised him with an appreciative smile rather than the loud rebuke he deserved for his lustful interest in her. Still, she quickly stood up and grinned mischievously as she turned to confront him with only a playful punch to his shoulder. What a silly little man he was!

"You've got a lovely bunch of balloons here, Bucko, all ready to hang! We'll keep them in this box until Sunday, okay, just in case the wind comes up and blows everything around," she strategized, enjoying his many levels of frustration. Like a pouncing lioness, she suddenly demanded of her garden boy, "How come this place is so dark?"

"Well duh...as you may have heard, Missy, we intend to dance during the afternoon, when we will have natural sunlight to guide our steps," Orwell snapped back like a smart aleck. He seemed to have quickly forgotten Kathleen's advice that dancing was more magical at night.

When Alicia gave him a dull look, Hughes repented for his cutting quip. He wanted her collaboration to last, and did not want to hurt her feelings, so he apologetically explained, "I intend to put out several lanterns on Sunday in strategic spots to light the corners of this deck, as well as guide people along the walkways after it gets dark. I'll light candles and put them inside coloured, plastic ice cream buckets that have their bottoms cut out. It makes a neat affect at night—you'll see."

"As long as you don't hide your light under a bushel," admonished Alicia jokingly. "That would never do! The Man Upstairs would disapprove!"

"Don't I know it."

"I can be a tad bossy sometimes," Alicia gravely acknowledged after an uncomfortable pause, offering her own apology of sorts.

They both giggled self-consciously. She pleasantly smiled and shook hands in truce with her knight. They strolled casually arm in arm about the deck, and then sat down together on a loveseat, to admire their handiwork and gaze towards the starry sky above. Alicia sidled against Orwell to seek warmth from the cool dry air. Laying her head affectionately on his shoulder, she sweetly asked, "I originally came looking for you, Orwell, because I hoped that you would make good on your promise to teach me how to dance. Can we start now?"

Orwell sighed that she really felt so helpless in that area and was taken aback that she asked so earnestly for his assistance. Why did she need private lessons now when he would have rather turned his thought to Georgina? But, since Alicia reminded him of his earlier promise, Hughes took the high road of chivalry and chose to tutor his guest.

"I can show you a few nifty moves I've learned, Alicia, but as JJ explained earlier, you move to the music. Listen to the beat and take inspiration from the mood of the lyrics. Why don't we go into the studio and choose a record, throw it on the turn table and crank up the sound. Then we'll dance to the music we like. What d'ya say, my sweet Seventeen?"

"...And never been kissed," laughed Alicia shyly as she accepted his helping hand and followed him back indoors. Kisses would come, she vowed to herself... all in God's perfect time.

"As you can see, our family enjoys a wide variety of musicians, bands, and genres—just like yours," Orwell chuckled as he opened the record cabinet with all the intrigue and pleasure of a showman unveiling a new art masterpiece for a rich, prospective buyer.

Her shadowy eyes lit up with amazement at the vast array of albums on display. She noted how carefully all the neatly aligned, vinyl discs were stored in jackets that appeared brand new, despite being old and regularly played by various members of the Hughes family or their many guests. Nothing was scratched or tattered! She impulsively pulled out a *Carpenters* record for closer inspection, featuring their 1973 hit song "Top of the World", which tickled her fancy.

"It's not just our family's music, my dear," Orwell informed this enthusiastic rover. "Anyone who visits our home—like you and Kathy for example—is welcome to play a song any time you like. Quite a few fellow Canadians who work or vacation in Zambia migrate here for a bit of R 'n' R, expat fellowship, and familiar flavours now and again. Who knows, maybe Tracy will wander into this oasis someday."

"*Que sera, sera*! And here, I thought Kathleen and I were your first live-in guests," chafed Alicia in mock deflation, though her very real sigh indicated that loneliness for Tracy was mutual.

"You are neither the first nor the last travellers to grace our home; after all, we have been here five years now," but worried that she might feel insulted by such levelling truth, Hughes chuckled, "However, you and Kathleen are our most interesting guests by far, I promise you."

"I hope so!"

"You and your sister are free to come and go as you please under this protective roof, Miss Alicia Pearl Rose MacDonachie."

"I know," Alicia beamed appreciatively at Orwell.

She gazed affectionately at him for several moments without blinking, daring this charming boy to pontificate with his resonant voice and entertain her with his dramatic gestures, which unnerved the supposedly calm, cool and collected host all the more. He obviously did not know what to do with her, particularly when she wore revealing clothes and was in such a lovey-dovey state. Orwell saw her at times as the lumbering kid he once knew and at others, the budding, deep young woman she was becoming. She, on the other hand, enjoyed how cluelessly he acted when thus she toyed with him. Alicia broke the silence, "Thank you so much for your splendid hospitality, my kind, caring host."

"Even our close family circle includes a troupe of temporary visitors here in this country," intoned Orwell robotically, still failing to head her off at the pass. "Most of our personal effects—dishes, furniture, bedding, tools, books, and music—were supplied by the Canadian High Commission when we arrived in Lusaka five years ago. Some things are more dearly personal than others, as you can well appreciate—a few are in fact collector's items to certain members of the Hughes family—like my *Classic Comics* or Rick's *Popular Science* magazines. As in a library, you just sign out whatever you want to borrow, so we know where to find it; just return the piece on loan to the collection when you're done, so that others can also enjoy it after you."

"Heard and noted, Orwell," Alicia replied. She then gurgled like a babbling brook as she marvelled at how this treasure trove of music was catalogued according to genre, each alphabetically arranged. "You are very dedicated and organized purveyor of home entertainment. Everything is so meticulously labelled: bluegrass, blues, classical, disco, folk, gospel, jazz, popular, rhythm 'n' blues, rock, sacred church music, and soul. So, Mr. Wolfman Jack[47] Deejay, what's the difference between rock and rock 'n' roll?"

When she let out a throaty howl before he could answer, Orwell looked askance at this boisterous kid, convinced that she did not want to learn anything from him.

---

47 *Robert Weston Smith* (1938 to 1995): disc jockey (DJ) who became famous as host of the *Wolfman Jack Radio Show* from 1963 to 1970 on Mexican stations XERF in Shreveport, and XERB in Los Angeles. His entertaining mix of rowdy rock and raw rhythm and blues music, plus his verbal antics, gravelly voice, high energy, and ability to work with and take on different DJ personas, made Wolfman Jack poplar to radio listeners across North America. In 1972, he became the announcer, interviewer, and co-host of NBC's late-night musical series *The Midnight Special.* Wolfman Jack made several TV and film appearances, including on the classic George Lucas-directed film *American Graffiti.* He was the subject of chart-topping hits during the 1960s and 1970s, written by major music artists like the *Guess Who.*

"Sorry", Alicia mumbled, blushing and zipping her mouth as she stood meekly with lowered eyes as if before a teacher. "I am all ears now, sir!"

Orwell worried that Alicia was just being congenial, but in order to handle her and yet stay sane, he took the unpredictable girl at face value. Orwell spoke normally, yet threw in dry humour as needed, "*Rock* and *rock 'n' roll* are like two siblings; they have the same mom and dad and share a similar home culture, but one is definitely the first born and forerunner. Example: Tracy and one of his younger siblings—like you, Chicka Babe!"

Orwell tried to be suave as he explained the clever parable. When this only drew a grunt of impatience from Mairam, who did not approve of his demeaning illustration, Orwell struggled to expound in more learned details upon his theme. "Rock 'n' roll came first, starting in the 1950s, whereas rock is what it grew into during the mid-1960s. Rock music sings about a variety of current social issues like drug use, sexual freedom, civil rights, and the Viet Nam War—and gets recognition widely from the population, whereas rock 'n' roll appealed mainly to young people when it first burst on the scene.

"Rock 'n' roll blends rhythm and blues, pop, and country music genres and often makes use of saxophone, brass, and piano in its instrumentation, whereas rock was influenced by urban folk music and the British invasion of the 1960s. Rock music is synthesized in a variety of new ways, but tends to go heavy on drums, base and electric guitar, and can therefore blow eardrums if cranked up too loud."

"Thank you, sir. I learned something very interesting from you," Princess Mairam assured her music guru by giving him a victory sign from her regal hand. Crisply ending his lecture, she moved on to other topics of her own interest. "African, European, Canadian, and American productions are all represented into this mix. Impressive! Most records are 33s, as can be expected, but you also have several little 45 singles, and even some big 78s. You've got a really cool musical library, Orwell—far more extensive than my father's, which is heavy on gospel! With such a wide range of musical interests and choices, we'll never fight over what to listen to!"

"Why fight over fun things like music?" Orwell reasoned. "I'd rather take turns, like share the wealth—you know what I mean?"

"It's an interesting concept," admitted Alicia, suddenly dismal. She claimed to live in a cardboard home where family members were supposed to love and respect each other, but actually gained the upper hand through ingenious tricks. Men ruled the roost; money spoke volumes. "I for one would like to adopt your softer ways."

Abruptly changing the topic before Orwell could follow her, Alicia effervescently asked, as she flashed his *MacDonachie Family Singers* album, "Hey, what are we doing in here?"

"I knew you were coming over to visit, so I bought the record a few weeks ago in Lusaka's finest music store. You guys all look really swell on the cover, with the gorgeous mountain forest backdrop," Orwell added, thankful that she gave him opportunity to show that he was on top of things—ahead of the game.

Aware that time was marching on without them, he stepped up his search for some hot dance music that they could turn onto, with growing impatience.

"Guys?" Alicia chafed, appearing miffed. "There's just as many women singing in the band...as you may have noticed by now, Oh-well!"

"I noticed, indeed!" Orwell assured her, gazing directly at the young filly as she swivelled her strong hips and tossed her wild mane, pleased that he admired her beauty.

He still hoped to rein Alicia in long enough to find that elusively suitable dance music, which he needed to get them both back on task. Determined not to be frustrated, Hughes suggested calmly, "Your family's music is certainly inspirational and uplifting, although it isn't really geared to dancing. We can play that record later for relaxation—if you aren't too tired!"

Alicia obediently stopped her cute primping and pretended to pout instead as she appeared to put away her family's album in proper place, but then she slyly tucked it under her arm together with *The Carpenters,* and sashayed back towards the deck once her would-be teacher turned back to his search.

Orwell tried to focus on business, but his eyes could not help but follow Alicia and her provocatively switching tail. He gulped in awe as the bright house lights revealed that Alicia's bottom was not only pleasingly plump and curvaceous, but that her skin-tight blue jeans erotically hugged the deep line that separated her ripe cheeks. Those succulent fruit must be 45 inches round and as long as they are wide, gulped Orwell! When Alicia turned at the top of the stairs and saw him ogling her awesome rear, she grinned smugly, pleased to know that he gladly understood she had purposely put her most luscious asset on display to entice only him, since he found her beautiful! It was their sexy little secret, she seemed to tell him with a sly wink—no one else needed to know about it.

Who had told her of his wicked little fetish for the curvaceous female bottom? Well, she happily knew he admired women with full, buxom figures: particularly those beautiful yet intelligent, charming girls like Georgina and Molly who were endowed with big breasts and shapely derrieres that wiggled provocatively with their every move. Such women were amazons: strong, athletic, healthy, and gloriously fertile...Alicia had noticed his looks, no matter how hard he tried to hide them...and now Alicia not only joined their enticing rank—she strutted to the head of the class!

Feeling daring yet hopelessly perverted, Orwell wondered if she respected him as a normal, Christian man of promise or just some carnal stud stallion, gleefully knowing his weak desires of the flesh? What would Tracy think of his burning lust for this not-so-innocent little sister? He would no doubt pound him out first, and then ask questions later about who started what! Orwell knew he would need to be ultra-creative, as well as show kindness and tremendous restraint now to keep things wholesome betwixt Mariam and himself from now on.

Others in their company, thankfully seemed blind to the raging fire Alicia had kindled in him! Bwana Hughes, seated in an easy chair not ten feet away from his spellbound son, remained oblivious to the sexy display and only saw print lines as he intently read the *Zambia Daily Mail* newspaper, opened like a huge book that hid his face. Mrs. Hughes was absorbed in her own happy thoughts as she knitted a cardigan for her hubby on the couch across from him. Laughter emanated from the games room, where Suzanne, JJ, Richard, and Kathleen were still playing the futures market game.

"Come along, Orwell," Alicia twittered invitingly to the lustful knave. "We have a dance date, remember."

"Right behind you, babe; hot on your heels!" answered Orwell daringly. When she laughed in appreciation of his desire, he smiled and appreciatively gave her enticing figure two thumbs-up, but said nothing more in front of the others, lest they take exception to their bold flirtations.

To put truth to fast words, Orwell held up his chosen *James Last* arrangement of nonstop party dance music, featuring a parade of rock and pop hits in easy listening style; and another compilation of music from *The Beatles, Rolling Stones,*

*Monkees,* and *Steppenwolf.* He made her laugh heartily by clowning about, and doing semaphores using the two albums like white flags. Hughes quickly signed the music out and raced after her.

Orwell found his eager dance pupil primly perched on the loveseat, waiting for him to teach her how to dance. Her wild, almond eyes followed his every move with fascination and anticipation. He felt like he was prey to a grinning lioness about to devour him, but choosing to give such worries up to God, he waved pleasantly in greeting. Like some suave playboy on the show business scene, Hughes brought her a glass of chilled Fanta orange pop to sip on while he set up the music machine.

"Why, thank you, kind sir," purred Alicia, demurely accepting his offering.

She smiled and watched with interest as Orwell adjusted the speakers, stacked *James Last* on the spindle, and started the record player at mid-range volume. He planned for a good time but not a long time, as he assumed that Alicia, a sensible child of God, would quit this fling once she saw how pagan was party dancing.

"Dad says I play everything at a dull roar, but I feel this will sound just right for us, seeing we're outside with the starry night as our glittering roof. I don't want to wake the neighbourhood, but the others may be drawn by the music... should I invite them to join us?"

"No!" Alicia growled, shocking him. Seeing Orwell shudder, she softly offered an explanation, "This is our secret fun, Orwell, not a block party! And you're supposed to be teaching *me*. I don't want to look like a fool in front of everyone...Think of it as a trial run for Sunday, just between you and me."

"Are you in the mood to dance then, pretty girl?" Orwell, tuned in politely as he bowed like a high-class gentleman before his haughty belle.

"With you, Mr. Orwell, I'll dance anytime," she sweetly agreed and rose smoothly to her feet to accept his chivalrously extended hand.

They strutted to the middle of the deck and then spun free of one another as if they had just come through an arch during an old-fashioned reel. Orwell explained to his intently listening student that they did not need to stay in step or even hold onto one another to dance contemporary style. They could occasionally face each other, but by all means, she should move freely to the beat. Alicia, already swaying airily to "Tie a Yellow Ribbon Round the Old Oak Tree", smiled broadly in agreement. Orwell learned quickly that he did not need to instruct Alicia, as she seemed to thrive on his simple encouragement. By returning her smiles, sharing the fun music, and participating in enjoyable dance, she impressively found her groove. She played it to the max! Orwell was energized by her artful rhythms.

Their mellow, hopeful ballet continued through "Those Were the Days", "Aquarius", and "Rose Garden". Then, at Orwell's deft signal to come closer to him, she eagerly jumped into his arms to polka to "Paloma Blanca". Orwell led the way of a bouncy two-step that Alicia, having tangled with him before and knowing his quirks, managed to follow after a somewhat choppy start that reminded both laughing youths of an uncoordinated three-legged race. They repeated the polka twice, just to prove Alicia's assertion that they could do better together with experience! "Chirpy, Chirpy, Cheep, Cheep" had Alicia and Orwell fluttering like birds, whereas "Knock Three Times" inspired them to mimic tapping on imaginary walls and water pipes in time with the beat.

"Popcorn", a fast and sassy piece, made Alicia twist, plummet, and rise energetically, and voluptuously shake her booty for her enraptured partner, as he strutted suavely and spun around like a macho man around her. They tried to only dance on the red tiles and avoid the grey ones with their nimble feet, then played a bizarre chase game with each other as they darted in and out of the shadows, along with the rushing currents of music. She wrapped herself around him like a silk scarf: side by side or back to back, close enough to rub her strong shoulders against his rugged yoke or bump her muscular bottom against his gyrating pelvis.

They suddenly noticed the kitchen windows darken with onlookers; lest everyone think that they were in love, Alicia and Orwell quickly switched to a rock mood with *Three Dog Night's* "Joy to the World" and *Steppenwolf's* signature pieces "Born to Be Wild" and "Magic Carpet Ride". "Honky-Tonk Women", "The Last Time", and "(I Can't Get No) Satisfaction" rolled out with the flippant defiance of Mick Jagger and *The Rolling Stones,* followed by the gleeful *Monkees'* hit "I'm a Believer" to finish up the set.

"Phew! What a workout!" Alicia exclaimed as she fanned her sweat-streaked face and rosy cheeks. They stood together as partners would, mutually pleased with one another and their great efforts made to come together. She exhaled with elation as Orwell, himself shiny from exercise, gazed upon her in admiration mixed with a healthy dose of fear. "Mr. Hughes, grand director of my magical mystery tour...that was great fun! Thank you so much!"

"Thank you too! I had a ball!" chortled Hughes, then added with amazement, "But you led me on, girl...I didn't realize how well you can already dance—like a pro in fact! Does your father know this?"

"Dad doesn't have a clue about my boring little life, nor does he need to, being a celebrated evangelist and globetrotting business tycoon, but as you already know by now, Bucko, I've been singing, playing, and moving to music all my life. I did tap dance, Highland flings, square and round stuff, jigs and reels...but it was all choreographed, controlled by tradition and old-fashioned parents who were watching me like hawks, demanding perfection for their own applause," grumbled Alicia against how she had been put on display as a child prodigy. How many times had *he* been her country dance partner or watched her recitals? She whispered deviously now, proud of her rebellious accomplishments. "When they sent me up to that private girls' school, my parents thought I would be reformed, like chained to a study cubicle for my waking hours. Little did they know that we clever girls smuggled in all the hit records and danced to rock and roll among ourselves? We perfected jive, bird dance, tango, and bunny hop.

"Some of our teachers even encouraged us for exercise as well as art; they prepared us to confidently handle ourselves in our future flings with men. They organized dance parties with the private boys' schools, but such exchanges were rigidly controlled. At last, I have a real live boy to dance with!"

"I would like to learn how to jive, Alicia. If you're game to mentor me, I think we have some *Bill Haley and the Comets* music in the house," suggested Orwell, as he got set to make a fifty-yards-dash to the music library to fetch it and any other album she wished from the jive section.

"I promise to teach you, but not right now, Orwell. Jive's not easy though I confess: you've worked me over good. I'm hot and sweaty all over, and pooped from all the moving and shaking we've done in this past hour," Alicia admitted huskily. For emphasis, she hiked up her sweater half a foot to show her admirer how her flat, muscular stomach glistened with perspiration. "Do you believe me now, mortal man?"

Then, seeming oblivious to his awe, she vigorously shook her top to let the cool night air circulate around her breasts. Alicia smiled foppishly when he watched her antics with interest, but she resolved to reveal no further secrets of her nubile body. Feeling the need to break Orwell's trance, she put him to work.

"I would be inclined towards some quieter, slower music to end our lesson. Could you make an appropriate selection, Orwell, while I sit down and drink the rest of my pop?" Princess Mairam stated her preference as she exquisitely reclined on the loveseat. She then mischievously added, winking at him with spicy invitation, "If you wish, Orwell, you may come and sit beside me for your own listening enjoyment."

"Your wish is my command, fair damsel," Hughes replied, bowing low as he jovially played along. "I'll be right back."

Alicia laughed merrily at his antics, then followed her selfless, caring friend with her gleaming eyes, admiring him even as she lounged about and drank greedily from her beverage. Alicia was a keen warrioress, however, and shouted out a stern warning when she saw, before Orwell could, the intrusion of their rowdy siblings upon this special little sanctuary.

"Who goes there? Identify yourself!"

Orwell plodded forward to protect the music machine, but before he could say Christopher Robin, Kathleen slipped some good vibrations *Beach Boys* music onto the record player and cranked the volume up full blast! Then, hand in hand with Rick, she raced jubilantly onto the tiled deck floor, followed close behind by Suzanne and JJ. The private dance studio was quickly overrun by fresh dancers cavorting to the sunny surf sound.

Orwell and Alicia, now well spent, were stunned by this new buzz of excitement! They sat together on the loveseat like grandparents, staring at the revellers and then blinking at each other, confused as to what to do next.

"Hey, Fannie! Orwell! Come on, get up—it's party time!" hailed Kathleen with exhilaration amid the tangle of flapping limbs and twisting bodies.

"We watched you two go-go dancing for the past half hour, bro—you're all broke in now", Rick ribbed his brother to jump start him. "Dance with us, eh!"

"What do you say?" Orwell asked Alicia, wanting her opinion.

"Let's show these stubble jumpers how it's done," Alicia shot back impudently. "Who do they think they are, Astaire and Rogers?"

She plopped her pop bottle sharply on the table and sprang deftly to her feet. Before Orwell knew what was happening, she hauled him resolutely into the fray. Rejuvenated by the others' challenge to put out, the now seasoned couple quickly found the beat.

The tunes Kathleen chose were just like her, jaunty and fun! Moving through the *Beach Boys'* "Sloop John B", "Silver Threads and Golden Needles" by Linda Ronstadt, Bobby Darin's "Splish Splash", and "Another Saturday Night" sung raucously plaintive by Cat Stevens, everyone energetically strutted their stuff. They sometimes worked like a synchronized dance troupe as they emulated each other's cool moves, but more often than not, each proud and artistic individual showed a unique interpretation that expressed one's unique style. They twisted or marched, shifted from side to side, drilled into the floor and spun back up, flung out their arms and legs, flapped their arms like birds, or appeared to float or glide around the room.

Suzanne and JJ, careless that they were the extra girls on the dance floor, impishly played the field. They jived splendidly with each other, but then one would swing her sister into the path of a different dancer, where each established a new rapport. The Hughes dainties flitted like fairies among the tall MacDonachies and their hulking dancing mates. Rick, whose eyes gazed into the stars, hardly knew his sisters existed. Although miffed by such disturbing children and oblivious to their desire to belong, Kathleen woodenly agreed to be replaced or claimed by them for a few moments; Alicia jived up a storm with JJ, while Orwell danced his heart out with Suzy. They switched partners again and again, yet kept dancing.

Rick shocked and awed the others, particularly his amused partner Kitty-Cat, as he performed athletic jumping jacks high in the air or frantically dropped and rolled on the floor as if he had parachuted in flames from a crashing aircraft. Kathleen called on her own Highland dancer's agility to daintily step and twirl over her hero. They appeared to be a hot item, but when Rick behaved more staidly and controlled in his dancing, Kitty seized the opportunities to tease her moonlit sister, who was moving elegantly in step with Orwell and gazing upward with enthrallment into his smiling face.

During one particularly fast section of Ronstadt's lament, Kathleen manoeuvred herself in front of Alicia and began to mischievously mirror the younger MacDonachie's spirited movements. Alicia sensed her annoying mimic, but grinning defiantly, took her on while Orwell and Rick tumbled in the background. They pranced like young fillies, sparring with each other in an unfenced pasture, but failed to rein each other in. When Alicia continued to enjoy the music, her playful copycat beckoned her close to whisper a happy secret, "Life is so wonderful when we're in love, Fannie!"

Then Kathleen strutted away and found Rick again, leaving her younger sister to ponder whether Kitty was sharing her own joy or could see into Alicia's twittering heart. Alicia watched as the obviously happy couple danced the last stanza of "Another Saturday Night" in blissful ignorance of the singer's frustration of having no one to talk to, no girl to date...*they* did! She must be happy for them, for were not Rick and Kathleen brought together by God's perfect timing? How wonderful it was that they were in love, Alicia marvelled as she watched the pair fit together like two peas in a pod and gradually regress toward the house.

Suddenly, as though they had been only a dream, the magical dancers were gone and Alicia was left on the quiet, shadowy stage with only Orwell idling beside her. The Cat Stevens album went lilting delightfully along: '*I'm being followed by a moon shadow ...*'

"What shall we do now?" she mused aloud. "I like the music, but I'm getting chilly just standing here. Should we go in with the others?"

"We could slow dance a little," Orwell offered gently, holding out his arms invitingly. "We can warm each other some and enjoy the music—you know, savour the moment?"

"Do you charge extra for overtime?" Alicia coyly inquired of her dance teacher before making any further move.

"The first lesson is always free," added Orwell, good-naturedly protesting her insinuation that he was giving her lessons out of a feeling of duty, for a set time, and that she was in fact imposing upon him. "I enjoy dancing with you, Alicia. You have excellent rhythm—a real knack, and a really good feel for dancing."

"I don't know how to slow dance, Bucko! You know I've lived a very sheltered life!"

"But you already know how to waltz. Slow dancing is just a casual form of waltzing. We just hold onto each other and move to the music, slowly. We can even stay in one place and just sway softly from side to side or back and forth. It's up to you girl, but I'm willing to give these slower songs a try if you are."

"Okay, Orwell, I'm all yours."

She gazed meaningfully at him to emphasize that he must be true to her. When Orwell gratefully nodded, Alicia smiled sweetly, then twirled playfully into his outstretched arms and trusted him to catch her, lead her, and treat her respectfully, not only in slow dancing but forever always. Orwell took her soft left hand inside his right and placed his left hand flat in the middle of her back, just below where her bra strap should be! She quivered at his touch but found it comforting; as usual, Orwell's respectful hands behaved themselves and did not go exploring where they were not invited. While he took charge, Hughes showed the spirited young woman that he was a careful rider who communicated his wishes gently and responded to her needs: a fine press on her back directed Alicia to follow him this way or that; a gentle tug on her hand signalled that he wanted to spin her. The masterful dance partner held her snugly without smothering her. At first, Alicia appeared rigid and shy, almost feisty in his embrace, but she softened into a receptive woman of beauty and grace the more they trusted and understood each other. She smiled, remembering how happily they had danced together but a few minutes ago, not to mention as children.

As "Moon Shadow" gave way to "Morning Has Broken", Alicia and Orwell continued to float about the deck, buoyed by the uplifting strains of the worship song and each other's pleasant company. She was as warm and soft as he was strong and comforting...Their smells intermingled...her scent of wild flowers blending with his manly *Old Spice*. Her ebony, oriental eyes sparkled and her wide smile expressed her contentment whenever she looked at him with her high cheek-boned face awash with cascades of wavy dark hair. Like the Biblical lovers in the *Song of Solomon*, he was a handsome, virile young stag who loved his doe.

Savouring this special time of deep connection, they talked sparingly, although Alicia, usually the quieter of the two, offered sweet nothings to her lover to nibble on. She observed that although Orwell was four inches taller, a foot broader and fifty pounds heavier than her, their hips reached equal height from the floor, meaning that they had legs of similar length. Did he now realize, in touching her strong back and sensing her flat, muscular stomach swishing so close to his own, that Alicia might be a buxom girl, but was all muscle...and definitely not fat? Alicia told her quiet listener that she was pleased he exercised regularly and ate healthy foods in order to stay trim and agile, rather than become lazy, like so many of his expat friends! She also mentioned that "Morning Has Broken"[48] had recently been sung as a folk hymn by the MacDonachies at St.

48 *"Morning Has Broken"*: popular and well-known Christian hymn, originated as the Scottish Gaelic

Andrew's church. She thought it interesting that an edgy rock star like Cat Stevens had chosen to sing such an inspired praise song. "Morning Has Broken" faded into "Here Comes the Sun", *The Beatles'* equally uplifting and hopeful tune. Alicia and Orwell cuddled as they took courage from the song that everything would be all right. She laid her head against his chest, and smiled blissfully as she hugged this tree of a man who danced so gently with her on this silent, peaceful end to a hallowed night. Rather than be offended or aroused, he allowed her breasts and stomach to cover his torso and melted a little in her embrace.

Although he felt guilty that he was planning on two-timing her with Georgina, Orwell did not know how to escape Alicia's intimate grip—nor did he really want to just now. Their little tryst might look silly in the morning, but tonight Orwell found himself affectionately drawn to his friend. He cherished her as a beautiful woman whom he knew and understood; he was blessed by not only her love but her caring awareness of him. He laid his chin gently atop her heap of thick hair and joined her on gossamer wings for that tranquil journey towards dreamland. If this was a dream, they hoped it would never end!

Yet, all good things must end, at least temporarily—so that the tantalizing experience might resume at another, more opportune and appropriate time. In the fairy tale case of Orwell and Alicia, the young poet was stirred from slumber by an increasingly urgent thought that he and his date had flouted their curfew; they should each find their separate, proper beds and get some real sleep before the busy morning shift at Hughes House found them out.

"Suzy—er uh, Alicia I mean, wake up," he whispered, rubbing her arm. "We need to get inside the house, you know...get some shuteye...sing some zeds. Wakey-wakey, my princess."

He gingerly unlaced her fingers that were tightly clasped in the small of his

---

folk song "Leanabh an Aigh", set to the tune "Bunessan" in the 1800s. It was first published in 1931 by author Eleanor Farjeon in *Songs of Praise*, edited by Percy Dearmer, who explained that the song reminded believers to give thanks to God, every day. Cat Stevens popularized "Morning Has Broken" on his 1971 record album *Teaser and the Firecat.* The piano arrangement for Steven's recording was composed and performed by Rick Wakeman, who said that "Morning Has Broken" was a very beautiful piece that brought people closer to religious truth. Cat Stevens, who earnestly sought religious truth himself, became a Muslim and changed his name to Yusuf Islam in 1977 after surviving a drowning accident; he credited God's help in saving his life, and vowed to serve Him.

back. Alicia seemed to weigh a ton when she was asleep, he muttered crossly as he finally extricated himself. By loosening her anchor, Orwell caused Alicia to slide down the front of his body. Not wanting his girlfriend to be embarrassed in any way, he moved with lightning speed and caught her before she landed on the floor. Alicia woke with a start to find herself cradled in his strong arms as he hoisted her up and steadied her on her feet. The amazon gave him a cross-eyed frown of bewilderment, then giggled foolishly, admitting to have no idea how she came to be where she was! Hughes assured Alicia that all was well—she had simply fallen asleep.

"Then I'm not drunk?" she laughed boisterously.

"No, just tired, like me. You've been a perfect angel all night, my dear. Alicia, I really liked being with you."

"Is it really you, Orwell?" yawned Alicia contentedly. She looked happily into her dream lover's eyes. "Thank you for such a wonderful evening."

They crept back into the darkened, silent house, but rather than disturb the others and be discovered as being up so late together by misunderstanding folks, they found a cozy little corner of the living room to bed down in for what little remained of night. Alicia curled up on the couch, swaddled in a warm, rainbow coloured, Hudson Bay blanket that Hughes brought her from the linen closet. Fatigued yet happy, she watched Orwell unfold a futon, on which he spread another blanket to make a bed for himself on the floor nearby. He set a wind-up travel clock to wake them at dawn, in time to skitter into their own bedrooms before anyone else up could question how they had spent the night together. Alicia smiled warmly as her protector tucked her in; they whispered the Lord's Prayer fervently together before drifting off to sleep.

Both night owls craved to dream serenely, but neither could find rest. Alicia tossed and turned until she became straight-jacketed by the blanket which had become tightly wrapped around her. Her thrashing turbulence, incoherent whimpers, and angry mutterings kept Orwell on edge. Dishevelled Alicia suddenly sat bolt upright and stared at him with such forlorn despair that Orwell thought she had seen a ghost! Then, as he anxiously watched her, she peeled herself free of her covers and sprang to her feet wearing only panties on her marvellous form. She practically mooned him with her round, white bum as she pilfered the cushions off the couch and splashed them on the floor beside him, but then she, oblivious to his worship, quickly wrapped herself again in her blanket and lay down next to him.

"Hold me, Orwell," Alicia begged the astounded youth with such lonely anguish that she broke his heart; though she said neither please or thank you, he in his compassion could do ought but comply.

Hughes gently gathered the distraught, shivering creature into his bosom and held her respectfully, warming and soothing her until both were finally able to settle themselves for two fleeting hours of quality sleep. They spooned together until morning.

Alicia stirred first, drawn kindly back to reality by birds singing in the rosy light of dawn. She stealthily slipped from Orwell's embrace, and hurriedly put on her clothes. She placed the cushions back on the couch, and lovingly draped her blanket over her still sleeping companion. Alicia gazed admiringly upon her knight for a long moment as she pondered how kind he had been to her in her joys and sorrows of previous days. She then knelt down beside Orwell's face, and bursting with love and gratitude, kissed him gently. Her fervent touch caused Orwell's eyes to flicker open; they smiled at each other before she flitted away like an angel. Thoughtfully alerted by his partner in crime that dawn had broken, Orwell swiftly got his own stuff together, and padded off to his bedroom.

# CHAPTER SEVENTEEN

EASTER SATURDAY WAS SPENT IN a frantic flurry of preparation for the grand Sunday feast. Martha Hughes, admired far and wide as the 'hostess with the mostest' among church, service, and expatriate communities, adhered meticulously to her plan as she deployed her household to make everything ready for comfort of their guests. Complaints and lethargy were not tolerated; buying into the big picture of fun times ahead, everyone pitched in to bring them on. Bwana Hughes poked out his head occasionally from his den like a groundhog checking for his shadow, and was pleased by the spartan efforts, enthusiastic compliance, and the traditional division of labour shown by today's youth—just like he had done as a lad on the farm.

"What does that old coot know?" Orwell wryly mused as the MacDonachie girls uttered nary a complaint about being pressed into labour or having their Sunday concert line-up altered, but chose to do yard work with their boyfriends—for the fee of manly pleasantries, attention, and respect—rather than remain sequestered inside, cleaning house with Martha Hughes, and be stuck doing 'women's work'!

Labouring in pairs, Rick with Kitty-Cat, and Orwell beside Alicia, harvested ripe peaches and loquats from fruit trees and a variety of vegetables from the family garden, bumper ready for such a feast: carrots, parsnips, tomatoes, green peppers, okra, onions, spinach, sweet and Irish potatoes—bounties from the soil to be washed in laundry tubs, then brought into the kitchen, to offer their colourful succulence to cook or process into salads, side dishes, and desserts. If either young man glibly thought he might shake off his mate, he was sorely mistaken! Worshipful Alicia earned her stripes with Orwell by helping him remove slimy snails climbing the mossy back wall of the house where the sink and bathtub drained into the septic system. Much as her highbrow model sister hated all creepy-crawly things, Kathleen helped Rick bag silver dollar-sized spiders from the living room walls.

Meanwhile, a whirlwind of fall cleaning blew throughout the house. In the houseboy's holiday absence, windows were washed, mantles dusted, bathrooms scrubbed, linens laundered and ironed, and stone or hardwood tile floors swept clean. Mrs. Hughes inventoried her cutlery and dishes—any piece that was even suspected of being dirty was washed until it gleamed like a mirror. A sweating galley swab might see his or her face reflected in English fine-bone china and real silverware...and be impressed!

When Orwell and Richard came inside, all sweaty and dirt-streaked, for a drink of water, they immediately chastised Suzanne for leading a bunch of nosy dames into their bedroom—their 'Holy of Holies'—supposedly to dust and vacuum, but really to snoop! Despite their protests, the Hughes boys were immediately ejected and put to work by their mother—the event's chairman of the board! Madame inspected for flaws every chair that Orwell and Richard obediently brought to her—be it a colonial armchair with carved teak frame and luxurious cushions covered in crushed velvet or a cardboard basin affair that the boys had built from a kit. She favoured the multi-use furniture that had come with the house: light-weight, wood-framed couches or easy chairs decked with red cushions stuffed with kapok, comfortably laid into laced sisal strapping. With the psychedelic 1970s sweeping out old-fashioned ways, however, Mrs. Hughes had recently acquired two stacks of green and brown plastic chairs from ZCBC [49]that could serve double duty as patio or living room furniture for just such a festive gathering of youths.

Pleased that the party venue had suitably taken shape, the worker bees moved purposefully into their choir practice, which played late into Saturday afternoon. People grew enthusiastic about both projects looming big and exciting for tomorrow—Easter service and party. They, despite inward uncertainties, were willing to let go and let God rather than fret; they found contentment to rest and reflect, prepare themselves—mentally, spiritually, and physically—for Sunday's zenith.

49 *ZCBC*: acronym for a high-end, local department store with Zambian ownership.

A courageous thought sprang to life from Orwell's brain: they should all go on the town Saturday night, and after a nice meal at Ridgeway Hotel, visit Evelyn Hone College to experience Easter from the radical point of view of *Jesus Christ Superstar*!

Alicia seemed intrigued—even liked the idea when, during a water break in their high-spirited, best-of-nine-games ping pong match, Orwell expressed his desire to watch the rock opera movie. She listened with intense interest, occasionally daring to smile as her flushed and sweaty opponent testified to how much he appreciated Rice and Lloyd Webber's modern take on the human side of Jesus: a man who struggled with religious hypocrisy, grew tired from healing so many blind and lame, taught a diverse bunch of promising—albeit sometimes dense—disciples, suffered under the rule of King Herod and Pontius Pilate, cared for his confused betrayer Judas, and most controversial of all, was loved by his comforter, Mary Magdalene.

The young poet went to great lengths to explain to his doe-eyed Christian girl that they would not actually see the Easter story re-enacted on stage or theatre screen, but rather, would watch maverick political pundits demonstrate against today's socioeconomic injustices. Alicia understood him, but then she got them both into hot water when she obediently sought her older and supposedly wiser sister's counsel. She was disappointed but not surprised when Kathleen, with tacit support from Mrs. Hughes, sternly vetoed the movie!

"Absolutely not! I abhor such vulgar depictions of our Saviour! They border on sacrilege!" growled Kitty-Cat as she sat on the couch. Her stern look returned, as a pleasant high tea with Mrs. Hughes and her daughters was grossly disturbed by Alicia's breathless intrusion and Orwell's shabby appearance looming behind her.

"The lyrics aren't evil, Kathleen—they speak to the heart and only make Jesus more human," protested Alicia, in an amazingly articulate effort. She wistfully looked to Orwell for support. "We believe in our heads that He is the Son of God, yet we ask with our hearts the age-old questions: *who* was our Lord, really? Why did He have to die? As mortal human beings, we can't understand God's divine plan, but we want to know what we should do, so as to be with our Creator always."

"*Jesus Christ Superstar* is a movie made by hippies strung out on drugs and into free love; it does not edify the sacred tenets of our Christian faith! Jesus rose from the dead; He is the Son of God! I will not go to this anti-Christian trash and neither shall you, Annie Fannie! That's final!"

"Orwell says that the filmmakers—cutting-edge and radical-thinking professors and their students from Evelyn Hone College right here in Lusaka, really want to reframe the story of Jesus as a study on current affairs—history, politics, economic development, geography of our mid-20th century world. They focus on civil rights, struggles against apartheid and colonialism, build-up of nuclear arms, meddling by Cold War super powers, unfair International Monetary Fund and exploitive plantations, sprawled by giant, multinational corporations in the Third World, and ensuring an equitable market place for all nations. Those topics really matter to both of us!"

"We viewed that controversial Norman Jewison flick in a downtown theatre last winter, against our parents' will, because Tracy took the church youth group there incognito! That got us into hot water with our parents and the church leaders, but Dad, in particular, was royally pee-ohed. You wouldn't believe all the debriefing and heavy lectures we *'rebellious tear-aways'* were subjected to, both through prayer counselling privately with Minister MacAlpine and public penitence in front of the shocked congregation. Tracy made an ass of himself, beaking off to justify our movie, but then he walked away unscathed, like it was a big joke!

"Left-wing religion shake-ups like *Jesus Christ Superstar* go against our family's deep-seated Christian moral values!" Kathleen explained with embarrassment to Mrs. Hughes and her intently listening daughters. She turned back to tongue-lash Alicia when she caught her smart-aleck junior sibling rolling her eyes and sighing belligerently at her, "Do you think for one minute, Fannie that you can mess around over here just because our parents aren't watching us? Dad'd give us both hard lickings if he found out we watched such smut again."

"Robert might, but then, he's a stone-age fanatic!"

"I told you not to lie about people behind their backs! Bearing false witness is a sin!"

"Mom and Dad would at least discuss the movie with us and listen to what we learned. You can't ban something unless you know what it's about," Alicia argued her case, whether or not her listeners judged her to be a sinner.

"This tempting devilry can simply pass us by—we have already seen the death and resurrection of Jesus re-enacted with dramatic style, but now it's time to stop acting like children and start working for our purpose in life. Fannie, don't you remember that we came to Africa on a mission? We are to present ourselves as holy and blameless before the Lord at all times, but especially if we are to honour Him during tomorrow's Easter church service, not to mention entertain a household full of *Oh-well*'s weird friends from the university!

"Don't get yourself all tired out again like last night, Fannie! You weren't exactly the sharpest tool in the shed this morning: sleeping in until ten o'clock like a spoiled princess when everyone else was up at seven for breakfast and doing all manner of household chores by eight. If I recall, you simply had to bathe and wash your hair before you could do anything useful."

"But then, I worked hard, for the rest of the day! Jesus taught that our Lord pays the same wages to those who labour for Him, whether they work all day in His vineyards or come onto the job late in the afternoon," reflected Alicia in rebuttal.

"What were you and Prince Charming doing in the living room at the crack of dawn?"

Kathleen smiled grimly at her sister, who blushed red as a beet and hung her head with shame in front of sombrely listening Mrs. Hughes and her daughters. Alicia gazed furtively at JJ, who shrugged her shoulders in a half-hearted attempt to look innocent of any betrayal. With a quick glance, Alicia begged Orwell to intervene.

"Alicia and I slept there instead of disturbing the rest of you at such a wee hour. We only danced a short while longer than you did, Kathy," Orwell admitted to their accuser, but then quickly reiterated, to convince her and the lolling crowd of their innocence, "Nothing bad happened—we were tired but restless, and needed to wind down from all the dancing. Okay, so we slept side by side, but in our underwear and under separate bedding, of course..."

"Of course," Kathleen chided him crossly. "You are a bad influence on my little sister, Oh-well. Should I watch you two like a hawk, to ensure that you stay on the straight and narrow?"

"You don't have to worry about us, Kathy," Orwell and Alicia asserted in unison. Orwell then surprised his partner in crime by courageously going further out on a limb for her. She smiled with pride as he turned tables on her autocratic sister, "And what about you and Rick? Do we question your motives, Kathleen, or spy on you guys like private eyes? I celebrate the deepening of your budding friendship! Obviously, you two seem to be in love...It must be a wonderful feeling, almost like being in Heaven!"

"We do fancy each other a lot—and we're going steady now. Down the road, we'll get married if everything works out," Kitty purred, her electric blue eyes growing soft. The blonde beauty smiled shyly as she divulged her special thoughts within earshot of her lover's siblings and his mother. Kitty seemed thankful that somebody—even if it was only this dolt—celebrated that she and Richard were a couple.

"Alicia and I, on the other hand, are just having a bit of holiday fun over here as friends—nothing more! So, give us a break, okay?" Orwell suffered to petition the powerful older sister of his intently listening pal, who seemed unmoved by their plight. Becoming increasingly uptight the more Kathleen smiled, smugly knowing at him, Orwell reasoned edgily, "Just because we want to have a movie date downtown doesn't mean that Alicia and I will be heavily kissing and petting, or getting our brains filled with worldly rubbish in some dark theatre. My idea was that we'd all go as a group to enjoy the movie together."

Kathleen stubbornly refused to budge on her position even if she relented about the impromptu living room sleepover. Mrs. Hughes backed her as did the Hughes daughters, who were exhausted after hours of housework and showed a blasé ambivalence at the idea of a movie night. Orwell and Alicia were soundly turned down as other plans for the evening, secretly made by the majority without their consultation, won out. As though on cue, Rick moseyed into the room from the wide blue yonder, all scrubbed, perfumed, and dressed in garish tourist garb; he grabbed a cupcake and reclined in a bean bag to eat it, seemingly oblivious to the recent hullabaloo. Mad at these square and narrow establishment types and inwardly blaming each other for their woes, Orwell and Alicia gloomily split and went their separate ways to sulk privately until supper time.

*****

LATER that evening, Orwell relaxed alone in his room, reading a good book while listening to the world news on his shortwave radio. His peace was short lived, however, as a hearty rap on the door heralded an exuberant invitation for him to come and play *Charades*. The young poet was torn; he craved his hard-won personal space for rest, relaxation, and spiritual renewal, yet was also feeling enticed by the sounds of laughter, singing, and clapping boisterously emanating from some distant part of the house. Orwell wanted to join the fun, but was squeamish about being the focus of the daughters of Eve who now jealously vied for his attention. In spite of his desire for a break from the challenge of being in their presence and his nagging thought that curiosity killed the cat, Orwell sighed as he laid down *Snows of Kilimanjaro* and sallied forth to partake in the silly parlour game. It was only after he opened his door to find nobody and blinked with confusion alone in the dark hallway that Orwell realized an entirely different kind of game was afoot!

Suddenly, a cackling, torch-wielding mob invaded his sanctuary from out of nowhere! He froze, blinded by a barrage of bright beams; two dark figures broke into his bedroom while two accomplices grabbed and quickly blindfolded him. He sensed light flashing and heard someone muttering about grabbing a mirror as they ransacked his room. A frantic urge to defend his turf was squelched when his captors plastered him face-first into a wall.

"Ow! Is this burglary a joke?" complained Hughes, knowing that something unfunny was up as he struggled haplessly to get free. "Just warning you thugs, I know judo, karate, and four other Chinese words!"

"Orwell, you are under arrest! No one will get hurt if you come quietly with us now to see your judge!" declared a deep, gruff voice near his ear. "Move it!"

The hands that spun him around and bandied him through the house were strong and firm. Hughes stopped fighting to bust out of their straightjacket grip as soon as he smelled Alicia's wild flowers perfume and heard JJ glibly whisper to him that all was well. He knew his life was safe among these allies who would not test him beyond his endurance, yet started to worry when his impish kidnappers bumped him rudely against furniture and sadistically rolled him down a staircase en route to some humiliating fate prepared just for him. Getting ominously closer, he could hear a rabble lustily chanting his name!

"Don't struggle. You shan't get away—we have ways to make you talk!" a female voice coarsely ordered this sweating, fidgeting blind man as she hovered stealthily beside him, guiding his close elbow with one rough hand while the other gripped his shoulder like a vice. "You are safe under our protection, right Sergeant Schultz?"

"I know nothing, Colonel Klink," huffed another voice—geez, Orwell chafed, this was a POW scene right out of *Hogan's Heroes*!

Someone clenched his right hand in hers and dragged him awkwardly forward as if the prisoner was a sack of bricks. Hughes sensed that they were trundling through the dining room and down into the living room where a jovial mob was now assembled and cheered their dramatic arrival. He heard others rushing past him, giggling under their breath as they carried what he could only imagine were props, while he was shunted against a wall none too gently by his escort. He believed his abductors were branching around him through the kitchen and entering the living room ahead of him, where they had laid some trap for him to stumble into. While he was the butt of their jokes, Alicia and JJ now gruffly pandered to him, to ensure that their victim arrived safely for his show trial.

"Stop here, Orwell!" Alicia the Warrior Girl commanded, as she firmly held him back, lest he fall over some precipice. "We're going to walk down these stairs now, to stand orderly in the judge's chambers. The lights are on. Everyone is watching you, so be a clever man, Orwell!"

He caught another whiff of Alicia's flowery scent as she embraced him, but she only applied pressure on his back to strategically direct him to stop, turn, or proceed, like she would firmly direct her horse by nudging its neck with leather reins. His fear of heights made him nervously imagine his worst nightmare: tip-toeing across Victoria Falls on a tightrope! Yet, because Alicia and JJ were calmly guiding him, the blindfolded prisoner trusted that they had brought a safety net to catch him, were he to fall into the foam. Tuning out the heckling audience, he gingerly inched forward with obedience to their life-saving direction.

"Carefully now, we wouldn't want to sprain an ankle or tumble into any sharp corner...Slide one foot over the step and plant it below, followed by the other. Easy does it...One step, two steps—one more step before we're done. Your feet are now on solid ground. Do you feel the cool breeze, hear the crackling hearth fire?" tenderly asked his smaller guard, as she held his trembling hand. "Good job, Orwell, you have arrived at the mercy seat."

"Bow before the judge now and kiss his ring. Lean forward in humble respect, mortal man!" Alicia grimly instructed him as the raucous gallery of spectators egged him on. "The court executioner is standing by, eager to punish any disobedience."

"Can I take my blindfold off?" cried the prisoner, flabbergasted by the wild hoots and handclapping of his audience. He had just kissed one fat and hairy ring finger! What did they see that he could not? What awful fate lay in store for him? Had he not already endured enough?

"Not yet," the bailiff tersely declared, while the jury giggled, so that the prisoner flinched nervously. "Listen to the judge while he passes sentence!"

"Orwell James Hughes, as punishment for reading a book in your bedroom instead of playing *Charades*, you must take an airplane ride to Zanzibar!" sombrely decreed the judge, from somewhere ahead of him. "I sentence you to five years transportation!"

"What, no trial? Where then shall I find this airplane, sir, since we are presently miles from Lusaka International Airport and night is upon us?" the convict despaired at his banishment in real bewilderment.

"Silence, boy!" thundered the bailiff indignantly. As someone clicked loudly into high gear a portable fan and several voices hummed like jet engines on cue, the judge tersely declared, "Your flying vehicle awaits you, sir, here in this courtroom. Bailiffs, escort the prisoner to his seat!"

Strong arms wrapped like grapple chains around Orwell where he stood and hoisted him onto a platform. Crudely setting him down like he was some heavy sack, other hands positioned his upon persons who flanked his platform. Orwell clung to these guardians in response to the judge's dismissive explanation. "These are your flight stewards, convict, who will guide you during your transcontinental journey. Obey them well and live. Goodbye, bon voyage. May God have mercy on your soul."

Although he understood that this drama was just an elaborate play, supposed to be fun and games, a dark foreboding now twanged at Orwell's heart as he recognized his father's calm voice dismissing him. As they separated, he longed to remove his blindfold and wave goodbye to his sire who had not really condemned him, he reminded himself...but he suddenly struggled just to keep his balance. As the jet lifted off, he felt his flight stewards rapidly falling away instead of serving him. Before long he couldn't even touch them, although he desperately stretched his long arms to their limit. The fan and hummed engine sounds grew in intensity and became powerful enough to bear him high above the ecstatic audience. Soon, only the ceiling hemmed him in! Was he dreaming or had the Rapture come? When his pilot calmly advised him that they had safely achieved maximum altitude and he could remove his seat belt for a while, the prisoner vividly imagined—nay, believed—that he had flown beyond confines of the house, broken free of all his troubles, and was now blissfully winging across East Africa.

"Orwell! One of our engines is on fire!" the pilot suddenly cried in alarm. "I can't hold the plane on course! We're losing altitude rapidly! We're going down!"

"What? Where am I? What can I do?" Orwell yelled, panic-stricken.

"Put on your parachute, open the cabin door, and jump out!"

"What parachute? Where is it?" demanded Hughes, clambering about, still blindfolded, in frantic search for his slim hope to escape from death. "I don't recall being issued a parachute. I don't even know how to use it, man!"

"Quickly now, but calmly. Put on that damn 'chute, Orwell," pleaded the pilot, sobbing now, so distraught was he with their predicament, "It's your only chance! Get ready, set, go!"

"Okay, thank you Lord" sighed Orwell breathlessly as he felt someone hand him a soft, bulky garment. "I'm coming home!"

"For the Love of Mike! The jet is burning; its fuel tanks will explode any second now...You must eject!"

In a death race against time, he tied the drawstring around his waist with flying fingers while the audience urged him on. With onlookers anxiously begging that he leap for his life, the reluctant skydiver flung open the cabin door and dove into thin air. He felt intense heat enveloping him, acrid smoke choking him, then was swept away by cool, refreshing air as he dropped into a free fall....

His ordeal lasted only a split second. Orwell was anxiously reaching behind his back to pull the ripcord when he landed hard on his feet on the tile floor. He hit and rolled to absorb the shock. He suddenly realized that he had only fallen a couple of inches and had neither left his living room nor beat this rollicking crowd who had been entertained by watching him making a total ass of himself!

Orwell stayed on the ground and played dead by rolling behind a couch, out of sight, out of mind. He refused to come out. His escape was foiled, however; pretending to care that he was alive, some of his tormentors rushed forward to revive him as nimble hands untied his blindfold. While he was still squinting against the limelight, a strong arm lifted him off the floor, then parked him into a soft chair. When he finally dared open his eyes, he saw Alicia kneeling before him, beaming with a mix of admiration and amusement as she offered this star actor a cold glass of water. The audience boisterously applauded his death-defying performance.

"You were magnificent, Orwell!" she exclaimed as she encouraged the frowning, mistrusting survivor to take a drink. "You really made us believe, true to life, man!"

"It was all very real to me," murmured Hughes glumly, as he stared into his water glass. "I felt like I truly was flying...feared that I would actually die in a fiery crash, like often in my dreams—is this water safe to drink?"

"What? Do you think I would poison you, Bucko?" demanded the amazon, perturbed by his childish insecurity. She leaned over him like a grumpy school teacher, eliciting incredulous laughter from the others as she followed his burrowing retreat deeper into the armchair. When Orwell flinched and paled, cowering in awareness that he had questioned her intentions, Alicia softened a tad, yet playfully assured him, "I brought that cool drink especially for you, my hero, straight from the water tap in the kitchen sink. See, no lipstick smudges on the glass, nor spit or floating cooties. I didn't even douse you with it, to shock you back into reality. I must care for the sick and injured, Oh-well!"

"Doctor, I believe you—I thank you from the bottom of my heart for this kindness," acknowledged Orwell humbly as he saluted his attendant made happy by him raising the glass in her honour before drinking deeply from it to quench his thirst.

Alicia stood and watched him critically, large hands on bountiful hips, as he drained her offering; only when he had finished was she convinced of her patient's stability, and went to take her own seat. Although Alicia sat across the room from him and conversed pleasantly with some Canuck strangers he vaguely recognized as having arrived at the airport on the same *Air Canada* flight, Orwell often felt her pensive gaze upon him during the rest of the social evening.

"I am totally befuddled that I only jumped a few inches off that plank," the young man, still confused, admitted aloud to anyone who would listen, although most by now had progressed from being his rowdy audience into chitchatting with one another on various sundry topics as they drank ice-chilled Cokes and munched on roasted ground nuts. His debacle was received as a vague afterthought as he interrupted someone's complaints about the quality of food and lodging at the hostel, "Seriously, I thought I was at least six feet up in the air. Did somebody levitate me?"

"Nobody hung you from the ceiling, silly boy," Kristi Stephenson, looking gorgeous in her white halter top and red-hot pants, scoffed from across the room, "You hardly left the ground. Maybe you were smoking a reefer in your room and took a trip without going anywhere..."

"I don't do drugs, Kristi, you know that. I was just taking a pleasurable reading break until I was so rudely interrupted!" Orwell protested, feeling the heat of Alicia's luminous, feline eyes stalking him again with concern. He then demanded to know, "Who were those pathetic airline stewardesses that were supposed to be escorting me to Zanzibar? I think they should get fired for deserting me!"

"I was one of them," chirped Suzanne, glibly raising her hand.

"I was the other and proud of it," declared feisty Kathleen. "Don't you get it yet, Orwell? Okay, child, let me explain. You placed your hands on our shoulders when you first stood on the plank, remember? Richard and Alicia stood at either end of the plank and lifted it all right, but you were raised less than a foot off the floor. They only confused and disoriented you. What made it seem like you were sent high in the air was that Suzy and I gradually squatted down."

"I guess I'll need to see that concept demonstrated with my eyes wide open before I can understand it. Physics isn't my strong suit—I'm a literature and African Studies buff," confessed Orwell, frowning as he struggled to get the gist of the apparently simple trick. "By the way, whose ring finger did I kiss?"

"Son, I was the appointed judge, although a totally fictitious and impotent one as you might have guessed," admitted Bwana Hughes, glancing at his namesake with a twinkle in his eyes.

"You didn't kiss Dad's finger, mind you," giggled JJ, pointing at her father's feet clad in knee-length socks and leather sandals. "He briefly went barefoot just for you...You paid homage to Dad's right-honourable big toe!"

"Ooh-la-la!" exclaimed Orwell, sparking a chuckle from multilingual Alicia with his crude outburst of French.

"Cheer up bro," dourly advised Richard. "At least these mullahs didn't have you chanting *Owa-tagoo-siam* like me when I was ordered to kneel down multiple times to kiss the judge's ring. I felt like some turkey about to get his head chopped off!"

"*C'est la vie!*" Kathleen dismissed this other crybaby with a wave of her hand. Then, springing to her feet as some bright-eyed feline with a winsome smile, she asked her boys to partake in yet another humiliating stunt to amuse the homesick Canadian newcomers. "Why don't you teach this smart college boy how to fly, Ricardo, since you're such a great pilot? How about it, Orwell? Want to take another jet trip? You can man the cockpit this time."

"I'll pass. I'm afraid of heights," mumbled the younger Hughes, nervously wise to her subtle wiles despite some goading from the other kids.

"No, no! You will be Captain this time, Orwell," insisted Kathleen, brimming with playful energy. "Come on now...if you learn this gag now, you'll have a gas trying it out on your African friends coming here tomorrow. It's just a harmless game! You can do it, Orwell, you're always the life of the party anyway!"

"Okay," sighed Hughes, taken in by Alicia smiling encouragingly behind her sister's back. "Ready for take-off, eh, bro!"

"That's the spirit!" cheered Kathleen, extending her elegant, long-nailed hand in congratulation. "Welcome aboard, mate!"

"So, do I get blindfolded, hogtied, and made to walk the plank again?" asked Orwell, ready now for any dangers she might throw at him. He glanced from Kathleen to Alicia, but these 'double trouble' sisters shrugged, seemingly confused by his worries, although they shared their low opinion of him through grins and winks they exchanged between them.

"None of the above," Kathleen schooled him. "No terrors this time—just go to your room and resume reading your novel, Captain James Kirk, until we call you to the bridge. Take your time, stretch out, drink some tea if you want..."

"Okay, fine. Call me when the jet is cleaned, fuelled up, and ready to go, eh Toby," playfully demanded Orwell, tossing his imaginary ignition keys to Rick before he clicked his heels and marched pompously away.

He fully expected Alicia to take this veiled invitation to follow him tightly as his self-appointed jail guard, but pouted from the hallway alone, instead to observe how smartly the sharp young lady stayed in her place as though she had suddenly found more important things to do than study him. Dressed nicely in a white cotton blouse and a beige *chitenge*[50] print wrap around skirt emblazoned with red flowers, her vibrant auburn hair well-coiffed, Alicia helped Suzanne and

50 *Chitenge* or *kitenge*: African fabric similar to sarong, often worn by women and wrapped around the waist or chest, over the head as a scarf or used as baby sling but was also worn as dresses, blouses or pants by expatriate women or men interested in the colourful local fashion. It is an inexpensive, informal piece of clothing that is often decorated with a huge variety of vibrant colours and patterns. The wax printings on the cloth was done by a traditional batik technique but in modern times is commercially prepared using rollers, such that designs may be less colourful on the observe side than previously.

JJ pass out snacks and pour tea for their parents' guests; she worked dutifully alongside Richard and Kathleen to prepare the room for the next game. Did Alicia not care that he was alone and vulnerable, in need of her support? Did she think he was some hardened veteran who must walk this lonesome valley by himself? Maybe she already had her eye on some new boy in the room—perhaps tall, dark, and handsome Chad who now grazed from the tray of sweets she was passing around. Alicia knew what awaited Orwell, yet she was entirely willing to leave him alone, with no sign of concern, totally trusting he would stay away until he was called....

A soft tap on his door, followed by a polite announcement from JJ that his jet was ready, brought Captain Orwell jauntily back on stage. He looked refreshed and at peace with the world as he sauntered into the room. As he strode between those seated to watch the show, people turned their heads with interest and applauded his arrival. Spotting new faces in the audience who had arrived during his brief hiatus, young Hughes nodded to each one in pleasant welcome like some savvy diplomat. His father smiled in glib approval.

"Hey, Orwell! Have a good trip!" Kristi heckled when he stumbled over her extended foot as he walked past his clever nemesis perched between two other platinum-blonde cuties—Karlee Bryant and Brandi Saunders—on a front-row couch.

"Yeah, last fall!" Orwell joked back, eliciting a gush of laughter from the three Barbie dolls.

His snappy one-liner seemed to hush Kristi, who had been rudely gossiping about him with her new friends, as Orwell straightened up and made his way to where the troupe of young actors was reassembling on stage. He blushed at the scintillating sight of these trendy girls looking peachy-keen in their hot, matching outfits; Karlee and Brandi, like their leader Kristi, were also lithe and tanned, which was surprising for being less than a week in the subtropics! The trio seemed too plastic to be real, except Karlee, who playfully grabbed the hem of Orwell's pant leg as he padded away. He whirled around and was met by her broad grin.

"Orwell, you're a swell actor!" applauded Karlee, her blue eyes twinkling with interest as she extended a hand to greet the gentle giant as best as she could. Unable to reach him and stay seated, the pretty pipsqueak giggled as she bounced to her feet to earnestly clasp his hand in friendship.

Orwell noted that Karla Eve was shapely, yet trim in all the right places, but he was also impressed by her energy and strong grip from such a short girl—her hands warmly wrapped around his own, which he prided to be as firm as iron from all his physical work and athletic feats. Orwell found no pen to write his autograph for the grinning Mighty Mouse, so he suavely drawled, "Thanks! I'm glad you're enjoying the show!"

"I know your airplane crash was a gag, but you played it so real," Karlee opined appreciatively. "I loved your great performance at the Ash Wednesday gig at the Anglican Church. It got me in the good mood to stay awhile in Zambia—at least long enough to enjoy Easter here."

"I am glad," replied Orwell, pleasantly taken aback by the pixie's kudos.

He would have chatted more with his upbeat fan, but was abruptly swept away and escorted on stage by Suzy and Kathy, who had grown tired of motioning to him to play his part in their act. Suzy glared back at Kristi when she smirked at her—obviously, there was no love lost between *those* two....

Girls were weird, conniving little foxes, thought Orwell to himself! Karlee smiled when he picked her out of the attentive crowd, but maybe she was just being nice to him now because she desperately needed his help to pass Grade Thirteen English. Yet, maybe Karlee was a Christian—had he not seen a cross dangling daintily from her necklace? She seemed different, a cut above the general female population—like Alicia for instance who, instead of berating his meet and greet style, politely noted that the would-be captain had combed his hair and donned a clean shirt during the intermission. Alicia waved to him from where she stood at attention, holding up a blanket with JJ beside Orwell's wall mirror, now propped vertically at the back of the room. Capturing his every movement and expression, the mirror reflected a confident, handsome young man riding on the cusp of a high adventure, where all the world delighted in him. The two blanket girls smiled approvingly as their willing 'victim' approached pleasantly, but what awful secrets did they know about his fate, he wondered as Suzy ushered him into a chair in front of them?

Kathleen strolled towards him on cue with sure steps of a topflight airline stewardess preparing to serve her captain before he flew their jet. Enraptured by Kitty-Cat's beauty and grace, Orwell barely heard the emcee as she richly purred, "Good evening, sir, and welcome aboard. I hope you feel comfortable?"

"Oh yes, I most certainly am."

"Excellent. Just make yourself at home. Can I get you anything?"

"Some peanuts would be nice, and a bottle of Schweppes's orange, if you don't mind."

Orwell played along although he was well aware that Kathy's sweetness could turn rancid at any time; he should not expect such favours in his wildest dreams from a spoiled, haughty brat like her! Expecting a slap, he was pleasantly surprised when Suzy, with but a sultry wink from Her Highness, crisply produced just such goodies for him on a serving tray. Orwell almost blushed for having thought so poorly of Kathleen; his discomfort with such pampering from pretty girls was caught in the mirror and observed with amusement by Alicia and JJ. He failed to see that Suzy had ducked behind the blanket.

The living screen the two girls were holding jovially shuffled over a foot to the right of the mirror to partially reveal a bulky, bespectacled oldster who, his face partially hidden beneath a huge floppy hat, was hunched over in a chair opposite the captain. Because this strange individual was sitting tightly against yet somewhat behind the mirror, Orwell could only see half of him, but oddly enough, caught the rest of him as a mirror image in the glass. Startled by the illusion, Orwell gave his head a shake. It must be all smoke and mirrors!

"Now, Captain, can you tell me who this person is?"

"I can't place him," acknowledged Hughes after a lengthy assessment. "Is he perchance our neighbour, Senhor Rodriguez flying to Portugal, or one of the new hires to the Canadian mission in Zambia?"

The rollicking crowd guffawed at Orwell's humorous acknowledgement, but not everyone was amused.

"Well, I declare!" chafed Mildred in a huff to Charlotte and Barbara, her red-faced couch mates who were equally appalled that the son of their host should characterize them so poorly. She glared at Orwell with mad, owlish eyes as she munched hard on her peanuts. "That boy has seen too much sun of late!"

"I don't think he means ill to any of us, dear," offered Dr. Jones, Mildred's patient husband, with a wry smile. "These kids are just trying to make us feel at home whilst we settle into our new stations. They were probably recruited on short notice into doing this play as comedy relief by Sir James when we showed up at his abode, bored, homesick, but unannounced at Easter. James and Martha are kind to us...They've got decent—and funny—children, compared to those spoiled, me-generation types we left back in Ontario!"

"Angela and Gabriel know how to behave in public, Robert," Mildred sternly reminded him. She clucked to her girlfriends, "Our children might have come down here with us, had Zambia's educational system been more suitable."

Orwell, outwardly ignored such nattering, let it flow like water off a duck's back. He was, however, inwardly pee-ohed by the disparaging comments he heard around him, yet what else could he do but lead by example as he slogged through his own tribulations? How little Mrs. Jones or her friends really knew about his personal situation, although he had heard them loudly complain, several times already since just arriving in Zambia...So far, they were determined to evangelize, modernize, or somehow 'fix' their African hosts, but these discontented Canadian women had not yet taken the time to learn anything about Zambians, nor did they want to. He hoped newcomers would talk to him again in more positive reflection after they were further into their service terms, that is, if they were able to survive so long! Without the comforts from home, three years could become an eternity! Oh well, back to the show!

"Is this person one of my learned university professors dropped in to wish me well during our special religious festivity?" asked Orwell pointedly.

"No, but he is a visitor, I will grant you that," explained the MC, moving the play along. "He came to your father's door while you were resting, drawn by our cheer, claiming to be stranded in town tonight after all commercial jetliners were suddenly grounded—I believe, he said, by loss of runway lights due to a power outage at the airport."

"Okay, such problems can happen, but they are temporary inconveniences that can be rectified by morning. What can I do to help?"

"I believe, Captain Orwell, that you could give this poor fellow a private flight to the Copperbelt. Are you not an experienced commercial pilot?"

"I've never been at the controls of any flying machine. You're talking to the wrong guy, lady—my brother Richard is the man you want."

"Rick is busy with another engagement and unavailable for such a mercy flight, but he assured me himself that you are a cinch for the job, because you are a better pilot than him."

"Rick said what? He's nuts."

"No, it's well documented that you, Captain Orwell, have plenty of wind beneath your wings. I've been assured from well-informed sources, and do now believe that you could lift this traveller right out of here with just a little puff of air."

"I don't have a clue what you're talking about," admitted Hughes cautiously, troubled by where the conversation was leading.

"Why, Orwell, don't be so modest! You're a fabulous bass singer. You can debate vigorously and drone for hours on any topic without ever stopping to breathe. I have seen first-hand your many acting accomplishments and how deftly you can project your voice. Let's not forget that you have blown up many balloons for your siblings' birthday celebrations over the years. I deduce that you have strong enough lungs to blow this little old man right off his rocker!"

"What do singing, public speaking, or inflating balloons have to do with flying a jetliner?"

"Let's find out! Captain Orwell, try to blow this guy away! Come on now, it's easier than dunking someone in a tank by throwing a baseball at a target, or driving a metal bar up a pole with a sledge hammer at Klondike Days. Just blast him with some of your hot air!"

"Okay, I get the picture," muttered Orwell darkly. "This is one of the dumbest things I have been asked to do, but I will indulge you."

He glanced at the crooked old man in the chair who stared anxiously back at him as Orwell stood up, took a deep breath, and exhaled loudly in his direction. To Orwell's amazement, the man's spectacles fluttered precariously on the bridge of his nose, then disappeared abruptly from view. Had the mirror turned magical and swallowed them up? The man blinked curiously at him like a mole coming into the light and seeing Orwell for the first time. The ridiculous saucer-sized, horn-rimmed spectacles looked as cheap as if it had come from a cereal box or some x-ray vision ad by *ACME Novelties* in the back of comic books. Both characters shuddered at the sound of glass tinkling as it hit the floor behind the blanket. Some folks in the audience, likening the accident to a waitress dropping dishes in a restaurant, clapped with congratulation, but Alicia and JJ grinned sheepishly, and the show went on.

"That was a feeble effort at best, Captain Orwell," Kathleen chastised. "You must help this poor gentleman with much more consideration if you expect to do anything useful for his journey! Try again please, but blow with more purpose, more intensity!"

"All right, here goes nothing," replied Hughes in gritty obedience. Gesturing to the traveller, who followed his every move with fear and trepidation, Orwell declared, "A gale is coming, so hang onto your seats folks—except you that is, my stranded friend!"

Orwell inhaled deeply once again and blasted the guy trembling in front of him. This time, the fellow's black walrus moustache took wing. Hughes, not to mention many in the audience, appeared stunned by such an escape. The stranger, flushed now, rubbed his face in pain.

"We'll lessen our friend's load blow by blow, so that eventually he must lift off because he has become lighter than air," offered Kathleen sarcastically, drawing snickers from the crowd. "Try again, Captain and please, do it like you mean it this time!"

With grim determination, Orwell put his full effort into the ridiculous task. He gulped in so much air that he looked like a bull frog about to croak love tomes to his mate. Then he leaped off his own chair and bellowed out his entire payload upon the seated victim. He gazed incredulously as the man's huge cowboy hat lifted off, passed behind the blanket, and rolled into the corner of the room like a tumble weed. The traveller grinned defiantly at Hughes as he clung to his seat. Orwell was red-faced and trembling near exhaustion, not to mention becoming very dizzy, as he staggered back and slumped into his own chair.

"Is that the best you can do—for a lady?" taunted Kathleen, unimpressed. "Why, the *Big Bad Wolf* could blow down houses of straw and sticks, and my own father has the faith to move mountains. Can you not succeed at this little task?"

Orwell recoiled at her critical lash, but spurred by the smug grin on Richard's face, whom he now recognized lounging pompously before him and refusing to accept failure, the blowhard girded his loins for a final attempt. As he charged forward to release one more volley of fierce wind and weather upon his brother, Orwell declared to him, "You're a goner, man!"

Orwell blew hard and long, urged on by all who witnessed his efforts. In an abrupt departure from Aesop's fable, *The Sun and the Wind*, Richard responded to the tempest. Firstly, his heavy cloak was peeled off and tossed into the lap of flabbergasted Dr. Jones. Then, his sandals went running down the hallway. Richard, now unable to hold onto his seat as it tumbled away, let the gale blow over him as he sank to his knees and shielded his head with his arms, but the smooth wooden floor tiles afforded him no protection. Succumbing to the fierce elements, Richard bravely began to flap his arms and kick out his long legs into the whistling current. Soon, he was flat out flying!

"You did it, Captain Orwell!" cheered Kathleen as Richard happily flew in place above his tipped over chair. "Our guest is on his way!"

Orwell, confused by the amazing flight of his brother and totally spent in his fierce efforts to make the impossible feat seem possible, shook his head as he collapsed with exhaustion, dizziness, embarrassment, and amusement on the floor. The dumbfounded audience responded with good-natured applause. When the wind died away, so did Richard comfortably come taxiing in to roost. He and Kathleen both hustled now to tend to Orwell; finding the lad safe and sound, they lifted him up and twirled him around to show him off as the tired but beaming star of this little pantomime. Alicia, Suzanne, and JJ dropped their blanket and stepped away from the mirror to join the cast in a group bow, where all received more kudos and accolades from the bubbly families they had entertained over snacks and soft drinks.

Performance done, the young people of Hughes House packed up their props and streamed from the living room followed by teenagers they had just entertained, who left parents chatting about schools, cars, and houses in the living room and mingled with their peers in the kitchen. Putting their own skit debrief aside, Orwell and Richard passed out soft drinks, while Alicia and JJ shared assorted fruit slices and roasted groundnuts, breaking ice with their curious visitors. Soon, youngsters from near and far enthusiastically chatted in their lingo about interesting topics they found in common: high school dating, rock bands, sports, movie stars, television, and the latest fads and fashions.

"Robert Redford and Paul Newman are so-o-o handsome!" cooed Kathleen, folding her hands together under her chin enthralled for the bevy of women gathered excitedly around her. She tossed her golden mane and fluttered her brilliant eyes at the young men ringing the room as she regaled everyone with air of a learned movie critic, "Redford and Newman starred together a few years ago in *Butch Cassidy and the Sundance Kid,* a great western movie about bank and train robbers! Just last year, they played *The Sting,* a story about con men who pulled a big heist in Chicago during the 1930s. Classic, man! "The Entertainer", the theme song for this crime movie, became a hit unto itself—it's totally more popular than the movie."

She began to hum a few lilting bars from Scott Joplin's ragtime score, and to the amazement of the wide-eyed Hughes children, was eagerly joined by others in the room. Orwell and his siblings lapped up odd colloquialisms, humour, and cultural trivia of these jet-set guests.

"I can play "The Entertainer" on the piano, Orwell," Alicia proudly informed her hero as she stood beside him while he soaked up the buzz of conversation. "Before I leave Zambia, I'll play that jaunty piece for you."

"That'd be great! I'd like to learn such popular music from a professional," Orwell welcomed her sweet offer. He blushed shyly in the radiance of Alicia's broad smile.

Orwell humbly accepted that, for a few minutes tonight, he was front and centre of the young people's powwow, being the Africanized son of Bwana Hughes as well as the star of some silly impromptu skits. Alicia was his patiently enduring friend; yet, neither he nor his fellow shy participant wanted their affection broadcast to random visitors. Karla Eve, jauntily perched on a counter to see better and study merriment more than she participated, caught on quickly that something special flowed between Orwell and Alicia. This intuitive observer turned glum when Kathleen, who thrived on celebrity status, yet seemed envious of Orwell's fifteen minutes of fame, shone her spotlight far down the line to ensure that everyone saw how this shy couple liked each other. How could Kathy even hear their obscure exchange above the din of exuberant chatter? Why did she care what Alicia and Orwell were saying to each other?

"You're always buttering up my sister...Don't act so hapless, Oh-well! Our Fannie is a raw talent who is still learning her notes; she generally plays back-up for me when we go on tour," gloated Kathleen. She leered at her now-embarrassed sister, and emboldened by her power play, bragged to others she thought listened breathlessly to her fount of entertainment knowledge, "Just ask me—I'm the one to sing and play for you when you need a professional musician!"

"Like wow, Kathy, you really rock as an emcee!" As though sweetening the discord, a lanky, shaggy-haired guy, basking like a lizard on the arborite countertop, toasted the gorgeous entertainer with a wave that seemed in keeping with his dozy voice. "You ought to perform on the *Ed Sullivan Show*."

"What's *your* name?" Kathleen demanded, feeling mocked by this pimple-faced hippie kid.

"Uh, Josh Roberts, ma'am—just call me Josh Rocket! Can I, like, have your autograph, Miss MacDonachie?"

"Later, Rocket Man," Kitty told her fan to cool his jets, "You've done *Charades* before?"

"Like, yeah," Brandi Saunders, Charlotte's daughter, affirmed the obvious when others laughed at what they thought was a joke.

"Kitty-Cat thinks she's still playing emcee," Orwell sighed in frustration to Alicia, who intuitively caught his drift, despite staring at the floor with glazed eyes.

"You're lead singer all right Kit, but Alicia plays accordion like Gaby Haas! What's more, she can bow the fiddle like Don Messer," pitched Orwell to defend his friend's artistic talents, but became worried when everyone gazed at him with clueless looks. Orwell made a comical bid to explain himself, lest these new kids think he was gonzo, "Those guys are Canadian music icons, like maple syrup and hockey—they had their own radio and television shows in the Sixties!"

"Never heard of such dudes," chirped Rocket Man, "They lost in space?"

Some listeners tittered, wondering if Orwell was out of touch, but Karlee laughed richly, amused by his dithering efforts to convince everybody of the validity of his reality; they must be close in age and interests, she quipped, remembering both musicians he trotted out. Karlee added her touch to Orwell's scene by suddenly hopping off the counter, but she stumbled as soon as her bare feet—delicately adorned with turquoise toenails—slipped on the tile floor! Orwell chivalrously rushed to Karlee's aid and caught her before she did a lip stand, for which the bewildered girl gave him a broad grin of appreciation. No fluff bunny this one—she was solid state!

"Heading out?" Orwell inquired.

He jested with Miss Bryant, recalling their earlier joke when he was tripped en route to the stage—like break a leg, man! Orwell chagrinned that he had embarrassed his new friend when Karlee giggled nervously, then sauntered around the kitchen humming Elton John's "Crocodile Rock" until she found a cup. She passed the sink, but did not pour a drink of water. Parading in tight red shorts, taking the scenic route, she smugly advertised her attractive bottom for every young man to drool over; Karla Eve was richly endowed for a short, white girl—a miniature Alicia, in fact! Orwell too feasted his eyes upon Karlee, amazed at how provocatively round and bouncy her bum cheeks were…for which she gave the erotic lad a sassy grin in passing. Returning to her perch, Karlee brazenly lit a cigarette, and used Mrs. Hughes' fine china cup as an ashtray!

Kristi gravitated to her new pal to share the cup as they smoked Zambia's finest tobacco and exhaled acrid blue clouds like cool kittens as the beat went on! Even if others around them had watery eyes or coughed on cigarette smoke, they dug this scene! It was, like, a 'laugh in'....

Orwell, however, was totally unimpressed by such rude behaviour! Kristi was being every bit the snobby bitch he expected her to be, but if Karla Eve thought she would gain brownie points with him by smudging his mother's spotless, Lysol-scented kitchen—especially after he had rescued her from falling in front of tons of her peers—this brassy girl had another think coming!

Stickler Orwell inwardly considered dousing Kristi and Karlee and hauling them back to the remote guesthouse for hard spankings, but the high-class MacDonachie sisters—pouting over how he had abandoned them to help a nothing girl like Karlee, joshingly ganged up on their fuming host: Kathleen murmured that he must have been watching black and white TV, not Technicolor, prior to coming to Africa, while Alicia insisted that she played the violin in youth orchestras, but *used* the fiddle in hoedowns. Orwell should chill out, forget Karlee, and remember who buttered his bread!

"I thought all child stars were born playing the piano, like Mozart," remarked Boyd Walker, a blonde youth dressed in blue jeans and a purple, tie-died shirt bearing the circular peace symbol that reminded woefully out of touch Orwell of a Mercedes Benz hood ornament.

Ignoring Boyd's off-beat comment and Orwell's baleful scrutiny, the Barbie girls chattered gaily to themselves about celebrities, fashion, and music in their trendy, tightly-knit clique. Their lingo was high-speed, shallow gibberish to many youths who thus quickly tuned out and turned onto real topics with others—but not Orwell. The bright trio seemed glad to be funky but annoying to him, as Orwell listened intently, with genuine interest—having learned African languages and pidgin English. He found their alien act fascinating. These haughty dames initially painted his undo attention as harassment, but they—Karlee in particular—were encouraged to banter with increased enthusiasm, energy, and laughter to entertain but not directly engage him, the more he paid them heed. As best Orwell could decipher, the Barbies' conversation went like this:

"Paul Newman has these beautiful blue eyes and winsome grin that melt a girl's heart."

"Robert Redford's brutal honesty, his dashing smile, brown eyes, tousled reddish-blond hair and sideburns, as well as his strength of body and character all came through in his love story with Barbara Streisand in *The Way We Were*. I liked their romance better than Ryan O'Neal and Ali McGraw's *Love Story*."

"Ryan and his daughter Tatum recently made a groovy flick in *Paper Moon,*" Karlee added, but then feeling Orwell's inquisitive gaze still upon her, turned her golden head around and spoke slowly to include the hovering lad and his sisters in her commentary. "It's a real tear jerker, Suzy and JJ, about these petty, Depression-era crooks. Tatum won an Academy Award as best supporting actress just this month for her performance—the youngest winner ever! Imagine, a ten-year old girl strolling amongst glamorous, talented women like Faye Dunaway, Shirley MacLaine, and Barbara Streisand! Can you believe it?"

"I thought *American Graffiti* was pretty cool, with hot-rods and beat tunes from the early Sixties," responded Boyd, still trying to make inroads. Like Orwell, he dug rock 'n' roll from beach parties and saxophone clubs more than the hard rock, acid rock, and heavy metal now pounding and screeching through the airwaves. Kristi and Brandi took no interest in his peripheral nattering, but Karlee seemed intrigued when, suddenly, Boyd broke Orwell's trance by asking him, "Like, dude, where were you in '62?"

"I was an eight-year-old boy, playing pirates or explorers on the river bank in a little fairytale village nestled among the poplar trees below the main town of Beverly, a hard-knocks place by comparison, built on coal mines, stockyards, and a garbage dump at the eastern outskirts of Edmonton," Hughes waxed lyrical.

"Where the heck is that?" demanded Boyd, who hailed from Toronto, centre of the Canadian universe. Suzanne and Richard also looked at their brother with dumb faces.

"I know," asserted Alicia, a mystery woman from Planet X for the Barbies, who looked askance at her in unison. Paying these manikins no heed, she proudly addressed Orwell, "I used to play on that riverbank with you ragamuffin Hughes kids, like I was one of you. It was fun... always an adventure! We scurried up storm sewers, collected fall leaves and driftwood, ate saskatoon berries and hazelnuts, and played plenty of snowball fights...Orwell showed me all the trophies he had gleaned from old cars strewn about the dump—radios, steering wheels, mirrors...We were all tomboys back then!"

She gave Orwell's calloused hand a squeeze in a show of affectionate solidarity. Then, changing the subject to take the focus away from Orwell, whom she knew was awkward with limelight, the youngest daughter of Reverend Wynnard MacDonachie testified about her Christian faith to the vaguely polite onlookers, "I loved both *Godspell* and *Jesus Christ Superstar*. They're plausible, albeit modern hippie musical versions of my Lord and Saviour's Biblical ministry. They show Jesus healing the sick and preaching the gospel, arguing with temple authorities, and breaking bread with his disciples in the upper room. *Godspell* is an urban legend, set amid the modern hustle and bustle of Gotham City, with its street gangs and hookers, cops and shopkeepers, rich white guys, preppy types, and poor people. The songs "Prepare Ye the Way of the Lord" and "Day By Day" really grabbed me! In *Superstar*, Jesus was brought as a prisoner by squeaky Annas and growling Caiaphas before long-nosed snob Pontius Pilate, and King Herod—he of the funky yellow glasses—and a bunch of powder-faced male dancers, no less!"

Alicia's cutting disapproval of the villainous clergy, queer Herod, and pompous Pontius Pilate, drew laughter from her audience, but then she brought her glib listeners crisply to heel as she steadfastly continued, "Jesus was crucified—no doubt! I did not see Him rise from the dead, although I believe with my whole heart that He died and was resurrected to save you and me. He touched many broken people; so many hurt and lost people craved His healing, cleansing touch and insightful teachings. Jesus certainly confused Judas Iscariot, a black man, who betrayed Him, but later committed suicide once he realized what a horrible thing he had done.

"Jesus is God, yet I saw all His suffering and struggles endured as a man. How his care for the poor and needy weighed Him down! He loved and was loved by Mary Magdalene, his closest friend. Whether she was a reformed prostitute from whom He had cast seven devils or a wealthy older woman who funded his ministry doesn't matter! Jesus allowed this cleansed believer of beautiful spirit to soothe and caress Him when he was tired, give him drink and food when He was thirsty and hungry. He needed her healing care. Mary ministered to Jesus and went on to be a mighty evangelist in her own right, after His resurrection."

JJ and Karlee were touched by Alicia's fervent testimony, but most of the other youth wondered where she was coming from or going with her proselytizing.

"I bet," muttered Rick, darkly amused. Sensing a general discomfort if not a disconnect in the room a bible-thumper who wore religion on her sleeve, this elder got everyone real again by playing devil's advocate, "I suppose *Jesus Christ*

*Superstar* was an antidote for folks who got messed up by *The Exorcist* and *The Godfather*. *Those* were five-star movies!"

Moving on, Rick snazzily asked the group, "What the hell has James Bond been doing lately? Anyone seen my hero in action? Is a new movie coming out?"

"In 1971, Sean Connery starred in *Diamonds Are Forever*, his last film as Double O Seven," informed a blonde, smiling youth who towered over Richard. He introduced himself as John Bryant, twin brother of Jim Bryant lounging yonder, draped over the ice box and breaking out more pops for everyone. How, Orwell wondered, could these giants be pipsqueak Karlee's younger brothers—or siblings at all? Ignoring him, John chattered on, "After Ernst Blofeld killed Tracy, Bond's lady love in his previous mission, *On Her Majesty's Secret Service,* 007 tracked his arch-enemy to Egypt in *Diamonds Are Forever* to avenge Tracy's death, and watched him die in a boiling mud pool—only Blofeld didn't die!

"This baddie created doubles of himself to confuse Bond, employed assassins to kill some diamond smugglers—like the crooked dentist working in a South African diamond mine who had a poisonous scorpion dropped down his shirt—and schemed to acquire enough diamonds to arm a satellite with a laser death ray capable of burning any target on earth! A smuggling ring supplied diamonds to a reclusive billionaire tycoon, only Blofeld held the tycoon captive, so he could use his high-tech company to build the super weapon...Are you laughing at me, Richard?"

"I just realized that Tracy was a *woman* in that flick. Orwell, did you hear that? *Tracy* was James Bond's girlfriend!" Richard roared with laughter.

""A Boy Named Sue"!" retorted Orwell, unintentionally provoking an exasperated, crossed-armed gesture from his sister Suzanne. Orwell dryly explained in his deep base voice to those who were clueless about the real Tracy, "As Johnny Cash sings, the boy's daddy named him Sue to make him grow up fighting for himself or die, 'cuz deadbeat Dad couldn't be there to raise Sue.

"I don't know whether Tracy MacDonachie can be explained as succinctly, but he's certainly more of a man than any of us boys here. Surely, you've heard about Tracy's title fight coming here next month, right here in Lusaka—it's the main event, man! If he was here tonight, like he was supposed to be, I'd be thrilled to introduce my best friend to you all. He's a boxing champion, yet so much more!"

"And," Alicia reminded, as she gestured to herself and Kathleen with sweeping pride for all to know, "Tracy is our best big brother, a married father to three strapping boys!"

"That means nothing nowadays! Tiptoe, his daddy called him! Tracy's a fake, and I doubt if he has the balls to ever show up here in Africa!" teased Richard, his neck proudly red as he played his glaring brother like sport fish hooked on a line. Orwell gasped for air in his desperate search for rebuttal.

The young strangers mingling in the room had never heard of The *MacDonachie Family Singers,* much less of *'Iron Horse'* the boxer, sportsman, singer, or adventurer. Orwell grimly debunked such ignorance in his heart as grossly un-Canadian, yet resolved to be patient with these fresh-off-the-jet newbies, who were now green students, but upon graduation from African Studies 101, might possibly become his peers. A polite lot, still wet behind the ears in their exotic surroundings and eager to bond with a veteran like himself, they were blissfully ignorant of the intrigues swirling about the Hughes household, especially those involving its celebrity guests.

"Moving right along," suggested Alicia sternly to the embattled Hughes boys, sweeping their squabble under the carpet with an invisible broom lest it envelope her.

"Yes, next," concurred Kathleen, giving Richard the evil eye.

Turning back to the Bryant twins, Rick suavely resumed their conversation, "I believe we were discussing Bond...James Bond. What kind of high-tech weapons did 007 use in *Diamonds Are Forever*?"

"Bond escaped across the Nevada desert in a moon buggy. Later, he was dropped, trapped inside a geodesic dome, into the ocean from an airplane. He walked on water inside this floating capsule towards Blofeld's oil-rig hideout, and actually stepped aboard after unzipping the capsule's plastic outer skin. Bond hijacked Blofeld's Bath-O-Sub and used it to disable the satellite death ray.

"In *Live and Let Die,* which came out last year, a new super villain named Dr. Kananga was introduced; he plotted to flood the USA with heroin grown on some Caribbean island that he ruled as a dictator. Roger Moore, who is now playing James Bond, battled against sharks and alligators, voodoo priests, a claw-armed thug, a corrupt CIA agent, and a clairvoyant named Solitaire. She later became Bond's lover, whom he rescued from being sacrificed by Dr. Kananga to a poisonous snake. James Bond eventually killed Dr. Kananga by blowing him up with a compressed air bullet he had forced into his enemy's mouth during an underwater fight in a shark tank. This M16 counter espionage mission featured a speed boat chase through the Louisiana bayous, an inflatable sofa, and Bond's magnetic wristwatch with a built-in buzz saw."

"Thanks John, that's my type of show!" concluded Richard, shaking the pitchman's hand with relish. "I look forward to *The Man with the Golden Gun,* due out later this year. We'll be back home in Canada by then to see it in a theatre."

"I'm Jim, he's John."

"Okay, Jim/John, now I'm confused. You got me. You guys should get into motion pictures, the circus, or some travelling exhibition," joked Rick, pointing good-naturedly at the identical twins with his gun finger. "Heck, people even mix up Orwell and me. Imagine that—but, with you guys, it's *The Twilight Zone* all over again!"

"Just remember, I'm the movie buff, but my bro is the television junkie. Ask John anything you want to know about shows playing on the tube—like, anything, man", dared Jim, baiting Richard with an intense grin.

"Okay John, which shows have the highest TV ratings right now?"

"I'm Jim."

"Yeah, I know. Boring...Just speak into the mike, John/Jim."

"*Hawaii 5-0* and *Kojak* are swell cop shows—tough and realistic!"

"As for 'quality' television shows," chirped in Brandi, snapping her fingers for emphasis, "We've got *The Brady Bunch,* the story of a widower with three boys who marries a widow with three girls; and *The Partridge Family,* where the entire family has their own groovy rock band. Keith, the oldest son, is totally dreamy, flashing his pearly whites every time he smiles—Keith's played by a *bona fide* singer/songwriter named David Cassidy."

"My mom likes the *Mary Tyler Moore Show,* about a recently divorced career woman, and soap operas: *All My Children* being the newest one. Dad watches comedy shows like *MASH,* about some US military bush hospital during the Korean War, and *All in the Family,* featuring a blue collar, loudmouthed bigot named Archie Bunker," added Karlee, smiling at intrigued Orwell.

"Sounds like a gas," deadpanned Richard, who knew none of these boring sitcoms, and was saddened to hear that his favourite espionage show, *Mission Impossible,* had recently been taken off air. He chuckled gloomily, "I guess now that Americans have walked on the moon, we won't watch science fiction marvels like *Star Trek, Voyage to the Bottom of the Sea,* and *The Outer Limits*—or even those kiddie sci-fi weeklies *Lost in Space* and *Dr. Who*—no more! At least *Bugs Bunny* and *Pink Panther* cartoons are still televised on Saturday mornings."

"How about *Sesame Street*?" offered one of the grinning Bryant twins.

"What?" interrupted JJ, appearing to be either deaf, totally out of touch, or just a royal pain in the butt. She broached the tall, gangly youth, "You mean, *Open Says-a-me*?"

"Like...me want a cookie!" rasped Josh Rocket, emulating Cookie Monster as he lifted three ginger snaps off a communal biscuit plate and shoved them in his mouth.

"Say what?" quizzed Bryant twin number one. The first newcomer to recall her real name, he kindly explained, "Janice Joanne, it's that Jim Henson puppet show from New York City for toddlers: you know, with Big Bird, Count Dracula, Kermit the Frog..."

"They're called muppets, and Kermit has an ugly girlfriend named Miss Piggy," chimed in Kathleen. This time, she grabbed no giggles by smugly cracking a joke at her 'Raggedy Anne' sister's expense, "She's Alicia's favourite character!"

Alicia, invigorated by the evening of fun and games despite her shy and serious nature, thrived upon the upbeat conversation until being suddenly slapped down again with another insult from Kitty. Rather than getting bent out of shape in front of so many handsome young men and buoyant women, however, she puckered her full red lips as big as Big Bird's beak and blew Kitty-Cat a kiss. Kathleen ducked, as though avoiding a snowball; she generated a few laughs with her clumsy retreat.

John/Jim explained *Sesame Street* to the dumbfounded Hughes kids. "Then, there's Oscar the Grouch, a grumpy, green, furry guy with huge eyebrows who lives in a garbage can and Ernie and Bert, two boyfriends who live together and keep a paperclip collection..."

He crossed his eyes fiercely and made his wrist go limp, causing the others to laugh. Alicia, perturbed that yet another fringe person was being mocked by these beautiful ones, explained to Orwell—the only person who would listen to her high ideals for more than five seconds in this giddy crowd. "The point of the show is to teach toddlers their ABCs, almost like they're in school, by introducing one letter from the alphabet and one number a day, through a series of animations and songs, and showing the subtle diversities of everyday objects. '*One of these things is not like the others, one of these things doesn't belong*' the teacher sings so sweetly, almost like a nursery rhyme.

"I know that *Sesame Street* is also trying to illustrate that every type of person, however different, is important in our neighbourhoods, like it's some happy urban melting pot, but I still feel sorry for the one who doesn't belong. I kind of know the feeling."

"Oh Lisa, lighten up, already!" JJ admonished her. "We're all Canadians here! You are part of this group!"

"You, young lady, are a unique individual," offered Orwell thoughtfully, sensing Alicia's sad loneliness even more now that his kid sister, supposedly her best friend, had dissed her.

Orwell gently stroked his friend's hand, though he worried inwardly at times that he was giving the wrong impression to Alicia and these other Canadians by paying the younger MacDonachie lass far too much attention, such that she might demand more of his time, talents, and allegiance—and next wish for him to be her boyfriend, then go steady, and finally get married—like Kathleen had already claimed Rick for all time! This could become a one-way train ticket to trouble! Orwell could not see down that track six months from now, or even tomorrow...

What would he do with Alicia tomorrow when beautiful, charming Georgina waltzed into his home as the belle of the ball, and commanded him to wait on her? Orwell had laboured for weeks just to receive Georgina's blessing of attendance as his Easter celebration guest. He hoped to receive her priceless jewels, not tumble and polish Mairam's ungraded ore! Much as he found Alicia refreshing and friendly, he could not allow this roughhewn girl to ruin his plans. He desired Alicia nonetheless, and did not wish to hurt her, enthralled as he was by her virgin beauty, brilliance, and the affection she cleverly unveiled only for him. He could tell she desired to be his alone—and might well someday be, if things perchance failed to work out for him with Georgie!

Orwell was haunted by the grief Alicia had so intimately shared with him late the previous night. Responding lovingly to her broken plea, he had held this majestic young woman, distraught to the point of turning wild, in his arms and comforted her. She had trusted him in her nakedness with her severe, though as yet unnamed distress, and now loved him forever by his freely-given kindness. How could he do anything other than uphold his childhood friend to grow into wonder woman, whatever the consequences? If God was testing him now, the Great Man Upstairs must help see him through his dilemma!

While the others largely ignored, missed, or thought drolly amusing the dark comment Alicia made about not belonging, the young poet acknowledged her concerns, but managed to stay cool without trotting out something glib or insulting. "Everyone here is unique and important. You, Alicia, were quite a mugger, bailiff, or whatever enforcer you played in those airplane skits, but I know you are much more intelligent and complex than that! You have much to offer, my dear; everyone would benefit from getting to know you better if they only try."

Alicia beamed speechlessly at her up-lifter, knowing of no other way to adequately accept his compliment. Most new arrivals, already forming their own network, took only a passing interest in this soap opera vignette, but Kathleen and Karla Eve looked on, woodenly amused.

Chad was educating him about the new Edmonton Oilers hockey team's entry into the World Hockey Association when Mrs. Hughes wandered into the kitchen with yet another request for entertainment by her adult guests.

"If you kids don't mind, we'd like you to sing for us old fogies some of those inspiring gospel songs you were practising last night. Kathy and Alicia, could you accompany with your instruments—I think Orwell's had enough limelight for one evening?"

"No problem, Mrs. Hughes, I'll be back in a jiffy with my violin," agreed Alicia gaily, as she skipped buoyantly out of the room. She meowed from somewhere down the hall, "Come on, Kitty-Cat, hustle your bustle!"

"I'll get my guitar," added Kathleen sedately but looking flushed as she strode through the crowd of the gawking youths.

"Suzanne and Janice Joanne, I also need help putting out these curried meatballs and sourdough buns warming in the oven," the elegant hostess informed her daughters, who then half-heartedly drew themselves into her service. She brightly commented to all the assembled young people, "You folks have certainly been gabbing great guns in here, for quite a while! I bet you're all excited about coming to live in Africa. I hope my children have encouraged you."

A chorus of "Oh yah! Right on! Amen! You betcha! It's cool, ma'am," rang out from various youths as she gathered up her goodies, then serenely paraded through them, followed briskly by her daughters laden with trays of hors d'oeuvres, and Orwell carrying a tea pot and coffee flask in either fist.

While mild-mannered Martha Hughes did not call out Karlee and Kristi for smoking in her kitchen and using one of her delicate bone china teacups for an ashtray, she gave these two ditzy blondes a stern look. Orwell, on his way out, nodded with appreciation at Karla Eve as she, having disposed of the girls' butts in the dust bin, eyed him contritely while she scrubbed the empty cup in warm soapy water.

The young guests did not immediately follow their refreshments-dispensing hosts, sensing that they must wait until Richard made his exit, and then followed his example. Smiling contentedly as he munched on a bun he had deftly lifted from JJ's passing tray, this dean of the fifteen to twenty-five-year-old crowd, an obvious role model among Canada's youths currently in Zambia, seemed in no hurry to join the old fogies in the living room.

Once Mrs. Hughes and her duty-bound youth were out of earshot, however, Richard addressed those who remained, "Thank you, guys for enlightening us about shiny gems we have missed during the past five years; it's true: we suffer withdrawals here, so far away. Now, I feel better prepared for what awaits me back home."

"No problem, man," replied Boyd, happy to help.

"Like, we really enjoyed your skit, Richard; you are an awesome flyer," Karlee exclaimed. "Your family and girlfriends are, like wow!"

Richard smiled congenially, but then became gravely sober as he did his due diligence and advised them of the rocky road upon which they would travel.

"We expats don't have all the technology, gadgets, and Hollywood diversions that you kids take for granted, although services are quite modern with telephones, running water, electricity—even TVs and theatres—but it is a simpler, old-fashioned, almost colonial way of life down here. White folks aren't in charge any more, even we are definitely a spoiled minority, so whatever odd things we do stick out like sore thumbs to Zambians. You may think you're basking in some tropical holiday at the moment, but you will soon wake up to the frustrating reality of being stuck in a different culture for the next four years! Home leave is a long two years away, and time will seem to drag on—you will find yourselves easily bored or frustrated if you don't have decent hobbies, or can't make friends and adjustments to this strange, new environment."

"God, I'm glad to be just visiting this jungle for a few days," muttered Kathleen, glumly amused from where she stood in the kitchen doorway, clutching her guitar and listening to Richard's grim diatribe. "I pity you kids who must live here forever because of your parents' work!"

Kathleen chose not to disclose to these newcomers that she was a daughter of Africa, having spent her first seven years playing with African children on a Christian missionary compound in Nigeria while her parents and grandparents had obediently served the Lord. Such was so long ago, she hardly remembered her strange past or cared about her beautiful Hausa birth name Aishatu. Now, basking amid her family's prestige and affluence garnered in Canada, Kathy wore status of missionary/preacher's kid like a millstone around her neck!

Her own view strengthened the legitimacy of her lover's speech for their receptive listeners. Like Jesus warning people that it was easier for a camel to pass through the eye of a needle than for a rich man to enter Heaven, Rick gave these new troops a stark reality check. Their buoyant enthusiasm was temporarily grounded and their careless swagger, hobbled as they took his pep talk to heart.

"What then can we do to survive?" Chad voiced in bewilderment what all were thinking, anxious to learn quickly from this polished veteran.

"Enjoy the vibrant new cultures swirling around you. Reach out to new friends, black and white. Bond with the land and its people, like my brother Orwell does so well! He won't advise you, but I am compelled to speak out. Don't hide away inside your cocoon, like I nearly did...until it's too late...until you are passed by or labelled. I tell you this without pride in my own accomplishments, because I care about what happens to each of you. Things do not always work out the way we want or expect, so you must adjust and find other stuff to do—formulate a plan B, even down to plan X if necessary, to become content where you are.

"I know from whence I speak...I'm 23 years old, and should have graduated from university by now, but I missed the boat because I was sick with malaria during my opportunity to write the British O-Level exams. My 20-year old brother made it through to university here in Lusaka and has surpassed me socially and academically. Should I sit here, feeling bummed out and rotting in this paradise? No! Rather than go to boarding school or stay with relatives back home, I completed my Canadian Grade Twelve senior matriculation program here by correspondence school. I then obtained my driver's and private pilot's licences. I currently work for *Blessings* book store, downtown, and am part of the pilot crew that does charter flights around Zambia for tourists through the Lusaka Flying Club. I obtained entrance into the University of Alberta, and will start my engineering degree there this fall, after our family finally returns to Canada at the end of my father's diplomatic term of service...This has been my own trajectory, and it shows how you can adapt and switch plans midstream... Okay, that's all for now—any questions or comments?"

"Thanks for sharing, man," whispered Josh Roberts, his pride taken down a peg by Richard's heartfelt testimony. He flashed frowning, reminiscing Hughes a peace sign with trembling fingers.

"Yay, far out!" seconded Boyd, bowing low as he shook Richard's hand.

"You're number one, Dick", the Bryant twins declared in unison as they came forward to pat their mentor on the shoulder.

"Well done. Now, let's get with the program," Richard grimly replied, shaking each kid's soft hand as she or he passed by to return to the living room.

"Nice going, Rick," Kitty purred approvingly as she escorted her general out of the war room. "These kids really listened; they look up to you."

Impressed by his courageous efforts to overcome adversity and nurtured by his respect towards her, Kathleen warmly held Rick's hand and let him carry her guitar in the other like he really was her boyfriend. That she would place him above her treasured instrument spoke volumes to Alicia, who followed them with a mixture of hope and trepidation.

# CHAPTER EIGHTEEN

EASTER DAWNED COOL BUT CLEAR. Not one to sleep in on Sunday—particularly this vital day—Orwell was rejuvenated by the rising sun and heard God speaking to him on the gentle breeze of His great salvation plan fulfilled. He savoured Easter's sacred peace, remembering how Jesus's followers had found His tomb empty, and learned of His resurrection from angels, nearly two thousand years ago.

Orwell, preparing for his morning run, loosened up stretching on the lawn as he waited for Alicia to join him, but she failed to show. He was disappointed, but respectfully understood if his jogging buddy wished to sleep in, what with her efforts eagerly spent all weekend preparing for today's celebrations...not to mention entertaining the already homesick Canadian newcomers on short notice until late last night. For all he knew, Alicia might be in the shower, styling her hair, or slipping into her pouffed Easter dress under Kathleen's stern supervision! He missed his chum's witty daybreak chatter; with Tug still in the dog house, Orwell sighed as he trotted out by his lonesome.

Oddly, he found the gate chained shut but not locked. The night watchman was no longer at his post; Orwell noted that his sturdy Raleigh bicycle was gone from beneath the jacaranda tree. He had not checked every bedroom before leaving the house, but young Bwana could not imagine anyone stirring before him as he slipped out of the compound. He promised to talk with his father at breakfast about this strange happening....

Turning his back to the street as he closed the gate, he was startled by someone whistling admiringly at his behind. He whirled around and found a tall powerful woman, dressed in a white tunic, standing on the approach before him.

At first, this young poet thought he was encountering an angel—he had no idea how else one so beautiful could suddenly arrive without detection! The majestic figure glowing in the sunlight, her golden hair and sparkling blue eyes, vividly reminded him of Kathleen.

"Well, well. Orwell, my boy, how are you? Where are you going on this fine Day of our risen Lord?" Kathy inquired, her normally stern face smiling brightly for him.

"I'm starting my morning jog," stammered Hughes nervously. "Alicia often accompanies me but she's not available today. Kathy, you look amazing! Already been out and about?"

"Yes, I have...Don't look so surprised, Orwell! I can do anything if I put my mind to it. I just got up and went for it, all by myself. I needed the fresh air."

"Good on you," approved Orwell of this fellow disciple for physical fitness. Kitty had modestly covered her model/actress curves in a white track suit, white terry towel socks and running shoes; he now understood how she kept herself looking so fit and trim. She glowed with health, prompting Orwell to invite her out, "Care to run an extra mile with me?"

Honoured as she appeared to be, Kathleen shook her head. "I'm tired and thirsty Orwell. I'm on my way back to base, where I'll sit on the sundeck and sip some hot lemon tea...What was your plan: take me down the same garden path where you and Fannie play together—or is that a secret route?"

"No lovers' lane where we privately steal away to neck, if that's what you think, Kathy," Hughes pshawed, suddenly feeling embarrassed beneath her cunning gaze.

"I never said it was," sang Kathleen, feigning innocence for his fluster.

"We could run anywhere you want, girl; I'd take you on a jogging tour of our high-class neighbourhood—all tranquil and above board, of course—Would you like the grand colonial view?"

Having teased him enough for an early Sunday morning, she released confused Orwell with a dainty wave of her hand, "Go running, stud! Another time, I'll come with you. We've got a date, mate, whether Fannie likes it or not."

Kathleen left him on the curb, and made her way into the compound. She expected that Orwell simply would jog away, but he tarried, watching her limp up the driveway and struggle to open the gate, all the while wearing a dark scowl on her beautiful face. Rather than gloat over Kathleen's discomfort, Orwell felt sorry for the brittle goddess; he shelved his fitness regimen and politely came to her aid. Unlike what her proudly independent sister would do, Kathleen smiled appreciatively and allowed this mere mortal to unlace the security chain and swing open the heavy wrought iron gate for her. She softly thanked him, then trudged to the back of the house. Preferring to walk softly on dewy grass rather than further bruise her feet on the laterite, Kathy gingerly skirted around flowering shrubs or ducked under the odd fruit tree. She supposed that Orwell would go merrily off now—to water flowers or feed his love birds—but, after turning around several times and finding him still following her, albeit at a respectful distance, the blonde bombshell smiled with amusement and beckoned him to pick up his pace.

Once they entered the kitchen, Kathleen sat on a stool and watched with baleful fascination as Orwell, taking charge of a place he knew well, fired up the propane stove and put a kettle of water on to boil. He poured the steaming water into his mother's fancy serving pot, then suspended into it a perforated metal ball he had filled with leaves of finest English breakfast tea, which he had spooned from a colourful plastic canister kept in the pantry. The canister might be *kitsch décor,* but her cultured host produced gold-rimmed cups and saucers with bright yet delicate floral designs from the china hutch and rounded up sugar cubes and cream, which he displayed for his guest's wide-eyed pleasure in crystal vessels.

"What would you like on the side, Kitty-Cat; fresh fruit? Or cheese and crackers, perhaps?" the improvised butler inquired with polished hospitality.

"Both!" Kathleen hungrily blurted out. When he stared incredulously at the raw humanity of this proud, sophisticated lady, Kathy rebuked him, "Don't gawk at me like that—I'm not a pig; I'm starved!"

"Sounds good to me! We'll chow down together," Hughes cheered. He packed the tea and condiments onto a carved teak serving tray, and directed Kathleen to snag the fruit bowl off the dining room table, and bring it along as they went out to the sun deck to enjoy their breakfast.

Chatting amicably and enjoying the peaceful twittering of birds as they ate together in the sunlight that filtered through the trees, Orwell sensed God's many blessings, one of which that he was finally connecting with Alicia's fiercely protective, older sister—Kathleen was really quite friendly and fun beneath her façade of stern snobbery. Orwell was lost in the midst of these pleasant reveries, when Kathleen brusquely brought him back to reality with her bubble-bursting news that she would not be attending church today!

"I can't abide the gross changes imposed upon our well-laid performance plans by your church's choral director. He did not consult us, and by dismissing the comprehensive program Fannie and I developed, Benjamin has insulted our musical heritage," Kathleen bitterly explained when Orwell begged to understand her unseemly decision.

"Please, reconsider," Orwell beseeched the scowling, standoffish prima donna. "My friends would never want to hurt your feelings. They feel duty-bound to host, with their utmost, such important visitors as the MacDonachies, and thus worked diligently for weeks to prepare their own music and songs to entertain and embrace you with during this special service..."

"Let them go ahead without me! I won't interfere with their little concert! I did not come 20,000 miles and suffer all this heat and confusion to be upstaged!" bitterly muttered Kathy, pouting like a spoiled child. "I was invited to perform in your church as an international guest artist. I am not some two-bit amateur singer, Oh-well—you know my quality, yet you side with Benjamin against me! I am so annoyed that I have lost my desire to sing today; all I want to do is go home!"

"Ben earnestly wishes to include you and Alicia in today's presentation—the entire congregation has looked forward to your participation with much enthusiasm for weeks, from the moment we learned you were coming to Lusaka."

"I doubt it! I'm just some crybaby to them! They don't need white people standing in their way anymore, overshadowing their independence parade. I don't want to oppress them!"

"Kathleen, I've been a choir member since we joined Trinity church five years ago. I share the excitement that buzzes over your coming. Nobody here is concerned that we are white—they are honoured that we collaborate with them to produce spiritual music for worship on any given Sunday, just as they feel blessed by your presence as a fellow Christian walking with them on the road to Heaven. These local choristers love The *MacDonachie Family Singers,* but they also believe that your fervent words well up from the heart. You and Alicia are spiritual messengers from God to them.

"Having heard you sing on Christian radio, Ben knows that you are the brilliant daughters of the famous evangelist, Rev. Wynnard MacDonachie. My friend wants to honour your father, Kathleen, to thank him for allowing you and Alicia to come all the way here in his name, to bless the people with your talent and worship. Churchgoers—black and white, old and young—deeply desire to embrace you ladies. Please, my beautiful friend, accept their hospitality. I invite you with all humility in my heart."

"Why should I consider you as a friend, Oh-well? You know nothing about me—in fact, you couldn't care less about me! Fannie is your pal and Tracy is your mentor; I am the odd one out. What have you ever done for me—or I for you—that you should ever like me?"

"I am here for Alicia and for you Kathy, because I love, respect, and care for you both as my sisters in the Lord, and because our families are long-time friends," testified Orwell, his face red and his voice quivering with emotion. "I am here for you, Kathleen Beulah MacDonachie...anytime, any way I can. If you *ever* need me to help you, please ask and I will do it, so far as it depends on me!"

She stared at him long and hard, frigidly hostile at first, but eventually warming and mellowing somewhat as Orwell quietly stayed with her, eyes lowered and showing her only humble patience. Seeing him finally as being entirely real, tears welled up in her eyes, which now looked tired if not remorseful.

As she acknowledged his kind hospitality and implored his understanding, Kathleen blushed hotly as she blubbered, "I did not expect Tracy to be a total deadbeat and leave me in charge of our mission. Not being the strongest of negotiators, I probably behaved like a foolish kid in everyone's eyes by protesting the situation. I feel like I insulted your friend and thus embarrassed you. I don't know how to face Mr. Mudenda or any of his songsters today."

Orwell solemnly testified as he held her trembling hands. "I will help you make amends with Ben, if needed. I will walk with you to him. Kathy, with God's help, everything is possible."

"No guy, not even your brother, has ever uttered such a heavy vow to me, or if they did, only spoke with glib cowboy infatuation; I doubt they ever meant or could actually deliver it," Kathleen sombrely declared. "I will hold you to your word, brave man."

Orwell, nodding obediently, accepted her response. Doing her father proud, she firmly shook his hand with typical MacDonachie assurance. The deal was sealed for all time.

They exchanged resolute smiles and hugged. The French windows suddenly slid open and roaring lioness Alicia, stuffed into a frilly gown, stormed onto the deck with her wet hair flapping unkemptly in the breeze followed boisterously by her handlers, Suzanne and JJ.

"Hey you guys, breakfast is getting cold on the dining room table; if you don't eat right now you'll be S.O.L.! It's almost time to go to church!" Alicia bellowed the announcement sent from Mrs. Hughes. The household had never heard the like!

Catching a sudden glimpse of the fancy tea set and dainty treats already consumed, wild Alicia stopped mid-flow and threw her sister a questioning look. Kathleen smirked back. Orwell politely greeted the burly princess, but she clenched her bright white teeth into a mad grin for him. Alicia seemed to reclaim the dolt rather than ignore him then, when she not so deftly leaned upon his shoulder with her large, warm hand even as she barraged her unamused sister with all sorts of petty requests. "Kitty, will you help me curl my hair? And I can't find my deodorant...also, this fancy dress you bought is really too small for me!"

"Well, suck it in with a girdle, you fat baby!" spat Kitty-Cat in exasperation. Alicia pulled a big lip pout and appeared ready to bawl. When Orwell wistfully panned her sauciness, Kathleen sighed and wearily departed her comfortable chair. "Okay, come along, child. I hope I find time to dress myself after fixing you."

As she followed Princess Alicia indoors and spied a red bra strap and milk chocolate flesh peeking through the yawning back of her dress, Kathleen rolled her eyes and berated, "*Oy*! You could have at least buttoned up before waltzing out here to brag about your measurements in mixed company!"

"I can button up Alicia's dress, Kathy, if you need time to get ready yourself," offered Orwell, gallantly he thought, as laden down with the leftovers from their meal, he dutifully joined the MacDonachies' train.

"You, Oh-well? Now really?" scoffed Kathleen, up to her old tricks again as she haughtily whirled upon him, and recalled some obscure failure from the eager lad's childhood. "You can't even tie balloons before they deflate!"

Orwell refused to take her bait and get frustrated, even when his normally supportive sisters piled on and teased him like pests.

"No wonder we went without fresh fruit for breakfast—you and Kitty hogged it all!" japed Suzanne as she swiped the fruit bowl off her brother like some pickpocket and ran ahead of him.

"Here's the cream for our corn flakes!" added disgruntled JJ, rescuing the glass pitcher before it fell off the tray Orwell was precariously bearing along.

"And just where do you think you're going, Mr. Man?" demanded Kathleen mischievously as she let his sisters traipse through the French windows, but barred entry to the roving young gentleman who had so recently entertained her like royalty. Alicia loomed behind, dark curved eyes gleaming with apprehension as she considered how Orwell might serve her if she was handed over to him.

"I've buttoned my mother's dress upon request from time to time, and I do have sisters of my own. If she wants, I can be gentle enough to secure Alicia's top buttons and clasp her necklace, better perhaps than my little sisters…"

He explained his credentials to smugly listening Kathy, keeping his gaze politely lowered, lest Alicia find out that he could see the luscious curves of her breasts and bum cheeks through the soft green fabric of her skin-tight dress. Indeed, her current outfit left little to his carnal imagination of what rich booty he had guarded the other night, but despite her obvious and provocative forms, Alicia revealed herself as an innocent young beauty in this magic dress. Even though she was strongly built, she was elegantly trim around the waist and Orwell also found her comely neck and supple limbs pleasing; her dark eyes, shaggy auburn hair, and sharpened cheek bones were balanced by sweet lips and a congenial smile. Orwell, having dutifully comforted his distressed friend out of love and compassion, having shared many interests as well as battles over the years, now realized he was seeing her with new eyes, and resolved in his heart that Alicia was an astounding lady! Rather than continue to feast upon her now with lust, Orwell strove to inwardly praise God for such unbridled beauty!

Alicia, smiling coyly in the sunlight, said nothing yet brimmed with gladness. Made aware that this young knight admired her enough to do even odd menial tasks to gain personal audience, she straightened up and refurbished her appearance to give her best for his gentle view.

"Okay, you're hired, Sir Galahad...but only if you also do right by me and fasten my dainties as well," Kathleen teased this suffering romantic and her quickly frowning sister. Laughing at Orwell's nervousness, she claimed to be kidding, then sternly hustled him along with circuitous orders, "Go in properly by the front door. Get yourself attired for church...We may call you if and when we need your help."

Orwell and Richard, anticipating a fulfilling church morning with their friends, quickly dressed into their Easter Sunday best: black slacks smartly pressed; blue socks and intricately latched leather sandals; festive cotton tunics with snazzy open collars, colourfully splashed with intricate floral bouquets about the neck and chest. Blonde-locked Orwell wore gold and Richard, turquoise to compliment his handsome shock of chestnut brown hair. They dabbed their freshly shaved faces with *English Leather* cologne. Having rolled on deodorant, combed hair and brushed their teeth, these handsome young men lounged in the living room and idly flipped between traditional dancing shows or re-runs of the university side losing badly at the national field hockey championship on the flying saucer TV that Rick had purchased from ZCBC, while they waited for their hot dates to appear. Although bored out of their minds, they easily became annoyed by the loud female clucking sounds emanating from the bathroom and bedrooms that drowned out the obscure, black and white television shows.

When Alicia appeared first on the landing, Orwell pleasantly noted that she had sensibly swapped her undersized, "see-what-I've-got" nightclub dress for a looser, traditional print gown and headdress of vibrant red, brown and black patterns. These elegant garments belonged to his mother, but Orwell was impressed by how well the girl wore them. Believing in his heart that this was a historic moment he should savour, Orwell returned Alicia's smile even as he motioned for Richard to switch off the orbital TV. Both Hughes boys clapped approvingly as Alicia gracefully descended the steps towards them, giving them an odd peek at tanned, shapely legs, her sturdy bare feet decked out in new leather sandals. Walking tall, she smiled serenely confident as she fixed her dark, almond eyes upon her admirers.

"Orwell, I have a little job for you to do," Alicia sweetly reminded the gawking younger brother as she perched on a foot stool in front of him and batted her big, black-lined eyes appealingly at him. Producing a braided rhinoceros hair hoop with a copper cross pendant dangling from it, she slapped the crude, locally fashioned jewellery into the outstretched hands of her helper. "As you offered ..."

"Anything for you, dear, anything," sang Hughes as he enthusiastically rose to the occasion. Complementing her, Orwell chirped, "That's a nice outfit you're wearing. I also like your cross—it's plain but wholesome."

Alicia basked in the attention he showered upon her, but rather than take the hoopla in good fun, she noted his promise remained to be fulfilled. Orwell moved swiftly behind her, where she could not see the worried look on his face as he struggled to decipher how to correctly adorn her. He determined that the necklace, already tied by the artisan, was simply meant to be slipped over the moody princess's big red head. While Alicia enjoyed his nervous respect toward her person, she intuitively pulled in, then drew back the rich, curly strands of her mane to help him guide the necklace down the smooth slope to where her comely neck curved into strong shoulders.

Rick had vaguely been watching this soap opera, but now he suddenly began to clap and cheer. His upward gaze dragged Orwell and Alicia curiously along, to glimpse Kathleen sashaying out of the cobblestone hallway, fashionably garbed in a blue wrapper dress and matching head tie. She smiled radiantly, pleased with her artistic transformation, and happy that the others noticed it.

"Kathleen, you look positively African now!" cheered Orwell. The outfit looked comfortable on her and was a good fit, but he knew that she too had borrowed it from Madame Hughes. When his mother and sisters, all colourfully attired in fashions of local women going out to celebrate, came skipping happily along behind Kathy, Orwell affirmed to Richard, "We're ready to go to church, bro."

"Right on! I'll fetch the car—and the camera," Rick gleefully concluded.

"Do we all look like freaks...or what?" demanded Alicia, suddenly worried.

"Oh no, my dear—I am so proud of all of you kids for embracing the local culture," Martha Hughes reassured her young lady as she calmly adjusted the head tie trying to contain her waterfall of curly hair, so that she looked more stylish and less like a baker, Orwell giggled to himself. "It's just that many of our white ladies still come to church wearing European midi skirts and high heels, trying to stay cool; they don't even cover their hair. Some expatriate men impeccably deck themselves out in dark suits and ties. Many Africans do the same, as though to keep up.

"And, while we worship at a multiracial church, in the heart of the capital city of a vibrant African nation, we are still very British—splendidly isolated, mostly white elite—in how we worship, not to mention how we play, work, and live. Things are bound to change though and must do, I believe, as Zambia asserts herself more and more..."

"I would like to style my hair like the African women do," Alicia added, equally solemn. "Both Kitty and I saw some gorgeous hairdos here among the black girls; we want to learn how, to try it out for ourselves. Maybe one of your friends can help us."

"We are establishing a new trend, Mrs. H! Let's go native—cuz *'that's the way, uh-huh, uh-huh, I like it, uh-huh, uh-huh*"[51] chortled Kathleen, energized by girl power blazing in the room.

Rick grinned and made Kathy blush, though she acted out all the more now for his amusement. Feeling frisky and wanting to get a rise out of dour Alicia, Kitty-Cat sidled playfully against her sister and dared Miss Sunday Dress-Up to primp in the mirror for her dashing lover boy, Orwell, who was standing attentively by.

"Oh no, I won't!" huffed Alicia, rightly outraged.

Aware, however, that Orwell was indeed admiring her from afar, Alicia answered the bell rather than insist Kathleen lay off. She knew that she looked good to him in her traditional feminine attire, but Alicia, inwardly embarrassed that he eagerly watched as she wiggled her big apple bum, smiled fiercely at Kathy as she met her challenge. Kitty giggled approvingly, and gave high fives to Alicia, Suzanne, and JJ, who had joined in the girls' dance.

As he edged out the room to attend to his duties, Rick drank up the creative colours, dainty curves, and joyous laughter of all the women who filled his home with fragrance on this Easter morning. They, who danced with hope and purpose, were a rowdy lot—the wonderful life of the festive holiday party—not drab looking guys who cowered on the edges of their view except when called to wait on them! The lords were leaping to a different tune now, though living in the land of women was not so bad. It domesticated, cultured him, he reasoned to himself.

With such an abundance of beauty and effervescence to bear all the way to church, it was only right that the family take two cars for their journey. That way, Mrs. Hughes whispered aside to her pensive husband, she could slip home ahead of the herd to set out lunch and get the house ready for the afternoon festivities, should the young people be detained by their many friends wanting to greet the MacDonachie girls. The splendid pair seemed so full of pep today!

In the midst of all the happy chatter, no further mention was made of the recital; indeed, they had nearly forgotten to take along their music or instruments!

---

51 Lyrics from "That's the Way (I Like It)" by *KC and The Sunshine Band* 1975.

"Oh, you can put my guitar in the boot...I may not even need it now," Kathleen airily waved him on when Orwell came running up to her window, clutching the guitar rigorously as if it was a suitcase filled with greenbacks he was transporting like a mule for the Mafia.

"I saw your music folder by the front door," divulged Hughes, diligently raising a trendy red briefcase he held in his other hand.

"Pack it beside my guitar. That way, I'm prepared if God calls upon me. It's all *copacetic* when we give the Lord charge of everything..."

Orwell did as he was told, albeit confused by Miss Sunshine blissfully forgetting all the sweat equity this hard taskmaster had boiled out of him to learn her trendy musical repertoire.

"Thanks already for loading my violin and Bwana's banjo, not to mention all those stuffy old hymnals in the other car. You boys are so sweet," Alicia twittered jovially as she reached over Suzanne and JJ, seated with her in the back, to blow her gallant young knight a kiss. Her broad smile sobered when Orwell, who had chivalrously loaded her cargo, now seemed miffed at all the shit and abuse he was getting. Desiring that he find peace, she sincerely wished, "God bless you, Orwell. Happy Easter!"

"Thank you, ma'am. You're highly welcome, ma'am," Orwell replied courteously, although he inwardly wondered why he was doing so much for these spoiled princesses when they had not even left room for him to sit with them, relegating him to ride by default as the lone youth in the old folk's car. His father's honking horn suddenly prodded him to mush!

Hughes rebuked his weird thoughts as he raced into his seat. Today marked the zenith of Christian faith. This afternoon, he would stand on a mountain top as he hosted beloved Georgina and all his friends. He now believed in his heart that this would be a glorious, uplifting festival. If God was in charge, there could be no doubt!

*****

THE Hughes party arrived in style. Breezing into the glad house of worship, they mingled with fellow believers, many brilliantly attired, gathered among the pruned gardens and freshly swept courtyard. While Bwana and Mrs. Hughes chatted with friends, the MacDonachies were buoyantly ushered by their peers into the sunny, busy choir room behind the sanctuary. JJ and Suzanne carefully stowed the girls' instruments against the side wall—out of harm's way but where they could be seen at all times—next to boxes of hymnals that Orwell and Richard had just carried in. As promised, Orwell made sure that Alicia and Kathleen were comfortably gathered into Ben's capable hands.

"You are very welcome, Miss Kathy! I am so thankful you came. Happy Easter to you, Miss Kathy," greeted Benjamin, heartily embracing Kitty's nervously outstretched hand with both of his while Orwell looked on, beaming with pride. Alicia, next in line, primly curtseyed for this regal gentleman. Ben graciously drew her to her feet with sweet assurance, "You also are highly welcome, Miss Alicia. Our choir is pleased that you both choose to join us today. We will share an exciting time together!

"Happy Easter, Mr. Orwell. Thank you for bringing us your lovely lady friends on this fine morning," remarked Mudenda exuberantly as the two friends exchanged holiday pleasantries. The music director had much ado on his mind, however, and shuffled the newcomers along so that he could continue his preparations. Ever polished and polite, Ben nonetheless shocked Orwell out of his tree by assigning him to accompaniment duties, "You must play organ today rather than sing, as Mr. Rosebury travelled to UK for the holidays to visit his sick mother."

"Okay," Hughes muttered obediently.

"I thought you knew this was coming. Did nobody tell you?"

"This is my first hearing of it, though I'm sad for Mr. Rosebury."

"This is Africa, my friend, but I think that you are able to stand in the gap for us today, like no one else can. You know very well the music we are singing. You play the organ and piano like a professional. Many times, you have come forward and done well when called upon. Are you prepared, sir?"

"I will do my best," promised Orwell, smiling resolutely.

He was buoyed up by Benjamin's glowing praise, delivered in the presence of the keenly attentive MacDonachie girls. They appeared worried at first but smiled admiringly, and gave him thumbs' up assurances when he demonstrated flexibility, courage, and faith in the Lord. Orwell nodded goodbye, convinced that everyone would be fine, before he ducked into the sanctuary to limber up the old pipe organ.

"Now, my young ladies, we too must roll up our sleeves and get down to business. See, some choir members are already rehearsing," Benjamin politely admonished those who gazed after Orwell's sudden departure.

Alicia studiously followed the sweeping gestures of Ben's manicured ebony hands, and was mesmerized by the malachite cufflinks that sparkled on white sleeve cuffs protruding from his tailored blue suit, as he motioned to several sharply dressed young Africans already gathered around and tuning their singing voices to the piano. They were pleasantly surprised by the commotion of the new arrivals.

"Come Lisa. Come Kathy. We'll introduce you ladies to the other singers," offered JJ cheerily. "They are eager to meet you."

"Sure thing. This is what we came for," agreed Kathleen, giving herself over to the situation, whatever it would be.

Kathleen walked boldly forward, hand in hand with Suzanne. Impressed that Richard had gone ahead and was already mingling jovially with his friends, she wished to join them. Alicia smiled at Benjamin before taking her leave of the seriously preoccupied conductor. She wondered now in passing, as she followed JJ and their sisters, where Orwell had disappeared to, but then the sacred drones of the "Hallelujah Chorus" rising out of the organ next door assured her that he had not gone far, and was simply fulfilling his liturgical duties.

"Here we are," Suzanne tinkled, presenting the impressive MacDonachie girls to those eagerly gathered and waiting to meet them. She gently touched the dangling arm of her tall, blonde companion—whose blue eyes now seemed subdued, warm, and willing to be led by her today. "This is my age-mate, Kathleen; we've been good friends since childhood. Now, at my invitation, she is visiting us here in Lusaka."

"This is Alicia, my friend and Kathleen's little sister," continued Janice Joanne, exuberantly promoting with sweeping gestures the brawny autumn girl who towered solemnly behind her. Drawing Her Shyness forward, JJ led Alicia on the obligatory rounds of introduction. "Here is Jenny; this is Hillary, and beside her is Yvonne. How are you ladies? And please, greet Beatrice, Alicia. How are you on this wonderful Easter morning? Finally, let me introduce you to Lalitha and Audrey. And now you've met everyone!"

"There will be a quiz on remembering names after we are done, girls, so you better take notes," Suzanne joked in warning as she followed behind with Kathleen. "I'm certain you'll do just fine, clever as you are."

The girls laughed at these comments. Alicia and Kathleen shook hands softly with each new acquaintance, and tried hard to put names to faces and commit them to memory.

Suzanne prodded Richard into action now, to take her cue and introduce his guy friends. Richard jauntily complied, touching base and generating connections for his guests with Godfrey, Crispin, Daniel, Winstone, Fwanya, and Augustinho. Her beau surely knew how to interact with his peers, Kathleen marvelled—he bantered with ease among them. Rick broke much ice when he adeptly parlayed the ritual of shaking hands the African way. They were a buoyant group, Kathleen had to admit, and if their singing was as boisterous as their banter, they would be formidable on any stage!

By now, Benjamin was pacing among them, perturbed by all the hullabaloo over what should have been simple greetings. Dressed like Count Dracula in a full-length black cape with red trim about the collar, the ultra-serious maestro suddenly seemed twice as old and learned as anyone else in the room as he tapped his cane impatiently on the piano box. It was time to get lined up in parts. Did everyone have their music sheets in hand? He seemed troubled that Godfrey was wearing a blue shirt instead of standard white. Why had people not yet donned their gowns? Where was the pianist and why was he late to accompany them? Where, for that matter, were the other choristers? Rather than single out any one person to chastise or demand explanations for these embarrassing shortfalls, Mudenda expected his choristers to mitigate them as he glared balefully through his horn-rimmed glasses beyond them all, and sought peace from the floral churchyard framed in the open window on the far wall of the room.

Ben patiently waited for the flurry of responses to calm down before bringing the group to order. Alicia sheepishly followed JJ and Suzy into the alto section, but Kathleen seemed lost in space after Richard left her to join his base fellows.

"Excuse, Madame. Excuse," murmured Lalitha softly, her dark soulful eyes soberly lowered as she hovered at Kathleen's side. When Kathy finally came to realization that this quiet girl was humbly broaching her attention, she looked at her sharply. Lalitha politely beckoned, "Excuse, Madame. Come with me. We must sing together now—like canaries."

"Okay, this should be fun," Kathleen agreed, smiling vaguely.

She let Lalitha take her by the hand to a close-knit group of giggling female admirers clustered in the far corner of the room. No sooner had she arrived, however, then Betty and Yvonne cloaked her in a heavy black gown. Kathleen pouted at the idea of her fancy wings being clipped, but glancing about her group, she gloomily noted that all the other sopranos had already gowned up for the big show. Were they all nuns singing in some convent? Why the dreary garb?

"What's the point of getting all dressed-up in colourful new outfits to celebrate Easter if we just get draped in black? Is this a funeral service?" Kathy complained to Yvonne as they rejoined the choristers assembling *en masse* before their maestro. The room seemed overcrowded now that more singers, including several white folks, had swelled the ranks.

"We wear these gowns to humbly serve God," Yvonne solemnly replied. Just when Kathy seemed discouraged at the implication that she, a world-celebrated evangelist's daughter, had somehow failed to respect the Lord, Yvonne suddenly guffawed, "But God requires we work in uniform only for one hour—then we are free to enjoy our Sundays as we like, blessed by Him!"

"Come along, ladies, we are not clocked to African time," Benjamin chided them as Kathy and Yvonne slipped into place before him.

Kathleen sensed Alicia smirking at her, yet found her sibling soberly robed just as she was and looking like a high-power trial lawyer, her gaze focused on the conductor when Kathy dared look for the dark white girl out of the corner of her precious blue eyes.

"Here are your starting notes," Benjamin directed as he plunked the appropriate notes from a chord on the piano keyboard. Though many choristers did not read music, Kathleen heard everyone instantly hum with resonant harmony. Their pitch was proven perfect when Mudenda reiterated, "Again, I am playing your notes."

Then, with a dynamic stroke of his cane, the conductor breathed life into the beautiful human musical instrument assembled before him. Daniel, appointed the song leader, belted out "Low in the Grave He Lay...Waiting the coming day" with his deep, rich voice, between which the choir responded with "Jesus my Saviour...Jesus my Lord." They resurrected each solemn verse by joyfully leaping into the chorus "Up from the Grave He arose, with a shout of triumph o'er His foes...He arose, He arose, Christ Jesus, He arose!"

Benjamin was pleased that the choristers impeccably followed his directions for timing and diction; they blended fluidly because each singer knew his or her notes by heart. They sang like a mighty angel band, yet without accompaniment or acoustics; their celebration danced and echoed throughout the room. No longer stiff or nervous about how they should best improve this group, Alicia and Kathleen hit their stride, and were soon easily swaying with others to the sounds of this old-time gospel rock.

The choir was marching through "Battle Hymn of the Republic" when Orwell made his appearance in the room, attired like an army general in his blue and white musician's regalia as he escorted the even more regally adorned Pastor Beausoleil. They strode in together, robust and congenial, in sharp contrast to Solly and Dave who, looking lost, meekly followed, but then quickly fled to the wardrobe to don their gowns under Benjamin's baleful glare. The maestro should rightly have reprimanded these latecomers for their blatant disrespect towards himself and fellow choristers. Rather than appear fractious in the eyes of the spiritual head of the church, particularly on this wonderful morning blessed by esteemed international visitors, Benjamin excused such riffraff as he greeted Pastor Beausoleil and was infused with his joviality.

"Is it already time to enter the sanctuary?" Benjamin sighed, as his eyes now met Orwell's. Without waiting for the organist to consult his wristwatch for the umpteenth time, Ben turned to the frozen choir and sounded their upward call to process. He admonished everyone filing past, before he briskly followed Orwell onto the end of the line, "Let's go—in quiet and orderly fashion, mind you! Remember: smile and be happy—Christ has risen!"

"Christ has risen indeed!" boisterously replied others on the liturgical train.

Beatrice, inspired by the pastor's enthusiasm for the Lord, jubilantly danced ahead to lead the stately troupe of worship participants into the sanctuary. The sea of Christian faithful arose, wave upon colourful wave, acknowledging their arrival and standing watch as the choir arrayed itself—to the right of the dais where Pastor Beausoleil and Benjamin ascended—and also behind and above the organ, where Orwell took his seat. Choir, conductor, and pastor then sat down together, followed by the congregation.

Glancing about her environs, Kathleen was amazed at this vast, cross-shaped sanctuary overflowing with people of all ages and colours; dozens more were visible through the open windows attentively seated on benches, lawn chairs, and mats outside the church. Her roving blue eyes noted that the blonde Bryants from last night's party also sprinkled the mainly African crowd. She recognized her nemesis—that splendidly dressed artist Madame Musakanya—who returned her demure smile of acknowledgement. Seated beside this esteemed bureaucrat was a dowdy white woman with her brood of ragamuffins in tow. An entire section of pews opposite the choir loft was alive with children under the hopeless oversight of Katrina and Andrea who—as Mrs. Granger, their dour Sunday school headmistress, came forward to explain—had earlier rolled dozens of painted, hard-boiled eggs down the lawns, in a playful re-enactment of angels rolling away the stone door of Christ's tomb. Afterwards, the children ate those eggs for breakfast, together with hot tea, freshly baked bread, and marmalade supplied by the church's Social Action Committee—a treat akin to the disciples' ladies discovering that Jesus' tomb was empty! Kathy smiled with her bench mate and new friend Yvonne on that concept.

Pastor Beausoleil effervescently embraced his people; welcoming everyone in fellowship with God on His great and glorious Day, he suggested they all take a few minutes to greet one another with peace and joy.

"Welcome the sojourners in our midst—I know there are many here today for various reasons—visiting friends or family, randomly stopped in for worship or perhaps, checking us out as a place to come back to next Sunday. Some may even be angels in disguise. You are all highly welcome! God wishes that we care about others, be they brethren or newcomers—for that is how we would want others to treat us when we travel," Beausoleil patiently taught above the din of hundreds of adherents already on their feet and gaily mingling. Not one to put the spotlight on strangers, he encouraged his flock to gently seek them out. He beckoned the shy MacDonachies with odd pleasure, causing observers to chuckle, "Some of our visitors from afar wish to bring greetings from their home congregations, and entertain us with song and dance later in the service."

Orwell, by pounding out the first few measures of the "Hallelujah Chorus" on the organ, drew everyone back into a semblance of order. He waited for Ben to announce the gathering hymn, then waded exuberantly into the joyous piece.

The maestro flamboyantly directed both the choristers and the congregation at every opportunity, though he had no need to, as everyone celebrated in unison. Benjamin startled the prudish Europeans in his audience by dancing on the podium in typical revival style, strutting about with eager rhythm, bouncing up and down, flailing his limbs, and calling out choir sections to sing. The choir did him proud through inspired renderings of "Low in the Grave He Lay" and "Battle Hymn of the Republic". Orwell enjoyed the choristers' splendid harmony, and was especially impressed to hear that extra little *pizzazz* delivered by guest members from Canada. He loved to hear his friends David and Solomon, stray sheep whom he had led into the fold today, sing lively. How he longed to join their chorus! A serious musician not known to smile when he was working, Orwell found himself grinning from ear to ear during these festive hymns. His antics caught Alicia's attention; her dark almond eyes sparkled with admiration at the young virtuoso who had come so far from their childhood drudgery of practising piano for her mother!

Orwell appreciated Alicia's interest, but her unblinking gaze unnerved him. Upon completion of his powerful music, rather than continue to glance back at his rapt admirer for affirmation, Hughes let his eyes amble about the sanctuary; from his high viewpoint of the organ seat, he was startled to find the temple awash with appreciative listeners, many of whom looked upon him for inspiration. Smiling serenely, Karla Eve enjoyed the hymns, though she lowered her sapphire eyes and shrank into the pew when she felt his gaze settle upon her.

Little Miss Bryant was nicely attired in a blue dress, her golden hair fashionably curled for Easter, but she looked tired and somewhat subdued today for one who had laughed boisterously, played enthusiastically, and pranced lively about in hot pants revealing her lush curves just hours earlier. Orwell found her attractive, though the straight-laced, snobby ladies of Hughes House complained later, after she had gone, that Karlee behaved like a slut—maybe they felt threatened by her as, Orwell surmised secretly (wisely on pain of death!), they might see her as competition. Karlee had shown her feisty side during a rowdy, late evening game of *Wink*—a musical chairs affair organized in the guest room made rumpus room by JJ and Alicia—whereby each girl sat in a circle with a boy behind her, except for one single boy who, on cue from some music—played on the flute by JJ (as she was not supposed to get excited in the dry winter air on account of her asthma)—winked at a girl to entice her to leave the partner, and sit on the empty chair in front of him. By rights, the attentive partner prevented his girl from crossing over, but he had to act quickly, persistently, in restraining her. The jilted guy then became the winker, until such time as he lured another to sit on his chair. All the girls were loosed when JJ flouted a special signal tune; yet a different ditty signalled that runners should switch with keepers.

Orwell had found jolly Alicia difficult to hold on to but tougher to escape from when roles were reversed; a winker barely volleyed before she sprang to her feet and burst through his tackle, or took him with her until he must let go or get thumped as she charged across the room. He dared not rumble with Kathleen, who was more sophisticated but less patient with male persuasion than her roughhousing sister. Either MacDonachie lass, catching a rival's alluring wink with eagle eyes before he did, decisively glued Orwell to his chair before he could get free.

Karla Eve, however, was an untameable foe: small but powerful, she wriggled from his tenacious grasp without fail. Orwell, respectful of all girls, tried to hold Mighty Mouse by her tiny waist or churning legs rather than wrap his arms around her full breasts or jiggling buttocks, but she completely foiled him by the time he figured out where to grab her. The spry gymnast squatted when he meant to hoop her from above, or jumped high when he bid to snare her legs. After one successful breakout, Karlee leered back, pumped her fist in the air as she yelled "*Yes!*" from the middle of the ring in haughty triumph over the chagrinned loser; she then strutted free on strong legs, provocatively grinning and switching her tail to and fro, showing off before she finally took a hard-earned, new chair to others' applause. Karlee, all lightning reflexes on defence, tenaciously held onto her man—even if it meant landing on Orwell's lap or running in front to check him down or block his path. Despite their struggle, she came to her opponent whenever he called her; Karlee obviously liked Orwell to want to restrain her. She often winked—deceptively dully or sternly at first, then more pleasingly or even provocatively defiant as their funny struggle went on, inviting Captain Orwell to sit before her—if he dared!

Surprisingly stalwart, yet always whooping and hollering, the blonde cutie kept Orwell on his toes and the other partiers, in stitches. Orwell clowned congenially, endearing himself to this colourful misfit. Like some hard rock groupie that would have gotten her mouth washed out with soap by any stern parent of the day, little Miss Bryant loudly cursed at any other male who dared to squeeze her. She put an abrupt end to the game by kicking Josh Rocket in the groin when he dared hold onto her churning torso for more than two seconds!

"He grabbed my ass!" gnashed Karlee in response to admonitions from Orwell as, her fierce eyes demanding he act, she stormed past and hit the bathroom for a pee and a smoke, while Alicia and Richard attended the crumpled Mr. Rocket.

The other disconcerted youths left the room; many drifted into the kitchen like so many confused sheep in search of food and water, but others sought their parents for direction. By the time Orwell's clan had revived Josh to where they could escort him into the main house, various families had collected themselves and were departing for home. Bryants went first out the door!

Yes, Orwell recalled as he glumly regarded Karlee now, a sober pipsqueak flanked by her towering twin brothers in the pew below him, they had partied heartily last night, but how could their budding friendship flourish when he and Karlee had not parted on good terms at evening's close? Their good-byes had been trite, awkward...indeed, fraught with embarrassing sting—but what else to expect when Orwell had publicly chastised his age-mate for insulting his other guests! Maybe, Karla Eve was feeling guilty now about her rash reaction and for having thoughtlessly left her plate under the living room couch, where he had found it later while cleaning up...A *decent* guest, Alicia could attest, washed her utensils in the sink after scraping half-eaten food into the slop pail for Orwell's compost heap! Karlee should repent, clean up her act, and get happy.

The high and mighty organist removed his glare from the obnoxious slob, and perused his next musical score. Later, from the edge of his vision, he caught Karlee watching him, fascinatingly amused! She, however, looked away when Orwell returned her gaze, yet renewed her interest as soon as he stalwartly concentrated on his playing. As Orwell pounded through "Stand Up, Stand Up for Jesus", he ignored her as a final attempt at showing that he refused to play her little game any longer, but when Karlee smiled broadly and waved at him as she rose and sang gladly with the congregation, Orwell decided to share a truce with her for this special day. Such odd flirtations were mere trifles in the grand scheme of church, but they were not lost on Alicia, who noted the exchange with concern as she pondered all things in her heart....

JJ read poignantly of Jesus' resurrection from the Bible, while Suzanne told the youngsters a parable about God's enduring love for all His children via *The Giving Tree,* penned by Shel Silverstein.

Pastor Beausoleil encouraged his listeners to trust in the miracle of Christ's resurrection, even in modern times of struggle and science. "Although oppression continues to foment, after mankind walked on the moon or eradicated ancient diseases like small pox, believers must still seek Jesus' truth when their hearts are troubled. He is the Promised One of the Old Testament; the Apostles, disciples, and witnesses of His teachings and actions, have given guidance through the past 1,900 years until today. Love the Lord with all your heart and love others as yourself, are still God's two greatest commandments. To let God open one's mind to understand the scriptures is still a relevant and wise strategy for daily living in our modern era."

The pastor exhorted his rapt brethren to remember Jesus' last words before He departed into Heaven:

"'*Thus it is written, that Christ should suffer and on the third day rise from the dead, and that repentance and forgiveness of sins should be preached in his name to all nations, beginning from Jerusalem. You are witnesses of these things. And behold, I send the promise of my Father upon you; but stay in the city, until you are clothed with power from on high.*'" (Luke 24: 46 to 50)

During the offering, people gave as they were able; gladly approaching the altar, they not only dropped cash but also tinned food, garden produce, or even dry goods and clothing, books or handicrafts into baskets as everyone sang favourite hymns like "What A Friend We Have in Jesus", "Higher Ground", and "Amazing Grace" accompanied by the organ's merry strains. Alicia and Kathleen also humbly came forward, following the lead of fellow choristers and offered all the currency they had on hand. Orwell grinned with pride.

The beautiful sisters were officially invited onto the podium a little later, seemingly last but certainly not forgotten, by beaming Pastor Beausoleil to bring greetings and gifts to the warmly anticipating congregation from their Canadian people. Blissfully lulled by the joyful service, the MacDonachies were suddenly confused by being recipients of such riveted attention. For the life of her, Kathleen could not remember where they had left their musical instruments, and Alicia wondered how she would manage to gather up all those blasted hymnals and lug them into the crowded sanctuary without looking like a total idiot! Lesser lights would have blown out at that level of stress, but Alicia and Kathleen adroitly girded each other as they made their way to the podium; they gained confidence from Orwell, who smiled admiringly upon them as they strode gracefully together to greet placid Beausoleil and Benjamin. The esteemed leaders looked happily expectant at the girls' approach. Why worry? All was hunky-dory!

"Good morning and Happy Easter to all of you!" greeted Kathleen, "My name is Kathleen Beulah, and this is my younger sister, Alicia Pearl Rose. We are the daughters of Reverend Wynnard and Pearl MacDonachie. We are pleased and honoured to worship with everyone here on this blessed Day of our Lord's resurrection! Thank you for inviting us to experience Africa. Christ has risen!"

"Christ has risen indeed!" buoyantly affirmed the massive congregation.

"We are also grateful to the Hughes family for many things: encouraging us to come and visit your wonderful country, hosting us so generously, showing us many interesting things...looking after us...putting up with us," Alicia effusively took up the baton. "Even though we wrote letters back and forth since they relocated here, we haven't seen one other for five long years, so it's been quite a rush getting reacquainted with our friends, let alone bonding with lovely Zambia and all wonderful peoples."

Kathleen started to speak again.

"As some of you may already know, Alicia and I are the youngest children of devoted Christian parents who love God, and provide us with the best role models for our own walk on His path. Our father, Rev. MacDonachie, is a renowned evangelist who has written many inspirational books as well as preached around the world on radio and television programs, but what you may not know is that, before this spotlight was placed on him, our parents served as Christian missionaries for ten years in Nigeria. All of their eight kids were born in that vibrant West African country, as was Dad. He and Mom put their trust in the Lord, and allowed us to travel so far from home as young ladies, because they understand we are safe in Africa with Africans."

"Our parents and other siblings are all well; they send their fond greetings and pray for you as fellow believers. They—indeed our entire congregation in Edmonton who sent us here as emissaries—encourage you to continue walking by faith in humble determination, serving God and helping other people in need," Alicia testified to the receptive congregation. "They ask God to bless you."

Kathy sighed in relief and nudged her sister when she glimpsed her guitar and Alicia's violin sitting intact, along with Bwana Hughes's banjo beside the podium, where unseen hands had placed them. Tears welled up in her beautiful sapphire eyes as Kathy confessed to hundreds of rapt listeners that she did not have in her hands the promised monetary gift to present the congregation today. St. Andrew's generous donation was coming with her brother, who was due any day in the country, but for unknown reasons, was not yet arrived. While this sophisticated, successful woman struggled to report her failure, three African boys brought in the hymnals and laid them like valuable treasures against the altar.

"But, we did bring written praise to God!" giggled Alicia, causing the sombre congregation to laugh and cheer with her. Orwell winced at Alicia, blushing and appealing with outstretched hands, as next she apologized for her petty past complaints, "Hymnals seemed so heavy when I carried them in my backpack to and from all those jets and through all those busy airports, but I see now that there really are only a few... so very few books to go around! Disciple John concluded his beautiful gospel, *'And there were many other things which Jesus did, which if they were written in detail, I suppose that even the world itself would not contain the books that would be written.'*

"I wish we could have filled the entire cargo hold with Bibles for you to read, but these are all that our mothers and grandmothers could give this time. On our next visit, we will bring as many as we can. Meanwhile, I hope that God will work miracles with what we brought, like He fed multitudes with one boy's five barley loaves and two fish."

"Thank you for your hospitality," Kathleen gratefully concluded. Together, the sisters chimed, "Thanks for letting us sing in the choir for today's Easter service. We are inspired!"

The gracious young visitors, not knowing what more to say, smiled and curtseyed to the solemnly watching congregation before heading back to their seats. They walked humbly, yet with poise and grace. Orwell smiled, certain on one hand that Reverend MacDonachie would be proud of his daughters' address, yet sensed with ominous chagrin that they were as fragile as fall leaves fluttering in a stiff breeze.

As he watched them recess, Orwell noticed that Benjamin was also enamoured with these elegant emissaries as he whispered something clever to Pastor Beausoleil. Benjamin was suddenly at the microphone, enthusiastically inviting Kathleen and Alicia back onto the podium!

"Are these two fine ladies not an integral part of that excellent Christian band The *MacDonachie Family Singers*? We are indeed privileged to have such accomplished musicians sojourning in our midst. I can happily testify that they have enriched my choir's presentation today." Then, turning with pleasure to his young guests, Mudenda crooned, "Dear Miss Kathy and Miss Alicia Mairam, may you please now sing something of your own choosing for all of us?"

Although the MacDonachie girls had polished their splendid talents to the nth degree for this vital moment, they now seemed taken aback by his request. Had Ben not already turned their morning upside down? Had they not followed God's leading obediently, sought to cooperate with their hosts as much as possible? Their own agenda, rendered petty in light of the bigger picture of working together with the Zambian choir for the common good of blessing the host congregation, seemed forgotten, lost in translation. The plucky MacDonachies had willingly humbled themselves to let God lead...but no shrinking violets were they! These brave girls had been taught by their parents from birth to go forward and serve willingly, walking in faith for good. With Benjamin and the choir, the pastor and the organist urging them on, Alicia and Kathy embraced this opportunity seemingly offered by God....

The music goddesses took their instruments onto the podium, then grinned radiantly at the congregation. Kathleen effervescently replied, "Well, since you asked...Please know, we are honoured to sing, anytime. How about an old gospel favourite to start with like—let me see—"There is Power in the Blood"? *Okay*! Feel free to join in, everyone!"

"That would be number 526 in our red hymnal," Orwell, shouting from the organ bench, reminded the buzzing congregation, although people knew the inspiring words by heart as they heartily rose to sing.

Kathleen, noting with concern that every three singers shared one hymnal, when these even existed, while others crowded around if they wished to follow the printed pages or simply had to wing it by memory, apologized for lack of helpful audio visuals. "When we had no formal songbooks back home at our Christian camps or Dad's tent meetings, one of us quickly wrote a selected chorus onto a piece of cellophane, and shone the words on the wall through an overhead projector for all to see and follow—no matter how many folks were present! I wish we were better prepared here, for you all."

Orwell chuckled, "You chose a very popular song, Kathy. We can do it!"

"Okay, let's praise the Lord together then," Kathleen encouraged everyone.

She tuned her guitar to Alicia's banjo, and they soon were belting out the great believers' hymn. The celestial girls did not need high-tech sound amplifiers, as their angelic voices and accompanying strums filled the sanctuary with the Lamb's wonder working power. The congregation eagerly sang along with the chorus, sharing their praise to Jesus with rich harmony and rhythmic clapping of hands. Orwell, Ben, and Pastor Beausoleil rocked to the beat. Everyone lifted up their praise to God!

"Wow, this is a blast! I could sing all day with you folks!" Kathleen exalted when they had rolled together through all four verses. She waited for chuckles to trail away before explaining, "Alicia and I really enjoyed worshipping God with everyone here today, but we know that Easter also has its after-church festivities of feasting and visiting. Most of us have places to go and people to see—I know we do, thanks to our wonderful hosts—but others may be lonely or sad; Jesus also rose from death for such folks far from home.

"Whatever your situation, may you find encouragement through "Put Your Hand in the Hand", a special number Alicia and I practised just for this important occasion. It's a fun, yet meaningful Christian folk song written in 1970 by Gene MacLellan, getting a lot of play these days back in North America, since the group *Ocean* and Canada's own Anne Murray made it into a pop hit."

Alicia coolly spoke into the microphone and explained for the benefit of all, "We must improvise now that our brother Tracy, an integral part of *The MacDonachie Family Singers,* can't be with us today. Since we've been practising "Put Your Hand in the Hand" all weekend at Hughes House, it would be swell if Orwell, Richard, Suzy, and JJ could join us now to sing. *Yoo-hoo*? Hughes clan, come up and help out!"

At her roll call, the others darted onto the platform, and six lively youngsters shuffled themselves into an impromptu folk band. They all provided mellow harmony on the choruses, but Kathleen, Alicia, and Orwell each soloed on a verse to testify to Jesus' miracles and exemplary living: the man who stilled the waters and calmed the seas...the carpenter who cleared the temple....Those turfed buyers and sellers were no different fellows than what Orwell professed to be, but through Jesus' teachings, he could look at himself and learn to love his brother or sister. Alicia encouraged her friend to pray for God's love; she felt closest to Heaven when kneeling in prayer. These were wonderful words, venerable amid selfishness and striving of the 'Me Generation' in the 1970s....

What a beautiful service! So many people had selflessly contributed; countless worshippers had been fed! Easter Sunday morning 1974 was a blessing from God that would be savoured, long after everyone departed these hallowed halls—yet, who wanted to leave, Orwell wondered? Wishing that all of His friends could be here together to receive the Lord's anointing, he prayed for Georgina that, wherever she was, whatever she was doing or thinking, God walked with her always! Professors Ibrahim and Muzorewa, Winter, Ben and Cepheus, David and Solomon, as well as his own family members, were offered up in prayer.

"And what of that wild rover, Tracy MacDonachie, Lord God?" Orwell begged to know, tears welling from his closed eyes as he was deeply moved by the popular new gospel praise chorus that Kathleen had recently taught him.

Just as he finished singing its final refrain, holding hands with Alicia and JJ, and swaying to the music, Orwell was drawn in the spirit to gaze upon the sunlit doorway to the sanctuary, where he glimpsed Tracy standing and nodding with approval at him. A thrill of hope jolted through him like a lightning bolt as Hughes exclaimed, "Tracy, you've made it, safe and sound! Hallelujah!"

Alicia glanced furtively at her ecstatic friend, but did not question his sanity as they walked hand in hand back to the choir loft. During the pastor's closing remarks, Alicia anxiously checked again on Orwell, even followed his euphoric gaze beyond the bemusedly basking crowds. Her suspicion turned to joy when she also saw Tracy, now standing inside the church and leaning against the back wall! Her wonderful big brother appeared like an angel dressed in his white safari suit; he smiled when she enthusiastically waved at him. Alicia, like Orwell, could hardly wait for the suddenly dragging service to end so that they could reunite with their long-lost mentor who, through much prayer, had finally been found! They would welcome him 'home' together!

With the final "Amen" chorus sounded and the benediction pronounced, the worship festival to our risen Lord reached its formal end. The choir and organist recessed out the back door while Pastor Beausoleil and Benjamin Mudenda marched down from the pulpit shoulder to shoulder and secured their stations at the front door of the sanctuary to greet departing church folk. The vast congregation followed, merrily flowing out through all four doors of the cross-shaped building. Those already gathered on the lawns welled up to meet the surf. Everyone mingled in the verdant churchyard to visit, reflect, and offer one another the peace of Christ before they went forth to embrace the sunny Sabbath day.

Many people tarried to glimpse, hopefully share a special word with, the beautiful MacDonachie girls. Orwell, having but briefly gone back into the sanctuary to retrieve their instruments, was accosted by several fans who asked him to broach the famous guest artists for autographs and memorabilia.

"Miss Alicia and Miss Kathy will come out shortly to meet everyone, after they change into their travelling clothes," Orwell pleasantly informed these seekers.

Hughes, who dared not speak for the MacDonachies, could promise nothing more. He was not their agent, just lucky to be a friend! Although too polite to say so, Orwell knew that everyone should make requests politely and in person.

Once inside the choir room, Hughes was amazed to find Alicia and Kathleen disrobed and ready to go, yet amicably chatting with several other choristers gathered around them. The African ladies in particular voiced an interest about their guests' home and family, their childhood in Nigeria, and how they had become so talented and accomplished as musicians. Kathleen and Alicia replied to all inquiries, but also returned the favour by asking about backgrounds and aspirations of their new friends. Yvonne and Beatrice were the most forthcoming in this mixed crowd, but Orwell observed how normally bashful Solomon and David also found nerve to interact. Sylvia Halliwell, a white woman looking on with reservation at the edge of the group, took note.

"We better go. I hope to see everyone here next Sunday," Alicia ended wistfully as she and Orwell exchanged meaningful glances.

Banter continued easily as Alicia and Kathleen were escorted *en masse* outside the church. The chivalrous Hughes boys carried instruments and opened doors, yet kept a shepherding eye on their girlfriends from afar, so that Alicia and Kathleen could stroll and mingle as they chose. Vibrant well-wishers surged about these lovely singing sisters and jovially bid to kidnap them, while Orwell, Richard, Suzy, and JJ tarried affably nearby, chatting with various acquaintances.

Orwell and Karla Eve passed one another, though could do ought but shrug and smile with chagrin as they were pulled away before they could explain their rough edges from last night's party: Karlee by her strict father to meet some welcoming Zambian church folk, and Orwell by looming Alicia, who butted in to tell him something apparently vital. During this fleeting moment where they still could hear each other amid the tumult, Orwell and Alicia promised each other to keep a look out for Tracy; whoever hooked that slippery fish first should reel him in for the other.

Although Tracy remained invisible, many other well-wishers of all ages—white, black, and brown—gaily greeted his celebrated sisters. Among the first to pay respects was Mrs. Musakanya, Minister for Arts and Culture. She was lavishly attired and of regal bearing, yet the esteemed politician celebrated this festive day to the max, and was ebullient with everyone she met.

"Well done, Miss Kathleen and Miss Alicia!" praised the great lady. She smiled gleefully and warmly clasped hands with these young white visitors as she blessed them with her own enthusiastic views. "I was deeply touched by your presentation. You are obviously talented and all praise is well-deserved, but I would say these people love you also for being so humble and caring in your interaction with everyone. Your parents would certainly be proud of you today—I know I am. Well done!"

"Thank you, Madame. I'm glad you enjoyed the service; we certainly did," Kathleen politely replied. She followed her junior sister in performing a curtsey to impress the dignitary.

"It was fun singing together with the church choir—we liked being part of the team; the harmony and rhythm were groovy!" Alicia spouted effervescently.

"You all really got down, and rocked it!" Veronica Musakanya chortled, surprising everyone with her hip lingo. When they blushed at having caused her to make such a Sixties scene, the arts maven enthusiastically clapped their hands, "Miss Kathleen and Miss Alicia, you dance like African girls now. Africa agrees with you. I am impressed!"

"Madame, you've made our day even more delightful!" Kathy breezily testified.

"Enjoy the rest of it then, and may God bless your household," Veronica generously offered. As she gracefully departed, she gave them a sweet promise, "We will be in touch about future engagements."

While the MacDonachies wondered, with tingling fear and dreamy anticipation, what Minister Musakanya had in mind for them, Sylvia duly came through the queue, accompanied by what looked like the old woman who lived in a shoe. Sylvia introduced this odd companion as her mother, whom Orwell already respectfully knew as Professor Halliwell, his physics instructor at the university.

"My dears, I gladly second the motion of my friend Veronica—what lovely, uplifting music you brought into our midst!" exclaimed the professor in jolly British as she clasped hands with both Alicia and Kathleen. "You deserve to be the talk of after-service conversation today."

"It was a pleasure singing with you girls. You twitter like canaries," added Sylvia, a plain spinster in her mid-twenties who smiled faintly now in her attempt to compliment supposed peers.

"You're quite a canary yourself," Kathleen merrily returned praise.

"I felt bolstered by your support," Sylvia continued, a shadow moving over her face. "I wish you could stay. With Suzanne and JJ scheduled to return to Canada soon, I will be the only white woman left in our choir."

"Then, you should recruit some replacements from the congregation in a hurry. Try Katrina and Andrea, or some of those Canucks newly arrived from the colonies," joked Kathleen, making Alicia blush when she suggested sassy Karla Eve.

"Those van der Merwe girls maybe can sing—in *Afrikaans*—but they are on loan from South Africa, just for the winter," muttered Sylvia dismissively. "They aren't allowed out much for socializing, and don't drive; choir practices during the week mean extra trips into Lusaka. When not doing farm chores, Katrina and Andrea work as café waitresses or chambermaids for their aunt Eulane, who owns Andrews Motel. I've offered them rides, but those girls won't speak to me; they're quite snobbish really."

"Orwell connects well with Katrina and Andrea," noted Alicia as she nodded at her friend chatting amicably nearby with the two South Africans, not so dowdy and grim looking now. "We found all the choir members to be very friendly and accepting. Just keep doing the best you can to interact, and you will do fine."

Alicia encouraged the downcast Sylvia, although prim Miss Halliwell, close to completing her degree in chemical engineering as a foreign student at the University of Zambia, quietly explained that she already was well-versed in such survival strategies.

Grey-haired and leathery-skinned, clothed in a beige dress that looked like gunnysacks coarsely sewn together, Professor Halliwell appeared plain as grass to the beautiful young MacDonachies. Kitty would later hear to her amazement from Alicia, who had heard it from Georgina during some idle chatter beside her uncle's pool, that Sylvia's strange mother was actually a brilliant scientist who had taught physics for years at various universities, conducted important research, and written many scholarly books. The whole notion seemed like an oxymoron to smart Kathleen, for whom beauty and wisdom went hand in hand. It shed some light on one mystery though, she smugly thought to herself: if such a drab character had taught Orwell about machines, energy, and refracted light, his doltish behaviour required no further explanation! Alicia, on the other hand, was drawn to the professor's broad smile and sparkling eyes, which like her own, floated behind thick glasses. The professor was far more intelligent than she looked!

"That's how I advise Sylvia, too," Dr. Edith Halliwell reiterated, sensing genuine respect and concern brewing in the dark, burly Canadian girl. Glancing fondly at her solemn daughter from time to time, she mentored the three younger women, "I'm glad she wants to be a participant, rather than a bystander, although one does not always know how to do so when tables keep getting turned over.

"Sylvia grew up in Lusaka, but her life of privilege changed with independence and continues to be revised as her adopted country develops. I am glad that she chose to attend the local university rather than go home to UK like all her friends did. Since my husband passed away, I don't know what I'd do without our oldest daughter here, to help take care of us all."

At that moment, Professor Halliwell's youngest son raced helter-skelter through the line, chased by his older brother and several Zambian boys. While the Africans appeared neatly dressed in their scout uniforms, both Halliwell children were barefoot and covered with leaves; their unkempt blonde heads bounced around like haystacks, and their impish faces were red-cheeked with energy.

"I think Jonathan and Gregory have been climbing trees again, pretending to be the 'Lost Boys' from *Peter Pan,*" Sylvia, sighing with good-natured frustration, apologized for such unruly behaviour. "I'll be mending their breeches this afternoon."

"Up to a year or so ago, that would be me, right Kitty-Cat," boasted Alicia.

Kathleen jovially recalled, "Right on, babe! You and Orwell used to play 'Cowboys and Indians' on the river bank like you were part of the Wild West."

"Orwell Hughes and you...playing savages in the forest? You don't say!" exclaimed Professor Halliwell, suppressing a giggle. "My dear, you both are such well-mannered and sophisticated up-and-comers, I can't imagine anything so odd!"

"I suppose I'd better round up the little twerps," Sylvia glumly excused herself from these pleasantries, distracted as she was by the *Lost Boys* boisterously kicking a football against the toolshed behind the church. "Mother, shall we meet you at the bus?"

"Yes, dear, I suppose you should; everyone's getting hungry for lunch," concurred Professor Halliwell. Smiling warmly, the good earth scientist bid Kathleen and Alicia adieu, "It was a treat to meet you ladies. Come again next Sunday?

"By the by, may we see you for a *braai* at our farm after the Campus Christian Fellowship work bee? We're all rolling up our sleeves in a fortnight to build a produce storehouse for some urban market gardeners in Kabwata. It gives UNZA students something useful to do, as well as a hot meal and social, while they wait for classes to resume. Remind Orwell to bring you along."

"We'd love to help out!" Alicia assured the great yet humble lady.

"If we are still here, Fannie, which I seriously doubt," Kathy qualified. Not wanting to be a party pooper, she added robustly, "But we do know how to work!"

Professor Halliwell smiled and bowed slightly in acknowledgement before moseying along. After she had unpretentiously passed by, her students David and Solomon respectfully stepped forward and saluted the MacDonachies. It was a fleeting moment of interaction, whereby the two Zambian lads timidly clasped hands, but barely spoke—yet showed vital signs of interest and respect, a beginning of friendship. They would mix again later today at Mr. Orwell's house.

Teenaged African girls flocked around their white age-mates, shyly broaching them to sign their *Orders of Service* or notebooks; the MacDonachies made lasting friends by asking Orwell to take out their trusty *Polaroid* camera and photograph them together with a bevy of these happy secondary school girls. Females of any kind fascinated him! They pranced about enthusiastically to take their positions, but then how sedately they posed, looking so gorgeously high-minded as they ignored the camera he trained upon them. He was amazed that he could barely decipher the two white celebrities amongst the locals! Mingling with the group was Tabatha, a junior niece of Benjamin Mudenda; she, on behalf of her esteemed uncle—whom Orwell wryly glimpsed across the yard engaged in a heated argument with two grim Englishmen—begged Alicia and Kathleen to sign Ben's new *MacDonachie Family Singers* album.

The elegant conductor paid his own visit to the MacDonachie lasses—fashionably late but exuding gallantry—as the young people from Hughes House placed themselves and their props into the car and prepared to head home.

Benjamin did not barge into them with his own busy agenda nor did he offer to help with theirs. Standing serenely under a shady flamboyant tree and proudly holding his autographed record album against his black suit coat, he patiently watched over the white youth with stoic amusement until their commotion dissipated. He calmly smiled when Alicia grinned and waved.

"Mr. Orwell and Mr. Richard, are you going to your house now? You are taking all your young ladies home to eat and get refreshed?" he inquired, pleased that these European guests in his country were doing as they should. Favoured by colourful backdrop of hibiscus hedges and poinsettia shrubs, Ben concluded his opening remarks with bouquets of admiration and thanks, "I say, you deserve some respite! Well done in today's service! The pleasure is all mine to thank everyone; your enthusiasm was enriching."

"It was a slice, sweet and juicy!" chirped Richard as he shook Benjamin's offered hand.

Behind the car, roadie Orwell nodded in agreement. Ben duly conversed with the white men, but he also wanted the young ladies they chaperoned to hear his praise. Although relieved to finally find a shady car seat with a hint of privacy wherein to rest in their weariness, the precious females basked in his princely attention.

"Thank you," JJ meekly vouched for everyone.

"Yes, this is indeed a very busy day," acknowledged Orwell when no further words were spoken. "We need to get back home to get ready for the big party we're hosting this afternoon. I hope you will be coming, Ben."

"Oh yes, absolutely I must come," Mudenda enthusiastically promised. He gazed meaningfully upon the MacDonachies, particularly merry Alicia, as he assured them, "I look forward to our fellowship."

"Hey, you bought one of our albums! Look, Kitty-Cat, we've got fans even here in southern Africa," Alicia impishly rooted, encouraging Mudenda to display the colourful package he held close to his breast.

"That's great, but I don't remember signing that album; he wasn't even in the greeting line!" joshed Kathleen, winking deviously at the maestro.

"Don't worry girls, your signatures are legit, no doubt," Orwell assured them. He chirped, "Benjamin, by his own ways and means, personally brought his album to you for autographs. I *saw* you sign it. I could recognize your artistic flourish anywhere—it's trademarked!"

"Okay, must be true," Alicia agreed as she examined the album that Benjamin duly handed her for proof. Fluttering dark eyes at her admiring fan, she airily posed, "Do you really like our music, sir?"

"I most certainly do. It is very inspirational," replied Ben with relish.

"God works in mysterious ways," she acknowledged. Sensing Orwell's growing anxiety to get home, Alicia brought down the curtain on their present act. "Mr. Mudenda, we must leave now, but we certainly look forward to seeing you later at the house. Are you perchance going our way now? Do you need a lift somewhere?"

"No, but thank you anyway, Miss Alicia. I will take my lunch at the church, where I still have work to close up, but then, after greeting my junior sister, I will travel to visit you by late afternoon."

They jovially parted company, but Benjamin remained a choice topic of conversation as the Hughes party, in their relief and tiredness, chattered and laughed over their morning adventures during their drive home.

"Does Ben always dance on stage?" inquired Kathleen incredulously. "Like, I mean, he was so into the music that he jolted us all with his energy!"

"He's had calmer days—particularly when he first came into the music ministry three years ago," acknowledged Rick, smiling as he eyed his front seat companion through his cool shades. "Benjamin didn't fly under the radar for long as our congregation quickly fell in love with his theatrics, which is odd because Ben's typically careful and thoughtful, but at times, an austere man. Mr. Eloquent Sophisticated tailors his gait to the mood of the music—today, he really rocked the place!"

"He sure did! Right on!" affirmed Kathleen, pumping her fist in the air.

"Some Europeans find him too radical, but they're just old fogies who need to get with the program. As Bob Dylan sings: '*The times they are a changing….*'"

"A visiting British prime minister told the white South African parliament a decade ago that winds of change were blowing across Africa," mused Suzanne, receiving a star on her forehead from Orwell for being up on world politics. "Like, *whatever*, man. White or black, *we* get along in our choir, and the love keeps growing under Ben's leadership. I prefer singing those stuffy old hymns the African way—it's livelier."

JJ added her two-bits' worth, "I heard some old biddies complaining about his frolicking and dancing, and his enthusiastic shouting of '*Amen!*' '*Praise the*

*Lord*' and '*Thank you, Jesus!*' but they keep coming back. Folks can say what they want, but I like Ben. He's no fanatic; *au contraire* he's one friendly prince of a guy! He can preach powerful sermons, write bestseller books, heal the sick, and speak political with verve.... Then he's willing to visit with kids like me."

"He's your dream idol," Suzy teased her kid sister, who frowned back.

"Mr. Mudenda is very lively, yet he always seems to be alone. Children flock around him, but none of them are his. Does Benjamin have a wife or even a girlfriend?" inquired Alicia of Orwell, whom she assumed knew this wonderful church man best of all, being his good friend and willing organist.

"I have only vague knowledge of Ben's personal life; it would make a very thin book for me to write," Hughes mumbled his confession at last. "Ben is popular with the ladies, but I've never seen any woman consistently by his side."

"Sir, you should become more involved with your friends," lectured baleful Miss A. MacDonachie, unimpressed by his lame excuse. Then, she cleverly cajoled, "Does Secret Agent Ben pay you to keep his secrets?"

"Benjamin leads a very orderly life, and is a very private person. I don't interfere unless he asks me...I just work here."

"That sassy young thing who pushed a record album under our noses for signatures," recalled Kathleen, amused by Orwell's bashful dithering under the pouting scrutiny of her nosy sister. Stirring the pot, Kathy saucily quipped, "Mr. God's-Gift-to-Women likely made her do it."

"You don't know that!" snapped Alicia, suddenly mad at both of them.

"Just like you, girl, who knows nothing about Tracy," Orwell grimly reined in Her Haughtiness. "We both saw him in the sanctuary only fifty minutes ago, holy rolling along with us all, but where is Tracy now? Nowhere, gonzo! Maybe he was just a mirage, an observing angel. For all my avid searching, I never found him after church let out, did you? What do you think, dear Mairam, about the strange situation of our Mr. Tracy Maurice MacDonachie?"

"*Touché*—away!" Alicia raised her big hand and uttered a feisty charge in recollection of some childhood TV cartoon hero, which drew laughter from everyone, but startled Orwell. Rather than run her victim through with her invisible sword, however, she pretended to nab him. Muttering darkly, Alicia declared, "I got you babe. We'll talk later!"

Alicia's comical release seemed to shatter the rising tension in the suddenly crowded, hot, and stuffy car.

"Well, I feel good. Life's is fine. I relaxed like you advised, Orwell, and rolled with the flow. I had a good time—I'm totally happy now," purred Kathleen. Pointing to her forehead peeking out from her golden curly bangs, Kitty testified, "Do you guys see that sign? It spells R-E-L-I-E-F...relief that my hot seat under the spotlight is finally over. I feel free as a bird; I can enjoy my holiday now in southern Africa instead of stewing and fuming about missionary obligations to perform.

"As for you and your party, Oh-well—good luck! Stay cool...Hey, there's Sylvia and Professor Halliwell! Howdy-do, folks!"

Kathleen giddily waved out her window at Halliwell's Volkswagen combi that was halted beside them at the traffic robot guarding busy crossroads near the Ridgeway Hotel. The greying professor smiled benignly in response, and waved delicately with her white handkerchief fluttering in hand, like Queen Elizabeth II was known to do for throngs of well-wishers. Sylvia seemed preoccupied with the jam of vehicles; she sombrely nodded to her neighbours, while all the little rascals bouncing inside her vehicle rambunctiously waved and cheered. Their chance meeting was fleeting; lights changed and all sped away.

"They look like a circus troupe!" Kathleen chuckled. "My God!"

Orwell astutely explained, "Sylvia comes from free-thinkers who value equality among all peoples and cultures. They suffered for striving to obey God's requirements to love mercy, do justice, and walk humbly before Him. Sylvia shared one Friday evening at the Campus Christian Fellowship how her parents came down to South Africa from Britain as young, idealistic professors in the 1950s to lecture at the University of Witwatersrand, but they were dismissed for demonstrating against the National Party's harsh apartheid policies. They later taught for a spell at the University College in Salisbury, but migrated further north when even living among fellow British colonials in bountiful Southern Rhodesia became insufferable with UDI. The couple finally settled in Lusaka, teaching first at Munali Secondary School and Evelyn Hone College, before joining UNZA's Science Faculty shortly after the university opened about five years ago. Both John and Edith Halliwell provided over a quarter–century to teaching physics and chemistry to African students. Dr. John passed away in 1972, but his wife and family stayed on here and became Zambian citizens."

"But they are white people, foreigners, hold-overs from the imperialistic

British colonial past! How can they become African?" protested Alicia, having up until now listened with enthrallment to Orwell's poignant oral history.

"And, if Sylvia worries about being the only white woman singing in church choir, she doesn't belong in an independent Zambia," harrumphed Kathleen.

"She has her anxieties, I grant you that, but Sylvia is right in there at university clubs like Campus Christian Fellowship. She has many African friends—Sylvia's even dated a couple of Zambian blokes during my time at UNZA."

"Excuse, Mr. Oh-well suh, excuse...Who in their right mind would fancy such a gloomy, skinny girl like her?" Kathleen cackled at what she thought was a preposterous supposition.

"I would never have guessed," acknowledged Alicia more solemnly, wondering how Benjamin saw Sylvia. Did her bold willingness to date across the colour line give Orwell hope with Georgina and Molly? Then Alicia asked her friend the obvious question. "Why didn't Professor Halliwell and her children simply go home after the husband died?"

"They *are* home, here in Lusaka. Where else would they go?"

"Jolly old England, of course—where they came from...to their people... their roots."

"As for Halliwells not belonging here—they have been part of Zambia for many moons and deservedly so, my dears. They do their civic duties, pay taxes, vote, employ and host Africans, support local charities, and give allegiance to the President. The Halliwells are card-carrying members of the governing United National Independence Party—*UNIP* to you! Nobody in that household travels to white minority countries anymore or has truck with supporters of those illegal regimes. Sylvia will be hired as soon as she graduates by a local engineering firm, since she's already taken a National Service stint with the Zambian army!"

"My word!" gasped Alicia. "The army? I could never point a gun at anything."

"They chose to stay and make a difference for good here—in this pleasant, but needy place. Sylvia, her mother and the younger children, all decided as a group to stay put, and help build Zambia. It isn't easy, but they have many friends and supporters here. They help out with so many things at church, in social action campaigns, at the university. African students in need of a hot meal and a friendly place to hang out go to their farm for a game of ping pong or to swim, sing, read, study, or get tutored in maths and sciences, and they do some yard work in return, no problem—they gladly flock to the Halliwell farm on any given day. Visitors are always welcome, as long as they take the Professor as she is, witty but cluttered and down-to-earth. I've been out there to study myself, as well as attend work bees and garden parties. There's a big happening at their home next month, after Campus Christian Fellowship folks lay some bricks and mortar to build a storage facility in Kabwata Township for some local market gardeners."

"That's right! I'm reminding you to take me along to help, Orwell, just like the dear old professor instructed after church today," Alicia piped in, despite Kathleen frowning at her to keep quiet. She thoughtfully placed her hand upon her breast as she pondered the Halliwells' difficult yet instructive odyssey. "Life is complicated! Rather than be black or white, it tends to have many shades of grey...or brown. We should never assume anything from first impressions."

"Better, we should walk a mile in their moccasins first, eh?" added Orwell, smiling appreciatively that they seemed to be back in tune with one another.

"Oh yes," nodded Alicia in agreement. She laughed merrily as she warmly shared, "We must talk more about what it means to belong. Orwell, you are so knowledgeable, so wise. I sometimes play the devil's advocate to stimulate conversation, but I love listening to you; I learn so much!"

"Fannie, you sound like Orwell is your Indian guru!" chided Kathleen.

"No, he's her hobby!" Suzanne declared impishly. "I've heard Alicia reveal that sweet tidbit more than a few times, with stars shining in her eyes. Orwell just laps all up this devotion. It's so rare, you see."

"Whatever, it's all true," sighed Alicia blissfully as she smiled out the window as some African children dressed in beautiful Easter garments gaily paraded down the leafy boulevard. When they waved back at her, Alicia reminded her teasing car mates, "We are all called to be nice to one another."

'Big Bertha Honey' seemed not to know or care that her boy-toy blushed and fidgeted as the others razzed them. Alicia sharply glared at JJ, however, after she obnoxiously led the group through a rousing rendition of:

"Orwell and Alicia, sitting in a tree, K-I-S-S-I-N-G!
First comes love, then comes marriage,
Last comes Alicia with a baby carriage!"

Fit to be tied, Orwell chastised these fighting words of his lippy kid sister, but Alicia stopped his loud mouth with a shrill whistle and an overriding signal for time out. Once she grabbed their attention, she frankly set the record straight.

"Orwell and I are good friends, but I am not his special girlfriend. Georgina is! *Répétez, s'il vous plait*: Georgina and Orwell are going together."

The others gazed incredulously at Alicia. Everyone thought she was joking or would soon break out in tears, but they dimly nodded in gradual accord when she stayed content in her clear, mature understanding of the situation. Orwell listened with relief, saddened yet impressed by her articulate sharing.

Alicia shocked him when she gently touched his arm.

"Oops," she murmured. They glanced at each other in surprise, then giggled together in solidarity. Smiling serenely now, Alicia seemed much older and wiser than him, Orwell marvelled, as she advocated on his behalf, "My friend has tried so sweetly and diligently throughout our stay, even while he made this morning go so well for Kathleen and me, to prepare a wonderful party for this afternoon, so that Georgina and all his other African friends can have a special Easter time—with us. I want to help Orwell host this *grande fête* as best I can."

"Okay, Lisa, we get your point," gnashed JJ, feeling bad about her recent outburst.

"You should become a lawyer or a shrink, not a doctor," Suzanne agreed.

Not so much unrepentant as surprised by her sister's selfless diplomacy, Kathleen covered her confusion by boisterously reminding Orwell of all manner of worries that had been churning already for hours like a washing machine inside his stomach.

"Now, it's your turn to sweat, eh Orwell? One big event down, but one still to go! It's almost party time, eh? All these eclectic friends are coming—you've got a honey to impress! Only three hours left to live, Oh-well?"

"Kitty-Cat, let up already!" scolded Alicia. "Give our brave man a break!"

"Get a grip, Annie Fannie!" Kathleen retorted. "Like, this party is all about some hot chick he's got coming by this afternoon? What about the rest of us—are we just cheap extras to decorate his romantic bash?"

"How embarrassing! We are all invited, so we must work together to have fun," Alicia lectured Kathleen sternly. She then pleaded with her host, "Orwell, I'm so sorry that you have to put up with such disrespectful and ungrateful guff after all the good things your family has done for us. You have really been kind and generous these past few days, and I can see it comes naturally out of the goodness of your hearts. Please accept my apologies if Kathleen and I don't measure up…"

"I'm okay, really," Orwell calmly countered. "You ladies are awesome! Just as 'The Man Upstairs' helped make a way for you today, He has given me the grace to hold a party for all my friends in your honour, before we all leave this wonderful place. Even Tracy has arrived and may attend! Everything will work out just fine if we all make the best of it together."

As he finished those words, they drove into the Hughes yard, where Easter splendidly bloomed.

# CHAPTER NINETEEN

WHEN THE HUGHES HOUSE YOUNG people returned home blessed from service, they devoured a sumptuous meal of fried chicken with rice and trimmings that Mama Hughes had prepared. Afterwards, there simply was no time to rest on one's laurels! Numerous guests, full of energy and expectations, soon would come...and another, sister festival was yet to be celebrated! Orwell told everyone to change into something more comfortable and get to work!

Tackling the first job on his long list, he fetched a tea chest from storage and fished out multi-coloured, plastic ice cream pails that he then laid out—one by one, staggered at ten-foot intervals—along both sides of the laterite driveway, down to the gate. Hughes knew why these pails had their bottoms missing, but he was irked that many were discoloured and melted from previous run-ins with fire. Orwell tossed the empty chest back in the store room, and ran into the house to get his supply of white paraffin candles from the pantry. In his frightful hurry, he spilled a large box of wooden match sticks on the floor, and gnashed his teeth as he quickly stuffed them into the pockets of his safari suit.

Orwell caught Alicia's eagle eye as he rushed through the kitchen carrying bundles of candles like so many sticks of dynamite, matches spilling from his bulging pockets. He glared at her stifling laughter at his comical sight, but Alicia, recognizing a man on a mission, wished him Godspeed and continued to wash dishes. After he stormed out of the house and disappeared around the corner of the carport, however, she left the hive of buzzing women and curiously followed Orwell. Keeping a safe distance, Alicia watched him feverishly installing sidewalk lanterns. She was impressed by his methodical layout, but in his urgency to complete the arduous task, Hughes' clumsy dithering amused the would-be spy.

Intrigued but wanting to help, Alicia crept closer and closer to the action until she leaned over Orwell as he squatted on the lawn, pairing jar lids with candles from respective piles.

"Since you absolutely must know, I'll spell out the obvious," teased Orwell, cross that the amazon should scrutinize his toil with such childlike fascination. "I'm counting out one candle for each plastic pail I'll use for a lampshade. Return to your scullery now, if your curiosity is satisfied."

"Let me help you here," pleaded Alicia, her bright eyes betraying genuine concern for him. Refusing to leave, she determinedly offered, "I'll set out each jar lid properly, so you can stand a lit candle in the dripping wax. Better yet, you set out the lids and I will follow behind, light each candle, melt a drop of wax onto its lid, and then set the candle in place."

"Girl, you know the drill inside out! You must have worked already on some factory assembly line where they make yard lanterns from recycled plastic pails," Hughes kidded, as he accepted her efficient scheme. "I'll lay out jar lids if you set candles. We'll be done in a jiffy."

"Like a well-oiled machine, my dear Watson."

Taking Alicia at her word, Hughes did what he said he would do; looking nervously over his shoulder, he was pleasantly surprised to see Alicia following closely behind and fulfilling her duties. Moving right along, these busy bees also set up the ping pong table and put final touches to decorations festooning the party deck. They intertwined streamers and mounted colourful balloons around the perimeter. A lava lamp, white gas lantern, and a large, battery-operated strobe light were strategically placed to provide more sensual glimmer after dark. They filled an ice-chilled cooler with pop bottles and piled assorted nuts, pretzels, and fruit into decoratively carved wooden bowls.

"What's this chunk of metal?" queried Alicia, as she performed forearm curls with a heavy metal box studded with electrical plug-ins. When Orwell calmly explained that the transformer was required to safely download Lusaka's 220-volt electrical current to 110-volts in order to run the stereo music system, Alicia appreciatively replied, "Oh, right. Let's not blow up this baby!"

"You got it, *Cadillac*!"

Faces flushed and glistening with sweat, the party planners stood back for a moment to appraise their ingenious handiwork. Alicia, content with the aesthetics so far, smiled at her collaborator, pleased to see that he also nodded and stuck up both thumbs affirmatively.

Unable to rest easy on any given day—let alone today when his beloved fairy princess, Georgina Amadu was due to cut the ribbon on festivities held in her honour—Orwell suddenly gasped at his watch and galloped away. Racing behind the house, he vaguely supposed that Alicia would take her cue to go help the women finish in the kitchen now. As principal planner, he knew how much more still needed to be done to make this gala fete completely right and fun....

Alicia ran after Orwell, determined to serve him; she had no intention of quitting the game until it was completed! Catching up to him as he dragged a heavy metal drum from the back garden, Alicia jumped right in by lifting the back end of his load and helped him carry it to a spot on the patio he had designated outside the guest room. Ignoring his admonitions that she should not get dirty—since he already had everything under control, thank you very much—Alicia again earned her keep when she hauled and stacked bricks to help make two pedestals upon which they carefully laid the drum horizontally. Orwell fascinated her when he inserted a crowbar into a secret hole and pried open the top half of the drum, revealing a barbecue!

Alicia was again impressed by the strength, ingenuity, and immensity both of her captain and his recycled cooking contraption, yet screwed up her face with disgust when she smeared her hand with greasy black soot after casually running it along the cylinder's ventilated interior. Orwell grimaced too when she opened a grate in the drum's bottom, causing a dusty pile of ash to spill onto the concrete below before he could catch it. Apologizing profusely, albeit glibly in Orwell's stern opinion, Alicia ran for a broom and dust pan before he could advise her to wait until more dirt and grime would surely be produced around the meat grilling station. She, grinning with satisfaction despite looking like a modern-day Cinderella, had already swept the old ashes into a can by the time Orwell returned to the scene, gingerly clutching the massive barbecue grill between his blackened, outstretched arms. Noting the cast-iron mesh was caked with remains from previous use, Alicia declared, "Orwell, this utensil is gritty with waste and reeks like an abattoir! Totally unhygienic—we can't use it like this! Put it away now, and buy a bucket of *Kentucky Fried Chicken* for your guests."

"A little crud ain't bad—adds grit to the diet!"

"Hah, hah! Very funny!"

"And just where would I find *Kentucky Fried Chicken* here on Easter Sunday? Don't worry, the grease'll boil off nicely, once the fire gets piping."

"We should clean this baby up before doing any cooking—unless you want to give people cancer or food poisoning!"

"We do things differently down here. Folks aren't so fussy when they're hungry, and all they have is a campfire to cook over. Besides, I don't have time to make everything sparkly clean!" wailed Orwell impatiently. Cross that his visitor proved so critical after barely arriving in Zambia, he ordered Alicia to go clean the soot off her hands and change her clothes.

"I'm still helping you; I'll clean up when we're done, thank you!" retorted the amazon, refusing to leave. "I'm not some spoiled princess, Bucko!"

"Okay, fine!" growled Orwell. "If you want to be useful, ask Mom for some steel wool and a bucket of hot, soapy water. Make that two buckets—we also need some hot rinse water, plus some rags for wiping everything down."

"And meanwhile, what are you going to do, pray tell?"

"Chop kindling...gather charcoal...manly things, you know."

"Humph, sounds like child's play to me!" huffed Alicia as she, feeling like his unappreciated servant, stamped angrily into the house, slamming the door behind her.

"You have no idea," gnashed Orwell from somewhere beneath her clatter.

Staring after this mad girl, he became mesmerized by her powerful legs pounding and rich bottom churning under her jumper. Alicia was stacked—a mighty steam engine well worth driving—but how would he ever manage her? Did he even want to? Why was this majestic yet fragile young lady even here to be such a thorn in his flesh when lovely Georgina was already made for him? Now that Alicia had sung her songs and celebrated Easter at church with her hosts, she should go home...get out of his face and stop messing with his mind... let him return to normal... find his academic and athletic programs, and resume his comfortable rhythms of life: music and writing, friends and girlfriends... Hopefully, such blessed reunions would begin in about two hours' time with Georgina's arrival. Alicia was in Zambia because of his sisters and Tracy, but where was he? Hopefully, the mighty Tracy would attend the party, to make all his strenuous preparations gloriously worthwhile.

"Where are your fire starter and fancy little charcoal briquettes?" Alicia asked, cheerily shattering his doldrums.

Blinking into the golden afternoon sunlight as though awakening from a dream, he found her leaning against the outside brick wall of the guest room, leering at him with amusement as he struggled to keep a piece of lumber upright long enough in the breeze to split it with his hatchet. Two steaming buckets of water, one foaming with soap bubbles, stood ready beside the barbecue, next to a neat stack of rags. For his part, soot-faced Orwell had rustled a man-sized burlap sack bulging with charred tree limbs from the storeroom, and pilfered several termite-riddled spruce studs from an airfreight box that had recently been discarded by a recent Canadian arrival. Orwell's contribution seemed pitiful by comparison, particularly when his axe swings hit the concrete or the head became stuck in a knot rather than sliced decisively through the soft, foreign wood. Orwell prided his woodsman skills learned early as a boy scout. Yet, he felt that Alicia, who keenly watched and patiently waited, judged him a feeble momma's boy when he took forever to finish the simple task of making a pretty pile of kindling.

"Let me help you, Orwell," Alicia, no longer able to hold her tongue, brazenly offered. She took advantage of his momentary pause between chops to grab, before he could, the mutilated two-by-four lying prone on the concrete, and wryly advised the fuming lad to use a proper chopping block. 'Bush-savvy Babe' set a slab of local hardwood from his wood pile beneath the much-hacked spruce stud, and sweetly broached, "Can I take a turn here?"

"Are you going to be careful? Do you even know how to hold an axe?" goaded Orwell, insulted by her fearless interference, even as he surrendered the tool to her insistently outstretched hands.

"Of course, man! I chopped cords of wood while cooking for Robert's wild bunch at *Bonne Chance*," snorted Alicia, a resolute look on her face as she gripped the axe like a tomahawk.

Rather than scalp him, however, Alicia yelled blood-curdling oaths as she grimly executed four boards—each one dispatched by one brutally precise swing. Orwell watched her with amazement and jealousy that this wonder woman could do everything well, while he bumbled even the simplest carpentry tasks his father expected all men should master....But he quickly shook these bleak thoughts from his head because he had no time to be a by-standing punk during the ever-shrinking preparation time. Sighing, Orwell trudged over to the waiting pails and rags and started cleaning the barbecue—a drudgery he had the staying power to endure. Alicia efficiently presented him with a fine bundle of kindling in short order, which he gratefully accepted. She grinned broadly before kneeling beside him to rinse and dry the portions of the drum Orwell had fiercely scrubbed clean with steel wool.

Orwell apparently made Alicia's day by trusting her with sharp tools! She pleasantly sang as she cleaned the grill, while he intricately fashioned a kindling pyre, ignited it with a single match, and gradually, carefully, added larger pieces of wood and then charcoal to fuel the flames. Alicia laughed rather than rebuked Orwell when he, by running the household vacuum cleaner with its hose connected to the exhaust port, ingeniously blew air onto the fire. Coals peacefully turned to embers by the time Alicia positioned the now shiny grill into place. She then stretched like a cat and strode happily into the house.

Minutes passed as Hughes, left by his lonesome, tidied up the cook shack. He heaved a sigh of relief to be finally free of Alicia's domineering presence, though he had to admit, as he stowed the charcoal and put away the vacuum cleaner, she had helped him like a Trojan through some thankless jobs. The feisty princess could not only work hard, but actually cooperate when she wanted to!

He rightly assumed that she had retired indoors to compose herself for the party, but he had barely admired the red-hot embers before his helper returned, bearing a platter heaped with raw sausages slathered in spicy red sauce for him to cook. His dutiful co-worker sported a healthy glow on her brown, freckled face that made her look beautiful, Orwell acknowledged to himself as he praised her return and was pleased to exchange smiles; he also noted approvingly that she had shed her flowing robes as well as her glasses. Beneath her flimsy kitchen apron, jolly Annie Fannie skipped around in a spiffy blue miniskirt and white cotton blouse that revealed her shapely legs and praised her luscious breasts and bottom. She, liberally batting her cutely lined eyes, relished his blatant observations, but brought adoring Orwell back to earth through easy banter, entertaining him while he sizzled the plump *boerewors*. Her sandals seemed to float upon the sidewalk while she glided away with the brazier heaped high with smoking, blackened meat that her brave hunter had cooked.

Playing the dutiful serving girl, Alicia came and went many times on kitchen business, but she surprised Orwell with treats—a glass of iced lemonade, slice of choice fruit or even a barbecued sausage blanketed with tomato sauce and wrapped in a bun—on various trips, while the other ladies laughed from the kitchen window at the scene. Winking to each other as they worked together preparing raw vegetables and baking sourdough buns, they noticed how the unusually chipper young woman took any opportunity to assist the broiling cook outback—it had to mean something! Some crazy little thing called love must be in the air! With a smile and a song on her soft red lips, the pleasant young lady also did her part of the inside chores, yet played oblivious to their curiosity as she went about chopping peppers and carrots, pouring drinks, and setting out plates and silverware in the dining room where Rick and Jim were adding the centre leaf to extend the table, and arranging extra seats for many invited guests.

As he watched her prance yet again back to the scullery, this time packing inside his dirty plate and cup, Orwell was agog at how Alicia worked her awesome feminine form. Her plump bum cheeks seemed to wink and smile daringly at him through her tight dress; their round curves cajoled him as Alicia set down her tray and conveniently bent over to adjust her sandal strap. Resisting a primal urge to reach for her shapely bottom with his grubby rough hands, Orwell sweated over the smoky barbecue instead, still allowing himself to whistle appreciatively at Alicia's fertile beauty.

"Naughty boy! You do *love* my plump apple bum!" the goddess giggled as she glanced back with a deliciously sassy grin at her shameless admirer.

Alicia primped in the kitchen doorway to honour Orwell's ribald attention and then chortled as the grimy, sweat-streaked boy stared at how energetically her bottom danced inside her dress. She revelled in his awe, pleased to catch him honestly looking—the only man she cared to entertain and wished would admire her ripe, buxom figure....

All good things must end, Orwell sighed as Alicia coyly waved goodbye and withdrew indoors. Kathleen and Suzanne, wondering why Alicia was puttering idly about, gawked smugly out the kitchen window. Orwell hoped to God they had not seen his bulging pants nor viewed her provocative display, which he knew he had encouraged through his own lusty response. Eventually, everyone went back to their own work without accosting him—a good sign! In rebuking his own weakness, Orwell wondered: what dangerous designs the amazon planned for him and his friends on this vital afternoon, now that he had let her imp out of the bottle? He resolved to stop encouraging her demons, but rather, tame Alicia with gentle pleasantries and stoic demeanour.

Orwell prayed he might see Alicia again and respectfully apologize to her before guests arrived. She returned at last, carrying a towel and a basin of hot soapy water. This must be for scrubbing clean his polluted mind, Orwell wryly concluded, but Alicia put her finger to her mouth to shush him when he began to babble all sorts of anguished excuses for his unseemly behaviour.

"I am pleased that you find me attractive, but I also appreciate that you respect me, Orwell," she solemnly replied. Smiling softly, she added, "We both love God and are obedient to Him above all else. Someday, if God wills and we both agree, opportunity may come when we may get to know each other better. I sincerely hope so, but not today, however, as you are entertaining many important guests, including a young woman who is your special friend."

Orwell cautiously nodded all while making sure not to hurt her feelings by agreeing too much with her analysis. Without her heavy glasses, her dark almond eyes gazed with fierce admiration upon him as she provided him with toiletries, and bid he wash himself. Orwell nodded and obeyed her directive as he nearly wept with joy over her merciful understanding of his needs. How selfless, how loving was this strange young woman! He wished he could not only eat his slice, but enjoy consuming the whole cake!

"Where are your glasses, Alicia?" he finally inquired, worried somehow that she would trip over her pouting lip or her misty eyes would become strained, squinting unprotected against the brilliant afternoon sun. "Like on that other day when you ambushed me at the compost heap? How can you see properly, especially when you're doing all this helpful work?" Hughes, mystified by the new invention, begged to know.

"I put in my new contact lenses!" she proudly informed him, chirping happily. "I'm trying them out again today. It's a new thing—all the rage back home—a wonderful liberation long in coming to four-eyed clowns like me," Alicia added. Then, winking and smiling deliciously at her bewildered admirer, she giggled, "The better to see you with, my dear!"

Orwell laughed heartily with his friend as they washed greasy utensils in the kitchen. Alicia, knowing the lateness of the hour from having heard the Westminster clock chime three times on the fireplace mantle...and from having been delegated by Mrs. Hughes to hurry her son along...playfully shooed the sooty figure into the bathroom to make himself quickly presentable, lest his elegant friends mistake him for a chimney sweep.

# CHAPTER TWENTY

FESTIVITIES STARTED PROMPTLY WITH HIGH tea at 3:00 pm, although guests arrived in gentle trickles throughout the afternoon. Orwell was changing into his striped bellbottom trousers and fluorescent flower shirt when Tug barked his muffled warnings from the garage. Articulating the dog's news, Alicia and JJ banged excitedly on their party captain's bedroom door to announce that two Zambians awaited him at the gate.

"Let them in, for Heaven's sake!" rumbled Orwell from deep within his sanctuary. Playing shy or just plain teasing him at a bad time, the girls disobediently tarried in the foyer, giggling nervously as they urged Orwell to hurry, and occasionally fiddled with his door knob or tapped on his window, then hid.

"What are you broads—antisocial bums? It's probably Solomon and David, whom you sang with only hours ago at church!" gnashed Hughes, nearly colliding with Alicia as he rushed out of his room, making the loitering girl gasp at his scrubbed face shiny from freshly-applied *Vaseline* cream, and his shirt unbuttoned to the breast bone to reveal a blond hairy chest rippling with muscles. He smelled abundantly of deodorant and expensive cologne, but this show of athletic masculinity was not for her!

The suddenly stern-faced girl refused to step out of his way. Appraising him keenly in the split second he allowed her, Alicia delayed the anxious host long enough to repair his haphazard condition. Orwell sighed impatiently as his stylist nimbly mopped his glistening face with her handkerchief and buttoned up his shirt a notch to restore his modesty.

After a seeming eternity, Alicia finally fell back, content with her mitigations, and released the host to engage his duties. "I'm done! Go get 'em, killer!"

"Where's JJ? She invited those guys!"

"She's already welcoming our friends, Solly and Dave. JJ is boy-crazy!" Alicia giggled, admonishing Orwell to lighten up.

"All right, it's our turn now!" growled Hughes. With urgency, he grabbed 'Big Bertha' by the hand and hauled her, laughing merrily, down the driveway. They eased into a stately walk when they saw the tall and brightly dressed Zambians incredulously studying their antics from afar.

"Good afternoon, Mr. Orwell," greeted David good-naturedly before he engaged his white friend in the gentle ritual of shaking hands, African style.

These UNZA lads did not hold each other in vice grips how Bwana Hughes acted on official Canadian service, or grapple like the MacDonachie men would do to cement a business deal, but softly parried for several clever seconds with their right hands: they clasped palms lightly, touched the backs of their hands together, then held hands somewhat more firmly in assurance of their connection. Orwell was a willing dance partner for David, a veteran at the game of culture.

"I think you've got it, Mr. Orwell," he laughed with appreciation of young Bwana's effort to learn how things were done in African. "Would you not agree, Mr. Solomon?"

"Yes," affirmed Solly with a broad grin as he went through the same hand dance with Orwell. "Well done, Mr. Orwell."

"Good afternoon to our lady friend, Miss MacDonachie," acknowledged David with a polite bow to Alicia.

"Welcome to you, Mr. David," replied the young woman who, suddenly self-conscious about the amount of skin and curves she was revealing to these virile strangers, curtseyed shyly in reply from a safe distance.

Where was her long dress, or at least a towel to wrap her bare legs with? JJ was right in the mix, sporting with David and Solomon, so could not discretely make a clothes run. From behind a bush, Alicia enjoyed the men's handshake game, and would have played it herself with Orwell's friends, had she known them better.

Mr. Sobukwe, already assured of her welcoming fellowship, praised Alicia, "I enjoyed singing with you and your sister at church today, Miss MacDonachie. You were brave and kind to sing our chosen pieces together with African choir voices, even with Zambian drums and shakers to accompany you. It was sweet for you ladies and Mr. Orwell to practice with us using the *so-fa* scales rather than piano notes. God has given you many gifts, Miss MacDonachie—notably the spirit of cooperation."

"Why, thank you sir. I enjoyed worshipping with all of you today. Everyone blessed me with welcoming spirits. It was fun to sing together; I was less nervous in the mass choir than when only Kathleen and I were presenting our duets. Of course, we'd have moved mountains, had Tracy sung with us like he was supposed to. Fortunately, Orwell proved excellent as Tracy's substitute on the bass harmony; he should replace Tracy at our future gigs!"

"Most definitely. The three of you sing very well together. Solomon and I already know that Mr. Orwell plays the piano and organ like a master musician, but he also shows his singing. Mr. Rick and their sisters—Miss Janice and Miss Suzanne—also assist splendidly as part of the choir that Mr. Benjamin directs for Sunday worship. We enjoy singing together in our rainbow choir!"

"I'm on the red band," laughed Orwell. "*Que sera, sera*[52]. I've been told before that I'm a red man by Professor Ibrahim, not to mention certain tall girls around here that I won't name. Now, ladies and gentlemen, let's stroll into the back garden and have some refreshments. I have everything prepared for you."

They were barely settled when Ali and Georgina drove with verve into the Hughes compound aboard their shiny green Volkswagen beetle. Stepping smartly forward, Orwell and Rick greeted Ali with respectful pleasantries befitting a foreign dignitary, while their sisters and sisters' girlfriends admired the pageantry from afar. Rick chatted with Ali about his neat set of wheels as they listened to Johnny Nash sing "I Can See Clearly Now" on the trend-setter's bracelet radio. Orwell gallantly held open Miss Amadu's door, glad that she gaily alighted into his bright, sun-shiny day.

"How nice of you," she offered, giving her adoring attendant a stack of records to carry into the house. Orwell thought Georgina expected him to play all this hot wax immediately, but when she saw his confused expression oh so familiar, the high-society lady airily explained, "I brought us some upbeat dance music for later on tonight—favourites from my own record collection...is that acceptable?"

"Of course, Georgina, thank you," Orwell assured her. Flipping with relish

52 French expression, meaning 'what will be, will be.'

through her assorted forty-fives as if they were a deck of playing cards, he remarked breathlessly even as he followed her up the driveway, "'The Twist' and "Let's Twist Again" by Chubby Checker, Little Eva singing "Loco-motion", *Mungo Jerry*'s "In the Summertime"! Wow! Let's see—you've also got famous hits by *Credence Clearwater Revival*; *The Rolling Stones, Beach Boys,* and *Supremes, Abbey Road and White Album* courtesy of *The Beatles*—even our own Canadian rock band *Steppenwolf,* pounding out "Born to Be Wild" and "Magic Carpet Ride"! Gosh, Georgina, did Wolfman Jack rate your records high?"

"Orwell, you *are* silly," Georgina laughed, then mischievously batted the long, silky lashes of her lovely eyes at him. His patron waved him charmingly onto the task at hand. "Take care of my records now, before your other guests arrive and distract you from your high purpose. We'll dance up a storm together later tonight, I promise you, now that I know how well you move to the beat. Remember our hip time dancing at the university? Of course, you excelled!"

While onlookers chuckled at how easily Orwell turned into a loaf of freshly baked bread in her hands, Georgina paraded regally ahead, and breezed into the company of warily watching Alicia, who lingered beneath the avocado tree and smiled politely only when their brown eyes briefly met. Georgie gently clasped the amazon's calloused hand with a vivacious grip as proof of her desire to be friends. Alicia blushed warmly but could not flee, since the bevy of young girls gracing the Hughes household now curiously gathered around her, fascinated to learn how she would deal with so splendid a rival.

"There you are my dear. I have been so looking forward to seeing you again since we reclined together like princesses in Uncle's limousine. Mairam, is this beautiful blonde lady not your sister, a famous singing partner?"

"She is indeed my sister, one of three, believe it or not!" exclaimed Alicia, wrapping her arm warmly around Kitty-Cat's slim waist and drawing her forward as moral support. "Kathy is my favourite pretty sister, who is next older above me; she's the clever one—my teacher whose example I follow!"

"I've heard such rumours from time to time," acknowledged Kathleen, woodenly humorous as she extended her elegant hand in welcome. "I wish they're all true."

"I wouldn't know; I don't have a sister, since my father wanted only me as a daughter," Georgina held her attentive female audience with her large brown eyes . Georgina smiled as she gestured at Ali, now strolling easily up the driveway hand in hand with Richard, discussing the advantages of Volkswagen's air-cooled, rear engine over run-of-the-mill American boats equipped with liquid coolant engines in front of the car.

"But I do have one brother from my same father and mother, who is wonderful to me," Georgina continued lushly.

As the lads dreamed of fast-driving sports cars, like Stingrays or Porsches, Kathleen and Suzanne suddenly ran to their boyfriends adoringly, leaving Georgina alone again with Alicia and JJ. These three girls, feeling bonded together by sensibility, laughed together.

"Whew, it's hot out here!" remarked JJ at length as she fanned herself with her dainty hand. "Come on, Georgina, let's take you to the patio for refreshments. Orwell can serve us tea...After all, you are the guest of honour — at least in his goo-goo eyes!"

"Janice Joanne!" chided Alicia, giving her friend a not so playful reprimand. When JJ quizzed the amazon, Alicia muttered as she purposefully led the way, "I better make myself useful, and give Orwell a hand behind the bar."

As expected, they found Orwell busy on deck, hosting his guests as he offered them dainty pastries, and poured English tea sweetened with condensed milk. Georgina comfortably reclined like Cleopatra in a plush lounge chair, smiling sedately while Orwell waited diligently on her every beck and call.

"Hey *garçon,* what about that Coke you promised me?" heckled Kitty-Cat at the blushing, sweaty waiter from her cushioned lawn chair beside Georgina. Amused by his tireless efforts to please the beautiful socialite, but also to impress her for Alicia's sake, Kathleen playfully pouted at Orwell, "Did you forget my order, *garçon*?"

"Righto, I'll get you next, Kathy," promised Hughes, clumsily upstaging Richard as he busily dashed around. Kathleen yelped deliciously at the risky thought while Rick, glancing at the soft, cloud-dappled sky, rolled his eyes in mock concern.

"I've got Kathleen's drink here, Orwell," offered Alicia smartly as she fished out one of the many glistening dark bottles swimming among ice cubes in the basin of cold water. Chuckling to mask her genuine concern, Alicia advised him, "Take a break before you die of heat stroke; I can bring my sister's dumb drink to her."

Orwell reluctantly obeyed, but then slapped his helper in the face by plopping himself down beside Georgina and entertaining her with all matter of curious questions about how she had spent her holidays thus far. Miffed but vowing not to be shaken, Alicia methodically placed Kathleen's bottle on the table and positioned the buck-toothed loop of the steel opener over the cap, to pry it off with her large hands. Suddenly, Ali and Suzanne loomed in front of her, apparently wanting to watch the strapping girl perform some magic trick.

"What would you folks like to drink?" barmaid Alicia gruffly demanded.

"A club soda and lime cordiale for Suzy and ginger beer for me—on the rocks!" ordered Ali jauntily. When Alicia appeared to be bending the puny bottle opener awkwardly in her balled fist, Ali bragged, "Here, let me do that for you, Hanoi Jane".

Ali grabbed the pop bottle away from Alicia, not caring how much he shook its volatile contents during the exchange. Her exasperation turned to shock as the playboy stuck the bottle sensually in his mouth and pried off the cap with his clenched teeth. He spit the projectile into a nearby basket before pushing the smoking bottle back into Alicia's outstretched hands. Suzanne gaily clapped for her showman as Ali quipped glibly, "That's how we open bottles here in Africa, Miss Jane."

"That's how you break your teeth," warned Alicia sternly. "Next thing you know, they'll be rolling on the floor like *Chicklets*!"

"Not mine—these pearly whites are strong and sharp!" boasted Ali as he selected another drink for himself, and brazenly opened it with his teeth.

"That's boneheaded, man! You're freaking me out!" gnashed Alicia as she strode away with Kathleen's drink nearly boiling in her hand.

Kathleen gave her frowning sister a quick check-up appraisal as if to demand, "What's up?" as she accepted the refreshment Alicia thrust in her face. Kathleen followed the buxom waitress with feline eyes, as Alicia glanced sadly at Orwell obliviously chatting with Georgina, before she retreated to the backstairs and sat down there to quench her own thirst with a glass of iced fruit juice, with her broad back to everyone.

Thus, Alicia was first to welcome Benjamin, who came strolling leisurely up from the open road, unannounced and single, yet luxuriously perfumed and dressed handsomely in a beige safari suit and polished black shoes.

"Good afternoon, Sir Benjamin," Alicia pleasantly quipped as, assuming the role of hostess in her adopted household since every Hughes was otherwise preoccupied, she attentively rose and clasped his hand with respectful greeting.

"Good afternoon to you, Miss Alicia?" replied Mudenda curiously who, normally oozing with charm and confidence, was stopped dead in his tracks by this tall, scantily-clad young woman, who bloomed gorgeously in contrast to the conservatively attired missionary's daughter he had conducted that very morning.

"It certainly is," she beckoned the dumbfounded churchman. "Come in."

Downplaying her buxom looks by staying true to her gentle inner spirit, Alicia brightly continued the ritual of welcome by asking Benjamin about his lunch and his journey as she ushered him into the deck party. Ben replied positively to every question offered by this hospitable girl. He beamed at her royal treatment as she introduced him round about, then led him to a comfortable chair in the shade, and served him a soothing cup of white tea with choice sweets and biscuits. Others greeted the dignified newcomer while Alicia took a moment to fill her own snack plate, but nobody took the liberty to sit in the empty chair beside Benjamin and chat at length with him. Benjamin was Orwell's friend, his musical director, Christian head, and writing tutor—that venerable seat belonged to Orwell—who else could dwell beside the learned man?

"Thank you for all your help, Alicia, especially for entertaining Benjamin," Orwell chirped gratefully as they briefly rubbed shoulders at the snacks table.

"No problem. I'm happy to help," Alicia pleasantly replied.

Energized by his timely but unexpected acknowledgement, she wished to touch base a tad longer, but Orwell had already dashed away to chivalrously present a combo platter of choice sweets to precious Georgina. Alicia, who could not bear to watch the object of her heart's desire make such display of servitude to another girl, rebuked her own bitter jealousy and asked God to help her cope—she had to mean what she had said about those two! With Orwell diligently trying to entertain all his friends while obviously favouring Georgina, Alicia dutifully sat beside Benjamin.

Physically and intellectually drawn to each other despite their obvious differences in age and culture, Benjamin and Alicia engaged in stimulating conversation. Mudenda, enamoured by his attractive and pleasant companion, wished to know about her special upbringing in Africa as well as in Canada under the Biblical headship of Rev. Wynnard MacDonachie. Explaining that he had been inspired from his youth by the sermons and writings of her famous father, Ben asked many questions about his work, life, faith journey, views on social justice and morality...Alicia tried to enlighten every question posed by the probing fellow Christian, but found to her chagrin that she simply did not know or understand her father well enough to satisfy this intense listener's thirst for information.

Alicia wanted Benjamin to learn about her, rather than focus on a celebrated family that alienated her, so she took every fleeting opportunity he gave to share her own viewpoint. She dared give him only favourable glimpses into her troubled life, however: playing with African children on her parent's missionary compound; flourishing in music and dance with her parents and siblings; earning sporting success in curling, softball, track and field, as well as table tennis. Alicia loved the exhilarating freedom of horseback riding through Alberta's wilderness on *Windchaser*, her most loyal companion...And, she enjoyed visiting her Cree grandmother with her mother and soul sister Evelyn, learning about traditional cooking, medicinal plants, and the old ways of her indigenous people. Alicia understood the Cree and Michif languages, danced fiddle jigs, and did intricate weavings and beadwork. Native spirituality was vitally important as they burned sweet grass and participated in sweat lodge ceremonies to cleanse their spirits before *Gichi Manitou*, the Great Creator.

Alicia's desire to celebrate and intertwine the various cultures that enriched her being fascinated Benjamin. He was surprised that she identified as a 'native' Canadian, holding to a heritage that valued her mixed Indian and European blood, rather than a white woman of founding European stock. She did not strike him as being a coloured girl like Georgina, but he wondered what it was like to be such a mixed-race child born in Africa—a totally different culture yet again. How could she bridge so many cultures and stay true to her own identity? Alicia articulately explained that her Christian faith was the constant, unifying force in her life. God, who is all-knowing, all-seeing, omnipresent, and unchanging, gave her purpose and guidance wherever she was. Benjamin lauded such devout belief, and wished that his own could be even half as strong!

Ben remained annoyingly mum about his own family, which caused Alicia consternation. Was she talking too much, and selfishly, about herself? Should she be more forward in learning about this beautiful, mysterious man? If he would not share, she would let go, for Ben was too old and sophisticated for her to interrogate or to change.

What Ben did share was as wonderful as it was provocative. He had promised God that, when his medical training was complete, he would obediently go wherever the Lord led, and do what He required of him. Ben heard God calling him to become a pastor, beyond his own decision to train as a medical doctor. The gallant prince spoke passionately of his deep desire to serve God in the African mission fields where, like Jesus, he could preach the gospel as well as heal the sick. With God's miraculous touch to his healing arts, he hoped to save souls as well as lives.

Ben desired not to continue the imperialistic methods of proselytizing the 'savage natives', a practice long flouted by foreign white missionaries upon his people. Impressive institutions built by Europeans had been useful in their day for establishing Christianity in the colonies, but the sun was now setting on the era of white missionaries, as it had already set upon colonialism. Missionary structures should be handed over to African churches forthwith, but American and European Christians must financially support their African brethren, so that vital outreach could continue to grow and mature in a culturally appropriate manner, in step with independence.

This being hard salt for Alicia to bear, she stalwartly debated with her keenly-listening yet unwavering opponent. She came from three generations of zealous white missionaries who had obeyed Jesus' parting exhortation to spread the gospel to all nations. Her father's religious affiliations faithfully operated a West African school and hospital, whereat she too had been born. She *also* harboured fervent desires to serve God as a medical doctor—at that long-established Christian hospital—if not elsewhere in Africa. She felt the Lord was calling her also to do grassroots service, be such purpose old-fashioned or not! Prayer and offerings made obliviously from afar did not cut it!

"My dear Miss MacDonachie, I am sorry to upset you!" apologized Ben, laughing nervously as he stepped back from the fray. He struggled to explain to the frustrated youngster, "I am simply broaching the question that must be asked someday, not demanding that you answer it now by somehow hurting yourself. We must work together, change together, so that we can effectively serve the Lord together. There should be a dialogue between equal partners. I believe that you are sensitive and open-minded enough to address such issues. You have a vital role to play. Please, think about what I have shared, even if now we agree to disagree?"

"Yes, I will meditate about it—a lot I'm sure", Alicia promised, albeit without enthusiasm. She shook his hand in truce. "I am still a young girl, Mr. Mudenda; I am a secondary school student, with much to learn before I can call myself a responsible adult woman, let alone be a competent medical doctor. Can we hold our peace today?"

"Agreed," chuckled Benjamin, relieved and happy. He made an appealing suggestion to restore their fellowship, "You said earlier that table tennis is one of your favourite sports, Miss Alicia. I also enjoy the game too much, and I noticed upon my arrival here this afternoon that Mr. Orwell has strategically placed a table and several racquets in the breezeway for his guests to partake in friendly matches. Would you care to join me in a game or two?"

"That would be a fun change of pace now, wouldn't it?" replied Alicia with a renewed spirit of joviality. She joked and tossed her flowing auburn mane as she bounced from her chair and enthusiastically followed Benjamin, "There's no point in getting all stiff-necked around here when we're supposed to be partying."

"Tennis, anyone?" Alicia invited David and Solomon, winking and smiling at those who gazed admiringly as she passed by.

The young men ambled after the attractive, inspiring female to watch her play table tennis with Benjamin, whom they knew to be a top player among the university students. They did not expect Alicia to survive, let alone match Benjamin—a crafty lion at racquet sports if there ever was one! He would likely go easy on the young white girl and chivalrously instruct her, but David and Solomon were amazed when they found the action already briskly underway, where Alicia and Ben were skillfully volleying the ball back and forth as equals. She ran around barefoot, caring not that these gawking men saw her shapely legs or watched her breasts or bottom jiggle every time she powerfully swerved to and fro to hit the ball. They quickly learned, with humility and joy, that Miss MacDonachie was no timid, politely-curtseying prude, but rather, a talented sportswoman of highest calibre!

Although she could be his protégé, Alicia battled Benjamin like she was his enemy, because he chose to be her stumbling block. This brazen amazon was almost manly in her strength, determination, and aggression. Whether with defensive backspins from deep in her court or lightning-reflex blocks at the net, Alicia crisply returned Ben's powerful topspin serves and bravely handled his famous smashes that had thwarted so many other opponents. Alicia could smash and loop as well as spin or push the ball; magically it seemed, she was always in position to give a smooth delivery. She could play any style her opponent wished, and achieve any level of difficulty that he suggested. He was pressed to play much more than his best just to stay with her, talk less of defeating her!

After they each won a hard-fought game, Benjamin good-naturedly called for a water break, which was assumed to be his prerogative to exercise, having invited the warrioress to play in the first place. Perhaps he feared for his life and wanted to be rescued? No one would ever know, but calling a draw was the best way to save face and stay friends. Both players were flushed and panting, drenched with sweat as they shook hands and congratulated one another as equals....

"Well done, Miss Alicia! You are superb at ping pong," praised Ben.

"So are you, sir, truly elite!" Alicia briskly returned the compliment. Sounding tougher than she meant as she placed her stippled rubber bat on the table, the tigress chortled, "Orwell is the only other guy who has given me such a challenging match. You should play him sometime, Ben!"

"I already have, and yes, he is a master!" politely countered Benjamin. Ready to saunter back to the deck, where the others were gaily socializing under the booming music of *The Rolling Stones,* he offered his racquet to Sollÿ or Dave, who appeared plastered against the wall, mesmerized by the international table tennis clinic they had just witnessed. "Do you two boys want to bat the ball around for a while?"

*"Aye,"* affirmed Solomon self-consciously as he accepted the warm racquet like a torch from his better. His sidekick, looking lost, gazed with big brown eyes at the amazon as he sought her guidance.

"David, you can use my paddle," offered Alicia with a winsome smile, "Or, if you want a different one, take your pick from those in the box beside you. Mind you, Ben and I chose the best paddles of the lot; others have worn rubber, none at all, or are covered with sand-paper instead, which just scratches the ball! Why don't you two guys warm up or have a game, while I take a break and watch you. Then we can play doubles together—that is, if Mr. Benjamin is up for it?"

"That would be grand," the dapper gentleman chuckled leisurely in reply.

A short while later, JJ, who had just finished setting up the croquet game on the front lawn and wondered where her friend Alicia—who was supposed to be helping her—had gone, came back to the deck to rest and have a drink. She found Georgina and Orwell, Ali and Suzanne, and Rick and Kathleen playing a feisty card game of *Hearts,* but they did not invite her to join their couples club, nor could she get a word in edge-wise with them.

"This is no fun! Why are people breaking into cliques?" pouted JJ upon deaf ears.

A tumult of raucous laughter and shouting suddenly erupted from the back garden! While the couples played on, JJ slipped away unnoticed and searched out the source of the bizarre noise. Skirting the hedge and descending the garden steps, she was shocked to find skimpily-dressed Alicia, playing a vigorous game of round-the-table ping pong with four enthusiastic and highly-entertained African men. Cepheus, having arrived at last, was loudly making his presence known as he challenged all comers at every opportunity, and placed shots at impossible angles for return. His circus antics caused everyone to guffaw and try extra hard to match him, particularly Alicia, whom he bumped, stretched, or bent with belly laughter. Seeing that the frisky white girl not only accepted such liberties, but generously returned the favour—all in good fun—the others relaxed and playfully roughhoused with her and each other as part of their frantic, seemingly endless and pointless round-game.

"Hey, there!" JJ hailed these rowdies. When they did not hear her, she put her fingers to her lips and rent the sultry afternoon air with a piercing whistle. The players momentarily froze, then melted into embarrassed children caught playing hooky by their frowning school mistress. As they quietly listened with lowered eyes, JJ made her pitch, "I can see that you're all having a whale of fun back here, but I want to draw attention to our planned Easter egg hunt, which is scheduled now to start. You are invited to take part, though being scavengers for half an hour is probably a little quieter and less strenuous, I'll wager...Well then, come along!"

With their game on pause, the players good-naturedly put away their paddles and strolled back to the deck, joking easily with one another; they shone with healthy glow, but appeared satisfied with being tired from their workout.

"Mr. Cepheus, good day, eh? Greetings to you upon your arrival," welcomed JJ as Belo sauntered past with jovial members of his company.

Cepheus politely replied in kind, but he seemed oddly out of place to the bright, stylish young woman, having shown up casually dressed in blue jeans, thongs, sun glasses, and a white T-shirt bearing Canada's centennial maple leaf to honour his Christian friends' home country. Yet, he bantered and strolled hand in hand with gentleman Ben, his polar opposite in clothing and manners, like they were close friends.

JJ fell in with Alicia, with whom she suddenly had a bone to pick. The social convener muttered crossly, "Lisa, I see you had quite a blast back there, out of sight and mind!"

"I did what Orwell asked me to do: entertain his friends so he could flirt privately with Georgina," replied Alicia with smug satisfaction as she moseyed up the leafy pathway with all her male admirers, barely giving lip service to her grim host marching beside her.

"Would you play in traffic or jump from a ten-storey window if Orwell asked you to?" demanded JJ. "Listen, ping pong was not part of the program, Lisa...I hid a pile of Easter eggs for the scavenger hunt, then spent the past half hour setting up the croquet game, all by myself. You were supposed to help me do those chores! Both mixers are ready to go, no thanks to you."

"We're pretty mixed up now. I helped by distracting all these fine young men, so they wouldn't see where you hid the eggs."

"I saw how you distracted them," rasped JJ, darkly amused. "By the way, Lisa, did you know your dress is ripped...in a tight place?"

Alicia, embarrassed now and needing some girl talk, took JJ firmly by the hand and stepped behind the bougainvillea hedge. Her escorts immediately stopped and glanced quizzically her way; David and Solomon tried to follow her, but Alicia chuckled and jauntily waved them on. "I'll see you later, fellows. Go have some drinks and munchies—you've earned it!"

"Is everything all right, Miss Alicia and Miss Janice?" asked Cepheus, almost derisively in his soft and musical voice, peering over the hedge.

Alicia ignored this impudent boy, but addressed his dashing companion, who respectfully held back and turned away to afford them some privacy.

"Would you wish to freshen up, Benjamin, after all our vigorous exercise? I know I should," Alicia giggled through the hedge at Mudenda as he tarried up the trail with Cepheus now in tow.

"After you, Miss Alicia," Ben, who already dry and cool, briskly replied.

"Okay, I'm first in line to use the toilet—or excuse me, the water closet?" she self-deprecatingly informed her incredulous listeners. "After I wash up, we'll hunt for Easter eggs together, as my friend JJ has announced."

"Lisa, can you please take a break from all your ridiculous jabbering?" JJ demanded as she dragged her boisterous but unsophisticated pal deeper into the ornamental shrubbery. "I've never seen you so vocal or on fire, for guys? You're turning into a vamp!"

But Alicia was distracted; she recognized Orwell's green thumb handiwork in the meticulous upkeep of these grounds. Just the other day, she had spied him toiling unawares, like some warrioress in prelude to battle. The two girls wanted no man to see or hear them now, as they decided how the rest of the day should go.

"Whew, it's hot all of a sudden today," Alicia remarked to the still scowling JJ as she fanned her flushed and perspiring face. As though to prove her point, the buxom girl unbuttoned her blouse to air out her sweaty breasts and stomach.

JJ blanched—but only momentarily. When again she found her voice, the little fireplug discretely cautioned Alicia, "I can plainly see that you're having fun today, Lisa, being the centre of attraction for all these exotic, hot guys...But be careful! This culture is different from ours, and you are too trusting and naïve to handle it presently. By flaunting yourself, guys here will think you are making yourself available. Next thing, they'll be asking Dad's permission to marry you! I am not kidding. Don't paint yourself into a corner."

"I'm not looking for boyfriends, far less a husband! I need a man cluttering my life like a fish needs a bicycle!" declared Alicia, offended by what she saw as jealous insinuations.

If this had been anyone else but Orwell's sister, she might have become belligerent. JJ would have been no match physically for the amazon, but she understood that the proper thing to do now was talk about feelings and work things out rather than fight; therefore, Alicia struggled to listen and learn.

"I care a lot about you, Lisa, and I don't want you embarrassing yourself around Orwell or his friends. Those guys are all at least ten years older than us, but according to their traditions, we are of proper age to marry them. No doubt, they would each love to bed a fresh white girl."

"Like Orwell pines to taste an exotic African girl? Has he taken her?"

"Shhh! I tried to warn you about Georgina," JJ whispered. "Read my lips, Lisa. Orwell has not made out with any girl to date, nor will he, unless they get married first. Orwell is very sensitive about cultural rules and doing what is right, especially in God's sight."

"Your brother sounds like my kind of guy," chirped Alicia, her dark eyes shining with admiration. "I already know and value his good points."

"That is why you and he would make a good match, but you must continue to be patient and understanding if you wish to succeed with Orly—nothing is a given. We are all so young, with so much yet to live for. Only God knows the future. Georgina keeps trying to tell my brother that, but he's worried he'll lose her altogether unless they get married before we leave Africa later this year. He's such a dreamer of a lover boy! I admire how reasonable you've been thus far, especially regarding Orwell. I think he secretly admires you, Lisa, but is not ready to come over to you."

"I'll wait. We are good friends, which is better than nothing. God knows."

"I also wish to be your good friend, Lisa."

"I look to you as my example for living in this culture, dear friend," vowed Alicia, feeling calmer now. "You certainly know more about Lusaka life than I do."

They both smiled knowingly and tapped fists in solidarity. As a show she heard her friend's message, Alicia buttoned her blouse and tucked it neatly into her skirt.

"Now, let's try to work together a bit longer, you know—stay on the same page, sing from the same song sheet—all that jazz," implored JJ with emphatic hand gestures.

"Always," agreed Alicia, feeling suitably chastised. She then sheepishly apologized, "Sorry I missed the boat with my assignments."

"*No problemo,*" JJ assured her.

The girls, good friends who mutually recognized that their relationship had strained with each added day of intimate contact, hugged one other before emerging together from hiding. Thank goodness, nobody was waiting for them on the trail!

"Can I quickly change my clothes before we start the scavenger hunt?" asked Alicia.

"By all means, go ahead, but hurry," JJ released her. "I'll check our party."

JJ skipped up the deck stairs, just in time to put out another fire. Indeed, while she had been parlaying with Alicia behind the azaleas, the conversation had grown tense on the patio where Georgina, vivaciously holding court, with a flourish produced Cepheus Belo for her brother, who was busy sketching Suzy while posed demurely for him against a backdrop of garden flowers, "Now Ali, let me introduce you to one of our compatriots who, like us, is eating his bread here in Zambia, a long way from home."

"*Salamu alaikum!*[53]" greeted Cepheus, before bowing slightly to Ali, whom he heralded both as a fellow Nigerian and brother Muslim.

When Georgina's well-heeled, world-travelling brother half-heartedly replied to Belo's Hausa salutation with "*Alaikum salam*" (May God's Peace also be with you), Cepheus pursued him further in the *lingua franca* of Northern Nigeria with "*Ina wuni?*" or "How are you this afternoon?"

Ali, not wishing to converse in his childhood tongue with this smart-aleck who was improperly dressed for the party, rudely replied with a question, "*Ya, ya?*"[54]

"I am very fine, Mallam Ali...or should I call you 'Muhammad Ali'," chattered Cepheus flippantly to hide his indignation. "Hah! Hah! Do you float like a butterfly and sting like a bee?"

"Sister, what should we do with this bizarre fellow?" demanded Ali then to Georgina, who was embarrassed by the loud, unseemly jousting of these two countrymen at her Romeo's party. "He is such a comedian!"

"We shall applaud his eclectic humour for a moment, and then move on," she solemnly counselled. Then, to Alhaji[55] Belo, the clever beauty threw her bouquet, "Sir, you must be quite the entertainer to make my brother laugh!"

"He is not laughing with me," corrected the owl-eyed observer. Darkly humorous, the brilliant writer seemed pleased that everyone was intently listening as he divulged his interpretation, "On the contrary, I believe Dr. Ali Mission is intending to remove me from the stage...but little does he know that such a mission, should he choose to accept it, is impossible. I have too much planting yet to do before the rains come."

"Why don't you find a shady spot somewhere in Orwell's garden and plant

---

53 Hausa greeting, adapted from Arabic, made upon arriving at or leaving a place, meaning "Peace of God to you; may you have relief from any difficulty."

54 *Ya, ya*: Hausa greeting "How are you?" This question can be used with familiarity or sometimes shows disdain by the speaker to the one he/she is talking to.

55 *Alhaji*: title given in Hausa to a Muslim who has made pilgrimage to Mecca.

some groundnuts? Then, you may write out your spy novel," Georgina boldly suggested as she ushered Belo aside with a sweeping gesture of her hands.

Insulted and enraged, Cepheus glared at this brazen woman who espoused feminism and flaunted wealth as she flew on the coattails of western modernity, to rise so far above her traditional station in Muslim African society as to attempt to bandy him about like a child.

"I say, Madam!" he snorted. "Where is Mr. Orwell now to control you?"

"People, people!" intervened JJ, arriving just in time to diffuse the building tension, "It's time for the games to begin!"

At JJ's joyful announcement, everyone jumped up and rejoined on the grounds, suddenly kids again, and hunted for hard-boiled, coloured eggs among the flowers and shrubbery. JJ spun her merry story as they all traipsed about, how the *Easter Rabbit* had painted and hidden these eggs for those who believed in birth, renewal, and magic to find. The others enjoyed her naïve fairy tale, although her sister and the MacDonachie girls winked at each other with insider knowledge, since they, rather than some glib rodent in pink tights, had decorated all those eggs as a tension reliever after the market fiasco Saturday. Even though she knew where all the eggs lay hidden, the imaginative pixie played along, jovially assisting clueless Solomon and David in their quest for garden goodies, while Alicia escorted the charming but unskilled egg hunters Benjamin and Cepheus about the sprawling, leafy grounds. As inquisitive but strictly-raised village boys, these gallant Africans had learned early on how to collect the eggs of chickens, guinea fowl, and ducks for food, but what of *rabbits*—mythical, pink bunnies from North America no less? JJ and Alicia played smashing[56] hostesses over the easy half hour, entertaining their gentlemen guests with banter and jokes even as they filled their baskets to overflowing with enough brightly coloured eggs to feed them well into next week!

Orwell was relieved that his friends were congenial together, so pleasantly attended by the good women of his boma. With his party unfurling successfully, he happily took opportunity to cultivate his budding relationship with Georgina. Joining two other bouncy young couples—Richard, Kathleen, Ali and Suzanne—Orwell and Georgina teamed up to search for Easter eggs, then

---

56 Informal British adjective meaning 'extraordinarily or unusually impressive or fine; wonderful; admirable'.

allowed their winning partnership to flourish as they played a leisurely game of croquet. Both students were intelligent learners; having worked together already on numerous physics projects, they quickly collaborated at these simple garden party games. Orly and Georgie breezed through the croquet circuit, hitting their wooden red ball with precision to strategic spots on the lawn, such that they cleared every wicket without a hitch, knocked posts squarely at either end, avoided rival balls, and sent to oblivion any unlucky one that got in their way. Playing with ease, comfortably ahead of the pack, bestowed an air of glorious blessing upon their lovely day.

Although inwardly they might ponder serious topics: why God needed a son—as if anyone could rise from the dead; black South Africans' increasingly brutal struggle against apartheid; news just in of the disappointing loss by UNZA's field hockey team at nationals; or how they would continue their studies when the university was closed indefinitely? Orwell and Georgina chose instead on this brilliant Easter Sunday to celebrate sweet morsels of God's goodness. Georgina threw her courtier many bouquets, enthusiastically expressing her pleasure with all the colourful flowers and shapely shrubs that his green thumbs so artistically cultivated round about them. Orwell praised his croquet partner's fluid swing and marvellous control; she shot boldly yet accurately. He liked her pink sun hat, striped tank top and whiter-than-white midi skirt that she had changed into from her silky fuchsia dress just for today's scheduled outdoor recreational activities. They basked in mild weather and thrived on the fun everyone was having together.

Orwell and Georgina finished so far ahead of other teams that they took a Coke break and lounged on the swing in the back yard, privately chatting while leisurely waiting for their rivals to complete the course. Georgie loved the iridescent fish that swam with carefree elegance in the pond he had built nearby; she was inspired by the peaceful cooing of doves and chatter of bulbuls perched above them amid the bottle brush trees, and she found delight in the weaver birds that ingeniously built their nests in this verdant Garden of Eden!

When they spoke of the upcoming semester so overdue to start, they asked each other not how they were coping now, but what they would do with the gift of free time if the university did not reopen for another six weeks? Georgina wished to go home to Nigeria for a fortnight, to visit her parents and look up old friends on Jos Plateau, after which she might follow Ali to UK, and check out the medical programs at graduate universities and hospitals in *Turai*. If things did not improve soon at UNZA, she might go abroad to complete her studies, rather than waste precious time waiting to return to her local schooling. Yet, such boldly desperate measures would take time and money to fulfill—the stuff of last resort! Meanwhile, she would take a job in one of Lusaka's tourist bureaus where—the sophisticated woman about town declared to her admirer with a clever twinkle in her eye—she could put her English language, natural charm, and knowledge of Zambia's hot spots to good use. Dutifully impressed, Orwell glibly accepted this fine lady's strategy as totally appropriate.

"Perhaps our extended vacation is really a blessing in disguise," he chirped. When Georgina looked sharply at him as though he should get his head examined, the young poet quickly backpedalled. He explained with concern, even while beaming with joy, "As the arrival of my friend Tracy MacDonachie is imminent, I am seriously in throes of planning how best to entertain this VIP! A shiny penny for your thoughts on where I should holiday with Tracy?"

"You must show him Zambia's finest tourist attractions! Luangwa Valley National Park offers fantastic viewing of a wide variety of big game African animals: elephants for certain, but there are also cape buffalo, rhinoceros, lions and leopards, all kinds of antelope and birds, even the rare Thornicroft giraffe," Georgina pep-talked him in her lilting way to get with the jet-set program. "Carry Alicia's senior brother south, Livingstone way, to marvel at Victoria Falls. Let him stand on the Knife-Edge Bridge and be amazed at how the wide and lazy Zambezi River suddenly plunges over a basalt lava cliff into a boiling chasm 350 feet below. Ensure that your illustrious Mr. MacDonachie brings his brolly and Wellingtons[57], however, or he will get drenched!"

"Drenched? Must Tracy jump over the water fall... During the cool, dry season?" quizzed Orwell, piqued by her laughter, bursting forth at his mentor's expense. Was she jealous of Tracy?

"Never, but... You will shiver for mercy in the billowing mists of *Mosi-oa-Tunya*—the Smoke that Thunders! This vast curtain of water is not a single cataract, but actually boasts a panorama of various falls separated by islands and channels: Eastern Cataract, Rainbow Falls, Horseshoe Falls, Main Falls, and

57 *Wellingtons*: British term for 'rubber boots'.

Devil's Cataract—the latter aptly named for the *Rhodesian* side. The Victoria Falls are truly a Seventh Wonder of the World, Orwell—a must see!"

"They dwarf Canada's own Niagara Falls, which Tracy has seen many times in his cross-country business trips and musical tours," Orwell reflected pensively. "Tracy is bored with Niagara now; he hates how the money changers have reduced her to a gaudy tourist trap!

"My friend admires the mighty power of Nature, wherein he glimpses God's majesty and finds hope from His creativity. Victoria Falls will enthrall him, but even that wonderful sight cannot satisfy his diverse interests. Tracy is a complicated mystic with rather eclectic tastes; he is also a scientist and businessman. MacDonachie appreciates culture and economic accomplishments, though he also strays off the beaten path to uncover secret little gems. I must prepare a very unique itinerary to tickle his fancies."

"While Mr. MacDonachie is sojourning in Lusaka, you should ensure that he becomes acquainted with all the amenities of our national capital, so that your friend can be impressed with how modern and thriving this city is. Show him the National Assembly building, with its burnished towers and square dome, a proud testimony to Zambia's place as one of the world's leading copper producers. Take him to other famous landmarks like the Anglican Cathedral and State House. If your man is as interested in mining as you say, and you don't have time to visit the Copperbelt, at least tour the Geological Survey Museum, where you will find exhibits on Zambia's copper and gem stone industries quite interesting. At the Gemstones Polishing Works, you will see how garnets, tourmalines, emeralds, amethysts, and malachite are polished, set, and sold. This savvy entrepreneur may wish to look into the tobacco auction floor, where fine Virginia or Burley tobacco are sold these days from central or southern Zambia. Should Mr. MacDonachie be partial to ornamental plants, by all means take him to *Munda Wanga*! I hope you have shown Alicia and Kathleen this beautiful park by now?"

"We intend to, but haven't had time as yet, what with our whirlwind schedule and bizarre little setbacks," groused Orwell vaguely, skipping the embarrassing details about their broad daylight robbery at the market.

Georgina sensed his frustration and showed concern, but did not press her suddenly downcast host to spill the beans. She realized that he bent over backwards to host the refined MacDonachie girls, like he was cultivating her and a gaggle of other high-maintenance friends here today. She reached out, encouraging him to try again.

"Then, you should make time soon, sir, even if it means taking the sisters there together with their brother. *Munda Wanga* is world-famous; it was recently featured in *Readers' Digest*! More than three hundred varieties of tropical and subtropical plants grow in that manicured oasis of colour, beauty, and fragrance. You simply must take your guests there soon! Girls like pretty things. They want to be rejuvenated."

"We will go to those botanical gardens next week, once the holiday crowd dwindles. We'll have a picnic, swim, play scrub softball on the lawn, wander about the artistic plant arrangements, watch proud male peacocks use colourful tail fans to court their females..."

Orwell, glimpsing envy and loneliness in Georgina's glossy, dark eyes, felt compelled to invite her along. While she contemplated such a sweet outing, he, not being perfect, fantasized how well this gorgeous woman would fill out a bikini. The proud beauty read his mind; refusing to give him an answer, she continued being his highly-capable tour guide. Such coy diversion stung the lad!

"What of Lundazi Castle, north of Chipata towards Nyika Plateau in Eastern Province? Not only does it look medieval, but some people think that old castle is haunted. By spending the night there, you could make your own conclusion, after your camp in Luangwa Valley. Then, you should climb Nyika Plateau, where you will find rare plants and butterflies, and still plenty of game animals—zebras, antelope, and the likes. At 7,000 feet above sea level, the air is crisp and refreshing, and the land is lush green with alpine grasses and thick, dark evergreen forests full of vines and ferns. Your Canadian friend will feel almost at home there. Mind you, it will be chilly in April at such high altitudes; better pack your cardigans and best hiking shoes—maybe bring Wellingtons and raincoats along in case of wet weather.

"Another trip destination to consider is Kasaba Bay on Lake Tanganyika. You branch north to Mbala off the Great North Road at Mpika. It's a bit far to drive to the lake by motor car, but no further I dare say than is Nyika Plateau! Perhaps Richard could fly you and Mr. MacDonachie up there by charter plane. Lake Tanganyika is Africa's second largest inland waterbody after Victoria, source of the Nile River. It is also the second oldest freshwater lake in the world, and the second deepest, after Lake Baikal in Siberia. Tanganyika is fine for swimming and has beautiful sandy beaches; you can also go boating and angle for Nile perch and tiger fish. Elephants and hippos wander freely about the grounds of the tourist lodge. Nearby is Kalombo Falls, the second highest waterfall in Africa! If you and Tracy are adventurous enough to hike into Kalombo Falls, you will likely see Marabou storks nesting on the cliffs that overlook the gorge. I've heard that Stone Age dwellings and cave paintings are located up there."

"I would love to take Tracy to all these fascinating places," Orwell breathlessly assured his companion, thanking her for so many suggestions about exotic travel destinations, and confirmed she would be a shoo-in at any travel agency in town! But then he apprehensively admitted, "He also speaks of travelling to Great Zimbabwe Ruins and Wankie National Park in Rhodesia, before visiting South Africa to see Witwatersrand gold mines and Johannesburg, the Drakensberg Mountains, Kruger National Park, and that mighty clash of three oceans east of Cape Town."

"My God!" swore Georgina with disgust. Jumping off the swing, she paced like a caged lioness before him. She suddenly stopped in front of her ashen-faced lover and balefully demanded, "What could possibly be the attraction of racist South Africa to Mr. MacDonachie? How can you even befriend such a man?"

"I don't think we should go down there, even to see world-renowned tourist attractions," mumbled Orwell, feeling his tight collar suddenly choking him with every word he blurted. "Rhodesia would be an impossible destination, since Canada has no diplomatic relations with Ian Smith's rebel regime..."

"Your friend need not pay homage to enemy states just to see elephants and lions. You can't seriously be considering to support him in this quest!" chided Georgina. "Have you ever visited South Africa, Orwell? Can you imagine how grievously black people suffer there under the yoke of apartheid? They must carry passes to travel in their own country! They are forced by the minority government's laws to stay off parks and buses that are reserved for whites; a black South African can't even drink from the same water fountain or use the same toilet as a white man. When the downtrodden protest, police cast them in jail or just shoot them! Orwell, you and I would not be able to eat together in the same restaurant, or date for a movie or a dance...And, because I am classified as coloured and you as white, we could never marry in South Africa!"

"I will persuade Tracy to holiday in Zambia," vowed Orwell obediently, desperate to please his mistress always and completely. He was also startled by

Georgina's mention of marriage, but managed to grasp onto the wonderful yet fleeting idea in time.

Her despair seemed quickly healed however by his loyal promise, to the point where she smiled and giggled soon after her impassioned plea. Georgina blushed shyly at him as she skipped forward and perched bravely on his knee. Her shapely bottom was cool and soft, but her whole body rippled with powerful agility as she arched her back against him. She turned to bathe the captured, red-faced youth with her adoring eyes and euphoric smile. Appreciative of his respectful restraint but smugly amused by his lack of experience, Georgina drew Orwell's trembling hand around her slim waist, that he might embrace her. When he affectionately kissed her, Georgina nodded with affirmation of his effort; Orwell was thrilled to oblige.

"You and I, we are free in Zambia to be close friends—even lovers," she murmured in a husky voice, heralding progress of their relationship. As they gently swung, intimately together and looked out from their tranquil glade upon other croquet players still stiffly competing in the dust and heat, Georgina cooed, "Look at these beautiful young people: black, white, and coloured between, yet they are all playing happily together. Croquet is such a pleasant social game. African boys have white girls as partners—they choose to be together because they like each other. Such is possible here in Zambia, proud and free!"

"Yes, I see what you mean," Orwell chuckled. "Your brother Ali and my sister Suzanne have obviously taken a shine to each other, but look at how Ben collaborates so well with my junior sister, Janice Joanne! Then, bringing up the rear, Alicia and Cepheus come plodding along!"

"They are the loud ones, always gesturing and arguing with each other!" laughed Georgina richly as she basked in his comfortable, attentive presence. "When Malam Belo is not fighting with Alicia, he gets them both into trouble by goading Ali. Why Alicia puts up with that blackguard, I can't imagine! She is so patient, so hospitable and understanding with all of us! Actually, Alicia and I hold much in common."

"You do—like what?" Orwell could not help but inquire.

"I can't tell any man our cherished female secrets!" giggled Georgina as she playfully slapped his fidgeting knee. When Hughes looked at her with dismay, the tease put her hand to her luscious lips and deftly fashioned her cunning grin into a more appropriate *Mona Lisa* pose, after which she stoically shared,

"Besides, she and I don't know everything about each other at this point nor may we ever. I need more opportunities to get to know Alicia better. In fact, I want your guest to be my best friend. I love her, Orwell."

"So do I," acknowledged Hughes, showing admiration for both women. When Georgina stiffened and stared coolly at him, he begged her to understand, "We've known each other from childhood, like...since forever."

"You do, do you?" Georgina gurgled deviously at him. She ground her plump bottom deeper into his lap and teased him all the more by unfurling her long, silky hair to brush upon his face. Her exquisite French perfume intoxicated him. "Do you know me better now, Orwell? Are you happy with me?"

"I am very happy that you came here today, Georgina. I am overjoyed to be holding you close like this. Going about with you has been a highlight of my life! I am a privileged man to be your special friend!"

"You certainly are!" the socialite reiterated haughtily. "You are blessed that I enjoy being with you, Orwell."

"Yes indeed, I truly am blessed, thank you." Hughes staunchly agreed.

Having grown uncomfortable with such bizarre debate, she slid off her perch and stood beside him, relieved. They fell into silence, to cool down and each to ponder their own turbulent thoughts alone.

"Why didn't you invite more women today?" Georgina asked at length, lodging a complaint now against her dumbfounded mate. "Look at Solomon and David, how they must awkwardly play together as a couple. Neither bloke has the slightest idea concerning this fancy European game of croquet! Kathleen, Alicia's older sister, obviously wants no truck with them; she cares only for your brother Richard. Does she wish for him to be her steady date?"

"Who knows?"

"Orwell, how can you permit such scandalous behaviour among fellow Christians, particularly from the daughter of a famous Christian leader visiting your home, or from the eldest son of a career Canadian diplomat, your senior brother, born like you to the same father and mother, devout Christians both?"

"Kathy is a nice girl, Georgina, once you get to know her, and my bro is awesome! Despite living cheek by jowl for most of the past week, Rick and Kathleen have done nothing immoral; they show much restraint and respect, as well as craft a deepening love bond for each other. We'll hear their wedding bells pealing shortly after we return to Canada, no doubt!"

"Respect? Love? What are those fine words?" Georgina, discontent and aloof, continued to gripe. "You earlier professed your pleasure that Suzanne and Ali are sparking with one another. No offence, Orwell, but I don't like such a union—Suzy is a bad match for my brother. She does not deserve him!"

"My dear, I'm sad to hear you be so disgruntled," murmured Hughes in sudden anguish as he watched Suzanne laughing and kidding with her suave partner, and noted aloud that this was the happiest he had seen his sister in months. Wanting love, joy, and peace to flourish everywhere for everyone in his world, the young poet felt hurt when his friend beseeched him.

"Your sister treated me rudely the last time I visited your home—she refused to acknowledge my presence, let alone talk with me. After the Christmas feast was eaten, Suzy snobbishly retired to her room, leaving her junior sister—a mere child—to entertain me! Today is no different. Am I invisible to her? Have I somehow offended Suzy because you choose to like me, a coloured girl? Have you talked badly about me behind my back?"

"Heavens, no! I would never be so inconsiderate! Please, Georgina my beloved, do not be troubled by such false ideas!" begged Orwell, now on his knees before this angry woman and her stinging words.

"It seems to me that Suzanne does not appreciate the ways how young African women—indeed any young women—socialize. Does your sister honestly believe that she can ever be part of my family when she behaves so shabbily around me now, when her relationship with Ali is fledgling? Besides, Ali follows the teachings of the Prophet Muhammad, peace be upon Him—Ali should marry a nice Muslim girl, preferably from Africa! My father insists."

"Your dad married a Christian white woman from England, didn't he?"

"Don't mock me, Orwell. Such things can happen, okay?"

"I am so sorry, Georgina. I did not realize my sister was making you so sad. I will implore Suzanne to be nice to you, starting this afternoon—right now!"

He jumped up, his face bright with anguish yet full of determination. He blasted off his mission to bring Suzanne to heel when Georgina wisely deterred him by emitting another albeit different complaint.

"You should have also invited Jasmine and Lovelace to balance out the sexes, the cultures. I would feel more comfortable if my African friends were here with me now."

"I did not think to ask them; I'm sorry, I didn't confer with you earlier about who you would like invited along with you. I invited Molly, who would happily have obliged, except that she is busy celebrating Easter festivals with her own church family today."

"Molly Nsamba? Hubbah! You can do better than her, Orwell!"

"Molly is a bright, friendly lady who fits in nicely with anyone. Whatever... we've got quite a jolly crowd here as it is, right?"

"You are right," Georgina conceded. She voiced her woman's intuition, "I think, however, that you would be happier if your friend Tracy was here."

"Of course I would," Hughes admitted touchily, although he was surprised by her insight. "He's my main man; this sunny little garden party was supposed to be a meet and greet for him with all my friends. Don't be cross with me, dear! I really wanted to introduce you to Tracy."

"I'm a big girl, Orwell—as old as you. I am not so vain as to think that the world revolves around me," sighed Miss Amadu. "I am dying to meet your great mentor after all the praises you have sung of him. I sense that you are disappointed, yet you take Tracy's unexplained absence in stride."

"I saw him at church today, Georgina, strangely enough. Although we did not actually speak in person, he conveyed to me his presence in spirit, as foreshadow that he will soon be coming into my life in person. God calmed my nerves by giving me such a wonderful promise."

"You saw a vision of Tracy today—or the actual man? Perhaps you were hallucinating, what with your aching desire to see him seeping through all your labours. You are tired, Orwell, and in dire need of rest. You have been striving like a house on fire for days!"

"I saw Tracy in the flesh, clear as I see you standing here beside me. God showed him to me. Ask Alicia; she also saw her brother. He smiled and waved at both of us while we were singing on stage."

"I'm sorry your hockey team lost the final yesterday," Georgina glumly said, shifting the subject, and applying salve on his frustration. Orwell continued to mystify her with his stoic outlook.

"It's okay, I glimpsed the grim score again in passing on tele," replied Orwell vaguely, surprised that Georgina should mention such a trivial event after bitching about so many other more pressing issues he could fix.

"You weren't even invited to go along. How rude, how short-sighted of those blockheads! Had you played goal keeper, the university side would have won the cup, hands down! You are stellar in net—everyone says so! I've seen you play many times, Orwell; I know you are a strong player. I'm not trying to butter you up, mate; my opinion counts, being a bona fide athlete myself!"

"Thanks for your vote of confidence," replied Hughes cheerily, feeling vindicated although the slight now seemed petty after all the good happenings that had occurred since, and this being such a hallowed day. He shared his thoughts with the intently listening young lady so dear to his heart, so blessed and yet troubled, "I was disappointed when the team decided to leave me behind—it seemed like racism in reverse!"

"That is odd," quipped Georgina with a hint of surprise in her melodious voice. She seemed amused, though she suppressed her smile.

"Odd?" the young poet felt hurt as he replied to delicious Miss Amadu. Of course, this coloured girl surely knew something about prejudice, despite her beauty, intellect, and privileged upbringing! Unlike Alicia when she was on the warpath demanding redress of native grievances, Georgina did not reprimand Orwell for stealing other peoples' land and heritage, or demand that he return to England if he could not hack receiving the trouble he deserved. Georgina articulated her deep-seated views calmly to her friend. She was a true gem!

"I never thought a white person could actually experience oppression or, if they did, whether such a feeling could ever be justified, considering the dominant position held by the white race in this world for the past two centuries. Bullies should get their come-uppance, Orwell, but you did not deserve to be mistreated at the university this past year by certain persons whom we know, though we shan't name them."

They both laughed at Georgina's diplomatic activism. Then Orwell shared, "I've learned to live with those hockey honchos' arbitrary decision. That frustration seems a long time ago in my life, almost forgotten now, — like my degrading experience with your uncle."

"You are a bigger man than any of them, Orwell Hughes, a good person...so kind and gentle that nobody knows what to do with you. My uncle likes you a lot, do you know? He asks about you every time we meet."

"I sense it. Otherwise, Professor Ibrahim would not engage me so vigorously in class or call me into his office to discuss the results of my tests or papers. He likes to converse with me in Swahili or Hausa; how many other students have been privileged to eat lunch at his mansion? By the way, how is the old duffer doing during these splendid holidays?"

"He utilizes the spare time wisely, cloistered in his private study or at the campus library, to catch up on his reading of history journals and treatises. Uncle also has begun to write his memoirs, which could be a good read someday, given that he is a man of letters, well-travelled, knowledgeable, and highly regarded by colleagues the world over. Uncle looks forward to return of the student crush, yet he also speaks of journeying away from Zambia in the near future, perhaps make *hajj*[58] to Mecca, go to Nigeria or the UK, even view some other country—whether to visit family and friends or attend some anthropological conference, none or all of the above, I don't know for certain, Orwell...Uncle has done well in his life, yet he seems restless now, worried for his future. He enjoys Ali being around for stimulation, but sometimes my brother irks him sorely with his carefree take on the world. I think the old lion prefers your company, Orwell, should you consider looking beyond how he belittled you in the past."

"God helps me forgive. When I leave matters with my Lord, He gives me other, better things to do and think about. A lot of good happened in my life over the past few weeks to heal the pain, as you might be aware. God knows what is best for me because He sees the big picture. How would I have enjoyed the MacDonachie girls at church this morning or hosted you and all my other important friends here this afternoon, had I played goalie for the UNZA field hockey team at Ndola? I would have missed a lot of important things here in Lusaka, for sure!"

"Well said," Georgina murmured appreciatively. She extended her hand now in a friendly truce, but instead of drawing herself back into Orwell's arms as he most wished, she assertively yanked him off the swing and landed him on his feet. "Let's go meet up with the others now, before they start to wonder about us."

Orwell and Georgina strolled leisurely hand in hand up the lawn to the deck, where some of their companions were gathered, socializing over soft drinks and snacks. Kathleen and Rick, who were passing out goodies and blaring *CCR's* "Bad Moon Arising" on the record player, looked rested in their denim safari suits and cool *Polaroid* shades. Benjamin and JJ were also home free and leaning

58 *Hajj*: pilgrimage by a Muslim to the holy city of Mecca in Saudi Arabia.

over the railing to boisterously congratulate Solly and Dave as the jovial gents finished the croquet course.

Then, everyone cheered on Ali and Suzanne versus Cepheus and Alicia as the last two couples battled each other down the stretch drive. For a while, it seemed like a dead heat—an exciting toss up as to who would finally win the race of also rans—but then Cepheus, zealous to forge ahead, made the grave error of laying his ball directly in the path of Ali's pursuit shot a scant yard from the final wickets. Ali could hardly contain his glee as he soundly hit his rival's gift ball. Both Alicia and Cepheus scowled and appeared to wilt, while Suzanne thrust her fist in the air with a triumphant "*Yes!*" as Ali deftly placed both wooden balls under his foot in strict accordance to the rules and severely whacked his, by which means he summarily discharged the doomed ball of his chafing rivals like a cannon shot, not only far down the lane but out of the yard!

"Sorry, old chap," Ali droned in mock apology to his frustrated opponent, as he blew the dust off his mallet into Belo's T-shirt. "I sent you down river with a blast that would make my Oxford polo mates proud. You left me no choice in the matter. Oh well, see you later on, my man. Goodbye, Hanoi Jane. You two must go find your ball in the rough, I'm afraid, while we play through to the end. Toodle-loo."

"Show offs! Smart-aleck Limey!" heckled Alicia fiercely, glaring red-faced with hands sternly akimbo, after Ali and Suzy leisurely tapped their ball against the end post and joined the applauding spectators on the viewing deck. She muttered to Belo without looking at her shocked partner as she strode past him, down the driveway, "Come on, you! We've got work to do!"

"Miss MacDonachie, where are you going now? What are you doing?" Cepheus, looking lost, begged to know.

Alicia whirled around and harshly briefed this high-maintenance dude who sapped her of every ounce of patience with his childish demands and verbal diarrhea. "We have to find our ball now, Bucko! Wherever the hell it landed, then hit it back here through the final wicket, if we're going to officially complete the game. I've got a bead on that ball now, but I need to get past the gate fast before I lose track. Are you coming to help me or what?"

Failing to wait for his reply, Alicia raced down the driveway. She did not care whether Cepheus followed or not, for the young filly was ready to ditch her troublesome rider and cash out altogether from this useless party after all the mind-boggling turmoil he and other bozo males had caused her today. The lioness fumed when, turning at the gate, she spied Cepheus still standing and staring at her forlornly on that miserable piece of turf from which their ball had been ejected. She also saw Orwell and Georgina, casually arm in arm, ambling to his aid while gazing curiously, possibly laughing, at her!

"Whatever...I'm so impressed—not!" growled Alicia as she darted wildly behind the hedge to begin her determined hunt for some stupid green ball.

Far up the lawn, Orwell and Georgina had indeed accosted Belo who, casually attired in tourist gear in stark contrast to the other, more respectable guests celebrating Easter at the esteemed diplomat's house, looked like some stranger trespassing in the yard or seeking employment as a garden boy. He played like the truant wedding guest Jesus taught about in Bible parables, who had crashed the celebration without wearing his gown! Yet, superficial things like clothing did not define the man! Orwell respected Cepheus and was too kind to cast him out, but how little did he really understand him!

"Mr. Orwell and Miss Amadu, how goes your afternoon? How was the croquet match for you? I ask only because I have not seen you for a while," sighed Cepheus with sing-song politeness as the happy young couple neared his outpost. He confided with his host, "Mr. Orwell, I think Miss MacDonachie is very angry now. She left us and went outside the compound."

"She wants to find your lost croquet ball," Hughes good-naturedly explained. "Come on, Cepheus. We should give Alicia a hand."

"You brave men search in the wilds down there. I'm going into the house to get properly dressed for supper," Georgina begged off from joining the pointless hunt. She smiled at Orwell, but he felt less assured of her contentment when he detected an edge of restless dissatisfaction on her normally airy voice.

"Okay, see you later?" Orwell playfully sought his beloved's promise as he released her hand. She nodded affirmatively as they parted, but did not look back. As the beautiful young woman made her way gracefully across the lawn, Orwell encouraged her, "I hope, gorgeous Georgie, to see you attired once again in your elegant fuchsia dress for our evening banquet. You will look wonderful."

"I'm sure I will," she giggled melodiously from far away.

Buoyed by charming Miss Amadu, Orwell and Cepheus now amicably strolled loosely hand in hand, as was the custom of friends, down the driveway and out the gate. He did not want to spoil this highlight of his day, but Orwell felt compelled to broach the subject of his manuscript again now that he was alone for a few fleeting moments with Cepheus. The president of the Writers' Club, although appearing oddly out of costume for such an august appointment, stayed true to character as he verbosely assured him that his poignant tale of *The Guard* was safely held under executive lock and key.

"I promise, Mr. Orwell, that your original writing will be returned to you as soon as we publish it in next volume of *Forum* magazine, to be issued May 10."

"What? You can't!" cried Hughes in dismay, then immediately felt immature and rude when Belo frowned quizzically at him.

"Do not be surprised, sir. *Forum*'s editorial staff is highly impressed with your skillful writing style, not to mention your timely choice of the brilliant theme on social consciousness: police corruption forced by poverty. It starkly parallels the suffering of all students presently oppressed by the intransigent university administration. Mr. Orwell, the decision to publish your story was unanimous!"

"I didn't realize that my writing was being considered for *Forum*. I thought you just wished to privately read the story simply out of interest and then would return it to me," mumbled Hughes, shocked by this stunning development. "I am honoured of course, but I feel I should touch things up before my work goes to press—you know, polish the grammar, check for spelling mistakes, make sure my ideas are legitimate...

"Imagine! My opinions typed and circulated for public review by any and all students, teachers and staff on campus and beyond! Learned professors like Muzorewa, Otis, and Ibrahim will take a serious read. Cepheus, I am quite nervous now."

"Your manuscript has passed all muster, Mr. Orwell. You will be impressed to read about *The Guard* very soon in *Forum*. It is in fact the centrefold of the next splendid literary anthology produced by UNZA Writers' Club. You will be the toast of your literary colleagues and fellow students—the talk of the campus!" cheered Cepheus rousingly.

"I will purchase the newest copy of the *Forum* hot off the press! I will read it with relish, and savour the entire offering as a collector's item to be framed on my bedroom wall," Orwell effervescently promised, caught up by Belo's genuine enthusiasm. Both elated and vexed by such unexpected limelight, he found himself pleading with his writing mentor, "Please return my original manuscript to me as soon as possible, is all I ask."

"Of course," Cepheus declared, appearing put-off by Orwell's insistent concerns. "To do otherwise is highly unethical among our fellowship."

By now the sun was setting; the cooling air was scented by cook fire smoke and delicious aromas of supper. The road was sprinkled with pedestrians going to and fro, but Alicia was nowhere to be seen. Only when he noticed the odd head turning curiously and he looked down himself in the direction of interest, did Orwell spy the burly white girl squatting barefoot at the bottom of a drain, meticulously rummaging for something among the reeds, mucky water, and blown-in rubbish! She reminded the startled lad of a bush woman about to give birth!

While his companion hung timidly back, Orwell immediately went to the rescue. He clambered down the bank and picked his way along the driest portions of the ditch bottom towards Alicia as if he was still a kid, playing *'Cowboys and Indians'* with her on the riverbank back home. Hearing him coming from afar, the amazon momentarily looked up with glittering eyes, but paid this harmless intruder no mind, and quickly returned to her grubby toil.

"What do you want?" Alicia grumbled miserably from the midst of her search as Orwell, stumbling and panting, reached her side.

"Alicia, how's it going? Can I help?" he cautiously broached the young woman's brawny, mud-splattered back.

"Do what you want, Bucko! You are free to stay or go—I don't care," her stack of auburn hair rasped in low, even terms.

"I choose to stay and help you find your ball. Like you, Alicia, I think it landed somewhere in this drain," Hughes gently concurred and began forthwith to search.

"Okay, suit yourself," she muttered, before inching forward on her hands and knees and trolling the slimy greenery further ahead. What with daylight rapidly waning and serious work still to be done, she cared less that her lovely bum cheeks wiggled through her wet, hip-hugging skirt and flowery panties for Hughes to stupidly admire.

Without speaking further, Orwell and Alicia combed the ditch bottom together for the missing croquet ball. At length, Cepheus approached them by following along the road above. Daring not to join the search, Cepheus studied it from higher ground, but freely offered his opinions and observations to those labouring with deaf ears in the trench beneath.

"Ah-hah! Here is that dratted ball!" Alicia exclaimed at last, holding the greasy, dripping orb triumphantly aloft with her grubby hand. Startling her male cohorts, she stood like some dark warrioress from outer space, mighty in conquest, near a culvert at the far end of the block.

"Hey, well done girl, that's great!" cheered Orwell. "You get extra points for diligence!"

"Miss MacDonachie, you have succeeded beyond all measure!" reiterated Cepheus loudly, clapping his hands somewhere in the shadows above. "Now we can finish our game!"

"No, thank you!" growled sweaty, slimy Alicia at the utterly inane suggestion as she scrambled up the far bank. She barely accepted Orwell's helping hand, and seemed perturbed when she grabbed her sandals that he had thoughtfully rounded up. Alicia complained bitterly to both males as she snapped on her footwear, "I'm all itchy with burs and algae! I need to bathe and change my clothes, for the third fricking time today. Men are nothing but trouble!"

With that rebuke, the amazon strode darkly back to the house. Chastened for what he knew not, Orwell felt crummy as he followed Alicia, but he could not lessen the distance between them as they hiked past the thorn hedge and entered the well-lit Hughes compound. He heard her, up ahead, softly greet the night watchman as she marched haughtily up the driveway without stopping to marvel at the honour guard of coloured pails—now lit by the candles they had painstakingly set out together just minutes before the arrival of party guests. Orwell wondered which helpful angel had fired all those candles during his ditch work, but Alicia, determined to avoid others now revelling blissfully in the bright living room, slipped quietly into the house through the back-kitchen door.

"Miss MacDonachie behaves like a wild lioness of the savannah!" marvelled Cepheus in confidence to Orwell as they trudged after her. "Is this savagery always her nature? Can any man tame her?"

"I don't know, but I don't think I should," sighed Hughes as he lost Alicia's trail completely somewhere in the carport.

"Someday, I shall tame this haughty lioness!" Cepheus vowed fiercely.

"Cepheus, Alicia is only a teenager!" Orwell reasoned. "She is young and naïve, but God has given her a tender soul to temper her fierce spirit."

"Where? She insults and bullies you, Mr. Orwell. Why do you allow this abuse, particularly under your own roof? That brazen female must learn her place and how to be subservient to men before she leaves her father's house, or she shall break his heart. Mairam needs to be beaten regularly. Do you know, Mr. Orwell, that a Muslim man in my culture can divorce his wife for improperly cooking his food? A traditional husband may bolt shut his wife's mouth if she becomes argumentative. An eligible woman behaves modestly—she covers herself in public and does not argue with men! Miss MacDonachie should learn humility."

"Alicia is a fine girl, Cepheus. I respect her," Orwell advocated for his friend to this other friend. "No man other than her father should assume he has any right to instruct a woman, particularly one as intelligent, talented, and sensitive as Mairam."

"Then, I shall wait until Mairam comes of age where she leaves her father's home, after which time I shall find and tame her, if she still has need of such vital training," Cepheus promised chillingly. After he had suitably shocked his naïve young listener, Belo broke into a laugh as he spoofed, "Then, I shall write about my harrowing adventures. My epic novel will become a best seller. I am certain that you, Mr. Orwell, will read and remember what I promised you tonight!"

"I will be waiting a long time for such a novel," Hughes bravely countered. Not wanting to go further down this runaway train of thought, he played the host card, "Since we're both hungry, why don't we go inside to eat."

"Yes, we must, for I am very hungry now, Mr. Orwell. I hope your father butchered a cow in my honour. I was born of princes in my own country."

"We tried—but we couldn't catch the cow...She ran away," mumbled Orwell dully.

The youth was frustrated by Belo's haughty self-opinion as well as his own dearth of offering for his guests. Rather than feel offended, however, Cepheus laughed heartily at this clever reply, and affectionately clasped Orwell's hand as they ambled together into the house.

Bwana Hughes, spiffily attired in his decorative gown, officiously greeted these late arrivals as head of the household, and ushered them into the cheery drawing room where the others were already eating.

"Orwell, we've laid out all the food and utensils buffet style on the dining room table. We've saved you seats, but what good is sitting without something to nourish you in your hands? There's plenty to eat, so why don't you and Mr. Belo fill your plates and join us," buoyantly invited the diplomat, a veteran of many dinner parties, yet pleased to host so many promising young people in his pad.

"Thank you, sir," agreed Orwell, becoming rejuvenated. To his solemn, owl-faced companion, he hospitably suggested, "Come along with me, Cepheus. We mustn't neglect the ladies' scrumptious home cooking."

When they reached the nearly depleted food table, Orwell took the lead; showing Cepheus what to do by example, he uncovered various serving bowls, took spoons or forks set aside, and enthusiastically sampled what was left of the grilled sausage, steamed vegetables, salad, and chutney sauce—and even buttered for each of them a fresh, piping-hot sourdough roll from a woven grass basket.

Having heaped his plate with food, the jolly host turned to see how his companion was faring, but was dismayed to find Belo still standing cluelessly, without plate or utensils, at the start of the line. Hughes suddenly felt embarrassed, like a glutton! Setting down his own portion, Orwell apologetically traipsed back to his friend's side and helped him get started: he showed him the stack of clean plates and the accompanying silverware tray, where pre-sorted knives, forks, and spoons wrapped in colourful serviettes fancily awaited the diner. When Belo would not take up his tools, Orwell humbly handed them to him. Cepheus seemed insulted by this patronizing gesture, yet he feebly took these provisions like one who was unaccustomed to feeding himself.

Cepheus followed Orwell apprehensively through the buffet and meticulously scrutinized every dish for potentially unhealthy flaws, but would take nothing. He demanded to know the value of Alicia now as a cook, "Did Mairam help Madame prepare this meal?"

"We all did—it was a team effort," admitted Orwell, detailing with pride what were obviously unusual circumstances to his listener. "I barbequed the meat. Kathleen and Suzanne cooked the carrots, peas and sweet potatoes. Alicia and JJ tossed a salad of shredded lettuce, diced tomatoes, okra and peppers, chopped garlic and green onions, and sliced avocado with lemon squeezed in for good measure. My mother, who oversaw the entire operation, also baked the sourdough buns with a famous recipe passed down from the Klondike gold rush through her pioneer forbearers. Eat and be merry, my friend."

"Are the sausages made of pork? I and Miss Georgina, not to mention her rake of a brother, are Muslims who believe that flesh of such cloven-hoofed animals is unclean. Surely you took into account our strict religious views."

"Yes we did, these are beef sausages," assured Orwell, smiling patiently, though he wondered where Cepheus had suddenly found religion. He kidded the other to lighten up, "You are allowed to eat cows, I hope."

"That and bush meat—my favourite from childhood where I was raised in the scrubby Sahel of Bornu State—you know, wild game: impala, wildebeest, gazelle, and the likes! Sheep and goats herded by village boys sufficed, and fish caught in Lake Chad were good in season. Sometimes, when food was scarce, we ate lizards or quails...Did your father invoke blessings from Allah upon the chosen bovine before he butchered it?"

"Mallam Cepheus, these sausages came wrapped from the supermarket! I do not know what cow gave up her life to provide such sausage. If it helps you put your concerns to bed about our Christian food being halal, my father prayed fervently over the entire spread before anyone ate a morsel. To thank God for His bounteous grace and blessings is a Hughes family tradition at meal times. The MacDonachie girls pray with us, for they too are diligent followers of Jesus. My father, no doubt, asked God to bless the people who eat as well as those who prepared tonight's feast, as such is his custom for every meal."

"So, he also blessed you," Cepheus deduced, pleased with such holy supplications. Remaining stubbornly unconvinced that he could partake now in the food and sit down to enjoy consuming it, this tiresome fellow added with disapproval, "You took your place in the kitchen as one of the women! That is highly irregular practice for a proper man, Mr. Orwell, highly irregular indeed!"

"I was happy to do my part; such duty is not unusual in my country."

"You should not feel happy doing Mairam's tasks. As a junior girl among the females, she should now prepare our suppers here and then bring choice helpings out to us while we sit together with the other men and discuss the affairs of the world. I notice that Mairam is not about her duties, nor has she bothered to return to our fellowship, Mr. Orwell. I would cane her sorely for this flagrant disobedience if she was of my household! Is she always so rude?"

"Alicia is likely showering, after which she will dress for dinner in a fresh evening gown. She soiled her clothing retrieving your croquet ball. Give her a break! The young lady has been doing her part with care and attention, all day."

"I don't care! Bathing? Dressing? Hubbah, Mr. Orwell, such lazy behaviour is unacceptable. She definitely needs correction. I demand that Mairam present herself at once and serve me my supper!" growled Cepheus, royally annoyed.

"Okay, all right. Take your coffee and sit down in the drawing room while I fetch Alicia to serve you," Hughes whispered calmly, trying to smooth things over.

As he respectfully drew a mug full of dark, chicory-flavoured brew from the urn, liberally whitened it with sweetened condensed milk, and carried the beverage for Cepheus while ushering his elder to a cushioned chair among the men, Orwell could not help but wonder whether this eccentric guest had any sisters, daughters, wife, or even a mother to teach him about women. Orwell ensured that this pompous Writers' Club president was comfortably seated, then placed at his elbow a TV tray with a copper-plated coaster to set his coffee mug upon. The demanding man was soon engaged in conversation with his cronies although, unlike the others, Cepheus had no food to eat. He simply shooed Orwell away to solve his minor problem.

As Hughes padded dutifully down the hallway to sound out Alicia, butterflies fluttered in his stomach as he pondered how to convince the powerful feminist to keep his tough promise to Master Belo—the ultimate male chauvinist pig! Should he kiss her amorously like Casanova, and agree to become her boyfriend? Should he humbly fall on his knees and beg for Alicia's cooperation? Would she take a pound of his flesh first, then consider his feeble petition while he kissed her curved ass? Why would she receive him now, when the last time they had interacted she had growled dismissively at his efforts to help her?

Nervously pondering his fate as he stopped outside the bathroom, Orwell noted that even though light glimmered beneath the locked door, no sounds emanated from behind it. He knocked and politely asked Alicia how she was doing, but nobody responded. Was she deaf or just playing another rude trick on him? Perhaps, he worried, someone else was using the loo—had he embarrassed another guest...and, worst of all, possibly Georgina?

"Heaven forbid!" Orwell swore under his breath as he turned away in frustration, and tiptoed further down the shadowy hallway towards the bedrooms.

He found every private room shut and dark, as should be the case when strange guests were visiting his house. Orwell felt foolish and increasingly awkward as he retraced his steps toward the distant gaiety of his party. He glimpsed Alicia leaving the bathroom ahead of him, but she offered him only a vague smile and then her back as she walked gracefully onward, barefoot and casually dressed in blue jeans and a print blouse. Surely, she knew his voice and had understood that he was looking for her, but now, was she pretending to not recognize him, let alone hear him?

This bountiful female certainly was a looker and obviously pleased to make him watch her, Orwell dejectedly acknowledged as he admired how her molten hair flowed onto broad shoulders and down her straight back; her plump tail swished provocatively beneath her narrow waist, daring him to follow. Alicia's perfume pleasantly wafted behind her, causing wild flowers to bloom rainbow colours in the grim stone passage as she traipsed along. The coy temptress smiled at her host as she turned the corner, but she kept moving, as though she wanted no time with such an awkward, tiresome lad or his petty problems. Hoping for an audience nonetheless, Orwell quickened his pace, yet Alicia had disappeared by the time he reached the kitchen.

He understood now that he was late for dinner and the girls, hungry and tired of waiting as well as culturally aware that African men and women ate separately, were likely eating together in another room. Alicia, apprised of their secret hideout, must have deftly joined her female collaborators. He noted with chagrin that his plate of delicious food had been scoffed from the buffet table. Refusing to be outfoxed, however, Orwell bravely searched until he found the ladies, gaily chattering and dining sumptuously, in his bedroom!

"Speaking of the devil, here he is!" teased Suzanne as the door was flung open, and Orwell's baleful hulk stood in the doorway, interrupting amusing tales she was spinning about him.

"Suzy, I told you he was coming", Alicia muttered with boisterous satisfaction from the lawn chair she had hurriedly crammed in beside Orwell's bed, where she devoured his carefully selected meal. Making light of the strange occupant of this den of fascinating secrets rather than wisely hiding from him, she added rowdily to the girls' tangled yarn, "Orwell was chasing me like some sailor just come to port from a long sea voyage, but I ditched him...or so I thought."

While the other girls congratulated Alicia for outwitting Orwell and heckled him for appearing lost in his own bedroom, JJ glibly quipped, "We don't live by the coast, Lisa; we're stuck inside Africa like ruddy landlubbers."

"Maybe Cap'n Oh-well just wanted to kiss you, Fannie. Why didn't you let him catch you?" needled Kathleen smugly. She laughed when Alicia glared fiercely at her, but then admonished the lioness, "I'm just joking, Honey, okay?"

Kitty-Cat, who beamed with delight for having reminisced many a vaunted girl tale about outwitting the awkward Hughes boys in Canada, glanced smartly at Georgina once again, but the dusky beauty sat demurely in her seat, and deigned not to be entertained further by such catty guff as she nibbled at her food with dainty grace. Master Orwell was now in the room, his ears undoubtedly burning! What would he say—what did he want now?

Orwell, afraid that Kathleen was craftily stirring up jealousy between Alicia and Georgina, interrupted the girls' fun with news of his urgent mission.

"I need assistance from a special lady with clever talents for service. Can somebody help me?" the young knight daringly requested, gazing upon Alicia.

"Are you really so helpless?" Suzanne baited her brother with a gleaming smile. She turned to the glamorous Miss Amadu, who seemed unable to comprehend that these apparent jabs were all just playful banter among siblings in the highbrow and Christian, Hughes household.

"I would come at once, but I have no talents for service," Georgina admitted, sighing as she shook her head and eyed her wannabe lover with feigned despair. "I believe that Miss Kathy is up to any test you have in mind."

"Not for a clod like him—send one of our junior girls to check things out!" insisted Kathleen haughtily, like a queen. "Alicia or JJ, go! Give this guy a hand!"

"Why am I always the gopher?" demanded JJ in rebellious frustration to her roomful of supposed fellow teens. "Go for this, go for that; darn my knickers, carry my satchel...while you ladies sit on your fat bums and eat peaches and cream! Who made you boss over me?"

"Enough, JJ — come on, we'll show 'em!" Alicia, bounding to her feet, grimly mustered her noisy sidekick with a stiff shoulder tap as she strode through the maze of shocked, sweltering girls stuck in their chairs, and reported to Sir Orwell.

Smartly saluting her commanding officer, Alicia followed him out of the room, dragging Janice Joanne along in her wake. Once outside, JJ demanded in a surly, ship deck bark that Orwell would have expected Alicia to use, which caused the discoursing men folk lounging like lords down yonder in the living room, to stare askance at her, "Okay Bucko, what do you want from us?"

Alicia shook her head at her gruff cohort, showing JJ a better way as she sweetly inquired of sweaty, anxious Orwell, "What service shall we talented ladies perform for you, gallant sir?"

"Miss, please take to Cepheus Belo his supper?" broached Orwell, giving all due respect to his esteemed mistress and her glowering lady in waiting.

"What! Why doesn't that egomaniac get off his duff and serve himself?" demanded Alicia, suddenly looking choked with her passive aggression outed, voiced the same obvious questions any normal, liberated female would pose in this crappy situation. "Does not Sir Cepheus have arms and legs of his own to engage the sumptuous food table we all prepared? Where are his manners, his gratitude?"

"Cepheus, despite his radical rhetoric, is a traditional African man..."

"He's a stone-age asshole, more like!" snorted Alicia, unimpressed by Hughes's pat excuse. "That guy needs a thorough tune up!"

"Please, Alicia," begged Hughes. "He asked specifically for you, just as I do now. Dearest Alicia, Cepheus is my friend. I don't know how else to mend this fence, but to humbly call upon my special, go-to girl—who is also my dear friend."

"All right, my lad; it's only because you're asking that I am even considering to help, but I have queries about this venture you need to answer first."

When Orwell agreed and showed a humble, listening spirit, Alicia drew him onto the relatively dark and secluded patio outside the brilliant kitchen, where she nervously asked her captain, "Must I sit with Mr. Belo? Do I entertain him while he eats?"

She explained her concerns in light of a rugged experience from earlier that day, when he had previously dispatched her to please Benjamin, "I argued badly with your friend about missions, then ripped my dress playing wild games of ping pong with him and several other guys."

"You are only required to smile as you deliver food to Cepheus. Whatever else you do above and beyond is totally your call, Alicia," instructed Orwell, after apologizing for getting her into trouble before. He praised Alicia's efforts in front of silent witness JJ, insisting that Ben appreciated her now all the more.

"That's swell by me," Alicia effervesced, dancing from relief for happy Orwell and his stony sister, who wisely held her tongue.

As she scampered over to the buffet table and gathered fixings of a hearty meal, Orwell, encouraged by her enthusiasm and beauty, offered Alicia thanks for such pleasant cooperation.

"You are sincerely welcome, dear, but I don't come free," she reminded him with a crafty wink and delicious grin. She dexterously handled her utensils to heap the plate with various foods like she was a drummer in a rock band. "You owe me big time."

"What? I do? How?" stammered Orwell, suddenly worried and flustered again. When this imp nodded convincingly despite all his protests, he could only acknowledge with a groan that he carried a debt unpaid, "So, I owe you. What shall I do to make things square between us, Alicia?"

"That's for me to know and for you to find out," she whispered delectably, tickling his fancy as she pranced away to complete the special errand for her gawking, famished host.

Standing with JJ and Mrs. Hughes above the stage and marvelling as he watched Alicia buoyantly perform her task with grace, tears he did not understand welled in Orwell's strained eyes. This unusual serving girl bowed elegantly and smiled pleasantly as she startled Cepheus with a generously laden plate. Princess Mairam, daughter to King Jesus, entertained all the men folk—including unusually chirpy Bwana Hughes—with jokes and banter, but flattered the magician specifically by bending low and sprinkling him with flower petals perfume and feathery dream catcher earrings dangling from her dainty earlobes before his wide eyes, while she whispered sweet nothings in his ear! The other men jovially acknowledged Cepheus's manly good fortune by singing "Tiyende Pamodzi" while he continued to stare with bewilderment upon her. Before any of these stallions might touch her, however, the frisky young filly gave Orwell a broad smile indicating mission accomplished; then she skipped freely out of their midst as they all rousingly applauded. Belo smiled and raised a thumbs-up to salute Orwell for fulfilling his duty.

"Brother, what task do you want me to do?" cried JJ, as though from behind the curtains of Orwell's dream. "Please, don't ask me to shake my booty for those dudes. They like me and I like them, but I'm not the kind of girl who puts on a provocative display to fete male company!"

"I would never ask you to either, just as I did not request Alicia to display herself! I don't think she really did, to tell you the truth, dear sister, but whatever her behaviour was, the young lady chose it—real and spunky—and my blokes loved it!" countered Orwell with rubbery lips, his throat dry. "As for you, please be decent as you determine who among our guests would like a fresh beverage. Then, with Suzy to help you, can you replenish supplies of assorted nuts and crisps? I would do the honours myself, but I haven't eaten anything yet. Thanks JJ."

"Okay, it's my party too. I invited this crowd and I will handle it—my way," murmured the brunette pixie as she purposefully tackled her duty.

Orwell heaved a sigh of relief as he scraped the last bits of food onto his own plate, and moseyed into the living room to join his cohorts. Plunking himself into a cardboard chair between Cepheus and Benjamin, he took a well-earned break; the jolly male contingent, including his father and brother, enthusiastically welcomed young bwana aboard. "Well done, Orwell! Right on, man!" Their well-earned kudos were music to his ears. He had run off his feet all day, trying to stroke and entertain...He deserved time now to rest, enjoy his mates who by now must truly respect him!

Although Orwell and his beloved Georgina were dining apart, he concluded that she had chosen to eat with women as expected by culture. Why be foolish and enter that hot henhouse again where he was not welcome, even if it was his bedroom? Once the meal was over, he knew that ardent social convener JJ would bring everyone back together for fun and games.

*****

Why should women rule the roost, Orwell wondered as he settled in with almost sleepy contentment amongst his proud and confident male comrades? Having squirmed to perform all day properly under the thumbs of demanding women, Orwell relished this palaver with his own kind. Their well-lit den was sprinkled with jovial banter, yet they conversed intelligently about the poignant affairs of the world. Well-dressed, clever lords they were: lounging in comfortable chairs...eating and drinking together...lauding one another's exploits...laughing at their jokes ...respecting everyone's credentials...listening to each knowledgeable opinion. They rode the cusp of life! Despite being gathered across onerous cultural, racial and religious divides, they were all *Orwell's* friends, his peers.

Bwana Hughes respectfully affirmed these eclectic visitors as such, although he was amazed that an odd chap like Orwell could gain friendship with so many impressive young gentlemen. They could have partied hearty just fine without the old establishment square hovering in their midst, but to their credit, these young bucks respected his wise diplomacy, much like Tracy and his biker hoods had done during tours to the Hughes acreage in years past. Sir Richard, awed by his little brother's society, was pleased at the opportunity to know him better through his choice of favourable and impressive friends!

They were of one blood, but Orwell was the first to acknowledge that God had made each as a different part of the same body. None of these fellows expected that a Hughes or MacDonachie should Africanize himself while living in Zambia: leave luxurious home for a thatched roof hovel; two-car lifestyle for a bicycle; American-run private schools for the austere public system; or democratic institutions for political uncertainty and social want. Orwell, Richard, and Bwana Hughes were welcome and respected in Africa, but they knew that they must earn these gifts by learning the cultures and aspirations of their hosts.

"Mr. James, I am glad that GRZ has partnered with Canada on so many projects, the most recent being the advancement of technical education. Zambia is a young country with much to learn. We know our awkwardness; we strive towards development, but need time to apprentice under good teachers. Work with us, share with us your knowledge at a level where we can comfortably negotiate, and we will do our best to blossom," appealed Ben, smiling at Bwana Hughes as everyone intently listened in the comfortable living room. "Mr. James, you are not only Dr. Kenneth Kaunda's friend, but you care deeply about all Zambians. The President is a devout Christian who cares for his people. Our government's doctrine of humanism is not some secular cult philosophy, but stems from KK's vision of a national brotherhood of caring, selfless citizens, working together in all aspects of life to keep our country strong and free."

"The copper industry is our bread and butter, although millions of dollars were spent to nationalize it, so that we, not foreign companies, could control our destiny," explained David, an economy student. Trying to be matter of fact without injecting gloominess into the party's enlightened atmosphere, Sobukwe espoused his view of the world with unusual boldness, "Now, we are in debt because the government has overspent in its stout efforts to build roads, schools, and hospitals quickly to help our people. We experience shortages of petrol and cooking oil. Many Zambians flock to the cities for amenities, where they must live in shantytowns without electricity or clean, running water. Why? Zambia is rich!

"These days, our economy is boosted by the favourable price of copper on the world market, but the boom will not last forever. We need to diversify our local manufacturing of goods. We must develop broadly our agricultural sector, which should be our economic back bone—our bread and butter! Mr. Orwell, I am pleased that you study the production of tropical crops— Zambian students need encouragement from your lead—but you are leaving us too soon!

"Our forefathers were successful subsistence farmers, but modern agricultural science, which advances production through use of machinery, fertilizers, and pesticides, must be learned. Theoretical management of large-scale commercial plantations must be taken from classrooms to the fields. As you know, Mr. Orwell, we are experimenting with cultivation of wheat to make better-quality bread flour for the masses. A wide variety of crops, both temperate and tropical, can be grown here, what with our fertile savannah soils and moderate climate, influenced by relatively high altitudes and seasonal rains. UNZA should also to turn out more teachers, doctors, engineers, and economists to fill many posts needed all over the country.

"We are forging ahead, and will not give up! We don't live under the oppression of Rhodesia and South Africa any more—though they wish to impose their rule forever! Rather, Zambia stands tall as a Front-Line State in conscientious objection against those illegal racist regimes. We have learned to circumvent our enemies even when they close their borders or delay the return of our rail cars. Soon, it won't matter what banditry happens to disrupt the Benguela Railway through Angola. My Canadian friends, do you realize that we built our own railway northeastward to Dar es Salaam with Chinese help? The Italians brought their technical advice in aviation, while other foreign experts from Europe or North America help us improve our commerce and industries. Kariba Dam and the Kafue Gorge Upper Power Station are generating hydroelectric power throughout the country, thanks to friends found in many quarters."

On cue, Solomon the political scientist, took the lead.

"The government does well to cultivate friendships with many countries in an international political alliance rather than tie itself exclusively to America or Britain. Zambia prides itself as a politically nonaligned nation, who adheres to the UN, yet reserves a special fondness for fellow free spirits like Yugoslavia and

Ethiopia. We are a member of the British Commonwealth of Nations, but not beholden to our former colonial master; Zambia is a republic, unlike Canada, who still reveres Elizabeth as her Queen.

"I do not mean to sling mud at Canada, for African nations admire Canadians as peacemakers, agents of development, and champions of human rights. Your country is rich, Mr. Orwell, but Canada does not flaunt its wealth by building showpiece development facilities. Your military does not bully weaker nations; Canada plays no war games in Third World countries for its own political and socioeconomic gain, unlike South Africa, the Soviet Union, and USA. You don't crush us by demanding swift repayment of loans at high interest. I believe that your people are different from Americans: you strike me as soft-spoken yet sincere, concerned but broad-minded, humble while progressive. White people, particularly those from the west, look alike to Africans, but Canadians stand out as being wholesome. We welcome you here."

Thus toasted Mr. Chona, as he and his countrymen rose in tribute to their rapt hosts. The Africans laughed in good-natured protest, however, when Orwell felt compelled to applaud their outpouring of recognition and gratitude. He made them all laugh by relating an encounter which he thought illustrated the difference between Canadians and Americans....

"Our family was on safari in East Africa and arrived in some dusty bush town, thirsty for minerals. No sooner had our baggage-laden Peugeot halted before the burg's only confectionary than we were mobbed by native children with pleading hands outstretched. We already knew about beggars! Upon closer examination of this horde, however, Dad and Rick determined that the waifs possessed hundreds of American dimes, which they said a caravan of Yankee tourists had given them while passing through en route to Serengeti National Park. With no bank around to convert their windfall into local currency, the children now appealed to us white strangers to play banker for them. Our family was moved to exchange all our Tanzanian shillings for as many dimes as we could carry, confident that we could trade American currency for Zambian, once back in Lusaka."

The Zambian men listened politely out of respect to their hosts as Orwell related this adventure, but were unable to laugh at his punch line, like Bwana and Richard Hughes did now in retrospect. Cepheus, however, became angry over what he perceived to be an insulting slap in the face of every African, but particularly Tanzania's esteemed socialist president, Julius Nyerere, who taught egalitarian, communal self-reliance as *Ujamaa.* A stony scowl masked his face, and he prepared to leave the otherwise chatty scene. When Orwell enquired after him, Cepheus would not reply, but seemed lost forever as a friend. Only after Alicia timely appeared, and stroked Belo's ego by filling his drink and serving him a plate of assorted sweets, did the owl-eyed activist articulate his turbulent feelings to the sobered listeners.

Flying into a tirade, Cepheus demanded that his white hosts accept the African's struggle for development, suffer with him in his poverty, but rejoice also in his successful breakthroughs—without condemning his one-party state, *Ujamaa* socialism, inability to repay huge IMF[59] loans...Listen and understand, don't patronize! Encourage, don't condemn! Africans are part of the civilized, space-aged world—they have always been! Was not Africa the cradle of civilization? Were whites afraid that even they, so far removed, still carried the genes of Africa? The time passed long ago for sending dour Christian missionaries with their English Bibles, followed by carpetbagger industrialists with loose environmental scruples, and shiploads of banned chemicals to dump...Stop exploiting the mother land and enslaving her people for gold and diamonds, copper and tin, mahogany and teak, cocoa and pyrethrum[60]! Imperialistic European and North American powers not only grew rich off Africa during the slave trade and colonial times, but barred African products from the international market place, to keep Africa poor! Cepheus related, that in his own lifetime, he had seen all of these injustices carried out, just as he had seen the time-honoured traditions and proven wisdom of his people warped by the same intruders who desired to civilize the so-called Dark Continent!

"And what, Miss MacDonachie, do you think about such blatant hypocrisy?" Cepheus irately demanded of Alicia as the serving girl grimly soaked up his fiery soapbox rhetoric from the doorway. "Is it not ironic that you should offer me food and drink tonight, when your powerful daddy dines daily on foodstuffs brought to his plate at the expense of peasants from all over the world? Are you not the rich, spoiled daughter of a tyrant?"

---

59 *IMF*: abbreviation for 'International Monetary Fund'.

60 *Pyrethrum*: botanical insecticide produced primarily from the flowers of *Tanacetum cinerariaefolium*, a species of chrysanthemum native to Dalmatia in Croatia. Pyrethrum plants have historically been grown in commercial quantities in Kenya, Tanzania, and Rwanda.

She should have been embarrassed by this unruly assault, yet Alicia calmly replied, "My father has many employees, but they are hired at generous wages with ample personal benefits, to carry out tasks needed to keep his companies running smoothly. They go home to bless their own families with money for food and shelter, clothing and education, medicine and transport, when the whistle blows at end of shift.

"We MacDonachie kids were raised to pull our weight around the house. I regularly cook and clean. Why would my parents need servants when they have eight children to do chores?"

"Why should you, a member of elite bourgeoisie who can afford servants, take away domestic jobs from those who need such work to feed their own families?" demanded Cepheus, confronting Alicia's rebuttal with an odd twist. When she argued that her father cared for the masses by employing hundreds of native workers in a dozen countries, Belo altered his stance by jovially making Hughes—who now fidgeted anxiously for Alicia, as well as others who did not understand Cepheus like he did—his whipping boy. "I've discussed this important socioeconomic issue many times with Mr. Orwell because he seems too busy to read his manuscripts at our bi-monthly Writers' Club. Mairam, why is our mutual friend so preoccupied?"

"Sir, I am only a high school girl, and not well-acquainted with the affairs of such distinguished older gentlemen as you or Orwell Hughes," replied Alicia, apologetically declining to comment; she drew laughs from the others nonetheless through her mock deferring tone.

"And, I presume, you are dutifully progressing towards passing with flying colours your Ordinary Level examinations in various subjects—Mathematics, Chemistry, Physics, Biology, Geography, History, English Grammar and Literature—that are foundational for completing one's secondary school education?" Cepheus smiled cleverly at his quarry as he listed fields of knowledge upon which all students her age were tested in the British Commonwealth of Nations. "But, I digress...

"Nonetheless Miss MacDonachie, it is well known around campus that Mr. Orwell is not only a full-time student, but that he also labours without pay on a daily basis as a garden boy in his family's compound. He defends such unseemly behaviour below his station by saying that he is helping his father—a high-ranking Canadian diplomat! As this honourable man also submits, he stays trim through physical exercise, so that he can continue to contribute athletically to UNZA's field hockey team. I find that his obsession with flowers takes away gainful employment from many young men presently languishing without work in this city. If Mr. Orwell would only give up his chores to a Zambian chap of suitable calibre, he could then concentrate on training for the field hockey team, as well as spend quality time writing for presentation at the Writers' Club. What say you, Miss MacDonachie?"

"Orwell, you would do well to heed the wisdom of your learned colleague," advised Alicia stoically, who then seemed to insult Cepheus by winking at Hughes and capriciously suggesting, "You might then find more time to spend with me!"

Everyone chuckled at Alicia's attempt at cheering the mood, but Orwell seemed caught like a deer in the headlights of an oncoming vehicle. Still reeling from the strained exchange with Cepheus and not knowing what else to do in response, he gave Alicia a dazed smile by which he telepathically promised to pay heed to her request. As she smiled back, admiration sparkling in her dark, oriental eyes turned slowly triumphant. The longer they gazed affectionately at one another, however, she melted into smouldering want and even sadness as her smile drained , leaving her awkwardly blushing and melancholy. Alicia shyly lowered her face and slipped away.

Hughes desired to follow Alicia now in her flight, but was foiled when Georgina, Kathleen, JJ, and Suzanne suddenly barged through the same doorway, demanding that the good old boys rise up to participate in the evening's planned social activities, which, from the stack of LPs Georgie held in her hands and the meaningful gaze she flashed at Orwell, translated into one thing: the girls wanted to dance! Orwell bounded up like a bunny ready to comply at once, but the other gents, older and wiser than he, eased more suavely into compliance. Bwana Hughes decided this a good time to retire to the den.

Soon, young people were milling about the deck under a starry night sky, giggling and chatting among the lava lamps and many candles flickering within their multi-coloured lanterns. At the first bold down-beat of rock 'n' roll music, Orwell and Richard assumed that they could take their adorable female partners onto the dance floor to enjoy a private fling, but Africans shied away from such intimacy, preferring instead to dance artistically within their genders or as one large, enthusiastic group. Georgina gently took Alicia by the hand, and bid her shy friend to dance beside her while Cepheus and Benjamin cavorted with Orwell. At times, Orwell's chaps moved fluidly about Alicia: she found herself in sights of shyly grinning David or enthusiastically shaking Solomon whenever the 'big cats' moseyed about JJ or Georgina. Suzanne and Ali preferred one another's company, as did Richard and Kathleen, but each couple jovially mingled as everyone danced together to a rhythmic reggae beat supplied by Ali's ghetto blaster.

Orwell marvelled at how his friends gravitated to Alicia. He found himself grinning and strutting his stuff for want of her pleasure too, as they also took opportunities to come together. Her forlorn desire was passé now as carefree Alicia frolicked barefoot with all around.

Georgina, however, sensed their special comradery; taking charge, the vixen drew Orwell away and requested he put on pounding, nonstop dance music she had brought to the party. Battle of the bands ensued between the *Beach Boys, Beatles,* and *Rolling Stones.* Vivacious Miss Amadu became the featured dancer for all to applaud and learn from, as she interpreted *Mungo Jerry*'s "In the Summertime" with high-octane energy!

Taking a well-earned rest at last from polishing the dance floor, the young people shared tea and crumpets in the warm glow of the parlour. Their fellowship was refuelled when Mrs. Hughes brought out a delicious platter of barbecued assorted meats, complete with bread and trimmings of garden vegetables. Solomon graciously responded by teaching his fellow guests and willing hosts a local game called *ayo,* a backgammon-like caper involving the strategic movement of small, smooth stones across two sets of bowls. Cepheus was versed in playing the *balafon,* a gourd xylophone, as was David with the thumb piano, both of which were decoratively stationed about the room. JJ and Alicia shook flamboyant pod rattles in accompaniment as they let down their hair long enough to help churn out a set of ancient tribal songs on instruments that had been purchased by their hosts as exotic tourist curios. The normally reserved Canucks became buoyantly coaxed by Ben into attempting the fancy footwork of a popular tribal dance. This cultural exchange ran its course as people swayed and stepped softly in rolling, bubbling circles to David's eerie chants and the rhythmic beat of Solomon's hand drum.

They took turns singing folk songs and sacred hymns to the accompaniment of Orwell's piano, Suzy's autoharp, Alicia's violin, JJ's flute, and Kathleen's guitar, which in a spirit of cooperation, she shared with Benjamin, who then strummed his own fine music. At Georgina's request, Ben led the group in a melodious rendition of "Kumbayah My Lord". Seated on the couch between two exotically beautiful women who loved, and were loved by him: Alicia singing, laughing and clapping her hands and Georgina smiling contentedly as she lay with her head upon his shoulder, Orwell could not have wished for a better party—save for Tracy to also be in attendance, to savour the festivities with him!

As the Westminster clock chimed ten, JJ came up with a crazy party game that squeezed the last ounce of energy from the mellow glow of satisfied tiredness. Asking puckishly for a clever volunteer and choosing dapper Ali as the obvious candidate, JJ gave this suave globetrotter a photograph to memorize, but *not*, she sternly instructed, share with anyone else! The ring mistress directed her victim to lie on the floor while Alicia draped him with an iconic Hudson Bay blanket. JJ then invited the stupefied audience to guess what was the mystery object depicted in Ali's photo. The performer must stay shrouded and sworn to silence, but he could nod, shake his head, or act out his answer to any question posed.

"Are the rules of this charade simple enough?" asked the tiny emcee with booming energy. When everyone on both sides of the blanket nodded politely, JJ christened the game to start with a hearty, "*Bon voyage*!"

The game started politely if not awkwardly, as the audience fiddled about asking appropriate yet strategic, close-ended questions. Some folks thought, if they concentrated hard enough on remembering all the details, they would see the photograph in their minds—if not somehow steal it from Ali's shrouded person. Cepheus suddenly broke ranks when he laughed at the clownish, burrowing shaman king! Georgina glared and clacked her tongue at Belo's bizarre amusement, then murmured her concern that Orwell take charge, lest her brother suffocate inside his heavy wraps.

Orwell, knowing this high intrigue was meant only to be a friendly parlour game, shattered the tense air by shouting out a strategic yes-no question, "Mr. Ali, does your photograph depict something alive?" When the shrouded figure nodded vigorously, causing Georgina to gasp as he generated snaps of static electricity, Orwell smartly followed up, "Is your creature a plant?"

Ali shook his head, then repeated this gesture more emphatically when Richard jumped in, "Are you a two-legged animal—a person, perchance?"

"Is it a four-legged animal?" inquired Alicia, looking like a scientist now with her heavy glasses on. She was well aware from biology class that insects had six legs, spiders skittered about on eight legs, and some creepy crawlers moved on dozens of limbs until caught and eaten by the locals for dietary protein.

Kathleen scowled unimpressed and gave her sister an F for asking such a dumb question when the game was on line for the boys to win. "Like, duh! Get with the program already, Fannie. Of course, it's obviously a four-legged animal! We have to get snappy here, cut to the chase—Mr. Ali, do you have a picture of a wild animal?"

"I was getting there, Kitty-Cat—I have to narrow down the options, you know, play the game intelligently," Alicia muttered aside to her sister.

Ali, as though to prove her strategic point, nodded vigorously before grabbing Alicia's leg and using it to lumber about on five legs; he extended the extra limb into the air and tried to pull down something huge. Alicia, dragged like a rag doll about the floor, shrieked that Ali was some famished alien who would drag her under the blanket to eat; she guffawed and squirmed until he released her. Alicia desperately clambered into her seat, but gave her stern sister a wild look; Kathleen, striving to concentrate and guess ahead of Richard and Orwell, waved Alicia off like she was some hyper-active child.

"Does this animal live in Africa?" demanded the Hughes brothers enthusiastically together. When Ali nodded, Georgina flashed Orwell a zesty grin, impressed that he was so animated...engaged...He was the life of the party!

Ali failed to respond immediately; he suddenly fell miserably behind! He sat slumped like a sad sack. Was he deeply pondering, or simply confused by the fusillade of questions? Was he getting too hot and tired, or was his brain finally fried? Cepheus found Ali's humbling predicament utterly hilarious. He so enjoyed the buzz of questions flying around that he saw no need to whip up his own to throw at his faltering nemesis.

"Is it a pet?" Suzanne asked girlishly, provoking laughter from the others. Cepheus practically fell off his seat at what he thought was a preposterous supposition, and rolled on the floor, laughing uproariously now as Ali vigorously negated that silly idea like one who felt totally insulted. The audience giggled with amused dismay at Cepheus's clownish antics, but Ali, provoked by this rude heckler, gained his second wind, and responded enthusiastically to Kathleen's musing that he was a large game animal like a lion or an elephant. Ali assumed a kneeling position, hunched his shoulders and outstretched curved arms below his head to form tusks. He laboriously dug at the floor until his knees gave way when tangled in the blanket.

"I know, brother, you're acting like an elephant! There must be an elephant in that photo!" shrieked Georgina with delight.

Ali threw off his sweltering wraps, and roundly congratulated her worthy guess. His relief to be free from confinement far outweighing any bitterness of having lost his secret, Ali bounded over to present his crumpled photo to Georgina, who was celebrating her clever win with Orwell and Alicia. Ali's face glistened with sweat and his voice was raspy as he exclaimed, "You are absolutely correct, my dear! Well done! Fabulous! How did you manage it?"

"I figured it out!" chortled Georgina triumphantly as she flashed the prized photograph of a huge grey pachyderm, bearing gleaming ivory tusks and a curling trunk as it grazed upon succulent tree shoots in the cool of the day, at her subdued rivals Kathleen, Suzanne and Richard. "I won the game!"

"You certainly did," acknowledged Kathleen icily, annoyed by the other's loud bragging. She insisted on calling a spade a spade, "With a little help from your friends, Georgie girl, to be fair. This game was likely rigged in your favour, just as croquet was earlier this afternoon for you and Orwell."

"*Ashe*[61], malama! I followed others' queries—that is true—but I made my own deductions," Georgina cunningly explained, while Orwell protested complaints of collusion.

"His sister can read Ali's mind. It was all planned, a trick," Suzanne teased.

Finding such a quip smart and stinging rather than clever, Georgina smiled fiercely even as she distilled her winning strategy to her detractors, "Yes, I plan all my moves very carefully—that is how I stay on the cutting-edge—ahead of the pack."

"Hear, hear," cheered Orwell, saluting the champion. He felt privileged to be on Georgina's winning side, though he did not tumble, as did Alicia and the other girls, that he was the winner's latest trophy. Orwell seemed more worried that he would need to stop a fight from breaking out between the girls, but he was barking up the wrong tree.

Suddenly, Cepheus threw a figurative pie in Ali's face.

"*Mallam, kai sarkin giwaye ne*—Ali, you are the king of the elephants!"

---

61 *Ashe*: Hausa term that expresses surprize or doubt, like 'really', or 'is that so?'

cackled Belo in Hausa and English, as he bowed mockingly before the blushing exhibitionist. Solomon and David found the exchange amusing, but the more mature Benjamin looked on soberly and the Hughes brothers became aghast. With Ali fuming, Belo rudely observed, "You did not, however, remember that your subjects live in Africa. How can this be? Even children know that elephants live in Africa! These beasts are more African than you are!"

"Ach, man, did you not see the photograph?" argued Ali. He crossly grabbed the picture from his startled sister and commanded this knave to look carefully, "See those high, barred walls behind the trees, my friend? This elephant lives in a *zoo*! Mr. Orwell's family could have snapped him at any urban zoo in North America or Europe—hence my hesitation."

"Ali is definitely correct," judged JJ with authority, as she moved between the disputants and examined the photograph with them. "That elephant was snapped years ago—before we came to Africa—he lived in captivity at the *Alberta Game Farm* near our home city of Edmonton."

"Then, Miss Hughes, you must have been a mere child," Cepheus turbulently mused.

"We all were. I have another photo from the same animal park that shows Rick, Orly, Suzy, and me riding together on a camel while she was being led by her trainer," JJ jovially bared another family secret, breaking ice for her guests, but dismaying her older siblings by circulating the odd childhood picture. She chattered engagingly as the others poured over her memories, "As kids, we went to the *Alberta Game Farm* for family, school, or church picnics, to look at exotic creatures collected from all over the world by Al Oeming, the famous Canadian wildlife conservationist. Lisa and Kathy, remember when we were together for Sunday school picnics?"

"That *was* a long time ago," Dame Kathleen reminisced to the sprightly kid.

"JJ, I sat with you on the camel, one kid on each of her humps. '*Sally the Camel had two humps, Sally the Camel had two humps, Sally the Camel had two humps, So ride Sally, ride*'," Alicia musically recalled a jolly camp song. Then, the big, frisky girl buffeted those crowded about with her hips and yelled, "*Boom, boom, boom!*"

She pushed far and wide the African blokes who had bumped her so liberally in the heat of ping pong. Cepheus was bowled onto a couch, while Benjamin sought safety in an easy chair beside the fireplace. Solomon and David, in trying to copy Alicia's energetic dance, bounced about with Suzy and Kathleen who, smiling darkly, gave back as much as they got. Georgina laughed with Alicia when she was vigorously boom-boomed by her roughhewn friend, but then apologized to Orwell when she jostled into him. He, enjoying their collision, playfully caught and swung Georgie around, making her shriek, for he knew this raucous song was meant to be a romp!

"Orwell, you could have at least offered us an African-born elephant," complained Georgina after he carefully set her down. She slapped the rumpled photos into his hands that she had rescued for him. "You are a complicated guy. Why do you make life so difficult?"

"My dear, I didn't know Janice Joanne would even play this bizarre game, especially so late at night. I have nothing to do with any of it," Hughes loudly replied above the party din, startling his lady love. "We tried to photograph wild elephants in the African game parks—Kafue, Luangwa Valley, Serengeti Plains—not a piece of cake!

"We couldn't get close enough to those great beasts in their natural habitat to get good photos. You need a powerful telescopic lens on the camera to do them justice, but you also must be careful, and ready to run—hard and fast! We were charged by a bull elephant while sitting in our car, last year in Luangwa! Elephants can damage people's farms when they rampage. I've developed a respectful fear of all wild creatures."

"You are so noble, Orwell Hughes. Who can doubt you? Who is like you?" Georgina asked with sultry breathlessness. Lest he hug and kiss her, Miss Amadu squeezed his hand as she deftly left him, "I need to use the restroom."

Orwell's eyes helplessly followed his dream girl as she coyly faded from view. He yawned with drowsiness, and became aware that others were also tired and preparing to retire. Kathleen took dirty dishes into the kitchen, while Richard collected the garbage. Alicia and JJ stood near the door with Benjamin, Solomon, and David, holding their coats and pleasantly chatting about plans for the coming week. The party, which had been a slice, was now a wrap. It was right to end on this high note, with midnight come. But not for everyone apparently, Orwell noted with gay trepidation; he was left wondering how to entertain Georgina as Ali suavely departed with Suzy for an intimate midnight stroll.

"Some fresh air will do us both—as you say, Suzy—a whale of good," suggested Ali to sweet Suzanne, laughing airily as he ushered the bubbly girl towards the doorway. In passing, he nodded to his almost brother, Orwell, "I say, are you coming along, my good man?"

"I'd like, but I have other friends to say goodbye to. I don't want to play tagalong, you know, be a fifth wheel, three-is-a-crowd, and that awkward sort of thing..."

"You and Georgie will join us. We'll be two happy couples sparking together," Ali explained to this blockhead. "I noticed you two love birds winking at each other all day. My sister tells me that you make her very happy. It's a good thing, Orwell. We four shall get along splendidly! Suzy and I will wait by the gate while you fetch your lady."

"Hurry along, Casanova," Suzanne twittered as they danced away.

"We'll catch up," promised Orwell, his heart soaring with joy, and not just for Suzy... He whispered ecstatically as he tidied the party room, while waiting for his lady love to return, "I praise you Lord for this wonderful gift."

Examining the intricately carved patterns on the thumb piano as he returned it to the mantel piece, Hughes grinned broadly as he realized how much Georgina really liked him. It was not a pipe dream. She had shared her heart's feelings with Ali; to be accepted now as her suitor by Georgina's big brother also was a big test passed! Ali understood the blossoming affection between him and Georgina, so it must be real and fruitful. Suzanne was her brother's ally—if only Georgina would join the circle wholeheartedly. But *where* was she? When was she coming back? Heavens' sakes, women took forever when they camped in the bathroom!

While Orwell waited by his lonesome for Georgina to return, and envisioned in his dreamy romantic mind how he would kiss and hug her down lover's lane, he watched with glazed detachment as Alicia and JJ gabbed with his almost forgotten university mates at the other end of the room. Cepheus, by joining the chipper group, ramped up their jocularity. What could they be joking about? The girls were guests, so not expected to help with clean-up. The men wore their coats now, but it was obvious they wanted to stay. Alicia and JJ looked like sweet honey to savour for these broke and lonely students without school or home. The teenaged girls were just being hospitable to these twenty-something men, but what jolly night owls they all were becoming together; no worries or commitments had they!

"Orwell, come join us," invited Alicia, smiling warmly at her friend when she found him admiring her. As one, her glassy-eyed companions followed the amazon's prompt.

"Yeah bro, boogie on over here," JJ briskly added. "You look lost."

"Sorry, I don't mean to be antisocial. Share your fun with me?" Orwell, snapping out of his trance, sheepishly apologized.

Georgina was still out of commission, he noted with dismay. Yet, glad to be wanted, and feeling energized by these others' interest in him, even after so many hours of ignoring them while toiling at the helm of their social, Orwell sauntered over to join the revellers. Everyone welcomed his arrival; Alicia's sparkling gaze encouraged him.

"We all agree, Mr. Orwell, that you are a wonderful host. Food, games, discussions, and singing made this Easter festival a true success!" exclaimed David, on behalf of his friends, who nodded solemnly in agreement. "You must thank your parents for us as we leave your home now.

"Mr. Orwell, we see you in the church and at university, but we honestly did not know how kind and generous you white people are until tonight; God bless you all. Miss Janice and Miss Alicia are very kind ladies too. May we all sleep well and rise up in the morning refreshed."

"Amen, may the Lord keep us all," replied Orwell, respecting God who provided everything.

"We African men are going back to the university now, Mr. Orwell, to find our beds. We must let you and your white ladies rest," announced Ben sombrely.

"How will you get there at this late hour?" asked Alicia with concern. She prodded Orwell into action, "Can't you drive your friends home?"

"By rights our family should, but I can't drive anyone myself—I don't have a driver's licence," Orwell stammered with embarrassment. This truth was tough enough to swallow, but how could he tell the prying girl in front of his gawking pals that he was waiting to take his hot date, Georgina Amadu for a walk? With female intuition, Alicia read his troubled mind.

"Ask Richard to take them", directed Alicia. It was a simple request in her mind, but sensing Orwell's increasing frustration while questioning his odd reticence, she gazed resolutely at him with eyes of a warrioress, "Or shall I?"

"I will ask my brother," Orwell declared, causing Alicia to smile proudly upon him, as if he was her hero, the hunter who would risk his life to bring home wild meat for her brood. Alicia's smile annoyed him because it brought back their connection to his mind, so Hughes blushed as he hurried into the kitchen, where Rick and Kathy were busy washing dishes.

Appalled at his colleague's slavery to the demanding girl, Cepheus called Orwell back from his needless quest. "Mr. Orwell, where are you going? We will hire a taxi to carry us ! The taxi park is very close now, beside the night market. No problem, we Africans can walk there easily. Come back, Mr. Orwell."

"Guys! It's okay, I'll fix it!" japed young Hughes from the kitchen door. "You live too far away to hitch a ride so late at night."

Kathleen suddenly blocked his entry and, grinning wildly, set Orwell square, "No way, Jose! Don't even think of asking any chauffeur favours from Richard unless you get your butt in here and dry these dishes!"

Benjamin, who saw that Orwell was caught between a rock and a hard place, politely allayed his host's anxieties, "Africans know how to manage in our own land, Mr. Orwell. We are going now to find a taxi. You may escort us to the gate if you wish."

"Oh, that sounds fun," agreed Alicia enthusiastically, winking at JJ.

"Let's go then," sighed Orwell. "Hopefully, the others won't miss us long."

Orwell inwardly despaired at Georgina's prolonged absence, even as he did the right thing and fell in with the jovial party that was leaving the house. He tried to enjoy the fleeting banter of his friends, but dismally noted as they sauntered down the candlelit driveway that Ali and Suzanne had stood him up; these true love birds were long gone somewhere in their car, having tired of waiting for him and Georgina to come along. They must have known all along that such a union was hopeless. What a horrible joke they had played on him!

Orwell also spied with sudden concern that a car idled near the gate, but it was not Ali's Volkswagen...Some big limousine full of strangers crouched beneath the jacaranda tree!

Playing the young bwana in his father's stead, Orwell stepped out of his group and looked for the night watchman, only to find him chatting amicably with the limousine driver. Two well-dressed male passengers, one white and one black, sat stiffly in their seats and stared sombrely straight ahead, as though waiting to be wound up for action by unseen handlers. Who were they? What was their purpose on the Hughes compound so late at night? Letting his friends pass by at a safe distance out the gate, Orwell crisply approached the purring vehicle to greet these mysterious newcomers. He courteously spoke to the driver while the white man glared stonily at him. The bespectacled black man seated in the back, under a fresh-off-the-rack Fedora hat, then rolled down his window to talk.

"Good evening sir," Hughes spoke firmly yet with respect. "I live here. Can I help you?"

"We's all fine here, son—just sitting tight, waitin' for our boss who's gone inside the house yonder to say howdy to y'all," replied the other harmlessly, in a soft drawl from deep in southern USA. He pleasantly reminded Hughes of Uncle Remus from childhood bedtime stories. "Ain't you met Tracy in there yet?"

"Tracy?" demanded Orwell excitedly. "Do you mean Tracy MacDonachie?"

"Why, o'course, son. We's all come t'Africa for the big boxin' match. Our fine fighter boy here, Karl Thompson, is challengin' for the heavy-weight title of the entire British Commonwealth! Surely you know dat, bein' Orwell Hughes 'n' such from Lusaka town!"

"What?"

"Hey, Uncle Rimond! How are you doing?" exuberantly hailed Alicia, from right beside Orwell's ear. When the old codger grinned broadly, showing an entire piano keyboard of pearly whites with his pleasure to see Tracy's fine kid sister, she extended her hand all friendly-like, and heartily shook the calloused ebony paw that pleased-as-punch Tracy Rimond extended through the open window.

"Glory be! Good to see you again, Honey Bunch! What a trip, what a trip we's had Miss Alicia, but we's all down here in one piece at last and accounted for. Your brother 'n' Rivard are in that house yonder right now, chattin' with ole Mr. Hughes!"

"Why don't you come inside as well, Uncle? Orwell's parents are very hospitable; they'd love to meet you. Bring your jolly friend along with you."

Thompson gave Alicia a forbidding scowl, like he wanted to eat her or worse, causing the amazon to step cautiously back into Hughes, her able protector. She took comfort from Orwell's warm presence to resume dialogue with her brother's long-time trainer. Although she knew he was here due to his boxing talent, Alicia upheld ageless Tracy Rimond as an accomplished trombone player from New Orleans, with whom she shared a love for nightclub jazz and country gospel music.

"I will sometime during our stay, Miss Alicia, but not t'night. Tracy tole us to stay put right here in this car. He don't want us cauliflower alley cats scarin' y'all and crowdin' out the place. He ain't visitin' long, and then we'll be hightailin' it to our hotel. We need our beauty sleep, as we's got lots of trainin' work to do with Mr. Thompson here for the next few days."

"Tracy's here!" Orwell, wildly ecstatic, hugged the woman merrily dancing beside him.

"*I* know! I saw Tracy coming in my mind since before church today. So did you! My big brother is safely here with me in Africa at last, thank you Lord!"

"We better go into the house right now and say hello!"

"Okay, Bucko, I'm right behind with you," Ms. MacDonachie gaily agreed, but then remembered where they had left off. Rimond laughed and Thompson scowled as Orwell broke free and ran toward the house, but then she rebuked him, "Hey, what about your pals back here? You'd best say goodbye to them first!"

"Good night guys. Safe trip home. Thanks for coming!" loudly saluted Orwell who, from the porch, dispatched his incredulous African friends between huge gulps of breath. Though his heart pounded with anxious excitement, he begged to be excused, "I gotta dash. A long-expected visitor has finally arrived, and I must attend to him."

Alicia sighed and shook her head as Orwell disappeared inside. She apologized for his rude behaviour to the African students, as well as to jovial Tracy Rimond and his glowering protégé, but everyone seemed to understand that the young poet was out of his mind with joy at finally receiving his most special friend: his illustrious mentor, Tracy MacDonachie! They saw that Orwell was still a raw lad in many ways, but knew he was nonetheless a good man, gentle and kind, who sincerely cared for them, as he did for all his fellow creatures. There would be other times to visit, say hello, and bid goodbye with cultural decorum. At the proper time, God would direct His believer to introduce Tracy MacDonachie to his friends in Lusaka.

# CHAPTER TWENTY-ONE

ORWELL THOUGHT HE WAS DREAMING as he wandered through quiet social rooms where lamps flickered low, and pleasant perfumes and spicy aromas lingered in the cool night air. The cacophony of party voices that had been so buoyant minutes ago had slipped away with departed revellers, but he heard real and new conversation nonetheless; warm bodies were up and about somewhere in the house! Kathleen chattered and laughed like uncorked bubbly high above the humoured rumblings of several men. Orwell, now playing detective, placed his ear to the wall, and recognized his father officiously droning with Tracy MacDonachie, whose clarion, engaging voice was unchanged despite warps of time and distance that had elapsed since last he heard it.

Eager to join their upbeat fellowship, Orwell hustled toward the light of his father's den. Seldom privileged to tarry inside this fortress of enlightenment and therefore unaccustomed to its layout, the excited lad slid on a floor mat near the door and crash-landed into his father's polished teak desk to mark his entry.

Tracy jovially held court with his stoic sidekick Rivard playing the straight-man, and regaled Bwana and Richard Hughes with harrowing adventures—servicing an oilfield drill rig in Nigeria, and turning sod on a huge wheat farm in Tanzania, while Kathleen and Georgina listened with rapt enthusiasm—when Orwell so rudely interrupted them. The animated gathering went instantly quiet, as everyone blinked quizzically at the wild-haired and blushing youth. The girls shared suppressed grins, but Rick, used to such shenanigans, simply rolled his eyes.

"Glad you dropped in, Son," saluted Bwana Hughes, smiling wryly from deep within his leather- cushioned chair. With a flourish of his manicured hand, he cleverly asked, "Do you know everyone here?"

"Well, the one on the left is Rivard Cummings, while the one on the right can be none other than Tracy!" Orwell, leaving ultra-serious, grinned at the two brawny adventurers who, clean-cut and impressively attired in business suits, spruced up the gathering of tired and sunburnt youths.

Such a show of false recall seemed ridiculous to Kathy...Rivard, who had been her big brother's friend since high school and had done everything with him—fixing cars, riding motorcycles, working on oil rigs and Dad's ranch, playing football, or dabbling in boxing and nightclub entertainment—was obviously the huge black dude sporting the Afro!

Orwell winced that Rivard enjoyed anew his unbridled youth. They had always gotten along in sharing Tracy, although Cummings was MacDonachie's best friend, while Orwell was like a kid brother with endless desire but so much to learn! These older guys loved to tease him, even while they taught him the ropes of life. The dynamic Tracy and Rivard show was well into its thirties now, but the good-natured black man seemed no different tonight than on that frigid December day when he and Tracy had helped Orwell's clan get their anxious selves and many cumbersome bags onto a jet bound for Africa, five long years ago. Rivard, a wise man of few words, was strong in so many ways: reliable and supportive—the steady, hands-on worker who made manifest Tracy's endless flights of fancy.

Tracy, the star mover and shaker, appeared suavely tanned and fit. His expensive European cologne gave him a pleasantly virile scent. His tailored, three-piece suit was very becoming, and one could not help but be impressed by other items he had chosen to complement his business attire: spotless white shirt with stiff collar and cuffs, all perfectly ironed: red, white and blue striped neck tie, crisply knotted and clipped in place by a gold band emblazoned with Canada's red maple leaf to match his cufflinks. On his powerful wrist, MacDonachie flashed a *Rolex* watch, yet no ring adorned his elegant, manicured fingers indicating that he belonged to any woman or society. His thick black hair, not long and wild as in his Absalom rebel days of the 1960s, was neatly barbered to reflect a mature and intelligent, successful man-about-town. Elvis sideburns and five o'clock shadow were shaved off to reveal chiselled cheek bones and a granite jaw. His dark eyebrows, piercing blue eyes, prominent sloping nose, manly lips, winning smile, jutting chin, and strong neck added to Tracy's rugged good looks. His telegenic face, charming personality and powerfully sculpted body aside, Orwell was attracted to MacDonachie for his strong inner light, fired by his unyielding determination, quest for adventure and knowledge, belief in social justice, and love of God and all His wonderful creation.

As Orwell glanced at Tracy, his anxiety was overcome by joy as his mentor grinned with pleasure at seeing him again. When Tracy enthusiastically rose and offered his hand in fellowship, Orwell eagerly ran to him, and was rejuvenated by his firm, electrifying grip.

"Tracy it's so great to see you, man! Thanks for coming!" Orwell cheered, almost sobbing with exultation. He-men were not supposed to cry or give hugs, but Orwell did both as he was pulled into a powerfully bonding embrace by his long-awaited friend. Energized, the young poet reached out to pump Cumming's huge paw, "And you too, Rivard. My God, I am so blessed that you guys have made it here at last! We're going to have a blast together."

"Let's do our best. That's what God asks of us, right?" MacDonachie concurred, albeit taken aback by their crazy outburst of passion. Breaking now from his bone-crushing grasp, Tracy appraised Orwell approvingly, "You've done well for being lost in the African jungle for the past five years. I barely recognize you, Orwell—you've grown from a runt boy into a strapping young man, a true *Adonis*!"

"I lift weights and run five miles per day!" Hughes, standing before Tracy and Rivard, reported proudly his manly regimen in stunned Georgina's presence. "I cycle or walk rather than drive to most places in this burg; I eat healthy foods. I march for social justice, and help our church and Campus Christian Fellowship build houses for the poor. Last year, Rick and I climbed Mt. Kilimanjaro. I box and play field hockey with the University of Zambia, where the calibre of organized sports is among the best in all Africa—as my good friend Georgina, Zambia's elite female tennis player, can ably attest to."

Georgina nodded, while Tracy and Rivard smiled approvingly at this effusive testimony, but Kathy, who claimed to know the current rendition of Orwell Hughes best, was less charitable.

"What a boastful bullfrog you are, Oh-well!" she chided, offering a smirk to challenge his wild claims. "Did your mother not teach you that pride cometh before a fall? Are you trying to impress us?"

"It's all true, I swear! UNZA has a premier sports program—very competitive, cutting-edge, and comprehensive. Orwell was cited this year as one of our best all-around athletes—as a *freshman,* nonetheless," Georgina rushed to her host's defence, earning brownie points for him in Tracy's deep blue eyes. When her wannabe lover blushed in surprise of her assertive support, Miss Amadu admonished young Hughes, "You must show your visitors that splendid trophy you won at assembly last term. Stop being so humble, Orwell!"

Though others had doubts, Tracy took detailed notes of Georgina's testimony, and thus caught the worshipful eyes of the young man yet again.

"So, Orwell, you continue to be a champion...and not only as an athlete, but also in the game of life! That's great—I would expect nothing less from a gem like you," said Tracy as he gave beaming Hughes a thumbs-up salute. He, who did not offer praises lightly, meant every word he said, although he always managed to pack them with humour.

Shifting over and enthusiastically patting the empty spot on the couch between him and Rivard, beckoning Tracy chortled, "I'm glad you listened at least a little bit to what I taught you in Sunday school when you were knee-high to a grasshopper! You do me proud, boy; you've done well! Come sit down beside me now, and keep quiet."

Taking such an order as compliment, despite others' laughter, Orwell eagerly obeyed these golden words! Not just was he sitting with his favourite people on the couch of his father's sacred grotto, Orwell was lounging on cloud nine, eating grapes! He had been validated by his beloved lady to his mentor, as well as honoured by him in full view of said lady. Life was sweet!

No sooner had Orwell sat down than Alicia and JJ, dressed in nighties and looking tired, entered the scene. Everyone gazed in amazement when Alicia ran to embrace her startled brother.

"Tracy, you really are here! Praise the Lord!" squealed Alicia affectionately as she draped herself around Tracy and gave him hugs and kisses. She would not let him loose while she blubbered like a baby into his fancy suit, "I missed you so much, and I got so worried for you, Tracy—you have no idea! Promise, don't you dare let go of Kathy and me, ever again!"

The roving adventurer grimaced with chagrin and embarrassment. He dearly loved Alicia, but her weepy harangue, following on the heels of Orwell's childishly emotional display, was marring his rugged male image before many admirers. With Georgina looking deeply touched by this family display, Tracy knew he must act quickly but appropriately to steer this ship along.

"It's okay Alicia, I hear you. The dangerous journey I took was not suited for you, my dear, so I did what I thought was best, and sent you and Kitty on ahead. I missed you all too and worried for you even as I struggled where I was, but I had faith that you'd manage fine and so you did, just as I also got through with flying colours—praise God! I'm just glad the gang's all here now.

"We belong together and therefore stick together—especially when we are in a strange land so far from home," the big brother softly reassured his little sister, as he kindly patted her back. Then, drawing back the curtain of shaggy auburn hair that spilled across Alicia's distraught face, Tracy gazed with manly composure into her dark, teary eyes and shared meaningfully, "I'm proud of how well you two girls handled yourselves in a tough situation."

"Okay, that's a first!" acknowledged Alicia happily, surprised by such a public compliment by a MacDonachie male.

She released her beloved brother and straightened up with pride and purpose, only to suddenly go weak-kneed as she realized that everyone was watching her intently, as if she and Tracy were enacting a soap opera. Alicia gazed around the room, making funny faces ranging from sheepish grins to frowns at her audience to jumpstart them out of their trances, and finally blurted, "I think I should sit down now...but there is no empty chair. Where can I sit? What do you think, JJ, is this some kind of message telling me it's past my bedtime?"

The group seemed amused at her clowning antics, but euphoric Orwell, who was laughing the loudest, became the butt of her joke when Alicia suddenly plopped down on his lap! Amazed that she would so casually do what she had vowed *never* to do with any man, he grabbed the buxom girl around her stomach with his strong arms and held her close against him, as though buckling her safely in place for a long, wild ride. Alicia firmly loosened the awkwardly intruding male hands and guided them downward to rest on the couch cushion at his sides where they belonged, lest Orwell wrongly assume he could put some claim on her. Since he understood and complied, the tall beauty did not try to escape, nor did she repent of her brazen act. With good old Orwell ever willing to accommodate, she took this special opportunity to be close to her friend as well as to fraternize with her brother and his pal.

Orwell sought permission to hold Alicia from Georgina, who was taking in the action from across the room. Miss Amadu just smiled, vaguely serene, seeming to bestow her blessing on the happy group in the room. Freed, yet disturbed by her glib ease, Hughes duly gave himself over to his task as the band played on; Alicia was an attractive burden. Although spent by her long busy day, she felt cool and dry against him, and smelled like freshly picked roses. The amazon applied surprisingly low ground pressure, as if she was trying to stay as light as possible out of duty and respect. Alicia really was a shy teenager and his equal for nervousness behind her tough exterior; yet, she did not squirm awkwardly on her seat, but peaceably offered her shapely bottom as a plush, warm cushion to calm his wobbly knees.

Alicia, pleased by Orwell's sweet acceptance, and glad to be an integral part of his inner circle, followed the pleasant banter alertly. Nearly hidden behind her hourglass figure, however, Hughes could hardly concentrate on the airy conversation swirling about them as he struggled to rein in his loin-teasing fantasies!

"You two seem to be getting on well! That's a recent development, I'll warrant—the sunny tropics encourage romance, don't they?" Tracy remarked glibly. "As I recall, you were fighting—tearing each other's clothes, actually—the last time you were thrown together in Canada!"

Orwell, still feeling guilty over this past battle and worried that Georgina, shocked to hear of such violence, might become jealous of Alicia and dump him, protested Tracy's amiable suggestion that he and the trickster's awkward kid sister were now hitched. Dodging Alicia's swishing hair long enough to deftly peek around her strong back, Orwell vigorously set the record straight for his keen observer and all the concurring witnesses.

"We're still strikingly different in our outlook, right down to how we eat breakfast! I am partial to *nshima*[62] with spicy groundnut and the spinach relish our houseboy cooks over the wood fire! Princess Mairam here, who has been pampered all her life, is a notoriously picky eater who craves only fast foods, which she knows from back home—like cornflakes and French fries!"

"I do not! I gratefully eat everything your mother sets before me," Alicia snorted. She gave her detractor a dark grin but Orwell babbled on.

"For coming from a king's household, Kitty-Cat and Annie Fannie know

62 *Nsima* (also spelled *nshima*): dish made from maize flour (white cornmeal) and water, and is a staple food in Zambia.

nothing about meaningful table conversation or keeping their bedrooms tidy. These spoiled rich kids are lazy and antisocial, not to mention always bellyaching about how drearily frontier everything is in Zambia compared to space-age Canada. With grace and flourish these high-class ladies completed their obligations of inspired singing and delivering hymnbooks brought from afar to the African church, but mostly they squabble and keep the rest of us on edge.

"I find it hilarious how your finicky sisters react with horror to chameleons basking in our flower beds, or stumble clumsily in their efforts to imitate African women carrying laundry baskets on their heads. They don't catch on to the simple trick of positioning a cloth roll on one's head to steady the load.

"I finally got even for all the times they smoked me when we were children, as I found them bewildered by all the exotic native foods displayed amid the riotous noise and vibrant colours of the open-air African Market. No chocolate *Smarties* for them, but earth-tone cowpeas, groundnuts and coffee beans, sun-dried and poured onto woven sisal sheets for the buyer's invitation to barter! Dried *kapenta* and larger fish like Nile perch, fighting tiger and tilapia gazing accusingly at shoppers and vendors alike with their dead eyes; maize cobs ground into flour or juicy stalks chewed for raw sugar; tomatoes, pumpkins, and peppers of strange shapes and hues; chickens squawking in wicker cages, and beef butchered while you wait...This is real Africa—in the raw—that your girls have never heard about, except in zealous missionary testimonies on their father's Bible broadcasts!"

"Mercy, son," cautioned Jim Hughes dourly from behind his desk.

"Listen to this bullshit! You are really shovelling it now, Oh-well!" gnashed Kathleen, red-faced with embarrassment. "Like, you forget that I was born in Africa?"

She glared at him accusingly and then at her brother, who seemed on the verge of laughing out loud at Orwell as he tried to listen intently to his tirade of half-truths, "Tracy, you have no idea what an ordeal you placed us through by arriving so late in Zambia! It's damn hard to soar like an eagle when you're stuck around such a turkey as Orwell."

MacDonachie sighed in frustration at this embarrassing, late-night spat by over-tired kids. To his sisters' dismay, he intervened now on behalf of Orwell by recalling Kathleen's glowing testimony, so recently made of the lad's exploits.

"Kitty-Cat, weren't you just praising my pal before he barged in here? You sounded highly impressed by his stellar singing, piano/organ playing, and acting abilities! You described my young man as sweet and considerate, which means a lot! Orwell, I heard you filled in for me just peachy-keen when I couldn't make our gig today at the church. Thanks a million, bud!"

Tracy grinned with relief, and affectionately tousled the already dishevelled mop of blond hair crowning Orwell's red face. With Alicia slumped dejectedly on his knee, Hughes felt awful for spouting off, but this golden praise from his mentor awarded him within Georgina's hearing, validated his concerns.

"I think I'm gonna hit the hay," yawned Alicia, after everyone endured a silence so heavy you could have heard a pin drop. As she jumped from his lap, she frowned at Orwell and grimly advised him, "You better get some rest too, Bucko...Try to feel happy tomorrow, okay?"

"Okay", replied Orwell solemnly, although he already felt overjoyed, now that Tracy had arrived. "Good night. Thanks for all your help."

Alicia smiled weakly as she trudged silently past this weird boy. JJ spoke volumes, however, as she gave Orwell a brutal glare while exiting with her dispirited friend.

"I'll call it a night as well," announced Tracy with leisurely satisfaction as he stretched his muscular arms towards Heaven. He nodded appreciatively at Georgina, as well as the other bleary-eyed folks waiting up with him. As Tracy and Rivard shook hands with the men of the Hughes House, silver-tongued charmer MacDonachie offered most of the parting words, "Good night, Richard. Thank you, Mr. Hughes for accommodating our late-night visit. Orwell, man, it's good to touch base with you again. Good night all."

"When will we see you again, Tracy? Let me escort you to your taxi," begged Orwell.

The goo-goo eyed youth cluelessly embarrassed his esteemed visitor by suggesting that Tracy travelled by cab rather than in a private limousine—as impressionable strangers like Georgina would have supposed. Leaving the lovely socialite to stare incredulously after them, Hughes anxiously chased after MacDonachie and Cummings as these broad-shouldered gentlemen strode purposefully out of the room.

Alicia reappeared, wrapped in Orwell's house coat, to give blessings of peaceful sleep to everyone, but showed a special concern for Georgina as she grabbed the hand reaching out for rescue from this bewildered lady of honour. Although gorgeous Miss Amadu outshone her in every facet, Alicia cared enough to ask her, "How are you getting home, Georgie?"

"Oh, dear Mairam, I hope you don't mind me hanging around this fairy tale castle just a bit longer before I get shunted back to my austere university residence," Georgina begged the prying lioness. "I like it here—this is where love in action is—a paradise compared to my threadbare concrete flat surrounded by prison walls and surly guards."

"It's not up to me to make your arrangements," Alicia muttered dryly, although not without sympathy. With a decisive nod of her head, she motioned to Orwell, who seemed tossed like flotsam upon some churning sea as he tried his best to entertain Tracy steaming ahead, but also turned back in his rough wake to attend to the equally vital needs of his lady love. "Ask that mouthy bloke what you should do, if you can pin him down for five seconds!"

"I shan't bother Orwell for a lift with his illustrious mentor in town. Ali is due to return shortly—he drives me about town these days, so that he can show off his sassy new love bug to all the fancy *Highlife* chicks!" purred Georgina, trying to be cool. "I arrived here with him earlier this afternoon, if you remember, so long ago?"

"I'll get your bed ready," Alicia grimly offered. "Who knows when those two love birds will finally fly in from where ever to roost!"

"Georgina shouldn't be sleeping here!" sternly ruled Orwell, more loudly than he wanted to, this late at night. The two girls were startled to find him suddenly standing behind them, listening to their discussion.

"As you wish, since you are our august master of ceremonies. You're too full at the inn—I get the picture," Georgina pouted, suddenly concerned that his reaction was due to the fact that coloured girls did not belong in his high-class European house, or that being Muslim, she followed the wrong God, even in her human circumstances of being potentially stranded upon his doorstep.

"I don't mean to be mean, ladies, honest," sputtered Hughes. After taking a vital moment to collect his thoughts, he explained, "You are welcome to sleep here in a pinch, of course, Georgina, but we don't have any spare beds. Nonetheless, it seems improper to me that such beautiful, talented, and unattached single woman should sleep here. You and Alicia could take our bedroom, while Rick and I would crash in the living room. Prudently, however, I should drive you back to the residence, or at least take you to your uncle's home."

"Orwell, show some hospitality! There is a fully-furnished guest suite, complete with several spare beds and a spacious sitting room—supplied with comfortable chairs, fireplace, tons of books, and a glistening bathroom next to your own holy abode—but with a separate entrance for privacy, of course. It's midnight! Georgina could happily sleep there for what remains of tonight; we could give her a nice breakfast before taking her home tomorrow," stoutly suggested Alicia. When he inquired how she knew about these special quarters, which were generally off-limits unless unlocked for official use by Bwana Hughes, the clever girl smiled deviously and whispered that the diplomat had showed her the suite when she wondered what laid behind that green door.

"What of Alicia or Kathleen?" begged Georgina, mortified. "They are visiting from faraway, yet you stuff them cheek by jowl with your sisters for days, where everyone in your household shares one communal bathroom, when such a wondrous guest suite exists? How can these beautiful MacDonachies keep any womanly secrets from you? Am I any different from these eligible *mademoiselles*?"

"I want to serve you utmost as a VIP, not inconvenience you in our crowded home," Orwell did mental gymnastics to articulate his intimate desires in a reasonable way to this blustery goddess. "If I take you home first class, perhaps you will feel happy to visit here again."

Alicia was glad for Orwell's chivalrous insistence to sweep her rival out of harm's way, but she still, like a thorn in the flesh, felt compelled to remind him of his glaring shortcomings, "Bucko, you seem to forget: you don't have a driver's licence—do you even know how to drive?"

Alicia gloated now as she taught this flustered boy how far behind her he really was, "I passed my Alberta driver's test shortly after my sixteenth birthday. I operate my own wheels, a durable pickup truck that I bought myself from part-time job earnings, to get around for school, sports, work, and errands. I chose the *Ford* half-ton over some sexy *Pontiac* ragtop that Robert wanted to buy me with his loose change, specifically so I could haul *Windchaser* in my horse trailer for country riding and boarding stuff. So there, Bucko! Now, you need to figure out what you want to do in life."

"Maybe you can teach me how to drive, Alicia—like starting tonight. We could take Georgina home now; I'll ride along to co-pilot if you agree...That would also let me start learning from you," suggested Hughes meekly. He felt duly chastised for all his earlier rebukes of her.

"That will be a treat, Bucko, me training you!" chortled Alicia, showing her sharp teeth in a savage smile of anticipation.

"Don't sweat it Orwell," Tracy, having observed this gong show for too long, gallantly stepped in to salvage the embarrassing situation for his protégé. Georgina, smiling brightly, was immediately drawn to Tracy and his tantalizing solution. "I'll drive your friend home. It's the least I can do to return the favours you've done: hosting my sisters, and playing my part today at church. Dad Hughes affirms you and the girls were stellar in representing The *MacDonachie Family Singers*; I couldn't improve a note upon your performance! What do you think, Rivard, can we make more room to help out Orwell's splendid young lady friend?"

"You bet," replied Cummings confidently. "I'll ask Jeeves to set up the third seat in back of the limo, where Karl and I can sit, no problem."

"Sounds like a plan!" MacDonachie conclusively gushed to his crowd of avid listeners. "We will pull out now with Miss Georgina Amadu on board, riding first class."

"Orwell, I am grateful for Mr. Tracy's offer. Let me go! You go and rest!" Georgina parlayed with Orwell. When Hughes seemed despondent at his own inability to serve his grand lady, she gave the dispirited youth a hug, followed by an affectionate kiss that warmed his cheek. As they embraced, she murmured in praise and gratitude, "You are a fantastic host, Orwell, but you were especially sweet and wonderful to me today! I enjoyed myself...You even arranged my transport. So, as you so articulately advised, my friend, I am going now—that I may return to embrace your uplifting fellowship at another time. God bless everyone!"

"Amen, my friend. May God bless you also, and may you all arrive safely at your homes. Let us all rest with tiredness tonight," said Hughes, slipping into Hausa , as he humbly praised the Lord on everyone's behalf.

"Malam Orwell, you are speaking like a *bahaushe*[63] now," lauded Georgina. Impressed that he tried so hard to please her, even to learn her language, she effervescently promised, "Someday, I will take you to Nigeria, where we will visit my father in Jos, and greet also my grandparents in their village of Pankshin. You shall be my interpreter..."

63 *Bahaushe*: Hausa term for 'a Hausa man.'

"That would be grand," Orwell cheered, feeling blessed for a lifetime.

In his weary jubilation, he did not care whether or not Georgina was joking, nor could he envision how such a wonderful journey would be accomplished, but the young poet believed in his heart that all good things were possible, since God was present. Tracy, after all, was here, witness to his joy; the great mentor had come, albeit via arduous ways, and had answered his invitation.

Like bubbly drink erupting from a vigorously shaken bottle of *Coca Cola*, visitors and hosts spilled out of the house and streamed across the lawn towards the waiting car. Tracy led the way, flanked by his loyal escorts. Alicia chatted amicably with her brother about his journey and her own adventures, yet found him charmingly vague when asked about his plans for coming days, even to know where he was staying, and why his pals had come with him to Africa. Orwell, strolling hand in hand with Georgina on the other side, enjoyed Miss Amadu's lovely presence even if they were not talking with each other; he kept his ear cupped, hoping to hear whatever vital tidbits Alicia could glean from his mentor without troubling the great man himself. Kathleen and Richard followed behind with Bwana and Mrs. Hughes, who marvelled that so much, like the myriads of beautiful stars glittering now in the heavens, could be packed into a single day.

"You were speaking Hausa back there, Orwell," remarked Tracy, turning to the starry-eyed lad and his girl as they reached the car—a big American *Chrysler*. MacDonachie explained to the incredulous pair, while Rivard rearranged the seating to accommodate another passenger, "I grew up on a missionary compound in Bornu State; although we spoke English at home, as well as in school and church, I talked Hausa with African kids like it was my first language."

"Mairam has already told me much about her African childhood," Georgina cleverly informed Tracy. She giggled at the bizarre situation, "Small world, eh?"

"Who is *Mairam*?"

"Like, duh, none other than your favourite, pesky little sister," muttered Alicia with feigned disgust, as she playfully punched Tracy in his shoulder. For a moment, the wily old boxer pretended to be badly bruised.

"Assuming that you and she have the same father and mother," Georgina teased out the tangled threads of MacDonachie family history. "Looking at the two of you together, I'd say you are definitely siblings!"

"I am totally Tracy's blood sister," Alicia, with her large hands gripping her stout hips, grimly reinforced this concept for Georgina. She schooled Orwell and Kathleen as well, "Kitty-Cat is also made from the same mould, though she may have been picked by God from a different part of His flower garden than me and Trace, which explains why she and I don't always get along!"

Big brother Tracy carried on more edifying conversation,. "It's been eons since I heard that musical language, but your frisky little conversations have tweaked many childhood memories. I'd like to dabble in the *lingua franca* with you guys while we're in town—get limbered up. Yet, Hausa is a West African tongue,[64]—why would you speak it way down south?"

Georgina, whose attention and energy were perked up by Tracy's astute observation, explained her equally odd situation for her fellow visitor to Zambia, even if MacDonachie claimed her homeland as his African birthplace.

"I am a Nigerian studying at the University of Zambia here in Lusaka. My father's senior brother, with whom I sometimes stay, is a Professor of *African Studies* at UNZA. We speak Hausa together, but my uncle is also mandated to teach his students all the great African languages and traditional cultures. Hausa is a vital language for this continent, sir; Orwell, although a foreign student like me—but white at that—is one of Professor Ibrahim's most earnest learners. He wants to learn, and tries well."

"We are all visitors here then—even my black companions Tracy and Rivard, whose ancestors were taken from Africa to the Americas as slaves, centuries ago. We are all visitors on planet Earth, but we come from the same Creator," Tracy concluded philosophically, just as Cummings returned to his side. "We ready to go, Rivard?"

"You bet, boss, all ready," confirmed Rivard. "...What?"

Lest Tracy's frowning sisters or anyone else gazing incredulously upon this midnight scene get the wrong impression, Rivard's serious face broke into a huge smile, and he laughed deeply with his lifelong friend. "C'mon, let's rock and roll!"

Cummings trotted around to the other side of the big, purring car, and burrowed into the passenger seat beside Karl and Tracy Rimond, who had been calming the surly white stranger all the while with soft-spoken small talk.

"You want to sit in now, Georgina?" invited MacDonachie as he chivalrously opened the front passenger door and ushered her inside.

64 *ko ba haka ba*: Hausa idiom meaning 'Is it not?'

Fancy Miss Amadu gratefully took her place on the front bench between the great man and his driver. Before making their grand exit, however, MacDonachie nonchalantly slipped some paper into Orwell's hand held out to shake his, in manly adieu. Hughes, initially thinking he was being paid off or sent on some petty errand, glumly felt like he had just been slapped in the face by his hero, until he realized that the rectangular pieces of paper were too stiff and small to be kwacha currency. He squinted hard in the ghostly light to read his gift, which appeared to be tickets! Orwell gazed worshipfully at his beaming mentor, who posed gallantly for him on the running board of the shiny new *Chrysler* before disappearing inside. Georgina, enthralled by his bravery, bent forward to whisper something chirpy in Tracy's ear that drew him into his seat. These cool, beautiful people then waved contentedly at their bewildered hosts.

"Tracy, what are these?" Orwell cried as he stood alone on the driveway, watching the luxury car curve smoothly backwards in preparation for take-off.

"Reserved seats, boy—for you and a friend! See you at the big bash!" Tracy encouraged him rousingly with a thumbs-up salute through the window as he rolled away.

With red tail lights zoomed away like a spaceship, the crowd of well-wishers left gawking behind began to disperse. JJ supported her mother as they hobbled tiredly, talking quietly, towards the house. Alicia wanted to know what treasure her brother had given Orwell, and shivering in the chilly night air, would have liked the handsome blonde student to escort her indoors, but shrieking with delight instead, he suddenly bolted into the house ahead of everyone, clasping the precious tickets—his own name artfully emblazed upon them—so masterfully presented by his gallant hero, Tracy MacDonachie! Alicia was thus left pouting in his dust, relegated to walk instead with her sardonically amused sister.

Bwana Hughes and Rick shrugged their shoulders at the bizarre course of events, then chatted easily about various science items as they shut the gate, locked the garage, and ambled about, torchlights in hand, inspecting the yard for anomalies. Going indoors, they assured the women—still abuzz over the Easter social, and Tracy MacDonachie's spectacular crashing of it—that they were safe and order was restored...Orwell was nowhere to be seen, but the others, who knew him well enough, believed that he would regain his sanity in the clear light of day. The family could now douse the lamps, open the windows to receive the cool night air, and find sleep.

# CHAPTER TWENTY-TWO

TRACY MACDONACHIE HAD FINALLY ARRIVED in Lusaka, more like a secret agent than a family friend...even so, let the bells ring out and the banners fly! He had overcome many obstacles through faith and ingenuity to reach his destination, just like his televangelist father would script in one of his powerful sermons, Bwana Hughes confided to his wife as they turned in to bed. She reminded her diplomat husband regarding Tracy: her best friend's son, albeit a black sheep who needed shepherding, was always welcome at Hughes House. Although Kathleen and Alicia might show dismay and Orwell pout that their long-awaited guest chose to sleep in the city's finest hotel rather than bunk in the *kraal*[65] of kith and kin, was it a blessing in disguise that garrulous, restless Tracy had other grand ideas still to orchestrate before he could finally join them in peace? Bwana Hughes sighed knowingly regarding Tracy: quite a talent, yet so full of mystery!

Next morning, Orwell waltzed joyously into the dining room, brightening the cool, overcast day where his parents, siblings, and guests dourly drank fruit juice or black coffee and ate a spartan brunch of sourdough buns, cheese, and mango jam. The *Mormon Tabernacle Choir* sang fervently from the living room's phonograph, but Bwana Hughes, dressed in dark suit and tie, austerely browsed the newspaper at one end of the table, while Martha Hughes read a familiar Bible passage—Jesus' *Sermon on the Mount*—aloud to unenthused children, who gazed at Orwell's noisy arrival with dark, hooded eyes.

"I knew in my heart that Tracy came here on a far more important quest

---

65 *Kraal*: Afrikaans for a traditional African village of huts or a livestock pen, typically enclosed by a fence.

than delivering old hymnbooks or singing gospel hymns!" cheered the beaming youngster, grinning from ear to ear. "Adventure at last! Let the good times roll!"

Kathleen, insulted that Orwell would trash her family's precious religion, glared at him crossly, but Alicia gazed with mixed amusement, curiosity, and chagrin at this clown, while Orwell raucously waved two ringside tickets to the Leopard Milongwe fight in the air as if they were colourful whirlybirds for the Edmonton *Klondike Days* parade.

"Those are noble causes in their own right, Orwell," chided Martha. "Our church is very thankful to receive such gifts; to have Kathleen and Alicia come from so far away to share in our Easter celebrations is a blessing from the Lord! These beautiful girls mingle well with our friends. Effort and faith are what God sees!"

"Tracy intends to defend his world ranking and the British Commonwealth boxing crown against Leopard Milongwe, Africa's heavy-weight champion!" Orwell devoutly announced to everyone as he read the main event described on the tickets. "Tracy's put together a successful stable of young boxers who are learning the ropes under his tutorage, two of whom have come here with him for preliminary cards against promising local fighters!"

"Great! Another brilliant idea comes trotting out! Another innovative project is in the works!" sarcastically applauded the High Commissioner's Chief of Staff, sternly slapping down his newspaper upon the table.

Bwana Hughes glowered at Orwell rather than the startled MacDonachie girls, but his message was also meant for Tracy's sisters, who intently watched this theatre unfold.

"Tracy sticks his finger in every pie he lays his hands on. He's already got a thick file going with the High Commission," Rick shared with Kathleen as he discretely explained his father's frustration.

He smiled diplomatically, but the blonde bombshell scowled she wanted no truck with either her gallivanting brother or this would-be suitor who glibly insulted him...at least not for now. Kathy had not been born yesterday!

"The last time I bumped into Tracy MacDonachie was at St. Andrew's church five years ago when I, after toiling long in the federal public service, had accepted our current overseas appointment and was saying goodbye to the congregation who lovingly held a tea in our honour," pontificated Hughes the Elder with scholarly recollection to two politely listening MacDonachie lasses, even as

Orwell chafed impatiently in the wings that his fuddy-duddy father was stealing his thunder. "Tracy had just been expelled from some big seminary down east minus his theology degree, but your brother, rather than try to finish, angrily derided his professors as glibly naïve and out of touch with turbulent social realities. He rejected the call to ministry in the institutional church foisted upon him by his old man!

"This angry young man was then drifting between careers, but had no time to be footloose and fancy-free—not with demands of a wife and three rambunctious sons in tow, and all the bills piling up to be paid! While your father fervently counselled him to keep the faith and serve his loving God as an African missionary, Tracy argued about taking time to clear his head and pay off his student loans—but not by working on the oil rigs up north as his oilman father-in-law instructed him. He then vaguely mentioned to me that he was continuing to earn his daily bread in the boxing ring! Your brother Robert, who had overheard our little conversation, scoffed that Tracy was just a petty brawler—a 'palooka' I believe he called him—who would never amount to anything. As for his big talk about mixing professional sports with pop music, Robert declared that Tracy was simply too lazy to wrestle drill pipes or punch steers like other young men building Alberta did. At best, Tiptoe would be singing in bars for change thrown his way by drunken builders! He had no talent or future; he'd blown everything at seminary!

"I am sure Tracy believes in his own ideas, but I wonder how this would-be gladiator handles the quiet routine of being a family man. His stock seems to be on the rise at the moment, so I give him credit for trying, albeit he always chooses the hard way! Mind you, I had no idea that Tracy had succeeded so well as a prize fighter that he should climb into the ring against Leopard Milongwe who, as son Orwell—a boxing buff of sorts will concur—pointed out, is acknowledged by many boxing commissions as an up-and-coming contender for the world heavy-weight title!"

Orwell grimaced in exasperation that his own father, a seasoned diplomat who knew the Prime Minister of Canada and Zambia's President on first name basis, should question Tracy's boxing prowess, particularly within earshot of the high-minded MacDonachie girls. Getting the wise teacher back on track, Orwell eagerly divulged more juicy tidbits from his hero's letter. "He wants to look us up after the big bout...take a road trip together, so we can show him the sights of this fabled corner of the earth!"

"I hope you didn't promise that yahoo I'd fly him and his goons to all the tourist hotspots in my single-engine Cessna!" grumbled Rick.

Ignoring Rick's outburst, goo-goo-eyed Orwell begged his father on bended knee for support. Kathleen stared at his outlandish antics in disbelief.

"Dad, I have to be at that big fight to cheer Tracy on to victory! He really needs my support! Let's see, who can I take with me? I would like to sit with Georgina, but I know she won't tolerate blood and guts that come with the territory! Maybe Benjamin will come."

By now, the parlour was reverberating with laughter at Orwell's breathless pitch, but Alicia suddenly looked sad that he was not choosing her. Orwell's patience rapidly wore thin when his mother actually wondered aloud whether she and all her girls should attend.

"Mom..." he objected fiercely, educating the smirking women with his rugged take on life, "A boxing arena is no place for church ladies!

"Most fighting men keep a small, closely-knit, and fiercely loyal entourage of supporting pals who know the ropes of their brutal trade at ring level. Tracy is surrounded by quality sparring partners who hone his skills by emulating every opponent; corner men who mend cuts between rounds better than any book-trained medical doctor with a little liniment and secret salve, smelling salts, sleight of hand, and water; a hardnosed trainer who keeps the gladiator's body and mind in keen fighting shape; a pompous manager who arranges key matches while avoiding palookas, giant killers, and the mob; and the odd movie starlet hanging around for kicks..."

"And I suppose Miss Amadu is your so-called movie starlet?" exploded Alicia, suddenly arising to her feet again, incensed by Orwell's balderdash.

Remonstrating him with wild eyes and appealing hands, Alicia testified that she had seen Georgina flaunting herself at Tracy last night when they were barely introduced. The floozy had eagerly accepted his invitation of a ride back to her university residence, so she could get closer to her admirer. Like Ali, Tracy seemed more concerned with grooming the interest of some eye candy than looking after his own sisters! Orwell, who had been diligently serving Georgina all day in hopes of pleasing her, had been upstaged!

Suzy, already chastised for her late-night tryst by her parents, bristled defiantly at Ali's name being dragged through the mud again, but when Rick and Kathleen laughed at the amazon's jealous observations, Alicia scowled and figuratively shook off the dust of her sandals against them all. She stuck out her tongue at ashen-faced Orwell, then bumped him brazenly aside with her ample, swaying derriere as she stormed out of the room.

"Don't camp in the loo all day, Fannie!" chortled Kitty as her sister slammed the bathroom door in a huff. "Others need to relieve themselves too!"

"What's her problem?" mumbled Orwell, dully gazing at the bathroom door, behind which he could hear Alicia whimpering, "Why do I even bother with those guys?"

"You are so utterly clueless, Oh-well!" Kathleen smugly concluded.

Orwell could not reconcile these spoiled girls' dramatic spirits in a month of Sundays! The few days they had already spent together had been surprisingly valuable and gone by in a blur, but he was still being stung daily by their annoying quirks, despite all his efforts and sacrifices made to help them feel comfortable in a strange land. Now, when he had finally found happiness, could the MacFemales not celebrate his joy? After all, Tracy was not only Orwell's mentor, but also their lost brother who had been found!

"Let me see those tickets!" demanded Rick, nearly tearing off the stubs as he wrestled the precious bits of pressboard from his embarrassing little brother. "You dumbo! It's not Tracy, but some dude named Karl Thompson who's gonna fight Milongwe!"

*****

ORWELL did not make the connection that Tracy MacDonachie was Thompson's manager until after the glowering brute was finally introduced to him as 'the contender', rather than simply a part of MacDonachie's ragtag entourage. Rivard Cummings, the goliath who served as chief trainer, and Tracy Rimond, the wise, ancient corner man with a raspy voice and cauliflower ears, were familiar faces from bygone years in the MacDonachie hood; they now shared with the manager and his fighter the finest accommodation that Zambia could offer! The supporting cast arrived quietly and piecemeal during the hectic pre-fight days following Easter. Orwell made several harried trips to the airport to bundle all manner of scary-looking thugs and their bulging gear bags into the hotel, with an almost manic Tracy fretting and haranguing him about myriad details and problems. Yet, this motley crew looked impressive once everyone was assembled for a boisterous pre-fight press conference broadcast on Zambia Television, which Orwell would have definitely attended, if only to stand beside Tracy, had his hero notified him!

The maestro then took his stable straight away into seclusion, far from prying eyes of the partisan media or meddlesome worries of kith and kin, to train at some secret camp for the big fight that was only a week away. Orwell and the girls were not invited, nor did anyone at Hughes House hear boo from MacDonachie again until one bizarre morning when he and his entourage stormed the compound with the rising sun and swept Orwell out of bed for some strenuous cross-country running. Tracy playfully roused the lad from dreamland, and got the groggy and protesting youth's Adrenalin pumping by showering him under a garden hose. He sicced drill sergeant Alicia upon him to chase Orwell into his jogging suit, and then, with her eager help, whipped him into shape down a gruelling course through the awakening city.

Such a unique sight as these spirited foreigners bounding through hardscrabble black townships brought out many spectators, particularly curious children, who hailed their energy and jogged excitedly alongside them over the dewy landscape. Tug, who got off-task from running proudly with his master to bark at phantom assailants, helped matters not, nor did bright-eyed Alicia when she persisted in glimpsing into brick compounds, and chatting with jolly natives as they breakfasted on tea and fried bean cakes. For all her bossy pep talk about running the good race to the finish—for Christ Jesus and His crown of life—this nosey girl tried the patience of her brother and host by impulsively stopping to explore and greet. Had she no shame? Had Big Bertha no inhibitions to guard her blooming innocence? She was curvy and buoyant, yet strong and fleet, Orwell marvelled as he toiled to keep up with his mentor's amazing sister!

Finally shaking their followers, the joggers paused, slumping and gasping for breath, beneath a towering *mofu* tree somewhere outside of Lusaka. Tracy, dismayed at his own apparent loss of conditioning and self-confidence that came with age, took Orwell aside—beyond earshot of curious Alicia—and begged his young attendant to pray for him.

MacDonachie then unloaded many burdens that were weighing on him: his marriage was in tatters; his bellicose father-in-law kept him away from his sons with a baseball bat; the opulent, self-serving church oppressed his ability to pastor the poor and needy; his self-righteously accusing father, a fellow man of the cloth, had publicly cast him out of his radio programs for being in league with the Devil! Tracy desired above all else to impress these powerful men who kept dismissing him, so that he too could be a winner.

They must therefore decisively win the upcoming fight, and move ever upward, not only to the highest echelon of the heavy-weight boxing division, but eventually buckle the coveted championship belt. He believed that Karl possessed the skills to make it to the top, but could Thompson's sometimes questionable drive sustain him under fire? Had he only been five years younger, Tracy MacDonachie vowed ardently to his avid pupil, he himself would be fighting Leopard Milongwe! Although he emphatically shook his head, the old gladiator smiled with fierce appreciation at Orwell's fervent assertion that Tracy could tame the Leopard, anytime, anywhere!

The high and mighty Reverend Wynnard MacDonachie knew not that his oldest son was managing the brutal contender now sitting over yonder and chatting amicably with Alicia—the old hypocrite understood much less that Tracy had dangerously brought Thompson to Africa to fight the local champion in a topflight match! How would Tracy explain his unseemly actions to God's Own once news of their high-risk adventure hit the international press? His blabbermouth sisters must be watched closely by Orwell, lest they leak any details to their father. Their noble task of delivering hymnbooks and singing gospel favourites at some far-flung mission church was Rev. MacDonachie's cup of tea, but the grumpy old codger squirmed uncomfortably at leaving these impressionable young ladies in a moment of sinful madness to the care of his black sheep son so far from home!

Tracy wearied of defending his sisters' honour as if it was their father's gold. Kathleen dallied around with many eager young studs anywhere, but should *not* on this safari while he devoted himself to preparing a valuable fighter to for the biggest payday of his career! Barely tolerating that Alicia was joking now with ruffians, felons, and womanizers as she innocently played *Concentration* in the shade with the boxers, Tracy shared with Orwell how carefully he sequestered them, lest these low-moral brutes gain opportunity to live out their sexual fantasies with either nubile, curvaceous female. What he could not do, Tracy grimly admitted, was ensure that Kathleen and Alicia resisted temptation under

Orwell's roof. He begged his avid listener's assurance that he—as his eyes and ears on the home front—would discourage any romantic tryst from developing between Kitty-Cat and Rick, since it was clear Orwell's bro stupidly worshipped her. Though he had promised to help Kathy in her need, Orwell doubted his fitness for the heavy task Tracy sought against his brother. MacDonachie dropped on him heavily with the other shoe: that he must protect the little sister, who really was a diamond in the rough, with his life! Orwell gulped like a fish out of water in making his solemn vow to do this double duty to the utmost. Tracy beamed with relief.

Embracing his mentor like a tamer holding onto a wild animal for dear life, Hughes felt humbled to pray for this great man who, like Jesus crying to God in the *Garden of Gethsemane*, suffered great tribulations as his disciples slept while he agreed to do the Father's will. He felt a warm, strong hand on his own shoulders; when they broke, Orwell and Tracy were both amazed to find Alicia sombrely standing with them. A breeze rustled through the magnificent tree whose crown danced cheerfully high above them, raising its branches in praise of Heaven and assuring those who looked up with delight that God carried them in their troubled times.

Having received Orwell's assurances that his requests would be honoured, Tracy reverted to his old jovial self as he escorted Orwell and Alicia over the hill, to where Tracy Rimond was waiting with a car. Against Orwell's loud protests and Alicia's dismay, Mighty MacDonachie sent them home with the grandfatherly trainer, lest they get thirsty and tired, while he and Rivard ran with the fighters back to his hideout.

"Stop being such a baby!" Alicia sternly rebuked Orwell when he reacted childishly, and practically threw a tantrum strapped in his car seat, while Tracy jauntily smiled and bade them adieu. Karl, Rivard, and several other gladiators followed their leader as he jogged away effortlessly; they gradually faded into the yellow savannah like a column of army ants.

The amazon glared at her distraught companion, barely masking her own pain as she silenced him in Tracy Rimond's stoic presence by demanding, "Why should my brother give you the time of day when you act so immature?"

Orwell had nothing polite or reasonable to say in response to her stinging remark, so in his rage, he hurled himself against the car door; finding it locked, he nonetheless sat as far away from her as he could. She, grunting in exasperation, did the same on her side. They huffed and puffed, wrathfully crossed arms, and stamped their feet in annoying, copycat fashion—they were not on the same page, although both were hurt and confused by Tracy's decision to send them packing. Orwell refused to meet Alicia's anguished gaze, and glared out his window in forbidding silence as Tracy Rimond pleasantly drove the long, winding road back to Lusaka.

*****

ORWELL suffered with double knowledge that, like Georgina, Tracy lived and breathed now so near, yet so far away from him. Buoyed by his mentor's presence in Zambia, he most unusually and bravely sought out Georgina by telephone, but his flowery calls to the Professor's mansion went unanswered. He wanted to follow-up what they had developed so far, while their promising affections were still fresh in her mind, but perhaps she had travelled or taken a job more quickly than discussed—or simply needed a break from it all. Georgina might be giving Orwell space for Tracy; whatever the reason, Orwell, without organized sports, university courses, or demanding girlfriends to detain him, ought to concentrate on that highest calling of helping Tracy succeed...He was a veteran of Lusaka life, but also spoke MacDonachie's rogue language, and knew the ropes of boxing. He was practically beside himself with anticipation, yet churned anxiously over Tracy's fortunes in the upcoming boxing extravaganza. Young bwana desired in his heart, beyond all telling, to help his beloved mentor succeed...with cards dealt, he must play!

After their recent, adventurous day of working out together on the road, Tracy disappeared off the map! Not even newspaper sleuths could find him. He did not telephone or come by the house, although both Orwell and Alicia, not to mention the old Hughes folks, had assured the wayward rover from the moment of his arrival that he was family...welcome, anytime. A place was permanently set for him at the dinner table, should he desire a home-cooked meal and Christian fellowship. Rivard, Tracy Rimond, and even rugged Karl Thompson and his sparring partners—who answered to such 'crayon' names as Bussy, Reddy, Greeny, and White-Eyes—were welcome to hang out at Hughes House. Martha's girls lovingly kept this wild bunch in their daily prayers, as Sundays came and went without any boxer attending church. Alicia and Orwell would gladly drive over care packages...if only they knew where Tracy was staying! Orwell—longing to share in MacDonachie's exciting venture, yet stewing over potential mistakes he must have made to embarrass his mentor—continued to extend invitations without replies. Having waited so long already for just a glimpse of Tracy, Orwell suffered as he waited alone in silence, hurt because he knew that Tracy now dwelt in his town.

Orwell searched for Tracy's friendly face or powerful frame every day: on the walkways, in shops, at social events, driving about traffic. He contacted Tracy's last-known lodging numerous times by wire and then in person, but was always pleasantly informed by some officious front desk clerk that Mr. MacDonachie was not present; he had gone downtown or was taking his meal. "*Yes, the very important resident of Penthouse Suite absolutely, positively could not come to the telephone—he had made express orders not to be disturbed,*" or "*He is resting or entertaining special guests.*" Who were *these* guests and what made *them* so special—more special than him obviously—Orwell anguished in his wounded heart?

The last time he tried, Hughes strode into the InterContinental Hotel clean-cut and wearing a business suit, escorting Alicia in a perky sun dress and high-heel shoes, only to learn that Mr. T.M. MacDonachie and his entourage had vacated the premises for other digs unknown. Orwell was temporarily soothed from feeling lost and downcast by Alicia, who looked quite fetching when she made the effort; she boldly invited her dapper young fellow for a drink of lime cordial on the café sundeck, before taking him downtown to watch a movie.

Orwell refused to answer any questions tossed out derisively by Bwana or Richard Hughes about Tracy MacDonachie's bizarre situation unfolding into their lives. He logically proposed to his doubtful interrogators that Tracy would provide the gift of money promised to the church in due course, after distractions of the big fight were over, and he found opportunity to attend a service arranged in his honour as an emissary from the Canadian brethren. Such a fete was desirable and prudent, yet out of Orwell's hands...beyond his control. Had any of the three B's—Beausoleil, Benjamin, or Bwana Hughes, the latter in his capacity as chairman of the church council—even contacted Tracy to make such invitations? Young Hughes believed that expressing worries would be unpopular and embarrassing during such a glorious time of fighting for victory and vindication; unlike his parents and siblings, he kept his own aching questions muzzled deep inside rather than voiced aloud. The devout fan deemed his own confusion as too feeble to divulge, and thus swept it under Tracy's red carpet.

Knowing full well—unlike pouting and anxious Orwell—that their brother must not be approached by family or friends during his pivotal appointment with destiny, Alicia and Kathleen stayed respectfully away. Having performed their required church duties well, they scheduled their time prudently and enjoyed the pleasant hospitality of Bwana Hughes' family, while they waited patiently for Tracy. These supposedly omnipotent sisters seemed blissfully unaware that their planned departure date was fast approaching—indeed, jaded Orwell eagerly counted the minutes before these pesky girls would be put on the plane for home, so he could then get back to his normal life of school, sports, writing, church, and Georgina...In hindsight, he would realize that his lady guests were brave and mature beyond their tender years; they knew not how or when Tracy would take them home to Canada, simply that he would call in due course, after he had achieved his glorious quest. While Orwell ignorantly suffered pain and humiliation, Alicia and Kathleen stoically did what their brother expected of them. They knew the drill, having performed it many times before to honour their privilege of being high-bred MacDonachie women.

Since they expected a long stay, Alicia and Kathleen refused to fritter away their downtime just lazing around, getting fat, or feeling bored. These efficient and well-organized honours students amazed the older Hughes boys when they unpacked their school books and worked through previously-set assignments in several courses, and exercised classroom regularity, despite the boys tooling about, to diligently keep abreast of their education as well as study for upcoming final exams that would soberly greet them upon returning to Canada. Settling in as members of Hughes's extended household, they joined their hosts in the everyday rhythms of life: doing domestic chores; participating in church services and High Commission functions; picnicking at *Munda Wanga* Botanical Gardens; cycling or swimming with Suzanne and JJ; golf or tennis with Orwell and Richard; helping in social action work at the local YWCA, church, and mission farm; providing musical entertainment when requested at various venues; and cultivating new friendships among the young people of the Canadian contingent as well as with others they met at church, school, or university.

Bwana Hughes, pleased by Wynnard's daughters' flexibility and collaboration, agreed to their reasonable petition—politely brought forward by Orwell—that Alicia and Kathleen relocate their digs to the guest quarters behind the house. The MacDonachies wished to make their remaining stay with their hosts as pleasant as possible until the end. They loved Suzy and JJ, but every girl needed personal space and privacy in order to stay friends; the entire household would benefit by spreading out yet sticking together! They were one.

Encouraged by the girls' resourcefulness, Orwell waited diligently for the weekend's boxing extravaganza, even without Tracy or Georgina to support him. He played tennis, went cycling with JJ and Alicia, thus continued childhood traditions of accompanying these bosom buddies in various adventures. When his parents tended to their diplomatic duties, Janice Joanne and Suzanne went to school, and Richard courted Kathleen, Orwell found himself solely interacting for hours each day with Miss Alicia Pearl Rose MacDonachie—a fascinating but risky past time to fill out the week!

Orwell, as he had promised Tracy, cared for Alicia although she, still stung from their recent spat, claimed to be self-sufficient: she read her school books, kept-up her black belts, and sustained new friends when not napping, reading an adventure novel, or vegetating in front of the TV. What did he want from her anyway? Orwell groused, was Fannie not a millstone around his neck? All posturing aside, however, they immersed themselves in mind-boggling scrabble games, played chess pretending to be duelling grandmasters Fischer and Spassky, fought many feisty table tennis or wrestling matches, and went driving around town—she to encourage her learning friend. They biked to the university and shot hoops on the outdoor basketball court, or kicked around the soccer ball in the grassed sports field nearby. They sang Christian hymns or folk songs; he jigged to her fiddle, she danced to his honky-tonk piano. They further entertained the house servants by playing creative duets on the family's upright piano. Orwell also escorted Alicia on walking tours of neighbourhood flower gardens, and long before others in the house were awake, the athletic pair jogged together every morning with Tug enthusiastically in stride.

Richard and Kathleen, perhaps feeling philanthropic or just plain bored with each other's lovey-dovey company, returned home from work at noon on Tuesday and took the younger couple golfing in Chainama Hills. This verdant course, although meticulously groomed and landscaped by uniformed gardeners, was located a good half-hour's drive east of Lusaka; with other golfers scarce and the café short on food service, the quiet club echoed a bygone era of colonial ease. It was a little gem that the Hughes clan had discovered and regularly patronized; they brought in their guests whenever possible for a round. The jolly Hughes boys, basking in their element on this fine sunny day, strutted along the fairways after each impressive drive, gaily accompanied by Kathleen in her spiffy white shorts and the more modestly-dressed Alicia twirling a multi-coloured umbrella. They extolled the picturesque scenery and exotic birds, raced their golf bag chariots, chatted and joked, and taught their gushing girlfriends how to hold and swing wooden drivers, choose the best iron for the height and length of shot needed to approach the green, and once at the flag, to sink that all important putt. Orwell, who claimed to have built his putting experience while watching Arnold Palmer and Sam Snead golf on *Wild World of Sports,* entertained flag girl Alicia, but boggled self-professed golf pro Kathy by lining up each final shot while flopped on the green, so he could eyeball the micro topography on the path his ball should travel to reach the cup.

Orwell cleared the deadly water ponds on the thirteenth hole only to have his hole-in-one kyboshed when some African children playing beside the green merrily ran off with his ball. Their lark soon ended; dropping the ball on some overgrown path, the would-be thieves fled in terror when pursued by a giant warrioress with flaming hair and booming voice! Alicia, an accomplished and talented sportswoman, naturally won the match. Runner up Rick, impressed with her smooth swing, powerful drive, and careful putting, let the amazon pilot the Peugeot home as her prize, while Orwell sat beside his beaming girl like her poodle, yapping pleasantly along as he guided her into town.

Despite her large presence and solemn, bespectacled gaze, Alicia showed her escort that she was fun to be with, popular and sociable as well as mysterious; she was determined, clever and athletic—darkly beautiful as a raw gem could be. He admired her courage and strength as of a legendary amazon from Greek mythology, yet found her to be strangely unnerving and unpredictable—a brilliant but untamed schemer who knew no limits, who sadly teetered between genius and madness...More than once, during what should have been a simple family outing to a park or downtown shops, he found himself desperately searching for Alicia, driven by fear that she was lost or hurt. Other times, even in his own yard, she stalked him like a lioness on the hunt; how he feared her then! She could be enthusiastically full of energy one moment, but then hide away to sleep or pout for hours...Before his duties were fulfilled, Alicia would seduce her protector and claim him as her husband!

Hughes toiled for Tracy at clever Mairam's bidding...if only Tracy could see and reward his diligent efforts to help the cause! Did Tracy know or care about his troubles with little sister that he was bound to uphold? Through all his aches and pains, Orwell wondered how The Great One would thank him, if ever he completed this arduous task....

# CHAPTER TWENTY-THREE

ALICIA BEGGED OFF FROM JOGGING Wednesday morning and cloistered herself in the guest room to complete a pressing math assignment, so Orwell was amazed, upon returning solo from the Lusaka Turf Club in Handsworth Park via a lengthy circuit, to meet his friend jogging along Addis Ababa Drive, with Tug bounding gaily at her side. The amazon veered neither right nor left, but kept high-stepping her long legs and pumping her bare, muscular arms fluidly towards him, a toothpaste grin plastered on her broad brown face. She was shapely in her revealing orange T-shirt and black gym shorts; although tied back in a ponytail, Alicia's lush auburn hair danced to drums of the powerful rhythm of her strides. Orwell halted and stood gaping in admiration at this young lioness as she raced towards him. Under better circumstances, Orwell would have whistled to salute her brawny beauty, but he could now only wonder how had she known where to find him in this sprawling, modern city of 250,000 people?

Tug recognized his master immediately, and barking his hello, bounded along the curbside towards him. What a dumkopf! The excited canine must have not read Orwell's fuming thoughts, for he pricked up his ears and sauntered forward, tail wagging. Did that stupid dog not realize that he was still in disgrace? Who had even given Alicia permission to bring him? Tug had yet again betrayed his master by leading this interfering female to a perfect rendezvous! Orwell, damn his male ego, fastidious control, and churning angst, was still pleased in some strange way that they had overcome all odds to reach him.

"Fancy meeting you, 'My-room'!" Orwell joked nervously as Tug licked his shaking hands. "Especially since this is not my normal route, nor do I routinely take runs at midday."

Alicia smiled, but not wanting to stiffen by standing still, jogged in place before him as she explained her motives between deep gulps of invigorating air.

"I felt compelled to seek you, Sir Oh-well when, by ten o'clock, I did not see you puttering about your prized flower gardens or writing in your study. I was concerned, knowing that you normally return within one hour from your brisk morning run, which you started shortly after breakfast! Intrigued by your cloak and dagger behaviour, yet worried for your safety, I thought as I put down my calculus figures and quickly donned my fitness uniform: a cross-country run is always good exercise...but more fun when one has a friend to run with."

"We are friends," Hughes happily assured her.

Orwell extended his hand to shake on that agreement, but Alicia, her almond eyes bubbling like fountains of boiling black oil within her reddened, sweaty face, fiercely performed a deep squat thrust, just missing him with her jabbing fist, shrieking, "*Hi-yah*, take that! I'm onto you now, Bucko!"

"You missed!" Orwell scoffed as he staggered backwards. He waited at a safe distance while she expressed her worries.

"I know we both miss Tracy terribly and are deeply concerned about him, but I also feel in my heart that I need to understand you better. I feel discouraged to see you so dissatisfied these days, but is it my fault if your university closes, Georgina stays not by the phone, or Tracy goes into hiding? Have I wronged you? I thought we agreed to be friends and had grown closer recently. You feel like Kathy and I have locked a ball and chain on your fancy-dandy legs to keep you under control—why not be thankful that your glass is half full instead of seeing it as half empty? And a penny for your thoughts now please, Orwell, so that I can make things right."

When he woodenly stood there refusing to answer, Alicia groaned in frustration. She bent down to massage her warm calves lest they cramp up and hobble her, leaving the proud huntress at the mercy of this bumbling fool. Hughes found himself gawking naughtily at her breasts as they heaved when she straightened back to full height. She placed a caring hand softly on his shoulder, and gazing sadly at him with glistening animal eyes, begged to share his pain.

Orwell could not articulate his feelings concerning Georgina, afraid that he would hurt Alicia, so he tenderly took her large, sweaty hand in his, raised it to his lips, and kissed it. He clasped her hand in his, and led her to a brick wall running along the perimeter of nearby *Long Acres Hostel*, where they sat down to drink water and rest momentarily on the protruding pedestal of a concrete fence post. Thus, gently attended to by her knight, Alicia shared her special news.

"Georgina came by the house for a visit this morning while you were out," she softly informed him, not wanting to upset the suddenly downcast lad. "She arrived unannounced, riding in that big, fancy Rolls we took last week at the market, but this time Georgie came alone, driven by her uncle's chauffeur."

"Okay, so what'd you regal dames do, have Joseph serve you tea and crumpets?" teased Orwell to cover his dismay and jealously.

"Since you weren't home, Oh-well," Alicia protested, rolling her eyes and screwing up her face, "Georgina and I engaged in female chatter. We talked about doing some girl stuff, you know, shop downtown for clothes or make-up, maybe take in a movie or fashion show, or even go for drinks together in some fancy restaurant.

"It was all girl talk, quite bitchy. Believe me, Orwell, you'd soon have gotten bored trying to follow our conversation," Alicia insisted sheepishly, making a funny face to make her sullen detractor laugh. "Georgina invited me to visit her where she stays now with Professor Ibrahim. We'll swim and sunbathe at the pool, likely play some tennis in the back yard."

"Hah! You'd better watch out, Alicia—Georgina is currently Zambia's women's singles champion. She'll either go easy on you or clean your clock!"

"Don't be so snotty, Bucko! Remember, I'm pretty good at ping pong and badminton. Georgina knows I play tennis—being a talented and keen, multi-sport athlete will help me give her a decent game on her own clay court."

"Don't get so competitive that you lose her friendship for me. Remember, Georgina knows where you live!"

"We plan to play friendly," Alicia assured her surprisingly feisty listener. She tried to relax him by presenting more staid images of women's socializing practices. "Later, we'll chat and listen to music over ginger tea and sweets in Georgina's private sitting room. Your girlfriend has an awesome record collection, eclipsing ours with all the latest pop, reggae, *Afrobeat,* and rock albums lining her shelves."

"The two of you two were feeling witty this morning. What were you gossiping about?"

"I didn't mean it like that. We didn't chatter about anyone per se," Alicia, miffed by his low insinuation, sternly corrected him while Tug lay contentedly, but always alert, at Orwell's feet. "We discussed young eligible men: movie stars, singers, sportsmen, race car drivers, political leaders...which is normal and healthy, though we didn't dwell on who is out of reach or sigh over them as if they were God's gifts to women. I'm sure you and Rick do the same, drooling over James Bond girls and hot models when nobody's watching you.

"Good looks and physical power don't last nor are they the only things that make a man attractive to women. We admire men who can laugh and have fun, but who also have strong principles, are reliable and honest. You see, both Georgina and I are feminists who can formulate intelligent opinions, and are determined to support good causes and fulfill goals that matter in this world. We demand to be treated with respect and equality, not as sex objects or bimbos. If you must know, Orwell James Hughes, your name came up in conversation as both Georgina and I find you to be an interesting topic."

"I'm pleased to hear that, as long as my image is not being burned in effigy or used as a dartboard. I hope my shortcomings were not too many for you fancy gals," Orwell chuckled self-depreciatively. His tone suddenly changed as he broached earnestly, "Does Georgina like me?"

"Yes, she does," Alicia admitted, elated yet subdued by his hopeful crush on their charming mutual acquaintance. Her own heart ached to see it!

She was about to speak more seriously, but then thought better of it, sensing that her views would seem selfish now and dampen his resurging hope in matters of the heart. He had returned to his bubbly, jovial and free self again, enough right now for she who loved him. Orwell was her friend first; his happiness must sustain her now while she waited patiently, and did her utmost to keep in touch with him.

Orwell was pleased to be affirmed as a young man of importance to Georgina. So, he was *liked* by this lily of the valley...his bright morning star! Hughes realized now the glory of her elusive, closely guarded secret: he had not only caught Georgina's notice, but had made the grade with her over these past rigorous months of pursuing her. He now feared to hear any juicy details of these expressly private girls' conversations, lest they give him false hopes or spur his erotic imagination. The last thing he sought was for Alicia to get written into Georgina's bad books by sharing as intimately with him as much as she had already, for he knew first-hand how awful life could be, languishing in banishment in the outer darkness of Georgina's sunny kingdom.

"Thank you, my friend, for being so candid with me," Orwell effervesced as, in the midst of his celebration, he impulsively hugged the stoically smiling Alicia. He was impressed that she was shapelier and sweeter than he had ever thought a scary amazon could be. Buoyed by their exchange of pleasantries, he added, "Thanks for finding me, Lisa. Shall we jog home now?"

"Why not?" replied Alicia in sweet surrender, storing her misgivings deep inside, and dying to herself as she relished the fresh breeze of his happiness. Trotting in a circle around him, she wildly tossed her mane as she shouted exuberantly, "Which way do we go from here, Bucko?"

Tug, sensing that the show was about to get back on the road, scrambled excitedly to his feet, and barked like some royal herald as he ran ahead of his human companions, but he did not head southward towards Hughes House, as expected. Instead, Tug raced into *Long Acres Hostel*, a warren of whitewashed sleep rooms and open-air hallways under red-brick roofing tiles, wherein he and Orwell had first met when the family was staying at the venerable guest house, upon arriving in Zambia five years ago. Orwell, worried that Tug would get lost in the sprawling maze, or would embarrass him by barking at some uniformed African housekeeper or stealing a beefsteak from the kitchen, chased him, closely followed by Alicia. They ran into Karla Eve who was just on her way to lunch in the dining room with her family.

"Well, hello there—aren't you the son of our illustrious Canadian leader in Zambia, James Hughes?" asked Mr. Ted Bryant, smiling broadly and looking comfortable in an open floral shirt that hung nearly to the crotch of his white cotton slacks. Karlee's father jovially detained the sweat-streaked lad in T-shirt and cut-off jeans from buzzing past in pursuit of Tug, who had skittered ahead on the red-painted, concrete floor and ducked into a side room.

"He's Captain Orwell, Dad," joked Jim, a blonde, blue-eyed youth who towered over Orwell, despite being two years younger. Gazing down from his lofty height, Jim kidded flustered Hughes, "Like, can you really fly, man?"

"No," corrected John, an identical lad inspecting Orwell from the left, "He's the hip organist from church—you know, that crowded, amen-praising place with the long name: Trinity United Lutheran Congregation of St. Luke—see: I got it right, first try!"

"And you must be Alicia MacDonachie, one of those beautiful singing sisters who entertained us so well on Easter Sunday...though, I must say, you look less dressed-up today," piped up Lisa Bryant, the spunky blonde mother of these two hulking lads, and their aloof and serious sister, pipsqueak Karlee. "It's a pleasure to talk with fellow Canadians any time in this strange new land," she effervesced to politely listening Alicia, "We really enjoyed the service and fell in love with the church, thanks in no small part to you kids. Trinity is a very welcoming place. Say, I see you're out jogging, but can you join us for lunch?"

"Um, er, that would be nice," Alicia nervously hesitated. "But, well, look at us ma'am in our grubby gear, all sweaty like, stinking up the posh dining room! Isn't there a dress code here? We've also got a dog running around loose that we need to catch."

"I've got no money to pay for our meals—they're several courses of fining dining as I recall from living here before," Orwell stammered, embarrassed.

"Be our guests today. Let us give back a little for all that your family has done for us greenhorns," generously offered Ted. "There's plenty of food, and many folks dine here in casual clothes—we're all inmates of this joint, trying to adjust to Africa. I'm sure the cooks won't mind feeding a few more strays."

"Okay, then yes...thanks," Orwell, unable to escape the invite, muttered his acceptance.

"Hey Orwell, I'll help you catch your dog," offered Karlee after she deftly made her way through the chatty crowd of tall people to stand beside him. Fondness for the willing lad gleamed in her large blue eyes as she gently touched his arm. "Come on, I think he's scampering about the lounge."

"What'll I do once I catch Tug? I don't have a leash, and he's not the most trained dog on the planet," Orwell appealed to Karlee, even as they traipsed into the lounge: a shadowy, yet refined and colonial gentlemen's retreat. Tug, who was laying low beneath the ping pong table, spied his master, and relieved, came meekly to greet him. Orwell replied with a "Hey, boy" and playfully tousled his canine head.

"I've got a plan, Orwell. Why don't you keep Tug here with you, while I go to the dining room and round up a plate of food for each of you?" suggested Karlee, showing a kinder side for one who was rumoured to have some sharp edges.

She chose for Orwell a comfortable easy chair, which though bigger and heavier than herself, this *Mighty Mouse*[66] dragged over hooked rugs and red

66 *Mighty Mouse*: American animated, super mouse character created by the *Terrytoons* studio for 20th Century Fox. He appeared in eighty theatrical films between 1942 and 1961, which were broadcast Saturday mornings on CBS television from 1955 to 1961. Mighty Mouse also appeared in comics and other media.

ceramic tiles to a polished mahogany games table nearby. Flushed but smiling at the incredulous lad as she patted the chair back, Karlee sweetly invited, "Here, Orwell, come sit down. Rest...Make yourself comfortable; read a magazine while you wait. Nobody will bother you and your dog for the next while, since they've all gone into the dining room to eat. I'll be back shortly with lunch."

Orwell smiled and did as she suggested, causing Karlee to blush as they passed. Rather than hot pants or a baggy track clothes, she wore a nifty blue and white sailor suit that revealed her muscular arms in healthy glow from a recent sunburn turning to tan. Her large, shapely behind—that she had provocatively displayed during the Canadian Saturday night hootenanny at Hughes House—wiggled lively inside her blue spandex pants as she enthusiastically went on her errand. Was her odd and humbling sacrifice a truce she called in apology for her previous bad behaviour? Orwell was appreciative, whatever Karlee's motive....

With Tug lying contentedly at his feet, Orwell sat gazing around the room, reacquainting himself with the comfortable old lounge. Although he had grown from a boy into a man over these last five years, this venerable recreation room had not changed one iota in his absence! A brick fireplace gaped like a cave in the far corner, waiting to roar during June winter days. The north wall was lined with books, while a dart board hung on the mahogany-panelled south wall, west of which was a large cabinet containing darts, table tennis paddles and balls, playing cards and various board games: chess, draughts[67] and cribbage, suitable for an upper crust, European drawing room. The east and west walls featured large windows with thick glass panels separated by inlaid lead lines drawn in square and diamond patterns. The grand windows were framed with carved brown wood and draped in red curtains that filtered incoming daylight. Morning ash trays had been emptied, but the room still reeked of recently-burned tobacco, as though several smokers had just vacated the premises for twelve o'clock lunch.

"We have ox-tail soup today! I also brought you Melba toast and assorted cheeses, cold cuts, and fruit to eat," pleasantly announced Karlee, returning with a tray so heaped with food that her blonde head was obscured from view.

Karlee bowed and carefully laid her offering before her esteemed visitor, deftly splitting her legs, bending her knees, and stretching across his view so that he could feast his eyes upon her lovely body—how her strong back tapered into

67 *Draughts*: British name for the game of checkers.

ample hips and then to strong, shapely legs, over which swelled pear-shaped mounds of her luscious bottom—that formed a cheeky-cute heart for him to relish, naughtily? Smiling through her flowing blonde hair as she noticed his admiration, Karlee slowly straightened up, exhaling a sigh of pleasure. Celebrating their connection, Karlee started a little dance for Orwell, stretching one hand sideways as if to wave at him, while pretending to bounce a ball with the other, in a silly attempt to entertain him. The lines of her chic sailor suit nicely accentuated the curves of her lush profile—she was tiny but strong—an enticing miniature of his acknowledged goddess, Alicia MacDonachie! They smiled at each other, savouring their fleeting, secret intimacy. Orwell affectionately dubbed her 'Mighty Mouse' and clapped for Karlee's cute little dance.

Giggling at all the commotion Orwell caused, Karlee merrily brought him to order, serving notice with her jewelled eyes as she informed him, "Alicia helped me select a suitable menu just for you, Orwell—based upon previous experience she says—so I hope you like what I brought. My family invited her to dine with them across the hall, but Alicia felt badly about leaving you alone, so she and I will come into your little hotspot here to eat with you."

"Hey, thanks a million to both you lovely ladies! This is great, Karla Eve—I feel like royalty. I must drop in to visit you more often!" chuckled Orwell, grinning with pleasure. He invited Karlee to sit and share the generous meal with him.

"It's true, Bucko! You and Tug are quite the high-maintenance celebrities," spoofed Alicia as she followed behind Karlee, and presented a bowl of water and some scrap meat to Tug, who appreciatively barked before ravenously gulping everything down.

Unlike Orwell, Alicia looked freshly coiffed and scrubbed via a pit stop in the ladies' room, care of concerned Mrs. Bryant. Taking her seat beside Orwell and opposite Karlee, the taller girl assured her peers, "This feels better, eating with my mates who brought me here, rather than sequestering myself with that genteel, highbrow crowd yonder."

"Cripes, so here's where you kids hang out, in the smoking room? You chose the venue, eh 'Sweets'—your favourite spot at Long Acres!" joshed Mr. Bryant with his daughter as he sauntered into the room, carrying lunch and joining the youth table. Karlee glared at her old man, unimpressed by his intruding presence, let alone his teasing use of her nickname.

Lisa and her lanky sons gregariously followed Ted. Mrs. Bryant further embarrassed Karlee by sighing, seemingly for her daughter's instruction, "These past few days living in Zambia have surely taught me to adapt and be flexible. Patience is certainly a virtue—it allows one to explore different ways of doing things, all equally valid I suppose, if they work—depending upon who does it."

After some initial stiltedness, the Canadian party chattered around the communal table as they enjoyed their savoury soup and side dishes: assorted crackers; sharp cheddar, smoked gouda wrapped in red wax, holey Swiss, and fermented blue Limburger cheeses; sliced salami, pastrami, smoked or spicy hams; and ox tongue. A Zambian waiter, dressed in white uniform complete with starched cap, came by to pour tea or coffee from shiny flasks, and serve cream or sugar, supplied in crystal vessels. He periodically returned to replenish drinks or clear away dishes.

Conversation seemed amicable at first, but Orwell sensed tensions rising between Karlee and her family. Having already been unflatteringly pegged by her parents as uncooperative, lazy, and addicted to cigarettes, Karlee endured further ridicule by her brothers in front of their visitors by being labelled a witch. John related how his sister drank tea prepared from various green leaves and pretty flowers she had collected around Long Acres, and brewed over a little wood stove that she had finagled from a chambermaid. Jim described the gory details of Karlee dripping a cup of poisonous white latex, tapped from poinsettia shrubs, into an ant nest she had found behind her room—the tiny warriors furiously erupted, only to be scorched by a beam of sunlight Karlee sadistically trained on them with her magnifying glass like some ray gun. Such bizarre revelations warned Orwell that he and Karla Eve should never be friends—she was totally messed up! Alicia stared anxiously upon the young female boiling opposite her.

"Liars—you freaking clods helped me! It was your damned idea as much as mine! Stop sticking pins into me!" Karlee shouted angrily at her brothers, making their day.

Her outburst made Karlee look like a foul-mouthed, high-strung junior-high teen rather than a cool and beautiful, twenty-two-year-old woman she wanted to be. Somebody should paddle her bum and wash her mouth out with soap! Karlee's vicious act of kicking Josh in the balls suddenly flashed into Orwell's raw memory; it was time for him, Alicia and Tug to leave—now!

The pesky lads giggled at their visitors' sudden reaction, and Mr. Bryant became enraged at Karla Eve, regardless of who else heard or saw.

"Is this how you waste your time, girl?" Karlee's livid father rebuked his distraught daughter. "I told you three days ago to get started on your school work. What's the matter? Do you need another spanking to make you set your priorities?"

"No! For God's sake, give me a break!" wailed Karlee, slapping the table in defiance and frustration. Tears streamed down her red, twisted face as she harangued her riled family, further airing its soiled laundry, before shocked Orwell and Alicia. "I did not ask to come to Zambia with you, and I certainly will not take any more shit and abuse here now. Goodbye to you all!"

Sobbing, Karlee fled from the room. Ted glared after her, but rather than follow in hot pursuit, Bwana Hughes's new agricultural engineer grimly held onto his seat and simmered down.

"Karla Eve's just being a brat, Orwell and Alicia; she's acting out to seek your attention, gain your sympathy," Lisa apologized on behalf of her speechless husband and glibly unashamed sons. "I'm sorry you had to witness such a tantrum. Karla Eve's not always so wild...She's usually quite pleasant when not stressed out. Hopefully, she'll settle down once we become more acclimatized, and get into our own house."

"Adjusting to new surroundings takes time," soberly acknowledged Orwell. Conferring with subdued, pale-faced Alicia, he suggested, "I think we better go."

"Please don't tell your parents about this little flare up," Lisa begged as she and her husband quickly ushered Orwell and Alicia from the hostel. "We're trying our best to fit in and get started on the Zambian scene by the right foot. Every family has problems—hopefully, they come and go."

"I understand," Orwell agreed, walking softly in the diplomatic shoes of his father on such delicate matters. Young Bwana attempted a chuckle as he winked at Alicia, "We at Hughes House act just as weird sometimes."

Alicia sheepishly laughed, catching her cohort's drift. She stopped with the others now at the gate to *Long Acres Hostel*. Before they parted, however, Lisa beseeched Orwell, not only on behalf of her daughter, but for the entire Bryant family's collective peace of mind. "Have you considered our need of a tutor for Karlee? She's a bit old and street-wise to enrol at the International School, but our little girl still needs to finish grade XIII—by correspondence this time around—in order to get anywhere decent in life. She has all the course materials here for English, Maths, Chemistry, Physics and Biology, which should keep her busy for months, but Karlee needs some face to face instruction and direction... at least to get started."

"She's got to get motivated and go forward, but how?" demanded Ted, looking totally mad and frustrated. "I can talk to my daughter until I'm blue in the face, but now she just needs a good boot in the backside to get moving."

"We've tried discipline and tough love, yet that's not the way either, especially for Christians," Lisa countered, glaring at her husband but refusing to escalate their argument. "Karlee's gone through enough hell in her young life already—we don't want to break her spirit or totally alienate her. She, like anyone, benefits from positive reinforcement.

"Karla Eve is actually a very clever student but she needs quality time from someone knowledgeable, with whom she can discuss her ideas, but also ask questions when she doesn't understand. Son, your mother thought you could tutor Karlee: help her start, keep trying, get through her courses...particularly in English."

"Mom has mentioned the idea to me already," Orwell admitted, showing empathy for Bryants' problem, but not much enthusiasm for solving it. "I will consider it, although I don't know exactly when or if I can tutor Karlee. I'm due back at university any day now, and I also have pressing prior commitments to fulfill."

Alicia gave her companion a questioning look, which weakened Orwell's argument in front of Karlee's parents, who grasped desperately for his help now as last resort. Orwell ground his teeth, but did not voice his frustrations. Had Alicia forgotten Saturday's big fight or exotic holiday excursions with Tracy in the offing? Orwell certainly did not need another crazy female bothering him—especially with Karlee behaving like a real piece of work; Georgina, Molly, Kathy, and Alicia were trouble enough! Perhaps the multi-talented daughters of Reverend and Pearl MacDonachie could consider being Karlee's study buddies—had not Kathleen aced high school before entering a Christian liberal arts college? Did not Alicia have a pile of her own Grade XII text books and assignments from a posh, private school to work through? They must talk later to solve this dilemma.

Not one to turn the poor away, however, Orwell gave Lisa and Ted some hope for now, promising to get back to them next week concerning their request. They thanked him profusely, relieved at potential sunshine breaking through the dark clouds that presently hung over their lives. Ted's jaunty smile returned and Lisa clung affectionately to her husband as they waved goodbye to their departing guests.

Orwell ran at full speed towards home, weaving through honking traffic like a speed demon across the busy, five-point roundabout, then raced south on Nationalist Road clear to Independence Avenue before stopping to take a breather. Sweat bathed his red face as he leaned, breathing hard, against a dormant jacaranda. Feeling sick, he teetered over and up-chucked into open drain, when a warm, comforting hand touched his shoulder. His nausea abated now that Alicia stood by his side, caring for him in his distress; Tug barked his concerns as he paced underfoot. It was the first time since the Long Acres debacle that Orwell had seen his mates—or even known they were still with him!

"Whew, that was close," Hughes whispered hoarsely as Alicia tenderly guided him back from the brink.

"What were you doing?" she beseeched him, "What were you thinking?"

"I needed some wind in my hair—you know, blow off the crud? Now I need a huge drink of Adam's Ale to quench my burning thirst!" Orwell cried as he grabbed the water canteen that Alicia offered him. He took a first gulp to rinse his dusty mouth, then swallowed fresh water. Able to speak, having whet his whistle, Orwell gnashed, "What an awful experience we had back there!"

"We all did...really Orwell, everyone lunching in that dive! How does that mother cope with such fricking BS?" Alicia, full of righteous anger, begged to know. She then chastised his father and the whole Canadian development mission in Zambia for hiring the Bryants and placing them in such a deplorable position. "That family is in trouble, guaranteed! They shouldn't have come here—or brought her along, anyway! Karla should go home, as she won't fit into Zambia!"

"I feel sorry for Karla Eve! It was decent of her to help me catch Tug and arrange to feed us...Somewhere, she's been hurt badly, but I don't know how to help her—if I even want to...or should. I must sleep on the matter, pray about it often over the next week before I can give the Bryants an intelligent answer."

"Don't bruise yourself lying about, procrastinating over a decision that doesn't take rocket science to figure out," Alicia advised Orwell. Perhaps against her better judgment, she considered which was the lesser of two evils—brazen and volatile Karla Bryant in class or the brutal fight game Tracy played—out of the pan and into the fire! She playfully needled him, "You've got a bigger fight to attend in two days, but we need to get home before you can do anything."

"Amen to that!" agreed Orwell. "We don't need to run helter-skelter the rest of the way, since we're only a mile from home, but we should keep moseying along, nonetheless. Getting a free meal at the proper time was toppers, eh what do you think, partner? Tug got filled as well, treated like royalty. We are blessed—why worry about what we should wear or will eat—God looks after us!"

"He certainly does, as the Lord will also help Karla and her family if they call diligently upon His name," affirmed Alicia, impressed at Orwell's ability to strategically quote scripture. She who loved the Lord and those who loved Him happily testified to her friend as they strolled leisurely towards home along the tree-lined boulevard of Independence Avenue, "Everyone has problems, but God can help us if we ask. I know...He helps me."

*****

UNDERWAY again, the trio kept an easy pace as they cut southward through the upscale neighbourhood of Hughes House. They enjoyed each other's light-hearted quips and observations. Orwell complimented how athletic his jogging mate looked in her skimpy uniform; Alicia whooped at his honest observation and voiced her appreciation of the amazingly smooth and effortless strokes of his brawny frame. They were both drawn to Tug's boundless energy as he led the way. Could they but bottle and drink the elixir of his mighty spirit!

The cool afternoon buzzed with the din of barking dogs as Tug and two white joggers ran the gauntlet through the canine's sworn enemies. For reasons known only to Tug, every postcard-perfect yard lining the route to his domain bristled with hounds that threatened retribution upon this swaggering charlatan. He held his tail high, and ignored such miserable rabble as he paraded by with his two humans in tow.

Three raging mongrels suddenly charged out from behind a spiked wall at the bottom of the hill and tore into this intruder! Tug was ambushed! The ensuing donnybrook gathered a baying mob of hounds that nipped sadistically at Tug as he valiantly struggled to escape. Bellowing curses, Orwell waded into the fray, but his superhuman efforts to separate such blood-lusting combatants were futile! These vengeful beasts were locked in mortal conflict, heedless of his puny efforts to pry Tug loose. Alicia, a lesser though wiser warrior, shouted advice from the sidelines, and took advantage of a few select opportunities to pull on a leg or whack a powerful torso in the dog pile with a stick.

Colonel Cedric Rainsforth, a starchy British neighbour whom Orwell vaguely knew as President of the Lusaka Flying Club, suddenly appeared with a troop of Zambian servants. Inflamed by this battle royal conflagrating outside his gate, Rainsforth ordered one of his men to turn a high-powered garden hose upon the brawling scrum of dogs. Grimly commanding from the curb, the English field general next ordered his platoon of stone-throwing, club-wielding servants to end the melee. He then fetched his lorry while his shouting storm-troopers slowly scattered the yelping brutes. Hurtling down his long, tree-lined driveway and wheeling aggressively onto the street, the commander screeched against the battlefield and ordered half-mutilated Orwell to hop aboard. Tug, although badly wounded, mustered his last ounce of fight, and scrambled into the rear freight box with his hobbling master.

"You, young lady, may sit in the cab with me. I will take you all home now," Colonel Rainsforth stiffly saluted Alicia, eying her tattered, water-soaked clothes and sweaty features with disdain. "Hurry now, Miss! My boys can't hold off those mongrels forever!"

He ordered rather than invited the beleaguered young woman to join him. Apprehensively, Alicia stood her ground, glancing furtively from her imposing rescuer to her battered friend in search of advice. Orwell shrugged, leaving the choice of where she rode entirely with the ever-ready warrioress, but also cautioned Alicia to make her decision quickly, so they could all get out of harm's way in one piece. Rainsforth muttered impatiently under his heavy breath at her balk. Then, in a crusty show of chivalry, the old knight climbed down from his mount, marched around the front of his lorry, and yanked open the far door. Compared to the half-naked female who warily studied his every move, this stalwart holdout from the British colonial empire was impeccably dressed for the subtropics in his starched khaki shirt and breeches, sporting leather sandals and grey knee stockings primly folded at the top.

Although seething with impatience, Sir Cedric bowed low, and with a sweeping gesture of his bare freckled arms, politely invited the maiden in distress to mount his steed. “Please enter, Miss, that we may swiftly get on our way.”

Colonel Rainsforth stared incredulously at Alicia when she stubbornly and silently stayed in place. He now inspected her full figure up and down, grading her braless breasts that protruded lusciously through her clinging wet T-shirt.

“I say, Miss, has the cat caught your tongue? I don’t bite, you know,” the wise old lion teased his quarry.

Picking on the older man’s leering ways and feeling very uncomfortable in her revealing attire, which had seemed adequate for cross-country running, Alicia now felt very exposed after her clothes had been drenched by the water hose.

“I’ll ride in the truck box with my boyfriend,” Alicia solemnly informed this randy lord. She, smiling vaguely but hesitantly in appreciation of his masculine attention, added with effort to smooth his ruffled feathers, “Thanks anyway, most kind sir.”

“Poppycock! Suit yourself then, foolish girl,” Rainsforth growled as he glared sternly at her. “I don’t think we’ve met before. What are you doing out here so wantonly displayed? If you really are a decent man’s daughter, you should dress more modestly and take better care of yourself...Men see you!”

“I am a decent man’s daughter—Orwell knows that,” Alicia firmly replied, nodding to Orwell for support as he gazed with mixed awe and trepidation at her from over the top of the truck. “That’s one of the reasons he likes me. And I am dressed for a jog, not for some social event.”

Alicia bowed her head and looked beyond Rainsforth, avoiding any further contact with this scowling rogue as she stepped resolutely past him. She could feel him leering at the full cheeks of her buttocks cavorting inside her skin-tight shorts as she energetically climbed into the truck box like some army private scaling a wall during an obstacle course. Orwell gave her an eager helping hand up.

“That lucky young bloke has every reason to be jolly with an untamed beauty like her for a mate,” the stodgy Brit muttered and shook his head at Inspector Thomas Mwila, his baleful Zambia Police colleague seated inside, as he climbed into the cab. . “She’s probably one of those militant Yankee womens’ libbers, who’ll enslave a gentleman and work him to the bone, before she finally tosses him some tail. If she was my daughter now, I’d teach her sassy bottom a thing or two with a buggy whip!”

The irate flyer drove his grateful rescues to their home while his footmen mopped up the baying canine pursuers. Rolling with the flow, but hanging on for dear life, Alicia and Orwell raged and grinned into the breeze. Tug silently hid, flat on the floorboards behind his master's feet.

"So, I'm your boyfriend now, am I?" Orwell winked as he good-naturedly chided his rough-riding companion. "Is that why you chose to tumble back here with me and Tug, forsaking padded comfort and the cultured company of that fine English gentleman?

"Sir Cedric gallantly served her Majesty in India during his youth before watching another sun go down on the British Empire here in southern Africa! He leads our Lusaka police force like Scotland Yard. He still plays cricket and polo, employs ten servants, and is First Lord of the Lusaka Flying Club."

"Where is Sir Cedric's wife? I'm afraid of his lecherous intentions, if you must know!" murmured Alicia defensively. "I felt like a bowl of plum pudding to that man. He undressed me in his vulgar mind! He must have x-ray glasses!"

Her fierce feline eyes softened as she complimented her friend, "You sir, on the other hand, shoot straight as an arrow, and always behave like a gentleman around women. I trust you, Orwell—so I invented you as my boyfriend to quell his dirty mind!"

"Okay, thanks," Hughes replied humbly, unused to such heartfelt female praise, and honoured to have been chosen as protection. They played shy for the rest of the journey, but smiled knowingly at each other when their soft eyes or fumbling hands met.

Colonel Cedric Rainsforth would have simply driven away after dumping his unwanted load in the Hughes front yard, but finding Bwana Hughes peacefully watering his flowers, the grumpy curmudgeon laid blame at the other man's feet when he queried the curious scene, concerning these incorrigible youths and their flea-bitten animal who had caused such a hullabaloo in his normally tranquil neighbourhood. Bwana Hughes tried his diplomatic best to listen like a quiet little beaver from the western colonies to bellowing John Bull, yet he could not help but momentarily turn away for respite and exchange glances of amused chagrin with Orwell, Alicia, and even Tug as the walking wounded beat a hasty retreat past the disputants, with tails dragging between their legs.

"Son, please ask your mother to brew Sir Cedric, Inspector Mwila, and me a spot of *Red Rose* tea—that special Canadian blend that can't be bought in

Britain? We keep it locked in the liquor cabinet for special occasions," Bwana Hughes calmly requested as the lad dully limped into the house.

It appeared to frowning Alicia, as she hurried Orwell to the loo, that Bwana Hughes failed to realize that his son and dog were torn and bloody, and required immediate medical attention!

The elder Hughes, seemingly to appease Her Sternness, added, "I see you 'men' have been through some ordeal but still able to walk, so I will assume you suffered surface wounds only, and are in good hands. Make sure that your mother tends to you nonetheless, Son… better safe than sorry! And ask Richard to bring us some chairs. We four musketeers will chat about vintage aircraft as we relax for a spell on the deck, while you get yourself bandaged up. Better give Tug a bath while you're at it?"

"Yes, Dad, we'll be fine!" the weary voice of Orwell Hughes acknowledged his father's many requests from somewhere inside the house.

"For Heaven's sakes, Orwell, I will pass on those petty errands," Alicia declared, detaining him only seconds longer as she knelt and swiftly untied the flustered youth's shoes. She then enlisted help from Suzy and JJ, who hovered over the now-collapsed Tug, anxiously voicing their concerns, "Can you girls bathe Tug? I'll bind his wounds after I've tended to Orwell."

"I'm usually tasked with washing Tug," Orwell griped as JJ obediently ran for a washtub and dog shampoo, while Suzanne gave the forlorn animal a drink.

Hushing his protests, Alicia shooed her patient down the hallway and into the bathroom. The would-be nurse inserted the plug and then ran hot water into the bathtub. She quickly pulled down a fresh towel and wash cloth from the linen cupboard, and placed them these in his hands as he stood there, helplessly admiring her every move. Alicia smiled sweetly when their eyes met, yet commanded him, "Clean yourself quickly now, so we can take you into the medical clinic for penicillin and a tetanus shot before they close! Come on, Orwell, strip off your clothes and step into that tub!"

She was almost family, being JJ's best friend and Tracy's kid sister dwelling long in their home; yet, Alicia was still a luscious female of mystery in her own right. Orwell was confused now by Alicia's motives, and shyly held back from going naked in front of her. Did not such a prudent daughter of missionaries and preachers understand his sticky predicament?

He babbled nervously, hoping she might get the hint to leave him some privacy, "A bit of infection I can stand, but I don't want lock jaw! I wouldn't be able to eat then, let alone sing or talk. Okay...I'll take my medicine, though I hate being jabbed with needles."

"It's just a reasonable precaution that you would be wise to follow," Alicia sombrely added. Then, cranking shut the water faucets, she set down further instructions as she prepared to leave the room to his private use, "This sanctuary is all yours now, Orwell; have a good bath, so we can see you clean and dressed in a few minutes."

"Where are you going?"

"To get your father on task, of course! He has to drive you to the medical clinic...after he plies the Colonel," Alicia retorted, as though she was offended that this ragged mortal man should question her comings and goings.

Men were all so needy and helpless! After a long, stern stare of appraisal, she smiled slyly as she assured her subdued patient, "I'll take out these torn clothes to the trash, and bring you back something clean and decent to wear..."

"You are hurt and dirty yourself, my lady. When and how will you bathe?"

"I'll make do with a sponge bath of sorts in my bedroom, safe from prying eyes. I'm not going to bathe with you, Oh-well, if that's what you expect from a naïve, pliant girl like me!" Alicia briskly added, as she bailed a gallon of the steamy water into a pail she had retrieved from under the sink.

Whether the amazon blushed from exertion or embarrassment he could not tell, but she seemed to appreciate his genuine concern for her own health. Alicia grinned as she proudly explained, "My mother gave me more than a few bucket baths while raising her kids in the West African bush! I can take care of myself, so don't you worry, Mr. Man! There are other ways to conserve water besides showering with a friend, although you are my friend! See you in five!"

"Peace at last!" Hughes sighed to himself after Alicia, with a fierce smile still crinkling her face, left him alone and closed the door securely behind her....

The young poet was barely thirty minutes into his restorative bath, and day-dreaming of playing in the wild South African surf with Tracy and Georgina, when Doctor Alicia dutifully returned on her rounds. She banged on the bathroom door. Hearing him splash about like some *Sea World* dolphin, the battle axe bluntly informed *Flipper* that she was not serving him his high tea! Clean clothes were waiting for him on the floor just outside his door; he thus should move his butt along, chop-chop, and get ready to go to the clinic.

Orwell was half-surprised to not find Alicia listening through the key hole or waiting for him in the hallway when he emerged, spic and span, from the steamy bathroom. He then checked the living room, expecting to find her sprawled ingloriously on the couch, reading without permission one of his prized *Orbit* magazines for young Zambians. Hughes then heard her deep, soothing voice and followed it into the dining room, where he found the budding doctor sitting Indian-style on the wood-tiled floor, carefully wrapping Tug's injured torso using strips of bed sheet that JJ cut for her with gleaming scissors, while wet-eyed Suzanne tenderly comforted their pet. With gauze, cotton swabs, and makeshift triangular bandages neatly piled at their elbows, and pans of clear water steaming nearby, the girls operated a makeshift sick-bay on the family's eating table! Ominous odours of soap and disinfectant overpowered the delicious aromas of supper that Kathleen and his mother were preparing in the kitchen. To get through that mayhem without being medicated was his goal, but Orwell was unable to make smooth crossing....

"That should do until a vet can see you," Alicia brightly assured Tug who, to Orwell's amazement, had not only lain obediently still in her hands throughout his ordeal, but now gave his caregiver a feeble lick of appreciation. Aware that he was finally free to go, Tug gingerly struggled to his feet, and gave Orwell a whimpered greeting upon seeing his master stiffly watching through the door way. He then hobbled into some dark place of quiet rest for the remainder of the evening.

Glimpsing Orwell nervously admiring their handiwork from the doorway, Alicia smiled as she jumped up to greet him.

"You're next, Bucko," she chirped sweetly, yet unnerved him as she smoothed down the bloodstained apron tied around her blue cotton dress, and reviewed his tardy arrival with dark, unblinking eyes. Suzanne and JJ grinned deviously with wraps and scissors in hand as the doctor, snappily donning a clean pair of rubber gloves, pleasantly beckoned Orwell to come in and sit down, "Let's see what wounds *you've* got to bind."

"Only aches and pains, I reckon—just flesh wounds."

Orwell's bid for an easy exit did not wash with his knowing caregiver. His attempt to appear strong and courageous sputtered like a failing engine as she guided him into the patient's chair.

"Orwell, now really," Alicia mused demurely, arching her brows at this foolish boy while she sat him down. After enjoining him to relax, she carefully unfolded and inspected his injured limbs one by one with great care.

Then, amazing everyone with her ability to calmly take charge and retain control, she supplied her grudgingly cooperative guinea pig with a more telling prognosis, "Now that all the dust smudged with blood and dog saliva is washed off, Orwell, I can see how scratched up you actually are. There aren't any puncture wounds from the bites, thank goodness, but those battling teeth and claws sure gave you some nasty lacerations. I will bandage the worst of the lot now before we take you to see Dr. Jones."

"Ouch, that hurts!" Hughes grouched, defensively pulling away as she lightly dabbed turpentine-smelling antiseptic on his slashed forearm with a Q-tip. Eying Alicia suspiciously, as if she was purposely tormenting him, he tried to wrestle himself free from the searing potion she had struck him with. He strenuously complained, "This stuff stings worse than iodine Mom painted our cuts with as kids!"

"Better a little remedial pain now than you getting sick with some awful bacterial infection," Alicia sang coarsely as she determinedly drew his arm back on the operating table. Despite his groans and grimaces, she worked skillfully to disinfect several more rips in what she marvelled to call his fine copper skin.

"I am not your sweet, soft chamois," snorted Orwell, insulted that this rough-hewn girl would somehow regard him as effeminate.

"I never said you were, my shiny new penny!" Alicia affectionately teased back as she continued to meticulously cleanse his battle wounds. Orwell gnashed his teeth but let her work.

He must be manlier than her, however tough and wild Alicia pretended to be! Yet, Alicia had a hot temper and a tenacious will; she, to his everlasting frustration, could beat him at sports, games, and arts. She came from a talented and powerful family, but Miss A. MacDonachie was just a roly-poly girl...He saw her female curves gorgeously displayed every day! Now he gulped nervously when, appearing to read his silly little mind, the amazon gazed upon him with benign amusement, as though she held many more secrets waiting for him to discover.

"Stop being such an *eway*![68]" chided Suzanne. "Honestly, Alicia, this guy

---

68 *Eway*: A word for 'little boy' or 'child' in the vernacular languages of Lusaka.

faints at the sight of paper cuts! He can only give blood or receive an injection while lying on a bed and keeping his eyes closed!"

"Your big brother acted like a brave warrior today when saving Tug from being ground into dog food!" Alicia softly praised Orwell now, to his amazement and chagrin. What did she want now from him? Nothing, it appeared when *She* appealed to her gloating assistants for proper bedside acumen by sternly asking for materials. "We need to apply dressings now, Suzy! JJ, bring the white adhesive tape!"

This first-aid goddess covered Orwell's first wound with a square block of medicated gauze that Suzanne had offered her using tongs; then she applied pressure with her rubberized hand until JJ taped the dressing in place. Alicia secured larger patches by wrapping them with long strips of gauze, the end of which she tucked in neatly and attached with a safety pin. This process was skillfully reiterated until every square inch of Orwell seemed stippled by compresses.

"What skill! What know how!" Hughes marvelled at the ease with which his medic nimbly carried out tasks that would have been awkward chores for him to fumble, especially had he been bandaging her.

"I believe we're done. That's that!" Alicia concluded after keen inspection of her handiwork, which heralded respite from her litany of demands for "dressing!"..."tape!"..."gauze!"..."pin!" with parroted responses from her two nurses. Sighing with relief, Alicia blushed as she offered, "Thank you all for your help. Let's tidy up here quickly now."

With all eyes curiously watching her, Alicia matter-of-factly closed up her medicine bottles and slipped off her gloves. Orwell, who hated wearing such clingy mitts to wash dishes in boiling bleach water, was amazed that this clever medicine woman could easily shed hers without turning them inside out. Unbeknownst to him, she had powdered her hands with talc prior to donning gloves. Alicia grinned as she planted a peace sign on her stunned admirer's face.

"Orwell, you look like a mummy!" giggled Suzanne as she walked past him towards the kitchen, bearing the water pan.

"A mummy in diapers," quipped JJ, jovially giving Orwell the once over as she reassembled the household First Aid kit. "Lisa, you showed lots of skill with diaper pins—you'll make a good mother someday!"

"Girl, I baby-sit tons of little nieces and nephews," Alicia briskly informed JJ as though she were a naïve child rather than a bosom buddy. Gazing distantly out the window at the setting sun, her mood suddenly darkening, Alicia muttered in almost supernatural tones, "I'll help others raise their children and do my best for these little ones to thrive, but as long as this world remains unsafe for children, I won't give birth to any of my own!"

The stern edge to her husky voice and the tears welling up in her flashing eyes startled Orwell and JJ when Alicia turned back to face them. She stared grimly in their direction, but these sun-kissed youths soon realized that the distraught young woman was gazing past them. She bore heavy burdens that she could not share with them now. As shadows drifted between them, Orwell fearfully saw Alicia struggle to calm the anguish raging within her; with concerned fascination, he watched her cover her wild, harried face with a mask of pleasant civility.

This was a mask Orwell had seen many times already, but he hoped to respect the lioness lurking beneath. In dancing the game of life with her, they wrestled as friends as well as rivals. Alicia had supported his Easter play with girlish delight. His spirit had soared to hear the God-gifted MacDonachie girls sing angelically in church, but he cherished them more when he saw how respectfully they joined his family and interacted with his African friends. Yet, Alicia was no naïve Sunday school girl visiting from back home!

"Besides," the feline princess purred softly, smiling now at Orwell. "I must first find a good man who can love me and our children."

"There are plenty of fish in the sea," blurted JJ reassuringly, trying to deflect Alicia's attention away from her helplessly squirming brother. "We are still school girls, you and I."

"So we are, today at least...best as we can be," Alicia begrudgingly agreed. Glancing anxiously at her watch and then at shadows seeping beneath fiery trees outside, she scolded everyone, "And, as typical school girls, we've wasted precious minutes gabbing pointlessly about boys, babies, bogeymen, and other such nonsense! Now, we really must go! Orwell, wrap yourself loosely in your bathrobe against the chill—and curious eyes! We'll meet you at the carport in five minutes max—be there or be square!"

"Yes doc, right away," Hughes meekly obeyed. He glimpsed a smile peeking out behind Alicia's frown as she watched him struggle to his feet and stiffly shuffle towards his bedroom.

Leaving him to catch his spinning head and get ready to roll, the girls moved quickly into the kitchen, where the budding doctor showed Mrs. Hughes that the medicine chest was properly reorganized before she allowed JJ to hang it back in place on the wall beside the refrigerator. Meanwhile, Alicia boldly ventured onto the back deck and called out the jaunty, men-only banter club to drive her and Orwell into town.

"You're all ready to come along with us, Doctor Alicia MD, having so efficiently bandaged up my son and ministered to our beloved Tug?" Bwana Hughes asked with dry humour, while Richard and Sir Cedric looked on with glassy-eyed amusement, but Thomas gazed sombrely and made keen observations.

"We await your able assistance, sir," Alicia solemnly replied, curtseying politely. They, Victorian lions all, appreciated her humble manners and modest dress, despite the urgency in her voice she could not completely hide.

"Then, as already discussed, I shall simply come with you," chuckled Bwana Hughes, rising to the occasion with bubbly acquiescence.

"I'm sorry to take you away from friends in the midst of your happy visit."

"Not to worry, my dear. Richard can entertain our esteemed coppers with account of his adventurous flight to Sanje Mountain today. I shall see you at the Flying Club's *braai* upcoming in June, eh Cedric?"

"Unless one of us gets his wings clipped!" chuckled Rainsforth, mellower now than either Richard or James could recall from past run-ins with the snobbish lord. Perhaps Alicia played a small part in lightening his usually dour mood, they mused, as Sir Cedric pleasantly addressed the young maiden with a nod of appreciation now that she had become presentable and shown her skills and manners. "You look comely tonight...it's Miss MacDonachie, I believe? I apologize if we got off on the wrong foot earlier, and I dare say: your blue skirt and white blouse compliment you quite elegantly! I hope you and your young man mend quickly."

"Thank you, sir," Alicia responded graciously, curtseying again for the pleasure of her betters. She jumped on the band wagon to mend fences with the crusty curmudgeon, "Thank you also, Colonel Rainsforth, for intervening in that dogfight to rescue Tug, Orwell, and I from even more serious damage!"

"Any time, Miss. Perhaps, we'll see you at the club's *braai*."

"If my hosts agree to bring me along, I'll talk with you then."

"I hope you will do more than talk," chuckled Rainsforth, throwing out his barrel chest and displaying his strong teeth and granite jaw like a baboon for the cautiously pleasant young woman. The three pilots laughed heartily at her shock.

"Pardon me?" Alicia, startled by the Colonel's brazen quip, burst forth with disgust, and forgetting herself, blurted, "Whatever do you mean, sir?"

To allay her sudden fears, however, the old man lifted his wine glass in toast to the world-famous child star of stage and screen as he casually invited her to perform at the club's fete.

"James informs me that you and your equally charming sister Kathleen are highly accomplished singers and musicians, of that lofty quality we aren't often entertained by here in southern Africa. Perhaps, you talented young ladies could provide a little program for club members some Saturday night? We're not a church crowd per se—more like a nightclub—where a little pop, jazz, or folk music will do fine. Think about it, Miss?"

"We provide only the most reputable entertainment. We've practised all sorts of songs lately for various venues," promised Alicia sweetly.

*****

MOMENTS later, Alicia and Bwana Hughes were driving downtown, resolutely conducting their vital medical mission. Seated miserably in the front seat beside his father and under strict supervision from Alicia in the seat behind, Orwell pouted over being pressganged by his uncaring foes. Richard raucously teased about the huge needle bro was about to receive in his backside! His pride was also stung because he had refused Alicia's advice to cover up, and now felt like a freak show to every passerby.

Suddenly, Orwell's worst nightmare came to life as Tracy MacDonachie drove past, going the other way in a big car full of people. Tracy gazed curiously at the mummy seated beside James Hughes, but Orwell stared straight ahead to avoid eye contact with his mentor. Alicia, who had also seen Tracy, smiled broadly, waved vigorously, and gaily hailed her brother through the open window as the vehicles passed by each other. Orwell groaned with embarrassment and tried to hide, deducing that if Tracy did not recognize the Canadian High Commission's black Mercedes Benz limousine, he certainly could not miss the boisterous cheers of his sister greeting him from inside it!

"By Jove, Orwell! I believe that was your pal, our illustrious boxing promoter, Tracy MacDonachie!" declared Bwana Hughes, turning to address the ball of gauze wrappings his son had morphed into. "Should I stop to greet him?"

"No, for God's sake Dad, don't!" wailed Orwell. "Drive to *Long Acres* as fast as you can, but lose Tracy, so he doesn't follow us. I don't want him to see me weak like this! He'd just bug me with all sorts of humiliating questions about my injuries!"

"Okay, Son. We'll keep just stay on track then. We're almost there. I can see the Freedom Fighters Roundabout up ahead, with the *Kentucky Fried Chicken* kiosk on the right," added Bwana as they motored steadily onward. He chuckled as he tossed out his otherwise dry, off-the-cuff remark, "Although I know it's popular back home, I don't have any craving to eat the Colonel's finger-licking, fried chicken over here! Zambian fast food seems like an oxymoron—out of place."

"Yes, we certainly are on an emergency mission now, but under better circumstances, Orwell, you know we would try our best to rendezvous with my brother," Alicia vowed, hurt by his avoidance. Had they not run like bosom buddies along these same roads just hours earlier? A dismal silence followed as both young people wrestled with their frustrations of missing Tracy.

Suddenly, Alicia squealed with joy, "Look, he's pursuing us now like a rally driver, weaving through traffic! Tracy is camped right on our bumper! Orwell, he's signalling us to pull over!"

"Suffering succotash, Alicia! Don't you understand English? I do not want your brother to see me like this!" roared Orwell as he turned wildly upon her, but his rage only entertained his wickedly grinning tormentor.

She enthusiastically pointed Tracy out for him, but by her swirling gestures, brought Orwell's bandaged face smack dab into the playboy's keen notice. Mentor and student then locked gaze on each other for what seemed like an eternity. The two fancy cars smoothly circled the roundabout in sequence, as if on a merry-go-round. While Alicia laughed madly at the joy ride, the frazzled young poet deduced that his father was purposely playing slowpoke in hopes that Tracy would overtake their car. After making several revolutions as a patient observer, MacDonachie poshly saluted Orwell's party with a toot of his horn, then aggressively pulled out and surged past.

"How's life, pal?" Tracy asked jovially through open windows, winking at Orwell with his eagle eyes as they rode abreast. "Dressing early for Hallowe'en?"

In one horrible, fleeting instant Orwell spied Georgina, dressed in her finery, gaily perched under the comfort of Tracy's wing. Ali sat regally next to her, riding shotgun and gazing dangerously at everyone through his cool mirror shades, while several nattily attired young men rocked to *Afrobeat* music in the big back seat. Tracy, dressed leisurely in a fluorescent beach shirt and sporting golden chains across his muscular chest, certainly was not toting a bunch of boxing stiffs to the gym! On the town for an evening of dining and dancing was more likely. They all smiled gaily and waved breezily at Orwell; when he did his best to lay low in utter embarrassment, Georgina greeted social butterfly Alicia, and wished she could join their party.

"We'll get together real soon, Orwell, I promise," Tracy insisted as he floated abreast with his downcast friend, "Then, you can tell me all about your wounds!"

"Sure, man," Orwell nodded gloomily. "I'll wait by the phone for your call."

Tracy zoomed out of the circle and disappeared, apparently unconvinced of the lad's sincerity, but bent on leaving their game to deal with other, more manly business.

Orwell brutally lost it then! Stamping down his swollen foot on the entire idiotic charade, he furiously declared to Tracy's mixed-up sister, "Annie Fannie, I'm totally fed up with you and Tiptoe! Get your fat butt out of this car!"

"What?! Why?" cried Alicia, shocked and dismayed by his blustery threat to abandon her . "I don't even know where I am, or how I'd get back to the house!"

"I couldn't care less! Figure something out quick," jeered Orwell at her huge watery eyes, which he assumed brimmed crocodile tears. "Put out your thumb to hitchhike—maybe Tracy, Benjamin, or that nice Colonel Rainsforth will ride by like knights in shining armour to give you a lift—all the way back to Canada!"

"Please, no!" she sobbed in profound frustration at his seemingly baseless rebuke. "I want to stay with you, Orwell."

"Lad, that's no way to talk to the young lady," chided Bwana Hughes as he turned their sleek limousine into the long, leafy driveway of *Long Acres Hostel*. Alicia intently listened, but with her luminous eyes respectfully lowered, as the crusty diplomat defended her. "She's innocent of any crime, just having fun with you and her brother after a hectic afternoon. I am surprised that you would stoop so low as to make Alicia walk the plank after all the gentle care she gave just now, bandaging you and Tug!

"Don't we stick together...reach our destination as a team? I know you are frustrated, Son, but you'd better think upon your words before blurting them out so harshly."

Heavy silence reigned as they rolled into the bastion of colonial tranquility still holding fast amid hubbub of the vibrant, modern city. Bwana Hughes greeted the sentry, who opened the gate to let them pass. Winding among bougainvillea hedges and beneath great umbrellas of jacaranda and flamboyant trees, they finally came to a stop before the stately welcome of *Long Acres'* great lobby doors, with their glimmering lamps, stone steps, and spacious verandas. Orwell knew that this sanctuary was as tenacious in upholding its culture as did the venerable old church that both he and Alicia had attended as children in the oil boom city of Edmonton. On a much happier day, he would be pleased to stroll with her around these lovely grounds dotted with brilliant flowers and succulent fruit trees, but he was now sorely disturbed; neither would he brook another encounter with weird Karlee or her needy family! African servants dressed in white uniforms glided over to attend to the arriving guests, but Orwell nearly whacked one dude when he threw open his door, whom he felt was patronizing him due to his ghastly appearance. He needed neither help nor pity, just a doctor!

"You children stay here and admire the fireflies, while I go in and fetch Doctor Jones. We'll be off again to the High Commission in a few minutes, so please don't stray," Bwana Hughes advised his crew, giving Orwell a sharp look before he followed the butler into the guest house.

"I can hardly wait!" Orwell groused as he discharged himself from the car. His purpose was strictly business—grab Jonesy, then get the hell out!

Still seething with stung pride and despising the idea of talking with Alicia, let alone looking at her, Orwell limped across the parking lot and sat down on an empty bench to cool off. He glared into space, trying to understand why he had seen the two people whom he loved most—and who *knew* his feelings—riding happily together without any thought of inviting him along. Why was Georgina suddenly taking an interest in Tracy, after all he, Orwell Hughes, had done to impress her at his recent Easter party held in her honour, after so many previous weeks of courting her on campus? Had he not already poured out his love to Georgina in heartfelt letters and through endless acts of affection, that she should understand without a shadow of a doubt, his love for her? He had already briefed Tracy via air mail about these deep feelings—why was his mentor taking his own run at the girl, when he was already married, and could have any starlet he chose at his beck and call? Tracy should be guiding Orwell into a fruitful relationship with Georgina, not claiming the belle for himself. Tied to boxing camp duties indeed—did Georgina keep Tracy too busy to come to Hughes House for supper? Was she that special guest he entertained instead of answering telephones at the hotel? No wonder Georgina was never available to speak with him when Orwell called at her uncle's mansion—she had found another, more suitable man to woo her! Hughes would die trying to understand how his mentor had weaseled his way in!

None of it made sense to Orwell, though the ethereal handiwork of the Lord fascinated the young poet now as he dejectedly watched the last glow of golden sunset scroll back to reveal a black night sky salted with twinkling stars. He noticed that not all lights were the same: some heavenly bodies blazed brighter than others; those that gazed unblinkingly upon him were planets. They all looked down and serenaded him like angels, as if pinned beside his name on the wall of his childhood Sunday school class. Orwell felt with a pang how remote they were, shining from millions of lightyears away, some a few eons closer to him than others, but none lamps screwed into a sculptured roof of the world. The *Southern Cross, Centaurus, Scorpio,* and other constellations were only fashioned in man's imagination – but where different legends were revered depending upon what culture one followed – not purposely grouped into animals, gods, or symbols by the Great Creator, who he hoped was still real out there, listening and caring about his puny life.

Why, of all those billions of rocks or gas balls out there, would God choose to place life on this little blue planet, third from the sun, instead of another planet orbiting Alpha Centauri, the closest star to the solar system, or brilliantly red Antares, or the Dog Star, the latter which shone with scorching brilliance, brighter than all other heavenly bodies? Humanity's sun warmed the earth, and brought light to life, but it was not much of a beacon for him now, a minor star in some backwater corner of the Milky Way! Those Greek tragedies and comedies that Kathy had so romantically spun for him, he had spoiled by hurting Alicia's feelings, demanding once too often that Sea Witch release his hero Tracy from her lair. Had not his mother advised him that he may not always want what he wished for? After seeing Tracy sparking with Georgina, Orwell never wanted to see either his phony mentor or that two-timing bitch alive, anymore!

"I arranged your appointment with Doctor Jones, Orwell. I telephoned to request that he check you out, and asked your dad to drive us here," Alicia quietly reminded him. Looking up, Hughes was startled to find the burly sister of his new rival curtseying before him as she humbly petitioned his favour.

"So, you did, Miss Fix-it!" grouched Orwell disdainfully from his throne. "Are you my fairy god mother? Why even bother waving your magic wand for me!"

"Because I care about you," Alicia blurted out. Then, catching her own girlish emotions lest this temperamental, older youth banish her in his rage, she qualified herself as professionally as possible under their trying circumstances. "As I do all of my friends."

"If you really cared about me, you would discourage Georgina from falling for your brother!"

"And, if you care one iota for me, Bucko, you would not be mad at me for something I have no control over, nor force me to choose between you and my brother!"

Orwell was rendered speechless by the brazen accusation Alicia hurled at him now from close range. Two could play the blame game! She stepped forward during their escalating exchange and now stood towering over him, with one hand firmly poised on her muscular hip and the other pointed menacingly like a pistol at him. She smiled triumphantly when he flinched like a scared rabbit.

"Do I ask you to choose between Georgina and me?" the amazon broached her quarry.

"What?" asked Orwell, dumbfounded by her apparent jest.

"I don't," Alicia firmly reminded him. "I never encourage Georgina, but she probes me about Tracy at any opportunity. It seems that your desired lady has taken a keen interest in him."

"Oh, I see," murmured Hughes with profound disappointment. He gnashed at Alicia, "How the hell does it happen that the girl of my dreams dumps me for my former Christian youth leader?"

"I'm sorry, Orwell." Alicia gently assured him, her voice softening now with genuine respect and concern. "I see how she pains you with such disloyal behaviour. I don't like talking to Georgina about Tracy, because I know that you want her."

She hardened now with resolve. "I shan't encourage her interest in my brother anymore, because it has swollen to the point where Tracy is all she talks about. I don't want to see her face another moment! Georgina is a foolish flirt, barking up the wrong tree. My brother is a father and husband, 'with fields and commitments that cost a pretty sum'[69], while Georgie is just a silly girl who wants fun and attention from handsome, well-heeled men!"

"Okay," murmured Orwell with parched lips, grey with abject despair. His eyes glazed over as he looked sadly upon this grim messenger.

"As I said before," Alicia murmured compassionately. "I am your friend, Orwell. I am here for you because I care about you. I love you."

"Thank you," whispered Hughes. While he held his aching head in his hands, he slid over and invited his friend to sit beside him on the bench.

She quietly joined him, but kept her respectful distance as they waited for Bwana Hughes and Doctor Jones to arrive. This fleeting respite brought some peace.

"There you kids are! I was beginning to worry that you two had eloped!" remarked Bwana Hughes as he came striding up, torch in hand, with Doctor and Mrs. Jones in tow. "Some teenagers do listen!"

"And some also know how to apply First Aid with skill and efficiency," marvelled Doctor Jones as he examined Orwell's plethora of neat but sturdy bandages under the spotlight that Bwana Hughes steadily held for him. He then straightened up and lightly shook Alicia's hand in appreciation. "You have done well, Miss MacDonachie. As a precaution, however, we'll take a closer look at your friend in good light down at the High Commission clinic. Is that okay with you?"

"Of course, sir," Alicia humbly deferred to the learned medical doctor, whom she hoped one day to emulate. "This is why I called you earlier. I want Orwell to receive the best care possible. I wish the same for any injured person."

"Heaven sakes, Robert, you're going to miss supper by dashing off. You know the dining room has strictly-set meal hours; I don't like eating alone!" Mrs. Jones beseeched her husband, unimpressed by the hubbub surrounding a few dog bites. "Surely, this young man who so daringly entertained us the other evening with his simulated airplane crash and flying lessons will heal quite well on his own!"

"I'm surprised he didn't break a leg during those death-defying stunts—almost Evel Knievel he was!" chuckled Doctor Jones without being swayed from

69 Lyrics of "The Wedding Banquet", a Christian folk hymn that gives credence to Jesus' cautionary parable, taught in Matthew 22:1 to 14 of the Bible's New Testament.

his duties as a physician by his wife's complaints. "Why don't you ask the cook to make me up a little doggie bag of assorted cold cuts, some cheese, and a few crackers to eat later in our room with tea when I return; I'd like some sliced ox tongue too if it's on the menu."

"Suit yourself!" retorted the annoyed woman, elegantly attired but looking lost. She snapped at Orwell as he limped past, following the two older men back to the car. "So, you were bit by a pack of wild dogs? Are you sure you don't have rabies now?"

"I think he's safe from that awful disease, but the doctor will make sure. Sometimes, problems we least expect to happen, happen, ma'am," murmured Alicia for her sullen patient.

"Miss MacDonachie, I believe that I met you and your sister while flying down to this subtropical paradise—some brazen stowaways on board our chartered government flight, you are, but a bit young nonetheless to be flying so far from home. You girls were certainly under aged to be drinking champagne! What would your parents think?" interjected the good doctor's wife with chilly sarcasm as she followed the youngsters like a shadow.

"I drank only fruit juices, Mrs. Jones," corrected Alicia, feeling embarrassed in front of curious Orwell. "Kathy, who is nineteen and more emancipated than I, wanted to taste some bubbly since it was being offered for free to any passenger who wished to imbibe. She only drank one glass, and then handled herself quite respectfully, I thought."

"Please! You were both drunk and disorderly!" spewed Mildred venomously, miffed that they were leaving her behind. "I understand you two golden girls sang in Hughes's church on Easter Sunday well enough, although I imagine it was a rather quaint affair for radio/television celebrities. You're likely used to being pampered by servants; it's amazing to see that you are still here...haven't yet become totally frustrated with this haphazard place, and packed your bags out of here for home-sweet-home!"

"I am enjoying my Zambian holiday, Mrs. Jones, even if it's been a bit longer than Kitty-Cat and I had originally planned," Alicia acknowledged with a sigh. Sweetly ignoring Mildred's bitter taunts, the amazon giggled knowingly with Orwell then as she walked easily with her friend. "My time here has been totally adventurous, an awesome learning experience—all I could hope for, Mrs. Jones!"

"Call me Mildred, dear! You're Fannie, if my memory serves me correct."

"That is a stupid childhood nickname that Kathleen still insists on calling me when she wants to belittle me—but I am no longer a child," Alicia briskly informed the stern older woman in Orwell's keen hearing, as she opened the car door for her patient, and enabled him to sit down on the front seat. "My real name is Alicia, which I prefer to go by to friends who choose to call me by my Christian name."

"You are a bold young lady. How is that African boyfriend of yours?"

"I don't know who you mean, Mildred," Alicia answered non-inquisitively.

"That well-dressed, black gentleman who took risqué pictures of you and the Hughes girl all around downtown the other day. I saw you!" Mildred confronted Alicia accusingly, baiting her, "Don't deny it!"

The teenager blushed, sorely taken aback. Rather than argue, she bit her lip, quickly retreated around the back end of the car, and slipped inside.

"You mean Cepheus, my student friend from the university," Orwell calmly interjected through his open window to explain the situation to Alicia's grateful relief. "He and I led a little walkabout, and escorted Alicia and Janice while the young ladies did their holiday shopping spree. Cepheus later visited us all in our home for Easter Sunday dinner."

"You are a trifle impertinent with me, young man!" scolded Mildred, miffed at Orwell's interruption. "My Angela and Gabriel were brought up to respect their elders. They both hold jobs to pay their way; my children rent their own apartments, and are studying hard at university to become useful as lawyer or engineer. They contribute to society, but what are you lot about? This pampered, neo-colonial lifestyle you CIDA kids enjoy down here has dulled your better judgment.

"Don't you get it? You are not on some hip back-packing trip abroad, where you work at odd jobs to get by, so you can party hearty with other prodigals on loose living and psychedelic drugs! Canadian youths like you should not behave so foolishly in a foreign country! You are ambassadors for Canada!"

"I hear you, totally. Every day that we live in this wonderful cross-cultural experience, we try to make the best interaction possible with our hosts," Orwell assured her, knowing painfully well what it was like to live in a fish bowl, as well as earn the right to swim there. Rather than describe his many poignant experiences, however, the young poet shared a heartfelt conviction that inadvertently slapped his detractor in the face. "Mrs. Jones, I am sorry if my behaviour offends you. I am a Christian, and as such, I follow the higher calling of being an ambassador for Jesus Christ. I am not perfect nor am I mature in my faith, but as much as it depends upon me, I try to live in harmony with those around me."

"I did not sign up to become a Christian missionary when my husband took his posting with the Canadian International Development Agency. My spirituality is a personal affair, and so it should be in a diverse, multicultural country like Canada. You will find your homeland much more cosmopolitan when you return there! It is no longer a white Christian land, ruled by men! I am not required to attend church back home, here, or anywhere, especially when I see all the destruction organized religion has foisted upon our world!" Mildred indignantly added, lest these Bible-belt fundamentalists judge her as unfit to serve now for the betterment of Africa. She challenged these two nervously listening young people, "I too can do many good things for social justice and human development—even if I don't believe in God."

"My dear, we should go now. I will see you later," promised Doctor Jones as he, having finally split off from discussing various sundry affairs of state with Bwana Hughes, ambled between the two arguing parties and took his place in the back seat, while his leader regained the steering wheel of the limousine.

"Sorry for the delay," the doctor joked with others already accustomed to African time, little realizing how grateful they were that he brought down the curtain on his wife's relentless tirade. His parting bouquet, tossed out the rear car window to her as they drove off, made Mildred smile if not relieve her stress, "You look splendid tonight, my dear! I savour the thought of nibbling ox tongue later in our quarters with you!"

Once at the clinic, Dr. Jones inspected Orwell as he lay naked on the table under bright overhanging lights in a clean, cool, modern, and well-stocked examination room that rivalled any medical office he had visited in Lusaka, while Alicia chatted with Bwana Hughes in an adjoining sitting room. The doctor marvelled again at the skilled manner in which Alicia had treated the lad's numerous lacerations. Understanding already how virulently infection could set into even the most superficial cut, Doctor Jones provided his patient with antibiotics, and stoically advised him to keep his wounds dry and bandaged while he rested at home for the next few days. He scheduled a follow-up appointment for the next week, unless Orwell came down with symptoms of either redness in any of the wounds or a fever, which could then warrant immediate hospitalization. Then it was time to get dressed and go.

Orwell nodded his head in dull agreement as he and his family consulted with Doctor Jones afterwards in Bwana Hughes' spacious office. Alicia took notes. Yet, Orwell inwardly argued to himself that Jones was either over reacting for Alicia's sake or humouring Bwana Hughes to earn brownie points early in his mission. An athletic man with many active pursuits to foster about town, Orwell felt that he was being severely curtailed by these cautious doctor's orders as if he was some convalescing weakling. By following the cited prescription, would he miss the big boxing match! And did this mean no more Tracy? Georgina be gone? End of glory!

# CHAPTER TWENTY-FOUR

FOR THE REST OF THE evening and through the following day, young Hughes despaired over his rotten luck as he languished in bed, swathed by gauze and woozy with penicillin. While other people went off to school or enjoyed themselves at the swimming pool, he was home-bound by a throbbing headache, and tottered about the house in search of a cool breeze, wearing sunglasses to conceal his swollen eyes and shield himself from the light. Almost delirious, he begged to visit Tracy at his boxing camp; he vowed to crawl to the university to rendezvous with Georgina when nobody would drive him there. Orwell tried to telephone his friends, but neither Tracy nor Georgina took his calls, which only compounded his misery.

Alicia appeared sympathetic, but when Orwell kept calling on her for his every little whim, she unceremoniously banished him to his bedroom, insisting that he must rest and pray to find peace and regain his health. Unless Orwell recovered, she refused to let him attend her brother's boxing extravaganza. Georgina, nurse Alicia sternly pronounced, was *verboten*; the enticing socialite would only torment him in his fragile state!

Nonetheless, stalwart Miss MacDonachie saw to his reasonable wants and needs with gladness. Taking time out from her studies, errands, chores, and social activities, Orwell's caregiver dutifully brought him his meals, and kept his room clean and fresh. She supplied him with the *Zambia Daily Mail,* as well as classic novel comics and *Orbit* magazines to read upon request. Alicia brought him biscuits and lemon tea with honey at mid-morning and during the late afternoon, when she listened to his rants, entertained him with a puppet show, read *The Last of the Mohicans* aloud or sang softly to him—like shepherd boy David had done for tormented King Saul—all freely given in an effort to restore his troubled spirit.

Friday morning, Orwell's promising convalescence was rudely interrupted by loud argument and feet running towards his door—suddenly, Georgina barged into the bedroom, hotly pursued by Alicia! Hughes, leisurely reclining on his bed stripped down to his briefs and expecting no interruptions for at least an hour as he read the newspaper and sipped his wake-up tea, barely had time to cover himself in blankets before the two young women so rudely invaded his privacy.

"I wish to see you, Orwell—I came here straight away when I heard from Suzanne that you had been injured!" Georgina explained breathlessly as she stood trembling before him, appealing for his favour. "Although Alicia tried to dissuade me—like she was paid to guard you as some high-profile political prisoner—it is only proper that I visit my suffering friend!"

Alicia blushed crossly at her rival's bleak insinuation, which adoring Orwell swallowed, hook, line, and sinker. Although astounded by her performance, Orwell smiled as he whispered, "Thanks for your concern, Georgie, but I am not suffering unduly. Alicia has been taking very good care of me, helping me mend."

"Really!" giggled the disarming beauty, flashing baleful nurse MacDonachie a daring smile. "Is she doing penance for being naughty?"

When Alicia glared at her with hooded eyes, Georgina clicked her tongue disparagingly at the pouty girl who was not willing to be her pal today. MacDonachie saw light glimmering at the end of the long dark tunnel, however, when Orwell defended her against the wily charms of her more glamorous rival.

"Georgina, I am very grateful for the kindness given me during this difficult time. My lady friend visiting me from Canada not only cleans my room and brings me goodies, but she entertains me with fun and games."

"Fun and games?" giggled Miss Amadu. As she gazed with wistful jealousy at the two friends, she felt the bond between them, and remarked with a simple, "My, my!"

"It's not what you think, Georgina, so forgive my clumsy explanation. No need to spark a fire with shame on us! Yes, we are close, but everything between us is wholesome and totally above board—just as Alicia and I like to behave. I've enjoyed much-needed respite while my injuries healed," Orwell assured his tempestuous visitor. "I feel like Alicia and I have been travelling on a vacation trip, experiencing a spiritual high for the last few days."

"And we never left this house," added Alicia, winking collaboratively at her upbeat patient. The strong young woman suddenly looked radiant in the morning sunlight from being softly brushed down by so many compliments after their long ride. "I am looking forward to that camping safari we will soon take together with your family, Orwell, before Kathy, Tracy, and I finally go home."

"Maybe you will take me along in your suitcase, my dears," Georgina pleaded. Gaining a crooked grin with *NO* gleaming all over it from the amazon as if she unabashedly asked for the moon, the coloured beauty insisted, "I know where all the best game viewing waterholes are in Kafue and Luangwa Valley parks. I have been there many times already with my uncle and brother—all part of my job as a travel agent. I get Grade A service from all the game wardens!

"Besides, I would love a chance to fix this coarse backstitch hairstyle that those gaggling servant ladies out back gave you the other day, Mairam! You resemble some plain school girl; I would even say that you look like Topsy from *Uncle Tom's Cabin*! You should let me plait your beautiful red hair into the exquisite fashions of West Africa! Orwell has seen them on me, and would approve."

"I'll think about it," Alicia muttered, giving her a wary look.

Charming Miss Amadu returned to her much easier task of brightening Orwell's day. He beamed with pleasure that she had come! He acknowledged the effort that this buoyant visitor had made without demanding more from her. The young poet seemed sensitive to her concerns, but would not confront her about them. Showing respect in kind, Georgina did not embarrass the young lion by asking how he had been wounded. Rather than bore him with trite reviews of shopping trips and parties, Georgina bid to cheer her avid listener with regaling news and a little dance, to illustrate how she had been using this forced vacation from academic studies to improve her physical fitness—he could only admire her impressively-toned figure. A new friend had recently taken her golfing, she added; at his nudging, she now swam every day for two hours at the Olympic swimming pool. Encouraged by Orwell's recent success with the university men's field hockey team, Georgina planned to try out for the women's team in the coming season. She felt such rigorous exercise would nicely augment her training regimen for competitive tennis, which still was her passion but not the only sport in her sights.

"Suzanne and I teamed up recently at Uncle's house to defeat Ali and his clever friends at billiards and ping pong! My fine old uncle taught me well those so-called gentlemanly sports during our many hours alone together in his mansion. He earnestly congratulated our victory, although he was not glad we made good on our challenge! Uncle worries we won a smashing victory for women's liberation, as big as Billy Jean King beating Bobby Riggs last year at lawn tennis! He discourages me from playing tennis against men. His venerable old-school mind finds it totally unnatural and unnecessary for women to prove themselves physically against bigger and stronger males, but Mairam and I disagree with Uncle, being adventurous and independent women with lofty goals to realize, and impressive achievements already banked."

"Move over, Helen Reddy!" Orwell cheered, reaching victoriously to the roof with his outstretched hands.

The two girls laughed at his rough rendition of the famous "I am Woman" singer, even as they marvelled at how his strong arms rippled despite being bandaged. Alicia clinically concurred that this display could only mean he must be healed! It would soon be time to get those distasteful coverings off!

"Professor Ibrahim warmly greets you, Orwell," Georgina impressed upon her animated listener. "He is tickled to this day that you, a privileged white foreigner, desire to learn so keenly about Africa—her languages, customs, history, modern struggles, and aspirations. Uncle invites you to have tea with him sometime when you are feeling better; perhaps the three of us could humour him before Alicia finally leaves this country...Think about it, Orwell, you are always highly welcome to visit Dr. Ibrahim."

Then, jokingly referring to the now seemingly ancient flap in African Studies class over a silly sheet of white paper, Georgina quipped, "When next he asks about you, I shall remind Uncle that you actually look quite pale when you are bedridden. Maybe, the proud old peacock will find his way down here to greet you in your sickness! I hope you get better soon, Orwell. You look more handsome when you are robust and happy!"

"As I am to be discharged from sick-bay very soon with a clean bill of health, I would be honoured to visit my venerable *African Studies* prof within the week," replied Hughes, pleasantly surprised after having suffered under the wizened educator's austere tutorage. "I like your idea of the three of us visiting him together. We could all chat on the back patio, maybe play some tennis."

"Maybe you could visit Uncle while Mairam trains with me for Zambia's upcoming international racquets tournament against Mauritius," countered Georgina, her serious plan pre-empting his ducky social outing. When Orwell appeared disappointed that he was being left on the sidelines, as though unworthy to engage this star athlete in even a friendly match, Georgina soberly explained, "I need to concentrate on honing my tennis skills, Orwell, not socializing. Mairam, a champion athlete in her own right, knows how to work hard with me, yet at my pace, and for my improvement. She has assigned herself to me for extra practice, over and above all I do at the Lusaka Tennis Club or with the Zambian national team to keep my high ranking.

"We are preparing for a summit tournament now, Orwell, not UNZA house leagues! Zambia, my sponsor, depends upon me to bring home a basket of gold medals for the country's glory. 'The rubber hits the road', to use our good friend Tracy MacDonachie's gritty words, which is why he privately surrounds himself with experienced boxers to rigorously prepare for his prize fight, and why I engage Mairam for personal training before my international tennis meet.

"My dear lad, don't look so glum! After our struggles are over, we can all partake in joyous celebrations together, I promise you. No doubt, you will watch Tracy's bout, but also, being my special friend, Orwell, of course I count on you to attend my tennis meet as an avid spectator, like you always do, to encourage me!"

With that, Georgina gaily bid her adieu and flitted out of the room like a multi-coloured butterfly. Orwell savoured her fleeting presence, but did not wish to keep her when they both could grow uncomfortable by the awkward situation of her new acquaintance. Had she lingered, Orwell would have asked Georgina what Tracy meant to her, but the women refused to countenance this dicey subject. Alicia dutifully escorted their impish visitor to the front yard, where her driver patiently waited in the shade beside Professor Ibrahim's gleaming car.

When Alicia returned ten minutes later, after vigilantly watching Georgina's departure, she shared with her patient that, in her educated opinion, he had recovered sufficiently to move onward and upward from the makeshift hospital. She dutifully removed his bandages and examined his scabbed-over wounds. The budding doctor was impressed by how well Orwell healed; she thanked him for cooperating so willingly while journeying towards recovery.

"Why don't you take a bath and get dressed?" Alicia suggested, smiling guardedly. "By then the others will be home for lunch. Maybe they've heard news about the great boxing extravaganza."

Hughes was pleased that Tracy's little sister was open to him going to Saturday's prizefight, now that he was healthy again. She helped him think less about Tracy, whom he did not contact again until that great and glorious day when he watched Mighty MacDonachie coach the fight of his life!

## CHAPTER

# TWENTY-FIVE

THE EPIC BATTLE WAS NOW at hand! Putting his jealousy aside, Orwell wished Tracy great victory, mighty success! He revelled in his mentor's red-letter day. He surmised that Karl Thompson, whom he knew nothing about, would win because he was a student of The Great One. With his own pride and heritage on the line, Orwell knew he must be present on the battlefield to support valiant MacDonachie, and share in his hero's splendour. The possibility of defeat was nowhere on his radar screen.

As much as Hughes floated on cloud nine, he found no one willing to fly with him on the magic carpet of Tracy's reserved ringside tickets. Benjamin, whom he had tracked down in his cluttered church office, decried boxing as an immoral spectacle, and compared its fans to Romans gorging themselves on food and wine while cheering raucously as Christians were thrown to lions, or gladiators slashed each other to death with swords. Cepheus was too busy ranting against UNZA's unjust labour practices to concern himself with foolish games. Georgina was out shopping for the day, or so explained her dour uncle before counselling Orwell, his apt pupil, to support Africa in her struggle for victory, rather than cheer for his unrated countryman.

Bwana and Mrs. Hughes had gone flying together like a pair of twitter-pated larks. Suzanne, feeling under the weather as she mourned Ali's immanent departure for the UK, would read a book in the shade of the back garden, rather than bake in some open-air arena as token blue-eyed, white girl in a raucous partisan crowd. Richard may have accompanied his brother to the fights in his previous life before Kathleen, but when the blonde bombshell turned up her nose at prospect of witnessing blood and guts, he good-naturedly begged off. Sensing the lad's despondency, however, Rick offered to drive him to Independence Stadium. JJ and Alicia, Orwell's loyal companions, were nowhere to be found.

Annoyed at being abandoned by family and close friends on such a vital day, Orwell ground his teeth as he ran to the car. Determined as he was to cheer Tracy—by his lonesome if necessary—he was utterly amazed to see Alicia rise, grinning like *The Great Pumpkin*[70], from her hiding place in the back seat.

"What do you want, 'My-Room'?" Hughes demanded, once he quieted his jumping heart.

"I want to go with you," she pleasantly replied. When Orwell chafed with frustration, the amazon's dark eyes gleamed with resolve as she seriously explained her mission. "I don't like seeing men hit each other, but I wish to support my brother in his serious endeavour."

"I am worried that Thompson will get murderlized!"

"He won't, since pugilistic masters have trained him. Tracy knows how to box, Orwell—you remember that he did well in his career. As a jock girl, I appreciate the strategy and athleticism of all sports he loves. I also feel that you wouldn't mind a companion to sit with, just as I would rather not sit alone. Can't we work this problem out?"

When Orwell studied her face for some inkling that she was teasing him, Alicia snapped in frustration, "This day is not about you, Bucko!"

Feeling immediately foolish for clipping his wings, the amazon begged, "Come on, Orwell, let me come with you. JJ thinks I'm nuts, but I want to go so bad! I care about Karl...but my heart is set on supporting the two Tracys and Rivard, my friends since childhood. I'll be good! I won't embarrass you with stupid questions or irritating chatter, promised."

"Fine," muttered Orwell, resigned. He then yelled out the window at his brother, who was frolicking across the lawn with Kathleen like two flower children high on LSD. "Let's go! We're gonna be late!"

---

70 *The Great Pumpkin:* a mythical creation by cartoonist Charles Schulz in his *Peanuts* comic strip, that became the subject of a 1966 American prime time animated television special called *It's the Great Pumpkin, Charlie Brown.* Linus van Pelt won't partake in Hallowe'en's weird cultural festivities (i.e. ghoulish costumes, trick-or-treating for candy, pumpkins carved into jack-o-lanterns, or spirited kids' parties) because he believes that *The Great Pumpkin* will visit him at his 'sincere' pumpkin patch on Hallowe'en Night. *The Great Pumpkin* does not reveal itself to him—maybe next year, Linus hopes.

Alicia assumed that anxious Orwell had accepted her companionship by uttering 'fine' one magical time. She sat softly near him and happily caressed his arm as Richard chauffeured them through the busy traffic.

It seemed to Orwell that everyone country-wide was going to the big bash. Long lines of would-be spectators waited like cattle outside the barred gates of Independence Stadium, where he and his date were dropped off for the event. The huge outdoor arena, built for the Commonwealth Games and used as the venue for all major political, athletic, and cultural events in Lusaka, was already crowded and buzzing excitedly an hour before fight time. Drums pounded and marching bands blasted upbeat tunes into the sultry air. Cultural dancers, clothed in thatched dresses and sporting elaborate masks, waited in the wings.

"We better go find our seats," Orwell grimly suggested, taking Alicia firmly by the hand.

The bright-eyed girl sensed his urgency and willingly followed, despite her penchant to pause every time she glimpsed or heard something new. Alicia was a noticeable young lady in the crowd of bystanders, with her auburn hair cascading down her shoulders complementing her red-lipped smile, golden brown tan, her chic white blouse, and pink cotton midi skirt. Alternately holding onto her sun hat or hand-woven tote bag, and slapping her sandals in the red dust as she ran, Alicia giggled playfully at Orwell's determination to lead her into the ring like some show pony as she trotted friskily along behind him.

Hughes tried not to appear too uppity as he breezed past the dully watching queues of walk-ins and presented his exclusive tickets at the gate. He was a minority in more ways than one, and certainly did not want to broadcast his enthusiastic support for the pariah *mzungu* fighter in front of the Leopard's rabid fans. Today was Orwell's big day to shine, particularly in company of the admiring sister of his hero, whom he now sought to impress.

To Hughes's utter dismay, the Zambian gatekeeper ordered him to the back of the line! When Orwell argued that his tickets had been reserved by a major player of the boxing event—Tracy MacDonachie's signature was emblazoned on them, for God's sake—the gatekeeper curtly replied that no tickets were valid unless stamped as paid by the vendor. This foolish white boy's notes were worthless pieces of paper in fact; only tickets purchased at Independence Stadium's sales counter on the day of the fight were official.

"Orwell, my friend, let's be polite and cooperative, and do what the nice man says. After all, he is the boss here," Alicia coolly advised her frustrated escort. The gatekeeper smiled benignly at her as the sensible girl ushered glowering Orwell aside.

"We've lost our place! Now, we'll never get inside!" Hughes berated Alicia with gulping breaths and gesturing hands as he hustled hard to keep up with her swift march to the rear of the line, which was now three blocks away!

"Oh, yes we will," Alicia replied with sing-song faith. Gently turning him around and pulling him into line with her, she promised, "God rewards those who believe in His grace when they do the right thing—sometimes in ways that we do not expect."

"Your jerk of a brother purposely set me up for this fiasco!" Hughes concluded irately, scowling red-faced at his companion. "He's the toast of Zambia's sports world—why does he need to embarrass me like this?"

"Although he tries hard, Tracy does not know all, nor can he control everything. He likely was unable to get you actual ringside tickets. Besides, Tracy is coaching a young man today in the biggest bout of his career—he does not have time to purposely mess with your life," Alicia solemnly muttered to her companion as their queue inched slowly but surely towards the gate.

When Orwell took comfort in her words of wisdom, and did not jaw further about Tracy's perceived slights against him, Alicia winked at him. Later, as their line of colourful fight fans shuffled into the shade under the stadium bleachers, she smiled appreciatively, and lovingly held his hand. They were, after all, only two of thousands of people who wanted to watch the epic bout; did others fret about waiting in long queues or not getting choice ringside seats? Hughes chivalrously bought two Cokes from a street vendor who sold chilled refreshments from an icebox lashed to his bicycle. Other vendors, balancing trays of merchandise on their heads, also plied their trade up and down the line of fans, selling everything from cigarettes to bananas, sweets to fried shish-kabobs. It was only Saturday afternoon, but folks were high on a party mood, decked out in their Sunday best, with many sporting the latest *Polaroid* sunglasses or flashy watches and listening to *Afrobeat* or American pop chart toppers—Johnny Nash's "Stir It Up"[71] and "Spirit in the Sky" by Norman Greenbaum—on their ghetto blasters before scheduled attractions should unfold.

---

71 "Stir It Up" was originally composed by Bob Marley in 1967, and sung by Marley's group "The

Alicia offered her beau a satisfied smile as they made it through the turnstiles, just in time. The gatekeeper was glad to see polite Alicia again, and warmed by her warm smile and pleasant banter. When contrite Orwell did not say a peep, he let them pass without incident after the lad humbly paid the fare. The young couple found two fairly decent seats near the middle of the stadium, close enough to ringside that they could see all the action...amazing, considering that the high-profile event was general admission, on a first-come, first-served basis. Orwell and Alicia were the only white people as far as their eyes could see, but even though they sat among total strangers, all those around them were festively cordial.

The crowds stood and cheered raucously for Leopard Milongwe when he entered the ring to fanfare and bold pronouncements, pounding drums and trumpet blasts. They lauded every move Milongwe made, every shadow punch he threw or dodged, but hissed as his sullen opponent and fierce handlers, anchored by wily Tracy MacDonachie, sauntered into view. The vast, partisan audience understood that Europeans followed Karl Thompson, so let Orwell and Alicia be when the youngsters politely applauded for him, the local favourite's unknown, long-shot challenger. Unlike those racists lurking south of the Zambezi River, entrenched by heavy, modern arms and draconian laws, Thompson and his two fans were not dangerous to black Africa's champion or his legions of followers gathered to witness the Leopard gallantly defend his turf!

Alicia was a good companion—much better than some blind date! She made sure they had essentials, like sun hats to protect them, water to drink, and peanuts to munch on. They enjoyed a strange assortment of entertainment provided between preliminary bouts featuring up-and-coming Zambian boxers: a band of men dressed in leopard skins and army boots stomping across the stage to the sounds of drums and horns; belly dancing by a deceptively heavy man in shorts; a choir of schoolgirls singing traditional songs, and as though aiming to specifically entertain the young white couple, Lusaka Regiment Band performed the lilting tune "Believe Me, If All Those Endearing Young Charms".

*The Rising Stars* performed their upbeat signature song "Tiyende Pamodzi", to the delight of all. Orwell's escort was favourably impressed when he showed

---

Wailers" as a single in 1967. The Wailers subsequently recorded "Stir It Up" on their album "Catch a Fire" in 1973. "Stir It Up" was also covered by Johnny Nash in his 1972 album "I Can See Clearly Now".

her how this buoyant troupe of African boys accompanied themselves with accordions, not to mention melodicas, a string bass, and various percussion instruments: drums, tambourines, and a triangle for the gala occasion. Orwell exclaimed that *The Rising Stars,* who played at virtually every important venue throughout the land—at the State House and five-star hotels, agricultural shows and fund-raising campaigns, as well as for private parties and hospitals to entertain the patients—were also famous performers on Zambian television and radio. What had begun as a scout group with natural musical aptitude had blossomed, through hard work and determination, into the country's brightest and most promising group of young musicians.

"I believe you, Orwell, I can see it!" assured this member of the world-famous *MacDonachie Family Singers,* smiling at his efforts to spark her interest. She celebrated with hand-smacking high fives that he knew how she loved accordion music!

Alicia was jovial and made small talk when appropriate, but she also got into the strategies and moves of the boxing matches. While Thompson and Milongwe relentlessly duked it out late into the afternoon, their expatriate fans became sunburned and dehydrated under the Zambian sun. Alicia fanned Orwell vigorously with her hat between rounds, then handed him a bottle of ice-cold Coke from her tote bag. She let Hughes fan her with the hat she had brought for him, while she drank deeply from her bottle of orange Schweppes and grinned with dreamy satisfaction. Her dark almond eyes sparkled and her full red lips enthralled him. Impulsively, Orwell snapped her black and white photo with his old box camera. He nodded, and tipping his hat dapperly to the amazon, exclaimed, "Hey babe, you are a beaut, not bad at all!"

Thompson and Milongwe fought hard and well for fifteen action-packed, championship rounds. Although Thompson was worthy, Milongwe won most of the early rounds because he was faster and more cunning than his lumbering opponent. Leopard stalked his prey warily like a wild cat, then suddenly moved in with lightning blows that caught Thompson flat-footed. Rocked early and often, Thompson was knocked down with a hammering left hook in the fifth round, bringing the huge, partisan crowd roaring to its feet for victory by Africa's hero, but then the no-name Canadian bounced off the canvas at the count of seven and never looked back.

Thompson counter-punched courageously. He parried Milongwe's jab and ducked underneath his vaunted left hook with powerful body shots. Thompson's secret uppercut suddenly lifted Milongwe off his feet and sent him crashing to the mat midway through the fight. Noisily urged on by thousands of fans, the African valiantly struggled his feet. Stumbling on rubbery legs, he desperately tied up his charging opponent in a clinch. Breaking free, the bigger and stronger Thompson cornered his opponent against the ropes, and laid a flurry of punches upon him to end of the round. He could not finish the Leopard off however; like the proverbial cat with nine lives, Milongwe not only weathered the storm, but came boldly back on the offensive. Karl was cut over the eye, yet refused to wilt as Leopard and his crowd of wild fans moved in for the kill. Thompson survived the round by dodging his opponent's blows, but would likely have quit on his stool had not Tracy implored his prized fighter to keep going, and shouted advice from his corner on how to protect himself when wounded in battle. Tracy Rimond and Rivard did a stellar patch job between rounds to stem the flow of blood, and kept Karl's aching arms supple with massage and ointments. Milongwe went after Thompson's bandaged laceration at every opportunity, causing his opponent to bleed again. The referee kept a vigilante eye on the cut, and threatened to stop the fight by technical knockout.

Karl, spurred on by Tracy's cracking whip and intense focus, seemed to fight better when hurt. He bloodied Milongwe's nose with a powerful right in the twelfth round, which he fiercely followed up with crashing hooks and uppercuts that turned the tide again in his favour. Both fighters landed many quality shots, but also took telling blows in stride. There was no time to backpedal; they were fighting toe to toe and swinging hard upon each other when the final bell rang. Exhausted, the two gladiators embraced, and raised each other's hands in mutual congratulation, to acknowledge the wildly cheering crowd, before fading to their respective corners to nervously await the judges' decision.

As each man had earned a win, their fight was rightly declared a draw—unprecedented in a heavy-weight boxing championship! Although Milongwe technically retained his belt, the dominantly black audience vociferously booed the unexpected outcome. Thompson had failed to knock out the Leopard, but the upstart white fighter had scored a tremendous upset nonetheless to catch the judges' eyes even in their partisan sight. He had powerfully risen to the occasion to grasp the most of his faint hope title shot. Neither fighter had won or lost outright, but unheralded Thompson had succeeded in claiming a satisfying moral victory: he had earned the draw by thwarting all notions of a home decision in favour of the champion.

Orwell brimmed with elation, but he kept a tight lid on his celebratory mood as he quickly shepherded Alicia away from the bleachers after the controversial decision was announced over the public-address system, lest they be confronted by angry partisan fans. Thank God, nobody bothered any of the expats in attendance. Orwell thought he glimpsed Georgina exiting the stadium with Ali a few rows away, but Alicia dissuaded him from going to them; she, like her escort, was more anxious to congratulate Tracy on his fighter's grand performance. The collaborative pair sought out Thompson's dressing room like blood hounds. Alicia asked her friend the gatekeeper for directions; kindly remembering the adventurous white youths despite backing a different horse, he directed them down the staircase behind him and follow the corridor. Orwell suspected that the gatekeeper might be sending them into a trap, but the old codger proved to be a great tipster. They found both dressing rooms empty, however, as fighters and their handlers had already debriefed, stripped their gear, showered, dressed in civvies, and left the building.

Disappointed but not discouraged, Orwell and Alicia raced towards the daylight gleaming at the far end of the tunnel, where they heard a tumult erupting. Like incorrigible children, Tracy's fans rushed into a billowing crowd gathered on the front steps of the stadium to hear impromptu post-fight interviews. Startled, they hung back against a wall but took everything in.

Thompson and Milongwe stood solemnly side by side, flanked by their respective managers; in the middle of the media scrum stood handsome, quick-thinking Tracy, plum for newsy quotes. A credible ambassador for white people in racially charged southern Africa, MacDonachie was not a brash American nor snobbish like a Brit; the seasoned manager was confident but gentle, unlike bullies who colonized Rhodesia and South Africa. The after-fight crowd grew enamoured by Tracy's grace and humility as much as it appreciated his boxing skills, cool-headedness, and competitive spirit displayed by his protégé in such a crucial match. Alicia and Orwell listened with pride as Tracy thanked Leopard Milongwe and his smiling coach, Isaac Chanda, for giving his own up-and-coming fighter a chance to prove himself against a great Commonwealth champion and worthy contender for the world heavy-weight title!

"Boxing is not a gentle sport; many fighters never enter the championship ring. As challengers to your Commonwealth heavy-weight title, Leopard, all that we asked for was the opportunity to compete; you were generous in accommodating us. We worked hard to honour the opportunity you gave us, and ran well for your money!" Tracy testified, breaking into a good-natured chuckle that spawned laughter from round about him.

Alicia, climbed up Orwell's side as if he was a public leaning post, then exuberantly cheered Tracy and gave him clasped hands of victory. Her hero gave a friendly wave back, but continued to congenially answer the flurry of reporters' questions. Some quick-thinking news camera man flashed Alicia perching precariously atop her human tree. At about that point in time, Georgina sashayed past all the hoopla of the crowd floating upon Ali's arm like some refined southern belle. They tarried to take in the spectacle, and received Tracy's nod of happy approval before gliding on their way. Georgina coyly slipped down her *Polaroid* sunglasses, so that Tracy could catch the meaningful look she gave him with her beautiful brown eyes. She did not seem to notice Orwell, which he thought strange indeed since he stuck out like a sore thumb, strapped with Tracy's weird sister swaying jovially on his shoulders!

"Maybe I seem too far under foot by this female I'm escorting, for gentle Miss Amadu's liking. Maybe she's jealous—who am I kidding...I just wish she was!" Orwell pouted dismally, nearly buckling under Alicia's weight. Georgina and Ali promenaded gaily away to meet their awaiting limousine, pursued by several paparazzi, who had recognized Zambia's premier tennis player and sought her opinion as a celebrity boxing spectator.

Orwell felt less like the sideshow that Tracy did not want, once the local tennis royalty had diverted attention away from him and Alicia. Tracy's little sister, thankfully an unknown compared to Georgina in the public eye, sensed her supporter's discomfort, and kindly relieved Orwell of his burden by slipping off his shoulder and down his front, where she landed exuberantly on the pavement. Hughes intuitively caught the teetering girl around her waist to steady her; Alicia, smiling cutely, gave Orwell a furtive kiss of gratitude before resting casually against him and letting him hold her from behind for the rest of the boxers' interview. Although she was modestly attired, he enjoyed the soft, cool pressure of her bottom pressing against his groin through her skirt, and was comforted by the gentle rise and fall of her flat stomach beneath his protective arms. Despite the heat, Alicia was pleasingly scented, and her curled auburn hair offered a silky caress to his chin and neck.

Protecting the girl who loved him, Orwell's distant eyes gleamed an oddly zealous light as he surveyed the interview scene with particularly personal privilege. Onlookers seemed surprised to learn from a subdued Leopard Milongwe that, while he had enjoyed the battle, Mr. Thompson had given him a serious challenge and been his most difficult opponent to date. When asked whether he would grant Thompson a return bout either in Canada or somewhere in Africa to settle their dispute , Milongwe winced at the thought, so soon after the epic match he had waged for most of the afternoon; he seemed reticent to pronounce himself on any future match. Mr. Chanda, more secure than his weary fighter, articulated defiantly that they would consider a rematch once other, equally worthy contenders had been put to bed. In order to qualify, Karl Thompson should stay polished by progressing through the British Commonwealth ranks.

When asked for a rebuttal, Thompson—a glowering brute of few words—nearly chomped on and spit out pieces of the microphone an Asian journalist stuck in his face. He growled as Tracy looked upon his diamond in the rough with smug satisfaction, "I'm ready to fight this Leopard man again, anytime. We just did a hell of a good brawl, my kind of game!

"Our phone is ringing all the time. Manager Tracy is lining up good opponents every day. Whoever the boss feeds me, bring him on—no sweat, man, I'll clobber the bum! If I get to meet Leopard again, that'd be sweet, man."

Neither boxing authorities nor the sporting press had ever heard of Tracy MacDonachie, but recognizing that some great fighter must have schooled journeyman Thompson, they now wished to detain and learn from him and his savvy crew. At an elegant wine and cheese reception held a few hours later, with entertainment provided by international artists in the Mkumbi Room of Lusaka's cosmopolitan InterContinental Hotel, the national boxing commission proposed to hire Tracy MacDonachie as a guest coach at an exhibition clinic for schoolboy boxers at the Lusaka Boxing Club, aimed to enrich the manly sport of boxing in the city. His expenses would be handsomely paid on government tab, and all club members, including Zambia's leading amateur and professional fighters—Milongwe, Paul Mulenga, Billy Soose, and Lotty Mwale (who had won the gold medal in his middle-weight class at the Commonwealth Games just last January)—would gladly be at Tracy's disposal. Karl Thompson, a proven boxer of merit now, was also encouraged to participate. Their collaboration would look good on the boxing resume, possibly leading to lucrative future bouts against other topflight boxers around the world. Tracy graciously accepted this offer, good-naturedly promising to do his best to help the clinic succeed.

Present among invited guests to see his friend celebrated and hear him accept the promising offer, Orwell congratulated Tracy about his coup as they mingled later on, full wine glass in one hand and hors d'oeuvres in the other. Tracy was happy with all the festivities swirling in his honour, but Orwell's enthrallment seemed to bother him. MacDonachie recoiled against Orwell's suggestion he should lodge with his sisters at Hughes House now that the big boxing match was done. Such an idea did not compute in Tracy's vast, razor-sharp mind; his adventures in Zambia were just beginning!

Even as Orwell struggled to celebrate with his mentor, bitter frustration welled up inside him against Tracy's continued distraction from engaging with him. Hughes inwardly fumed, "God knows, I mean well...Yet, I embarrass Tracy in his moment of glory by acting like some goo-goo-eyed groupie! I appear too eager. Georgina's 'situation' aside, am I pestering him with too many naïve questions instead of drawing intelligent conclusions? He seems to be looking through me, past me, in search of someone better to share his new prestige with."

When Tracy wondered out loud where the hell his sisters were, and why they had forgone attending the gala held in his honour, Hughes blurted out that Kathleen and Richard had not watched the bout on ZTV, let alone in person, and now were off for an evening flight! The great man's other sister had purposely stayed home to patch some girlie things up with her friend JJ, whom she did not see much of late due to yours truly! And, Orwell laughed as he added to frowning Tracy, Alicia did not enjoy these strutting rooster shows anyways, even if a loved one was the centre of attention.

He then shared that prudent Alicia's fetching alter-ego Mairam had been diligently practising her musical repertoire with him at home, since they were invited to perform a nightclub-style song and instrumental routine for a full house of enthusiastic fans at June's Flying Club barbecue—would Tracy like to attend as their special guest? His boxing troupe might enjoy a tasty steak dinner and some relaxing music as a reward and wind down to all their hard work. All the club facilities: swimming pool, table tennis, darts, billiards, card tables, and tavern were open to members and guests.

Tracy seemed appalled at how far his innocent little sisters had fallen without him around to guide them! What had Orwell done with all the talents MacDonachie had given him to utilize for good during his absence? Had he forgotten everything the master had taught him?

Unfortunately, Alicia had not been there to help her lover keep his foot out of his mouth, and if Thompson talked with his fists, Orwell babbled through rented lips! Tracy's reaction was one of frustration rather than fizzy good humour.

"Orwell! Why don't you have things on the home front under control?" barked MacDonachie. "I specifically instructed you to keep Ricky and Kitty-Cat apart! As for Alicia...Yes, she looks good on your arm, needs to get out more, and singing in church is right up her alley, but I never suggested that you get her a gig as some cheap burlesque entertainer. She'll get eaten alive by a bunch of drunk, obnoxious dudes whistling at her booty, and cat-calling her to perform ever livelier. Know what I mean, Orwell? Dad will croak if he finds out."

Orwell promised nothing bad would happen to the girls while he was around, "The Lusaka Flying Club is above reproach. Singing for the airmen, their ladies and families is Alicia's baby, but I and the other youths at our house are providing back-up vocals and accompaniment.

"Your little sister eagerly accepted the invitation to entertain from the club president himself—a stodgy old Brit who's taken a shine to her, but who also happens to be the commander of Lusaka's police force. Dad and Richard, who know Colonel Rainsforth well, being avid flyers and club members, have no issues with us performing. They totally encourage the concert! Rainsforth has a knack for finding stage talent; Alicia feels she owes him for seeing good in her, and aims to please, like sing for her supper. I can't dissuade her from doing ought but her best."

"Of course, who wouldn't—but that's how the wide road leads to ruin!" debunked Tracy bitterly, from personal experience. He demanded as he gripped Orwell hard by the arm, "What does Kathy think of this schmozzle?"

"She's in now, but admittedly had to pray about the idea before agreeing that the MacDonachie girls would show."

"I am glad one of you punks has some sense!"

"Listen Tracy, our little jug band has been vigorously practising a wealth of music for all kinds of venues. Kathy is our hard-driving maestro. Word has gotten out about your glamorous singing sisters being in town, and everyone wants to hear them now, from the Flying Club to local churches, YWCA to Campus Christian Fellowship, from school teachers and the Ministry of Arts, Culture, and Antiquities...to our Canadian contingent!"

"Sounds like you've been far busier than I have," conceded MacDonachie as he shook his head, incredulously yet knowingly. "They're my sisters—God bless them! Life goes on…"

"So, you'll come to the *braai* and listen to our music?" Orwell concluded.

Tracy rebuked him, "You should really consider joining *Toast Masters*; you could learn to speak properly in public, a good skill to learn at your age."

Rather than protest these insults from his mentor, Orwell tried to revel in their high-jinks adventures of bygone youth, hoping that Tracy would mellow out, but his steely mentor had other, more important things on his mind than family matters! Tracy sternly advised the younger man that, since the visas of many in his entourage were about to expire, and the crew would soon be leaving the country, his clinic was now short-staffed. He needed Orwell to pick up the slack, and help him demonstrate the sweet science to Zambia's youth.

Although Hughes lived for such glorious opportunities to work shoulder to shoulder with Tracy on manly projects, he was stunned by his request. When Orwell hesitated, pooh-poohing his own boxing skills as being rudimentary at best, while citing tutor work for Karla Eve, musical gigs with Alicia and other previous engagements, Tracy insisted that he was more than able to spar with anyone in these friendly exhibitions with local amateurs. He had full confidence in Orwell's fighting abilities. Had he not personally taught him how to box, then coached him successfully in many junior amateur tournaments back home?

When Orwell tried to bargain with this icon like Moses pleading to God at the burning bush, MacDonachie's good nature lost its lustre. Becoming impatient with his former student, he bluntly told him that this is where the rubber hit the road! This was their chance to spend quality time together before he returned to Canada, so Orwell should take the opportunity being handed out if the lad considered him to be his friend. Orwell owed his mentor a few favours, after all. Where was his gratitude to Tracy for making him into a self-confident man? Who the hell was some dumb broad named Karla Eve that she took precedence over him, not to mention a government-sponsored boxing clinic led by world-class fighters?

"What about all that hardware gleaming in your trophy case? You should have more guts, take pride and courage in your skill set!" Tracy berated the incredulous youth like he was still his hard-as-nails trainer. "According to what Alicia boasts to me, you hone your pugilistic skills as an active member of the university boxing club."

Smiling and lowering his voice to a congenial murmur without relenting from his campaign when he sensed Orwell's cringing dismay, Tracy promised, "This travelling road show will be fun as well as educational. I'll make it worth your while!"

Intrigued, Orwell happily capitulated; despite water flowing silently under the bridge between them concerning Georgina, he felt morally obligated to assist his friend. Tracy made him an offer he could not refuse. Robert MacDonachie was a snake oil salesman, and his august Dad preached hellfire, but Tracy was more considerate, and knew when to ice his campaign.

*****

Speaking of *MacDonachie & Son,* they were so anxious to find out how Alicia and Kathleen were doing, and what was keeping them so long in Africa, that they laid down some serious coin and telephoned the Hughes home all the way from Edmonton, the very evening when mighty Tracy was being wined and dined in Lusaka's five-star hotel by the high-rolling boxing crowd.

Holed up in Bwana Hughes's normally tranquil study, Alicia was loudly fielding their hot-line international call as Orwell came sauntering into the house, flush with his own wonderful news, dropped off by his victorious mentor. Alicia was the first one Orwell wished to share his good fortune with, but judging by her agitated voice and red face glaring past him when he barged excitedly into her private space, Orwell sensed that the conversation was not going well! Kathleen sat, cross-armed and scowling, on the velvet-covered ottoman. Feeling he was intruding, he took his cue to leave.

Princess Mairam, despite her misery, motioned for her friend to stay, to quietly sit down and wait—her eyes pled for him to pray for her while she tried to conclude this call with civility!

"Robert, I've already told you everything I know, many times and in various ways. I'm sorry—I have no detailed schedule for our return!"

Alicia, tears of anguish glistening in her eyes and frustration rising in her voice, beseeched her despotic older brother to show some understanding, but his incessant shouting over thousands of telephone miles only made Alicia cringe like a shackled prisoner.

"You're lying, Fannie! Don't play games with me, you stupid bitch, or I'll tan your hide within an inch of your life when I get you shipped back here!"

"I'm *not* a liar! Dad loves me, and you are not my father, Robert. You will never lay a hand on me again!" angrily retorted the amazon. She stopped short of threatening him, but Robert could be heard demanding to know her intentions, however feeble he dismissed them to be.

Orwell was impressed that Alicia had taken his encouragement, given a scant few weeks ago after he and the young lioness had played *manhunt* in the back garden, to stand her ground against her tormentor. Yet, as he looked on aghast, she banged down the telephone receiver like a judge's gavel on his father's polished mahogany desk, and paused to recompose herself, lest she break down sobbing or fire back her own retaliatory volley of profane jibes.

Having pushed Robert back, she spoke now to him in low, measured words that summarized her case with finality, "Despite the misinformation Kathy just reported to you, she and I have really enjoyed our African holiday! It's true, we've stayed longer than expected, but *hey*—that's okay. We do our homework, help out with chores, and generally fit in—every day!

"Orwell's family has been very hospitable to us. They've taken us on many interesting excursions around the countryside. We had a fine Easter season, when we sang and provided the gift of hymnals while holding a meet and greet at their church. Orwell and his folks are happy for us to stay as long as we wish, for they love us. They understand that we must wait patiently until Tracy is finally ready to take us home with him to Canada. I think that Tracy's commitments are nearly over, so we will likely leave here together in a few days."

"Is our illustrious Orwell Hughes there in the room with you, Fannie?"

"Yes, he is—and he's heard everything!"

"Put him on then, my sweet papoose with the big caboose! Hah! Hah! Just kidding, sissy babe...Hello? Where are you? Alicia, don't hang up on us!"

"I have only this left to say to you, Bucko: leave Orwell out of this!"

"I just want to congratulate your new boyfriend for putting up with you for so long—sweet seventeen and never been kissed, indeed," snickered Robert derisively, unconcerned for her embarrassment.

Alicia rolled her eyes and sighed with profound indignation. She stared grimly at Orwell as she thrust the telephone towards him with resolute hands. Then she stamped away, and plopped herself down heavily beside her equally unhappy sister, the momentum of her crash landing causing the ottoman to scrape backwards on the tile floor and bring a snarl of irritation from Kathleen. Orwell gazed incredulously at these wild sisters, who glared defiantly back at him as they intently waited for him to perform a mission of intervention upon their behalf.

"Hello?" Orwell began hesitantly, fearing the worst. "How are you, Bruce?"

"Richly blessed by the Lord, as always," caressed a bounteous voice that the young poet recognized with awe as belonging to none other than Reverend Wynnard MacDonachie, the greatest Christian leader of his time. "Orly Hughes, how are you, my fine, plucky lad? Have you turned black yet, as you feared you might upon leaving Edmonchuk five years ago? I am surprised that you have a functioning telephone in your home. It's likely an old black rotary model, eh? We'll get you one of those new touch tone phones as soon as they come out later this year. I already have digital clocks...

"A sweet birdie told me that you were saved last year. Do you wear that quaint little crucifix Annie Fannie lovingly made you from the nail of her dear departed pony? What was that animal's name, Bruce? Oh yes, *Windchaser*—a sleek, golden buckskin he was, who could fly like Pegasus and jump over the moon, but only when Annie Fannie rode him. She loved him more than any boy! Sad to say, *Windchaser* broke his leg in a riding accident at our *Bonne Chance* Ranch, and had to be put down!"

When Orwell, stunned silent by this august presence, hung awkwardly on the line all while twiddling the nail crucifix dangling from his neck, Rev. MacDonachie knotted shut his joke bag and posed his vital question, "Son, what is the Lord doing in your life these precious days?"

"Despite closure of the university, I'm enjoying an extended Easter vacation, sir, made more interesting by companionship of your daughters, who share my interest for Africa, and are helping me embrace this diverse land, its cultured peoples, and exotic animals with renewed heart. I also tutor Karlee, a recently arrived Canadian lady who's struggling to finish high school."

"Helping others is an honourable service, for which God will bless you. How eloquently but succinctly you put your thoughts together, Orly. What a clear, strong voice you have—perfect for teaching now, but there's more you can do. You ought to be in radio; you'd also make a fine preacher! We must talk more about your future career path when you return to civilization."

"Thank you, sir," replied young Hughes, trying his best to sound polite without fawning before the great man, whom he knew did not suffer yes-men gladly. "I recently acted and sang in an ecumenical musical on Ash Wednesday to a packed audience, which your daughters attended. That was two weeks ago! I guess time flies when you're having fun!"

"We're wondering how you could still have fun with three of my children living in your home, mooching off your generous hospitality, which is why we telephoned you."

"We're getting on famously, sir. I read scriptures behind the pulpit, sing in the choir, and play organ at church. Alicia and Kathy fully support our choir and youth group."

"Excellent, Orly. You are a true disciple of Jesus—a credit to your Christian parents, and always a welcome guest in our home!"

"Did you know that Alicia and Kathleen joined our enthusiastic multiracial choir for several rousing hallelujah anthems on Easter Sunday—"Jesus Christ is Risen Today!", "Low in the Grave He Lay", and "Battle Hymn of the Republic"—to name three?"

"Wonderful, traditional Easter hymns they are, and still meaningful today!"

"Church folk remark effervescently about your girls' beautiful voices."

"Chips of the old block, eh boy? You play a solid, deep tune yourself," praised wise, old MacDonachie, chuckling fondly. "My daughters had you sing with them, which is a feather in your cap. Was Tracy performing too?"

"No sir. Tracy was too busy preparing for a boxing match to join us in church," Orwell chafed with brutal honesty.

Alicia and Kathleen, who had mellowed somewhat as they soaked up his amusing dialogue, gazed sharply at Orwell now. Alicia shook her head furiously as she planted a finger to her iron lips to quiet this announcement, but her dire warning came too late!

"A boxing match! My son, playing professional sports on Sunday?" incredulously protested Rev. MacDonachie. "I taught my children to remember the Sabbath, and keep it holy!"

"Sir, I believe that Tracy took time out to pray and read his Bible, and he didn't fight himself," Orwell tried desperately to assure the distraught theologian, but riled him all the more by clumsily justifying Tracy's rebellious actions. "Your son, my friend, came down here with Karl Thompson in tow, a young prizefighter he manages, to challenge the local hero Leopard Milongwe for his Commonwealth heavy-weight championship. They were definite underdogs, but Tracy trained Karl exceedingly well, and he fought valiantly to a draw in this very important battle. I believe that God was with Tracy and Karl all the way."

"You do? How remarkable!" groused the elderly pastor. "Was our Lord seen supporting those renegades in the ring, or cheering them from the stands with the lolling crowd? Was God pleased with the outcome?"

"I only know the decisions of the earthly judges, sir. The two fighters fought to a draw over fifteen excellent rounds of boxing."

"Nothing was really accomplished then—except to diminish the Lord's Name—to take it in vain. Tracy continues his rebellion in open defiance against both his Heavenly and earthly fathers, and therefore reaps futility in all his cursed endeavours."

"Milongwe retained his crown, but Thompson's ranking improved significantly. A rematch in Canada for next year is seriously discussed! Your son is the toast of the international boxing community. His leadership and knowledge of the sport became so quickly admired here that the Zambian boxing authorities asked him to stay another week, so that he might teach a clinic aimed at improving the skills of local prospects. Tracy will demonstrate many valuable boxing techniques for these kids, along with several top-class Zambian boxers in attendance...and myself?"

"You must not indulge in this folly, Orly. God does not mean for an intelligent, artistic boy like you to be bruised by pugs. Keep yourself pure, as unto the Lord, lest Tracy poison your spirit with his own iniquities," Reverend MacDonachie soberly counselled him. When Orwell protested, insisting that his friend was all alone and needed companionship, Wynnard fervently gave him a sermon, "To quote the reasoning preacher of Ecclesiastes, my naïve lad: '*Vanity of vanities; all is vanity! What does a man gain from all his labour, at which he toils under the sun?*'

"King Solomon was renowned in the ancient world for his wisdom. He devoted himself to study, and wisely explored all that is done under Heaven. He undertook great projects, like building palaces and planting vineyards, as well as establishing fruit orchards, vegetable gardens and woodlots; he also irrigated these plantations with pools of water that he had constructed. The great king pastured huge herds of cattle, and possessed legendary treasures of gold and silver. His vast household was run by many servants, while talented singers and musicians entertained in his splendid court. If this wealth of blessing was not enough, Solomon also took many wives and concubines, who produced children, as well as provided him with pleasures untold. Have you not read *Song of Solomon*, Orly, where the King and his Shulammite bride loved each other so beautifully as to inspire lovers throughout the ages—how God loves his creation?

"Even this glorious romance brought Solomon no lasting joy. Although he was uplifted in fame, possessions and wisdom, enjoyed many pleasures, and accomplished every undertaking, this glorious monarch learned at the end of the day that all was vanity and vexation to his spirit; there was no profit to be gained under the sun. Among his harem were many foreign women who dulled the King's faith in our holy God with their own perverse, idolatrous religions, a failing which led to the break-up of his bounteous kingdom Israel through civil war among the royal sons. Solomon's legacy was tarnished by this sad ending, although he was one of the greatest rulers of the ancient world. His wisdom has been revered for over 3,000 years!

"What noble or practical thing has Tracy done for his generation, with his many God-given talents, and advantages of upbringing? Nothing! He is an utter embarrassment to our family. Truly, Orwell, if I had to rate my eldest son on a scale of one to ten for his value to mankind, I would give Tracy Maurice MacDonachie a big fat zero!" railed Reverend MacDonachie, nearly choking with rage and despair. "At times, I regret to have sired him!"

"I am sorry to hear that, sir," murmured Hughes over and over again in effort to console the elderly man and to keep him coherent, fearful now for Rev. MacDonachie's health as he listened in shock to his plaintive cries to Jesus amid heavy breathing and background clatter.

"Orly, it is no use. I have tried my best to help him for 35 years, but Tracy will never change of his own accord. I have given up fighting with him, although I continue to pray for his soul. Perhaps Tracy can yet be salvaged now that he is bound and handed over to Satan to learn repentance for the error of his ways."

Orwell, unable to bear such a horrifying sentence for his friend that he still loved, tried to bargain with Reverend MacDonachie by testifying to the many poignant experiences he had enjoyed in their church because of Tracy's imaginative youth ministry. The modern Christian leader had pricked Orwell's interest in Jesus through his dedication, flexibility, ingenuity, and most compelling, his *love* for people—especially for searching young people who were turned off by the crusty institutional church! *He* promised to walk with Tracy, and seek God's help and guidance for this struggling fellow believer. God must have planned such vital intervention by giving Tracy and Orwell the special opportunity to sojourn together in Africa...

Robert's sharp, irritated voice on the other end of the phone now refuted such purpose by cynically revealing that Tracy's socialist rhetoric and civil disobedience tarnished his lofty plans, by continually miring him in conflict with church leaders and educators.

"Dad got so upset with your argument, Orly that he went to his bedroom to lie down. I just brought him an Aspirin to drink with warm milk to comfort his headache," lectured Robert sternly. "He seems to have a soft spot for you, but don't take him for granted...Better watch what you say, boy! Dad's done more great things in his life than you could dream of doing in 1,000 years!"

"Tracy told me he made a detour to look at some oil leases, grain farms, and tin mines wherein *Silver Lining Corporation* has invested in both east and West Africa, which delayed him from arriving in Lusaka for our Easter Sunday church service," protested Hughes on his mentor's behalf, anguished that he had foolishly disturbed Tracy's famous father, an icon in Christian and business circles.

"We don't deal in that part of the world, Orly. It's too remote, too unstable," Robert said bluntly, wishing to educate the impressionable lad who would follow his pied-piper brother anywhere. "Don't let Tracy explain away his irresponsibility by selling you a fake bill of goods! He's good at lying and cheating, like Fannie."

"Please keep Alicia out of this, Bob; she is my friend," Orwell parried bravely, for the gratitude of his intently listening princess, against the rapier thrusts of the bully who would inherit all of Wynnard's empire. When Robert guffawed like a baboon, goading the cocky lad to swing with him, Orwell asserted, "Karl Thompson nearly won that big fight today, thanks to excellent training and coaching by Tracy and his elite team. Karl's going to advance, man! You'll see him contending for the world title soon."

He may have downed Reverend MacDonachie, but Robert the Bruce[72] was

72 *Robert the Bruce*: heroic Scottish king (1274 to 1329) who defeated the English at Bannockburn in

no nobleman to follow in his regal father's footsteps. He was a blowhard about everything, including boxing!

"Tracy may be doing a good thing in your deluded eyes, but he is wasting his time on a goon who will never amount to anything except being a punching bag for up-and-coming contenders!" Robert haughtily schooled Orwell, as if the lad was a total idiot. "Unpolished is a kind overstatement on Thompson, Orly, to be sure! He's a total unknown, as are Tracy and his hoodlum friends—even in Canada. Performing in that back-alley cockfight you attended today, somewhere lost in the jungle, did nothing to help their ratings!

"Tracy's goon is just a stepping stone—a journeyman—a bum of the month for legitimate prospects who try to pad their records. Thompson got very lucky today! Tracy likely bribed the referees to gain a favourable result...This Leopard dude barely retained his belt; he was a damn fool to let a snake in the grass like Tracy get him into the ring with his no-name thug! No wonder legitimate contenders are hopping mad! Had Karl won, he would have ruined the better fighter's career—Milongwe is damaged goods to avoid now, after scraping to draw against this pile of shit!

"Why Tracy bothers with creeps and bums like Karl Thompson, Rivard Cummings, and Tracy Rimond, I can't for the life of me imagine. All those biker hoods do is fix cars by day and carouse by night—they could be gangsters or pimps, for God's sake! As Dad says, 'Tiptoe' is chasing after the wind...He should clean up his own bad act instead of trying to save the world from sin and oppression!"

"I thought you tycoons admired brave young men who took up their calling and pursued it to the end—against all odds," Orwell argued fiercely. "So, Tracy and Karl are not household boxing names with records a mile long against name opponents. They confronted Leopard's loud boast that he could whip any fighter on the planet; my guys trained diligently, followed a strategic game plan, and proved to Milongwe's camp that they could successfully meet his challenge.

"Tracy and Karl have both paid their dues, toiling for years in obscurity. They, having learned the ropes well, made the best of a golden opportunity given them, earned Milongwe's respect, and will likely get another shot at him.

---

1314 to retain independence for Scotland.

They also received the upward call to bigger and better matches. This is the big break the boys wanted. I say, well done! Good luck!"

"Those bozos will get ground into hamburger soon enough, hopefully next fight out—if the cops don't bust 'em first for fraud," predicted Robert dismissively as he sang, "Too bad, so sad."

"Bob, I know how proud your father is with your own accomplishments," Orwell countered slyly. "You dropped out of engineering at university, but that little glitch has not stopped one of the world's premier entrepreneurs from grooming you to become an able helmsman of his empire. You were given a second chance and proved yourself, became a highly successful businessman on merit, Bob. You, who possess flare, energy, insight, and fatherly mentorship to manage a soaring multinational firm, can hire as many engineers as you need now to complete various strategic projects aggressively on the go.

"What is a degree after all but a piece of paper? You succeeded by applying your own superb leadership qualities, as well as your own ingenuity to run the rat race to glorious completion, regardless of what experts determine you can or cannot do. The mark of a man is how he achieves his goals and meets challenges in the way of those goals, when given hope."

"Okay, Orly, okay; you've made your point," Robert glumly called a truce after pondering this eloquent missive. He chuckled dryly, "Don't burn up my phone line with a sermon—I hear enough of those around here. For now, we'll agree to disagree; I leave my brother to his fate. Have a good time being part of this epic sports clinic—just don't agree to be a punching bag. We'll probably cross trails again when you return to Canada, which is not long to wait, I take it?"

"Four months and counting," sighed Orwell with mixed emotions. "Did you want to speak anymore with your sisters?"

"There's no need; they understand the drill: be good and get home ASAP! You may need to prod them if they get stubborn, so take charge. Bye."

"Right," acknowledged Hughes solemnly as the stern ruler broke off with a click of MacDonachie's gold-plated receiver.

He assumed that Robert was joking, but one never knew what crossed the razor mind of the ruthless business tycoon with the winsome grin and iron handshake. Still tingling from this unique audience with giants, but concerned that he had disturbed Alicia's ailing father, Orwell carefully hung up the telephone. He gazed pensively upon his reflection in Bwana Hughes's polished mahogany table before lifting his eyes towards the two young women who, still sitting together on the couch, remained his captive audience. They stared at him with teary-eyed admiration.

"Well? ...How now?" quizzed Alicia, watching him anxiously with her luminous brown eyes.

"What's new with you?" drolly teased Orwell, fishing for her sweet smile that hid in deep but stormy waters.

Kathleen, who had been brooding in the shadows throughout this bizarre exchange, now sprang menacingly to her feet and confronted him.

"Dad is really concerned about us because we overstayed our visas and did not return home when supposed to! He felt he had to look for us. Robert threatened to ground us, to give us lickings like we were naughty little girls—how embarrassing! At least Dad realizes now that we're doing the best we can with this bad situation. He knows what going on... it's all Tracy's fault!

"Oh-well, I can't believe you would not only help Tracy make our lives miserable, but shamelessly boast to our father about your joined exploits!" yowled the enraged lioness, her electric blue eyes sparkling dangerously at him. "No wonder everyone is upset; guys are jerks!"

Having vented her spleen, Kathleen turned and stamped out of the room. Alicia gazed wide-eyed after her. Dismayed, Hughes smarted and wanted revenge for this unwarranted slap in the face. Did the junior lioness, by lingering with him, seem torn between haughtily following the pride, or trying to comfort him?

"Alicia, I'm not trying to cause problems for you ladies. It was not my wish to rile Bob or upset your father," Orwell cautiously defended himself in advance against her untamed fury.

"You seem to be in your glory now that Tracy has finally called for you," she grimly replied, understanding Orwell's deep yearnings better than he did. "Go with your hero. Having fun with Tracy is what you crave above all else; manly adventure shared with him is all you dream of.

"After all the good times we simple females have already enjoyed with your caring family, Kathy and I can afford to wait a few more days, cooking and cleaning, until our roving cavalier brother has finished playing all his high-stakes games. You, who are his most loyal follower, should gladly accept Sir Tracy's special invitation to join his fabled company! Orwell, you must go to him at once!"

Laughter broke out as even sombre Alicia recognized the theatrical humour of her performance. Her urging should have led him to immediately suit up with armour, saddle his war horse, pierce the sky with his sword, and ride hard for Tracy's secret camp, but Hughes was stymied by bitterness he could hear in her voice, which made her encouragement ring hollow.

What was this self-promotion to her dad about him being a tutor? Did Orwell intend to spend his spare time with that devious vixen, Karla Eve? Alicia appreciated his care for the troubled and needy, blonde girl, but the amazon's almond eyes were sad that he was abandoning her altogether in search of greener pastures. Orwell offered no comforting words on this odd topic.

"I want to be with Tracy, but I wish that Kathleen and Richard—as well as Suzy and JJ, Ben and Georgina—but especially you Alicia could also join our party," he blurted, anxious that his caring companion should be certain of his concern for her. "I don't want to leave anyone out; I hope none my friends feel disappointed by my selfishness."

"You are being true to yourself as you answer that upward call to arms. I understand. I am happy for you."

"Are you? Really?" Hughes begged to silence his nagging doubts. When she grinned broadly and energetically nodded, he gave her a hug. "Thank you, Alicia, for being such a good sport—a true friend. This clinic is a big chance for Tracy, and definitely a highlight in my life—I'm elated to help him out!"

She allowed him to hold her for a fleeting moment of tenderness, but then playing shy, wriggled free of his grasp, and made a dash for freedom. Orwell, who impulsively desired to know Alicia better, could barely restrain himself from chasing after her...He would love to catch and win her...make her day complete as well! Had Alicia not only said, but shown that she loved him? This strange girl seemed to have multiple personalities—was she mad? More likely, she played a game to throw people off—portraying herself sometimes as a tough broad, other times as the intelligent, strait-laced preacher's kid, and yet again, as a wild and beautiful warrior princess. Mairam now revealed herself as a cool but luscious female to his touch, except that she refused to let him close. Comfortably wrapped in a pink housecoat, freshly scrubbed and perfumed like a field of wild flowers, Alicia was ready for bed—did she want him to sleep with her? Alicia smiled coyly at the awkward suitor as she placed her strong frame protectively against the door, and turned the doorknob deftly with one hand behind her back.

"That's great, Orwell! You both will do your best," Alicia promised as she swung open the door. Motioning him out of the room with a sweeping gesture of her free hand, Alicia prattled briskly along behind him as they trod the shadowy hallway, "We who await your glorious return from battle can manage the home front just fine! Why have dysfunctional soldiers clanging noisily around the house, getting in the way because they have nothing chivalrous to do....

"Mark my words and read my lips; men are expendable, Oh-well," she brashly informed him, unsubtly warning him as she stopped with finality at her bedroom.

"Would you like a drink of pop?" Hughes pleasantly offered Alicia a virgin nightcap, hoping to draw her into the well-lit kitchen for further discussion. "I've ten flavours, all ice-cold!"

"No...but thank you," she murmured from the safe ambiguity of the guest room, her smile gleaming in the dark as she gazed benignly upon him from behind her glasses. "I'm going to brush my teeth now, and go back to bed. Do you know that I was awakened from a pleasant dream to answer that miserable, long-distance blast from Canada?"

"What were you dreaming about?"

"Wouldn't you like to know!" she teased him. "I can't remember all the sweet details, but I was really enjoying a sunny afternoon strolling hand in hand with you among the flower gardens at *Munda Wanga*."

"That sounds fun! Maybe you were having a vision of good times ahead," Orwell chirped. "We should go out there sometime, and walk about! We could take a picnic lunch, and go swimming too, before you folks leave for Canada. Georgina insisted that I show you that world-famous park as soon as possible—it's a must see!"

"True enough, we'll visit that park—especially if Georgina recommends it," saluted Alicia, as a pout suddenly possessed her pretty face.

"Dear, I could take you to *Munda Wanga* next week, after the clinic gets done. I want to show you all my special plant friends. Yet, how can I do this when Georgina has you booked daily as her special trainer?"

"You'll be busy soon, schooling Karla B—an equally vital task," Alicia reminded him, cleverly tit for tat. "We both have our little duties to do each day, so let's brighten our corners where we are..."

"Okay, since I'm not back at university, I'm using my time productively for what seems right for now: help Karlee make some progress...demonstrate my boxing skills for your brother at his clinic...play organ at church...That's what good Christians and diplomats do, right? Help those in need. It's legitimate service. All said, I will think of and miss you."

"Really?" Alicia giggled, touched by his affection. Then, parrying his advance with her large elegant hands, lest they become needlessly lovey-dovey so late at night, the amazon seriously advised him, "We should get some sleep now, so we can both stay in top shape for whatever tomorrow brings."

"Alicia, my supporting your brother is for him to do so well at his clinic that he can then retire rich and happy, and willingly come home with me to you forever. I promise you, we'll be together soon to enjoy life in Africa! I'd like him to come to *Munda Wanga,* and even accompany us to watch Georgina whip some Mauritian ass at tennis. Tracy and his guys will attend our show at the Flying Club, billed as a fitting wind-up barbecue social for everyone."

"Oh...kay," she drawled, playfully unconvinced, though she found his reference to Georgina 'whipping ass' amusing. Acknowledging at last that his vow was fervent and earnestly dedicated to her, she urged him, "Just make sure you two pugs come home in one piece, and not too beat up. That is your mission from me, should you choose to accept it. I don't want to play doctor again before our musical debut, Orwell. It's all bonus to me if Tracy comes to the *braai.*"

Alicia waved goodbye and turned in, but not before giving him a wistful gaze when she caught him admiring her through the guest room threshold. Soft backlighting of her refuge revealed Alicia's secret: the princess was wondrously naked under her nightie! Incredulously, Orwell glimpsed her jutting breasts and round buttocks that curved sensuously away from her flat stomach, and quivered daintily with the smooth gait of her long, powerful legs. Orwell felt his penis swell warmly with carnal desire, but he obediently looked away, not wanting to embarrass his friend. She, noting his worshipful stare, smiled in appreciation as she disappeared inside her bedroom, closing her door quietly behind her.

After the goddess was gone, Orwell stepped into the coolness of the night garden, to ponder the Lord's amazing creation under the comforting light of the moon. What a wonderful surprise was Alicia! A flannel nightgown loosely draped over her hourglass figure was a mere convenience, more to protect its lustrous finish from dust than hide her magnificent curves from avid eyes—until the strategic time of her unveiling? Was this not his needed time? They could satisfy their mad love for one another, here and now, if only Alicia would come to the garden or invite him into her sanctuary—but she, being a good girl, hid in God's protective hands.

He stood convicted, foolishly deceived, desiring to have torrid sex with Alicia now when he should not! God had killed several Old Testament princes who had offended Him by illicitly sampling the first fruit if His garden, but how would Orwell flee evermore temptation when it loomed deliciously before him? If Alicia truly loved him, they should get married soon, like Rick and Kathy were, and legitimize his wild fantasies in her regard.

Angry that he could behave so wrongly against Georgina, his true flame, or slander Karla Eve, who wanted more from him than mere book learning, Orwell slapped himself severely to get his mind out of the gutter, away from the temptress pretending to sleep now in the hallowed guest room. Even if only one brick wall separated them, he must cloister in his own bedroom now, to pray and repent, before hopefully finding sleep, lest his carnal male lusts take hold and lead him where he should not go. Why must he see Alicia's breathtaking beauty if she pretended not to recognize it? As Kathleen and Robert admonished him, Alicia was no innocent child! Why was she always tempting poor guys she had the hots for when she knew it was dangerously wrong to mess with their minds? She seemed pleased by his worship, yet disdained such weakness, and would fiercely explain tonight's risqué state tomorrow as having jumped out of bed to obediently speak with her father. There was no ulterior motive, no invitation on her part to partake in some vulgar tryst—oh no! Oh yes! After giving him an enticing show, Alicia had brushed him off, and gone to bed alone—as a good Christian girl should.

Orwell vowed to respect her choice, as he and Alicia were friends, who cared for one another as friends and fellow Christians should. They would come together again tomorrow, when another hopeful African day would dawn!

**THE END**

# ABOUT THE AUTHOR

ROBERT PROUDFOOT, AN EDMONTON, ALBERTA-BASED creative writer, tutor, and editor, was born and raised in Alberta, but spent four years as a high school and university student (1969 to 1973) in Lusaka, Zambia; and subsequently worked as an agro forester in Nigeria, west Africa from 1988 to 1991. Robert is also a professional environmental scientist and is married to Valerie, with whom they have two daughters, Annora and Alicia.

Robert writes about diverse, often controversial topics that interest him, including: mental health; truth and reconciliation; building bridges with, rather than walls against, other cultures and faiths; social justice; enjoyment of sports and nature; and relations between humans, the environment, and their Creator. He continues to learn about African as well as indigenous Canadian history, culture, concerns, and socioeconomics. Robert believes in Canada but he also feels that we all can do better to care about one another, as well as protect the world's environment, which are all interconnected but unique to stakeholders and time.

Robert Proudfoot is a member of the Writers' Guild of Alberta. In February 2019, he published "Enduring Art, Active Faith - 3 Generations Create!", a poignant collection of short stories, essays, poetry, and depictions of physical art work created by three generations of his family. Robert researched and wrote the background document for a CD prepared in 2009 to celebrate the 50th anniversary of Edmonton's First Mennonite Church. Mr. Proudfoot presented a biography of his grandparents who lived/worked in Edmonton during the early 1900s, called "A Playful Policeman Meets the Citizen-Making Teacher", in May 1994 for "Come and Know Your History" project that celebrated the 200th anniversary of the City of Edmonton.

Printed in Canada